GREAT AMERICAN WRITERS

THE

WILD WEST

RIDERS OF THE PURPLE SAGE
BY ZANE GREY

TENNESSEE'S PARTNER
THE LUCK OF ROARING CAMP
BY BRET HARTE

THE CABALLERO'S WAY
THE PIMIENTA PANCAKES
A CALL LOAN
BY O. HENRY

THE LAST OF THE MOHICANS
(an extract)
BY JAMES FENIMORE COOPER

Riders of the Purple Sage by Zane Grey was first published in 1912
'Tennessee's Partner' and 'The Luck of Roaring Camp' by Bret Harte were
first published in *The Luck of Roaring Camp* in 1870
'The Caballero's Way', 'The Pimienta Pancakes' and 'A Call Loan' by
O. Henry were first published in *Heart of the West* in 1907
The Last of the Mohicans by James Fenimore Cooper was first published
in 1826

This volume first published in 1989 by
The Octopus Group Limited
Michelin House, 81 Fulham Road, London SW3 6RB

This edition published in 1989 by Gallery Books
An imprint of W. H. Smith Publishers Inc.
112 Madison Avenue, New York, New York 10016

CONTENTS

RIDERS
OF THE
PURPLE SAGE

BY

ZANE GREY

CHAPTER ONE
Lassiter

A SHARP CLIP-CLOP OF iron-shod hoofs deadened and died away, and clouds of yellow dust drifted from under the cottonwoods out over the sage.

Jane Withersteen gazed down the wide purple slope with dreamy and troubled eyes. A rider had just left her and it was his message that held her thoughtful and almost sad, awaiting the churchmen who were coming to resent and attack her right to befriend a Gentile.

She wondered if the unrest and strife that had lately come to the little village of Cottonwoods was to involve her. And then she sighed, remembering that her father had founded this remotest border settlement of southern Utah and that he had left it to her. She owned all the ground and many of the cottages. Withersteen House was hers, and the great ranch, with its thousands of cattle, and the swiftest horses of the sage. To her belonged Amber Spring, the water which gave verdure and beauty to the village and made living possible on that wild purple upland waste. She could not escape being involved by whatever befell Cottonwoods.

That year, 1871, had marked a change which had been gradually coming in the lives of the peace-loving Mormons of the border. Glaze – Stone Bridge – Sterling, villages to the north, had risen against the invasion of Gentile settlers and the forays of rustlers. There had been opposition to the one and fighting with the other. And now Cottonwoods had begun to wake and bestir itself and grow hard.

Jane prayed that the tranquillity and sweetness of her life would not be permanently disrupted. She meant to do so much more for her people than she had done. She wanted the sleepy quiet pastoral days to last always. Trouble between the Mormons and the Gentiles of the community would make her unhappy. She was Mormon-born, and she was a friend to poor and unfortunate Gentiles. She wished only to go on doing good and being happy. And she thought of what that great ranch meant to her. She loved it all – the grove of cottonwoods, the old stone house, the amber-tinted water, and the droves of shaggy, dusty horses and mustangs, the sleek, clean-limbed, blooded racers, and the browsing herds of cattle and the lean, sun-browned riders of the sage.

While she waited there she forgot the prospect of untoward change. The bray of a lazy burro broke the afternoon quiet, and it was comfortingly suggestive of the drowsy farmyard, and the open corrals, and the green alfalfa fields. Her clear sight intensified the purple sage-slope as it rolled before her. Low swells of prairie-like ground sloped up to the west. Dark, lonely cedar-trees, few and far between, stood out strikingly, and at long distances ruins of red rocks. Farther on, up the gradual slope, rose a broken wall, a huge monument, looming dark purple and stretching its solitary, mystic way, a wavering line that faded in the north. Here to the westward was the light and color and beauty. Northward the slope descended to a dim line of cañons from which rose an up-flinging of the earth, not mountainous, but a vast heave of purple uplands, with ribbed and fan-shaped walls, castle-crowned cliffs, and gray escarpments. Over it all crept the lengthening, waning afternoon shadows.

The rapid beat of hoofs recalled Jane Withersteen to the question at hand. A group of riders cantered up the lane, dismounted, and threw their bridles. They were seven in number, and Tull, the leader, a tall, dark man, was an elder of Jane's church.

'Did you get my message?' he asked, curtly.

'Yes,' replied Jane.

'I sent word I'd give that rider Venters half an hour to come down to the village. He didn't come.'

'He knows nothing of it,' said Jane. 'I didn't tell him. I've been waiting here for you.'

'Where is Venters?'

'I left him in the courtyard.'

'Here, Jerry,' called Tull, turning to his men, 'take the gang and fetch Venters out here if you have to rope him.'

The dusty-booted and long-spurred riders clanked noisily into the grove of cottonwoods and disappeared in the shade.

'Elder Tull, what do you mean by this?' demanded Jane. 'If you must arrest Venters you might have the courtesy to wait till he leaves my home. And if you do arrest him it will be adding insult to injury. It's absurd to accuse Venters of being mixed up in that shooting fray in the village last night. He was with me at the time. Besides, he let me take charge of his guns. You're only using this as a pretext. What do you mean to do to Venters?'

'I'll tell you presently,' replied Tull. 'But first tell me why you defend this worthless rider.'

'Worthless!' exclaimed Jane, indignantly. 'He's nothing of the kind. He was the best rider I ever had. There's not a reason why I shouldn't champion him and every reason why I should. It's no little shame to me, Elder Tull, that through my friendship he has roused the enmity of my people and become an outcast. Besides, I owe him eternal gratitude for saving the life of little Fay.'

'I've heard of your love for Fay Larkin and that you intend to adopt her. But – Jane Withersteen, the child is a Gentile!'

'Yes. But, Elder, I don't love the Mormon children any less because I love a Gentile child. I shall adopt Fay if her mother will give her to me.'

'I'm not so much against that. You can give the child Mormon teaching,' said Tull. 'But I'm sick of seeing this fellow Venters hang around you. I'm going to put a stop to it. You've so much love to throw away on these beggars of Gentiles that I've an idea you might love Venters.'

Tull spoke with the arrogance of a Mormon whose power could not be brooked and with the passion of a man in whom jealousy had kindled a consuming fire.

'Maybe I do love him,' said Jane. She felt both fear and anger stir her heart. 'I'd never thought of that. Poor fellow! He certainly needs some one to love him.'

'This'll be a bad day for Venters unless you deny that,' returned Tull, grimly.

Tull's men appeared under the cottonwoods and led a young man out into the lane. His ragged clothes were those of an outcast. But he stood tall and straight, his wide shoulders flung back, with the muscles of his bound arms rippling and a blue flame of defiance in the gaze he bent on Tull.

For the first time Jane Withersteen felt Venters's real spirit. She wondered if she would love this splendid youth. Then her emotion cooled to the sobering sense of the issue at stake.

'Venters, will you leave Cottonwoods at once and forever?' asked Tull, tensely.

'Why?' rejoined the rider.

'Because I order it.'

Venters laughed in cool disdain.

The red leaped to Tull's dark cheek.

'If you don't go it means your ruin,' he said, sharply.

'Ruin!' exclaimed Venters, passionately. 'Haven't you already ruined me? What do you call ruin? A year ago I was a rider. I had horses and cattle of my own. I had a good name in Cottonwoods. And now when I come into the village to see this woman you set your men on me. You hound me. You trail me as if I were a rustler. I've no more to lose – except my life.'

'Will you leave Utah?'

'Oh! I know,' went on Venters, tauntingly, 'it galls you, the idea of beautiful Jane Withersteen being friendly to a poor Gentile. You want her all yourself. You're a wiving Mormon. You have use for her – and Withersteen House and Amber Spring and seven thousand head of cattle!'

Tull's hard jaw protruded, and rioting blood corded the veins of his neck.

'Once more. Will you go?'

'No!'

'Then I'll have you whipped within an inch of your life,' replied Tull, harshly. 'I'll turn you out in the sage. And if you ever come back you'll get worse.'

Venters's agitated face grew coldly set and the bronze changed to gray.

Jane impulsively stepped forward. 'Oh! Elder Tull!' she cried. 'You won't do that!'

Tull lifted a shaking finger toward her.

'That'll do from you. Understand, you'll not be allowed to hold this boy to a friendship that's offensive to your Bishop. Jane Withersteen, your father left you wealth and power. It has turned your head. You haven't yet come to see the place of Mormon women. We've reasoned with you, borne with you. We've patiently waited. We've let you have your fling, which is more than I ever saw granted to a Mormon woman. But you haven't come to your senses. Now, once for all, you can't have any further friendship with Venters. He's going to be whipped, and he's got to leave Utah!'

'Oh! Don't whip him! It would be dastardly!' implored Jane, with slow certainty of her failing courage.

Tull always blunted her spirit, and she grew conscious that she had feigned a boldness which she did not possess. He loomed up now in different guise, not as a jealous suitor, but embodying the mysterious despotism she had known from childhood – the power of her creed.

'Venters, will you take your whipping here or would you rather go out in the sage?' asked Tull. He smiled a flinty smile that was more than inhuman, yet seemed to give out of its dark aloofness a gleam of righteousness.

'I'll take it here – if I must,' said Venters. 'But by God! – Tull, you'd better kill me outright. That'll be a dear whipping for you and your praying Mormons. You'll make me another Lassiter!'

The strange glow, the austere light which radiated from Tull's face, might have been a holy joy at the spiritual conception of exalted duty. But there was something more in him, barely hidden, a something personal and sinister, a deep of himself, an engulfing abyss. As his religious mood was fanatical and inexorable, so would his physical hate be merciless.

'Elder, I – I repent my words,' Jane faltered. The religion in her, the long habit or obedience, of humility, as well as agony of fear, spoke in her voice. 'Spare the boy!' she whispered.

'You can't save him now,' replied Tull, stridently.

Her head was bowing to the inevitable. She was grasping the truth, when suddenly there came, in inward construction, a hardening of gentle forces within her breast. Like a steel bar it was, stiffening all that had been soft and weak in her. She felt a birth in her of something new and unintelligible. Once more her strained gaze sought the sage-slopes. Jane Withersteen loved that wild and purple wilderness. In times of sorrow it had been her strength, in happiness its beauty was her continual delight. In her extremity she found herself murmuring, 'Whence cometh my help!' It was a prayer, as if forth from those lonely purple reaches and walls of red and clefts of blue might ride a fearless man, neither creed-bound nor creed-mad, who would hold up a restraining hand in the faces of her ruthless people.

The restless movements of Tull's men suddenly quieted down. Then followed a low whisper, a rustle, a sharp exclamation.

'Look!' said one, pointing to the west.

'A rider!'

Jane Withersteen wheeled and saw a horseman, silhouetted against the western sky, come riding out of the sage. He had ridden down from the left, in the golden glare of the sun, and had been unobserved till close at hand. An answer to her prayer!

'Do you know him? Does any one know him?' questioned Tull, hurriedly.

His men looked and looked, and one by one shook their heads.

'He's come from far,' said one.

'Thet's a fine hoss,' said another.

'A strange rider.'

'Huh! He wears black leather,' added a fourth.

With a wave of his hand, enjoining silence, Tull stepped forward in such a way that he concealed Venters.

The rider reined in his mount, and with a lithe forward slipping action appeared to reach the ground in one long step. It was a peculiar movement in its quickness and inasmuch that while performing it the rider did not swerve in the slightest from a square front to the group before him.

'Look!' hoarsely whispered one of Tull's companions. 'He packs two black-butted guns – low down – they're hard to see – black agin them black chaps.'

'A gun-man!' whispered another. 'Fellers, careful now about movin' your hands.'

The stranger's slow approach might have been a mere leisurely manner of gait or the cramped short steps of a rider unused to walking; yet, as well, it could have been the guarded advance of one who took no chances with men.

'Hello, stranger!' called Tull. No welcome was in this greeting, only a gruff curiosity.

The rider responded with a curt nod. The wide brim of a black sombrero cast a dark shade over his face. For a moment he closely regarded Tull and his comrades, and then, halting in his slow walk, he seemed to relax.

'Evenin', ma'am,' he said to Jane, and removed his sombrero with quaint grace.

Jane, greeting him, looked up into a face that she trusted instinctively and which riveted her attention. It had all the characteristics of the range rider's – the leanness, the red burn of the sun, and the set changelessness that came from years of silence and solitude. But it was not these which held her; rather the intensity of his gaze, a strained weariness, a piercing wistfulness of keen, gray sight, as if the man was forever looking for that which he never found. Jane's subtle woman's intuition, even in that brief instant, felt a sadness, a hungering, a secret.

'Jane Withersteen, ma'am?' he inquired.

'Yes,' she replied.

'The water here is yours?'

'Yes.'

'May I water my horse?'

'Certainly. There's the trough.'

'But mebbe if you knew who I was—' He hesitated, with his glance on the listening men. 'Mebbe you wouldn't let me water him – though I ain't askin' none for myself.'

'Stranger, it doesn't matter who you are. Water your horse. And if you are thirsty and hungry come into my house.'

'Thanks, ma'am. I can't accept for myself – but for my tired horse—'

Trampling of hoofs interrupted the rider. More restless movements on the part of Tull's men broke up the little circle, exposing the prisoner Venters.

'Mebbe I've kind of hindered somethin' – for a few moments, perhaps?' inquired the rider.

'Yes,' replied Jane Withersteen, with a throb in her voice.

She felt the drawing power of his eyes; and then she saw him look at the bound Venters, and at the men who held him, and their leader.

'In this here country all the rustlers an' thieves an' cut-throats an' gun-throwers an' all-round no-good men jest happen to be Gentiles. Ma'am, which of the no-good class does that young feller belong to?'

'He belongs to none of them. He's an honest boy.'

'You *know* that, ma'am?'

'Yes – yes.'

'Then what has he done to get tied up that way?'

His clear and distinct question, meant for Tull as well as for Jane Withersteen, stilled the restlessness and brought a momentary silence.

'Ask him,' replied Jane, her voice rising high.

The rider stepped away from her, moving out with the same slow, measured stride in which he had approached, and the fact that his action placed her wholly to one side, and him no nearer to Tull and his men, had a penetrating significance.

'Young feller, speak up,' he said to Venters.

'Here, stranger, this's none of your mix,' began Tull. 'Don't try any interference. You've been asked to drink and eat. That's more than you'd have got in any other village on the Utah border. Water your horse and be on your way.'

'Easy – easy – I ain't interferin' yet,' replied the rider. The tone of his voice had undergone a change. A different man had spoken. Where, in addressing Jane, he had been mild and gentle, now, with his first speech to Tull, he was dry, cool, biting. 'I've jest stumbled onto a queer deal. Seven Mormons all packin' guns, an' a Gentile tied with a rope, an' a woman who swears by his honesty! Queer, ain't that?'

'Queer or not, it's none of your business,' retorted Tull.

'Where I was raised a woman's word was law. I ain't quite outgrowed that yet.'
Tull fumed between amaze and anger.

'Meddler, we have a law here something different from woman's whim –
Mormon law! . . . Take care you don't transgress it.'

'To hell with your Mormon law!'

The deliberate speech marked the rider's further change, this time from kindly
interest to an awakening menace. It produced a transformation in Tull and his
companions. The leader gasped and staggered backward at a blasphemous affront
to an institution he held most sacred. The man Jerry, holding the horses, dropped
the bridles and froze in his tracks. Like posts the other men stood, watchful-eyed,
arms hanging rigid, all waiting.

'Speak up now, young man. What have you done to be roped that way?'

'It's a damned outrage!' burst out Venters. 'I've done no wrong. I've offended
this Mormon Elder by being a friend to that woman.'

'Ma'am, is it true – what he says?' asked the rider of Jane; but his quiveringly
alert eyes never left the little knot of quiet men.

'True? Yes, perfectly true,' she answered.

'Well, young man, it seems to me that bein' a friend to such a woman would be
what you wouldn't want to help an' couldn't help. . . . What's to be done to you
for it?'

'They intend to whip me. You know what that means – in Utah!'

'I reckon,' replied the rider, slowly.

With his gray glance cold on the Mormons, with the restive bit-champing of
the horses, with Jane failing to repress her mounting agitation, with Venters
standing pale and still, the tension of the moment tightened. Tull broke the spell
with a laugh, a laugh without mirth, a laugh that was only a sound betraying fear.

'Come on, men!' he called.

Jane Withersteen turned again to the rider.

'Stranger, can you do nothing to save Venters?'

'Ma'am, you ask me to save him – from your own people?'

'Ask you? I beg of you!'

'But you don't dream who you're askin?.'

'Oh, sir, I pray you – save him!'

'These are Mormons, an' I . . .'

'At – at any cost – save him. For I – I care for him!'

Tull snarled. 'You love-sick fool! Tell your secrets. There'll be a way to teach
you what you've never learned. . . . Come men, out of here!'

'Mormon, the young man stays,' said the rider.

Like a shot his voice halted Tull.

'What!'

'He stays.'

'Who'll keep him? He's my prisoner!' cried Tull, hotly. 'Stranger, again I tell
you – don't mix here. You've meddled enough. Go your way now or—'

'Listen! . . . He stays.'

Absolute certainty, beyond any shadow of doubt, breathed in the rider's low
voice.

'Who are you? We are seven here.'

The rider dropped his sombrero and made a rapid movement, singular in that it
left him somewhat crouched, arms bent and stiff, with the big black gun-sheaths
swung round to the fore.

'Lassiter!'

It was Venters's wondering, thrilling cry that bridged the fateful connection between the rider's singular position and the dreaded name.

Tull put out a groping hand. The life of his eyes dulled to the gloom with which men of his fear saw the approach of death. But death, while it hovered over him, did not descend, for the rider waited for the twitching fingers, the downward flash of hand that did not come. Tull, gathering himself together, turned to the horses, attended by his pale comrades.

CHAPTER TWO

Cottonwoods

VENTERS APPEARED TOO DEEPLY moved to speak the gratitude his face expressed. And Jane turned upon the rescuer and gripped his hands. Her smiles and tears seemingly dazed him. Presently, as something like calmness returned, she went to Lassiter's weary horse.

'I will water him myself,' she said, and she led the horse to a trough under a huge old cottonwood. With nimble fingers she loosened the bridle and removed the bit. The horse snorted and bent his head. The trough was of solid stone, hollowed out, moss-covered and green and wet and cool, and the clear brown water that fed it spouted and splashed from a wooden pipe.

'He has brought you far to-day?'

'Yes, ma'am, a matter of over sixty miles, mebbe seventy.'

'A long ride – a ride that – Ah, he is blind!'

'Yes, ma'am,' replied Lassiter.

'What blinded him?'

'Some men once roped an' tied him, an' then held white-iron close to his eyes.'

'Oh! Men? You mean devils. . . . Were they your enemies – Mormons?'

'Yes, ma'am.'

'To take revenge on a horse! Lassiter, the men of my creed are unnaturally cruel. To my everlasting sorrow I confess it. They have been driven, hated, scourged till their hearts have hardened. But we women hope and pray for the time when our men will soften.'

'Beggin' your pardon, ma'am – that time will never come.'

'Oh, it will! . . . Lassiter, do you think Mormon women wicked? Has your hand been against them, too?'

'No. I believe Mormon women are the best and noblest, the most long-sufferin', and the blindest, unhappiest women on earth.'

'Ah!' She gave him a grave, thoughtful look. 'Then you will break bread with me?'

Lassiter had no ready response, and he uneasily shifted his weight from one leg to another, and turned his sombrero round and round in his hands. 'Ma'am,' he began, presently, 'I reckon your kindness of heart makes you overlook things. Perhaps I ain't well known hereabouts, but back up North there's Mormons who'd rest uneasy in their graves at the idea of me sittin' to table with you.'

'I dare say. But – will you do it, anyway?' she asked.

'Mebbe you have a brother or relative who might drop in an' be offended, an' I wouldn't want to—'

'I've not a relative in Utah that I know of. There's no one with a right to question my actions.' She turned smilingly to Venters. 'You will come in, Bern, and Lassiter will come in. We'll eat and be merry while we may.'

'I'm only wonderin' if Tull an' his men'll raise a storm down in the village,' said Lassiter, in his last weakening stand.

'Yes, he'll raise the storm – after he has prayed,' replied Jane. 'Come.'

She led the way, with a bridle of Lassiter's horse over her arm. They entered a grove and walked down a wide path shaded by great low-branching cottonwoods. The last rays of the setting sun sent golden bars through the leaves. The grass was deep and rich, welcome contrast to sage-tired eyes. Twittering quail darted across the path, and from a tree-top somewhere a robin sang its evening song, and on the still air floated the freshness and murmur of flowing water.

The home of Jane Withersteen stood in a circle of cottonwoods, and was a flat, long, red-stone structure with a covered court in the center through which flowed a lively stream of amber-colored water. In the massive blocks of stone and heavy timbers and solid doors and shutters showed the hand of a man who had built against pillage and time; and in the flowers and mosses lining the stone-bedded stream, in the bright colors of rugs and blankets on the court floor, and the cozy corner with hammock and books, and the clean-linened table, showed the grace of a daughter who lived for happiness and the day at hand.

Jane turned Lassiter's horse loose in the thick grass. 'You will want him to be near you,' she said, 'or I'd have him taken to the alfalfa fields.' At her call appeared women who began at once to bustle about, hurrying to and fro, setting the table. Then Jane, excusing herself, went within.

She passed through a huge low-ceiled chamber, like the inside of a fort, and into a smaller one where a bright wood-fire blazed in an old open fireplace, and from this into her own room. It had the same comfort as was manifested in the home-like outer court; moreover, it was warm and rich in soft hues.

Seldom did Jane Withersteen enter her room without looking into her mirror. She knew she loved the reflection of that beauty which since early childhood she had never been allowed to forget. Her relatives and friends, and later a horde of Mormon and Gentile suitors, had fanned the flame of natural vanity in her. So that at twenty-eight she scarcely thought at all of her wonderful influence for good in the little community where her father had left her practically its beneficent landlord; but cared most for the dream and the assurance and the allurement of her beauty. This time, however, she gazed into her glass with more than the usual happy motive, without the usual slight conscious smile. For she was thinking of more than the desire to be fair in her own eyes, in those of her friend; she wondered if she were to seem fair in the eyes of this Lassiter, this man whose name had crossed the long, wild brakes of stone and plains of sage, this gentle-voiced, sad-faced man who was a hater and a killer of Mormons. It was not now her usual half-conscious vain obsession that actuated her as she hurriedly changed her riding-dress to one of white, and then looked long at the stately form with its gracious contours, at the fair face with its strong chin and full firm lips, at the dark-blue, proud, and passionate eyes.

'If by some means I can keep him here a few days, a week – he will never kill another Mormon,' she mused. 'Lassiter! . . . I shudder when I think of that name, of him. But when I look at the man I forget who he is – I almost like him. I remember only that he saved Bern. He has suffered. I wonder what it was – did he love a Mormon woman once? How splendidly he championed us poor misunderstood souls! Somehow he knows – much.'

Jane Withersteen joined her guests and bade them to her board. Dismissing her woman, she waited upon them with her own hands. It was a bountiful supper and a strange company. On her right sat the ragged and half-starved Venters; and though blind eyes could have seen what he counted for in the sum of her happiness, yet he looked the gloomy outcast his allegiance had made him, and about him there was the shadow of the ruin presaged by Tull. On her left sat the black-leather-garbed Lassiter looking like a man in a dream. Hunger was not with him, nor composure, nor speech, and when he twisted in frequent unquiet movements the heavy guns that he had not removed knocked against the table-legs. If it had been otherwise possible to forget the presence of Lassiter those telling little jars would have rendered it unlikely. And Jane Withersteen talked and smiled and laughed with all the dazzling play of lips and eyes that a beautiful, daring woman could summon to her purpose.

When the meal ended, and the men pushed back their chairs, she leaned closer to Lassiter and looked square into his eyes.

'Why did you come to Cottonwoods?'

Her question seemed to break a spell. The rider arose as if he had just remembered himself and had tarried longer than his wont.

'Ma'am, I have hunted all over southern Utah and Nevada for – somethin'. An' through your name I learned where to find it – here in Cottonwoods.'

'My name! Oh, I remember. You did know my name when you spoke first. Well, tell me where you heard it and from whom?'

'At the little village – Glaze, I think it's called – some fifty miles or more west of here. An' I heard it from a Gentile, a rider who said you'd know where to tell me to find—'

'What?' she demanded, imperiously, as Lassiter broke off.

'Milly Erne's grave,' he answered low, and the words came with a wrench.

Venters wheeled in his chair to regard Lassiter in amazement, and Jane slowly raised herself in white, still wonder.

'Milly Erne's grave?' she echoed, in a whisper. 'What do you know of Milly Erne, my best-beloved friend – who died in my arms? What were you to her?'

'Did I claim to be anythin'?' he inquired. 'I know people – relatives – who have long wanted to know where she's buried. That's all.'

'Relatives? She never spoke of relatives, except a brother who was shot in Texas. Lassiter, Milly Erne's grave is in a secret burying-ground on my property.'

'Will you take me there? . . . You'll be offendin' Mormons worse than by breakin' bread with me.'

'Indeed yes, but I'll do it. Only we must go unseen. Tomorrow perhaps.'

'Thank you, Jane Withersteen,' replied the rider, and he bowed to her and stepped backward out of the court.

'Will you not stay – sleep under my roof?' she asked.

'No, ma'am, an' thanks again. I never sleep indoors. An' even if I did there's that gatherin' storm in the village below. No, no. I'll go to the sage. I hope you won't suffer none for your kindness to me.'

'Lassiter,' said Venters, with a half-bitter laugh, 'my bed, too, is the sage. Perhaps we may meet out there.'

'Mebbe so. But the sage is wide an' I won't be near. Good night.'

At Lassiter's low whistle the black horse whinnied, and carefully picked his blind way out of the grove. The rider did not bridle him, but walked beside him,

leading him by touch of hand, and together they passed slowly into the shade of
the cottonwoods.

'Jane, I must be off soon,' said Venters. 'Give me my guns. If I'd had my guns—'

'Either my friend or the Elder of my church would be lying dead,' she
interposed.

'Tull would be – surely.'

'Oh, you fierce-blooded, savage youth! Can't I teach you forebearance, mercy?
Bern, it's divine to forgive your enemies. "Let not the sun go down upon the
wrath." '

'Hush! Talk to me no more of mercy or religion – after today. Today this strange
coming of Lassiter left me still a man, and now I'll die a man! . . . Give me my
guns.'

Silently she went into the house, to return with a heavy cartridge-belt and gun-
filled sheath and a long rifle; these she handed to him, and as he buckled on the
belt she stood before him in silent eloquence.

'Jane,' he said, in gentler voice, 'don't look so. I'm not going out to murder your
churchman. I'll try to avoid him and all his men. But can't you see I've reached the
end of my rope? Jane, you're a wonderful woman. Never was there a woman so
unselfish and good. Only you're blind in one way. . . . Listen!'

From behind the grove came the clicking sound of horses in a rapid trot.

'Some of your riders,' he continued. 'It's getting time for the night shift. Let us
go out to the bench in the grove and talk there.'

It was still daylight in the open, but under the spreading cottonwoods shadows
were obscuring the lanes. Venters drew Jane off from one of these into a shrub-
lined trail, just wide enough for the two to walk abreast, and in a roundabout way
led her far from the house to a knoll on the edge of the grove. Here in a secluded
nook was a bench from which, through an opening in the tree-tops, could be seen
the sage slope and the wall of rock and the dim lines of cañons. Jane had not
spoken since Venters had shocked her with his first harsh speech; but all the way
she had clung to his arm, and now, as he stopped and laid his rifle against the
bench, she still clung to him.

'Jane, I'm afraid I must leave you.'

'Bern!' she cried.

'Yes, it looks that way. My position is not a happy one – I can't feel right – I've
lost all—'

'I'll give you anything you—'

'Listen, please. When I say loss I don't mean what you think. I mean loss of
good-will, good name – that which would have enabled me to stand up in this
village without bitterness. Well, it's too late. . . . Now, as to the future, I think
you'd do best to give me up. Tull is implacable. You ought to see from his
intention today that – But you can't see. Your blindness – your damned religion!
. . . Jane, forgive me – I'm sore within and something rankles. Well, I fear that
invisible hand will turn its hidden work to your ruin.'

'Invisible hand? Bern!'

'I mean your Bishop.' Venters said it deliberately and would not release her as
she started back. 'He's the law. The edict went forth to ruin me. Well, look at me!
It'll now go forth to compel you to the will of the Church.'

'You wrong Bishop Dyer. Tull is hard, I know. But then he has been in love
with me for years.'

'Oh, your faith and your excuses! You can't see what I know – and if you did see
it you'd not admit it to save your life. That's the Mormon of you. These elders and

bishops will do absolutely any deed to go on building up the power and wealth of their church, their empire. Think of what they've done to the Gentiles here, to me – think of Milly Erne's fate!'

'What do you know of her story?'

'I know enough – all, perhaps, except the name of the Mormon who brought her here. But I must stop this kind of talk.'

She pressed his hand in response. He helped her to a seat beside him on the bench. And he respected a silence that he divined was full of woman's deep emotion, beyond his understanding.

It was the moment when the last ruddy rays of the sunset brightened momentarily before yielding to twilight. And for Venters the outlook before him was in some sense similar to a feeling of his future, and with searching eyes he studied the beautiful purple, barren waste of sage. Here was the unknown and the perilous. The whole scene impressed Venters as a wild, austere, and mighty manifestation of nature. And as it somehow reminded him of his prospect in life, so it suddenly resembled the woman near him, only in her there were greater beauty and peril, a mystery more unsolvable, and something nameless that numbed his heart and dimmed his eye.

'Look! A rider!' exclaimed Jane, breaking the silence. 'Can that be Lassiter?'

Venters moved his glance once more to the west. A horseman showed dark on the sky-line, then merged into the color of the sage.

'It might be. But I think not – that fellow was coming in. One of your riders, more likely. Yes, I see him clearly now. And there's another.'

'I see them, too.'

'Jane, your riders seem as many as the bunches of sage. I ran into five yesterday 'way down near the trail to Deception Pass. They were with the white herd.'

'You still go to that cañon? Bern, I wish you wouldn't. Oldring and his rustlers live somewhere down there.'

'Well, what of that?'

'Tull has already hinted of your frequent trips into Deception Pass.'

'I know.' Venters uttered a short laugh. 'He'll make a rustler of me next. But, Jane, there's no water for fifty miles after I leave here, and the nearest is in the cañon. I must drink and water my horse. There! I see more riders. They are going out.'

'The red herd is on the slope, towards the Pass.'

Twilight was fast falling. A group of horsemen crossed the dark line of low ground to become more distinct as they climbed the slope. The silence broke to a clear call from an incoming rider, and, almost like the peal of a hunting-horn, floated back the answer. The outgoing riders moved swiftly, came sharply into sight as they topped a ridge to show wild and black above the horizon, and then passed down, dimming into the purple of the sage.

'I hope they don't meet Lassiter,' said Jane.

'So do I,' replied Venters. 'By this time the riders of the night shift know what happened today. But Lassiter will likely keep out of their way.'

'Bern, who is Lassiter? He's only a name to me – a terrible name.'

'Who is he? I don't know, Jane. Nobody I ever met knows him. He talks a little like a Texan, like Milly Erne. Did you note that?'

'Yes. How strange of him to know of her! And she lived here ten years and has been dead two. Bern, what do you know of Lassiter? Tell me what he has done – why you spoke of him to Tull – threatening to become another Lassiter yourself?'

'Jane, I only heard things, rumors, stories, most of which I disbelieved. At

Glaze his name was known, but none of the riders or ranchers I knew there ever met him. At Stone Bridge I never heard him mentioned. But at Sterling and villages north of there he was spoken of often. I've never been in a village which he had been known to visit. There were many conflicting stories about him and his doings. Some said he had shot up this and that Mormon village, and others denied it. I'm inclined to believe he has, and you know how Mormons hide the truth. But there was one feature about Lassiter upon which all agree – that he was what riders in this country call a gunman. He's a man with marvelous quickness and accuracy in the use of a Colt. And now that I've seen him I know more. Lassiter was born without fear. I watched him with eyes which saw him my friend. I'll never forget the moment I recognized him from what had been told me of his crouch before the draw. It was then I yelled his name. I believe that yell saved Tull's life. At any rate, I know this, between Tull and death then there was not the breadth of the littlest hair. If he or any of his men had moved a finger downward . . .'

Venters left his meaning unspoken, but at the suggestion Jane shuddered.

The pale afterglow in the west darkened with the merging of twilight into night. The sage now spread out black and gloomy. One dim star glimmered in the southwest sky. The sound of trotting horses had ceased, and there was silence broken only by a faint, dry pattering of cottonwood leaves in the soft night wind.

Into this peace and calm suddenly broke the high-keyed yelp of a coyote, and from far off in the darkness came the faint answering note of a trailing mate.

'Hello! the sage-dogs are barking,' said Venters.

'I don't like to hear them,' replied Jane. 'At night, sometimes, when I lie awake, listening to the long mourn or breaking bark or wild howl, I think of you asleep somewhere in the sage, and my heart aches.'

'Jane, you couldn't listen to sweeter music, nor could I have a better bed.'

'Just think! Men like Lassiter and you have no home, no comfort, no rest, no place to lay your weary heads. Well! . . . Let us be patient. Tull's anger may cool, and time may help us. You might do some service to the village – who can tell? Suppose you discovered the long-unknown hiding place of Oldring and his band, and told it to my riders? That would disarm Tull's ugly hints and put you in favor. For years my riders have trailed the tracks of stolen cattle. You know as well as I how dearly we've paid for our ranges in this wild country. Oldring drives our cattle down into that network of deceiving cañons, and somewhere far to the north or east he drives them up and out to Utah markets. If you will spend time in Deception Pass try to find the trails.'

'Jane, I've thought of that. I'll try.'

'I must go now. And it hurts, for now I'll never be sure of seeing you again. But tomorrow, Bern?'

'Tomorrow surely. I'll watch for Lassiter and ride in with him.'

'Good night.'

Then she left him and moved away, a white, gliding shape that soon vanished in the shadows.

Venters waited until the faint slam of a door assured him she had reached the house; and then, taking up his rifle, he noiselessly slipped through the bushes, down the knoll, and on under the dark trees to the edge of the grove. The sky was now turning from gray to blue; stars had begun to lighten the earlier blackness; and from the wide flat sweep before him blew a cool wind, fragrant with the breath of sage. Keeping close to the edge of the cottonwoods, he went swiftly and silently westward. The grove was long, and he had not reached the end when he heard something that brought him to a halt. Low padded thuds told him horses were coming his way. He sank down in the gloom, waiting, listening. Much before he had expected, judging from sound, to his amazement he descried horsemen near at hand. They were riding along the border of the sage, and instantly he knew the hoofs of the horses were muffled. Then the pale starlight afforded him indistinct sight of the riders. But his eyes were keen and used to the dark, and by peering closely he recognized the huge bulk and black-bearded visage of Oldring and the lithe, supple form of the rustler's lieutenant, a masked rider. They passed on; the darkness swallowed them. Then, farther out on the sage, a dark, compact body of horsemen went by, almost without sound, almost like specters, and they, too, melted into the night.

CHAPTER THREE

Amber Spring

NO UNUSUAL CIRCUMSTANCE was it for Oldring and some of his men to visit Cottonwoods in the broad light of day, but for him to prowl about in the dark with the hoofs of his horses muffled meant that mischief was brewing. Moreover, to Venters the presence of the masked rider with Oldring seemed especially ominous. For about this man there was mystery; he seldom rode through the village, and when he did ride through it was swiftly; riders seldom met him by day on the sage; but wherever he rode there always followed deeds as dark and mysterious as the mask he wore. Oldring's band did not confine themselves to the rustling of cattle.

Venters lay low in the shade of the cottonwoods, pondering this chance meeting, and not for many moments did he consider it safe to move on. Then, with sudden impulse, he turned the other way and went back along the grove. When he reached the path leading to Jane's home he decided to go down to the village. So he hurried onward, with quick soft steps. Once beyond the grove he entered the one and only street. It was wide, lined with tall poplars, and under each row of trees, inside the foot-path, were ditches where ran the water from Jane Withersteen's spring.

Between the trees twinkled lights of cottage candles, and far down flared bright windows of the village stores. When Venters got closer to these he saw knots of men standing together in earnest conversation. The usual lounging on the corners and benches and steps was not in evidence. Keeping in the shadow, Venters went closer and closer until he could hear voices. But he could not distinguish what was said. He recognized many Mormons, and looked hard for Tull and his men, but looked in vain. Venters concluded that the rustlers had not passed along the village street. No doubt these earnest men were discussing Lassiter's coming. But Venters felt positive that Tull's intention toward himself that day had not been and would not be revealed.

So Venters, seeing there was little for him to learn, began retracing his steps. The church was dark, Bishop Dyer's home next to it was also dark, and likewise

Tull's cottage. Upon almost any night at this hour there would be lights here, and Venters marked the unusual omission.

As he was about to pass out of the street to skirt the grove, he once more slunk down at the sound of trotting horses. Presently he descried two mounted men riding toward him. He hugged the shadow of a tree. Again the starlight, brighter now, aided him, and he made out Tull's stalwart figure, and beside him the short, frog-like shape of the rider Jerry. They were silent, and they rode on to disappear.

Venters went his way with busy, gloomy mind, revolving events of the day, trying to reckon those brooding in the night. His thoughts overwhelmed him. Up in that dark grove dwelt a woman who had been his friend. And he skulked about her home, gripping a gun stealthily as an Indian, a man without place or people or purpose. Above her hovered the shadow of grim, hidden, secret power. No queen could have given more royally out of a bounteous store than Jane Withersteen gave her people, and likewise to those unfortunates whom her people hated. She asked only the divine right of all women – freedom; to love and to live as her heart willed. And yet prayer and her hope were vain.

'For years I've seen a storm clouding over her and the village of Cottonwoods,' muttered Venters, as he strode on. 'Soon it'll burst. I don't like the prospect.' That night the villagers whispered in the street – and night-riding rustlers muffled horses – and Tull was at work in secret – and out there in the sage hid a man who meant something terrible – Lassiter!

Venters passed the black cottonwoods, and, entering the sage, climbed the gradual slope. He kept his direction in line with a western star. From time to time he stopped to listen and heard only the usual familiar bark of coyote and sweep of wind and rustle of sage. Presently a low jumble of rocks loomed up darkly somewhat to his right, and, turning that way, he whistled softly. Out of the rocks glided a dog that leaped and whined about him. He climbed over rough, broken rock, picking his way carefully, and then went down. Here it was darker, and sheltered from the wind. A white object guided him. It was another dog, and this one was asleep, curled up between a saddle and a pack. The animal awoke and thumped his tail in greeting. Venters placed the saddle for a pillow, rolled in his blankets, with his face upward to the stars. The white dog snuggled close to him. The other whined and pattered a few yards to the rise of ground and there crouched on guard. And in that wild covert Venters shut his eyes under the great white stars and intense vaulted blue, bitterly comparing their loneliness to his own, and fell asleep.

When he awoke, day had dawned and all about him was bright steel-gray. The air had a cold tang. Arising, he greeted the fawning dogs and stretched his cramped body, and then, gathering together bunches of dead sage sticks, he lighted a fire. Strips of dried beef held to the blaze for a moment served him and the dogs. He drank from a canteen. There was nothing else in his outfit; he had grown used to a scant fare. Then he sat over the fire, palms outspread, and waited. Waiting had been his chief occupation for months, and he scarcely knew what he waited for, unless it was the passing of the hours. But now he sensed action in the immediate present; the day promised another meeting with Lassiter and Jane, perhaps news of the rustlers; on the morrow he meant to take the trail to Deception Pass.

And while he waited he talked to his dogs. He called them Ring and Whitie; they were sheep-dogs, half collie, half deer-hound, superb in build, perfectly trained. It seemed that in his fallen fortunes these dogs understood the nature of their value to him, and governed their affection and faithfulness accordingly.

Whitie watched him with somber eyes of love, and Ring, crouched on the little rise of ground above, kept tireless guard. When the sun rose, the white dog took the place of the other, and Ring went to sleep at his master's feet.

By and by Venters rolled up his blankets and tied them and his meager pack together, then climbed out to look for his horse. He saw him, presently, a little way off in the sage, and went to fetch him. In that country, where every rider boasted of a fine mount and was eager for a race, where thoroughbreds dotted the wonderful grazing ranges, Venters rode a horse that was sad proof of his misfortunes.

Then, with his back against a stone, Venters faced the east, and stick in hand and idle blade, he waited. The glorious sunlight filled the valley with purple fire. Before him, to left, to right, waving, rolling, sinking, rising, like low swells of a purple sea, stretched the sage. Out of the grove of cottonwoods, a green patch on the purple, gleamed the dull red of Jane Withersteen's old stone house. And from these extended the wide green of the village gardens and orchards marked by the graceful poplars; and farther down shone the deep, dark richness of the alfalfa fields. Numberless red and black and white dots speckled the sage, and these were cattle and horses.

So, watching and waiting, Venters let the time wear away. At length he saw a horse rise above a ridge, and he knew it to be Lassiter's black. Climbing to the highest rock, so that he would show against the skyline, he stood and waved his hat. The almost instant turning of Lassiter's horse attested to the quickness of that rider's eye. Then Venters climbed down, saddled his horse, tied on his pack, and, with a word to his dogs, was about to ride out to meet Lassiter, when he concluded to wait for him there, on higher ground, where the outlook was commanding.

It had been long since Venters had experienced friendly greeting from a man. Lassiter's warmed in him something that had grown cold from neglect. And when he had returned it, with a strong grip of the iron hand that held his, and met the gray eyes, he knew that Lassiter and he were to be friends.

'Venters, let's talk awhile before we go down there,' said Lassiter, slipping his bridle. 'I ain't in no hurry. Them's sure fine dogs you've got.' With a rider's eye he took in the points of Venters's horse, but did not speak his thought. 'Well, did anythin' come off after I left you last night?'

Venters told him about the rustlers.

'I was snug hid in the sage,' replied Lassiter, 'an' didn't see or hear no one. Oldrin's got a high hand here, I reckon. It's no news up in Utah how he holes in cañons an' leaves no track.' Lassiter was silent a moment. 'Me an' Oldrin' wasn't exactly strangers some years back when he drove cattle into Bostil's Ford, at the head of the Rio Virgin. But he got harassed there an' now he drives some place else.'

'Lassiter, you knew him? Tell me, is he Mormon or Gentile?'

'I can't say. I've knowed Mormons who pretended to be Gentiles.'

'No Mormon ever pretended that unless he was a rustler,' declared Venters.

'Mebbe so.'

'It's a hard country for any one, but hardest for Gentiles. Did you ever know or hear of a Gentile prospering in a Mormon community?'

'I never did.'

'Well, I want to get out of Utah. I've a mother living in Illinois. I want to go home. It's eight years now.'

The older man's sympathy moved Venters to tell his story. He had left Quincy, run off to seek his fortune in the gold fields, had never gotten any farther than Salt

Lake City, wandered here and there as helper, teamster, shepherd, and drifted southward over the divide and across the barrens and up the rugged plateau through the passes to the last border settlements. Here he became a rider of the sage, had stock of his own, and for a time prospered, until chance threw him in the employ of Jane Withersteen.

'Lassiter, I needn't tell you the rest.'

'Well, it'd be no news to me. I know Mormons. I've seen their women's strange love an' patience an' sacrifice an' silence an' what I call madness for their idea of God. An' over against that I've seen the tricks of the men. They work hand in hand, all together, an' in the dark. No man can hold out against them, unless he takes to packin' guns. For Mormons are slow to kill. That's the only good I ever seen in their religion. Venters, take this from me, these Mormons ain't just right in their minds. Else could a Mormon marry one woman when he already had a wife, an' call it duty?'

'Lassiter, you think as I think,' returned Venters.

'How'd it come then that you never throwed a gun on Tull or some of them?' inquired the rider, curiously.

'Jane pleaded with me, begged me to be patient, to overlook. She even took my guns from me. I lost all before I knew it,' replied Venters, with the red color in his face. 'But, Lassiter, listen. Out of the wreck I saved a Winchester, two Colts, and plenty of shells. I packed these down into Deception Pass. There, almost every day for six months, I have practiced with my rifle till the barrel burnt my hands. Practiced the draw – the firing of a Colt, hour after hour!'

'Now that's interestin' to me,' said Lassiter, with a quick uplift of his head and a concentration of his gray gaze on Venters. 'Could you throw a gun before you began that practicin'?'

'Yes. And now . . .' Venters made a lightning-swift movement.

Lassiter smiled, and then his bronzed eyelids narrowed till his eyes seemed mere gray slits. 'You'll kill Tull!' He did not question; he affirmed.

'I promised Jane Withersteen I'd try to avoid Tull. I'll keep my word. But sooner or later Tull and I will meet. As I feel now, if he even looks at me I'll draw!'

'I reckon so. There'll be hell down there, presently.' He paused a moment and flicked a sage-brush with his quirt. 'Venters, seein' as you're considerable worked up, tell me Milly Erne's story.'

Venters's agitation stilled to the trace of suppressed eagerness in Lassiter's query.

'Milly Erne's story? Well, Lassiter, I'll tell you what I know. Milly Erne had been in Cottonwoods years when I first arrived there, and most of what I tell you happened before my arrival. I got to know her pretty well. She was a slip of a woman, and crazy on religion. I conceived an idea that I never mentioned – I thought she was at heart more Gentile than Mormon. But she passed as a Mormon, and certainly she had the Mormon woman's locked lips. You know, in every Mormon village there are women who seem mysterious to us, but about Milly there was more than the ordinary mystery. When she came to Cottonwoods she had a beautiful little girl whom she loved passionately. Milly was not known openly in Cottonwoods as a Mormon wife. That she really was a Mormon wife I have no doubt. Perhaps the Mormon's other wife or wives would not acknowledge Milly. Such things happen in these villages. Mormon wives wear yokes, but they get jealous. Well, whatever had brought Milly to this country – love or madness of religion – she repented of it. She gave up teaching the village school. She quit the church. And she began to fight Mormon upbringing for her baby girl. Then the

Mormons put on the screws – slowly, as is their way. At last the child disappeared. Lost, was the report. The child was stolen, I know that. So do you. That wrecked Milly Erne. But she lived on in hope. She became a slave. She worked her heart and soul and life out to get back her child. She never heard of it again. Then she sank. . . . I can see her now, a frail thing, so transparent you could almost look through her – white like ashes – and her eyes! . . . Her eyes have always haunted me. She had one real friend – Jane Withersteen. But Jane couldn't mend a broken heart, and Milly died.'

For moments Lassiter did not speak, or turn his head.

'The man!' he exclaimed, presently, in husky accents.

'I haven't the slightest idea who the Mormon was,' replied Venters; 'nor has any Gentile in Cottonwoods.'

'Does Jane Withersteen know?'

'Yes. But a red-hot running iron couldn't burn that name out of her!'

Without further speech Lassiter started off, walking his horse, and Venters followed with his dogs. Half a mile down the slope they entered a luxuriant growth of willows, and soon came into an open space carpeted with grass like deep green velvet. The rushing of water and singing of birds filled their ears. Venters led his comrade to a shady bower and showed him Amber Spring. It was a magnificent outburst of clear, amber water pouring from a dark, stone-lined hole. Lassiter knelt and drank, lingered there to drink again. He made no comment, but Venters did not need words. Next to his horse a rider of the sage loved a spring. And this spring was the most beautiful and remarkable known to the upland riders of southern Utah. It was the spring that made old Withersteen a feudal lord and now enabled his daughter to return the toll which her father had exacted from the toilers of the sage.

The spring gushed forth in a swirling torrent, and leaped down joyously to make its swift way along a willow-skirted channel. Moss and ferns and lilies overhung its green banks. Except for the rough-hewn stones that held and directed the water, this willow thicket and glade had been left as nature had made it.

Below were artificial lakes, three in number, one above the other in banks of raised earth; and round about them rose the lofty green-foliated shafts of poplar trees. Ducks dotted the glassy surface of the lakes; a blue heron stood motionless on a water-gate; kingfishers darted with shrieking flight along the shady banks; a white hawk sailed above; and from the trees and shrubs came the song of robins and catbirds. It was all in strange contrast to the endless slopes of lonely sage and the wild rock environs beyond. Venters thought of the woman who loved the birds and the green of the leaves and the murmur of water.

Next on the slope, just below the third and largest lake, were corrals and a wide stone barn and open sheds and coops and pens. Here were clouds of dust, and cracking sounds of hoofs, and romping colts and hee-hawing burros. Neighing horses trampled to the corral fences. And from the little windows of the barn projected bobbing heads of bays and blacks and sorrels. When the two men entered the immense barnyard, from all around the din increased. This welcome, however, was not seconded by the several men and boys who vanished on sight.

Venters and Lassiter were turning toward the house when Jane appeared in the lane leading a horse. In riding-skirt and blouse she seemed to have lost some of her statuesque proportions, and looked more like a girl rider than the mistress of Withersteen. She was bright, smiling, and her greeting was warmly cordial.

'Good news,' she announced. 'I've been to the village. All is quiet. I expected –

I don't know what. But there's no excitement. And Tull has ridden out on his way to Glaze.'

'Tull gone?' inquired Venters, with surprise. He was wondering what could have taken Tull away. Was it to avoid another meeting with Lassiter that he went? Could it have any connection with the probable nearness of Oldring and his gang?

'Gone, yes, thank goodness,' replied Jane. 'Now I'll have peace for a while. Lassiter, I want you to see my horses. You are a rider, and you must be a judge of horseflesh. Some of mine have Arabian blood. My father got his best strain in Nevada from Indians who claimed their horses were bred down from the original stock left by the Spaniards.'

'Well, ma'am, the one you've been ridin' takes my eye,' said Lassiter, as he walked round the racy, clean-limbed, and fine-pointed roan.

'Where are the boys?' she asked, looking about. 'Jerd, Paul, where are you? Here, bring out the horses.'

The sound of dropping bars inside the barn was the signal for the horses to jerk their heads in the windows, to snort and stamp. Then they came pounding out of the door, a file of thoroughbreds, to plunge about the barnyard, heads and tails up, manes flying. They halted afar off, squared away to look, came slowly forward with whinnies for their mistress, and doubtful snorts for the strangers and their horses.

'Come – come – come,' called Jane, holding out her hands. 'Why Bells – Wrangle, where are your manners? Come, Black Star – come, Night. Ah, you beauties! My racers of the sage!'

Only two came up to her; those she called Night and Black Star. Venters never looked at them without delight. The first was soft dead black, the other glittering black, and they were perfectly matched in size, both being high and long-bodied, wide through the shoulders, with lithe, powerful legs. That they were a woman's pets showed in the gloss of skin, the fineness of mane. It showed, too, in the light of big eyes and the gentle reach of eagerness.

'I never seen their like,' was Lassiter's encomium, 'an' in my day I've seen a sight of horses. Now, ma'am, if you was wantin' to make a long an' fast ride across the sage – say to elope—'

Lassiter ended there with dry humor, yet behind that was meaning. Jane blushed and made arch eyes at him.

'Take care, Lassiter, I might think that a proposal,' she replied, gaily. 'It's dangerous to propose elopement to a Mormon woman. Well, I was expecting you. Now will be a good hour to show you Milly Erne's grave. The day-riders have gone, and the night-riders haven't come in. Bern, what do you make of that? Need I worry? You know I have to be made to worry.'

'Well, it's not usual for the night shift to ride in so late,' replied Venters, slowly, and his glance sought Lassiter's. 'Cattle are usually quiet after dark. Still, I've known even a coyote to stampede your white herd.'

'I refuse to borrow trouble. Come,' said Jane.

They mounted, and, with Jane in the lead, rode down the lane, and, turning off into a cattle trail, proceeded westward. Venters's dogs trotted behind them. On this side of the ranch the outlook was different from that on the other; the immediate foreground was rough and the sage more rugged and less colorful; there were no dark-blue lines of cañons to hold the eye, nor any up-rearing rock walls. It was a long roll and slope into gray obscurity. Soon Jane left the trail and rode into the sage, and presently she dismounted and threw her bridle. The men did likewise. Then, on foot, they followed her, coming out at length on the rim of a low escarpment. She passed by several little ridges of earth to halt before a faintly defined mound. It lay in the shade of a sweeping sage-brush close to the edge of the promontory; and a rider could have jumped his horse over it without recognizing a grave.

'Here!'

She looked sad as she spoke, but she offered no explanation for the neglect of an unmarked, uncared-for grave. There was a little bunch of pale, sweet lavender daisies, doubtless planted there by Jane.

'I only come here to remember and to pray,' she said. 'But I leave no trail!'

A grave in the sage! How lonely this resting-place of Milly Erne! The cottonwoods or the alfalfa fields were not in sight, nor was there any rock or ridge or cedar to lend contrast to the monotony. Gray slopes, tinging the purple, barren and wild, with the wind waving the sage, swept away to the dim horizon.

Lassiter looked at the grave and then out into space. At that moment he seemed a figure of bronze.

Jane touched Venters's arm and led him back to the horses.

'Bern!' cried Jane, when they were out of hearing. 'Suppose Lassiter were Milly's husband – the father of that little girl lost so long ago!'

'It might be, Jane. Let us ride on. If he wants to see us again he'll come.'

So they mounted and rode out to the cattle trail and began to climb. From the height of the ridge, where they had started down, Venters looked back. He did not see Lassiter, but his glance, drawn irresistibly farther out on the gradual slope, caught sight of a moving cloud of dust.

'Hello, a rider!'

'Yes, I see,' said Jane.

'That fellow's riding hard. Jane, there's something wrong.'

'Oh yes, there must be. . . . How he rides!'

The horse disappeared in the sage, and then puffs of dust marked his course.

'He's short-cut on us – he's making straight for the corrals.'

Venters and Jane galloped their steeds and reined in at the turning of the lane. This lane led down to the right of the grove. Suddenly into its lower entrance flashed a bay horse. Then Venters caught the fast rhythmic beat of pounding hoofs. Soon his keen eyes recognized the swing of the rider in his saddle.

'It's Judkins, your Gentile rider!' he cried. 'Jane, when Judkins rides like that it means hell!'

CHAPTER FOUR

Deception Pass

THE RIDER THUNDERED UP and almost threw his foam-flecked horse in the sudden stop. He was of giant form, and with fearless eyes.

'Judkins, you're all bloody!' cried Jane, in affright. 'Oh, you've been shot!'

'Nothin' much, Miss Withersteen. I got a nick in the shoulder. I'm some wet an' the hoss's been throwin' lather, so all this ain't blood.'

'What's up?' queried Venters, sharply.

'Rustlers sloped off with the red herd.'

'Where are my riders?' demanded Jane.

'Miss Withersteen, I was alone all night with the herd. At daylight this mornin' the rustlers rode down. They began to shoot at me on sight. They chased me hard an' far, burnin' powder all the time, but I got away.'

'Jud, they meant to kill you,' delcared Venters.

'Now I wonder,' returned Judkins. 'They wanted me bad. An' it ain't regular for rustlers to waste time chasin' one rider.'

'Thank Heaven you got away,' said Jane. 'But my riders – where are they?'

'I don't know. The night-riders weren't there last night when I rode down, an' this mornin' I met no day-riders.'

'Judkins! Bern, they've been set upon – killed by Oldring's men!'

'I don't think so,' replied Venters, decidedly. 'Jane, your riders haven't gone out in the sage.'

'Bern, what do you mean?' Jane Withersteen turned deathly pale.

'You remember what I said about the unseen hand?'

'Oh! . . . Impossible!'

'I hope so. But I fear—' Venters finished, with a shake of his head.

'Bern, you're bitter; but that's only natural. We'll wait to see what's happened to my riders. Judkins, come to the house with me. Your wound must be attended to.'

'Jane, I'll find out where Oldring drives the herd,' vowed Venters.

'No, no! Bern, don't risk it now – when the rustlers are in such shooting mood.'

'I'm going. Jud, how many cattle in that red herd?'

'Twenty-five hundred head.'

'Whew! What on earth can Oldring do with so many cattle? Why, a hundred head is a big steal. I've got to find out.'

'Don't go,' implored Jane.

'Bern, you want a hoss thet can run. Miss Withersteen, if it's not too bold of me to advise, make him take a fast hoss or don't let him go.'

'Yes, yes, Judkins. He must ride a horse that can't be caught. Which one – Black Star – Night?'

'Jane, I won't take either,' said Venters, emphatically. 'I wouldn't risk losing one of your favorites.'

'Wrangle, then?'

'Thet's the hoss,' replied Judkins. 'Wrangle can outrun Black Star an' Night. You'd never believe it, Miss Withersteen, but I know. Wrangle's the biggest an' fastest hoss on the sage.'

'Oh no, Wrangle can't beat Black Star. But, Bern, take Wrangle, if you will go. Ask Jerd for anything you need. Oh, be watchful, careful. . . . God speed you!'

She clasped his hand, turned quickly away, and went down the lane with the rider.

Venters rode to the bar, and, leaping off, shouted for Jerd. The boy came running. Venters sent him for meat, bread, and dried fruits, to be packed in saddle-bags. His own horse he turned loose into the nearest corral. Then he went for Wrangle. The giant sorrel had earned his name for a trait the opposite of amiability. He came readily out of the barn, but once in the yard he broke from Venters, and plunged about with ears laid back. Venters had to rope him, and then he kicked down a section of fence, stood on his hind legs, crashed down and fought the rope. Jerd returned to lend a hand.

'Wrangle don't git enough work,' said Jerd, as the big saddle went on. 'He's unruly when he's corralled, an' wants to run. Wait till he smells the sage!'

'Jerd, this horse is an iron-jawed devil. I never straddled him but once. Run? Say, he's swift as wind!'

When Venters's boot touched the stirrup the sorrel bolted, giving him the rider's flying mount. The swing of this fiery horse recalled to Venters days that were not really long past, when he rode into the sage as the leader of Jane Witherseen's riders. Wrangle pulled hard on a tight rein. He galloped out of the lane, down the shaky border of the grove, and hauled up at the watering-trough, where he pranced and champed his bit. Venters got off and filled his canteen while the horse drank. The dogs, Ring and Whitie, came trotting up for their drink. Then Venters remounted and turned Wrangle toward the sage.

A wide, white trail wound away down the slope. One keen, sweeping glance told Venters that there was neither man nor horse nor steer within the limit of his vision, unless they were lying down in the sage. Ring loped in the lead and Whitie loped in the rear. Wrangle settled gradually into an easy swinging canter, and Venters's thoughts, now that the rush and flurry of the start were past, and the long miles stretched before him, reverted to a calm reckoning of late singular coincidences.

There was the night ride of Tull's, which, viewed in the light of subsequent events, had a look of his covert machinations; Oldring and his Masked Rider and his rustlers riding muffled horses; the report that Tull had ridden out that morning with his man Jerry on the trail to Glaze, the strange disappearance of Jane Witherseen's riders, the unusually determined attempt to kill the one Gentile still in her employ, an intention frustrated, no doubt, only by Judkins's magnificent riding of her racer, and lastly the driving of the red herd. These events, to Venters's color of mind, had a dark relationship. Remembering Jane's accusation of bitterness, he tried hard to put aside his rancor in judging Tull. But it was bitter knowledge that made him see the truth. He had felt the shadow of an unseen hand; he had watched till he saw its dim outline, and then he had traced it to a man's hate, to the rivalry of a Mormon Elder, to the power of a Bishop, to the long, far-reaching arm of a terrible creed. That unseen hand had made its first move against Jane Witherseen. Her riders had been called in, leaving her without help to drive seven thousand head of cattle. But to Venters it seemed extraordinary that the power which had called in these riders had left so many cattle to be driven by rustlers and harried by wolves. For hand in glove with that power was an insatiate greed; they were one and the same.

'What can Oldring do with twenty-five hundred head of cattle?' muttered Venters. 'Is he a Mormon? Did he meet Tull last night? It looks like a black plot to me. But Tull and his churchmen wouldn't ruin Jane Witherseen unless the Church was to profit by that ruin. Where does Oldring come in? I'm going to find out about these things.'

Wrangle did twenty-five miles in three hours and walked little of the way. When he had gotten warmed up he had been allowed to choose his own gait. The afternoon had well advanced when Venters struck the trail of the red herd and found where it had grazed the night before. Then Venters rested the horse and used his eyes. Near at hand were a cow and a calf and several yearlings, and farther out in the sage some struggling steers. He caught a glimpse of coyotes skulking near the cattle. The slow, sweeping gaze of the rider failed to find other living things within the field of sight. The sage about him was breast-high to his horse, oversweet with its warm, fragrant breath, gray where it waved to the light, darker where the wind left it still, and beyond the wonderful haze-purple lent by distance. Far across that wide waste began the slow lift of uplands through which Deception Pass cut its tortuous many-cañoned way.

Ventors raised the bridle of his horse and followed the broad cattle trail. The crushed sage resembled the path of a monster snake. In a few miles of travel he passed several cows and calves that had escaped the drive. Then he stood on the last high bench of the slope with the floor of the valley beneath. The opening of the cañon showed in a break of the sage, and the cattle trail paralleled it as far as he could see. That trail led to an undiscovered point where Oldring drove cattle into the pass, and many a rider who had followed it had never returned. Venters satisfied himself that the rustlers had not deviated from their usual course, and then he turned at right angles off the cattle trail and made for the head of the pass.

The sun lost its heat and wore down to the western horizon, where it changed from white to gold and rested like a huge ball about to roll on its golden shadows down the slope. Venters watched the lengthening of the rays and bars, and marveled at his own league-long shadow. The sun sank. There was instant shading of brightness about him, and he saw a kind of cold purple bloom creep ahead of him to cross the cañon, to mount the opposite slope and chase and darken and bury the last golden flare of sunlight.

Venters rode into a trail that he always took to get down into the cañon. He dismounted and found no tracks but his own made several days previous. Nevertheless he sent the dog Ring ahead and waited. In a little while Ring returned. Whereupon Venters led his horse on to the break in the ground.

The opening into Deception Pass was one of the remarkable natural phenomena in a country remarkable for vast slopes of sage, uplands insulated by gigantic red walls, and deep cañons of mysterious source and outlet. Here the valley floor was level, and here opened a narrow chasm, a ragged vent in yellow walls of stone. The trail down the five hundred feet of sheer depth always tested Venters's nerve. It was bad going for even a burro. But Wrangle, as Venters led him, snorted defiance or disgust rather than fear, and, like a hobbled horse on the jump, lifted his ponderous iron-shod fore hoofs and crashed down over the first rough step. Venters warmed to greater admiration of the sorrel; and, giving him a loose bridle, he stepped down foot by foot. Oftentimes the stones and shale started by Wrangle buried Venters to his knees; again he was hard put to it to dodge a rolling boulder; there were times when he could not see Wrangle for dust, and once he and the horse rode a sliding shelf of yellow, weathered cliff. It was a trail on which there could be no stops, and, therefore, if perilous, it was at least one that did not take long in the descent.

Venters breathed lighter when that was over, and felt a sudden assurance in the success of his enterprise. For at first it had been a reckless determination to achieve something at any cost, and now it resolved itself into an adventure worthy of all his reason and cunning, and keenness of eye and ear.

Piñon pines clustered in little clumps along the level floor of the pass. Twilight had gathered under the walls. Venters rode into the trail and up the cañon. Gradually the trees and caves and objects low down turned black, and this blackness moved up the walls till night enfolded the pass, while day still lingered above. The sky darkened; and stars began to show, at first pale and then bright. Sharp notches of the rim-wall, biting like teeth into the blue, were landmarks by which Venters knew where his camping site lay. He had to feel his way through a thicket of slender oaks to a spring where he watered Wrangle and drank himself. Here he unsaddled and turned Wrangle loose, having no fear that the horse would leave the thick, cool grass adjacent to the spring. Next he satisfied his own hunger, fed Ring and Whitie, and, with them curled beside him, composed himself to await sleep.

There had been a time when night in the high altitude of these Utah uplands had been satisfying to Venters. But that was before the oppression of enemies had made the change in his mind. As a rider guarding the herd he had never thought of the night's wildness and loneliness; as an outcast, now when the full silence set in, and the deep darkness, and trains of radiant stars shone cold and calm, he lay with an ache in his heart. For a year he had lived as a black fox, driven from his kind. He longed for the sound of a voice, the touch of a hand. In the daytime there was riding from place to place, and the gun practice to which something drove him, and other tasks that at least necessitated action; at night, before he won sleep, there was strife in his soul. He yearned to leave the endless sage slopes, the wilderness of cañons; and it was in the lonely night that this yearning grew unbearable. It was then that he reached forth to feel Ring or Whitie, immeasurably grateful for the love and companionship of two dogs.

On this night the same old loneliness beset Venters, the old habit of sad thought and burning unquiet had its way. But from it evolved a conviction that his useless life had undergone a subtle change. He had sensed it first when Wrangle swung him up to the high saddle, he knew it now when he lay in the gateway of Deception Pass. He had no thrill of adventure, rather a gloomy perception of great hazard, perhaps death. He meant to find Oldring's retreat. The rustlers had fast horses, but none that could catch Wrangle. Venters knew no rustlers could creep upon him at night when Ring and Whitie guarded his hiding-place. For the rest, he had eyes and ears, and a long rifle and an unerring aim, which he meant to use. Strangely his foreshadowing of change did not hold a thought of the killing of Tull. It related only to what was to happen to him in Deception Pass; and he could no more lift the veil of that mystery than tell where the trails led to in that unexplored cañon. Moreover, he did not care. And at length, tired out by stress of thought, he fell asleep.

When his eyes unclosed, day had come again, and he saw the rim of the opposite wall tipped with the gold of sunrise. A few moments sufficed for the morning's simple camp duties. Near at hand he found Wrangle, and to his surpise the horse came to him. Wrangle was one of the horses that left his viciousness in the home corral. What he wanted was to be free of mules and burros and steers, to roll in dust-patches, and then to run down the wide, open, windy sage-plains, and at night browse and sleep in the cool wet grass of a spring-hole. Jerd knew the sorrel when he said of him, 'Wait till he smells the sage!'

Venters saddled and led him out of the oak thicket, and, leaping astride, rode up the cañon, with Ring and Whitie trotting behind. An old grass-grown trail followed the course of a shallow wash where flowed a thin stream of water. The cañon was a hundred rods wide; its yellow walls were perpendicular; it had abundant sage and a scant growth of oak and piñon. For five miles it held to a comparatively straight bearing, and then began a heightening of rugged walls and a deepening of the floor. Beyond this point of sudden change in the character of the cañon Venters had never explored, and here was the real door to the intricacies of Deception Pass.

He reined Wrangle to a walk, halted now and then to listen, and then proceeded cautiously with shifting and alert gaze. The cañon assumed proportions that dwarfed those of its first ten miles. Venters rode on and on, not losing in the interest of his wide surroundings any of his caution or keen search for tracks or sight of living thing. If there ever had been a trail here, he could not find it. He rode through sage and clumps of piñon trees and grassy plots where long-petaled purple lilies bloomed. He rode through a dark constriction of the pass no wider than the lane in the grove at Cottonwoods. And he came out into a great amphitheater into which jutted huge towering corners of a confluence of intersection cañons.

Venters sat his horse, and, with a rider's eye, studied this wild cross-cut of huge stone gullies. Then he went on, guided by the course of running water. If it had not been for the main stream of water flowing north he would never have been able to tell which of those many openings was a continuation of the pass. In crossing this amphitheater he went by the mouths of five cañons, fording little streams that flowed into the larger one. Gaining the outlet which he took to be the pass, he rode on again under overhanging walls. One side was dark in shade, the other light in sun. This narrow passageway turned and twisted and opened into a valley that amazed Venters.

Here again was a sweep of purple sage richer than upon the higher levels. The valley was miles long, several wide, and enclosed by unscalable walls. But it was the background of this valley that so forcibly struck him. Across the sage-flat rose a strange upflinging of yellow rocks. He could not tell which were close and which were distant. Scrawled mounds of stone, like mountain waves, seemed to roll up to steep bare slopes and towers.

In this plain of sage Venters flushed birds and rabbits, and when he had proceeded about a mile he caught sight of the bobbing white tails of a herd of running antelope. He rode along the edge of the stream which wound toward the western end of the slowly looming mounds of stone. The high slope retreated out of sight behind the nearer projection. To Venters the valley appeared to have been filled in by a mountain of melted stone that had hardened in strange shapes of rounded outline. He followed the stream till he lost it in a deep rut. Therefore Venters quit the dark slit which baffled further search in that direction, and rode out along the curved edge of stone where it met the sage. It was not long before he came to a low place, and here Wrangle readily climbed up.

All about him was ridgy roll of wind-smoothed, rain-washed rock. Not a tuft of grass or a bunch of sage colored the dull rust-yellow. He saw where, to the right, this uneven flow of stone ended in a blunt wall. Leftward, from the hollow that lay at his feet, mounted a gradual slow-swelling slope to a great height topped by leaning, cracked, and ruined crags. Not for some time did he grasp the wonder of that acclivity. It was no less than a mountainside, glistening in the sun like polished granite, with cedar-trees springing as if by magic out of the denuded surface. Winds had swept it clear of weathered shale, and rains had washed it free of dust. Far up the curved slope its beautiful lines broke to meet the vertical rim-wall, to lose its grace in a different order and color of rock, a stained yellow cliff of cracks and caves and seamed crags. And straight before Venters was a scene less striking but more significant to his keen survey. For beyond a mile of the bare, hummocky rock began the valley of sage, and the mouths of cañons, one of which surely was another gateway into the pass.

He got off his horse, and, giving the bridle to Ring to hold, he commenced a search for the cleft where the stream ran. He was not successful and concluded the water dropped into an underground passage. Then he returned to where he had left Wrangle, and led him down off the stone to the sage. It was a short ride to the opening cañons. There was no reason for a choice of which one to enter. The one he rode into was a clear, sharp shift in yellow stone a thousand feet deep, with wonderful wind-worn caves low down and high above buttressed and turreted ramparts. Farther on Venters came into a region where deep indentations marked the line of cañon walls. These were huge, cove-like blind pockets extending back to a sharp corner with a dense growth of underbrush and trees.

Venters penetrated into one of these offshoots, and, as he had hoped, he found abundant grass. He had to bend the oak saplings to get his horse through. Deciding to make this a hiding-place if he could find water, he worked back to the limit of the shelving walls. In a little cluster of silver spruces he found a spring. This enclosed nook seemed an ideal place to leave his horse and to camp at night, and from which to make stealthy trips on foot. The thick grass hid his trail; the dense growth of oaks in the opening would serve as a barrier to keep Wrangle in, if, indeed, the luxuriant browse would not suffice for that. So Venters, leaving Whitie with the horse, called Ring to his side, and, rifle in hand, worked his way out to the open. A careful photographing in mind of the formation of the bold outlines of rim-rock assured him he would be able to return to his retreat, even in the dark.

Bunches of scattered sage covered the center of the cañon, and among these Venters threaded his way with the step of an Indian. At intervals he put his hand on the dog and stopped to listen. There was a drowsy hum of insects, but no other sound disturbed the warm midday stillness. Venters saw ahead a turn, more abrupt than any yet. Warily he rounded this corner, once again to halt bewildered.

The cañon opened fan-shaped into a great oval of green and gray growths. It was the hub of an oblong wheel, and from it, at regular distances, like spokes, ran the outgoing cañons. Here a dull red color predominated over the fading yellow. The corners of wall bluntly rose, scarred and scrawled, to taper into towers and serrated peaks and pinnacled domes.

Venters pushed on more heedfully than ever. Toward the center of this circle the sage-brush grew smaller and farther apart. He was about to sheer off to the right, where thickets and jumbles of fallen rock would afford him cover, when he ran right upon a broad cattle trail. Like a road it was, more than a trail; and the cattle tracks were fresh. What surprised him more, they were wet! He pondered over this feature. It had not rained. The only solution to this puzzle was that the cattle had been driven through water, and water deep enough to wet their legs.

Suddenly Ring growled low. Venters rose cautiously and looked over the sage. A band of straggling horsemen were riding across the oval. He sank down, startled and trembling. 'Rustlers!' he muttered. Hurriedly he glanced about for a place to hide. Near at hand there was nothing but sage-brush. He dared not risk crossing the open patches to reach the rocks. Again he peeped over the sage. The rustlers – four – five – seven – eight in all, were approaching, but not directly in line with him. That was relief for a cold deadness which seemed to be creeping inward along his veins. He crouched down with bated breath and held the bristling dog.

He heard the click of iron-shod hoofs on stone, the coarse laughter of men, and then voices gradually dying away. Long moments passed. Then he rose. The rustlers were riding into a cañon. Their horses were tired, and they had several pack animals; evidently they had traveled far. Venters doubted that they were the rustlers who had driven the red herd. Oldring's band had split. Venters watched these horsemen disappear under a bold cañon wall.

The rustlers had come from the northwest side of the oval. Venters kept a steady gaze in that direction, hoping, if there were more, to see from what cañon they rode. A quarter of an hour went by. Reward for his vigilance came when he descried three more mounted men, far over to the north. But out of what cañon they had ridden it was too late to tell. He watched the three ride across the oval and round the jutting red corner where the others had gone.

'Up that cañon!' exclaimed Venters. 'Oldring's den! I've found it!'

A knotty point for Venters was the fact that the cattle tracks all pointed west. The broad trail came from the direction of the cañon into which the rustlers had ridden, and undoubtedly the cattle had been driven out of it across the oval. There were no tracks pointing the other way. It had been in his mind that Oldring had driven the red herd toward the rendezvous, and not from it. Where did that broad trail come down into the pass, and where did it lead? Venters knew he wasted time in pondering the question, but it held a fascination not easily dispelled. For many years Oldring's mysterious entrance and exit to Deception Pass had been all-absorbing topics to sage-riders.

All at once the dog put an end to Venters's pondering. Ring sniffed the air, turned slowly in his tracks with a whine, and then growled. Venters wheeled. Two horsemen were within a hundred yards, coming straight at him. One, lagging behind the other, was Oldring's Masked Rider.

Venters cunningly sank, slowly trying to merge into sage-brush. But, guarded as his action was, the first horse detected it. He stopped short, snorted, and shot up his ears. The rustler bent forward, as if keenly peering ahead. Then, with a swift sweep, he jerked a gun from its sheath and fired.

The bullet zipped through the sage-brush. Flying bits of wood struck Venters, and the hot, stinging pain seemed to lift him in one leap. Like a flash the blue barrel of his rifle gleamed level and he shot once – twice.

The foremost rustler dropped his weapon and toppled from his saddle, to fall with his foot catching in a stirrup. The horse snorted wildly and plunged away, dragging the rustler through the sage.

The Masked Rider huddled over his pommel, slowly swaying to one side, and then, with a faint, strange cry, slipped out of the saddle.

CHAPTER FIVE
The Masked Rider

VENTERS LOOKED QUICKLY from the fallen rustlers to the cañon where the others had disappeared. He calculated on the time needed for running horses to return to the open, if their riders heard shots. He waited breathlessly. But the estimated time dragged by and no riders appeared. Venters began presently to believe that the rifle report had not penetrated into the recesses of the cañon, and felt safe for the immediate present.

He hurried to the spot where the first rustler had been dragged by his horse. The man lay in deep grass, dead, jaw fallen, eyes protruding – a sight that sickened Venters. The first man at whom he had ever aimed a weapon he had shot through the heart. With the clammy sweat oozing from every pore Venters dragged the rustler in among some boulders and covered him with slabs of rock. Then he smoothed out the crushed trail in grass and sage. The rustler's horse had stopped a quarter of a mile off and was grazing.

When Venters rapidly strode toward the Masked Rider not even the cold nausea that gripped him could wholly banish curiosity. For he had shot Oldring's infamous lieutenant, whose face had never been seen. Venters experienced a grim pride in the feat. What would Tull say to this achievement of the outcast who rode too often to Deception Pass?

Venters's curious eagerness and expectation had not prepared him for the shock he received when he stood over a slight, dark figure. The rustler wore the black mask that had given him his name, but he had no weapons. Venters glanced at the drooping horse; there were no gun-sheaths on the saddle.

'A rustler who didn't pack guns!' muttered Venters. 'He wears no belt. He couldn't pack guns in that rig. . . . Strange!'

A low, gasping intake of breath and a sudden twitching of body told Venters the rider still lived.

'He's alive! . . . I've got to stand here and watch him die. And I shot an unarmed man.'

Shrinkingly Venters removed the rider's wide sombrero and the black cloth mask. This action disclosed bright chestnut hair, inclined to curl, and a white, youthful face. Along the lower line of cheek and jaw was a clear demarcation, where the brown of tanned skin met the white that had been hidden from the sun.

'Oh, he's only a boy! . . . What! Can he be Oldring's Masked Rider?'

The boy showed signs of returning consciousness. He stirred; his lips moved; a small brown hand clenched in his blouse.

Venters knelt with a gathering horror of his deed. His bullet had entered the rider's right breast, high up to the shoulder. With hands that shook, Venters untied a black scarf and ripped open the blood-wet blouse.

First he saw a gaping hole, dark red against a whiteness of skin, from which welled a slender red stream. Then the graceful, beautiful swell of a woman's breast!

'A woman!' he cried. 'A girl! . . . I've killed a girl!'

She suddenly opened her eyes that transfixed Venters. They were fathomless blue. Consciousness of death was there, a blended terror and pain, but no consciousness of sight. She did not see Venters. She stared into the unknown.

Then came a spasm of vitality. She writhed in a torture of reviving strength, and in her convulsions she almost tore from Venter's grasp. Slowly she relaxed and sank partly back. The ungloved hand sought the wound, and pressed so hard that her wrist half buried itself in her bosom. Blood trickled between her spread fingers. And she looked at Venters with eyes that saw him.

He cursed himself and the unerring aim of which he had been so proud. He had seen that look in the eyes of a crippled antelope which he was about to finish with his knife. But in her it had infinitely more – a revelation of mortal spirit. The instinctive clinging to life was there, and the driving helplessness and the terrible accusation of the stricken.

'Forgive me! I didn't know!' burst out Venters.

'You shot me – you've killed me!' she whispered, in panting gasps. Upon her lips appeared a fluttering, bloody froth. By that Venters knew the air in her lungs was mixing with blood. 'Oh, I knew – it would – come – some day! . . . Oh, the burn! . . . Hold me – I'm sinking – it's all dark. . . . Ah, God! . . . Mercy—'

Her rigidity loosened in one long quiver and she lay back limp, still, white as snow, with closed eyes.

Venters thought then that she died. But the faint pulsation of her breast assured him that life yet lingered. Death seemed only a matter of moments, for the bullet had gone clear through her. Nevertheless, he tore sage-leaves from a bush, and, pressing them tightly over her wounds, he bound the black scarf round her shoulder, tying it securely under her arm. Then he closed the blouse, hiding from his sight that blood-stained, accusing breast.

'What – now?' he questioned, with flying mind. 'I must get out of here. She's dying – but I can't leave her.'

He rapidly surveyed the sage to the north and made out no animate object. Then he picked up the girl's sombrero and mask. This time the mask gave him as great a shock as when he first removed it from her face. For in the woman he had forgotten the rustler, and this black strip of felt-cloth established the identity of Oldring's Masked Rider. Venters had solved the mystery. He slipped his rifle under her, and, lifting her carefully upon it, he began to retrace his steps. The dog trailed in his shadow. And the horse, that had stood drooping by, followed without a call. Venters chose the deepest tufts of grass and clumps of sage on his return. From time to time he glanced over his shoulder. He did not rest. His concern was to avoid jarring the girl and to hide his trail. Gaining the narrow cañon, he turned and held close to the wall till he reached his hiding-place. When he entered the dense thicket of oaks he was hard put to it to force a way through. But he held his burden almost upright, and by slipping sidewise and bending the saplings he got in. Through sage and grass he hurried to the grove of silver spruces.

He laid the girl down, almost fearing to look at her. Though marble pale and cold, she was living. Venters then appreciated the tax that long carry had been to his strength. He sat down to rest. Whitie sniffed at the pale girl and whined and crept to Venters's feet. Ring lapped the water in the runway of the spring.

Presently Venters went out to the opening, caught the horse, and, leading him through the thicket, unsaddled him and tied him with a long halter. Wrangle left his browsing long enough to whinny and toss his head. Venters felt that he could not rest easily till he had secured the other rustler's horse; so, taking his rifle and calling for Ring, he set out. Swiftly yet watchfully he made his way through the cañon to the oval and out to the cattle trail. What few tracks might have betrayed him he obliterated, so only an expert tracker could have trailed him. Then, with many a wary backward glance across the sage, he started to round up the rustler's horse. This was unexpectedly easy. He led the horse to lower ground, out of sight from the opposite side of the oval, along the shadowy western wall, and so on into his cañon and secluded camp.

The girl's eyes were open; a feverish spot burned in her cheeks; she moaned something unintelligible to Venters, but he took the movement of her lips to mean that she wanted water. Lifting her head, he tipped the canteen to her lips. After that she again lapsed into unconsciousness or a weakness which was its counterpart. Venters noted, however, that the burning flush had faded into the former pallor.

The sun set behind the high cañon rim, and a cool shade darkened the walls. Venters fed the dogs and put a halter on the dead rustler's horse. He allowed Wrangle to browse free. This done, he cut spruce boughs and made a lean-to for the girl. Then, gently lifting her upon a blanket, he folded the sides over her. The other blanket he wrapped about his shoulders and found a comfortable seat against a spruce-tree that upheld the little shack. Ring and Whitie lay near at hand, one asleep, the other watchful.

Venters dreaded the night's vigil. At night his mind was active, and this time he had to watch and think and feel beside a dying girl whom he had all but murdered. A thousand excuses he invented for himself, yet not one made any difference in his act or his self-reproach.

It seemed to him that when night fell black he could see her white face so much more plainly.

'She'll go, presently,' he said, 'and be out of agony – thank God!'

Every little while certainty of her death came to him with a shock; and then he would bend over and lay his ear on her breast. Her heart still beat.

The early night blackness cleared to the cold starlight. The horses were not moving, and no sound disturbed the deathly silence of the cañon.

'I'll bury her here,' thought Venters, 'and let her grave be as much a mystery as her life was.'

For the girl's few words, the look of her eyes, the prayer, had strangely touched Venters.

'She was only a girl,' he soliloquized. 'What was she to Oldring? Rustlers don't have wives nor sisters nor daughters. She was bad – that's all. But somehow . . . well, she may not have willingly become the companion of rustlers. That prayer of hers to God for mercy! . . . Life is strange and cruel. I wonder if other members of Oldring's gang are women? Likely enough. But what was his game? Oldring's Masked Rider! A name to make villagers hide and lock their doors. A name credited with a dozen murders, a hundred forays, and a thousand stealings of cattle. What part did the girl have in this? It may have served Oldring to create mystery.'

Hours passed. The white stars moved across the narrow strip of dark-blue sky above. The silence awoke to the low hum of insects. Venters watched the immovable white face, and as he watched, hour by hour waiting for death, the infamy of her passed from his mind. He thought only of the sadness, the truth of the moment. Whoever she was – whatever she had done – she was young and she was dying.

The after-part of the night wore on interminably. The starlight failed and the gloom blackened to the darkest hour. 'She'll die at the gray of dawn,' muttered Venters, remembering some old woman's fancy. The blackness paled to gray, and the gray lightened and day peeped over the eastern rim. Venters listened at the breast of the girl. She still lived. Did he only imagine that her heart beat stronger, ever so slightly, but stronger? He pressed his ear closer to her breast. And he rose with his own pulse quickening.

'If she doesn't die soon – she's got a chance – the barest chance – to live,' he said.

He wondered if the internal bleeding had ceased. There was no more film of blood upon her lips. But no corpse could have been whiter. Opening her blouse, he untied the scarf, and carefully picked away the sage-leaves from the wound in her shoulder. It had closed. Lifting her lightly, he ascertained that the same was true of the hole where the bullet had come out. He reflected on the fact that clean wounds closed quickly in the healing upland air. He recalled instances of riders who had been cut and shot, apparently to fatal issues; yet the blood had clotted, the wounds closed, and they had recovered. He had no way to tell if internal hemorrhage still went on, but he believed that it had stopped. Otherwise she would surely not have lived so long. He marked the entrance of the bullet and concluded that it had just touched the upper lobe of her lung. Perhaps the wound in the lung had also closed. As he began to wash the blood stains from her breast and carefully rebandage the wound, he was vaguely conscious of a strange, grave happiness in the thought that she might live.

Broad daylight and a hint of sunshine high on the cliff-rim to the west brought him to consideration of what he had better do. And while busy with his few camp tasks he revolved the thing in his mind. It would not be wise for him to remain long in his present hiding place. And if he intended to follow the cattle trail and try to find the rustlers he had better make a move at once. For he knew that rustlers, being riders, would not make much of a day's or night's absence from camp for one or two of their number; but when the missing ones failed to show up in reasonable time there would be a search. And Venters was afraid of that.

'A good tracker could trail me,' he muttered. 'And I'd be cornered here. Let's see. Rustlers are a lazy set when they're not on the ride. I'll risk it. Then I'll change my hiding-place.'

He carefully cleaned and reloaded his guns. When he rose to go he bent a long glance down upon the unconscious girl. Then, ordering Whitie and Ring to keep guard, he left the camp.

The safest cover lay close under the wall of the cañon, and here through the dense thickets Venters made his slow, listening advance toward the oval. Upon gaining the wide opening he decided to cross it and follow the left wall till he came to the cattle trail. He scanned the oval as keenly as if hunting for antelope. Then, stooping, he stole from one cover to another, taking advantage of rocks and bunches of sage, until he had reached the thickets under the opposite wall. Once there, he exercised extreme caution in his surveys of the ground ahead, but increased his speed when moving. Dodging from bush to bush, he passed the mouths of two cañons, and in the entrance of a third cañon he crossed a wash of swift, clear water, to come abruptly upon the cattle trail.

It followed the low bank of the wash, and, keeping it in sight, Venters hugged the line of sage and thicket. Like the curves of a serpent, the cañon wound for a mile or more and then opened into a valley. Patches of red showed clear against the purple of sage, and farther out on the level dotted strings of red led away to the wall of rock.

'Ha, the red herd!' exclaimed Venters.

Then dots of white and black told him there were cattle of other colors in this enclosed valley. Oldring, the rustler, was also a rancher. Venters's calculating eye took count of stock that outnumbered the red herd.

'What a range!' went on Venters. 'Water and grass enough for fifty thousand head, and no riders needed!'

After his first burst of surprise and rapid calculation Venters lost no time there, but slunk again into the sage on his back trail. With the discovery of Oldring's hidden cattle-range had come enlightenment on several problems. Here the rustler kept his stock; here was Jane Withersteen's red herd; here were the few cattle that had disappeared from the Cottonwoods slopes during the last two years. Until Oldring had driven the red herd his thefts of cattle for that time had not been more than enough to supply meat for his men. Of late no drives had been reported from Sterling or the villages north. And Venters knew that the riders had wondered at Oldring's inactivity in that particular field. He and his band had been active enough in their visits to Glaze and Cottonwoods; they always had gold; but of late the amount gambled away and drunk and thrown away in the villages had given rise to much conjecture. Oldring's more frequent visits had resulted in new saloons, and where there had formerly been one raid or shooting fray in the little hamlets there were now many. Perhaps Oldring had another range farther on up the pass, and from there drove the cattle to distant Utah towns where he was little known. But Venters came finally to doubt this. And, from what he had learned in the last few days, a belief began to form in Venters's mind that Oldring's intimidations of the villages and the mystery of the Masked Rider, with his alleged evil deeds, and the fierce resistance offered any trailing riders, and the rustling of cattle – these things were only the craft of the rustler-chief to conceal his real life and purpose and work in Deception Pass.

And like a scouting Indian Venters crawled through the sage of the oval valley, crossed trail after trail on the north side, and at last entered the cañon out of which headed the cattle trail, and into which he had watched the rustlers disappear.

If he had used caution before, now he strained every nerve to force himself to creeping stealth and to sensitiveness of ear. He crawled along so hidden that he could not use his eyes except to aid himself in the toilsome progress through the brakes and ruins of cliff-wall. Yet from time to time, as he rested, he saw the massive red walls growing higher and wilder, more looming and broken. He made note of the fact that he was turning and climbing. The sage and thickets of oak and brakes of alder gave place to piñon pine growing out of rocky soil. Suddenly a low, dull murmur assailed his ears. At first he thought it was thunder, then the slipping of a weathered slope of rock. But it was incessant, and as he progressed it filled out deeper and from a murmur changed into a soft roar.

'Falling water,' he said. 'There's volume to that. I wonder if it's the stream I lost.'

The roar bothered him, for he could hear nothing else. Likewise, however, no rustlers could hear him. Emboldened by this, and sure that nothing but a bird could see him, he arose from his hands and knees to hurry on. An opening in the piñons warned him that he was nearing the height of slope.

He gained it, and dropped low with a burst of astonishment. Before him stretched a short cañon with rounded stone floor bare of grass or sage or tree, and with curved, shelving walls. A broad rippling stream flowed toward him, and at the back of the cañon a waterfall burst from a wide rent in the cliff, and, bounding down in two green steps, spread into a long white sheet.

If Venters had not been indubitably certain that he had entered the right cañon his astonishment would not have been so great. There had been no breaks in the walls, no side cañons entering this one where the rustlers' tracks and the cattle trail had guided him, and, therefore, he could not be wrong. But here the cañon ended, and presumably the trails also.

'That cattle trail headed out of here,' Venters kept saying to himself. 'It headed out. Now what I want to know is how on earth did cattle ever get in here?'

If he could be sure of anything it was of the careful scrutiny he had given that cattle track, every hoofmark of which headed straight west. He was now looking east at an immense round boxed corner of cañon down which tumbled a thin, white veil of water, scarcely twenty yards wide. Somehow, somewhere, his calculations had gone wrong. For the first time in years he found himself doubting his rider's skill in finding tracks, and his memory of what he had actually seen. In his anxiety to keep under cover he must have lost himself in this offshoot of Deception Pass, and thereby, in some unaccountable manner, missed the cañon with the trails. There was nothing else for him to think. Rustlers could not fly, nor cattle jump down thousand-foot precipices. He was only proving what the sage-riders had long said of this labyrinthine system of deceitful cañons and valleys – trails led down into Deception Pass, but no rider had ever followed them.

On a sudden he heard above the soft roar of the waterfall an unusual sound that he could not define. He dropped flat behind a stone and listened. From the direction he had come swelled something that resembled a strange muffled pounding and splashing and ringing. Despite his nerve the chill sweat began to dampen his forehead. What might not be possible in this stone-walled maze of mystery? The unnatural sound passed beyond him as he lay gripping his rifle and fighting for coolness. Then from the open came the sound, now distinct and different. Venters recognized a hobble-bell of a horse, and the cracking of iron on submerged stones, and the hollow splash of hoofs in water.

Relief surged over him. His mind caught again at realities, and curiosity prompted him to peep from behind the rock.

In the middle of the stream waded a long string of packed burros driven by three superbly mounted men. Had Venters met these dark-clothed, dark-visaged, heavily armed men anywhere in Utah, let alone in this robbers' retreat, he would have recognized them as rustlers. The discerning eye of a rider saw the signs of a long, arduous trip. These men were packing in supplies from one of the northern villages. They were tired, and their horses were almost played out, and the burros plodded on, after the manner of their kind when exhausted, faithful and patient, but as if every weary, splashing, slipping step would be their last.

All this Venters noted in one glance. After that he watched with a thrilling eagerness. Straight at the waterfall the rustlers drove the burros, and straight through the middle, where the water spread into a fleecy, thin film like dissolving smoke. Following closely, the rustlers rode into this white mist, showing in bold black relief for an instant, and then they vanished.

Venters drew a full breath that rushed out in brief and sudden utterance.

'Good Heaven! Of all the holes for a rustler! . . . There's a cavern under that waterfall, and a passageway leading out to a cañon beyond. Oldring hides in there. He needs only to guard a trail leading down from the sage-flat above. Little danger of this outlet to the pass being discovered. I stumbled on it by luck, after I had given up. And now I know the truth of what puzzled me most – why that cattle trail was wet!'

He wheeled and ran down the slope, and out to the level of the sage-brush. Returning, he had no time to spare, only now and then, between dashes, a moment when he stopped to cast sharp eyes ahead. The abundant grass left no trace of his trail. Short work he made of the distance to the circle of cañons. He doubted that he would ever see it again; he knew he never wanted to; yet he looked at the red corners and towers with the eyes of a rider picturing landmarks never to be forgotten.

Here he spent a panting moment in a slow-circling gaze of the sage-oval and the gaps between the bluffs. Nothing stirred except the gentle wave of the tips of the brush. Then he pressed on past the mouths of several cañons and over ground new to him, now close under the eastern wall. This latter part proved to be easy traveling, well screened from possible observation from the north and west, and he soon covered it and felt safer in the deepening shade of his own cañon. Then the huge, notched bulge of red rim loomed over him, a mark by which he knew again the deep cove where his camp lay hidden. As he penetrated the thicket, safe again for the present, his thoughts reverted to the girl he had left there. The afternoon had far advanced. How would he find her? He ran into camp, frightening the dogs.

The girl lay with wide-open, dark eyes, and they dilated when he knelt beside her. The flush of fever shone in her cheeks. He lifted her and held water to her dry lips, and felt an inexplicable sense of lightness as he saw her swallow in a slow, choking gulp. Gently he laid her back.

'Who – are – you?' she whispered, haltingly.

'I'm the man who shot you,' he replied.

'You'll – not – kill me – now?'

'No, no.'

'What – will – you – do – with me?'

'When you get better – strong enough – I'll take you back to the cañon where the rustlers ride through the waterfall.'

As with a faint shadow from a flitting wing overhead, the marble whiteness of her face seemed to change.

'Don't – take – me – back – there!'

CHAPTER SIX

The Mill-Wheel of Steers

MEANTIME, AT THE RANCH, when Judkins's news had sent Venters on the trail of the rustlers, Jane Withersteen led the injured man to her house and with skilled fingers dressed the gunshot wound in his arm.

'Judkins, what do you think happened to my riders?'

'I – I'd rather not say,' he replied.

'Tell me. Whatever you'll tell me I'll keep to myself. I'm beginning to worry about more than the loss of a herd of cattle. Venters hinted of – but tell me, Judkins.'

'Well, Miss Withersteen, I think as Venters thinks – your riders have been called in.'

'Judkins! . . . By whom?'

'You know who handles the reins of your Mormon riders.'

'Do you dare insinuate that my churchmen have ordered in my riders?'

'I ain't insinuatin' nothin', Miss Withersteen,' answered Judkins, with spirit. 'I know what I'm talking about. I didn't want to tell you.'

'Oh, I can't believe that! I'll not believe it! Would Tull leave my herds at the mercy of rustlers and wolves just because – because – ? No, no! It's unbelievable.'

'Yes, thet particular thing's onheard of around Cottonwoods. But, beggin' pardon, Miss Withersteen, there never was any other rich Mormon woman here on the border, let alone one thet's taken the bit between her teeth.'

That was a bold thing for the reserved Judkins to say, but it did not anger her. This rider's crude hint of her spirit gave her a glimpse of what others might think. Humility and obedience had been hers always. But had she taken the bit between her teeth? Still she wavered. And then, with a quick spurt of warm blood along her veins, she thought of Black Star when he got the bit fast between his iron jaws and ran wild in the sage. If she ever started to run! Jane smothered the glow and burn within her, ashamed of a passion for freedom that opposed her duty.

'Judkins, go to the village,' she said, 'and when you have learned anything definite about my riders please come to me at once.'

When he had gone Jane resolutely applied her mind to a number of tasks that of late had been neglected. Her father had trained her in the management of a hundred employees and the working of gardens and fields; and to keep record of the movement of cattle and riders. And beside the many duties she had added to this work was one of extreme delicacy, such as required all her tact and ingenuity. It was an unobtrusive, almost secret aid which she rendered to the Gentile families of the village. Though Jane Withersteen never admitted so to herself, it amounted to no less than a system of charity. But for her invention of numberless kinds of employment, for which there was no actual need, these families of Gentiles, who had failed in a Mormon community, would have starved.

In aiding these poor people Jane thought she deceived her keen churchmen, but it was a kind of deceit for which she did not pray to be forgiven. Equally as difficult was the task of deceiving the Gentiles, for they were as proud as they were poor. It had been a great grief to her to discover how these people hated her people; and it had been a source of great joy that through her they had come to soften in hatred. At any time this work called for a clearness of mind that precluded anxiety and worry; but under the present circumstances it required all her vigor and obstinate tenacity to pin her attention upon her task.

Sunset came, bringing with the end of her labor a patient calmness and power to wait that had not been hers earlier in the day. She expected Judkins, but he did not appear. Her house was always quiet; tonight, however, it seemed unusually so. At supper her women served her with a silent assiduity; it spoke what their sealed lips could not utter – the sympathy of Mormon women. Jerd came to her with the key of the great door of the stone stable, and to make his daily report about the horses. One of his daily duties was to give Black Star and Night and the other racers a ten-mile run. This day it had been omitted, and the boy grew confused in explanations that she had not asked for. She did inquire if he would return on the morrow, and Jerd, in mingled surprise and relief, assured her he would always work for her. Jane missed the rattle and trot, canter and gallop of the incoming riders on the hard trails. Dusk shaded the grove where she walked; the birds ceased singing; the wind sighed through the leaves of the cottonwoods, and the running water murmured down its stone-bedded channel. The glimmering of the first star was like the peace and beauty of the night. Her faith welled up in her heart and said that all would soon be right in her little world. She pictured Venters about his lonely camp-fire sitting between his faithful dogs. She prayed for his safety, for the success of his undertaking.

Early the next morning one of Jane's women brought in word that Judkins wished to speak to her. She hurried out, and in her surprise to see him armed with rifle and revolver, she forgot her intention to inquire about his wound.

'Judkins! Those guns? You never carried guns.'

'It's high time, Miss Withersteen,' he replied. 'Will you come into the grove? It ain't jest exactly safe for me to be seen here.'

She walked with him into the shade of the cottonwoods.

'What do you mean?'

'Miss Withersteen, I went to my mother's house last night. While there, someone knocked, an' a man asked for me. I went to the door. He wore a mask. He said I'd better not ride any more for Jane Withersteen. His voice was hoarse an' strange, disguised, I reckon, like his face. He said no more, an' ran off in the dark.'

'Did you know who he was?' asked Jane, in a low voice.

'Yes.'

Jane did not ask to know; she did not want to know; she feared to know. All her calmness fled at a single thought.

'Thet's why I'm packin' guns,' went on Judkins. 'For I'll never quit ridin' for you, Miss Withersteen, till you let me go.'

'Judkins, do you want to leave me?'

'Do I look thet way? Give me a hoss – a fast hoss, an' send me out on the sage.'

'Oh, thank you, Judkins! You're more faithful than my own people. I ought not accept your loyalty – you might suffer more through it. But what in the world can I do? My head whirls. The wrong to Venters – the stolen herd – these masks, threats, this coil in the dark! I can't understand! But I feel something dark and terrible closing in around me.'

'Miss Withersteen, it's all simple enough,' said Judkins, earnestly. 'Now please listen – an' beggin' your pardon – jest turn thet deaf Mormon ear aside, an' let me talk clear an' plain in the other. I went around to the saloons an' the stores an' the loafin' places yesterday. All your riders are in. There's talk of a vigilance band organized to hunt down rustlers. They call themselves "The Riders." Thet's the report – thet's the reason given for your riders leavin' you. Strange thet only a few riders of other ranchers joined the band! An' Tull's man, Jerry Card – he's the leader. I seen him an' his hoss. He ain't been to Glaze. I'm not easy to fool on the looks of a hoss thet's traveled the sage. Tull an' Jerry didn't ride to Glaze! . . . Well, I met Blake an' Dorn, both good friends of mine, usually, as far as their Mormon lights will let 'em go. But these fellers couldn't fool me, an' they didn't try very hard. I asked them, straight out like a man, why they left you like thet. I didn't forget to mention how you nursed Blake's poor old mother when she was sick, an' how good you was to Dorn's kids. They looked ashamed, Miss Withersteen. An' they jest froze up – thet dark set look thet makes them strange an' different to me. But I could tell the difference between thet first natural twinge of conscience an' the later look of some secret thing. An' the difference I caught was thet they couldn't help themselves. They hadn't no say in the matter. They looked as if their bein' unfaithful to you was bein' faithful to a higher duty. An' there's the secret. Why, it's as plain as – as sight of my gun here.'

'Plain! . . . My herds to wander in the sage – to be stolen! Jane Withersteen a poor woman! Her head to be brought low and her spirit broken! . . . Why, Judkins, it's plain enough.'

'Miss Withersteen, let me get what boys I can gather, an' hold the white herd. It's on the slope now, not ten miles out – three thousand head, an' all steers. They're wild, an' likely to stampede at the pop of a jack-rabbit's ears. We'll camp right with them, an' try to hold them.'

'Judkins, I'll reward you some day for your service, unless all is taken from me. Get the boys and tell Jerd to give you pick of my horses, except Black Star and Night. But – do not shed blood for my cattle nor heedlessly risk your lives.'

Jane Withersteen rushed to the silence and seclusion of her room, and there could no longer hold back the bursting of her wrath. She went stone-blind in the fury of a passion that had never before showed its power. Lying upon her bed, sightless, voiceless, she was a writhing, living flame. And she tossed there while her fury burned and burned, and finally burned itself out.

Then, weak and spent, she lay thinking, not of the oppression that would break her, but of this new revelation of self. Until the last few days there had been little in her life to rouse passions. Her forefathers had been Vikings, savage chieftains who bore no cross and brooked no hindrance to their will. Her father had inherited that temper; and at times, like antelope fleeing before fire on the slope, his people fled from his red rages. Jane Withersteen realized that the spirit of wrath and war had lain dormant in her. She shrank from black depths hitherto unsuspected. The one thing in man or woman that she scorned above all scorn, and which she could not forgive, was hate. Hate headed a flaming pathway straight to hell. All in a flash, beyond her control there had been in her a birth of fiery hate. And the man who had dragged her peaceful and loving spirit to this degradation was a minister of God's word, an Elder of her church, the counselor of her beloved Bishop.

The loss of herds and ranges, even of Amber Spring and the Old Stone House, no longer concerned Jane Withersteen; she faced the foremost thought of her life, what she now considered the mightiest problem – the salvation of her soul.

She knelt by her bedside and prayed; she prayed as she had never prayed in all her life – prayed to be forgiven for her sin; to be immune from that dark, hot hate; to love Tull as her minister, though she could not love him as a man; to do her duty by her church and people and those dependent upon her bounty; to hold reverence of God and womanhood inviolate.

When Jane Withersteen rose from that storm of wrath and prayer for help she was serene, calm, sure – a changed woman. She would do her duty as she saw it, live her life as her own truth guided her. She might never be able to marry a man of her choice, but she certainly never would become the wife of Tull. Her churchmen might take her cattle and horses, ranges and fields, her corrals and stables, the house of Witherssteen and the water that nourished the village of Cottonwoods; but they could not force her to marry Tull, they could not change her decision or break her spirit. Once resigned to further loss, and sure of herself, Jane Withersteen attained a peace of mind that had not been hers for a year. She forgave Tull, and felt a melancholy regret over what she knew he considered duty, irrespective of his personal feeling for her. First of all, Tull, as he was a man, wanted her for himself; and secondly, he hoped to save her and her riches for his church. She did not believe that Tull had been actuated solely by his minister's zeal to save her soul. She doubted her interpretation of one of his dark sayings – that if she were lost to him she might as well be lost to heaven. Jane Withersteen's common sense took arms against the binding limits of her religion; and she doubted that her Bishop, whom she had been taught had direct communication with God – would damn her soul for refusing to marry a Mormon. As for Tull and his churchmen, when they had harassed her, perhaps made her poor, they would find her unchangeable, and then she would get back most of what she had lost. So she reasoned, true at last to her faith in all men, and in their ultimate goodness.

The clank of iron hoofs upon the stone courtyard drew her hurriedly from her retirement. There, beside his horse, stood Lassiter, his dark apparel and the great black gun-sheaths contrasting singularly with his gentle smile. Jane's active mind took up her interest in him and her half-determined desire to use what charm she had to foil his evident design in visiting Cottonwoods. If she could mitigate his hatred of Mormons, or at least keep him from killing more of them, not only would she be saving her people, but also be leading back this blood-spiller to some semblance of the human.

'Mornin', ma'am,' he said, black sombrero in hand.

'Lassiter, I'm not an old woman, or even a madam,' she replied, with her bright smile. 'If you can't say Miss Witherssteen – call me Jane.'

'I reckon Jane would be easier. First names are always handy for me.'

'Well, use mine, then. Lassiter, I'm glad to see you. I'm in trouble.'

Then she told him of Judkins's return, of the driving of the red herd, of Venters's departure on Wrangle, and the calling-in of her riders.

"Pears to me you're some smilin' an' pretty for a woman with so much trouble,' he remarked.

'Lassiter! Are you paying me compliments? But, seriously, I've made up my mind not to be miserable. I've lost much, and I'll lose more. Nevertheless, I won't be sour, and I hope I'll never be unhappy – again.'

Lassiter twisted his hat round and round, as was his way, and took his time in replying.

'Women are strange to me. I got to back-trailin' myself from them long ago. But I'd like a game woman. Might I ask, seein' as how you take this trouble, if you're goin' to fight?'

'Fight! How? Even if I would, I haven't a friend except that boy who doesn't dare stay in the village.'

'I make bold to say, ma'am – Jane – that there's another, if you want him.'

'Lassiter! . . . Thank you. But how can I accept you as a friend? Think! Why, you'd ride down into the village with those terrible guns and kill my enemies – who are also my churchmen.'

'I reckon I might be riled up to jest about that,' he replied, dryly.

She held out both hands to him.

'Lassiter! I'll accept your friendship – be proud of it – return it – if I may keep you from killing another Mormon.'

'I'll tell you one thing,' he said bluntly, as the gray lightning formed in his eyes. 'You're too good a woman to be sacrificed as you're goin' to be. . . . No, I reckon you an' me can't be friends on such terms.'

In her earnestness she stepped closer to him, repelled yet fascinated by the sudden transition of his moods. That he would fight for her was at once horrible and wonderful.

'You came here to kill a man – the man whom Milly Erne—'

'The man who dragged Milly Erne to hell – put it that way! . . . Jane Witherseen, yes, that's why I came here. I'd tell so much to no other livin' soul. . . . There're things such a woman as you'd never dream of – so don't mention her again. Not till you tell me the name of the man!'

'Tell you! I? Never!'

'I reckon you will. An' I'll never ask you. I'm a man of strange beliefs an' ways of thinkin', an' I seem to see into the future an' feel things hard to explain. The trail I've been followin' for so many years was twisted an' tangled, but it's straightenin' out now. An', Jane Witherseen, you crossed it long ago to ease poor Milly's agony. That, whether you want or not, makes Lassiter your friend. But you cross it now strangely to mean somethin' to me – God knows what! – unless by your noble blindness to incite me to greater hatred of Mormon men.'

Jane felt swayed by a strength that far exceeded her own. In a clash of wills with this man she would go to the wall. If she were to influence him it must be wholly through womanly allurement. There was that about Lassiter which commanded her respect; she had abhorred his name; face to face with him, she found she feared only his deeds. His mystic suggestion, his foreshadowing of something that she was to mean to him, pierced deep into her mind. She believed fate had thrown in her way the lover or husband of Milly Erne. She believed that through her an evil man might be reclaimed. His allusion to what he called her blindness terrified her. Such a mistaken idea of his might unleash the bitter, fatal mood she sensed in him. At any cost she must placate this man; she knew the die was cast, and that if

Lassiter did not soften to a woman's grace and beauty and wiles, then it would be because she could not make him.

'I reckon you'll hear no more such talk from me,' Lassiter went on, presently. 'Now, Miss Jane, I rode in to tell you that your herd of white steers is down on the slope behind them big ridges. An' I seen somethin' goin' on that'd be mighty interestin' to you, if you could see it. Have you a field-glass?'

'Yes, I have two glasses. I'll get them and ride out with you. Wait, Lassiter, please,' she said, and hurried within. Sending word to Jerd to saddle Black Star and fetch him to the court, she then went to her room and changed to the riding-clothes she always donned when going into the sage. In this male attire her mirror showed her a jaunty, handsome rider. If she expected some little meed of admiration from Lassiter, she had no cause for disappointment. The gentle smile that she liked, which made of him another person, slowly overspread his face.

'If I didn't take you for a boy!' he exclaimed. 'It's powerful queer what difference clothes make. Now I've been some scared of your dignity, like when the other night you was all in white, but in this rig—'

Black Star came pounding into the court, dragging Jerd half off his feet, and he whistled at Lassiter's black. But at sight of Jane all his defiant lines seemed to soften, and with tosses of his beautiful head he whipped his bridle.

'Down, Black Star, down,' said Jane.

He dropped his head, and, slowly lengthening, he bent one foreleg, then the other, and sank to his knees. Jane slipped her left foot in the stirrup, swung lightly into the saddle, and Black Star rose with a ringing stamp. It was not easy for Jane to hold him to a canter through the grove, and like the wind he broke when he saw the sage. Jane let him have a couple of miles of free running on the open trail, and then she coaxed him in and waited for her companion. Lassiter was not long in catching up, and presently they were riding side by side. It reminded her how she used to ride with Venters. Where was he now? She gazed far down the slope to the curved purple lines of Deception Pass, and involuntarily shut her eyes with a trembling stir of nameless fear.

'We'll turn off here,' Lassiter said, 'an' take to the sage a mile or so. The white herd is behind them big ridges.'

'What are you going to show me?' asked Jane. 'I'm prepared – don't be afraid.'

He smiled as if he meant that bad news came swiftly enough without being presaged by speech.

When they reached the lee of a rolling ridge Lassiter dismounted, motioning to her to do likewise. They left the horses standing, bridles down. Then Lassiter, carrying the field glasses, began to lead the way up the slow rise of ground. Upon nearing the summit he halted her with a gesture.

'I reckon we'd see more if we didn't show ourselves against the sky,' he said. 'I was here less than a hour ago. Then the herd was seven or eight miles south, an' if they ain't bolted yet—'

'Lassiter! . . . Bolted?'

'That's what I said. Now let's see.'

Jane climbed a few more paces behind him and then peeped over the ridge. Just beyond began a shallow swale that deepened and widened into a valley and then swung to the left. Following the undulating sweep of sage, Jane saw the straggling lines and then the great body of the white herd. She knew enough about steers, even at a distance of four or five miles, to realize that something was in the wind. Bringing her field-glass into use, she moved it slowly from left to right, which action swept the whole herd into range. The stragglers were restless; the more compactly massed steers were browsing. Jane brought the glass back to the big sentinels of the herd, and she saw them trot with quick steps, stop short and toss wide horns, look everywhere, and then trot in another direction.

'Judkins hasn't been able to get his boys together yet,' said Jane. 'But he'll be there soon. I hope not too late. Lassiter, what's frightening those big leaders?'

'Nothin' jest on the minute,' replied Lassiter. 'Them steers are quietin' down. They've been scared, but not bad yet. I reckon the whole herd has moved a few miles this way since I was here.'

'They didn't browse that distance – not in less than an hour. Cattle aren't sheep.'

'No, they jest run it, an' that looks bad.'

'Lassiter, what frightened them?' repeated Jane, impatiently.

'Put down your glass. You'll see at first better with a naked eye. Now look along them ridges on the other side of the herd, the ridges where the sun shines bright on the sage. . . . That's right. Now look an' look hard an' wait.'

Long-drawn moments of straining sight rewarded Jane with nothing save the low, purple rim of ridge and the shimmering sage.

'It's begun again!' whispered Lassiter, and he gripped her arm. 'Watch. . . . There, did you see that?'

'No, no. Tell me what to look for?'

'A white flash – a kind of pin-point of quick light – a gleam as from sun shinin' on somethin' white.'

Suddenly Jane's concentrated gaze caught a fleeting glint. Quickly she brought her glass to bear on the spot. Again the purple sage, magnified in color and size and wave, for long moments irritated her with its monotony. Then from out of the sage on the ridge flew up a broad, white object, flashed in the sunlight and vanished. Like magic it was, and bewildered Jane.

'What on earth is that?'

'I reckon there's someone behind that ridge throwin' up a sheet or a white blanket to reflect the sunshine.'

'Why?' queried Jane, more bewildered than ever.

'To stampede the herd,' replied Lassiter, and his teeth clicked.

'Ah!' She made a fierce, passionate movement, clutched the glass tightly, shook as with the passing of a spasm, and then dropped her head. Presently she raised it to greet Lassiter with something like a smile. 'My righteous brethren are at work again,' she said, in scorn. She had stifled the leap of her wrath, but for perhaps the first time in her life a bitter derision curled her lips. Lassiter's cool gray eyes seemed to pierce her. 'I said I was prepared for anything; but that was hardly true. But why would they – anybody stampede my cattle?'

'That's a Mormon's godly way of bringin' a woman to her knees.'

'Lassiter, I'll die before I ever bend my knees. I might be led; I won't be driven. Do you expect the herd to bolt?'

'I don't like the looks of them big steers. But you can never tell. Cattle sometimes stampede as easily as buffalo. Any little flash or move will start them. A rider gettin' down an' walkin' toward them sometimes will make them jump an' fly. Then again nothin' seems to scare them. But I reckon that white flare will do the biz. It's a new one on me, an' I've seen some ridin' an' rustlin'. It jest takes one of them God-fearin' Mormons to think of devilish tricks.'

'Lassiter, might not this trick be done by Oldring's men?' asked Jane, ever grasping at straws.

'It might be, but it ain't,' replied Lassiter. 'Oldrin's an honest thief. He don't skulk behind ridges to scatter your cattle to the four winds. He rides down on you, an' if you don't like it you can throw a gun.'

Jane bit her tongue to refrain from championing men who at the very moment were proving to her that they were little and mean compared even with rustlers.

'Look! . . . Jane, them leadin' steers have bolted! They're drawin' the stragglers, an' that'll pull the whole herd.'

Jane was not quick enough to catch the details called out by Lassiter, but she saw the line of cattle lengthening. Then, like a stream of white bees pouring from a huge swarm, the steers stretched out from the main body. In a few moments, with astonishing rapidity, the whole herd got into motion. A faint roar of trampling hoofs came to Jane's ears, and gradually swelled; low, rolling clouds of dust began to rise above the sage.

'It's a stampede, an' a hummer,' said Lassiter.

'Oh, Lassiter! The herd's running with the valley! It leads into the cañon! There's a straight jump-off!'

'I reckon they'll run into it, too. But that's a good many miles yet. An' Jane, this valley swings round almost north before it goes east. That stampede will pass within a mile of us.'

The long, white, bobbing line of steers streaked swiftly through the sage, and a funnel-shaped dust-cloud arose at a low angle. A dull rumbling filled Jane's ears.

'I'm thinkin' of millin' that herd,' said Lassiter. His gray glance swept up the slope to the west. 'There's some specks an' dust way off toward the village. Mebbe that's Judkins an' his boys. It ain't likely he'll get here in time to help. You'd better hold Black Star here on this high ridge.'

He ran to his horse and, throwing off saddle-bags and tightening the cinches, he leaped astride and galloped straight down across the valley.

Jane went for Black Star and, leading him to the summit of the ridge, she mounted and faced the valley with excitement and expectancy. She had heard of milling stampeded cattle, and knew it was a feat accomplished by only the most daring riders.

The white herd was now strung out in a line two miles long. The dull rumble of thousands of hoofs deepened into continuous low thunder, and as the steers swept swiftly closer the thunder became a heavy roll. Lassiter crossed in a few moments the level of the valley to the eastern rise of ground and there waited the coming of the herd. Presently, as the head of the white line reached a point opposite to where Jane stood, Lassiter spurred his black into a run.

Jane saw him take a position on the off side of the leaders of the stampede, and there he rode. It was like a race. They swept on down the valley, and when the end of the white line neared Lassiter's first stand the head had begun to swing round to the west. It swung slowly and stubbornly, yet surely, and gradually assumed a long, beautiful curve of moving white. To Jane's amaze she saw the leaders swinging, turning till they headed back toward her and up the valley. Out to the right of these wild, plunging steers ran Lassiter's black, and Jane's keen eye appreciated the fleet stride and sure-footedness of the blind horse. Then it seemed that the herd moved in a great curve, a huge half-moon, with the points of head and tail almost opposite, and a mile apart. But Lassiter relentlessly crowded the leaders, sheering them to the left, turning them little by little. And the dust-blinded wild followers plunged on madly in the tracks of their leaders. This ever-moving, ever-changing curve of steers rolled toward Jane, and when below her, scarce half a mile, it began to narrow and close into a circle. Lassiter had ridden parallel with her position, turned toward her, then aside, and now he was riding directly away from her, all the time pushing the head of that bobbing line inward.

It was then that Jane, suddenly understanding Lassiter's feat, stared and gasped at the riding of this intrepid man. His horse was fleet and tireless, but blind. He had pushed the leaders around and around till they were about to turn in on the inner side of the end of that line of steers. The leaders were already running in a circle; the end of the herd was still running almost straight. But soon they would be wheeling. Then, when Lassiter had the circle formed, how would he escape? With Jane Withersteen prayer was as ready as praise; and she prayed for this man's safety. A circle of dust began to collect. Dimly, as through a yellow veil, Jane saw Lassiter press the leaders inward to close the gap in the sage. She lost sight of him in the dust; again she thought she saw the black, riderless now, rear and drag himself and fall. Lassiter had been thrown – lost! Then he reappeared running out of the dust into the sage. He had escaped, and she breathed again.

Spellbound, Jane Withersteen watched this stupendous mill-wheel of steers. Here was the milling of the herd. The white running circle closed in upon the open space of sage. And the dust circles closed above into a pall. The ground quaked and the incessant thunder of pounding hoofs rolled on. Jane felt deafened, yet she thrilled to a new sound. As the circle of sage lessened the steers began to bawl, and when it closed entirely there came a great upheaval in the center, and a terrible thumping of heads and clicking of horns. Bawling, climbing, goring, the great mass of steers on the inside wrestled in a crashing din, heaved and groaned under the pressure. Then came a deadlock. The inner strife ceased, and the hideous roar and crash. Movement went on in the outer circle, and that, too, gradually stilled. The white herd had come to a stop, and the pall of yellow dust began to drift away on the wind.

Jane Withersteen waited on the ridge, with full and grateful heart. Lassiter appeared, making his weary way toward her through the sage. And up on the slope Judkins rode into sight with his troop of boys. For the present, at least, the white herd would be looked after.

When Lassiter reached her and laid his hand on Black Star's mane, Jane could not find speech.

'Killed – my – hoss,' he panted.

'Oh! I'm sorry,' cried Jane. 'Lassiter! I know you can't replace him, but I'll give you any one of my racers – Bells, or Night, even Black Star.'

'I'll take a fast hoss, Jane, but not one of your favorites,' he replied. 'Only – will you let me have Black Star now an' ride him over there an' head off them fellers who stampeded the herd?'

He pointed to several moving specks of black and puffs of dust in the purple sage.

'I can head them off with this hoss, an' then—'

'Then, Lassiter?'

'They'll never stampede no more cattle.'

'Oh! No! No! . . . Lassiter, I won't let you go!'

But a flush of fire flamed in her cheeks, and her trembling hands shook Black Star's bridle, and her eyes fell before Lassiter's.

CHAPTER SEVEN

The Daughter of Withersteen

'LASSITER WILL YOU BE my rider?' Jane had asked him.

'I reckon so,' he had replied.

Few as the words were, Jane knew how infinitely much they implied. She wanted him to take charge of her cattle and horses and ranges, and save them if that were possible. Yet, though she could not have spoken aloud all she meant, she was perfectly honest with herself. Whatever the price to be paid, she must keep Lassiter close to her; she must shield from him the man who had lured Milly Erne to Cottonwoods. In her fear she so controlled her mind that she did not whisper this Mormon's name to her own soul, she did not even think it. Besides, beyond this thing she regarded as a sacred obligation thrust upon her, was the need of a helper, of a friend, of a champion in this critical time. If she could rule this gun-man, as Venters had called him, if she could even keep him from shedding blood, what strategy to play his name and his presence against the game of oppression her churchmen were waging against her? Never would she forget the effect upon Tull and his men when Venters shouted Lassiter's name. If she could not wholly control Lassiter, then what she could do might put off the fatal day.

One of her safe racers was a dark bay, and she called him Bells because of the way he struck his iron shoes on the stones. When Jerd led out this slender, beautifully built horse Lassiter suddenly became all eyes. A rider's love of a thoroughbred shone in them. Round and round Bells he walked, plainly weakening all the time in his determination not to take one of Jane's favorite racers.

'Lassiter, you're half horse, and Bells sees it already,' said Jane, laughing. 'Look at his eyes. He likes you. He'll love you, too. How can you resist him? Oh, Lassiter, but Bells can run! It's nip and tuck between him and Wrangle, and only Black Star can beat him. He's too spirited a horse for a woman. Take him. He's yours.'

'I jest am weak where a hoss is concerned,' said Lassiter. 'I'll take him, an' I'll take your orders, ma'am.'

'Well, I'm glad, but never mind the ma'am. Let it still be Jane.'

From that hour, it seemed, Lassiter was always in the saddle, riding early and late; and coincident with his part in Jane's affairs the days assumed their old tranquillity. Her intelligence told her this was only the lull before the storm, but her faith would not have it so.

She resumed her visits to the village, and upon one of these she encountered Tull. He greeted her as he had before any trouble came between them, and she, responsive to peace if not quick to forget, met him halfway with manner almost cheerful. He regretted the loss of her cattle; he assured her that the vigilantes which had been organized would soon rout the rustlers; when that had been accomplished her riders would likely return to her.

'You've done a headstrong thing to hire this man Lassiter,' Tull went on, severely. 'He came to Cottonwoods with evil intent.'

'I had to have somebody. And perhaps making him my rider may turn out best in the end for the Mormons of Cottonwoods.'

'You mean to stay his hand?'

'I do – if I can.'

'A woman like you can do anything with a man. That would be well, and would atone in some measure for the errors you have made.'

He bowed and passed on. Jane resumed her walk with conflicting thoughts. She resented Elder Tull's cold, impassive manner that looked down upon her as one who had incurred his just displeasure. Otherwise he would have been the same calm, dark-browed, impenetrable man she had known for ten years. In fact, except when he had revealed his passion in the matter of the seizing of Venters, she had never dreamed he could be other than the grave, reproving preacher. He stood out now a strange, secretive man. She would have thought better of him if he had picked up the threads of their quarrel where they had parted. Was Tull what he appeared to be? The question flung itself involuntarily over Jane Withersteen's inhibitive habit of faith without question. And she refused to answer it. Tull could not fight in the open. Venters had said, Lassiter had said, that her Elder shirked fight and worked in the dark. Just now in this meeting Tull had ignored the fact that he had sued, exhorted, demanded that she marry him. He made no mention of Venters. His manner was that of the minister who had been outraged, but who overlooked the frailties of a woman. Beyond question he seemed unutterably aloof from all knowledge of pressure being brought to bear upon her, absolutely guiltless of any connection with secret power over riders, with night journeys, with rustlers and stampedes of cattle. And that convinced her again of unjust suspicions. But it was convincement through an obstinate faith. She shuddered as she accepted it, and that shudder was the nucleus of a terrible revolt.

Jane turned into one of the wide lanes leading from the main street and entered a huge, shady yard. Here were sweet-smelling clover, alfalfa, flowers, and vegetables, all growing in happy confusion. And like these fresh green things were the dozens of babies, tots, toddlers, noisy urchins, laughing girls, a whole multitude of children of one family. For Collier Brandt, the father of all this numerous progeny, was a Mormon with four wives.

The big house where they lived was old, solid, picturesque, the lower part built of logs, the upper of rough clapboards, with vines growing up the outside stone chimneys. There were many wooden-shuttered windows, and one pretentious window of glass, proudly curtained in white. As this house had four mistresses, it likewise had four separate sections, not one of which communicated with another, and all had to be entered from the outside.

In the shade of a wide, low, vine-roofed porch Jane found Brandt's wives entertaining Bishop Dyer. They were motherly women, of comparatively similar ages, and plain-featured, and just at this moment anything but grave. The Bishop was rather tall, of stout build, with iron-gray hair and beard, and eyes of light blue. They were merry now; but Jane had seen them when they were not, and then she feared him as she had feared her father.

The women flocked around her in welcome.

'Daughter of Withersteen,' said the Bishop, gaily, as he took her hand, 'you have not been prodigal of your gracious self of late. A Sabbath without you at service! I shall reprove Elder Tull.'

'Bishop, the guilt is mine. I'll come to you and confess,' Jane replied, lightly; but she felt the undercurrent of her words.

'Mormon love-making!' exclaimed the Bishop, rubbing his hands. 'Tull keeps you all to himself.'

'No. He is not courting me.'

'What? The laggard! If he does not make haste, I'll go a-courting myself up to Withersteen House.'

There was laughter and further bantering by the Bishop, and then mild talk of village affairs, after which he took his leave, and Jane was left with her friend, Mary Brandt.

'Jane, you're not yourself. Are you sad about the rustling of the cattle? But you have so many, you are so rich.'

Then Jane confided in her, telling much, yet holding back her doubts and fears.

'Oh, why don't you marry Tull and be one of us?'

'But, Mary, I don't love Tull,' said Jane, stubbornly.

'I don't blame you for that. But, Jane Withersteen, you've got to choose between the love of man and love of God. Often we Mormon women have to do that. It's not easy. The kind of happiness you want I wanted once. I never got it, nor will you, unless you throw away your soul. We've all watched your affair with Venters in fear and trembling. Some dreadful thing will come of it. You don't want him hanged or shot – or treated worse, as that Gentile boy was treated in Glaze for fooling round a Mormon woman. Marry Tull. It's your duty as a Mormon. You'll feel no rapture as his wife – but think of Heaven! Mormon women don't marry for what they expect on earth. Take up the cross, Jane. Remember your father founded Amber Spring, built these old houses, brought Mormons here, and fathered them. You are the daughter of Withersteen!'

Jane left Mary Brandt and went to call upon other friends. They received her with the same glad welcome as had Mary, lavished upon her the pent-up affection of Mormon women, and let her go with her ears ringing of Tull, Venters, Lassiter, of duty to God and glory in Heaven.

'Verily,' murmured Jane, 'I don't know myself when, through all this, I remain unchanged – nay, more fixed of purpose.'

She returned to the main street and bent her thoughtful steps toward the center of the village. A string of wagons drawn by oxen was lumbering along. These 'sage-freighters,' as they were called, hauled grain and flour and merchandise from Sterling; and Jane laughed suddenly in the midst of her humility at the thought that they were her property, as was one of the three stores for which they freighted goods. The water that flowed along the path at her feet, and turned into each cottage-yard to nourish garden and orchard, also was hers, no less her private property because she chose to give it free. Yet in this village of Cottonwoods, which her father had founded and which she maintained, she was not her own mistress; she was not to abide by her own choice of a husband. She was the daughter of Withersteen. Suppose she proved it, imperiously! But she quelled that proud temptation at its birth.

Nothing could have replaced the affection which the village people had for her; no power could have made her happy as the pleasure her presence gave. As she went on down the street, past the stores with their rude platform entrances, and the saloons, where tired horses stood with bridles dragging, she was again assured of what was the bread and wine of life to her – that she was loved. Dirty boys playing in the ditch, clerks, teamsters, riders, loungers on the corners, ranchers on dusty horses, little girls running errands, and women hurrying to the stores all looked up at her coming with glad eyes.

Jane's various calls and wandering steps at length led her to the Gentile quarter of the village. This was at the extreme southern end, and here some thirty Gentile families lived in huts and shacks and log-cabins and several dilapidated cottages. The fortunes of these inhabitants of Cottonwoods could be read in their abodes.

Water they had in abundance, and therefore grass and fruit-trees and patches of alfalfa and vegetable gardens. Some of the men and boys had a few stray cattle, others obtained such intermittent employment as the Mormons reluctantly tendered them. But none of the families was prosperous, many were very poor, and some lived only by Jane Withersteen's beneficence.

As it made Jane happy to go among her own people, so it saddened her to come in contact with these Gentiles. Yet that was not because she was unwelcome; here she was gratefully received by the women, passionately by the children. But poverty and idleness, with their attendant wretchedness and sorrow, always hurt her. That she could alleviate this distress more now than ever before proved the adage that it was an ill wind that blew nobody good. While her Mormon riders were in her employ she had found few Gentiles who could stay with her, and now she was able to find employment for all the men and boys. No little shock was it to have man after man tell her that he dare not accept her kind offer.

'It won't do,' said one Carson, an intelligent man who had seen better days. 'We've had our warning. Plain and to the point! Now there's Judkins, he packs guns, and he can use them, and so can the daredevil boys he's hired. But they've little responsibility. Can we risk having our homes burned in our absence?'

Jane felt the stretching and chilling of the skin of her face as the blood left it.

'Carson, you and the others rent these houses?' she asked.

'You ought to know, Miss Withersteen. Some of them are yours.'

'I know? . . . Carson, I never in my life took a day's labor for rent or a yearling calf or a bunch of grass, let alone gold.'

'Bivens, your store-keeper, sees to that.'

'Look here, Carson,' went on Jane, hurriedly, and now her cheeks were burning. 'You and Black and Willet pack your goods and move your families up to my cabins in the grove. They're far more comfortable than these. Then go to work for me. And if aught happens to you there I'll give you money – gold enough to leave Utah!'

The man choked and stammered, and then, as tears welled into his eyes, he found the use of his tongue and cursed. No gentle speech could ever have equaled that curse in eloquent expression of what he felt for Jane Withersteen. How strangely his look and tone reminded her of Lassiter!

'No, it won't do,' he said, when he had somewhat recovered himself. 'Miss Withersteen, there are things that you don't know, and there's not a soul among us who can tell you.'

'I seem to be learning many things, Carson. Well, then, will you let me aid you – say till better times?'

'Yes, I will,' he replied, with his face lighting up. 'I see what it means to you, and you know what it means to me. Thank you! And if better times ever come I'll be only too happy to work for you.'

'Better times will come. I trust God and have faith in man. Good day, Carson.'

The lane opened out upon the sage-enclosed alfalfa fields, and the last habitation, at the end of that lane of hovels, was the meanest. Formerly it had been a shed; now it was a home. The broad leaves of a wide-spreading cottonwood sheltered the sunken roof of weathered boards. Like an Indian hut, it had one floor. Round about it were a few scanty rows of vegetables, such as the hand of a weak woman had time and strength to cultivate. This little dwelling-place was just outside the village limits, and the widow who lived there had to carry her water from the nearest irrigation ditch. As Jane Withersteen entered the unfenced yard a child saw her, shrieked with joy, and came tearing toward her with curls flying. This child was a little girl of four called Fay. Her name suited her, for she was an elf, a sprite, a creature so fairy-like and beautiful that she seemed unearthly.

'Muvver sended for oo,' cried Fay, as Jane kissed her, 'an' oo never tome.'

'I didn't know, Fay; but I've come now.'

Fay was a child of outdoors, of the garden and ditch and field, and she was dirty and ragged. But rags and dirt did not hide her beauty. The one thin little bedraggled garment she wore half covered her fine, slim body. Red as cherries were her cheeks and lips; her eyes were violet blue, and the crown of her childish loveliness was the curling golden hair. All the children of Cottonwoods were Jane Witheristeen's friends; she loved them all. But Fay was dearest to her. Fay had few playmates, for among the Gentile children there were none near her age, and the Mormon children were forbidden to play with her. So she was a shy, wild, lonely child.

'Muvver's sick,' said Fay, leading Jane toward the door of the hut.

Jane went in. There was only one room, rather dark and bare, but it was clean and neat. A woman lay upon a bed.

'Mrs Larkin, how are you?' asked Jane, anxiously.

'I've been pretty bad for a week, but I'm better now.'

'You haven't been here all alone – with no one to wait on you?'

'Oh no! My women neighbors are kind. They take turns coming in.'

'Did you send for me?'

'Yes, several times.'

'But I had no word – no messages ever got to me.'

'I sent the boys, and they left word with your women that I was ill and would you please come.'

A sudden deadly sickness seized Jane. She fought the weakness, as she fought to be above suspicious thoughts, and it passed, leaving her conscious of her utter impotence. That, too, passed as her spirit rebounded. But she had again caught a glimpse of dark underhand domination, running its secret lines this time into her own household. Like a spider in the blackness of night an unseen hand had begun to run these dark lines, to turn and twist them about her life, to plait and weave a web. Jane Witheristeen knew it now, and in the realization further coolness and sureness came to her, and the fighting courage of her ancestors.

'Mrs Larkin, you're better, and I'm so glad,' said Jane. 'But may I not do something for you – a turn at nursing, or send you things, or take care of Fay?'

'You're so good. Since my husband's been gone what would have become of Fay and me but for you? It was about Fay that I wanted to speak to you. This time I thought surely I'd die, and I was worried about Fay. Well, I'll be around all right shortly, but my strength's gone and I won't live long. So I may as well speak now. You remember you've been asking me to let you take Fay and bring her up as your daughter?'

'Indeed yes, I remember. I'll be happy to have her. But I hope the day—'

'Never mind that. The day'll come – sooner or later. I refused your offer, and now I'll tell you why.'

'I know why,' interposed Jane. 'It's because you don't want her to be brought up as a Mormon.'

'No, it wasn't altogether that.' Mrs Larkin raised her thin hand and laid it appealingly on Jane's. 'I don't like to tell you. But – it's this: I told all my friends what you wanted. They know you, care for you, and they said for me to trust Fay to you. Women will talk, you know. It got to the ears of Mormons – gossip of your love for Fay and your wanting her. And it came straight back to me, in jealousy, perhaps, that you wouldn't take Fay as much for love of her as because of your religious duty to bring up another girl for some Mormon to marry.'

'That's a damnable lie!' cried Jane Withersteen.

'It was what made me hesitate,' went on Mrs Larkin, 'but I never believed it at heart. And now I guess I'll let you—'

'Wait! Mrs Larkin, I may have told little white lies in my life, but never a lie that mattered, that hurt anyone. Now believe me. I love little Fay. If I had her near me I'd grow to worship her. When I asked for her I thought only of that love. . . . Let me prove this. You and Fay come to live with me. I've such a big house, and I'm so lonely. I'll help nurse you, take care of you. When you're better you can work for me. I'll keep little Fay and bring her up – without Mormon teaching. When she's grown, if she should want to leave me, I'll send her, and not empty-handed, back to Illinois where you came from. I promise you.'

'I knew it was a lie,' replied the mother, and she sank back upon her pillow with something of peace in her white, worn face. 'Jane Withersteen, may Heaven bless you! I've been deeply grateful to you. But because you're a Mormon I never felt close to you till now. I don't know much about religion as religion, but your God and my God are the same.'

CHAPTER EIGHT

Surprise Valley

BACK IN THAT STRANGE cañon, which Venters had found indeed a valley of surprises, the wounded girl's whispered appeal, almost a prayer, not to take her back to the rustlers crowned the events of the last few days with a confounding climax. That she should not want to return to them staggered Venters. Presently, as logical thought returned, her appeal confirmed his first impression – that she was more unfortunate than bad – and he experienced a sensation of gladness. If he had known before that Oldring's Masked Rider was a woman his opinion would have been formed and he would have considered her abandoned. But his first knowledge had come when he lifted a white face quivering in a convulsion of agony; he had heard God's name whispered by blood-stained lips; through her solemn and awful eyes he had caught a glimpse of her soul. And just now had come the entreaty to him, 'Don't – take – me – back – there!'

Once for all Venters's quick mind formed a permanant conception of this poor girl. He based it, not upon what the chances of life had made her, but upon the revelation of dark eyes that pierced the infinite, upon a few pitiful, halting words that betrayed failure and wrong and misery, yet breathed the truth of a tragic fate rather than a natural leaning to evil.

'What's your name?' he inquired.

'Bess,' she answered.

'Bess what?'

'That's enough – just Bess.'

The red that deepened in her cheeks was not all the flush of fever. Venters marveled anew, and this time at the tint of shame in her face, at the momentary drooping of long lashes. She might be a rustler's girl, but she was still capable of shame; she might be dying, but she still clung to some little remnant of honor.

'Very well, Bess. It doesn't matter,' he said. 'But this matters – what shall I do with you?'

'Are – you – a rider?' she whispered.

'Not now. I was once. I drove the Withersteen herds. But I lost my place – lost all I owned – and now I'm – I'm a sort of outcast. My name's Bern Venters.'

'You won't – take me – to Cottonwoods – or Glaze? I'd be – hanged.'

'No, indeed. But I must do something with you. For it's not safe for me here. I shot that rustler who was with you. Sooner or later he'll be found, and then my tracks. I must find a safer hiding-place where I can't be trailed.'

'Leave me – here.'

'Alone – to die!'

'Yes.'

'I will not.' Venters spoke shortly with a kind of ring in his voice.

'What – do you want – to do – with me?' Her whispering grew difficult, so low and faint that Venters had to stoop to hear her.

'Why, let's see,' he replied, slowly. 'I'd like to take you some place where I could watch by you, nurse you, till you're all right again.'

'And – then?'

'Well, it'll be time to think of that when you're cured of your wound. It's a bad one. And – Bess, if you don't want to live – if you don't fight for life – you'll never—'

'Oh! I want – to live! I'm afraid – to die. But I'd rather die – than go back – to – to—'

'To Oldring?' asked Venters, interrupting her in turn.

Her lips moved in an affirmative.

'I promise not to take you back to him or to Cottonwoods or to Glaze.'

The mournful earnestness of her gaze suddenly shone with unutterable gratitude and wonder. And as suddenly Venters found her eyes beautiful as he had never seen or felt beauty. They were as dark blue as the sky at night. Then the flashing changed to a long, thoughtful look, in which there was wistful, unconscious searching of his face, a look that trembled on the verge of hope and trust.

'I'll try – to live,' she said. The broken whisper just reached his ears. 'Do what – you want – with me.'

'Rest then – don't worry – sleep,' he replied.

Abruptly he arose, as if her words had been decision for him, and with a sharp command to the dogs he strode from the camp. Venters was conscious of an indefinite conflict of change within him. It seemed to be a vague passing of old moods, a dim coalescing of new forces, a moment of inexplicable transition. He was both cast down and uplifted. He wanted to think and think of the meaning, but he resolutely dispelled emotion. His imperative need at present was to find a safe retreat, and this called for action.

So he set out. It still wanted several hours before dark. This trip he turned to the left and wended his skulking way southward a mile or more to the opening of the valley, where lay the strange scrawled rocks. He did not, however, venture boldly out into the open sage, but clung to the right-hand wall and went along that till its perpendicular line broke into the long incline of bare stone.

Before proceeding farther he halted, studying the strange character of this slope and realizing that a moving black object could be seen far against such back-ground. Before him ascended a gradual swell of smooth stone. It was hard, polished and full of pockets worn by centuries of eddying rain-water. A hundred yards up began a line of grotesque cedar-trees, and they extended along the slope clear to its most southerly end. Beyond that end Venters wanted to get, and he concluded the cedars, few as they were, would afford some cover.

Therefore he climbed swiftly. The trees were farther up than he had estimated, though he had from long habit made allowance for the deceiving nature of distances in that country. When he gained the cover of cedars he paused to rest and look, and it was then he saw how the trees sprang from holes in the bare rock. Ages of rain had run down the slope, circling, eddying in depressions, wearing deep round holes. There had been dry seasons, accumulations of dust, wind-blown seeds, and cedars rose wonderfully out of solid rock. But these were not beautiful cedars. They were gnarled, twisted into weird contortions, as if growth were torture, dead at the tops, shrunken, gray, and old. Theirs had been a bitter fight, and Venters felt a strange sympathy for them. This country was hard on trees – and men.

He slipped from cedar to cedar, keeping them between him and the open valley. As he progressed, the belt of trees widened, and he kept to its upper margin. He passed shady pockets half full of water, and, as he marked the location for possible future need, he reflected that there had been no rain since the winter snows. From one of these shady holes a rabbit hopped out and squatted down, laying its ears flat.

Venters wanted fresh meat now more than when he had only himself to think of. But it would not do to fire his rifle there. So he broke off a cedar branch and threw it. He crippled the rabbit, which started to flounder up the slope. Venters did not wish to lose the meat, and he never allowed crippled game to escape, to die lingeringly in some covert. So after a careful glance below, and back toward the cañon, he began to chase the rabbit.

The fact that rabbits generally ran uphill was not new to him. But it presently seemed singular why this rabbit, that might have escaped downward, chose to ascend the slope. Venters knew then that it had a burrow higher up. More than once he jerked over to seize it, only in vain, for the rabbit by renewed effort eluded his grasp. Thus the chase continued on up the bare slope. The farther Venters climbed the more determined he grew to catch his quarry. At last, panting and sweating, he captured the rabbit at the foot of a steeper grade. Laying his rifle on the bulge of rising stone, he killed the animal and slung it from his belt.

Before starting down he waited to catch his breath. He had climbed far up that wonderful smooth slope, and had almost reached the base of yellow cliff that rose skyward, a huge scarred and cracked bulk. It frowned down upon him as if to forbid further ascent. Venters bent over for his rifle, and, as he picked it up from where it leaned against the steeper grade, he saw several little nicks cut in the solid stone.

They were only a few inches deep and about a foot apart. Venters began to count them – one – two – three – four – on up to sixteen. That number carried his glance to the top of this first bulging bench of cliff-base. Above, after a more level offset, was still steeper slope, and the line of nicks kept on, to wind round a projecting corner of wall.

A casual glance would have passed by these little dents; if Venters had not known what they signified he would never have bestowed upon them the second glance. But he knew they had been cut there by hand, and, though age-worn, he recognized them as steps cut in the rock by the cliff-dwellers. With a pulse beginning to beat and hammer away his calmness, he eyed that indistinct line of steps, up to where the buttress of wall hid further sight of them. He knew that behind the corner of stone would be a cave or a crack which could never be suspected from below. Chance, that had sported with him of late, now directed him to a probable hiding-place. Again he laid aside his rifle, and, removing boots and belt, he began to walk up the steps. Like a mountain goat, he was agile, sure-footed, and he mounted the first bench without bending to use his hands. The next ascent took grip of fingers as well as toes, but he climbed steadily, swiftly, to reach the projecting corner, and slipped around it. Here he faced a notch in the cliff. At the apex he turned abruptly into a ragged vent that split the ponderous wall clear to the top, showing a narrow streak of blue sky.

At the base this vent was dark, cool, and smelled of dry, musty dust. It zigzagged so that he could not see ahead more than a few yards at a time. He noticed tracks of wildcats and rabbits in the dusty floor. At every turn he expected to come upon a huge cavern full of little square stone houses, each with a small aperture like a staring dark eye. The passage lightened and widened, and opened at the foot of a narrow, steep, ascending chute.

Venters had a moment's notice of the rock, which was of the same smoothness and hardness as the slope below, before his gaze went irresistibly upward to the precipitous walls of this wide ladder of granite. These were ruined walls of yellow sandstone, and so split and splintered, so overhanging with great sections of balancing rim, so impending with tremendous crumbling crags, that Venters caught his breath sharply, and, appalled, he instinctively recoiled as if a step upward might jar the ponderous cliffs from their foundation. Indeed, it seemed that these ruined cliffs were but awaiting a breath of wind to collapse and come tumbling down. Venters hesitated. It would be a foolhardy man who risked his life under the leaning, waiting avalanches of rock in that gigantic split. Yet how many years had they leaned there without falling! At the bottom of the incline was an immense heap of weathered sandstone all crumbling to dust, but there were no huge rocks as large as houses, such as rested so lightly and frightfully above, waiting patiently and inevitably to crash down. Slowly split from the parent rock by the weathering process, and carved and sculptured by ages of wind and rain, they waited their moment. Venters felt how foolish it was for him to fear these broken walls; to fear that, after they had endured for thousands of years, the moment of his passing should be the one for them to slip. Yet he feared it.

'What a place to hide!' muttered Venters. 'I'll climb – I'll see where this thing goes. If only I can find water!'

With teeth tight shut he essayed the incline. And as he climbed he bent his eyes downward. This, however, after a little grew impossible; he had to look to obey his eager, curious mind. He raised his glance and saw light between row on row of shafts and pinnacles and crags that stood out from the main wall. Some leaned against the cliff, others against each other; many stood sheer and alone; all were crumbling, cracked, rotten. It was a place of yellow, ragged ruin. The passage narrowed as he went up; it became a slant, hard for him to stick on; it was smooth as marble. Finally he surmounted it, surprised to find the walls still several hundred feet high, and a narrow gorge leading down on the other side. This was a divide between two inclines, about twenty yards wide. At one side stood an enormous rock. Venters gave it a second glance, because it rested on a pedestal. It attracted closer attention. It was like a colossal pear of stone standing on its stem. Around the bottom were thousands of little nicks just distinguishable to the eye. They were marks of stone hatchets. The cliff-dwellers had chipped and chipped away at this boulder till it rested its tremendous bulk upon a mere pin-point of its surface. Venters pondered. Why had the little stone-men hacked away at that big boulder? It bore no semblance to a statue or an idol or a godhead or a sphinx. Instinctively he put his hands on it and pushed; then his shoulder and heaved. The stone seemed to groan, to stir, to grate, and then to move. It tipped a little downward and hung balancing for a long instant, slowly returned, rocked slightly, groaned, and settled back to its former position.

Venters divined its significance. It had been meant for defense. The cliff-dwellers, driven by dreaded enemies to this last stand, had cunningly cut the rock until it balanced perfectly, ready to be dislodged by strong hands. Just below it leaned a tottering crag that would have toppled, starting an avalanche on an acclivity where no sliding mass could stop. Crags and pinnacles, splintered cliffs, and leaning shafts and monuments, would have thundered down to block forever the outlet to Deception Pass.

'That was a narrow shave for me,' said Venters, soberly. 'A balancing rock! The cliff-dwellers never had to roll it. They died, vanishished, and here the rock stands, probably little changed. . . . But it might serve another lonely dweller of the cliffs. I'll hide up here somewhere, if I can only find water.'

He descended the gorge on the other side. The slope was gradual, the space narrow, the course straight for many rods. A gloom hung between the up-sweeping walls. In a turn the passage narrowed to scarce a dozen feet, and here was darkness of night. But light shone ahead; another abrupt turn brought day again, and then wide open space.

Above Venters loomed a wonderful arch of stone bridging the cañon rims, and through the enormous round portal gleamed and glistened a beautiful valley shining under sunset gold reflected by surrounding cliffs. He gave a start of surprise. The valley was a cove a mile long, half that wide, and its enclosing walls were smooth and stained, and curved inward, forming great caves. He decided that its floor was far higher than the level of Deception Pass and the intersecting cañons. No purple sage colored this valley floor. Instead there were the white of aspens, streaks of branch and slender trunk glistening from the green of leaves, and the darker green of oaks, and through the middle of this forest, from wall to wall, ran a winding line of brilliant green which marked the course of cottonwoods and willows.

'There's water here – and this is the place for me,' said Venters. 'Only birds can peep over those walls. I've gone Oldring one better.'

Venters waited no longer, and turned swiftly to retrace his steps. He named the cañon Surprise Valley and the huge boulder that guarded the outlet Balancing Rock. Going down he did not find himself attended by such fears as had beset him in the climb; still, he was not easy in mind and could not occupy himself with plans of moving the girl and his outfit until he had descended to the notch. There he rested a moment and looked about him. The pass was darkening with the approach of night. At the corner of the wall, where the stone steps turned, he saw a spur of rock that would serve to hold the noose of a lasso. He needed no more aid to scale that place. As he intended to make the move under cover of darkness, he wanted most to be able to tell where to climb up. So, taking several small stones with him, he stepped and slid down to the edge of the slope where he had left his rifle and boots. Here he placed the stones some yards apart. He left the rabbit lying upon the bench where the steps began. Then he addressed a keen-sighted, remembering gaze to the rim-wall above. It was serrated, and between two spears of rock, directly in line with his position, showed a zigzag crack that at night would

let through the gleam of sky. This settled, he put on his belt and boots and
prepared to descend. Some consideration was necessary to decide whether or not
to leave his rifle there. On the return, carrying the girl and a pack, it would be
added encumbrance; and after debating the matter he left the rifle leaning against
the bench. As he went straight down the slope he halted every few rods to look up
at his mark on the rim. It changed, but he fixed each change in his memory. When
he reached the first cedar-tree, he tied his scarf upon a dead branch, and then
hurried toward camp, having no more concern about finding his trail upon the
return trip.

Darkness soon emboldened and lent him greater speed. It occurred to him, as
he glided into the grassy glade near camp and heard the whinny of a horse, that he
had forgotten Wrangle. The big sorrel could not be gotten into Surprise Valley.
He would have to be left there.

Venters determined at once to lead the other horses out through the thicket
and turn them loose. The farther they wandered from this cañon the better it
would suit him. He easily descried Wrangle through the gloom, but the others
were not in sight. Venters whistled low for the dogs, and when they came trotting
to him he sent them out to search for the horses, and followed. It soon developed
that they were not in the glade nor the thicket. Venters grew cold and rigid at the
thought of rustlers having entered his retreat. But the thought passed, for the
demeanor of Ring and Whitie reassured him. The horses had wandered away.

Under the clump of silver spruces hung a denser mantle of darkness, yet not so
thick that Venters's night-practiced eyes could not catch the white oval of a still
face. He bent over it with a slight suspension of breath that was both caution lest
he frighten her and chill uncertainty of feeling lest he find her dead. But she slept,
and he arose to renewed activity.

He packed his saddle-bags. The dogs were hungry, they whined about him and
nosed his busy hands; but he took no time to feed them nor to satisfy his own
hunger. He slung the saddle-bags over his shoulders and made them secure with
his lasso. Then he wrapped the blankets closer about the girl and lifted her in his
arms. Wrangle whinnied and thumped the ground as Venters passed him with the
dogs. The sorrel knew he was being left behind, and was not sure whether he liked
it or not. Venters went on and entered the thicket. Here he had to feel his way in
pitch blackness and to wedge his progress between the close saplings. Time meant
little to him now that he had started, and he edged along with slow side movement
till he got clear of the thicket. Ring and Whitie stood waiting for him. Taking to
the open aisles and patches of the sage, he walked guardedly, careful not to
stumble or step in dust or strike against spreading sage-branches.

If he were burdened he did not feel it. From time to time, when he passed out of
the black lines of shade into the wan starlight, he glanced at the white face of the
girl lying in his arms. She had not awakened from her sleep or stupor. He did not
rest until he cleared the black gate of the cañon. Then he leaned against a stone
breast-high to him and gently released the girl from his hold. His brow and hair
and the palms of his hands were wet, and there was a kind of nervous contraction
of his muscles. They seemed to ripple and string tense. He had a desire to hurry
and no sense of fatigue. A wind blew the scent of sage in his face. The first early
blackness of night passed with the brightening of the stars. Somewhere back on
his trail a coyote yelped, splitting the dead silence. Venters's faculties seemed
singularly acute.

He lifted the girl again and pressed on. The valley afforded better traveling than
the cañon. It was lighter, freer of sage, and there were no rocks. Soon, out of the

pale gloom shone a still paler thing, and that was the low swell of slope. Venters mounted it, and his dogs walked beside him. Once upon the stone he slowed to snail pace, straining his sight to avoid the pockets and holes. Foot by foot he went up. The weird cedars, like great demons and witches chained to the rock and writhing in silent anguish, loomed up with wide and twisting naked arms. Venters crossed this belt of cedars, skirted the upper border, and recognized the tree he had marked, even before he saw his waving scarf.

Here he knelt and deposited the girl gently, feet first, and slowly laid her out full length. What he feared was to reopen one of her wounds. If he gave her a violent jar, or slipped and fell! But the supreme confidence so strangely felt that night admitted of no such blunders.

The slope before him seemed to swell into obscurity, to lose its definite outline in a misty, opaque cloud that shaded into the over-shadowing wall. He scanned the rim where the serrated points speared the sky, and he found the zigzag crack. It was dim, only a shade lighter than the dark ramparts; but he distinguished it, and that served.

Lifting the girl, he stepped upward, closely attending to the nature of the path under his feet. After a few steps he stopped to mark his line with the crack in the rim. The dogs clung closer to him. While chasing the rabbit this slope had appeared interminable to him; now, burdened as he was, he did not think of length or height or toil. He remembered only to avoid a misstep and to keep his direction. He climbed on, with frequent stops to watch the rain, and before he dreamed of gaining the bench he bumped his knees into it, and saw, in the dim gray light, his rifle and the rabbit. He had come straight up without mishap or swerving off his course, and his shut teeth unlocked.

As he laid the girl down in the shallow hollow of the little ridge, with her white face upturned, she opened her eyes. Wide, staring, black, at once like both the night and the stars, they made her face seem still whiter.

'Is – it – you?' she asked, faintly.

'Yes,' replied Venters.

'Oh! Where – are we?'

'I'm taking you to a safe place where no one will ever find you. I must climb a little here and call the dogs. Don't be afraid. I'll soon come for you.'

She said no more. Her eyes watched him steadily for a moment and then closed. Venters pulled off his boots and then felt for the little steps in the rock. The shade of the cliff above obscured the point he wanted to gain, but he could see dimly a few feet before him. What he had attempted with care he now went at with surpassing lightness. Buoyant, rapid, sure, he attained the corner of wall and slipped around it. Here he could not see a hand before his face, so he groped along, found a little flat space, and there removed the saddle-bags. The lasso he took back with him to the corner and looped the noose over the spur of rock.

'Ring – Whitie – come,' he called softly.

Low whines came up from below.

'Here! Come, Whitie – Ring,' he repeated, this time sharply.

Then followed scraping of claws and pattering of feet; and out of the gray gloom below him swiftly climbed the dogs to reach his side and pass beyond.

Venters descended, holding to the lasso. He tested its strength by throwing all his weight upon it. Then he gathered the girl up, and holding her securely in his left arm, he began to climb, at every few steps jerking his right hand upward along the lasso. It sagged at each forward movements he made, but he balanced himself lightly during the interval when he lacked the support of a taut rope. He climbed as if he had wings, the strength of a giant, and knew not the sense of fear. The sharp corner of cliff seemed to cut out of the darkness. He reached it and the protruding shelf, and then, entering the black shade of the notch, he moved blindly but surely to the place where he had left the saddle-bags. He heard the dogs, though he could not see them. Once more he carefully placed the girl at his feet. Then, on hands and knees, he went over the little flat space, feeling for stones. He removed a number, and, scraping the deep dust into a heap, he unfolded the outer blanket from around the girl and laid her upon this bed. Then he went down the slope again for his boots, rifle, and the rabbit, and, bringing also his lasso with him, he made short work of that trip.

'Are – you – there?' The girl's voice came low from the blackness.

'Yes,' he replied, and was conscious that his laboring breast made speech difficult.

'Are we – in a cave?'

'Yes.'

'Oh, listen! . . . The waterfall! . . . I hear it! You've brought me back!'

Venters heard a murmuring moan that one moment swelled to a pitch almost softly shrill and the next lulled to a low, almost inaudible sigh.

'That's – wind blowing – in the – cliffs,' he panted. 'You're far – from Oldring's – cañon.'

The effort it cost him to speak made him conscious of extreme lassitude following upon great exertion. It seemed that when he lay down and drew his blanket over him the action was the last before utter prostration. He stretched inert, wet, hot, his body one great strife of throbbing, stinging nerves and bursting veins. And there he lay for a long while before he felt that he had begun to rest.

Rest came to him that night, but no sleep. Sleep he did not want. The hours of strained effort were now as if they had never been, and he wanted to think. Earlier in the day he had dismissed an inexplicable feeling of change; but now, when there was no longer demand on his cunning and strength and he had time to think, he could not catch the illusive thing that had sadly perplexed as well as elevated his spirit.

Above him, through a V-shaped cleft in the dark rim of the cliff, shone the lustrous stars that had been his lonely accusers for a long, long year. Tonight they were different. He studied them. Larger, whiter, more radiant they seemed; but that was not the difference he meant. Gradually it came to him that the distinction was not one he saw, but one he felt. In this he divined as much of the baffling change as he thought would be revealed to him then. And as he lay there, with the singing of the cliff-winds in his ears, the white stars above the dark, bold vent, the difference which he felt was that he was no longer alone.

CHAPTER NINE

Silver Spruce and Aspens

THE REST OF THAT NIGHT seemed to Venters only a few moments of starlight, a dark overcasting of sky, an hour or so of gray gloom, and then the lighting of dawn.

When he had bestirred himself, feeding the hungry dogs and breaking his long fast, and had repacked his saddle bags, it was clear daylight, though the sun had not tipped the yellow wall in the east. He concluded to make the climb and descent into Surprise Valley in one trip. To that end he tied his blanket upon Ring and gave Whitie the extra lasso and the rabbit to carry. Then, with the rifle and saddle-bags slung upon his back, he took up the girl. She did not awaken from heavy slumber.

That climb up under the rugged, menacing brows of the broken cliffs, in the face of a grim, leaning boulder that seemed to be weary of its age-long wavering, was a tax on strength and nerve that Venters felt equally with something sweet and strangely exulting in its accomplishment. He did not pause until he gained the narrow divide and there he rested. Balancing Rock loomed huge, cold in the gray light of dawn, a thing without life, yet it spoke silently to Venters: 'I am waiting to plunge down, to shatter and crash, roar and boom, to bury your trail, and close forever the outlet to Deception Pass!'

On the descent of the other side Venters had easy going, but was somewhat concerned because Whitie appeared to have succumbed to temptation, and while carrying the rabbit was also chewing on it. And Ring evidently regarded this as an injury to himself, especially as he had carried the heavier load. Presently he snapped at one end of the rabbit and refused to let go. But his action prevented Whitie from further misdoing, and then the two dogs pattered down, carrying the rabbit between them.

Venters turned out of the gorge, and suddenly paused stock-still, astounded at the scene before him. The curve of the great stone bridge had caught the sunrise, and through the magnificent arch burst a glorious stream of gold that shone with a long slant down into the center of Surprise Valley. Only through the arch did any sunlight pass, so that all the rest of the valley lay still asleep, dark green, mysterious, shadowy, merging its level into walls as misty and soft as morning clouds.

Venters then descended, passing through the arch, looking up at its tremendous height and sweep. It spanned the opening to Surprise Valley, stretching in almost perfect curve from rim to rim. Even in his hurry and concern Venters could not but feel its majesty, and the thought came to him that the cliff-dwellers must have regarded it as an object of worship.

Down, down, down Venters strode, more and more feeling the weight of his burden as he descended, and still the valley lay below him. As all other cañons and coves and valleys had deceived him, so had this deep, nesting oval. At length he passed beyond the slope of weathered stone that spread fan-shape from the arch, and encountered a grassy terrace running to the right and about on a level with the tips of the oaks and cottonwoods below. Scattered here and there upon this shelf were clumps of aspens, and he walked through them into a glade that surpassed, in beauty and adaptability for a wild home, any place he had ever seen. Silver spruces bordered the base of a precipitous wall that rose loftily. Caves indented its surface, and there were no detached ledges or weathered sections that might dislodge a stone. The level ground, beyond the spruces, dropped down into a little ravine. This was one dense line of slender aspens from which came the low splashing of water. And the terrace, lying open to the west, afforded unobstructed view of the valley of green tree-tops.

For his camp Venters chose a shady, grassy plot between the silver spruces and the cliff. Here, in the stone wall, had been wonderfully carved by wind or washed by water several deep caves above the level of the terrace. They were clean, dry, roomy. He cut spruce boughs and made a bed in the largest cave and laid the girl there. The first intimation that he had of her being aroused from sleep or lethargy was a low call for water.

He hurried down into the ravine with his canteen. It was a shallow, grass-green place with aspens growing up everywhere. To his delight he found a tiny brook of swift-running water. Its faint tinge of amber reminded him of the spring at Cottonwoods, and the thought gave him a little shock. The water was so cold it made his fingers tingle as he dipped the canteen. Having returned to the cave, he was glad to see the girl drink thirstily. This time he noted that she could raise her head slightly without his help.

'You were thirsty,' he said. 'It's good water. I've found a fine place. Tell me – how do you feel?'

'There's pain – here,' she replied, and moved her hand to her left side.

'Why, that's strange! Your wounds are on your right side. I believe you're hungry. Is the pain a kind of dull ache – a gnawing?'

'It's like – that.'

'Then it's hunger.' Venters laughed, and suddenly caught himself with a quick breath and felt again the little shock. When had he laughed? 'It's hunger,' he went on. 'I've had that gnaw many a time. I've got it now. But you mustn't eat. You can have all the water you want, but no food just yet.'

'Won't I – starve?'

'No, people don't starve easily. I've discovered that. You must lie perfectly still and rest and sleep – for days.'

'My hands – are dirty; my face feels – so hot and sticky; my boots hurt.' It was her longest speech as yet, and it trailed off in a whisper.

'Well, I'm a fine nurse!'

It annoyed him that he had never thought of these things. But then, awaiting her death and thinking of her comfort were vastly different matters. He unwrapped the blanket which covered her. What a slender girl she was! No wonder he had been able to carry her miles and pack her up that slippery ladder of stone. Her boots were soft, fine leather, reaching clear to her knees. He recognized the make as one of a bootmaker in Sterling. Her spurs, that he had stupidly neglected to remove, consisted of silver frames and gold chains, and the rowels, large as silver dollars, were fancifully engraved. The boots slipped off rather hard. She wore heavy woollen rider's stockings, half length, and these were pulled up over the ends of her short trousers. Venters took off the stockings to note her little feet were red and swollen. He bathed them. Then he removed his scarf and bathed her face and hands.

'I must see your wounds now,' he said, gently.

She made no reply, but watched him steadily as he opened her blouse and untied the bandage. His strong fingers trembled a little as he removed it. If the wounds had reopened! A chill struck him as he saw the angry red bullet-mark, and a tiny stream of blood winding from it down her white breast. Very carefully he lifted her to see that the wound in her back had closed perfectly. Then he washed the blood from her breast, bathed the wound, and left it unbandaged, open to the air.

Her eyes thanked him.

'Listen,' he said earnestly. 'I've had some wounds, and I've seen many. I know a little about them. The hole in your back has closed. If you lie still three days the one in your breast will close and you'll be safe. The danger from hemorrhage will be over.'

He had spoken with earnest sincerity, almost eagerness.

'Why – do you – want me – to get well?' she asked, wonderingly.

The simple question seemed unanswerable except on grounds of humanity. But the circumstances under which he had shot this strange girl, the shock and realization, the waiting for death, the hope, had resulted in a condition of mind wherein Venters wanted her to live more than he had ever wanted anything. Yet he could not tell why. He believed the killing of the rustler and the subsequent excitement had disturbed him. For how else could he explain the throbbing of his brain, the heat of his blood, the undefined sense of full hours, charged, vibrant with pulsating mystery where once they had dragged in loneliness?

'I shot you,' he said, slowly, 'and I want you to get well so I shall not have killed a woman. But – for your own sake, too—'

A terrible bitterness darkened her eyes, and her lips quivered.

'Hush,' said Venters. 'You've talked too much already.'

In her unutterable bitterness he saw a darkness of mood that could not have been caused by her present weak and feverish state. She hated the life she had led, that she probably had been compelled to lead. She had suffered some unforgivable wrong at the hands of Oldring. With that conviction Venters felt a flame throughout his body, and it marked the rekindling of fierce anger and ruthlessness. In the past long year he had nursed resentment. He had hated the wilderness – the loneliness of the uplands. He had waited for something to come to pass. It had come. Like an Indian stealing horses he had skulked into the recesses of the cañons. He had found Oldring's retreat; he had killed a rustler; he had shot an unfortunate girl, then had saved her from this unwitting act, and he meant to save her from the consequent wasting of blood, from fever and weakness. Starvation he had to fight for her and for himself. Where he had been sick at the letting of blood, now he remembered it in grim, cold calm. And as he lost that softness of nature, so he lost his fear of men. He would watch for Oldring, biding his time, and he would kill this great black-bearded rustler who had held a girl in bondage, who had used her to his infamous ends.

Venters surmised this much of the change in him – idleness had passed; keen, fierce vigor flooded his mind and body; all that had happened to him at Cottonwoods seemed remote and hard to recall; the difficulties and perils of the present absorbed him, held him in a kind of spell.

First, then, he fitted up the little cave adjoining the girl's room for his own comfort and use. His next work was to build a fireplace of stones and to gather a store of wood. That done, he spilled the contents of his saddle-bags upon the grass and took stock. His outfit consisted of a small-handled axe, a hunting-knife, a large number of cartridges for rifle or revolver, a tin plate, a cup, and a fork and spoon, a quantity of dried beef and dried fruits, and small canvas bags containing tea, sugar, salt, and pepper. For him alone this supply would have been bountiful to begin a sojourn in the wilderness, but he was no longer alone. Starvation in the uplands was not an unheard-of thing; he did not, however, worry at all on that score, and feared only his possible inability to supply the needs of a woman in a weakened and extremely delicate condition.

If there was no game in the valley – a contingency he doubted – it would not be a great task for him to go by night to Oldring's herd and pack out a calf. The exigency of the moment was to ascertain if there were game in Surprise Valley. Whitie still guarded the dilapidated rabbit, and Ring slept near by under a spruce. Venters called Ring and went to the edge of the terrace, and there halted to survey the valley.

He was prepared to find it larger than his unstudied glances had made it appear; for more than a casual idea of dimensions and a hasty conception of oval shape and singular beauty he had not had time. Again the felicity of the name he had given the valley struck him forcibly. Around the red perpendicular walls, except under the great arc of stone, ran a terrace fringed at the cliff-base by silver spruces; below that first terrace sloped another wider one densely overgrown with aspens; and the center of the valley was a level circle of oaks and alders, with the glittering green line of willows and cottonwood dividing it in half. Venters saw a number and variety of birds flitting among the trees. To his left, facing the stone bridge, an enormous cavern opened in the wall; and low down, just above the tree-tops, he made out a long shelf of cliff-dwellings, with little black, staring windows or doors. Like eyes they were, and seemed to watch him. The few cliff-dwellings he had seen – all ruins – had left him with haunting memory of age and solitude and of something past. He had come, in a way, to be a cliff-dweller himself, and those silent eyes would look down upon him, as if in surprise that after thousands of years a man had invaded the valley.

Venters felt sure that he was the only white man who had ever walked under the shadow of the wonderful stone bridge, down into that wonderful valley with its circle of caves and its terraced rings of silver spruce and aspens.

The dog growled below and rushed into the forest. Venters ran down the declivity to enter a zone of light shade streaked with sunshine. The oak-trees were slender, none more than half a foot thick, and they grew close together, intermingling their branches. Ring came running back with a rabbit in his mouth. Venters took the rabbit and, holding the dog near him, stole softly on. There were fluttering of wings among the branches and quick bird-notes, and rustling of dead leaves and rapid patterings. Venters crossed well-worn trails marked with fresh tracks; and when he had stolen on a little farther he saw many birds and running quail, and more rabbits than he could count. He had not penetrated the forest of oaks for a hundred yards, had not approached anywhere near the line of willows and cottonwoods which he knew grew along a stream. But he had seen enough to know that Surprise Valley was the home of many wild creatures.

Venters returned to camp. He skinned the rabbits, and gave the dogs the one they had quarreled over, and the skin of this he dressed and hung up to dry, feeling that he would like to keep it. It was a particularly rich, furry pelt with a beautiful white tail. Venters remembered that but for the bobbing of that white tail catching his eye he would not have espied the rabbit, and he would never have discovered Surprise Valley. Little incidents of chance like this had turned him here and there in Deception Pass; and now they had assumed to him the significance and direction of destiny.

His good fortune in the matter of game at hand brought to his mind the necessity of keeping it in the valley. Therefore he took the axe and cut bundles of aspens and willows, and packed them up under the bridge to the narrow outlet of the gorge. Here he began fashioning a fence, by driving aspens into the ground and lacing them fast with willows. Trip after trip he made down for more building material, and the afternoon had passed when he finished the work to his satisfaction. Wildcats might scale the fence, but no coyote could come in to search for prey, and no rabbits or other small game could escape from the valley.

Upon returning to camp he set about getting his supper at ease, around a fine fire, without hurry or fear of discovery. After hard work that had definite purpose, this freedom and comfort gave him peculiar satisfaction. He caught himself often, as he kept busy round the camp-fire, stopping to glance at the quiet form in the cave, and at the dogs stretched cozily near him, and then out across the beautiful valley. The present was not yet real to him.

While he ate, the sun set beyond a dip in the rim of the curved wall. As the morning sun burst wondrously through a grand arch into this valley, in a golden, slanting shaft, so the evening sun, at the moment of setting, shone through a gap of cliffs, sending down a broad red burst to brighten the oval with a blaze of fire. To Venters both sunrise and sunset were unreal.

A cool wind blew across the oval, waving the tips of oaks, and, while the light lasted, fluttering the aspen leaves into millions of facets of red, and sweeping the graceful spruces. Then with the wind soon came a shade and a darkening, and suddenly the valley was gray. Night came there quickly after the sinking of the sun. Venters went softly to look at the girl. She slept, and her breathing was quiet and slow. He lifted Ring into the cave, with stern whisper for him to stay there on guard. Then he drew the blanket carefully over her and returned to the camp-fire.

Though exceedingly tired, he was yet loath to yield to lassitude, but this night it was not from listening, watching vigilance; it was from a desire to realize his position. The details of his wild environment seemed the only substance of a strange dream. He saw the darkening rims, the gray oval turning black, the undulating surface of forest, like a rippling lake, and the spear-pointed spruces. He heard the flutter of aspen-leaves and the soft, continuous splash of falling water. The melancholy note of a cañon bird broke clear and lonely from the high cliffs. Venters had no name for this night singer, and he had never seen one; but the few notes, always pealing out just at darkness, were as familiar to him as the cañon silence. Then they ceased, and the rustle of leaves and the murmur of water hushed in a growing sound that Venters fancied was not of earth. Neither had he a name for this, only it was inexpressibly wild and sweet. The thought came that it might be a moan of the girl in her last outcry of life, and he felt a tremor shake him. But no! This sound was not human, though it was like despair. He began to doubt his sensitive perceptions, to believe that he half-dreamed what he thought he heard. Then the sound swelled with the strengthening of the breeze, and he realized it was the singing of the wind in the cliffs.

By and by a drowsiness overcame him, and Venters began to nod, half asleep, with his back against a spruce. Rousing himself and calling Whitie, he went to the cave. The girl lay barely visible in the dimness. Ring crouched beside her, and the patting of his tail on the stone assured Venters that the dog was awake and faithful to his duty. Venters sought his own bed of fragrant boughs; and as he lay back, somehow grateful for the comfort and safety, the night seemed to steal away from him and he sank softly into intangible space and rest and slumber.

Venters awakened to the sound of melody that he imagined was only the haunting echo of dream music. He opened his eyes to another surprise of this valley of beautiful surprises. Out of his cave he saw the exquisitely fine foliage of the silver spruces crossing a round space of blue morning sky; and in this lacy leafage fluttered a number of gray birds with black and white stripes and long tails.

They were mocking-birds, and they were singing as if they wanted to burst their throats. Venters listened. One long, silver-tipped branch drooped almost to his cave, and upon it, within a few yards of him, sat one of the graceful birds. Venters saw the swelling and quivering of its throat in song. He arose, and when he slid down out of his cave the birds fluttered and flew farther away.

Venters stepped before the opening of the other cave and looked in. The girl was awake, with wide eyes and listening look, and she had a hand on Ring's neck.

'Mocking-birds!' she said.

'Yes,' replied Venters, 'and I believe they like our company.'

'Where are we?'

'Never mind now. After a little I'll tell you.'

'The birds woke me. When I heard them – and saw the shiny trees – and the blue sky – and then a blaze of gold dropping down – I wondered—'

She did not complete her fancy, but Venters imagined he understood her meaning. She appeared to be wandering in mind. Venters felt her face and hands and found them burning with fever. He went for water, and was glad to find it almost as cold as if flowing with ice. That water was the only medicine he had, and he put faith in it. She did not want to drink, but he made her swallow, and then he bathed her face and head and cooled her wrists.

The day began with a heightening of the fever. Venters spent the time reducing her temperature, cooling her hot cheeks and temples. He kept close watch over her, and at the least indication of restlessness, that he knew led to tossing and rolling of the body, he held her tightly, so no violent move could reopen her wounds. Hour after hour she babbled and laughed and cried and moaned in delirium; but whatever her secret was she did not reveal it. Attended by something somber for Venters, the day passed. At night in the cool winds the fever abated and she slept.

The second day was a repetition of the first. On the third he seemed to see her wither and waste away before his eyes. That day he scarcely went from her side for a moment, except to run for fresh, cool water; and he did not eat. The fever broke on the fourth day and left her spent and shrunken, a slip of a girl with life only in her eyes. They hung upon Venters with a mute observance, and he found hope in that.

To rekindle the spark that had nearly flickered out, to nourish the little life and vitality that remained in her, was Venters's problem. But he had little resource other than the meat of the rabbits and quail; and from these he made broths and soups as best he could, and fed her with a spoon. It came to him that the human body, like the human soul, was a strange thing and capable of recovering from terrible shocks. For almost immediately she showed faint signs of gathering strength. There was one more waiting day, in which he doubted, and spent long hours by her side as she slept, and watched the gentle swell of her breast rise and fall in breathing, and the wind stir the tangled chestnut curls. On the next day he knew that she would live.

Upon realizing it he abruptly left the cave and sought his accustomed seat against the trunk of a big spruce, where once more he let his glance stray along the sloping terraces. She would live, and the somber gloom lifted out of the valley, and he felt relief that was pain. Then he roused to the call of action, to the many things he needed to do in the way of making camp fixtures and utensils, to the necessity of hunting food, and the desire to explore the valley.

But he decided to wait a few more days before going far from camp, because he fancied that the girl rested easier when she could see him near at hand. And on the first day her languor appeared to leave her in a renewed grip of life. She awoke stronger from each short slumber; she ate greedily, and she moved about in her bed of boughs; and always, it seemed to Venters, her eyes followed him. He knew now that her recovery would be rapid. She talked about the dogs, about the caves, the valley, about how hungry she was, till Venters silenced her, asking her to put off further talk till another time. She obeyed, but she sat up in her bed, and her eyes roved to and fro, and always back to him.

Upon the second morning she sat up when he awakened her, and would not permit him to bathe her face and feed her, which actions she performed for herself. She spoke little, however, and Venters was quick to catch in her the first intimations of thoughtfulness and curiosity and appreciation of her situation. He left camp and took Whitie out to hunt for rabbits. Upon his return he was amazed and somewhat anxiously concerned to see his invalid sitting with her back to a corner of the cave and her bare feet swinging out. Hurriedly he approached, intending to advise her to lie down again, to tell her that perhaps she might overtax her strength. The sun shone upon her, glinting on the little head with its tangle of bright hair and the small, oval face with its pallor, and dark-blue eyes underlined by dark-blue circles. She looked at him and he looked at her. In that exchange of glances he imagined each saw the other in some different guise. It seemed impossible to Venters that this frail girl could be Oldring's Masked Rider. It flashed over him that he had made a mistake which presently she would explain.

'Help me down,' she said.

'But – are you well enough?' he protested. 'Wait – a little longer.'

'I'm weak – dizzy. But I want to get down.'

He lifted her – what a light burden now! – and stood her upright beside him, and supported her as she essayed to walk with halting steps. She was like a stripling of a boy; the bright, small head scarcely reached his shoulder. But now, as she clung to his arm, the rider's costume she wore did not contradict, as it had done at first, his feeling of her femininity. She might be the famous Masked Rider of the uplands, she might resemble a boy; but her outline, her little hands and feet, her hair, her big eyes and tremulous lips, and especially a something that Venters felt as a subtle essence rather than what he saw, proclaimed her sex.

She soon tired. He arranged a comfortable seat for her under the spruce that overspread the camp-fire.

'Now tell me – everything,' she said.

He recounted all that had happened from the time of his discovery of the rustlers in the cañon up to the present moment.

'You shot me – and now you've saved my life?'

'Yes. After almost killing you I've pulled you through.'

'Are you glad?'

'I should say so!'

Her eyes were unusually expressive, and they regarded him steadily; she was unconscious of that mirroring of her emotions, and they shone with gratefulness and interest and wonder and sadness.

'Tell me – about yourself?' she asked.

He made this a briefer story, telling of his coming to Utah, his various occupations till he became a rider, and then how the Mormons had practically driven him out of Cottonwoods, an outcast.

Then, no longer able to withstand his own burning curiosity, he questioned her in turn.

'Are you Oldring's Masked Rider?'

'Yes,' she replied, and dropped her eyes.

'I knew it – I recognized your figure – and mask, for I saw you once. Yet I can't believe it! . . . But you never *were* really that rustler, as we riders knew him? A thief – a marauder – a kidnapper of women – a murderer of sleeping riders!'

'No! I never stole – or harmed any one – in all my life. I only rode and rode—'

'But why – why?' he burst out. 'Why the name? I understand Oldring made you ride. But the black mask – the mystery – the things laid to your hands – the threats in your infamous name – the night-riding credited to you – the evil deeds deliberately blamed on you and acknowledged by rustlers – even Oldring himself! Why? Tell me why!'

'I never knew that,' she answered low. Her drooping head straightened, and the large eyes, larger now and darker, met Venters's with a clear, steadfast gaze in which he read truth. It verified his own conviction.

'Never knew? That's strange! Are you a Mormon?'

'No.'

'Is Oldring a Mormon?'

'No.'

'Do you – care for him?'

'Yes. I hate his men – his life – sometimes I almost hate him!'

Venters paused in his rapid-fire questioning, as if to brace himself to ask for a truth that would be abhorrent for him to confirm, but which he seemed driven to hear.

'What are – what *were* you to Oldring?'

Like some delicate thing suddenly exposed to blasting heat, the girl wilted; her head dropped, and into her white, wasted cheeks crept the red of shame.

Venters would have given anything to recall that question. It seemed so different – his thought when spoken. Yet her shame established in his mind something akin to the respect he had strangely been hungering to feel for her.

'D – n that question! – forget it!' he cried, in a passion of pain for her and anger at himself. 'But once and for all – tell me – I know it, yet I want to hear you say so – you couldn't help yourself?'

'Oh no.'

'Well, that makes it all right with me,' he went on, honestly. 'I – I want you to feel that . . . you see – we've been thrown together – and – and I want to help you – not hurt you. I thought life had been cruel to me, but when I think of yours I feel mean and little for my complaining. Anyway, I was a lonely outcast. And now! . . . I don't see very clearly what it all means. Only we are here – together. We've got to stay here, for long, surely till you are well. But you'll never go back to Oldring. And I'm sure helping you will help me, for I was sick in mind. There's something now for me to do. And if I can win back your strength – then get you away, out of this wild country – help you somehow to a happier life – just think how good that'll be for me!'

CHAPTER TEN

Love

DURING ALL THESE WAITING days Venters, with the exception of the afternoon when he had built the gate in the gorge, had scarcely gone out of sight of camp and never out of hearing. His desire to explore Surprise Valley was keen, and on the morning after his long talk with the girl he took his rifle and, calling Ring, made a move to start. The girl lay back in a rude chair of boughs he had put together for her. She had been watching him, and when he picked up the gun and called the dog Venters thought she gave a nervous start.

'I'm only going to look over the valley,' he said.

'Will you be gone long?'

'No,' he replied, and started off. The incident set him thinking of his former impression that, after her recovery from fever, she did not seem at ease unless he was close at hand. It was fear of being alone, due, he concluded, most likely to her weakened condition. He must not leave her much alone.

As he strode down the sloping terrace, rabbits scampered before him, and the beautiful valley quail, as purple in color as the sage on the uplands, ran fleetly along the ground into the forest. It was pleasant under the trees, in the gold-flecked shade, with the whistle of quail and twittering of birds everywhere. Soon he had passed the limit of his former excursions and entered new territory. Here the woods began to show open glades and brooks running down from the slope, and presently he emerged from shade into the sunshine of a meadow. The shaking of the high grass told him of the running of animals, what species he could not tell, but from Ring's manifest desire to have a chase they were evidently some kind wilder than rabbits. Venters approached the willow and cottonwood belt that he had observed from the height of slope. He penetrated it to find a considerable stream of water and great half-submerged mounds of brush and sticks, and all about him were old and new gnawed circles at the base of the cottonwoods.

'Beaver!' he exclaimed. 'By all that's lucky! The meadow's full of beaver! How did they ever get here?'

Beaver had not found a way into the valley by the trail of the cliff-dwellers, of that he was certain; and he began to have more than curiosity as to the outlet or inlet of the stream. When he passed some dead water, which he noted was held by a beaver-dam, there was a current in the stream, and it flowed west. Following its course, he soon entered the oak forest again, and passed through to find himself before massed and jumbled ruins of cliff-wall. There were tangled thickets of wild plum-trees and other thorny growths that made passage extremely laborsome. He found innumerable tracks of wildcats and foxes. Rustlings in the thick under-growth told him of stealthy movements of these animals. At length his further advance appeared futile, for the reason that the stream disappeared in a split at the base of immense rocks over which he could not climb. To his relief he concluded that though beaver might work their way up the narrow chasm where the water rushed, it would be impossible for men to enter the valley there.

This western curve was the only part of the valley where the walls had been split asunder, and it was a wildly rough and inaccessible corner. Going back a little way, he leaped the stream and headed toward the southern wall. Once out of the oaks he found again the low terrace of aspens, and above that the wide, open terrace fringed by silver spruces. This side of the valley contained the wind or water worn caves. As he pressed on, keeping to the upper terrace, cave after cave opened out of the cliff; now a large one, now a small one. Then yawned, quite suddenly and wonderfully above him, the great cavern of the cliff-dwellers.

It was still a goodly distance, and he tried to imagine, if it appeared so huge from where he stood, what it would be when he got there. He climbed the terrace and then faced a long, gradual ascent of weathered rock and dust, which made climbing too difficult for attention to anything else. At length he entered a zone of shade, and looked up. He stood just within the hollow of a cavern so immense that he had no conception of its real dimensions. The curved roof, stained by ages of leakage, with buff and black and rust-colored streaks, swept up and loomed higher and seemed to soar to the rim of the cliff. Here again was a magnificent arch, such as formed the grand gateway to the valley, only in this instance it formed the dome of a cave instead of the span of a bridge.

Venters passed onward and upward. The stones he dislodged rolled down with strange, hollow crack and roar. He had climbed a hundred rods inward, and yet he had not reached the base of the shelf where the cliff-dwellings rested, a long half-circle of connected stone house, with little dark holes that he had fancied were eyes. At length he gained the base of the shelf, and here found steps cut in the rock. These facilitated climbing, and as he went up he thought how easily this vanished race of men might once have held that stronghold against an army. There was only one possible place to ascend, and this was narrow and steep.

Venters had visited cliff-dwellings before, and they had been in ruins, and of no great character or size but this place was of proportions that stunned him, and it had not been desecrated by the hand of man, nor had it been crumbled by the hand of time. It was a stupendous tomb. It had been a city. It was just as it had been left by its builders. The little houses were there, the smoke-blackened stains of fires, the pieces of pottery scattered about cold hearths, the stone hatchets; and stone pestles and mealing-stones lay beside round holes polished by years of grinding maize – lay there as if they had been carelessly dropped yesterday. But the cliff-dwellers were gone!

Dust! They were dust on the floor or at the foot of the shelf, and their habitations and utensils endured. Venters felt the sublimity of that marvelous vaulted arch, and it seemed to gleam with a glory of something that was gone. How many years had passed since the cliff-dwellers gazed out across the beautiful valley as he was gazing now? How long had it been since women ground grain in those polished holes? What time had rolled by since men of an unknown race lived, loved, fought, and died there? Had an enemy destroyed them? Had disease destroyed them, or only that greatest destroyer – time? Venters saw a long line of blood-red hands painted low down upon the yellow roof of stone. Here was strange portent, if not an answer to his queries. The place oppressed him. It was light, but full of a transparent gloom. It smelled of dust and musty stone, of age and disuse. It was sad. It was solemn. It had the look of a place where silence had become master and was now irrevocable and terrible and could not be broken. Yet, at the moment, from high up in the carved crevices of the arch, floated down the low, strange wail of wind – a knell indeed for all that had gone.

Venters, sighing, gathered up an armful of pottery, such pieces as he thought strong enough and suitable for his own use, and bent his steps toward camp. He mounted the terrace at an opposite point to which he had left. He saw the girl looking in the direction he had gone. His footsteps made no sound in the deep grass, and he approached close without her being aware of his presence. Whitie lay on the ground near where she sat, and he manifested the usual actions of welcome, but the girl did not notice them. She seemed to be oblivious to everything near at hand. She made a pathetic figure drooping there, with her sunny hair contrasting so markedly with her white, wasted cheeks and her hands listlessly clasped and her little bare feet propped in the framework of the rude seat. Venters could have sworn and laughed in one breath at the idea of the connection between this girl and Oldring's Masked Rider. She was the victim of more than accident of fate – a victim to some deep plot the mystery of which burned him. As he stepped forward with a half-formed thought that she was absorbed in watching for his return, she turned her head and saw him. A swift start, a change rather than rush of blood under her white cheeks, a flashing of big eyes that fixed their glance upon him, transformed her face in that single instant of turning; and he knew she had been watching for him, that his return was the one thing in her mind. She did not smile; she did not flush, she did not look glad. All these would have meant little compared to her indefinite expression. Venters grasped the peculiar, vivid, vital something that leaped from her face. It was as if she had been in a dead, hopeless clamp of inaction and feeling, and had been suddenly shot through and through with quivering animation. Almost it was as if she had returned to life.

And Venters thought with lightning swiftness, 'I've saved her – I've unlinked her from that old life – she was watching as if I were all she had left on earth – she belongs to me!' The thought was startlingly new. Like a blow it was in an unprepared moment. The cheery salutation he had ready for her died unborn and he tumbled the pieces of pottery awkwardly on the grass, while some unfamiliar, deep-seated emotion, mixed with pity and glad assurance of his power to succor her, held him dumb.

'What a load you had!' she said. 'Why, they're pots and crocks! Where did you get them?'

Venters laid down his rifle, and, filling one of the pots from his canteen, he placed it on the smoldering camp-fire.

'Hope it'll hold water,' he said, presently. 'Why, there's an enormous cliff-dwelling just across here. I got the pottery there. Don't you think we needed something? That tin cup of mine has served to make tea, broth, soup – everything.'

'I noticed we hadn't a great deal to cook in.'

She laughed. It was the first time. He liked that laugh, and though he was tempted to look at her, he did not want to show his surprise or his pleasure.

'Will you take me over there, and all around in the valley – pretty soon when I'm well?' she added.

'Indeed I shall. It's a wonderful place. Rabbits so thick you can't step without kicking one out. And quail, beaver, foxes, wildcats. We're in a regular den. But – haven't you ever seen a cliff-dwelling?'

'No. I've heard about them, though. The – the men say the Pass is full of old houses and ruins.'

'Why, I should think you'd have run across one in all your riding around,' said Venters. He spoke slowly, choosing his words carefully, and he essayed a perfectly casual manner, and pretended to be busy sorting pieces of pottery. She must have no cause again to suffer shame for curiosity of his. Yet never in all his days had he been so eager to hear the details of anyone's life.

'When I rode – I rode like the wind,' she replied, 'and never had time to stop for anything.'

'I remember that day I – I met you in the Pass – how dusty you were, how tired your horse looked. Were you always riding?'

'Oh, no. Sometimes not for months, when I was shut up in the cabin.'

Venters tried to subdue a hot tingling.

'You were shut up, then?' he asked, carelessly.

'When Oldring went away on his long trips – he was gone for months sometimes – he shut me up in the cabin.'

'What for?'

'Perhaps to keep me from running away. I always threatened that. Mostly, though, because the men got drunk at the villages. But they were always good to me. I wasn't afraid.'

'A prisoner! That must have been hard on you.'

'I liked that. As long as I can remember I've been locked up there at times, and those times were the only happy ones I ever had. It's a big cabin, high up on a cliff, and I could look out. Then I had dogs and pets I had tamed, and books. There was a spring inside, and food stored, and the men brought me fresh meat. Once I was there one whole winter.'

It now required deliberation on Venters's part to persist in his unconcern and to keep at work. He wanted to look at her, to volley questions at her.

'As long as you can remember – you've lived in Deception Pass?' he went on.

'I've a dim memory of some other place, and women and children; but I can't make anything of it. Sometimes I think till I'm weary.'

'Then you can read – you have books?'

'Oh yes, I can read, and write, too, pretty well. Oldring is educated. He taught me, and years ago an old rustler lived with us, and he had been something different once. He was always teaching me.'

'So Oldring takes long trips,' mused Venters. 'Do you know where he goes?'

'No. Every year he drives cattle north of Sterling – then does not return for months. I heard him accused once of living two lives – and he killed the man. That was at Stone Bridge.'

Venters dropped his apparent task and looked up with an eagerness he no longer strove to hide.

'Bess,' he said, using her name for the first time, 'I suspected Oldring was something besides a rustler. Tell me, what's his purpose here in the Pass? I believe much that he has done was to hide his real work here.'

'You're right. He's more than a rustler. In fact, as the men say, his rustling cattle is now only a bluff. There's gold in the cañons!'

'Ah!'

'Yes, there's gold, not in great quantities, but gold enough for him and his men. They wash for gold week in and week out. Then they drive a few cattle and go into the villages to drink and shoot and kill – to bluff the riders.'

'Drive a few cattle! But, Bess, the Withersteen herd, the red herd – twenty-five hundred head! That's not a few. And I tracked them into a valley near here.'

'Oldring never stole the red herd. He made a deal with Mormons. The riders were to be called in, and Oldring was to drive the herd and keep it till a certain time – I don't know when – then drive it back to the range. What his share was I didn't hear.'

'Did you hear why that deal was made?' queried Venters.

'No. But it was a trick of Mormons. They're full of tricks. I've heard Oldring's men tell about Mormons. Maybe the Withersteen woman wasn't minding her halter! I saw the man who made the deal. He was a little, queer-shaped man, all humped up. He sat his horse well. I heard one of our men say afterward there was no better rider on the sage than this fellow. What was the name? I forget.'

'Jerry Card?' suggested Venters.

'That's it. I remember – it's a name easy to remember – and Jerry Card appeared to be on fair terms with Oldring's men.'

'I shouldn't wonder,' replied Venters, thoughtfully. Verification of his suspicions in regard to Tull's underhand work – for the deal with Oldring made by Jerry Card assuredly had its inception in the Mormon Elder's brain, and had been accomplished through his orders – revived in Venters a memory of hatred that had been smothered by press of other emotions. Only a few days had elapsed since the hour of his encounter with Tull, yet they had been forgotten and now seemed far off, and the interval one that now appeared large and profound with incalculable change in his feelings. Hatred of Tull still existed in his heart; but it had lost its white heat. His affection for Jane Withersteen had not changed in the least; nevertheless, he seemed to view it from another angle and see it as another thing – what, he could not exactly define. The recalling of these two feelings was to Venters like getting glimpses into a self that was gone; and the wonder of them – perhaps the change which was too illusive for him – was the fact that a strange irritation accompanied the memory and a desire to dismiss it from mind. And straightway he did dismiss it, to return to thoughts of his significant present.

'Bess, tell me one more thing,' he said. 'Haven't you known any women – any young people?'

'Sometimes there were women with the men; but Oldring never let me know them. And all the young people I ever saw in my life was when I rode fast through the villages.'

Perhaps that was the most puzzling and thought-provoking thing she had yet said to Venters. He pondered, more curious the more he learned, but he curbed his inquisitive desires, for he saw her shrinking on the verge of that shame, the causing of which had occasioned him such self-reproach. He would ask no more. Still he had to think, and he found it difficult to think clearly. This sad-eyed girl was so utterly different from what it would have been reason to believe such a remarkable life would have made her. On this day he had found her simple and frank, as natural as any girl he had ever known. About her there was something sweet. Her voice was low and well modulated. He could not look into her face, meet her steady, unabashed, yet wistful eyes, and think of her as the woman she had confessed herself. Oldring's Masked Rider sat before him, a girl dressed as a man. She had been made to ride at the head of infamous forays and drives. She had been imprisoned for many months of her life in an obscure cabin. At times the most vicious of men had been her companions; and the vilest of women, if they had not been permitted to approach her, had, at least, cast their shadows over her. But – but in spite of all this – there thundered at Venters some truth that lifted its voice higher than the clamoring facts of dishonor, some truth that was the very life of her beautiful eyes; and it was innocence.

In the days that followed, Venters balanced perpetually in mind this haunting conception of innocence over against the cold and sickening fact of an unintentional yet actual gift. How could it be possible for the two things to be true? He believed the latter to be true, and he would not relinquish his conviction of the former; and these conflicting thoughts augmented the mystery that appeared to be a part of Bess. In those ensuing days, however, it became clear as clearest light that Bess was rapidly regaining strength; that, unless reminded of her long association with Oldring, she seemed to have forgotten it; that, like an Indian who lives solely from moment to moment, she was utterly absorbed in the present.

Day by day Venters watched the white of her face slowly change to brown, and the wasted cheeks fill out by imperceptible degrees. There came a time when he could just trace the line of demarcation between the part of her face once hidden by a mask and that left exposed to wind and sun. When that line disappeared in clear bronze tan it was as if she had been washed clean of the stigma of Oldring's Masked Rider. The suggestion of the mask always made Venters remember; now that it was gone he seldom thought of her past. Occasionally he tried to piece together the several stages of strange experience and to make a whole. He had shot a masked outlaw the very sight of whom had been ill omen to riders; he had carried off a wounded woman whose bloody lips quivered in prayer; he had nursed what seemed a frail, shrunken boy; and now he watched a girl whose face had become strangely sweet, whose dark-blue eyes were ever upon him without boldness, without shyness, but with a steady, grave, and growing light. Many times Venters found the clear gaze embarrassing to him, yet, like wine, it had an exhilarating effect. What did she think when she looked at him so? Almost he believed she had no thought at all. All about her and the present there in Surprise Valley, and the dim yet subtly impending future, fascinated Venters and made him thoughtful as all his lonely vigils in the sage had not.

Chiefly it was the present that he wished to dwell upon; but it was the call of the future which stirred him to action. No idea had he of what that future had in store for Bess and him. He began to think of improving Surprise Valley as a place to live in, for there was no telling how long they would be compelled to stay there. Venters stubbornly resisted the entering into his mind of an insistent thought that, clearly realized, might have made it plain to him that he did not want to leave Surprise Valley at all. But it was imperative that he consider practical matters; and whether or not he was destined to stay long there, he felt the immediate need of a change of diet. It would be necessary for him to go farther afield for a variety of meat, and also that he soon visit Cottonwoods for a supply of food.

It occurred again to Venters that he could go to the cañon where Oldring kept his cattle, and at little risk he could pack out some beef. He wished to do this, however, without letting Bess know of it till after he had made the trip. Presently he hit upon the plan of going while she was asleep.

That very night he stole out of camp, climbed up under the stone bridge, and entered the outlet to the Pass. The gorge was full of luminous gloom. Balancing Rock loomed dark and leaned over the pale descent. Transformed in the shadowy light, it took shape and dimensions of a spectral god waiting – waiting for the moment to hurl himself down upon the tottering walls and close forever the outlet to Deception Pass. At night more than by day Venters felt something fearful and fateful in that rock, and that it had leaned and waited through a thousand years to have somehow to deal with his destiny.

'Old man, if you must roll, wait till I get back to the girl, and then roll!' he said, aloud, as if the stones were indeed a god.

And those spoken words, in their grim note to his ear, as well as contents to his mind, told Venters that he was all but drifting on a current which he had not power nor wish to stem.

Venters exercised his usual care in the matter of hiding tracks from the outlet, yet it took him scarcely an hour to reach Oldring's cattle. Here sight of many calves changed his original intention, and instead of packing out meat he decided to take a calf out alive. He roped one, securely tied its feet, and swung it up over his shoulder. Here was an exceedingly heavy burden, but Venters was powerful – he could take up a sack of grain and with ease pitch it over a pack-saddle – and he made long distance without resting. The hardest work came in the climb up to the outlet and on through to the valley. When he had accomplished it, he became fired with another idea that again changed his intention. He would not kill the calf, but keep it alive. He would go back to Oldring's herd and pack out more calves. Thereupon he secured the calf in the best available spot for the moment and turned to make a second trip.

When Venters got back to the valley with another calf, it was close upon daybreak. He crawled into his cave and slept late. Bess had no inkling that he had been absent from camp nearly all night, and only remarked solicitously that he appeared to be more tired than usual, and more in the need of sleep. In the afternoon Venters built a gate across a small ravine near camp, and here corralled the calves; and he succeeded in completing his task without Bess being any the wiser.

That night he made two more trips to Oldring's range, and again on the following night, and yet another on the next. With eight calves in his corral, he concluded that he had enough; but it dawned upon him then that he did not want to kill one. 'I've rustled Oldring's cattle,' he said, and laughed. He noted then that all the calves were red. 'Red!' he exclaimed. 'From the red herd. I've stolen Jane Withersteen's cattle! . . . That's about the strangest thing yet.'

One more trip he undertook to Oldring's valley, and this time he roped a yearling steer and killed it and cut out a small quarter of beef. The howling of coyotes told him he need have no apprehension that the work of his knife would be discovered. He packed the beef back to camp and hung it upon a spruce-tree. Then he sought his bed.

On the morrow he was up bright and early, glad that he had a surprise for Bess. He could hardly wait for her to come out. Presently she appeared and walked under the spruce. Then she approached the camp-fire. There was a tinge of healthy red in the bronze of her cheeks, and her slender form had begun to round out in graceful lines.

'Bess, didn't you say you were tired of rabbit?' inquired Venters. 'And quail and beaver?'

'Indeed I did.'

'What would you like?'

'I'm tired of meat, but if we have to live on it I'd like some beef.'

'Well, how does that strike you?' Venters pointed to the quarter hanging from the spruce tree. 'We'll have fresh beef for a few days, then we'll cut the rest into strips and dry it.'

'Where did you get that?' asked Bess, slowly.

'I stole that from Oldring.'

'You went back to the cañon – you risked—' While she hesitated the tinge of bloom faded out of her cheeks.

'It wasn't any risk, but it was hard work.'

'I'm sorry I said I was tired of rabbit. Why! How – When did you get that beef?'

'Last night.'

'While I was asleep?'

'Yes.'

'I woke last night sometime – but I didn't know.'

Her eyes were widening, darkening with thought, and whenever they did so the steady, watchful, seeing gaze gave place to the wistful light. In the former she saw as the primitive woman without thought; in the latter she looked inward, and her

gaze was the reflection of a troubled mind. For long Venters had not seen that dark
change, that deepening of blue, which he thought was beautiful and sad. But now
he wanted to make her think.

'I've done more than pack in that beef,' he said. 'For five nights I've been
working while you slept. I've got eight calves corralled near a ravine. Eight calves,
all alive and doing fine!'

'You went five nights!'

All that Venters could make of the dilation of her eyes, her slow pallor, and her
exclamation, was fear – fear for herself or for him.

'Yes. I didn't tell you, because I knew you were afraid to be alone.'

'Alone?' She echoed his word, but the meaning of it was nothing to her. She
had not even thought of being left alone. It was not, then, fear for herself, but for
him. This girl, always slow of speech and action, now seemed almost stupid. She
put forth a hand that might have indicated the groping of her mind. Suddenly she
stepped swiftly to him, with a look and touch that drove from him any doubt of her
quick intelligence or feeling.

'Oldring has men watch the herds – they would kill you. You must never go
again!'

When she had spoken, the strength and the blaze of her died, and she swayed
towards Venters.

'Bess, I'll not go again,' he said, catching her.

She leaned against him, and her body was limp and vibrated to a long,
wavering tremble. Her face was upturned to his. Woman's face, woman's eyes,
woman's lips – all acutely and blindly and sweetly and terribly truthful in their
betrayal! But as her fear was instinctive, so was her clinging to this one and only
friend.

Venters gently put her from him and steadied her upon her feet; and all the
while his blood raced wild, and a thrilling tingle unsteadied his nerve, and
something – that he had seen and felt in her – that he could not understand –
seemed very close to him, warm and rich as a fragrant breath, sweet as nothing had
ever before been sweet to him.

With all his will Venters strove for calmness and thought and judgment
unbiased by pity, and reality unswayed by sentiment. Bess's eyes were still fixed
upon him with all her soul bright in that wistful light. Swiftly, resolutely he put
out of mind all of her life except what had been spent with him. He scorned
himself for the intelligence that made him still doubt. He meant to judge her as
she had judged him. He was face to face with the inevitableness of life itself. He
saw destiny in the dark, straight path of her wonderful eyes. Here was the
simplicity, the sweetness of a girl contending with new and strange and enthral-
ling emotions; here the living truth of innocence; here the blind terror of a woman
confronted with the thought of death to her savior and protector. All this Venters
saw, but, besides, there was in Bess's eyes a slow-dawning consciousness that
seemed about to break out in glorious radiance.

'Bess, are you thinking?' he asked.

'Yes – oh yes!'

'Do you realize we are here alone – man and woman?'

'Yes.'

'Have you thought that we may make our way out to civilization, or we may
have to stay here – alone – hidden from the world all our lives?'

'I never thought – till now.'

'Well, what's your choice – to go – or to stay here – alone with me?'

'Stay!' New-born thought of self, ringing vibrantly in her voice, gave her answer singular power.

Venters trembled, and then swiftly turned his gaze from her face – from her eyes. He knew what she had only half divined – that she loved him.

CHAPTER ELEVEN
Faith and Unfaith

AT JANE WITHERSTEEN'S HOME the promise made to Mrs Larkin to care for little Fay had begun to be fulfilled. Like a gleam of sunlight through the cottonwoods was the coming of the child to the gloomy house of Withersteen. The big, silent halls echoed with childish laughter. In the shady court, where Jane spent many of the hot July days, Fay's tiny feet pattered over the stone flags and splashed in the amber stream. She prattled incessantly. What difference, Jane thought, a child made in her home! It had never been a real home, she discovered. Even the tidiness and neatness she had so observed, and upon which she had insisted to her women, became, in the light of Fay's smile, habits that now lost their importance. Fay littered the court with Jane's books and papers, and other toys her fancy improvised, and many a strange craft went floating down the little brook.

And it was owing to Fay's presence that Jane Withersteen came to see more of Lassiter. The rider had for the most part kept to the sage. He rode for her, but he did not seek her except on business; and Jane had to acknowledge in pique that her overtures had been made in vain. Fay, however, captured Lassiter the moment he first laid eyes on her.

Jane was present at the meeting, and there was something about it which dimmed her sight and softened her toward this foe of her people. The rider had clanked into the court, a tired yet wary man, always looking for the attack upon him that was inevitable and might come from any quarter; and he had walked right upon little Fay. The child had been beautiful even in her rags and amid the surroundings of the hovel in the sage, but now, in a pretty white dress, with her shining curls brushed and her face clean and rosy, she was lovely. She left her play and looked up at Lassiter.

If there was not an instinct for all three of them in that meeting, an unreasoning tendency toward a closer intimacy, then Jane Withersteen believed she had been subject to a queer fancy. She imagined any child would have feared Lassiter. And Fay Larkin had been a lonely, a solitary elf of the sage, not at all an ordinary child, and exquisitely shy with strangers. She watched Lassiter with great, round, grave eyes, but showed no fear. The rider gave Jane a favorable report of cattle and horses; and as he took the seat to which she invited him, little Fay edged as much as half an inch nearer. Jane replied to his look of inquiry and told Fay's story. The rider's gray, earnest gaze troubled her. Then he turned to Fay and smiled in a way that made Jane doubt her sense of the true relation of things. How could Lassiter smile so at a child when he had made so many children fatherless? But he did smile, and to the gentleness she had seen a few times he added something that was infinitely sad and sweet. Jane's intuition told her that Lassiter had never been a father; but if life ever so blessed him he would be a good one. Fay, also, must have found that smile singularly winning. For she edged closer and closer, and then, by way of feminine capitulation, went to Jane, from whose side she bent a beautiful glance upon the rider.

Lassiter only smiled at her.

Jane watched them, and realized that now was the moment she should seize, if she was ever to win this man from his hatred. But the step was not easy to take. The more she saw of Lassiter the more she respected him, and the greater her respect the harder it became to lend herself to mere coquetry. Yet as she thought of her great motive, of Tull, and of that other whose name she had schooled herself never to think of in connection with Milly Erne's avenger, she suddenly found she had no choice. And her creed gave her boldness far beyond the limit to which vanity would have led her.

'Lassiter, I see so little of you now,' she said, and was conscious of heat in her cheeks.

'I've been ridin' hard,' he replied.

'But you can't live in the saddle. You come in sometimes. Won't you come here to see me – oftener?'

'Is that an order?'

'Nonsense! I simply ask you to come to see me when you find time.'

'Why?'

The query once heard was not so embarrassing to Jane as she might have imagined. Moreover, it established in her mind a fact that there existed actually other than selfish reasons for her wanting to see him. And as she had been bold, so she determined to be both honest and brave.

'I've reasons – only one of which I need mention,' she answered. 'If it's possible I want to change you toward my people. And on the moment I can conceive of little I wouldn't do to gain that end.'

How much better and freer Jane felt after that confession! She meant to show him that there was one Mormon who could play a game or wage a fight in the open.

'I reckon,' said Lassiter, and he laughed.

It was the best in her, if the most irritating, that Lassiter always aroused.

'Will you come?' She looked into his eyes, and for the life of her could not quite subdue an imperiousness that rose with her spirit. 'I never asked so much of any man – except Bern Venters.'

'Pears to me that you'd run no risk, or Venters, either. But mebbe that doesn't hold good for me.'

'You mean it wouldn't be safe for you to be often here? You look for ambush in the cottonwoods?'

'Not that so much.'

At this juncture little Fay sidled over to Lassiter.

'Has oo a little dirl?' she inquired.

'No, lassie,' replied the rider.

Whatever Fay seemed to be searching for in Lassiter's sun-reddened face and quiet eyes she evidently found. 'Oo tan tum to see me,' she added, and with that, shyness gave place to friendly curiosity. First his sombrero with its leather band and silver ornaments commanded her attention; next his quirt, and then the clinking, silver spurs. These held her for some time, but presently, true to childish fickleness, she left off playing with them to look for something else. She laughed in glee as she ran her little hands down the slippery, shiny surface of Lassiter's leather chaps. Soon she discovered one of the hanging gun-sheaths, and she dragged it up and began tugging at the huge black handle of the gun. Jane Withersteen repressed an exclamation. What significance there was to her in the little girl's efforts to dislodge that heavy weapon! Jane Withersteen saw Fay's play and her beauty and her love as most powerful allies to her own woman's part in a game that suddenly had acquired a strange zest and a hint of danger. And as for the rider, he appeared to have forgotten Jane in the wonder of this lovely child playing about him. At first he was much the shyer of the two. Gradually her confidence overcame his backwardness, and he had the temerity to stroke her golden curls with a great hand. Fay rewarded his boldness with a smile, and when he had gone to the extreme of closing that great hand over her little brown one, she said, simple, 'I like oo!'

Sight of his face then made Jane oblivious for the time of his character as a hater of Mormons. Out of the mother longing that swelled her breast she divined the child hunger in Lassiter.

He returned the next day, and the next; and upon the following he came both at morning and at night. Upon the evening of this fourth day Jane seemed to feel the breaking of a brooding struggle in Lassiter. During all these visits he had scarcely a word to say, though he watched her and played absent-mindedly with Fay. Jane had contented herself with silence. Soon little Fay substituted for the expression of regard, 'I like oo,' a warmer and more generous one, 'I love oo.'

Thereafter Lassiter came oftener to see Jane and her little protégée. Daily he grew more gentle and kind, and gradually developed a quaintly merry mood. In the morning he lifted Fay upon his horse and let her ride as he walked beside her to the edge of the sage. In the evening he played with the child at an infinite variety of games she invented, and then, oftener than not, he accepted Jane's invitation to supper. No other visitor came to Withersteen House during those days. So that in spite of watchfulness he never forgot, Lassiter began to show he felt at home there. After the meal they walked into the grove of cottonwoods or up by the lakes, and little Fay held Lassiter's hand as much as she held Jane's. Thus a strange relationship was established, and Jane liked it. At twilight they always returned to the house, where Fay kissed them and went in to her mother. Lassiter and Jane were left alone.

Then, if there were anything that a good woman could do to win a man and still preserve her self-respect, it was something which escaped the natural subtlety of a woman determined to allure. Jane's vanity, that after all was not great, was soon satisfied with Lassiter's silent admiration. And her honest desire to lead him from his dark, blood-stained path would never have blinded her to what she owed herself. But the driving passion of her religion, and its call to save Mormons' lives, one life in particular, bore Jane Withersteen close to an infringement of her womanhood. In the beginning she had reasoned that her appeal to Lassiter must be through the senses. With whatever means she possessed in the way of adornment she enhanced her beauty. And she stooped to artifices that she knew were unworthy of her, but which she deliberately chose to employ. She made of herself a girl in every variable mood wherein a girl might be desirable. In those moods she was not above the methods of an inexperienced though natural flirt. She kept close to him whenever opportunity afforded; and she was forever playfully, yet passionately underneath the surface, fighting him for possession of the great black guns. These he would never yield to her. And so in that manner their hands were often and long in contact. The more of simplicity that she sensed in him the greater the advantage she took.

She had a trick of changing – and it was not altogether voluntary – from this gay, thoughtless, girlish coquettishness to the silence and the brooding, burning mystery of a woman's mood. The strength and passion and fire of her were in her eyes, and she so used them that Lassiter had to see this depth in her, this haunting promise more fitted to her years than to the flaunting guise of a willful girl.

The July days flew by. Jane reasoned that if it were possible for her to be happy during such a time, then she was happy. Little Fay completely filled a long aching void in her heart. In fettering the hands of this Lassiter she was accomplishing the greatest good of her life, and to do good even in a small way rendered happiness to Jane Withersteen. She had attended the regular Sunday services of her church; otherwise she had not gone to the village for weeks. It was unusual that none of her churchmen or friends had called upon her of late; but it was neglect for which she was glad. Judkins and his boy riders had experienced no difficulty in driving the white herd. So these warm July days were free of worry, and soon Jane hoped she had passed the crisis; and for her to hope was presently to trust, and then to believe. She thought often of Venters, but in a dreamy, abstract way. She spent hours teaching and playing with little Fay. And the activity of her mind centered around Lassiter. The direction she had given her will seemed to blunt any branching off of thought from that straight line. The mood came to obsess her.

In the end, when her awakening came, she learned that she had built better than she knew. Lassiter, though kinder and gentler than ever, had parted with his quaint humor and his coldness and his tranquillity to become a restless and unhappy man. Whatever the power of his deadly intent toward Mormons, that passion now had a rival, and one equally burning and consuming. Jane Withersteen had one moment of exultation before the dawn of a strange uneasiness. What if she had made of herself a lure, at tremendous cost to him and to her, and all in vain!

That night in the moonlit grove she summoned all her courage and, turning suddenly in the path, she faced Lassiter and leaned close to him, so that she touched him and her eyes looked up to his.

'Lassiter! . . . Will you do anything for me?'

In the moonlight she saw his dark, worn face change, and by that change she seemed to feel him immovable as a wall of stone.

Jane slipped her hands down to the swinging gun-sheaths, and when she had locked her fingers around the huge, cold handles of the guns, she trembled as with a chilling ripple over all her body.

'May I take your guns?'

'Why?' he asked, and for the first time to her his voice carried a harsh note. Jane felt his hard, strong hands close around her wrists. It was not wholly with intent that she leaned toward him, for the look of his eyes and the feel of his hands made her weak.

'It's no trifle – no woman's whim – it's deep – as my heart. Let me take them?'

'Why?'

'I want to keep you from killing more men – Mormons. You must let me save you from more wickedness – more wanton bloodshed—' Then the truth forced itself falteringly from her lips. 'You must – let – me – help me to keep my vow to Milly Erne. I swore to her – as she lay dying – that if ever any one came here to avenge her – I swore I would stay his hand. Perhaps I – I alone can save the – the man who – who – Oh, Lassiter! . . . I feel that if I can't change you – then soon you'll go out to kill – and you'll kill by instinct – and among the Mormons you kill will be the one – who . . . Lassiter, if you care a little for me – let me – for my sake – let me take your guns!'

As if her hands had been those of a child, he unclasped their clinging grip from the handles of his guns, and, pushing her away, he turned his gray face to her in one look of terrible realization and then strode off into the shadows of cottonwoods.

When the first shock of her futile appeal to Lassiter had passed, Jane took his cold, silent condemnation and abrupt departure not so much as a refusal to her entreaty as a hurt and stunned bitterness for her attempt at his betrayal. Upon further thought and slow consideration of Lassiter's past actions, she believed he would return and forgive her. The man could not be hard to a woman, and she doubted that he could stay away from her. But at the point where she had hoped to find him vulnerable she now began to fear he was proof against all persuasion. The iron and stone quality that she had early suspected in him had actually cropped out as an impregnable barrier. Nevertheless, if Lassiter remained in Cottonwoods she would never give up her hope and desire to change him. She would change him if she had to sacrifice everything dear to her except hope of heaven. Passionately devoted as she was to her religion, she had yet refused to marry a Mormon. But a situation had developed wherein self paled in the great white light of religious duty of the highest order. That was the leading motive, the divinely spiritual one; but there were other motives, which, like tentacles, aided in drawing her will to the acceptance of a possible abnegation. And through the watches of that sleepless night Jane Withersteen, in fear and sorrow and doubt, came finally to believe that if she must throw herself into Lassiter's arms to make him abide by 'Thou shalt not kill!' she would yet do well.

In the morning she expected Lassiter at the usual hour, but she was not able to go at once to the court, so she sent little Fay. Mrs Larkin was ill and required attention. It appeared that the mother, from the time of her arrival at Withersteen House, had relaxed and was slowly losing her hold on life. Jane had believed that absence of worry and responsibility coupled with good nursing and comfort would mend Mrs Larkin's broken health. Such, however, was not the case.

When Jane did get out to the court, Fay was there alone, and at the moment embarking on a dubious voyage down the stoned-lined amber stream upon a craft of two brooms and a pillow. Fay was as delightfully wet as she could possibly get.

Clatter of hoofs distracted Fay and interrupted the scolding she was gleefully receiving from Jane. The sound was not the light-spirited trot that Bells made when Lassiter rode him into the outer court. This was slower and heavier, and Jane did not recognize in it any of the other horses. The appearance of Bishop Dyer startled Jane. He dismounted with his rapid, jerky motion, flung the bridle, and, as he turned toward the inner court and stalked up on the stone flags, his boots rang. In his authoritative front, and in the red anger unmistakably flaming in his face, he reminded Jane of her father.

'Is that the Larkin pauper?' he asked bruskly, without any greeting to Jane.

'It's Mrs Larkin's little girl,' replied Jane, slowly.

'I hear you intend to raise the child?'

'Yes.'

'Of course you mean to give her Mormon bringing-up?'

'No!'

His questions had been swift. She was amazed at a feeling that someone else was replying for her.

'I've come to say a few things to you.' He stopped to measure her with stern, speculative eye.

Jane Withersteen loved this man. From earliest childhood she had been taught to revere and love bishops of her church. And for ten years Bishop Dyer had been the closest friend and counselor of her father, and for the greater part of that period her own friend and Scriptural teacher. Her interpretation of her creed and her religious activity in fidelity to it, her acceptance of mysterious and holy Mormon truths, were all invested in this Bishop. Bishop Dyer as an entity was next to God. He was God's mouthpiece to the little Mormon community at Cottonwoods. God revealed himself in secret to this mortal.

And Jane Withersteen suddenly suffered a paralyzing affront to her consciousness of reverence by some strange, irresistible twist of thought wherein she saw this Bishop as a man. And the train of thought hurdled the rising, crying protests of that other self whose poise she had lost. It was not her Bishop who eyed her in curious measurement. It was a man who tramped into her presence without removing his hat, who had no greeting for her, who had no semblance of courtesy. In looks, as in action, he made her think of a bull stamping cross-grained into a corral. She had heard of Bishop Dyer forgetting the minister in the fury of a common man, and now she was to feel it. The glance by which she measured him in turn momentarily veiled the divine in the ordinary. He looked a rancher; he was booted, spurred, and covered with dust; he carried a gun at his hip, and she remembered that he had been known to use it. But during the long moment while he watched her there was nothing commonplace in the slow-gathering might of his wrath.

'Brother Tull has talked to me,' he began. 'It was your father's wish that you marry Tull, and my order. You refused him?'

'Yes.'

'You would not give up your friendship with that tramp Venters?'

'No.'

'But you'll do as I order!' he thundered. 'Why, Jane Withersteen, you are in danger of becoming a heretic! You can thank your Gentile friends, for that. You face the damning of your soul to perdition.'

In the flux and reflux of the whirling torture of Jane's mind, that new daring spirit of hers vanished in the old habitual order of her life. She was a Mormon, and the Bishop regained ascendance.

'It's well I got you in time, Jane Withersteen. What would your father have said to these goings-on of yours? He would have put you in a stone cage on bread and water. He would have taught you something about Mormonism. Remember, you're a born Mormon. There have been Mormons who turned heretic – damn their souls! – but no born Mormon ever left us yet. Ah, I see your shame. Your faith is not shaken. You are only a wild girl.' The Bishop's tone softened. 'Well, it's enough that I got to you in time. . . . Now tell me about this Lassiter. I hear strange things.'

'What do you wish to know?' queried Jane.

'About this man. You hired him?'

'Yes, he's riding for me. When my riders left me I had to have any one I could get.'

'Is it true what I hear – that he's a gun-man, a Mormon-hater, steeped in blood?'

'True – terribly true, I fear.'

'But what's he doing here in Cottonwoods? This place isn't notorious enough for such a man. Sterling and the villages north, where there's universal gun-packing and fights every day – where there are more men like him, it seems to me they would attract him most. We're only a wild, lonely border settlement. It's only recently that the rustlers have made killings here. Nor have there been saloons till lately, nor the drifting in of outcasts. Has not this gun-man some special mission here?'

Jane maintained silence.

'Tell me,' ordered Bishop Dyer, sharply.

'Yes,' she replied.

'Do you know what it is?'

'Yes.'

'Tell me that.'

'Bishop Dyer, I don't want to tell.'

He waved his hand in an imperative gesture of command. The red once more leaped to his face, and in his steel-blue eyes glinted a pin-point of curiosity.

'That first day,' whispered Jane, 'Lassiter said he came here to find – Milly Erne's grave!'

With downcast eyes Jane watched the swift flow of the amber water. She saw it and tried to think of it, of the stones, of the ferns; but, like her body, her mind was in a leaden vise. Only the Bishop's voice could release her. Seemingly there was silence of longer duration than all her former life.

'For what – else?' When Bishop Dyer's voice did cleave the silence it was high, curiously shrill, and on the point of breaking. It released Jane's tongue, but she could not lift her eyes.

'To kill the man who persuaded Milly Erne to abandon her home and her husband – and her God!'

With wonderful distinctness Jane Withersteen heard her own clear voice. She heard the water murmur at her feet and flow on to the sea; she heard the rushing of all the waters in the world. They filled her ears with low, unreal murmurings – these sounds that deadened her brain and yet could not break the long and terrible silence. Then, from somewhere – from an immeasurable distance – came a slow, guarded, clinking, clanking step. Into her it shot electrifying life. It released the weight upon her numbed eyelids. Lifting her eyes she saw – ashen, shaken, stricken – not the Bishop but the man! And beyond him, from round the corner came that soft, silvery step. A long black boot with a gleaming spur swept into sight – and then Lassiter! Bishop Dyer did not see, did not hear: he stared at Jane in the throes of sudden revelation.

'Ah, I understand!' he cried, in hoarse accents. 'That's why you made love to this Lassiter – to bind his hands!'

It was Jane's gaze riveted upon the rider that made Bishop Dyer turn. Then clear sight failed her. Dizzily, in a blur, she saw the Bishop's hand jerk to his hip. She saw gleam of blue and spout of red. In her ears burst a thundering report. The court floated in darkening circles around her, and she fell into utter blackness.

The darkness lightened, turned to slow-drifting haze, and lifted. Through a thin film of blue smoke she saw the rough-hewn timbers of the court roof. A cool, damp touch moved across her brow. She smelled powder, and it was that which galvanized her suspended thought. She moved, to see that she lay prone upon the stone flags with her head on Lassiter's knee, and he was bathing her brow with water from the stream. The same swift glance, shifting low, brought into range of her sight a smoking gun and splashes of blood.

'Ah-h!' she moaned, and was drifting, sinking again into darkness, when Lassiter's voice arrested her.

'It's all right, Jane. It's all right.'

'Did – you – kill – him?' she whispered.

'Who? That fat party who was here? No. I didn't kill him.'

'Oh! . . . Lassiter!'

'Say! It was queer for you to faint. I thought you were such a strong woman, not faintish like that. You're all right now – only some pale. I thought you'd never come to. But I'm awkward round women folks. I couldn't think of anythin'.'

'Lassiter! . . . the gun there! . . . the blood!'

'So that's troublin' you. I reckon it needn't. You see it was this way. I come round the house an' seen that fat party an' heard him talkin' loud. Then he seen me, an' very impolite goes straight for his gun. He oughtn't have tried to throw a gun on me – whatever his reason was. For that's meetin' me on my own grounds. I've seen runnin' molasses that was quicker'n him. Now I didn't know who he was, visitor or friend or relation of yours, though I seen he was a Mormon all over, an' I couldn't get serious about shootin'. So I winged him – put a bullet through his arm as he was pullin' at his gun. An' he dropped the gun there, an' a little blood. I told him he'd introduced himself sufficient, an' to please move out of my vicinity. An' he went.'

Lassiter spoke with slow, cool, soothing voice, in which there was a hint of levity, and his touch, as he continued to bathe her brow, was gentle and steady. His impassive face, and the kind, gray eyes, further stilled her agitation.

'He drew on you first, and you deliberately shot to cripple him – you wouldn't kill him – you – *Lassiter?*'

'That's about the size of it.'

Jane kissed his hand.

All that was calm and cool about Lassiter instantly vanished.

'Don't do that! I won't stand it! An' I don't care a d———n who that fat party was.'

He helped Jane to her feet and to a chair. Then with the wet scarf he had used to bathe her face he wiped the blood from the stone flags and, picking up the gun, he threw it upon a couch. With that he began to pace the court, and his silver spurs jangled musically, and the great gun-sheaths softly brushed against his leather chaps.

'So – it's true – what I heard him say?' Lassiter asked, presently halting before her. 'You made love to me – to bind my hands?'

'Yes,' confessed Jane. It took all her woman's courage to meet the gray storm of his glance.

'All these days that you've been so friendly an' like a pardner – all these evenin's that have been so bewilderin' to me – your beauty – an' – an' the way you looked an' came close to me – they were woman's tricks to bind my hands?'

'Yes.'

'An' your sweetness that seemed so natural, an' your throwin' little Fay an' me so much together – to make me love the child – all that was for the same reason?'

'Yes.'

Lassiter flung his arms – a strange gesture for him.

'Mebbe it wasn't much in your Mormon thinkin', for you to play that game. But to bring the child in – that was hellish!'

Jane's passionate, unheeding zeal began to loom darkly.

'Lassiter, whatever my intention in the beginning, Fay loves you dearly – and I – I've grown to – to like you.'

'That's powerful kind of you, now,' he said. Sarcasm and scorn made his voice that of a stranger. 'An' you sit there an' look me straight in the eyes! You're a wonderful strange woman, Jane Withersteen.'

'I'm not ashamed, Lassiter. I told you I'd try to change you.'

'Would you mind tellin' me just what you tried?'

'I tried to make you see beauty in me and be softened by it. I wanted you to care for me so that I could influence you. It wasn't easy. At first you were stone-blind. Then I hoped you'd love little Fay, and through that come to feel the horror of making children fatherless.'

'Jane Withersteen, either you're a fool or noble beyond my understandin'. Mebbe you're both. I know you're blind. What you meant is one thing – what you *did* was to make me love you.'

'Lassiter!'

'I reckon I'm a human bein', though I never loved any one but my sister, Milly Erne. That was long –'

'Oh, are you Milly's brother?' .

'Yes, I was, an' I loved her. There never was anyone but her in my life till now. Didn't I tell you that long ago I back-trailed myself from women? I was a Texas ranger till – till Milly left home, an' then I became somethin' else – Lassiter! For years I've been a lonely man set on one thing. I came here an' met you. An' now I'm not the man I was. The change was gradual, an' I took no notice of it. I understand now that never-satisfied longin' to see you, listen to you, watch you, feel you near me. It's plain now why you were never out of my thoughts. I've had no thoughts but of you. I've lived an' breathed for you. An' now when I know what it means – what you've done – I'm burnin' up with hell's fire!'

'Oh, Lassiter – no – no – you don't love me that way!' Jane cried.

'If that's what love is, then I do.'

'Forgive me! I didn't mean to make you love me like that. Oh, what a tangle of our lives! You – Milly Erne's brother! And I – heedless, mad to melt your heart toward Mormons. Lassiter, I may be wicked, but not wicked enough to hate. If I couldn't hate Tull, could I hate you?'

'After all, Jane, mebbe you're only blind – Mormon blind. That only can explain what's close to selfishness –'

'I'm not selfish. I despise the very word. If I were free –'

'But you're not free. Not free of Mormonism. An' in playin' this game with me you've been unfaithful.'

'Unfaithful!' faltered Jane.

'Yes, I said unfaithful. You're faithful to your Bishop an' unfaithful to yourself. You're false to your womanhood an' true to your religion. But for a savin' innocence you'd have made yourself low an' vile – betrayin' yourself, betrayin' me – all to bind my hands an keep me from snuffin' out Mormon life. It's your damned Mormon blindness.'

'Is it vile – is it blind – is it only Mormonism to save human life? No, Lassiter, that's God's law, divine, universal for all Christians.'

'The blindness I mean is blindness that keeps you from seein' the truth. I've known many good Mormons. But some are blacker than hell. You won't see that even when you know it. Else, why all this blind passion to save the life of that – that. . . .'

Jane shut out the light, and the hands she held over her eyes trembled and quivered against her face.

'Blind – yes, an' let me make it clear an' simple to you,' Lassiter went on, his voice losing its tone of anger. 'Take, for instance, that idea of yours last night when you wanted my guns. It was good an' beautiful, an' showed your heart – but – why, Jane, it was crazy. Mind I'm assumin' that life to me is as sweet as to any other man. An' to preserve that life is each man's first an' closest thought. Where would any man be on this border without guns? Where, especially, would Lassiter be? Well, I'd be under the sage with thousands of other men now livin' an' sure better men than me. Gun-packin' in the West since the Civil War has growed into a kind of moral law. An' out here on this border it's the difference between a man an' somethin' not a man. Look what your takin' Venters's guns from him all but made him! Why, your churchmen carry guns. Tull has killed a man an' drawed on others. Your Bishop has shot a half dozen men, an' it wasn't through prayers of his that they recovered. An' today he'd have shot me if he'd been quick enough on the draw. Could I walk or ride down into Cottonwoods without my guns? This is a wild time, Jane Withersteen, this year of our Lord eighteen seventy-one.'

'No time – for a woman!' exclaimed Jane, brokenly. 'Oh, Lassiter, I feel helpless – lost – and don't know where to turn. If I *am* blind – then – I need some one – a friend – you, Lassiter – more than ever!'

'Well, I didn't say nothin' about goin' back on you, did I?'

CHAPTER TWELVE

The Invisible Hand

JANE RECEIVED A LETTER from Bishop Dyer, not in his own handwriting, which stated that the abrupt termination of their interview had left him in some doubt as to her future conduct. A slight injury had incapacitated him from seeking another meeting at present, the letter went on to say, and ended with a request which was virtually a command, that she call upon him at once.

The reading of the letter acquainted Jane Withersteen with the fact that something within her had all but changed. She sent no reply to Bishop Dyer nor did she go to see him. On Sunday she remained absent from the service – for the second time in years – and though she did not actually suffer there was a dead-lock of feelings deep within her, and the waiting for a balance to fall on either side was almost as bad as suffering. She had a gloomy expectancy of untoward circumstances, and with it a keen-edged curiosity to watch developments. She had a half-formed conviction that her future conduct – as related to her churchmen – was beyond her control and would be governed by their attitude toward her. Something was changing in her, forming, waiting for decision to make it a real and fixed thing. She had told Lassiter that she felt helpless and lost in the fateful tangle of their lives; and now she feared that she was approaching the same chaotic condition of mind in regard to her religion. It appalled her to find that she questioned phases of that religion. Absolute faith had been her serenity. Though leaving her faith unshaken, her serenity had been disturbed, and now it was broken by open war between her and her ministers. That something within her – a whisper – which she had tried in vain to hush had become a ringing voice, and it called to her to wait. She had transgressed no laws of God. Her churchmen, however invested with the power and the glory of a wonderful creed, however they sat in inexorable judgment of her, must now practice toward her the simple, common, Christian virtue they professed to preach, 'Do unto others as you have others do unto you!'

Jane Withersteen, waiting in darkness of mind, remained faithful still. But it was darkness that must soon be pierced by light. If her faith were justified, if her churchmen were trying only to intimidate her, the fact would soon be manifest, as would their failure, and then she would redouble her zeal toward them and toward what had been the best work of her life – work for the welfare and happiness of those among whom she lived. Mormon and Gentile alike. If that secret, intangible power closed its toils round her again, if that great invisible hand moved here and there and everywhere, slowly paralyzing her with its mystery and its inconceivable sway over her affairs, then she would know beyond doubt that it was not chance, nor jealousy, nor intimidation, nor ministerial wrath at her revolt, but a cold and calculating policy thought out long before she was born, a dark, immutable will of whose empire she and all that was hers was but an atom.

Then might come her ruin. Then might come her fall into black storm. Yet she would rise again, and to the light. God would be merciful to a driven woman who had lost her way.

A week passed. Little Fay played and prattled and pulled at Lassiter's big black guns. The rider came to Withersteen House oftener than ever. Jane saw a change in him, though it did not relate to his kindness and gentleness. He was quieter and more thoughtful. While playing with Fay or conversing with Jane he seemed to be possessed of another self that watched with cool, roving eyes, that listened, listened always as if the murmuring amber stream brought messages, and the moving leaves whispered something. Lassiter never rode Bells into the court any more, nor did he come by the lane or the paths. When he appeared it was suddenly and noiselessly out of the dark shadow of the grove.

'I left Bells out in the sage,' he said one day at the end of that week. 'I must carry water to him.'

'Why not let him drink at the trough or here?' asked Jane, quickly.

'I reckon it'll be safer for me to slip through the grove. I've been watched when I rode in from the sage.'

'Watched? By whom?'

'By a man who thought he was well hid. But my eyes are pretty sharp. An', Jane,' he went on, almost in a whisper, 'I reckon it'd be a good idea for us to talk low. You're spied on here by your women.'

'Lassiter!' she whispered in turn. 'That's hard to believe. My women love me.'

'What of that?' he asked. 'Of course they love you. But they're Mormon women.'

Jane's old, rebellious loyalty clashed with her doubt.

'I won't believe it,' she replied, stubbornly.

'Well then, just act natural an' talk natural, an' pretty soon – give them time to hear us – pretend to go over there to the table, an' then quick-like make a move for the door an' open it.'

'I will,' said Jane, with heightened color. Lassiter was right; he never made mistakes; he would not have told her unless he positively knew. Yet Jane was so tenacious of faith that she had to see with her own eyes, and so constituted that to employ even such small deceit toward her women made her ashamed, and angry for her shame as well as theirs. Then a singular thought confronted her that made her hold up this simple ruse – which hurt her, though it was well justified – against the deceit she had wittingly and eagerly used toward Lassiter. The difference was staggering in its suggestion of that blindness of which he had accused her. Fairness and justice and mercy, that she had imagined were anchor-cables to hold fast her soul to righteousness, had not been hers in the strange, biased duty that had so exalted and confounded her.

Presently Jane began to act her little part, to laugh and play with Fay, to talk of horses and cattle to Lassiter. Then she made deliberate mention of a book in which she kept records of all pertaining to her stock, and she walked slowly toward the table, and when near the door she suddenly whirled and thrust it open. Her sharp action nearly knocked down a woman who had undoubtedly been listening.

'Hester,' said Jane, sternly, 'you may go home, and you need not come back.'

Jane shut the door and returned to Lassiter. Standing unsteadily, she put her hand on his arm. She let him see that doubt had gone, and how this stab of disloyalty pained her.

'Spies! My own women! . . . Oh, miserable!' she cried, with flashing, tearful eyes.

'I hate to tell you,' he replied. By that she knew he had long spared her. 'It's begun again – that work in the dark.'

'Nay, Lassiter – it never stopped!'

So bitter certainty claimed her at last, and trust fled Withersteen House and fled forever. The women who owed much to Jane Withersteen changed not in love for her, nor in devotion to their household work, but they poisoned both by a thousand acts of stealth and cunning and duplicity. Jane broke out once and caught them in strange, stone-faced, unhesitating falsehood. Thereafter she broke out no more. She forgave them because they were driven. Poor, fettered, and sealed Hagars, how she pitied them! What terrible thing bound them and locked their lips, when they showed neither consciousness of guilt toward their benefactress nor distress at the slow wearing apart of long-established and dear ties?

'The blindness again!' cried Jane Withersteen. 'In my sisters as in me! . . . Oh, God!'

There came a time when no words passed between Jane and her women. Silently they went about their household duties, and secretly they went about the underhand work to which they had been bidden. The gloom of the house and the gloom of its mistress, which darkened even the bright spirit of little Fay, did not pervade these women. Happiness was not among them, but they were aloof from gloom. They spied and listened; they received and sent secret messengers; and they stole Jane's books and records, and finally the papers that were deeds of her possessions. Through it all they were silent, rapt in a kind of trance. Then one by one, without leave or explanation or farewell, they left Withersteen House, and never returned.

Coincident with this disappearance Jane's gardeners and workers in the alfalfa fields and stable men quit her, not even asking for their wages. Of all her Mormon employees about the great ranch only Jerd remained. He went on with his duty, but talked no more of the change than if it had never occurred.

'Jerd,' said Jane, 'what stock you can't take care of turn out in the sage. Let your first thought be for Black Star and Night. Keep them in perfect condition. Run them every day and watch them always.'

Though Jane Withersteen gave with such liberality, she loved her possessions. She loved the rich, green stretches of alfalfa, and the farms, and the grove, and the old stone house, and the beautiful, ever-faithful amber spring, and every one of a myriad of horses and colts and burros and fowls down to the smallest rabbit that nipped her vegetables; but she loved best her noble Arabian steeds. In common with all riders of the upland sage Jane cherished two material things – the cold, sweet, brown water that made life possible in the wilderness and the horses which were a part of that life. When Lassiter asked her what he would be without his guns he was assuming that his horse was part of himself. So Jane loved Black Star and Night because it was her nature to love all beautiful creatures – perhaps all living things; and then she loved them because she herself was of the sage and in her had been born and bred the rider's instinct to rely on his four-footed brother. And when Jane gave Jerd the order to keep her favorites trained down to the day it was a half-conscious admission that presaged a time when she would need her fleet horses.

Jane had now, however, no leisure to brood over the coils that were closing round her. Mrs Larkin grew weaker as the August days began; she required constant care; there was little Fay to look after; and such household work as was imperative. Lassiter put Bells in the stable with the other racers, and directed his efforts to a closer attendance upon Jane. She welcomed the change. He was always at hand to help, and it was her fortune to learn that his boast of being awkward around women had its root in humility and was not true.

His great, brown hands were skilled in a multiplicity of ways which a woman might have envied. He shared Jane's work, and was of especial help to her in nursing Mrs Larkin. The woman suffered most at night, and this often broke Jane's rest. So it came about that Lassiter would stay by Mrs Larkin during the day, when she needed care, and Jane would make up the sleep she lost in night-watches. Mrs Larkin at once took kindly to the gentle Lassiter, and, without ever asking who or what he was, praised him to Jane. 'He's a good man and loves children,' she said. How sad to hear this truth spoken of a man whom Jane thought lost beyond all redemption! Yet ever and ever Lassiter towered above her, and behind or through his black, sinister figure shone something luminous that strangely affected Jane. Good and evil began to seem incomprehensibly blended in her judgment. It was her belief that evil could not come forth from good; yet here was a murderer who dwarfed in gentleness, patience, and love any man she had ever known.

She had almost lost track of her more outside concerns when early one morning Judkins presented himself before her in the courtyard.

Thin, hard, burnt, bearded, with the dust and sage thick on him, with his leather wrist-bands shining from use, and his boots worn through on the stirrup side, he looked the rider of riders. He wore two guns and carried a Winchester.

Jane greeted him with surprise and warmth, set meat and bread and drink before him; and called Lassiter out to see him. The men exchanged glances, and the meaning of Lassiter's keen inquiry and Judkins's bold reply, both unspoken, was not lost upon Jane.

'Where's your hoss?' asked Lassiter, aloud.

'Left him down the slope,' answered Judkins. 'I footed it in a ways, an' slept last night in the sage. I went to the place you told me you 'most always slept, but didn't strike you.'

'I moved up some, near the spring, an' now I go there nights.'

'Judkins – the white herd?' queried Jane, hurriedly.

'Miss Withersteen, I make proud to say I've not lost a steer. Fer a good while after thet stampede Lassiter milled we hed no trouble. Why, even the sage dogs left us. But it's begun agin – thet flashin' of lights over ridge tips, an' queer puffin' of smoke, an' then at night strange whistles an' noises. But the herd's acted magnificent. An' my boys, say, Miss Withersteen, they're only kids, but I ask no better riders. I got the laugh in the village fer takin' them out. They're a wild lot, an' you know boys hev more nerve than grown men, because they don't know what danger is. I'm not denyin' there's danger. But they glory in it, an' mebbe I like it myself – anyway, we'll stick. We're goin' to drive the herd on the far side of the first break of Deception Pass. There's a great round valley over there, an' no ridges or piles of rocks to aid these stampeders. The rains are due. We'll hev plenty of water fer a while. An' we can hold thet herd from anybody except Oldrin'. I come in fer supplies. I'll pack a couple of burros an' drive out after dark tonight.'

'Judkins, take what you want from the store-room. Lassiter will help you. I – I can't thank you enough . . . but – wait.'

Jane went to the room that had once been her father's, and from a secret chamber in the thick stone wall she took a bag of gold, and, carrying it back to the court, she gave it to the rider.

'There, Judkins, and understand that I regard it as little for your loyalty. Give what is fair to your boys, and keep the rest. Hide it. Perhaps that would be wisest.'

'Oh . . . Miss Withersteen!' ejaculated the rider. 'I couldn't earn so much in – in ten years. It's not right – I oughtn't take it.'

'Judkins, you know I'm a rich woman. I tell you I've few faithful friends. I've fallen upon evil days. God only knows what will become of me and mine! So take the gold.'

She smiled in understanding of his speechless gratitude, and left him with Lassiter. Presently she heard him speaking low at first, then in louder accents emphasized by the thumping of his rifle on the stones. 'As infernal a job as even you, Lassiter, ever heerd of.'

'Why, son,' was Lassiter's reply, 'this breakin' of Miss Withersteen may seem bad to you, but it ain't bad – yet. Some of these wall-eyed fellers who look jest as if they was walkin' in the shadow of Christ himself, right down the sunny road, now they can think of things an' do things that are really hell-bent.'

Jane covered her ears and ran to her own room, and there like a caged lioness she paced to and fro till the coming of little Fay reversed her dark thoughts.

The following day, a warm and muggy one threatening rain, while Jane was resting in the court, a horseman clattered through the grove and up to the hitching-rack. He leaped off and approached Jane with the manner of a man determined to execute a difficult mission, yet fearful of its reception. In the gaunt, wiry figure and the lean, brown face Jane recognized one of her Mormon riders, Blake. It was he of whom Judkins had long since spoken. Of all the riders ever in her employ Blake owed her the most, and as he stepped before her, removing his hat and making manly efforts to subdue his emotion, he showed that he remembered.

'Miss Withersteen, mother's dead,' he said.

'Oh – Blake!' exclaimed Jane, and she could say no more.

'She died free from pain in the end, and she's buried – resting at last, thank God! . . . I've come to ride for you again, if you'll have me. Don't think I mentioned mother to get your sympathy. When she was living and your riders quit, I had to also. I was afraid of what might be done – said to her. . . . Miss Withersteen, we can't talk of – of what's going on now—'

'Blake, do you know?'

'I know a great deal. You understand, my lips are shut. But without explanation or excuse I offer my services. I'm a Mormon – I hope a good one. But – there are some things! . . . It's no use, Miss Withersteen, I can't say any more – what I'd like to. But will you take me back?'

'Blake! . . . You know what it means?'

'I don't care. I'm sick of – of – I'll show you a Mormon who'll be true to you!'

'But, Blake – how terribly you might suffer for that!'

'Maybe. Aren't you suffering now?'

'God knows indeed I am!'

'Miss Withersteen, it's a liberty on my part to speak so, but I know you pretty well – know you'll never give in. I wouldn't if I were you. And I – I must – Something makes me tell you the worst is yet to come. That's all. I absolutely can't say more. Will you take me back – let me ride for you – show everybody what I mean?'

'Blake, it makes me happy to hear you. How my riders hurt me when they quit!' Jane felt the hot tears well to her eyes and splash down upon her hands. 'I thought so much of them – tried so hard to be good to them. And not one was true. You've made it easy to forgive. Perhaps many of them really feel as you do, but dare not return to me. Still, Blake, I hesitate to take you back. Yet I want you so much.'

'Do it, then. If you're going to make your life a lesson to Mormon women, let me make mine a lesson to the men. Right is right. I believe in you, and here's my life to prove it.'

'You hint it may mean your life!' said Jane, breathless and low.

'We won't speak of that. I want to come back. I want to do what every rider aches in his secret heart to do for you. . . . Miss Withersteen, I hoped it'd not be necessary to tell you that my mother on her deathbed told me to have courage. She knew how the thing galled me – she told me to come back. . . . Will you take me?'

'God bless you, Blake! Yes, I'll take you back. And will you – will you accept gold from me?'

'Miss Withersteen!'

'I just gave Judkins a bag of gold. I'll give you one. If you will not take it you must not come back. You might ride for me a few months – weeks – days till the storm breaks. Then you'd have nothing, and be in disgrace with your people. We'll forearm you against poverty, and me against endless regret. I'll give you gold which you can hide – till some future time.'

'Well, if it pleases you,' replied Blake. 'But you know I never thought of pay. Now, Miss Withersteen, one thing more. I want to see this man Lassiter. Is he here?'

'Yes, but, Blake – what – Need you see him? Why?' asked Jane, instantly worried. 'I can speak to him – tell him about you.'

'That won't do. I want to – I've got to tell him myself. Where is he?'

'Lassiter is with Mrs Larkin. She is ill. I'll call him,' answered Jane, and going to the door she softly called for the rider. A faint, musical jingle preceded his step – then his tall form crossed the threshold.

'Lassiter, here's Blake, an old rider of mine. He has come back to me and he wishes to speak to you.'

Blake's brown face turned exceedingly pale.

'Yes, I had to speak to you,' he said, swiftly. 'My name's Blake. I'm a Mormon and a rider. Lately I quit Miss Withersteen. I've come to beg her to take me back. Now I don't know you, but I know – what you are. So I've this to say to your face. It would never occur to this woman to imagine – let alone suspect me to be a spy. She couldn't think it might just be a low plot to come here and shoot you in the back. Jane Withersteen hasn't that kind of a mind. . . . Well, I've not come for that. I want to help her – to pull a bridle along with Judkins and – and you. The thing is – do you believe me?'

'I reckon I do,' replied Lassiter. How this slow, cool speech contrasted with Blake's hot, impulsive words! 'You might have saved some of your breath. See here, Blake, cinch this in your mind. Lassiter has met some square Mormons! An' mebbe –'

'Blake,' interrupted Jane, nervously anxious to terminate a colloquy that she perceived was an ordeal for him. 'Go at once and fetch me a report of my horses.'

'Miss Withersteen! . . . You mean the big drove – down in the sage-cleared fields?'

'Of course,' replied Jane. 'My horses are all there, except the blooded stock I keep here.'

'Haven't you heard – then?'

'Heard? No! What's happened to them?'

'They're gone, Miss Withersteen, gone these ten days past. Dorn told me, and I rode down to see for myself.'

'Lassiter – did you know?' asked Jane, whirling to him.

'I reckon so. . . . But what was the use to tell you?'

It was Lassiter turning away his face and Blake studying the stone flags at his feet that brought Jane to the understanding of what she betrayed. She strove desperately, but she could not rise immediately from such a blow.

'My horses! My horses! What's become of them?'

'Dorn said the riders report another drive by Oldring. . . . And I trailed the horses miles down the slope toward Deception Pass.'

'My red herd's gone! My horses gone! The white herd will go next. I can stand that. But if I lost Black Star and Night, it would be like parting with my own flesh and blood. Lassiter – Blake – am I in danger of losing my racers?'

'A rustler – or – or anybody stealin' hosses of yours would most of all want the blacks,' said Lassiter. His evasive reply was affirmation enough. The other rider nodded gloomy acquiescence.

'Oh! Oh!' Jane Withersteen choked, with violent utterance.

'Let me take charge of the blacks?' asked Blake. 'One more rider won't be any great help to Judkins. But I might hold Black Star and Night, if you put such store on their value.'

'Value! Blake, I love my racers. Besides, there's another reason why I mustn't lose them. You go to the stables. Go with Jerd every day when he runs the horses, and don't let them out of your sight. If you would please me – win my gratitude, guard my black racers.'

When Blake had mounted and ridden out of the court Lassiter regarded Jane with the smile that was becoming rarer as the days sped by.

''Pears to me, as Blake says, you do put some store on them hosses. Now I ain't gainsayin' that the Arabians are the handsomest hosses I ever seen. But Bells can beat Night, an' run neck an' neck with Black Star.'

'Lassiter, don't tease me now. I'm miserable – sick. Bells is fast, but he can't stay with the blacks, and you know it. Only Wrangle can do that.'

'I'll bet that big raw-boned brute can more'n show his heels to your black racers. Jane, out there in the sage, on a long chase, Wrangle could kill your favorites.'

'No, no,' replied Jane, impatiently. 'Lassiter, why do you say that so often? I know you've teased me at times, and I believe it's only kindness. You're always trying to keep my mind off worry. But you mean more by this repeated mention of my racers?'

'I reckon so.' Lassiter paused, and for the thousandth time in her presence moved his black sombrero round and round, as if counting the silver pieces on the band. 'Well, Jane, I've sort of read a little that's passin' in your mind.'

'You think I might fly from my home – from Cottonwoods – from the Utah border?'

'I reckon. An' if you ever do an' get away with the blacks I wouldn't like to see Wrangle left here on the sage. Wrangle could catch you. I know Venters had him. But you can never tell. Mebbe he hasn't got him now. . . . Besides – things are happenin', an' somethin' of the same queer nature might have happened to Venters.'

'God knows you're right! . . . Poor Bern, how long he's gone! In my trouble I've been forgetting him. But, Lassiter, I've little fear for him. I've heard my riders say he's as keen as a wolf. . . . As to your reading my thoughts – well, your suggestion makes an actual thought of what was only one of my dreams. I believe I dreamed of flying from this wild borderland, Lassiter. I've strange dreams. I'm not always practical and thinking of my many duties, as you said once. For instance – if I dared – if I dared I'd ask you to saddle the blacks and ride away with me – and hide me.'

'Jane!'

The rider's sunburnt face turned white. A few times Jane had seen Lassiter's cool calm broken – when he had met little Fay, when he had learned how and why he had come to love both child and mistress, when he had stood beside Milly Erne's grave. But one and all they could not be considered in the light of his present agitation. Not only did Lassiter turn white – not only did he grow tense, not only did he lose his coolness, but also he suddenly, violently, hungrily took her into his arms and crushed her to his breast.

'Lassiter!' cried Jane, trembling. It was an action for which she took sole blame. Instantly, as if dazed, weakened, he released her. 'Forgive me!' went on Jane. 'I'm always forgetting your – your feelings. I thought of you as my faithful friend. I'm always making you out more than human . . . only, let me say – I meant that – about riding away. I'm wretched, sick of this – this – Oh, something bitter and black grows on my heart!'

'Jane, the hell – of it,' he replied, with deep intake of breath, 'is you *can't* ride away. Mebbe realizin' it accounts for my grabbin' you – that way, as much as the crazy boy's rapture your words gave me. I don't understand myself. . . . But the hell of this game is – you *can't* ride away.'

'Lassiter! . . . What on earth do you mean? I'm an absolutely free woman.'

'You ain't absolutely anythin' of the kind. . . . I reckon I've got to tell you!'

'Tell me all. It's uncertainty that makes me a coward. It's faith and hope – blind love, if you will, that makes me miserable. Every day I awake believing – still believing. The day grows, and with it doubts, fears, and that black bat hate that bites hotter and hotter into my heart. Then comes night – I pray – I pray for all, and for myself – I sleep – and I awake free once more, trustful, faithful, to believe – to hope! Then, Oh, my God! I grow and live a thousand years till night again! . . . But if you want to see me a woman, tell me why I can't ride away – tell me what more I'm to lose – tell me the worst.'

'Jane, you're watched. There's no single move of yours, except when you're hid in your house, that ain't seen by sharp eyes. The cottonwood grove's full of creepin', crawlin' men. Like Indians in the grass. When you rode, which wasn't often lately, the sage was full of sneakin' men. At night they crawl under your windows, into the court, an' I reckon into the house. Jane Withersteen, you know, never locked a door! This here grove's a hummin' bee-hive of mysterious happenin's. Jane, it ain't so much that these spies keep out of my way as me keepin' out of theirs. They're goin' to try to kill me. That's plain. But mebbe I'm as hard to shoot in the back as in the face. So far I've seen fit to watch only. This all means, Jane, that you're a marked woman. You can't get away – not now. Mebbe later, when you're broken, you might. But that's sure doubtful. Jane, you're to lose the cattle that's left – your home an' ranch – an' Amber Spring. You can't even hide a sack of gold! For it couldn't be slipped out of the house, day or night, an' hid or buried, let alone be rid off with. You may lose all. I'm tellin' you, Jane, hopin' to prepare you, if the worst does come. I told you once before about that strange power I've got to feel things.'

'Lassiter, what can I do?'

'Nothin', I reckon, except know what's comin' an' wait an' be game. If you'd let me make a call on Tull, an' a long-deferred call on –'

'Hush! . . . Hush!' she whispered.

'Well, even that wouldn't help you any in the end.'

'What does it mean? Oh, what does it mean? I am my father's daughter – a Mormon, yet I can't see! I've not failed in religion – in duty. For years I've given with a free and full heart. When my father died I was rich. If I'm still rich it's because I couldn't find enough ways to become poor. What am I, what are my possessions to set in motion such intensity of secret oppression?'

'Jane, the mind behind it all is an empire builder.'

'But, Lassiter, I would give freely – all I own to avert this – this wretched thing. If I gave – that would leave me with faith still. Surely my – my churchmen think of my soul? If I lose my trust in them –'

'Child, be still!' said Lassiter, with a dark dignity that had in it something of pity. 'You are a woman, fine an' big an' strong, an' your heart matches your size. But in mind you're a child. I'll say a little more – then I'm done. I'll never mention this again. Among many thousands of women you're one who has bucked against your churchmen. They tried you out, an' failed of persuasion, an' finally of threats. You meet now the cold steel of a will as far from Christlike as the universe is wide. You're to be broken. Your body's to be held, given to some man, made, if possible, to bring children into the world. But your soul? . . . What do they care for your soul?'

CHAPTER THIRTEEN

Solitude and Storm

IN HIS HIDDEN VALLEY Venters awakened from sleep, and his ears rang with innumerable melodies from full-throated mocking-birds, and his eyes opened wide upon the glorious golden shaft of sunlight shining through the great stone bridge. The circle of cliffs surrounding Surprise Valley lay shrouded in morning mist, a dim blue low down along the terraces, a creamy, moving cloud along the ramparts. The oak forest in the center was a plumed and tufted oval of gold.

He saw Bess under the spruces. Upon her complete recovery of strength she always rose with the dawn. At the moment she was feeding the quail she had tamed. And she had begun to tame the mocking-birds. They fluttered among the branches overhead, and some left off their songs to flit down and shyly hop near the twittering quail. Little gray and white rabbits crouched in the grass, now nibbling, now laying long ears flat and watching the dogs.

Venters's swift glance took in the brightening valley, and Bess and her pets, and Ring and Whitie. It swept over all to return again and rest upon the girl. She had changed. To the dark trousers and blouse she had added moccasins of her own make, but she no longer resembled a boy. No eye could have failed to mark the rounded contours of a woman. The change had been to grace and beauty. A glint of warm gold gleamed from her hair, and a tint of red shone in the clear dark brown of cheeks. The haunting sweetness of her lips and eyes, that earlier had been illusive, a promise, had become a living fact. She fitted harmoniously into that wonderful setting; she was like Surprise Valley – wild and beautiful.

Venters leaped out of his cave to begin the day.

He had postponed his journey to Cottonwoods until after the passing of the summer rains. The rains were due soon. But until their arrival and the necessity for his trip to the village he sequestered in a far corner of mind all thought of peril, of his past life, and almost that of the present. It was enough to live. He did not want to know what lay hidden in the dim and distant future. Surprise Valley had enchanted him. In this home of the cliff-dwellers there were peace and quiet and solitude, and another thing, wondrous as the golden morning shaft of sunlight, that he dared not ponder over long enough to understand.

The solitude he had hated when alone he had now come to love. He was assimilating something from this valley of gleams and shadows. From this strange girl he was assimilating more.

The day at hand resembled many days gone before. As Venters had no tools with which to build, or to till the terraces, he remained idle. Beyond the cooking of the simple fare there were no tasks. And as there were no tasks, there was no system. He and Bess began one thing, to leave it; to begin another, to leave that; and then do nothing but lie under the spruces and watch the great cloud-sails majestically move along the ramparts, and dream and dream. The valley was a golden, sunlit world. It was silent. The sighing wind and the twittering quail and the singing birds, even the rare and seldom-occurring hollow crack of a sliding weathered stone, only thickened and deepened that insulated silence.

Venters and Bess had vagrant minds.

'Bess, did I tell you about my horse Wrangle?' inquired Venters.

'A hundred times,' she replied.

'Oh, have I? I'd forgotten. I want you to see him. He'll carry us both.'

'I'd like to ride him. Can he run?'

'Run? He's a demon. Swiftest horse on the sage! I hope he'll stay in that canõn.'

'He'll stay.'

They left camp to wander along the terraces, into the aspen ravines, under the gleaming walls. Ring and Whitie wandered in the fore, often turning, often trotting back, open-mouthed and solemn-eyed and happy. Venters lifted his gaze to the grand archway over the entrance to the valley, and Bess lifted hers to follow his, and both were silent. Sometimes the bridge held their attention for a long time. Today a soaring eagle attracted them.

'How he sails!' exclaimed Bess. 'I wonder where his mate is?'

'She's at the nest. It's on the bridge in a crack near the top. I see her often. She's almost white.'

They wandered on down the terrace, into the shady, sun-flecked forest. A brown bird fluttered crying from a bush. Bess peeped into the leaves.

'Look! A nest and four little birds. They're not afraid of us. See how they open their mouths. They're hungry.'

Rabbits rustled the dead brush and pattered away. The forest was full of a drowsy hum of insects. Little darts of purple, that were runnning quail, crossed the glades. And a plaintive, sweet peeping came from the coverts. Bess's soft step disturbed a sleeping lizard that scampered away over the leaves. She gave chase and caught it, a slim creature of nameless color but of exquisite beauty.

'Jewel eyes,' she said. 'It's like a rabbit – afraid. We wont eat you. There – go.'

Murmuring water drew their steps down into a shallow shaded ravine where a brown brook brawled softly over mossy stones. Multitudes of strange, gray frogs with white spots and black eyes lined the rocky bank and leaped only at close approach. Then Venters's eye descried a very thin, very long green snake coiled round a sapling. They drew closer and closer till they could have touched it. The snake had no fear and watched them with scintillating eyes.

'It's pretty,' said Bess. 'How tame! I thought snakes always ran.'

'No. Even the rabbits didn't run here till the dogs chased them.'

On and on they wandered to the wild jumble of massed and broken fragments of cliff at the west end of the valley. The roar of the disappearing stream dinned in their ears. Into this maze of rocks they threaded a tortuous way, climbing, descending, halting to gather wild plums and great lavender lilies, and going on at the will of fancy. Idle and keen perceptions guided them equally.

'Oh, let us climb there!' cried Bess, pointing upward to a small space of terrace left green and shady between huge abutments of broken cliff. And they climbed to the nook and rested and looked out across the valley to the curling column of blue smoke from their campfire. But the cool shade and the rich grass and the fine view were not what they had climbed for. They could not have told, although whatever had drawn them was all-satisfying. Light, sure-footed as a mountain goat, Bess pattered down at Venters's heels; and they went on, calling the dogs, eyes dreamy and wide, listening to the wind and the bees and the crickets and the birds.

Part of the time Ring and Whitie led the way, then Venters, then Bess; and the direction was not an object. They left the sun-streaked shade of the oaks, brushed the long grass of the meadows, entered the green and fragrant swaying willows, to stop, at length, under the huge old cottonwoods where the beavers were busy.

Here they rested and watched. A dam of brush and logs and mud and stones backed the stream into a little lake. The round, rough beaver houses projected from the water. Like the rabbits, the beavers had become shy. Gradually, however, as Venters and Bess knelt low, holding the dogs, the beavers emerged to swim with logs and gnaw at cottonwoods and pat mud walls with their paddle-like tails, and, glossy and shiny in the sun, to go on with their strange, persistent industry. They were the builders. The lake was a mud-hole, and the immediate environment a scarred and dead region, but it was a wonderful home of wonderful animals.

'Look at that one – he puddles in the mud,' said Bess. 'And there! See him dive! Hear them gnawing! I'd think they'd break their teeth. How's it they can stay out of the water and under the water?'

And she laughed.

Then Venters and Bess wandered farther, and, perhaps not all unconsciously this time, wended their slow steps to the cave of the cliff-dwellers, where she liked best to go.

The tangled thicket and the long slant of dust and little chips of weathered rock and the steep bench of stone and the worn steps all were arduous work for Bess in the climbing. But she gained the shelf, gasping, hot of cheek, glad of eye, with her hand in Venters's. Here they rested. The beautiful valley glittered below with its millions of wind-turned leaves bright-faced in the sun, and the mighty bridge towered heavenward, crowned with blue sky. Bess, however, never rested for long. Soon she was exploring, and Venters followed; she dragged forth from corners and shelves a multitude of crudely fashioned and painted pieces of pottery, and he carried them. They peeped down into the dark holes of the kivas, and Bess gleefully dropped a stone and waited for the long-coming hollow sound to rise. They peeped into the little globular houses, like mud-wasp nests, and wondered if these had been store-places for grain, or baby cribs, or what; and they crawled into the larger houses and laughed when they bumped their heads on the low roofs, and they dug in the dust of the floors. And they brought from dust and darkness armloads of treasure which they carried to the light. Flints and stones and strange curved sticks and pottery they found; and twisted grass rope that crumbled in their hands, and bits of whitish stone which crushed to powder at a touch and seemed to vanish in the air.

'That white stuff was bone,' said Venters, slowly. 'Bones of a cliff-dweller.'

'No!' exclaimed Bess.

'Here's another piece. Look! . . . Whew! dry, powdery smoke! That's bone.'

Then it was that Venters's primitive, childlike mood, like a savage's, seeing, yet unthinking, gave way to the encroachment of civilized thought. The world had not been made for a single day's play or fancy or idle watching. The world was old. Nowhere could be gotten a better idea of its age than in this gigantic silent tomb. The gray ashes in Venters's hand had once been bone of a human being like himself. The pale gloom of the cave had shadowed people long ago. He saw that Bess had received the same shock – could not in moments such as this escape her feeling, living, thinking destiny.

'Bern, people have lived here,' she said, with wide, thoughtful eyes.

'Yes,' he replied.

'How long ago?'

'A thousand years and more.'

'What were they?'

'Cliff-dwellers. Men who had enemies and made their homes high out of reach.'

'They had to fight?'

'Yes.'

'They fought for – what?'

'For life. For their homes, food, children, parents – for their women!'

'Has the world changed any in a thousand years?'

'I don't know – perhaps very little.'

'Have men?'

'I hope so – I think so.'

'Things crowd into my mind,' she went on, and the wistful light in her eyes told Venters the truth of her thoughts. 'I've ridden the border of Utah. I've seen people – know how they live – but they must be few of all who are living. I had my books and I studied them. But all that doesn't help me any more. I want to go out into the big world and see it. Yet I want to stay here more. What's to become of us? Are we cliff-dwellers? We're alone here. I'm happy when I don't think. These – these bones that fly into dust – they make me sick and a little afraid. Did the people who lived here once have the same feelings as we have? What was the good of their living at all? They're gone! What's the meaning of it all – of us?'

'Bess, you ask more than I can tell. It's beyond me. Only there was laughter here once – and now there's silence. There was life – and now there's death. Men cut these little steps, made these arrow-heads and mealing-stones, plaited the ropes we found, and left their bones to crumble in our fingers. As far as time is concerned it might all have been yesterday. We're here today. Maybe we're higher in the scale of human beings – in intelligence. But who knows? We can't be any higher in the things for which life is lived at all.'

'What are they?'

'Why – I suppose relationship, friendship – love.'

'Love!'

'Yes. Love of man for woman – love of woman for man. That's the nature, the meaning, the best of life itself.'

She said no more. Wistfulness of glance deepened into sadness.

'Come, let us go,' said Venters.

Action brightened her. Beside him, holding his hand, she slipped down the shelf, ran down the long, steep slant of sliding stones, out of the cloud of dust, and likewise out of the pale gloom.

'We beat the slide,' she cried.

The miniature avalanche cracked and roared, and rattled itself into an inert mass at the base of the incline. Yellow dust like the gloom of the cave, but not so changeless, drifted away on the wind; the roar clapped in echo from the cliff, returned, went back, and came again to die in the hollowness. Down on the sunny terrace there was a different atmosphere. Ring and Whitie leaped around Bess. Once more she was smiling, gay, and thoughtless, with the dream-mood in the shadow of her eyes.

'Bess, I haven't seen that since last summer. Look!' said Venters, pointing to the scalloped edge of rolling purple clouds that peeped over the western wall. 'We're in for a storm.'

'Oh, I hope not. I'm afraid of storms.'

'Are you? Why?'

'Have you ever been down in one of these walled-up pockets in a bad storm?'

'No, now I think of it, I haven't.'

'Well, it's terrible. Every summer I get scared to death and hide somewhere in the dark. Storms up on the sage are bad, but nothing to what they are down here in the cañons. And in this little valley – why, echoes can rap back and forth so quick they'll split our ears.'

'We're perfectly safe here, Bess.'

'I know. But that hasn't anything to do with it. The truth is I'm afraid of lightning and thunder, and thunder-claps hurt my head. If we have a bad storm, will you stay close by me?'

'Yes.'

When they got back to camp the afternoon was closing, and it was exceedingly sultry. Not a breath of air stirred the aspen leaves, and when these did not quiver the air was indeed still. The dark-purple clouds moved almost imperceptibly out of the west.

'What have we for supper?' asked Bess.

'Rabbit.'

'Bern, can't you think of another new way to cook rabbit?' went on Bess, with earnestness.

'What do you think I am – a magician?' retorted Venters.

'I wouldn't dare tell you. But, Bern, do you want me to turn into a rabbit?'

There was a dark-blue, merry flashing of eyes and a parting of lips; then she laughed. In that moment she was naïve and wholesome.

'Rabbit seems to agree with you,' replied Venters. 'You are well and strong – and growing very pretty.'

Anything in the nature of compliment he had never before said to her, and just now he responded to a sudden curiosity to see its effect. Bess stared as if she had not heard aright, slowly blushed, and completely lost her poise in happy confusion.

'I'd better go right away,' he continued, 'and fetch supplies from Cottonwoods.'

A startlingly swift change in the nature of her agitation made him reproach himself for his abruptness.

'No, no, don't go!' she said. 'I didn't mean – that about the rabbit. I – I was only trying to be – funny. Don't leave me all alone!'

'Bess, I must go sometime.'

'Wait then. Wait till after the storms.'

The purple cloud-bank darkened the lower edge of the setting sun, crept up and up, obscuring its fiery red heart, and finally passed over the last ruddy crescent of its upper rim.

The intense dead silence awakened to a long, low, rumbling roll of thunder.

'Oh!' cried Bess, nervously.

'We've had big black clouds before this without rain,' said Venters. 'But there's no doubt about that thunder. The storms are coming. I'm glad. Every rider on the sage will hear that thunder with glad ears.'

Venters and Bess finished their simple meal and the few tasks around the camp, then faced the open terrace, the valley, and the west, to watch and await the approaching storm.

It required keen vision to see any movement whatever in the purple clouds. By infinitesimal degrees the dark cloud-line merged upward into the golden-red haze of the afterglow of sunset. A shadow lengthened from under the western wall across the valley. As straight and rigid as steel rose the delicate spear-pointed silver spruces; the aspen leaves, by nature pendant and quivering, hung limp and heavy; no slender blade of grass moved. A gentle splashing of water came from the ravine. Then again from out of the west sounded the low, dull, and rumbling roll of thunder.

A wave, a ripple of light, a trembling and turning of the aspen leaves, like the approach of a breeze on the water, crossed the valley from the west; and the lull and the deadly stillness and the sultry air passed away on a cool wind.

The night bird of the canõn, with his clear and melancholy notes, announced the twilight. And from all along the cliffs rose the faint murmur and moan and mourn of the wind singing in the caves. The bank of clouds now swept hugely out of the western sky. Its front was purple and black, with gray between, a bulging, mushrooming, vast thing instinct with storm. It had a dark, angry, threatening aspect. As if all the power of the winds were pushing and piling behind, it rolled ponderously across the sky. A red flare burned out instantaneously, flashed from west to east, and died. Then from the deepest black of the purple cloud burst boom. It was like the bowling of a huge boulder along the crags and ramparts, and seemed to roll on and fall into the valley to bound and bang and boom from cliff to cliff.

'Oh!' cried Bess, with her hands over her ears. 'What did I tell you?'

'Why, Bess, be reasonable!' said Venters.

'I'm a coward.'

'Not quite that, I hope. It's strange you're afraid. I love a storm.'

'I tell you a storm down in these cañons is an awful thing. I know Oldring hated storms. His men were afraid of them. There was one who went deaf in a bad storm, and never could hear again.'

'Maybe I've lots to learn, Bess. I'll lose my guess if this storm isn't bad enough. We're going to have heavy wind first, then lightning and thunder, then the rain. Let's stay out as long as we can.'

The tips of the cottonwoods and the oaks waved to the east, and the rings of aspens along the terraces twinkled their myriad of bright faces in fleet and glancing gleam. A low roar rose from the leaves of the forest, and the spruces swished in the rising wind. It came in gusts, with light breezes between. As it increased in strength the lulls shortened in length till there was a strong and steady blow all the time, and violent puffs at intervals, and sudden whirling currents. The clouds spread over the valley, rolling swiftly and low, and twilight faded into a sweeping darkness. Then the singing of the wind in the caves drowned the swift roar of rustling leaves; then the song swelled to a mourning, moaning wail; then with the gathering power of the wind the wail changed to a shriek. Steadily the wind strengthened and constantly the strange sound changed.

The last bit of blue sky yielded to the onsweep of clouds. Like angry surf the pale gleams of gray, amid the purple of that scudding front, swept beyond the eastern rampart of the valley. The purple deepened to black. Broad sheets of lightning flared over the western wall. There were not yet any ropes or zigzag streaks darting down through the gathering darkness. The storm center was still beyond Surprise Valley.

'Listen! . . . Listen!' cried Bess, with her lips close to Venters's ear. 'You'll hear Oldring's knell!'

'What's that?'

'Oldring's knell. When the wind blows a gale in the caves it makes what the rustlers call Oldring's knell. They believe it bodes his death. I think he believes so, too. It's not like any sound on earth . . . It's beginning. Listen!'

The gale swooped down with a hollow unearthly howl. It yelled and pealed and shrilled and shrieked. It was made up of a thousand piercing cries. It was a rising and moving sound. Beginning at the western break of the valley, it rushed along each gigantic cliff, whistling into the caves and cracks, to mount in power, to bellow a blast through the great stone bridge. Gone, as into an engulfing roar of surging waters, it seemed to shoot back and begin all over again.

It was only wind, thought Venters. Here sped and shrieked the sculptor that carved out the wonderful caves in the cliffs. It was only a gale, but as Venters listened, as his ears became accustomed to the fury and strife, out of it all or through it or above it pealed low and perfectly clear and persistently uniform a strange sound that had no counterpart in all the sounds of the elements. It was not of earth or of life. It was the grief and agony of the gale. A knell of all upon which it blew!

Black night enfolded the valley. Venters could not see his companion, and knew of her presence only through the tightening hold of her hand on his arm. He felt the dogs huddle closer to him. Suddenly the dense, black vault overhead split asunder to a blue-white, dazzling streak of lightning. The whole valley lay vividly clear and luminously bright in his sight. Up-reared, vast and magnificent, the stone bridge glimmered like some grand god of storm in the lightning's fire. Then all flashed black again – blacker than pitch – a thick, impenetrable coal-blackness. And there came a ripping, crashing report. Instantly an echo resounded with clapping crash. The initial report was nothing to the echo. It was a terrible, living, reverberating, detonating crash. The wall threw the sound across, and could have made no greater roar if it had slipped in avalanche. From cliff to cliff the echo went in crashing retort and banged in lessening power, and boomed in thinner volume, and clapped weaker and weaker till a final clap could not reach across to waiting cliff.

In the pitchy darkness Venters led Bess, and, groping his way, by feel of hand found the entrance to her cave and lifted her up. On the instant a blinding flash of lightning illumined the cave and all about him. He saw Bess's face white now, with dark, frightened eyes. He saw the dogs leap up, and he followed suit. The golden glare vanished; all was black; then came the splitting crack and the infernal din of echoes.

Bess shrank closer to him and closer, found his hands, and pressed them tightly over her ears, and dropped her face upon his shoulder, and hid her eyes.

Then the storm burst with a succession of ropes and streaks and shafts of lightning, playing continuously, filling the valley with a broken radiance; and the cracking shots followed each other swiftly till the echoes blended in one fearful, deafening crash.

Venters looked out upon the beautiful valley – beautiful now as never before – mystic in its transparent, luminous gloom, weird in the quivering, golden haze of lightning. The dark spruces were tipped with glimmering lights; the aspens bent low in the winds, as waves in a tempest at sea; the forest of oaks tossed wildly and shone with gleams of fire. Across the valley the huge cavern of the cliff-dwellers yawned in the glare, every little black window as clear as at noonday; but the night and storm added to their tragedy. Flung arching to the black clouds, the great stone bridge seemed to bear the brunt of the storm. It caught the full fury of the rushing wind. It lifted its noble crown to meet the lightnings. Venters thought of the eagles and their lofty nest in a niche under the arch. A driving pall of rain, black as the clouds, came sweeping on to obscure the bridge and the gleaming walls and the shining valley. The lightning played incessantly, streaking down through opaque darkness of rain. The roar of the wind, with its strange knell and the recrashing echoes, mingled with the roar of the flooding rain, and all seemingly were deadened and drowned in a world of sound.

In the dimming pale light Venters looked down upon the girl. She had sunk into his arms, upon his breast, burying her face. She clung to him. He felt the softness of her, and the warmth, and the quick heave of her breast. He saw the dark, slender, graceful outline of her form. A woman lay in his arms! And he held her closer. He who had been alone in the sad, silent watches of the night was not now and never must be again alone. He who had yearned for the touch of a hand felt the long tremble and the heartbeat of a woman. By what strange chance had she come to love him! By what change – by what marvel had she grown into a treasure!

No more did he listen to the rush and roar of the thunder-storm. For with the touch of clinging hands and the throbbing bosom he grew conscious of an inward storm – the tingling of new chords of thought, strange music of unheard, joyous bells, sad dreams dawning to wakeful delight, dissolving doubt, resurging hope, force, fire, and freedom, unutterable sweetness of desire. A storm in his breast – a storm of real love.

CHAPTER FOURTEEN
West Wind

WHEN THE STORM ABATED Venters sought his own cave, and late in the night, as his blood cooled and the stir and throb and thrill subsided, he fell asleep.

With the breaking of dawn his eyes unclosed. The valley lay drenched and bathed, a burnished oval of glittering green. The rain-washed walls glistened in the morning light. Waterfalls of many forms poured over the rims. One, a broad, lacy sheet, thin as smoke, slid over the western notch and struck a ledge in its downward fall, to bound into broader leap, to burst far below into white and gold and rosy mist.

Venters prepared for the day, knowing himself a different man.

'It's a glorious morning,' said Bess, in greeting.

'Yes. After the storm the west wind,' he replied.

'Last night was I – very much of a baby?' she asked, watching him.

'Pretty much.'

'Oh, I couldn't help it!'

'I'm glad you were afraid.'

'Why?' she asked, in slow surprise.

'I'll tell you some day,' he answered, soberly. Then around the camp-fire and through the morning meal he was silent; afterward he strolled thoughtfully off alone along the terrace. He climbed a great yellow rock raising its crest among the spruces, and there he sat down to face the valley and the west.

'I love her!'

Aloud he spoke – unburdened his heart – confessed his secret. For an instant the golden valley swam before his eyes, and the walls waved, and all about him whirled with tumult within.

'I love her! . . . I understand now.'

Reviving memory of Jane Withersteen and thought of the complications of the present amazed him with proof of how far he had drifted from his old life. He discovered that he hated to take up the broken threads, to delve into dark problems and difficulties. In this beautiful valley he had been living a beautiful dream. Tranquillity had come to him, and the joy of solitude, and interest in all the wild creatures and crannies of this incomparable valley – and love. Under the shadow of the great stone bridge God had revealed himself to Venters.

'The world seems very far away,' he muttered, 'but it's there – and I'm not yet done with it. Perhaps I never shall be . . . Only – how glorious it would be to live here always and never think again!'

Whereupon the resurging reality of the present, as if in irony of his wish, steeped him instantly in contending thought. Out of it all he presently evolved these things: he must go to Cottonwoods; he must bring supplies back to Surprise Valley; he must cultivate the soil and raise corn and stock, and, most imperative of all, he must decide the future of the girl who loved him and whom he loved. The first of these things required tremendous effort, the last one, concerning Bess, seemed simply and naturally easy of accomplishment. He would marry her. Suddenly, as from roots of poisonous fire, flamed up the forgotten truth concerning her. It seemed to wither and shrivel up all his joy on its hot, tearing way to his heart. She had been Oldring's Masked Rider. To Venters's question, 'What were you to Oldring?' she had answered with scarlet shame and drooping head.

'What do I care who she is or what she was!' he cried, passionately. And he knew it was not his old self speaking. It was this softer, gentler man who had awakened to new thoughts in the quiet valley. Tenderness, masterful in him now, matched the absences of joy and blunted the knife-edge of entering jealousy. Strong and passionate effort of will, surprising to him, held back the poison from piercing his soul.

'Wait . . . Wait!' he cried, as if calling. His hand pressed his breast, and he might have called to the pang there. 'Wait! It's all so strange – so wonderful. Anything can happen. Who am I to judge her? I'll glory in my love for her. But I can't tell it – can't give up to it.'

Certainly he could not then decide her future. Marrying her was impossible in Surprise Valley and in any village south of Sterling. Even without the mask she had once worn she would easily have been recognized as Oldring's Rider. No man who had ever seen her would forget her, regardless of his ignorance as to her sex. Then more poignant than all other argument was the fact that he did not want to take her away from Surprise Valley. He resisted all thought of that. He had brought her to the most beautiful and wildest place of the uplands; he had saved her, nursed her back to strength, watched her bloom as one of the valley lilies; he knew her life there to be pure and sweet – she belonged to him, and he loved her. Still these were not all the reasons why he did not want to take her away. Where could they go? He feared the rustlers – he feared the riders – he feared the Mormons. And if he should ever succeed in getting Bess safely away from these immediate perils, he feared the sharp eyes of women and their tongues, the big outside world with its problems of existence. He must wait to decide her future, which, after all, was deciding his own. But between her future and his something hung impending. Like Balancing Rock, which waited darkly over the steep gorge, ready to close forever the outlet to Deception Pass, that nameless thing, as certain yet intangible as fate, must fall and close forever all doubts and fears of the future.

'I've dreamed,' muttered Venters, as he rose. 'Well, why not? . . . To dream is happiness! But let me just once see this clearly, wholly; then I can go on dreaming till the things fall. I've got to tell Jane Withersteen. I've dangerous trips to take. I've work here to make comfort for this girl. She's mine. I'll fight to keep her safe from that old life. I've already seen her forget it. I love her. And if a beast ever rises in me I'll burn my hand off before I lay it on her with shameful intent. And, by God! sooner or later I'll kill the man who hid her and kept her in Deception Pass!'

As he spoke the west wind softly blew in his face. It seemed to soothe his passion. That west wind was fresh, cool, fragrant, and it carried a sweet, strange burden of far-off things – tidings of life in other climes, of sunshine asleep on other walls – of other places where reigned peace. It carried, too, sad truth of human hearts and mystery – of promise and hope unquenchable. Surprise Valley was only a little niche in the wide world whence blew that burdened wind. Bess was only one of millions at the mercy of unknown motive in nature and life. Content had come to Venters in the valley; happiness had breathed in the slow, warm air; love as bright as light had hovered over the walls and descended to him; and now on the west wind came a whisper of the eternal triumph of faith over doubt.

'How much better I am for what has come to me!' he exclaimed. 'I'll let the future take care of itself. Whatever falls, I'll be ready.'

Venters retraced his steps along the terrace back to camp, and found Bess in the old familiar seat, waiting and watching for his return.

'I went off by myself to think a little,' he explained.

'You never looked that way before. What – what is it? Won't you tell me?'

'Well, Bess, the fact is I've been dreaming a lot. This valley makes a fellow dream. So I forced myself to think. We can't live this way much longer. Soon I'll simply have to go to Cottonwoods. We need a whole pack train of supplies. I can get – '

'Can you go safely?' she interrupted.

'Why, I'm sure of it. I'll ride through the Pass at night. I haven't any fear that Wrangle isn't where I left him. And once on him – Bess, just wait till you see that horse!'

'Oh, I want to see him – to ride him. But – but, Bern, this is what troubles me,' she said. 'Will – will you come back?'

'Give me four days. If I'm not back in four days you'll know I'm dead. For that only shall keep me.'

'Oh!'

'Bess, I'll come back. There's danger – I wouldn't lie to you – but I can take care of myself.'

'Bern, I'm sure – oh, I'm sure of it! All my life I've watched hunted men. I can tell what's in them. And I believe you can ride and shoot and see with any rider of the sage. It's not – not that I – fear.'

'Well, what is it, then?'

'Why – why – why should you come back at all?'

'I couldn't leave you here alone.'

'You might change your mind when you get to the village – among old friends – '

'I won't change my mind. As for old friends – ' He uttered a short, expressive laugh.

'Then – there – there must be a – a woman!' Dark red mantled the clear tan of temple and cheek and neck. Her eyes were eyes of shame, upheld a long moment by intense, straining search for the verification of her fear. Suddenly they drooped, her head fell to her knees, her hands flew to her hot cheeks.

'Bess – look here,' said Venters, with a sharpness due to the violence with which he checked his quick, surging emotion.

As if compelled against her will – answering to an irresistible voice – Bess raised her head, looked at him with sad, dark eyes, and tried to whisper with tremulous lips.

'There's no woman,' went on Venters, deliberately holding her glance with his. 'Nothing on earth, barring the chances of life, can keep me away.'

Her face flashed and flushed with the glow of a leaping joy; but like the vanishing of a gleam it disappeared to leave her as he had never beheld her.

'I am nothing – I am lost – I am nameless!'

'Do you *want* me to come back?' he asked, with sudden stern coldness. 'Maybe *you* want to go back to Oldring!'

That brought her erect, trembling and ashy pale, with dark, proud eyes and mute lips refuting his insinuation.

'Bess, I beg your pardon. I shouldn't have said that. But you angered me. I intend to work – to make a home for you here – to be a – a brother to you as long as ever you need me. And you must forget what you are – were – I mean, and be happy. When you remember that old life you are bitter, and it hurts me.'

'I was happy – I shall be very happy. Oh, you're so good that – that it kills me! If I think, I can't believe it. I grow sick with wondering *why*. I'm only a – *let me say it* – only a lost, nameless – girl of the rustlers. *Oldring's Girl*, they called me. That you should save me – be so good and kind – want to make me happy – why, it's beyond belief. No wonder I'm wretched at the thought of your leaving me. But I'll be wretched and bitter no more. I promise you. If only I could repay you even a little – '

'You've repaid me a hundredfold. Will you believe me?'

'Believe you! I couldn't do else.'

'Then listen! . . . Saving you, I saved myself. Living here in this valley with you, I've found myself. I've learned to think while I was dreaming. I never troubled myself about God. But God, or some wonderful spirit, has whispered to me here. I absolutely deny the truth of what you say about yourself. I can't explain it. There are things too deep to tell. Whatever the terrible wrongs you've suffered, God holds you blameless. I see that – feel that in you every moment you are near me. I've a mother and a sister 'way back in Illinois. If I could I'd take you to them – tomorrow.'

'*If it were true!* Oh, I might – I might lift my head!' she cried.

'Lift it then – you child. For I swear it's true.'

She did lift her head with the singular wild grace always a part of her actions, with that old unconscious intimation of innocence which always tortured Venters, but now with something more – a spirit rising from the depths that linked itself to his brave words.

'I've been thinking – too,' she cried, with quivering smile and swelling breast. 'I've discovered myself – too. I'm young – I'm alive – I'm so full – oh! I'm a woman!'

'Bess, I believe I can claim credit of that last discovery – before you,' Venters said, and laughed.

'Oh, there's more – there's something I must tell you.'

'Tell it, then.'

'When will you go to Cottonwoods?'

'As soon as the storms are past, or the worst of them.'

'I'll tell you before you go. I can't now. I don't know how I shall then. But it must be told. I'd never let you leave me without knowing. For in spite of what you say there's a chance you mightn't come back.'

Day after day the west wind blew across the valley. Day after day the clouds clustered gray and purple and black. The cliffs sang and the caves rang with Oldring's knell, and the lightning flashed, the thunder rolled, the echoes crashed and crashed, and the rains flooded the valley. Wild flowers sprang up everywhere, swaying with the lengthening grass of the terraces, smiling wanly from shady nooks, peeping wondrously from year-dry crevices of the walls. The valley bloomed into a paradise. Every single moment, from the breaking of the gold bar through the bridge at dawn on to the reddening of rays over the western wall, was one of colorful change. The valley swam in thick, transparent haze, golden at dawn, warm and white at noon, purple in the twilight. At the end of every storm a rainbow curved down into the leaf-bright forest to shine and fade and leave lingeringly some faint essence of its rosy iris in the air.

Venters walked with Bess, once more in a dream, and watched the lights change on the walls, and faced the wind from out of the west.

Always it brought softly to him strange, sweet tidings of far-off things. It blew from a place that was old and whispered of youth. It blew down the grooves of time. It brought a story of the passing hours. It breathed low of fighting men and praying women. It sang clearly the song of love. That ever was the burden of its tidings – youth in the shady woods, waders through the wet meadows, boy and girl at the hedgerow stile, bathers in the booming surf, sweet, idle hours on grassy, windy hills, long strolls down moonlit lanes – everywhere in far-off lands, fingers locked and bursting hearts and longing lips – from all the world tidings of unquenchable love.

Often, in these hours of dreams he watched the girl, and asked himself of what was she dreaming? For the changing light of the valley reflected its gleam and its color and its meaning in the changing light of her eyes. He saw in them infinitely more than he saw in his dreams. He saw thought and soul and nature – strong vision of life. All tidings the west wind blew from distance and age he found deep in those dark-blue depths, and found them mysteries solved. Under their wistful shadow he softened, and in the softening felt himself grow a sadder, a wiser, and a better man.

While the west wind blew its tidings, filling his heart full, teaching him a man's part, the days passed, the purple clouds changed to white, and the storms were over for that summer.

'I must go now,' he said.

'When?' she asked.

'At once – tonight.'

'I'm glad the time has come. It dragged at me. Go – for you'll come back the sooner.'

Late in the afternoon, as the ruddy sun split its last flame in the ragged notch of the western wall, Bess walked with Venters along the eastern terrace, up the long, weathered slope, under the great stone bridge. They entered the narrow gorge to climb around the fence long before built there by Venters. Farther than this she had never been. Twilight had already fallen in the gorge. It brightened to waning shadow in the wider ascent. He showed her Balancing Rock, of which he had often told her, and explained its sinister leaning over the outlet. Shuddering, she looked down the long, pale incline with its closed-in, toppling walls.

'What an awful trail! Did you carry me up here?'

'I did, surely,' replied he.

'It frightens me, somehow. Yet I never was afraid of trails. I'd ride anywhere a horse could go, and climb where he couldn't. But there's something fearful here. I feel as – as if the place was watching me.'

'Look at this rock. It's balanced here – balanced perfectly. You know I told you the cliff-dwellers cut the rock, and why. But they're gone and the rock waits. Can't you see – feel how it waits here? I moved it once, and I'll never dare again. A strong heave would start it. Then it would fall and bang, and smash that crag, and jar the walls, and close forever the outlet to Deception Pass!'

'Ah! When you come back I'll steal up here and push and push with all my might to roll the rock and close forever the outlet to the Pass!' She said it lightly, but in the undercurrent of her voice was a heavier note, a ring deeper than any ever given mere play of words.

'Bess . . . You can't dare me! Wait till I come back with supplies – then roll the stone.'

'I – was – in – fun.' Her voice now throbbed low. 'Always you must be free to go when you will. Go now . . . this place presses on me – stifles me.'

'I'm going – but you had something to tell me?'

'Yes . . . Will you – come back?'

'I'll come if I live.'

'But – but you mightn't come?'

'That's possible, of course. It'll take a good deal to kill me. A man couldn't have a faster horse or keener dog. And, Bess, I've guns, and I'll use them if I'm pushed. But don't worry.'

'I've faith in you. I'll not worry until after four days. Only – because you mightn't come – I *must* tell you – '

She lost her voice. Her pale face, her great, glowing, earnest eyes, seemed to stand alone out of the gloom of the gorge. The dog whined, breaking the silence.

'I *must* tell you – because you mightn't come back,' she whispered. 'You *must* know what – what I think of your goodness – of you. Always I've been tongue-tied. I seemed not to be grateful. It was deep in my heart. Even now – if I were other than I am – I couldn't tell you. But I'm nothing – only a rustler's girl – nameless – infamous. You've saved me – and I'm – I'm yours to do with as you like . . . With all my heart and soul – I love you!'

CHAPTER FIFTEEN

Shadows on the Sage-Slope

IN THE CLOUDY, THREATENING, waning summer days shadows lengthened down the sage-slope, and Jane Withersteen likened them to the shadows gathering and closing in around her life.

Mrs Larkin died, and little Fay was left an orphan with no known relative. Jane's love redoubled. It was the saving brightness of a darkening hour. Fay turned now to Jane in childish worship. And Jane at last found full expression for the mother-longing in her heart. Upon Lassiter, too, Mrs Larkin's death had some subtle reaction. Before, he had often, without explanation, advised Jane to send Fay back to any Gentile family that would take her in. Passionately and reproachfully and wonderingly Jane had refused even to entertain such an idea. And now Lassiter never advised it again, grew sadder and quieter in his contemplation of the child, and infinitely more gentle and loving. Sometimes Jane had a cold, inexplanable sensation of dread when she saw Lassiter watching Fay. What did the rider see in the future? Why did he, day by day, grow more silent, calmer, cooler, yet sadder in prophetic assurance of something to be?

No doubt, Jane thought, the rider, in his almost superhuman power of foresight, saw behind the horizon the dark, lengthening shadows that were soon to crowd and gloom over him and her and little Fay. Jane Withersteen awaited the long-deferred breaking of the storm with a courage and embittered calm that had come to her in her extremity. Hope had not died. Doubt and fear, subservient to her will, no longer gave her sleepless nights and tortured days. Love remained. All that she had loved she now loved the more. She seemed to feel that she was defiantly flinging the wealth of her love in the face of misfortune and of hate. No day passed but she prayed for all – and most fervently for her enemies. It troubled her that she had lost, or had never gained, the whole control of her mind. In some measure reason and wisdom and decision were locked in a chamber of her brain, awaiting a key. Power to think of some things was taken from her. Meanwhile, abiding a day of judgment, she fought ceaselessly to deny the bitter drops in her cup, to tear back the slow, the intangibly slow growth of a hot, corrosive lichen eating into her heart.

On the morning of August 10th, Jane, while waiting in the court for Lassiter, heard a clear, ringing report of a rifle. It came from the grove, somewhere toward the corrals. Jane glanced out in alarm. The day was dull, windless, soundless. The leaves of the cottonwoods drooped, as if they had foretold the doom of Withersteen House and were now ready to die and drop and decay. Never had Jane seen such shade. She pondered on the meaning of the report. Revolver shots had of late cracked from different parts of the grove – spies taking snap-shots of Lassiter from a cowardly distance! But a rifle report meant more. Riders seldom used rifles. Judkins and Venters were the exceptions she called to mind. Had the men who hounded her hidden in her grove, taken to the rifle to rid her of Lassiter, her last friend? It was probable – it was likely. And she did not share his cool assumption that his death would never come at the hands of a Mormon. Long had she expected it. His constancy to her, his singular reluctance to use the fatal skill for which he was famed – both now plain to all Mormons – laid him open to inevitable assassination. Yet what charm against ambush and aim and enemy he seemed to bear about him! No, Jane reflected, it was not charm; only a wonderful training of eye and ear, and sense of impending peril. Nevertheless that could not forever avail against secret attack.

That moment a rustling of leaves attracted her attention; then the familiar clinking accompaniment of a slow, soft, measured step, and Lassiter walked into the court.

'Jane, there's a fellow out there with a long gun,' he said, and, removing his sombrero, showed his head bound in a bloody scarf.

'I heard the shot; I knew it was meant for you. Let me see – you can't be badly injured?'

'I reckon not. But mebbe it wasn't a close call! . . . I'll sit here in this corner where nobody can see me from the grove.' He untied the scarf and removed it to show a long, bleeding furrow above his left temple.

'It's only a cut,' said Jane. 'But how it bleeds! Hold your scarf over it just a moment till I come back.'

She ran into the house and returned with bandages; and while she bathed and dressed the wound Lassiter talked.

'That fellow had a good chance to get me. But he must have flinched when he pulled the trigger. As I dodged down I saw him run through the trees. He had a rifle. I've been expectin' that kind of gun play. I reckon now I'll have to keep a little closer hid myself. These fellers all seem to get chilly or shaky when they draw a bead on me, but one of them might jest happen to hit me.'

'Won't you go away – leave Cottonwoods as I've begged you to – before someone does happen to hit you?' she appealed to him.

'I reckon I'll stay.'

'But, oh, Lassiter – your blood will be on my hands!'

'See here, lady, look at your hands now, right now. Aren't they fine, firm, white hands? Aren't they bloody now? Lassiter's blood! That's a queer thing to stain your beautiful hands. But if you could only see deeper you'd find a redder color of blood. Heart color, Jane!'

'Oh! . . . My friend!'

'No, Jane, I'm not one to quit when the game grows hot, no more than you. This game, though, is new to me, an' I don't know the moves yet, else I wouldn't have stepped in front of that bullet.'

'Have you no desire to hunt the man who fired at you – to find him – and – kill him?'

'Well, I reckon I haven't any great hankerin' for that.'

'Oh, the wonder of it! . . . I knew – I prayed – I trusted. Lassiter, I almost gave – all myself to soften you to Mormons. Thank God, and thank you, my friend . . . But, selfish woman that I am, this is no great test. What's the life of one of those sneaking cowards to such a man as you? I think of your great hate toward him who – I think of your life's implacable purpose. Can it be – '

'Wait! . . . Listen!' he whispered. 'I hear a hoss.'

He rose noiselessly, with his ear to the breeze. Suddenly he pulled his sombrero down over his bandaged head and, swinging his gun-sheaths round in front, he stepped into the alcove.

'It's a hoss – comin' fast,' he added.

Jane's listening ear soon caught a faint, rapid, rhythmic beat of hoofs. It came from the sage. It gave her a thrill that she was at a loss to understand. The sound rose stronger, louder. Then came a clear, sharp difference when the horse passed from the sage trail to the hard-packed ground of the grove. It became a ringing run – swift in its bell-like clatterings, yet singular in longer pause than usual between the hoof-beats of a horse.

'It's Wrangle! . . . It's Wrangle!' cried Jane Withersteen. 'I'd know him from a million horses!'

Excitement and thrilling expectancy flooded out all Jane Withersteen's calm. A tight band closed round her breast as she saw the giant sorrel flit in reddish-brown flashes across the openings in the green. Then he was pounding down the lane – thundering into the court – crashing his great iron-shod hoofs on the stone flags. Wrangle it was surely, but shaggy and wild-eyed, and sage-streaked, with dust-caked lather staining his flanks. He reared and crashed down and plunged. The rider leaped off, threw the bridle, and held hard on a lasso looped round Wrangle's head and neck. Jane's heart sank as she tried to recognize Venters in the rider. Something familiar struck her in the lofty stature, in the sweep of the powerful shoulders. But this bearded, long-haired, unkempt man, who wore ragged clothes patched with pieces of skin, and boots that showed bare legs and feet – this dusty, dark and wild rider could not possibly be Venters

'Whoa, Wrangle, old boy! Come down. Easy now. So – so – so. You're home, old boy, and presently you can have a drink of water you'll remember.'

In the voice Jane knew the rider to be Venters. He tied Wrangle to the hitching-rack and turned to the court.

'Oh, Bern! . . . You wild man!' she exclaimed.

'Jane – Jane, it's good to see you! Hello, Lassiter! Yes, it's Venters.'

Like rough iron his hard hand crushed Jane's. In it she felt the difference she saw in him. Wild, rugged, unshorn – yet how splendid! He had gone away a boy – he had returned a man. He appeared taller, wider of shoulder, deeper-chested, more powerfully built. But was that only her fancy – he had always been a young giant – was the change one of spirit? He might have been absent for years, proven by fire and steel, grown like Lassiter, strong and cool and sure. His eyes – were they keener, more flashing than before? – met hers with clear, frank, warm regard, in which perplexity was not, nor discontent, nor pain.

'Look at me long as you like,' he said, with a laugh. 'I'm not much to look at. And, Jane, neither you nor Lassiter, can brag. You're paler than I ever saw you. Lassiter, here, he wears a bloody bandage under his hat. That reminds me. Someone took a flying shot at me down in the sage. It made Wrangle run some . . . Well, perhaps you've more to tell me than I've got to tell you.'

Briefly, in few words, Jane outlined the circumstances of her undoing in the weeks of his absence.

Under his beard and bronze she saw his face whiten in terrible wrath.

'Lassiter – what held you back?'

No time in the long period of fiery moments and sudden shocks had Jane Withersteen ever beheld Lassiter as calm and serene and cool as then.

'Jane had gloom enough without my addin' to it by shootin' up the village,' he said.

As strange as Lassiter's coolness was Venters's curious, intent scrutiny of them both, and under it Jane felt a flaming tide wave from bosom to temples.

'Well – you're right,' he said, with slow pause. 'It surprises me a little, that's all.'

Jane sensed than a slight alteration in Venters, and what it was, in her own confusion, she could not tell. It had always been her intention to acquaint him with the deceit she had fallen to in her zeal to move Lassiter. She did not mean to spare herself. Yet now, at the moment, before these riders, it was an impossibility to explain.

Venters was speaking somewhat haltingly, without his former frankness. 'I found Oldring's hiding-place and your red herd. I learned – I know – I'm sure there was a deal between Tull and Oldring.' He paused and shifted his position and his gaze. He looked as if he wanted to say something that he found beyond him. Sorrow and pity and shame seemed to contend for mastery over him. Then he raised himself and spoke with effort. 'Jane, I've cost you too much. You've almost ruined yourself for me. It was wrong, for I'm not worth it. I never deserved such friendship. Well, maybe it's not too late. You must give me up. Mind, I haven't changed. I am just the same as ever. I'll see Tull while I'm here, and tell him to his face.'

'Bern, it's too late,' said Jane.

'I'll *make* him believe!' cried Venters, violently.

'You ask me to break our friendship?'

'Yes. If you don't, I shall!'

'Forever?'

'Forever!'

Jane sighed. Another shadow had lengthened down the sage-slope to cast further darkness upon her. A melancholy sweetness pervaded her resignation. The boy who had left her had returned a man, nobler, stronger, one in whom she divined something unbending as steel. There might come a moment later when she would wonder why she had not fought against his will, but just now she yielded to it. She liked him as well – nay, more, she thought, only her emotions were deadened by the long, menacing wait for the bursting storm.

Once before she had held out her hand to him – when she gave it; now she stretched it tremblingly forth in acceptance of the decree circumstance had laid upon them. Venters bowed over it, kissed it, pressed it hard, and half stifled a sound very like a sob. Certain it was that when he raised his head tears glistened in his eyes.

'Some – women – have a hard lot,' he said, huskily. Then he shook his powerful form, and his rags lashed about him. 'I'll say a few things to Tull – when I meet him.'

'Bern – you'll not draw on Tull? Oh, that must not be! Promise me – '

'I promise you this,' he interrupted, in stern passion that thrilled while it terrorized her. 'If you say one more word for that plotter I'll kill him as I would a mad coyote!'

Jane clasped her hands. Was this fire-eyed man the one whom she had once made as wax to her touch? Had Venters become Lassiter and Lassiter Venters?

'I'll – say no more,' she faltered.

'Jane, Lassiter once called you blind,' said Venters. 'It must be true. But I won't upbraid you. Only don't rouse the devil in me by praying for Tull! I'll try to keep cool when I meet him. That's all. Now there's one more thing I want to ask of you – the last. I've found a valley down in the Pass. It's a wonderful place. I intend to stay there. It's so hidden I believe no one can find it. There's good water, and browse, and game. I want to raise corn and stock. I need to take in supplies. Will you give them to me?'

'Assuredly. The more you take the better you'll please me – and perhaps the less my – my enemies will get.'

'Venters, I reckon you'll have trouble packin' anythin' away,' put in Lassiter.

'I'll go at night.'

'Mebbe that wouldn't be best. You'd sure be stopped. You'd better go early in the mornin' – say, just after dawn. That's the safest time to move round here.'

'Lassiter, I'll be hard to stop,' returned Venters, darkly.

'I reckon so.'

'Bern,' said Jane, 'go first to the riders' quarters and get yourself a complete outfit. You're a – a sight. Then help yourself to whatever else you need – burros, packs, grain, dried fruits, and meat. You must take coffee and sugar and flour – all kinds of supplies. Don't forget corn and seeds. I remember how you used to starve. Please – please take all you can pack away from here. I'll make a bundle for you, which you musn't open till you're in the valley. How I'd like to see it! To judge by you and Wrangle, how wild it must be!'

Jane walked down into the outer court and approached the sorrel. Upstarting, he laid back his ears and eyed her.

'Wrangle – dear old Wrangle,' she said, and put a caressing hand on his matted mane. 'Oh, he's wild, but he knows me! Bern, can he run as fast as ever?'

'Run? Jane, he's done sixty miles since last night at dark, and I could make him kill Black Star right now in a ten-mile race.'

'He never could,' protested Jane. 'He couldn't even if he was fresh.'

'I reckon mebbe the best hoss'll prove himself yet,' said Lassiter, 'an', Jane, if it ever comes to that race I'd like you to be on Wrangle.'

'I'd like that, too,' rejoined Venters. 'But, Jane, maybe Lassiter's hint is extreme. Bad as your prospects are, you'll surely never come to the running point.'

'Who knows!' she replied, with mournful smile.

'No, no, Jane, it can't be so bad as all that. Soon as I see Tull there'll be a change in your fortunes. I'll hurry down to the village . . . Now don't worry.'

Jane retired to the seclusion of her room. Lassiter's subtle forecasting of disaster, Venters's forced optimism, neither remained in mind. Material loss weighed nothing in the balance with other losses she was sustaining. She wondered dully at her sitting there, hands folded listlessly, with a kind of numb deadness to the passing of time and the passing of her riches. She thought of Venters's friendship. She had not lost that, but she had lost him. Lassiter's friendship – that was more than love – it would endure, but soon he, too, would be gone. Little Fay slept dreamlessly upon the bed, her golden curls streaming over the pillow. Jane had the child's worship. Would she lose that, too? And if she did, what then would be left? Conscience thundered at her that there was left her religion. Conscience thundered that she should be grateful on her knees for this baptism of fire; that through misfortune, sacrifice, and suffering her soul might be fused pure gold. But the old, spontaneous, rapturous spirit no more exalted her. She wanted to be a woman – not a martyr. Like the saint of old who mortified his flesh, Jane

Withersteen had in her the temper for heroic martyrdom, if by sacrificing herself she could save the souls of others. But here the damnable verdict blistered her that the more she sacrificed herself the blacker grew the souls of her churchmen. There was something terribly wrong with her soul, something terribly wrong with her churchmen and her religion. In the whirling gulf of her thought there was yet one shining light to guide her, to sustain her in her hope; and it was that, despite her errors and her frailties and her blindness, she had one absolute and unfaltering hold on ultimate and supreme justice. That was love. 'Love your enemies as yourself!' was a divine word, entirely free from any church or creed.

Jane's meditations were disturbed by Lassiter's soft, tinkling step in the court. Always he wore the clinking spurs. Always he was in readiness to ride. She passed out and called him into the huge, dim hall.

'I think you'll be safer here. The court is too open,' she said.

'I reckon,' replied Lassiter. 'An' it's cooler here. The day's sure muggy. Well, I went down to the village with Venters.'

'Already! Where is he?' queried Jane, in quick amaze.

'He's at the corrals. Blake's helpin' him get the burros an' packs ready. That Blake is a good fellow.'

'Did – did Bern meet Tull?'

'I guess he did,' answered Lassiter, and he laughed dryly.

'Tell me! Oh, you exasperate me! You're so cool, so calm! For heaven's sake, tell me what happened!'

'First time I've been in the village for weeks,' went on Lassiter, mildly. 'I reckon there ain't been more of a show for a long time. Me an' Venters walkin' down the road! It was funny. I ain't sayin' anybody was particular glad to see us. I'm not much thought of hereabouts, an' Venters he sure looks like what you called him, a wild man. Well, there was some runnin' of folks before we got to the stores. Then everybody vamoosed except some surprised rustlers in front of a saloon. Venters went right in the stores an' saloons, an' of course I went along. I don't know which tickled me the most – the actions of many fellers we met, or Venters's nerve. Jane, I was downright glad to be along. You see *that* sort of thing is my element, an' I've been away from it for a spell. But we didn't find Tull in one of them places. Some Gentile feller at last told Venters he'd find Tull in that long buildin' next to Parson's store. It's a kind of meetin'-room; and sure enough, when we peeped in, it was half full of men.

'Venters yelled: "Don't anybody pull guns! We ain't come for that!" Then he tramped in, an' I was some put to keep alongside him. There was a hard, scrapin' sound of feet, a loud cry, an' then some whisperin', an' after that stillness you could cut with a knife. Tull was there, an' that fat party who once tried to throw a gun on me, an' other important-lookin' men, an' that little frog-legged feller who was with Tull the day I rode in here. I wish you could have seen their faces, 'specially Tull's an' the fat party's. But there ain't no use of me tryin' to tell you how they looked.

'Well, Venters an' I stood there in the middle of the room, with that batch of men all in front of us, an' not a blamed one of them winked an eyelash or moved a finger. It was natural, of course, for me to notice many of them packed guns. That's a way of mine, first noticin' them things. Venters spoke up, an' his voice sort of chilled an' cut, an' he told Tull he had a few things to say.'

Here Lassiter paused while he turned his sombrero round and round, in his familiar habit, and his eyes had the look of a man seeing over again some thrilling spectacle, and under his red bronze there was strange animation.

'Like a shot, then, Venters told Tull that the friendship between you an' him was all over, an' he was leaving your place. He said you'd both of you broken off in the hope of propitiatin' your people, but you hadn't changed your mind otherwise, an' never would.

'Next he spoke up for you. I ain't goin' to tell you what he said. Only – no other woman who ever lived ever had such tribute! You had a champion, Jane, an' never fear that those thick-skulled men don't know you now. It couldn't be otherwise. He spoke the ringin', lightnin' truth. . . . Then he accused Tull of the underhand, miserable robbery of a helpless woman. He told Tull where the red herd was, of a deal made with Oldrin', that Jerry Card had made the deal. I thought Tull was goin' to drop, an' that little frog-legged cuss, he looked some limp an' white. But Venters's voice would have kept anybody's legs from bucklin'. I was stiff myself. He went on an' called Tull – called him every bad name ever known to a rider, an' then some. He cursed Tull. I never heard a man get such a cursin'. He laughed in scorn at the idea of Tull bein' a minister. He said Tull an' a few more dogs of hell builded their empire out of the hearts of such innocent an' God-fearin' women as Jane Withersteen. He called Tull a binder of women, a callous beast who hid behind a mock mantle of righteousness – an' the last an' lowest coward on the face of the earth. To prey on weak women through their religion – that was the last unspeakable crime!

'Then he finished, an' by this time he'd almost lost his voice. But his whisper was enough. "Tull," he said, "*she* begged me not to draw on you today. *She* would pray for you if you burned her at the stake. . . . But listen! . . . I swear if you and I ever come face to face again, I'll kill you!"

'We backed out of the door then, an' up the road. But nobody follered us.'

Jane found herself weeping passionately. She had not been conscious of it till Lassiter ended his story, and she experienced exquisite pain and relief in shedding tears. Long had her eyes been dry, her grief deep; long had her emotions been dumb. Lassiter's story put her on the rack; the appalling nature of Venters's act and speech had no parallel as an outrage; it was worse than bloodshed. Men like Tull had been shot, but had one ever been so terribly denounced in public? Over-mounting her horror, an uncontrollable, quivering passion shook her very soul. It was sheer human glory in the deed of a fearless man. It was hot, primitive instinct to live – to fight. It was a kind of mad joy in Venters's chivalry. It was close to the wrath that had first shaken her in the beginning of this war waged upon her.

'Well, well, Jane, don't take it that way,' said Lassiter, in evident distress. 'I had to tell you. There's some things a feller jest can't keep. It's strange you give up on hearin' that, when all this long time you've been the gamest woman I ever seen. But I don't know women. Mebbe there's reason for you to cry. I know this – nothin' ever rang in my soul an' so filled it as what Venters did. I'd like to have done it, but – I'm only good for throwin' a gun, an' it seems you hate that. . . . Well, I'll be goin' now.'

'Where?'

'Venters took Wrangle to the stable. The sorrel's shy a shoe, an' I've got to help hold the big devil an' put on another.'

'Tell Bern to come for the pack I want to give him – and – and to say good-bye,' called Jane, as Lassiter went out.

Jane passed the rest of that day in a vain endeavor to decide what and what not to put in the pack for Venters. This task was the last she would ever perform for him, and the gifts were the last she would ever make him. So she picked and chose and rejected, and chose again, and often paused in sad revery, and began again, till at length she filled the pack.

It was about sunset, and she and Fay had finished supper and were sitting in the court, when Venters's quick steps rang on the stones. She scarcely knew him, for he had changed the tattered garments, and she missed the dark beard and long hair. Still he was not the Venters of old. As he came up the steps she felt herself pointing to the pack, and heard herself speaking words that were meaningless to her. He said good-bye; he kissed her, released her, and turned away. His tall figure blurred in her sight, grew dim through dark, streaked vision, and then he vanished.

Twilight fell around Withersteen House, and dusk and night. Little Fay slept; but Jane lay with strained, aching eyes. She heard the wind moaning in the cottonwoods and mice squeaking in the walls. The night was interminably long, yet she prayed to hold back the dawn. What would another day bring forth? The blackness of her room seemed blacker for the sad, entering gray of morning light. She heard the chirp of awakening birds, and fancied she caught a faint clatter of hoofs. Then low, dull, distant, throbbed a heavy gunshot. She had expected it, was waiting for it; nevertheless, an electric shock checked her heart, froze the very living fiber of her bones. That vise-like hold on her faculties apparently did not relax for a long time, and it was a voice under her windows that released her.

'Jane! . . . Jane!' softly called Lassiter.

She answered somehow.

'It's all right. Venters got away. I thought mebbe you'd heard that shot, an' I was worried some.'

'What was it – who fired?'

'Well – some fool feller tried to stop Venters out there in the sage – an' he only stopped lead! . . . I think it'll be all right. I haven't seen or heard of any other fellers around. Venters'll go through safe. An', Jane, I've got Bells saddled, an' I'm going to trail Venters. Mind, I won't show myself unless he falls foul of somebody an' needs me. I want to see if this place where he's goin' is safe for him. He says nobody can track him there. I never seen the place yet I couldn't track a man to. Now, Jane, you stay indoors while I'm gone, an' keep close watch on Fay. Will you?'

'Yes! Oh yes!'

'An' another thing, Jane,' he continued, then paused for long – 'another thing – if you ain't here when I come back – if you're gone – don't fear, I'll trail you – I'll find you.'

'My dear Lassiter, where could I be gone – as you put it?' asked Jane, in a curious surprise.

'I reckon you might be somewhere. Mebbe tied in an old barn – or corralled in some gulch – or chained in a cave! Milly Erne was – till she gave in! Mebbe that's news to you . . . Well, if you're gone I'll hunt for you.'

'No, Lassiter,' she replied, sadly and low. 'If I'm gone just forget the unhappy woman whose blinded selfish deceit you repaid with kindness and love.'

She heard a deep, muttering curse, under his breath, and then the silvery tinkling of his spurs as he moved away.

Jane entered upon the duties of that day with a settled, gloomy calm. Disaster hung in the dark clouds, in the shade, in the humid west wind. Blake, when he reported, appeared without his usual cheer; and Jerd wore a harassed look of a worn and worried man. And when Judkins put in appearance, riding a lame horse, and dismounted with the cramp of a rider, his dust-covered figure and his darkly grim, almost dazed expression told Jane of dire calamity. She had no need of words.

'Miss Withersteen, I have to report – loss of the – white herd,' said Judkins, hoarsely.

'Come, sit down; you look played out,' replied Jane, solicitously. She brought him brandy and food, and while he partook of refreshments, of which he appeared badly in need, she asked no questions.

'No one rider – could hev done more – Miss Withersteen,' he went on, presently.

'Judkins, don't be distressed. You've done more than any other rider. I've long expected to lose the white herd. It's no surprise. It's in line with other things that are happening. I'm grateful for your service.'

'Miss Withersteen, I knew how you'd take it. But if anythin', that makes it harder to tell. You see, a feller wants to do so much fer you, an' I'd got fond of my job. We hed the herd a ways off to the north of the break in the valley. There was a big level an' pools of water an' tip-top browse. But the cattle was in a high nervous condition. Wild – as wild as antelope! You see, they'd been so scared they never slept. I ain't a-goin' to tell you of the many tricks that were pulled off out there in the sage. But there wasn't a day fer weeks thet the herd didn't get started to run. We allus managed to ride 'em close an' drive 'em back an' keep 'em bunched. Honest, Miss Withersteen, them steers was *thin*. They was *thin* when water and grass was everywhere. *Thin* at this season – thet'll tell you how your steers was pestered. Fer instance, one night a strange runnin' streak of fire run right through the herd. That streak was a coyote – *with an oiled an' blazin' tail!* Fer I shot it an' found out. We hed hell with the herd that night, an' if the sage an' grass hedn't been wet – we, hosses, steers, an' all would hev burned up. But I said I wasn't goin' to tell you any of the tricks. . . . Strange now, Miss Withersteen, when the stampede did come it was from natural cause – jest a whirlin' devil of dust. You've seen the like often. An' this wasn't no big whirl, fer the dust was mostly settled. It had dried out in a little swale, an' ordinarily no steer would ever hev run fer it. But the herd was nervous an' wild. An' jest as Lassiter said, when that bunch of white steers got to movin' they was as bad as buffalo. I've seen some buffalo stampedes back in Nebraska, an' this bolt of the steers was the same kind.

'I tried to mill the herd jest as Lassiter did. But I wasn't equal to it, Miss Withersteen. I don't believe the rider lives who could hev turned thet herd. We kept along of the herd fer miles, an' more'n one of my boys tried to get the steers a-millin'. It wasn't no use. We got off level ground, goin' down, an' then the steers ran somethin' fierce. We left the little gullies an' washes level-full of dead steers. Finally I saw the herd was makin' to pass a kind of low pocket between ridges. There was a hog-back – as we used to call'em – a pile of rocks stickin' up, and I saw the herd was goin' to split round it, or swing out to the left. An' I wanted 'em to go to the right so mebbe we'd be able to drive 'em into the pocket. So, with all my boys except three, I rode hard to turn the herd a little to the right. We couldn't budge 'em. They went on, an' split round the rocks, an' the most of 'em was turned sharp to the left by a deep wash we hedn't seen – had no chance to see.

'The other three boys – Jimmy Vail, Joe Wills, an' thet little Cairns boy – a nervy kid! they, with Cairns leadin', tried to buck thet herd round to the pocket. It was a wild, fool idee. I couldn't do nothin'. The boys got hemmed in between the steers an' the wash – thet they hedn't no chance to see, either. Vail an' Wills was run down right before our eyes. An' Cairns, who rode a fine hoss, he did some ridin' I never seen equaled, an' would hev beat the steers if there'd been any room to run in. I was high up an' could see how the steers kept spillin' by twos and threes over into the wash. Cairns put his hoss to a place thet was too wide fer any hoss, an' broke his neck an' the hoss's too. We found that out after, an' as fer Vail an' Wills – two thousand steers ran over the poor boys. There was't much left to pack home fer buryin! . . . An', Miss Withersteen, thet all happened yesterday, an' I believe, if the white herd didn't run over the wall of the Pass, it's runnin' yet.'

On the morning of the second day after Judkins's recital, during which time Jane remained indoors a prey to regret and sorrow for the boy riders, and a new and now strangely insistent fear for her own person, she again heard what she had missed more than she dared honestly confess – the soft, jingling step of Lassiter. Almost overwhelming relief surged through her, a feeling as akin to joy as any she could have been capable of in those gloomy hours of shadow, and one that suddenly stunned her with the significance of what Lassiter had come to mean to her. She had begged him, for his own sake, to leave Cottonwoods. She might yet beg that, if her weakening courage permitted her to dare absolute loneliness and helplessness, but she realized now that if she were left alone her life would become one long, hideous nightmare.

When his soft steps clinked into the hall, in answer to her greeting, and his tall, black-garbed form filled the door, she felt an inexpressible sense of immediate safety. In his presence she lost her fear of the dim passageways of Withersteen House and of every sound. Always it had been that, when he entered the court or the hall, she had experienced a distinctly sickening but gradually lessening shock at sight of the huge black guns swinging at his sides. This time the sickening shock again visited her, it was, however, because a revealing flash of thought told her that it was not alone. Lassiter who was thrillingly welcome, but also his fatal weapons. They meant so much. How she had fallen – how broken and spiritless must she be – to have still the same old horror of Lassiter's guns and his name, yet feel somehow a cold, shrinking protection in their law and might and use.

'Did you trail Venters – find this wonderful valley?' she asked, eagerly.

'Yes, an' I reckon it's sure a wonderful place.'

'Is he safe there?'

'That's been botherin' me some. I tracked him an' part of the trail was the hardest I ever tackled. Mebbe there's a rustler or somebody in this country who's as good at trackin' as I am. If that's so Venters ain't safe.'

'Well – tell me all about Bern and his valley.'

To Jane's surprise Lassiter showed disinclination for further talk about his trip. He appeared to be extremely fatigued. Jane reflected that one hundred and twenty miles, with probably a great deal of climbing on foot, all in three days, was enough to tire any rider. Moreover, it presently developed that Lassiter had returned in a mood of singular sadness and preoccupation. She put it down to a moodiness over the loss of her white herd and the now precarious condition of her fortune.

Several days passed, and, as nothing happened, Jane's spirits began to brighten. Once in her musings she thought that this tendency of hers to rebound was as sad as it was futile. Meanwhile, she had resumed her walks through the grove with little Fay.

One morning she went as far as the sage. She had not seen the slope since the beginning of the rains, and now it bloomed a rich deep purple. There was a high wind blowing, and the sage tossed and waved and colored beautifully from light to dark. Clouds scudded across the sky and their shadows sailed darkly down the sunny slope.

Upon her return toward the house she went by the lane to the stables, and she had scarcely entered the great open space with its corrals and sheds when she saw Lassiter hurriedly approaching. Fay broke from her and, running to a corral fence, began to pat and pull the long, hanging ears of a drowsy burro.

One look at Lassiter armed her for a blow.

Without a word he led her across the wide yard to the rise of the ground upon which the stable stood.

'Jane – look!' he said, and pointed to the ground.

Jane glanced down, and again, and upon steadier vision made out splotches of blood on the stones, and broad, smooth marks in the dust, leading out toward the sage.

'What made these?' she asked.

'I reckon somebody has dragged dead or wounded men out to where there was hosses in the sage.'

'Dead – or – wounded – men!'

'I reckon – Jane, are you strong? Can you bear up?'

His hands were gently holding hers, and his eyes – suddenly she could no longer look into them. 'Strong?' she echoed, trembling. 'I – I will be.'

Up on the stone-flag drive, nicked with the marks made by the iron-shod hoofs of her racers, Lassiter led her, his grasp ever growing firmer.

'Where's Blake – and – and Jerd?' she asked, haltingly.

'I don't know where Jerd is. Bolted, most likely,' replied Lassiter, as he took her through the stone door.

'But Blake – poor Blake! He's gone forever! . . . Be prepared, Jane.'

With a cold prickling of her skin, with a queer thrumming in her ears, with fixed and staring eyes, Jane saw a gun lying at her feet with chamber swung and empty, and discharged shells scattered near.

Outstretched upon the stable floor lay Blake, ghastly white – dead – one hand clutching a gun and the other twisted in his bloody blouse.

'Whoever the thieves were, whether your people or rustlers – Blake killed some of them!' said Lassiter

'Thieves?' whispered Jane.

'I reckon. Hoss-thieves! . . . Look!' Lassiter waved his hand toward the stalls.

The first stall – Bells's stall – was empty. All the stalls were empty. No racer whinnied and stamped greeting to her. Night was gone! Black Star was gone!

CHAPTER SIXTEEN

Gold

As LASSITER HAD REPORTED to Jane, Venters 'went through' safely, and after a toilsome journey reached the peaceful shelter of Surprise Valley. When finally he lay wearily down under the silver spruces, resting from the strain of dragging packs and burros up the slope and through the entrance to Surprise Valley, he had leisure to think, and a great deal of the time went in regretting that he had not been frank with his loyal friend, Jane Withersteen.

But, he kept continually recalling, when he had stood once more face to face with her and had been shocked at the change in her and had heard the details of her adversity, he had not had the heart to tell her of the closer interest which had entered his life. He had not lied; yet he had kept silence.

Bess was in transports over the stores of supplies and the outfit he had packed from Cottonwoods. He had certainly brought a hundred times more than he had gone for; enough, surely, for years, perhaps to make permanent home in the valley. He saw no reason why he need ever leave there again.

After a day of rest he recovered his strength and shared Bess's pleasure in rummaging over the endless packs, and began to plan for the future. And in this planning, his trip to Cottonwoods, with its revived hate of Tull and consequent unleashing of fierce passions, soon faded out of mind. By slower degrees his friendship for Jane Withersteen and his contrition drifted from the active preoccupation of his present thought to a place in memory, with more and more infrequent recalls.

And as far as the state of his mind was concerned, upon the second day after his return, the valley, with its golden hues and purple shades, the speaking west wind and the cool, silent night, and Bess's watching eyes with their wonderful light, so wrought upon Venters that he might never have left them at all.

That very afternoon he set to work. Only one thing hindered him upon beginning, though it in no wise checked his delight, and that was that in the multiplicity of tasks planned to make a paradise out of the valley he could not choose the one with which to begin. He had to grow into the habit of passing from one dreamy pleasure to another, like a bee going from flower to flower in the valley, and he found his wandering habit likely to extend to his labors. Nevertheless, he made a start.

At the outset he discovered Bess to be both a considerable help in some ways and a very great hindrance in others. Her excitement and joy were spurs, inspirations; but she was utterly impracticable in her ideas, and she flitted from one plan to another with bewildering vacillation. Moreover, he fancied that she grew more eager, youthful, and sweet; and he marked that it was far easier to watch her and listen to her than it was to work. Therefore he gave her tasks that necessitated her going often to the cave where he had stored his packs.

Upon the last of these trips, when he was some distance down the terrace and out of sight of camp, he heard a scream, and then the sharp barking of the dogs.

For an instant he straightened up, amazed. Danger for her had been absolutely out of his mind. She had seen a rattlesnake – or a wildcat. Still she would not have been likely to scream at sight of either; and the barking of the dogs was ominous. Dropping his work, he dashed back along the terrace. Upon breaking through a clump of aspens he saw the dark form of a man in the camp. Cold, then hot, Venters burst into frenzied speed to reach his guns. He was cursing himself for a thoughtless fool when the man's tall form became familiar and he recognized Lassiter. Then the reversal of emotions changed his run to a walk; he tried to call out, but his voice refused to carry; when he reached camp there was Lassiter staring at the white-faced girl. By that time Ring and Whitie had recognized him.

'Hello, Venters! I'm makin' you a visit,' said Lassiter, slowly. 'An' I'm some surprised to see you've a – a young feller for company.'

One glance had sufficed for the keen rider to read Bess's real sex, and for once his cool calm had deserted him. He stared till the white of Bess's cheeks flared into crimson. That, if it were needed, was the concluding evidence of her femininity; for it went fittingly with her sun-tinted hair and darkened, dilated eyes, the sweetness of her mouth, and the striking symmetry of her slender shape.

'Heavens! Lassiter!' panted Venters, when he caught his breath. 'What relief – it's only you! How – in the name of all – that's wonderful – did you ever get here?'

'I trailed you. We – I wanted to know where you was, if you had a safe place. So I trailed you.'

'Trailed me!' cried Venters, bluntly.

'I reckon. It was some of a job after I got to them smooth rocks. I was all day trackin' you up to them little cut steps in the rock. The rest was easy.'

'Where's your hoss? I hope you hid him.'

'I tied him in them queer cedars down on the slope. He can't be seen from the valley.'

'That's good. Well, well! I'm completely dumbfounded. It was my idea that no man could track me in here.'

'I reckon. But if there's a tracker in these uplands as good as me he can find you.'

'That's bad. That'll worry me. But, Lassiter, now you're here I'm glad to see you. And – my companion here is not a young fellow! . . . Bess, this is a friend of mine. He saved my life once.'

The embarrassment of the moment did not extend to Lassiter. Almost at once his manner, as he shook hands with Bess, relieved Venters and put the girl at ease. After Venters's words and one quick look at Lassiter, her agitation stilled, and, though she was shy, if she were conscious of anything out of the ordinary in the situation, certainly she did not show it.

'I reckon I'll only stay a little while,' Lassiter was saying. 'An' if you don't mind troublin', I'm hungry. I fetched some biscuits along, but they're gone. Venters, this place is sure the wonderfullest ever seen. Them cut steps on the slope! That outlet into the gorge! An' it's like climbin' up through hell into heaven to climb through that gorge into this valley! There's a queer-lookin' rock at the top of the passage. I didn't have time to stop. I'm wonderin' how you ever found this place. It's sure interestin'.'

During the preparation and eating of dinner Lassiter listened mostly, as was his wont, and occasionally he spoke in his quaint and dry way. Venters noted, however, that the rider showed an increasing interest in Bess. He asked her no questions, and only directed his attention to her while she was occupied and had no opportunity to observe his scrutiny. It seemed to Venters that Lassiter grew more and more absorbed in his study of Bess, and that he lost his coolness in some strange, softening sympathy. Then, quite abruptly, he arose and announced the necessity for his early departure. He said good-bye to Bess in a voice gentle and somewhat broken, and turned hurriedly away. Venters accompanied him, and they had traversed the terrace, climbed the weathered slope, and passed under the stone bridge before either spoke again.

Then Lassiter put a great hand on Venters's shoulder and wheeled him to meet a smoldering fire of gray eyes.

'Lassiter, I couldn't tell Jane! I couldn't,' burst out Venters, reading his friend's mind. 'I tried. But I couldn't. She wouldn't understand, and she has troubles enough. And I love the girl!'

'Venters, I reckon this beats me. I've seen some queer things in my time, too. This girl – who is she?'

'I don't know.'

'Don't know! What is she, then?'

'I don't know that, either. Oh, it's the strangest story you ever heard. I must tell you. But you'll never believe.'

'Venters, women were always puzzles to me. But for all that, if this girl ain't a

child, an' as innocent, I'm no fit person to think of virtue an' goodness in anybody.
Are you goin' to be square with her?'

'I am – so help me God!'

'I reckoned so. Mebbe my temper oughtn't led me to make sure. But, man, she's
a woman in all but years. She's sweeter'n the sage.'

'Lassiter, I know, I know. And the *hell* of it is that in spite of her innocence and
charm she's – she's not what she seems!'

'I wouldn't want to – of course, I couldn't call you a liar, Venters,' said the older
man.

'What's more, she was Oldring's Masked Rider!'

Venters expected to floor his friend with that statement, but he was not in any
way prepared for the shock his words gave. For an instant he was astounded to see
Lassiter stunned; then his own passionate eagerness to unbosom himself, to tell
the wonderful story, precluded any other thought.

'Son, tell me all about this,' presently said Lassiter as he seated himself on a
stone and wiped his moist brow.

Thereupon Venters began his narrative at the point where he had shot the
rustler and Oldring's Masked Rider, and he rushed through it, telling all, not
holding back even Bess's unreserved avowal of her love or his deepest emotions.

'That's the story,' he said, concluding. 'I love her, though I've never told her. If
I did tell her I'd be ready to marry her, and that seems impossible in this country.
I'd be afraid to risk taking her anywhere. So I intend to do the best I can for her
here.'

'The longer I live the stranger life is,' mused Lassiter, with downcast eyes. 'I'm
reminded of somethin' you once said to Jane about hands in her game of life.
There's that unseen hand of power, an' Tull's black hand, an' my red one, an' your
indifferent one, an' the girl's little brown, helpless one. An', Venters, there's
another one that's all-wise an' all-wonderful. *That's* the hand guidin' Jane
Withersteen's game of life! . . . Your story's one to daze a far clearer head than
mine. I can't offer no advice, even if you asked for it. Mebbe I can help you.
Anyway, I'll hold Oldrin' up when he comes to the village, an' find out about this
girl. I knew the rustler years ago. He'll remember me.'

'Lassiter, if I ever meet Oldring I'll kill him!' cried Venters, with sudden
intensity.

'I reckon that'd be perfectly natural,' replied the rider.

'Make him think Bess is dead – as she is to him and that old life.'

'Sure, sure, son. Cool down now. If you're goin' to begin pullin' guns on Tull an'
Oldrin' you want to be cool. I reckon, though, you'd better keep hid here. Well, I
must be leavin'.'

'One thing, Lassiter. You'll not tell Jane about Bess? Please don't!'

'I reckon not. But I wouldn't be afraid to bet that after she'd got over anger at
your secrecy – Venters, she'd be furious once in her life! – she'd think more of you.
I don't mind sayin' for myself that I think you're a good deal of a man.'

In the further ascent Venters halted several times with the intention of saying
good-bye, yet he changed his mind and kept on climbing till they reached
Balancing Rock. Lassiter examined the huge rock, listened to Venters's idea of its
position and suggestion, and curiously placed a strong hand upon it.

'Hold on!' cried Venters. 'I heaved at it once and have never gotten over my
scare.'

'Well, you do seem uncommon nervous,' replied Lassiter, much amused. 'Now,
as for me, why I always had the funniest notion to roll stones! When I was a kid I

did it, an' the bigger I got the bigger stones I'd roll. Ain't that funny? Honest – even now I often get off my hoss just to tumble a big stone over a precipice, an' watch it drop, an' listen to it bang an' boom. I've started some slides in my time, an' don't you forget it. I never seen a rock I wanted to roll as bad as this one! Wouldn't there jest be roarin' crashin' hell down that trail?'

'You'd close the outlet forever!' exclaimed Venters. 'Well, good-bye, Lassiter. Keep my secret and don't forget me. And be mighty careful how you get out of the valley below. The rustlers' cañon isn't more than three miles up the Pass. Now you've tracked me here, I'll never feel safe again.'

In his descent to the valley, Venters's emotion, roused to stirring pitch by the recital of his love story, quieted gradually, and in its place came a sober, thoughtful mood. All at once he saw that he was serious, because he would never more regain his sense of security while in the valley. What Lassiter could do another skillful cracker might duplicate. Among the many riders with whom Venters had ridden he recalled no one who could have taken his trail at Cottonwoods and have followed it to the edge of the bare slope in the pass, let alone up that glistening smooth stone. Lassiter, however, was not an ordinary rider. Instead of hunting cattle tracks he had likely spent a goodly portion of his life tracking men. It was not improbable that among Oldring's rustlers there was one who shared Lassiter's gift for trailing. And the more Venters dwelt on this possibility the more perturbed he grew.

Lassiter's visit, moreover, had a disquieting effect upon Bess, and Venters fancied that she entertained the same thought as to future seclusion. The breaking of their solitude, though by a well-meaning friend, had not only dispelled all its dream and much of its charm, but had instilled a canker of fear. Both had seen the footprint in the sand.

Venters did no more work that day. Sunset and twilight gave way to night, and the cañon bird whistled its melancholy notes, and the wind sang softly in the cliffs, and the camp-fire blazed and burned down to red embers. To Venters a subtle difference was apparent in all of these, or else the shadowy change had been in him. He hoped that on the morrow this slight depression would have passed away.

In that measure, however, he was doomed to disappointment. Furthermore, Bess reverted to a wistful sadness that he had not observed in her since her recovery. His attempt to cheer her out of it resulted in dismal failure, and consequently in a darkening of his own mood. Hard work relieved him; still, when the day had passed, his unrest returned. Then he set to deliberate thinking, and there came to him the startling conviction that he must leave Surprise Valley and take Bess with him. As a rider he had taken many chances, and as an adventurer in Deception Pass he had unhesitatingly risked his life; but now he would run no preventable hazard of Bess's safety and happiness, and he was too keen not to see that hazard. It gave him a pang to think of leaving the beautiful valley just when he had the means to establish a permanent and delightful home there. One flashing thought tore in hot temptation through his mind – why not climb up into the gorge, roll Balancing Rock down the trail, and close forever the outlet to Deception Pass? 'That was the beast in me – showing his teeth!' muttered Venters, scornfully. 'I'll just kill him good and quick! I'll be fair to this girl, if it's the last thing I do on earth!'

Another day went by, in which he worked less and pondered more and all the time covertly watched Bess. Her wistfulness had deepened into downright unhappiness, and that made his task to tell her all the harder. He kept the secret another day, hoping by some chance she might grow less moody, and to his exceeding anxiety she fell into far deeper gloom. Out of his own secret and the torment of it he divined that she, too, had a secret and the keeping of it was torturing her. As yet he had no plan thought out in regard to how or when to leave the valley, but he decided to tell her the necessity of it and to persuade her to go. Furthermore, he hoped his speaking out would induce her to unburden her own mind.

'Bess, what's wrong with you?' he asked.

'Nothing,' she answered, with averted face.

Venters took hold of her and gently, though masterfully, forced her to meet his eyes.

'You can't look at me and lie,' he said. 'Now – what's wrong with you? You're keeping something from me. Well, I've got a secret, too, and I intend to tell it presently.'

'Oh – I *have* a secret. I was crazy to tell you when you came back. That's why I was so silly about everything. I kept holding my secret back – gloating over it. But when Lassiter came I got an idea – that changed my mind. Then I hated to tell you.'

'Are you going to now?'

'Yes – yes. I was coming to it. I tried yesterday, but you were so cold. I was afraid. I couldn't keep it much longer.'

'Very well, most mysterious lady, tell your wonderful secret.'

'You needn't laugh,' she retorted, with a first glimpse of reviving spirit. 'I can take the laugh out of you in one second.'

'It's a go.'

She ran through the spruces to the cave, and returned carrying something which was manifestly heavy. Upon nearer view he saw that whatever she held with such evident importance had been bound up in a black scarf he well remembered. That alone was sufficient to make him tingle with curiosity.

'Have you any idea what I did in your absence?' she asked.

'I imagine you lounged about, waiting and watching for me,' he replied, smiling. 'I've my share of conceit, you know.'

'You're wrong. I worked. Look at my hands.' She dropped on her knees close to where he sat, and, carefully depositing the black bundle, she held out her hands. The palms and inside of her fingers were white, puckered, and worn.

'Why, Bess, you've been fooling in the water,' he said.

'Fooling? Look here!' With deft fingers she spread open the black scarf, and the bright sun shone upon a dull, glittering heap of gold.

'Gold!' he ejaculated.

'Yes, gold! See, pounds of gold! I found it – washed it out of the stream – picked it out grain by grain, nugget by nugget!'

'Gold!' he cried.

'Yes. Now – now laugh at my secret!'

For a long minute Venters gazed. Then he stretched forth a hand to feel if the gold was real.

'*Gold!*' he almost shouted. 'Bess, there are hundreds – thousands of dollars' worth here!'

He leaned over to her, and put his hand, strong and clenching now, on hers.

'Is there more where this came from?' he whispered.

'Plenty of it, all the way up the stream to the cliff. You know I've often washed for gold. Then I've heard the men talk. I think there's no great quantity of gold here, but enough for – for a fortune for *you.*'

'That – was – your – secret!'

'Yes. I hate gold. For it makes men mad. I've seen them drunk with joy and dance and fling themselves around. I've seen them curse and rave. I've seen them fight like dogs and roll in the dust. I've seen them kill each other for gold.'

'Is that why you hated to tell me?'

'Not – not altogether.' Bess lowered her head. 'It was because I knew you'd never stay here long after you found gold.'

'You were afraid I'd leave you?'

'Yes.'

'Listen! . . . You great, simple child! Listen . . . You sweet, wonderful, wild, blue-eyed girl! I was tortured by my secret. It was that I knew we – we must leave the valley. We can't stay here much longer. I couldn't think how we'd get away – out of the country – or how we'd live, if we ever got out. I'm a beggar. That's why I kept my secret. I'm poor. It takes money to make way beyond Sterling. We couldn't ride horses or burros or walk forever. So while I knew we must go, I was distracted over how to go and what to do. Now! We've gold! Once beyond Sterling, we'll be safe from rustlers. We've no others to fear.

'Oh! Listen! Bess!' Venters now heard his voice ringing high and sweet, and he felt Bess's cold hands in his crushing grasp as she leaned toward him pale, breathless. 'This is how much I'd leave you! You made me live again! I'll take you away – far away from this wild country. You'll begin a new life. You'll be happy. You shall see cities, ships, people. You shall have anything your heart craves. All the shame and sorrow of your life shall be forgotten – as if they had never been. This is how much I'd leave you here alone – you sad-eyed girl. I love you! Didn't you know it? How could you fail to know it? I love you! I'm free! I'm a man – a man you've made – no more a beggar! . . . Kiss me! This is how much I'd leave you here alone – you beautiful, strange, unhappy girl. But I'll make you happy. What – what do I care for – your past! I love you! I'll take you home to Illinois – to my mother. Then I'll take you to far places. I'll make up all you've lost. Oh, I know you love me – knew it before you told me. And it changed my life. And you'll go with me, not as my companion as you are here, nor my sister, but, Bess, darling! . . . As my wife!'

CHAPTER SEVENTEEN

Wrangle's Race Run

THE PLAN EVENTUALLY decided upon by the lovers was for Venters to go to the village, secure a horse and some kind of a disguise for Bess, or at least less striking apparel than her present garb, and to return post-haste to the valley. Meanwhile, she would add to their store of gold. Then they would strike the long and perilous trail to ride out of Utah. In the event of his inability to fetch back a horse for her, they intended to make the giant sorrel carry double. The gold, a little food, saddle blankets, and Venters's guns were to compose the light outfit with which they would make the start.

'I love this beautiful place,' said Bess. 'It's hard to think of leaving it.'

'Hard! Well, I should think so,' replied Venters. 'Maybe – in years – ' But he did not complete in words his thought that it might be possible to return after many years of absence and change.

Once again Bess bade Venters farewell under the shadow of Balancing Rock, and this time it was with whispered hope and tenderness and passionate trust. Long after he had left her, all down through the outlet to the Pass, the clinging clasp of her arms, the sweetness of her lips, and the sense of a new and exquisite birth of character in her remained hauntingly and thrillingly in his mind. The girl who had sadly called herself nameless and nothing had been marvelously transformed in the moment of his avowal of love. It was something to think over, something to warm his heart, but for the present it had absolutely to be forgotten so that all his mind could be addressed to the trip so fraught with danger.

He carried only his rifle, revolver, and a small quantity of bread and meat; and thus lightly burdened, he made swift progress down the slope and out into the valley. Darkness was coming on, and he welcomed it. Stars were blinking when he reached his old hiding-place in the split of cañon wall, and by their aid he slipped through the dense thickets to the grassy enclosure. Wrangle stood in the center of it with his head up, and he appeared black and of gigantic proportions in the dim light. Venters whistled softly, began a slow approach, and then called. The horse snorted and, plunging away with dull, heavy sound of hoofs, he disappeared in the gloom. 'Wilder than ever!' muttered Venters. He followed the sorrel into the narrowing split between the walls, and presently had to desist because he could not see a foot in advance. As he went back toward the open Wrangle jumped out of an ebony shadow of cliff and like a thunderbolt shot huge and black past him down into the starlit glade. Deciding that all attempts to catch Wrangle at night would be useless, Venters repaired to the shelving rock where he had hidden saddle and blanket, and there went to sleep.

The first peep of day found him stirring, and as soon as it was light enough to distinguish objects, he took his lasso off his saddle and went out to rope the sorrel. He espied Wrangle at the lower end of the cove and approached him in a perfectly natural manner. When he got near enough, Wrangle evidently recognized him, but was too wild to stand. He ran up the glade and on into the narrow lane between the walls. This favored Venters's speedy capture of the horse, so coiling his noose ready to throw, he hurried on. Wrangle let Venters get to within a hundred feet and then he broke. But as he plunged by, rapidly getting into his stride, Venters made a perfect throw with the rope. He had time to brace himself for the shock; nevertheless, Wrangle threw him and dragged him several yards before halting.

'You wild devil,' said Venters, as he slowly pulled Wrangle up. 'Don't you know me? Come now – old fellow – so – so – '

Wrangle yielded to the lasso and then to Venters's strong hand. He was as straggly and wild-looking as a horse left to roam free in the sage. He dropped his long ears and stood readily to be saddled and bridled. But he was exceedingly sensitive, and quivered at every touch and sound. Venters led him to the thicket, and, bending the close saplings to let him squeeze through, at length reached the open. Sharp survey in each direction assured him of the usual lonely nature of the cañon; then he was in the saddle, riding south.

Wrangle's long, swinging canter was a wonderful ground-gainer. His stride was almost twice that of an ordinary horse, and his endurance was equally remarkable. Venters pulled him in occasionally, and walked him up the stretches of rising ground and along the soft washes. Wrangle had never yet shown any indication of distress while Venters rode him. Nevertheless, there was now reason to save the horse; therefore Venters did not resort to the hurry that had characterized his former trip. He camped at the last water in the Pass. What distance that was to Cottonwoods he did not know; he calculated, however, that it was in the neighborhood of fifty miles.

Early in the morning he proceeded on his way, and about the middle of the forenoon reached the constricted gap that marked the southerly end of the Pass, and through which led the trail up to the sage-level. He spied out Lassiter's tracks in the dust, but no others, and dismounting, he straightened out Wrangle's bridle and began to lead him up the trail. The short climb, more severe on beast than on man, necessitated a rest on the level above, and during this he scanned the wide purple reaches of slope.

Wrangle whistled his pleasure at the smell of the sage. Remounting, Venters headed up the white trail with the fragrant wind in his face. He had proceeded for perhaps a couple of miles when Wrangle stopped with a suddenness that threw Venters heavily against the pommel.

'What's wrong, old boy?' called Venters, looking down for a loose shoe or a snake or a foot lamed by a picked-up stone. Unrewarded, he raised himself from his scrutiny. Wrangle stood stiff, head high, with his long ears erect. Thus guided, Venters swiftly gazed ahead to make out a dust-clouded, dark group of horsemen riding down the slope. If they had seen him, it apparently made no difference in their speed or direction.

'Wonder who they are!' exclaimed Venters. He was not disposed to run. His cool mood tightened under grip of excitement as he reflected that, whoever the approaching riders were, they could not be friends. He slipped out of the saddle and led Wrangle behind the tallest sage-brush. It might serve to conceal them until the riders were close enough for him to see who they were; after that he would be indifferent to how soon they discovered him.

After looking to his rifle and ascertaining that it was in working order, he watched, and as he watched, slowly the force of a bitter fierceness, long dormant, gathered ready to flame into life. If those riders were not rustlers he had forgotten how rustlers looked and rode. On they came, a small group, so compact and dark that he could not tell their number. How unusual that their horses did not see Wrangle! But such failure, Venters decided, was owing to the speed with which they were traveling. They moved at a swift canter affected more by rustlers than by riders. Venters grew concerned over the possibility that these horsemen would actually ride down on him before he had a chance to tell what to expect. When they were within three hundred yards he deliberately led Wrangle out into the trail.

Then he heard shouts, and the hard scrape of sliding hoofs, and saw horses rear and plunge back with up-flung heads and flying manes. Several little white puffs of smoke appeared sharply against the black background of riders and horses, and shots rang out. Bullets struck far in front of Venters, and whipped up the dust and then hummed low into the sage. The range was great for revolvers, but whether the shots were meant to kill or merely to check advance, they were enough to fire that waiting ferocity in Venters. Slipping his arm through the bridle, so that Wrangle could not get away, Venters lifted his rifle and pulled the trigger twice.

He saw the first horseman lean sideways and fall. He saw another lurch in his saddle and heard a cry of pain. Then Wrangle, plunging in fright, lifted Venters and nearly threw him. He jerked the horse down with a powerful hand and leaped into the saddle. Wrangle pulled again, dragging his bridle, that Venters had not had time to throw in place. Bending over with a swift movement, he secured it and dropped the loop over the pommel. Then, with grinding teeth, he looked to see what the issue would be.

The band had scattered so as not to afford such a broad mark for bullets. The riders faced Venters, some with red-belching guns. He heard a sharper report, and just as Wrangle plunged again he caught the whizz of a leaden missile that would have hit him but for Wrangle's sudden jump. A swift, hot wave, turning cold, passed over Venters. Deliberately he picked out the one rider with a carbine, and killed him. Wrangle snorted shrilly and bolted into the sage. Venters let him run a few rods, then with iron arm checked him.

Five riders, surely rustlers, were left. One leaped out of the saddle to secure his fallen comrade's carbine. A shot from Venters, which missed the man but sent the dust flying over him, made him run back to his horse. Then they separated. The crippled rider went one way; the one frustrated in his attempt to get the carbine rode another; Venters thought he made out a third rider, carrying a strange-appearing bundle and disappearing in the sage. But in the rapidity of action and vision he could not discern what it was. Two riders with three horses swung out to the right. Afraid of the long rifle – a burdensome weapon seldom carried by rustlers or riders – they had been put to rout.

Suddenly Venters discovered that one of the two men last noted was riding Jane Withersteen's horse Bells – the beautiful bay racer she had given to Lassiter. Venters uttered a savage outcry. Then the small, wiry, frog-like shape of the second rider, and the ease and grace of his seat in the saddle – things so strikingly incongruous – grew more and more familiar in Venters's sight.

'Jerry Card!' cried Venters.

It was indeed Tull's right-hand man. Such a white-hot wrath inflamed Venters that he fought himself to see with clearer gaze.

'It's Jerry Card!' he exclaimed, instantly. 'And he's riding Black Star and leading Night!'

The long-kindling, stormy fire in Venters's heart burst into flame. He spurred Wrangle, and as the horse lengthened his stride Venters slipped cartridges into the magazine of his rifle till it was once again full. Card and his companion were now half a mile or more in advance, riding easily down the slope. Venters marked the smooth gait, and understood it when Wrangle galloped out of the sage into the broad cattle trail, down which Venters had once tracked Jane Withersteen's red herd. This hard-packed trail, from years of use, was as clean and smooth as a road. Venters saw Jerry Card look back over his shoulder; the other rider did likewise. Then the three racers lengthened their stride to the point where the swinging canter was ready to break into a gallop.

'Wrangle, the race's on,' said Venters, grimly. 'We'll canter with them and gallop with them and run with them. We'll let them set the pace.'

Venters knew he bestrode the strongest, swiftest, most tireless horse ever ridden by any rider across the Utah uplands. Recalling Jane Withersteen's devoted assurance that Night could run neck and neck with Wrangle, and Black Star could show his heels to him, Venters wished that Jane were there to see the race to recover her blacks and in the unqualified superiority of the giant sorrel. Then Venters found himself thankful that she was absent, for he meant that race to end in Jerry Card's death. The first flush, the raging of Venters's wrath, passed, to leave him in sullen, almost cold possession of his will. It was a deadly mood, utterly foreign to his nature, engendered, fostered, and released by the wild passions of wild men in a wild country. The strength in him then – the thing rife in him that was not hate, but something as remorseless – might have been the fiery fruition of a whole lifetime of vengeful quest. Nothing could have stopped him.

Venters thought out the race shrewdly. The rider on Bells would probably drop behind and take to the sage. What he did was of little moment to Venters. To stop Jerry Card, his evil, hidden career as well as his present flight, and then to catch the blacks – that was all that concerned Venters. The cattle trail wound for miles and miles down the slope. Venters saw with a rider's keen vision ten, fifteen, twenty miles of clear purple sage. There were no on-coming riders or rustlers to aid Card. His only chance to escape lay in abandoning the stolen horses and creeping away in the sage to hide. In ten miles Wrangle could run Black Star and Night off their feet, and in fifteen he could kill them outright. So Venters held the sorrel in, letting Card make the running. It was a long race that would save the blacks.

In a few miles of that swinging canter Wrangle had crept appreciably closer to the three horses. Jerry Card turned again, and when he saw how the sorrel had gained, he put Black Star to a gallop. Night and Bells, on either side of him, swept into his stride.

Venters loosened the rein on Wrangle and let him break into a gallop. The sorrel saw the horses ahead and wanted to run. But Venters restrained him. And in the gallop he gained more than in the canter. Bells was fast in that gait, but Black Star and Night had been trained to run. Slowly Wrangle closed the gap down to a quarter of a mile, and crept closer and closer.

Jerry Card wheeled once more. Venters distinctly saw the red flash of his red face. This time he looked long. Venters laughed. He knew what passed in Card's mind. The rider was trying to make out what horse it happened to be that thus gained on Jane Withersteen's peerless racers. Wrangle had so long been away from the village that not improbably Jerry had forgotten. Besides, whatever Jerry's qualifications for his fame as the greatest rider of the sage, certain it was that his best point was not far-sightedness. He had not recognized Wrangle. After what must have been a searching gaze he got his comrade to face about. This action gave Venters amusement. It spoke so surely of the fact that neither Card nor the rustler actually knew their danger. Yet if they kept to the trail – and the last thing such men would do would be to leave it – they were both doomed.

This comrade of Card's whirled far around in his saddle, and he even shaded his eyes from the sun. He, too, looked long. Then, all at once, he faced ahead again and, bending lower in the saddle, began to fling his right arm up and down. That flinging Venters knew to be the lashing of Bells. Jerry also became active. And the three racers lengthened out into a run.

'Now, Wrangle!' cried Venters. 'Run, you big devil! Run!'

Venters laid the reins on Wrangle's neck and dropped the loop over the pommel. The sorrel needed no guiding on that smooth trail. He was surer-footed in a run than at any other fast gait, and his running gave the impression of something devilish. He might now have been actuated by Venters's spirit; undoubtedly his savage running fitted the mood of his rider. Venters bent forward, swinging with the horse, and gripped his rifle. His eye measured the distance between him and Jerry Card.

In less than two miles of running Bells began to drop behind the blacks, and Wrangle began to overhaul him. Venters anticipated that the rustler would soon take to the sage. Yet he did not. Not improbably he reasoned that the powerful sorrel could more easily overtake Bells in the heavier going outside of the trail. Soon only a few hundred yards lay between Bells and Wrangle. Turning in his saddle, the rustler began to shoot, and the bullets beat up little whiffs of dust.

Venters raised his rifle, ready to take snap shots, and waited for favorable opportunity when Bells was out of line with the forward horses. Venters had it in him to kill these men as if they were skunk-bitten coyotes, but also he had restraint enough to keep from shooting one of Jane's beloved Arabians.

No great distance was covered, however, before Bells swerved to the left, out of line with Black Star and Night. Then Venters, aiming high and waiting for the pause between Wrangle's great strides, began to take snap shots at the rustler. The fleeing rider presented a broad target for rifle, but he was moving swiftly forward and bobbing up and down. Moreover, shooting from Wrangle's back was shooting from a thunderbolt. And added to that was the danger of a low-placed bullet taking effect on Bells. Yet, despite these considerations, making the shot exceedingly difficult, Venters's confidence, like his implacability, saw a speedy and fatal termination of that rustler's race. On the sixth shot the rustler threw up his arms and took a flying tumble off his horse. He rolled over and over, hunched himself to a half-erect position, fell, and then dragged himself into the sage. As Venters went thundering by he peered keenly into the sage, but caught no sign of the man. Bells ran a few hundred yards, slowed up, and had stopped when Wrangle passed him.

Again Venters began slipping fresh cartridges into the magazine of his rifle, and his hand was so sure and steady that he did not drop a single cartridge. With the eye of a rider and the judgment of a marksman he once more measured the distance between him and Jerry Card. Wrangle had gained, bringing him into rifle range. Venters was hard put to it now not to shoot, but thought it better to withhold his fire. Jerry, who, in anticipation of a running fusillade, had huddled himself into a little twisted ball on Black Star's neck, now surmising that this pursuer would make sure of not wounding one of the blacks, rose to his natural seat in the saddle.

In his mind perhaps, as certainly as in Venters's, this moment was the beginning of the real race.

Venters leaned forward to put his hand on Wrangle's neck; then backward to put it on his flank. Under the shaggy, dusty hair trembled and vibrated and rippled a wonderful muscular activity. But Wrangle's flesh was still cold. What a cold-blooded brute, thought Venters, and felt in him a love for the horse he had never given to any other. It would not have been humanly possible for any rider, even though clutched by hate or revenge or a passion to save a loved one or fear of his own life, to be astride the sorrel, to swing with his swing, to see his magnificent stride and hear the rapid thunder of his hoofs, to ride him in that race and not glory in the ride.

So, with his passion to kill still keen and unabated, Venters lived out that ride, and drank a rider's sage-sweet cup of wildness to the dregs.

When Wrangle's long mane, lashing in the wind, stung Venters in the cheek, the sting added a beat to his flying pulse. He bent a downward glance to try to see Wrangle's actual stride, and saw only twinkling, darting streaks and the white rush of the trail. He watched the sorrel's savage head, pointed level, his mouth still closed and dry, but his nostrils distended as if he were snorting unseen fire. Wrangle was the horse for a race with death. Upon each side Venters saw the sage merged into a sailing, colorless wall. In front sloped the lay of ground with its purple breadth split by the white trail. The wind, blowing with heavy, steady blast into his face, sickened him with enduring, sweet odor, and filled his ears with a hollow, rushing roar.

Then for the hundredth time he measured the width of space separating him from Jerry Card. Wrangle had ceased to gain. The blacks were proving their fleetness. Venters watched Jerry Card, admiring the little rider's horsemanship. He had the incomparable seat of the upland rider, born in the saddle. It struck Venters that Card had changed his position, or the position of the horses. Presently Venters remembered positively that Jerry had been leading Night on the right-hand side of the trail. The racer was now on the side to the left. No – it was Black Star. But, Venters argued in amaze, Jerry had been mounted on Black Star. Another clearer, keener gaze assured Venters that Black Star was really riderless. Night now carried Jerry Card.

'He's changed from one to the other!' ejaculated Venters, realizing the astounding feat with unstinted admiration. 'Changed at full speed! Jerry Card, that's what you've done unless I'm drunk on the smell of sage. But I've got to see the trick before I believe it.'

Thenceforth, while Wrangle sped on, Venters glued his eyes to the little rider. Jerry Card rode as only he could ride. Of all the daring horsemen of the uplands, Jerry was the one rider fitted to bring out the greatness of the blacks in that long race. He had them on a dead run, but not yet at the last strained and killing pace. From time to time he glanced backward, as a wise general in retreat calculating his chances and the power and speed of pursuers, and the moment for the last desperate burst. No doubt, Card, with his life at stake, gloried in that race, perhaps more wildly than Venters. For he had been born to the sage and the saddle and the wild. He was more than half horse. Not until the last call – the sudden up-flashing instinct of self-preservation – would he lose his skill and judgment and nerve and the spirit of that race. Venters seemed to read Jerry's mind. That little crime-stained rider was actually thinking of his horses, husbanding their speed, handling them with knowledge of years, glorying in their beautiful, swift, racing stride, and wanting them to win the race when his own life hung suspended in quivering balance. Again Jerry whirled in his saddle and the sun flashed red on his face. Turning, he drew Black Star closer and closer toward Night, till they ran side by side, as one horse. Then Card raised himself in the saddle, slipped out of the stirrups, and, somehow twisting himself, leaped upon Black Star. He did not even lose the swing of the horse. Like a leech he was there in the other saddle, and as the horses separated, his right foot, that had been apparently doubled under him, shot down to catch the stirrup. The grace and dexterity and daring of that rider's act won something more than admiration from Venters.

For the distance of a mile Jerry rode Black Star and then changed back to Night. But all Jerry's skill and the running of the blacks could avail little more against the sorrel.

Venters peered far ahead, studying the lay of the land. Straightaway for five miles the trail stretched, and then it disappeared in hummocky ground. To the right, some few rods, Venters saw a break in the sage, and this was the rim of Deception Pass. Across the dark cleft gleamed the red of the opposite wall. Venters imagined that the trail went down into the Pass somewhere north of those ridges. And he realized that he must and would overtake Jerry Card in this straight course of five miles.

Cruelly he struck his spurs into Wrangle's flanks. A light touch of spur was sufficient to make Wrangle plunge. And now, with a ringing, wild snort, he seemed to double up in muscular convulsions and to shoot forward with an impetus that almost unseated Venters. The sage blurred by, the trail flashed by, and the wind robbed him of breath and hearing. Jerry Card turned once more. And the way he shifted to Black Star showed he had to make his last desperate running. Venters aimed to the side of the trail and sent a bullet puffing the dust beyond Jerry. Venters hoped to frighten the rider and get him to take to the sage. But Jerry returned the shot, and his ball struck dangerously close in the dust at Wrangle's flying feet. Venters held his fire then, while the rider emptied his revolver. For a mile, with Black Star leaving Night behind and doing his utmost, Wrangle did not gain; for another mile he gained little, if at all. In the third he caught up with the now galloping Night and began to gain rapidly on the other black.

Only a hundred yards now stretched between Black Star and Wrangle. The giant sorrel thundered on – and on – and on. In every yard he gained a foot. He was whistling through his nostrils, wringing wet, flying lather, and as hot as fire. Savage as ever, strong as ever, fast as ever, but each tremendous stride jarred Venters out of the saddle! Wrangle's power and spirit and momentum had begun to run him off his legs. Wrangle's great race was nearly won – and run. Venters seemed to see the expanse before him as a vast, sheeted, purple plain sliding under him. Black Star moved in it as a blur. The rider, Jerry Card, appeared a mere dot bobbing dimly. Wrangle thundered on – on – on! Venters felt the increase in quivering, straining shock after every leap. Flecks of foam flew into Venters's eyes, burning him, making him see all the sage as red. But in that red haze he saw, or seemed to see, Black Star suddenly riderless and with broken gait. Wrangle thundered on to change his pace with a violent gallop. Then Venters pulled him hard. From run to gallop, gallop to canter, canter to trot, trot to walk, and walk to stop, the great sorrel ended his race.

Venters looked back. Black Star stood riderless in the trail. Jerry Card had taken to the sage. Far up the white trail Night came trotting faithfully down. Venters leaped off, still half blind, reeling dizzily. In a moment he had recovered sufficiently to have a care for Wrangle. Rapidly he took off the saddle and bridle. The sorrel was reeking, heaving, whistling, shaking. But he had still the strength to stand, and for him Venters had no fears.

As Venters ran back to Black Star he saw the horse stagger on shaking legs into the sage and go down in a heap. Upon reaching him Venters removed the saddle and bridle. Black Star had been killed on his legs, Venters thought. He had no hope for the stricken horse. Black Star lay flat, covered with bloody froth, mouth wide, tongue hanging, eyes glaring, and all his beautiful body in convulsions.

Unable to stay there to see Jane's favorite racer die, Venters hurried up the trail to meet the other black. On the way he kept a sharp lookout for Jerry Card. Venters imagined the rider would keep well out of range of the rifle, but, as he would be lost on the sage without a horse, not improbably he would linger in the vicinity on the chance of getting back one of the blacks. Night soon came trotting up, hot and wet and run out. Venters led him down near the others, and, unsaddling him, let him loose to rest. Night wearily lay down in the dust and rolled, proving himself not yet spent.

Then Venters sat down to rest and think. Whatever the risk, he was compelled to stay where he was, or comparatively near, for the night. The horses must rest and drink. He must find water. He was now seventy miles from Cottonwoods, and, he believed, close to the canõn where the cattle trail must surely turn off and go down into the Pass. After a while he rose to survey the valley.

He was very near to the ragged edge of a deep canõn into which the trail turned. The ground lay in uneven ridges divided by washes, and those sloped into the canõn. Following the canõn line, he saw where its rim was broken by other intersecting canõns, and farther down red walls and yellow cliffs leading toward a deep blue cleft that he made sure was Deception Pass. Walking out a few rods to a promontory, he found where the trail went down. The descent was gradual, along a stone-walled trail, and Venters felt sure that this was the place where Oldring drove cattle into the Pass. There was, however, no indication at all that he ever had driven cattle out at this point. Oldring had many holes to his burrow.

In searching round in the little hollows Venters, much to his relief, found water. He composed himself to rest and eat some bread and meat, while he waited for a sufficient time to elapse so that he could safely give the horses a drink. He judged the hour to be somewhere around noon. Wrangle lay down to rest and Night followed suit. So long as they were down Venters intended to make no move. The longer they rested the better, and the safer it would be to give them water. By and by he forced himself to go over to where Black Star lay, expecting to find him dead. Instead he found the racer partially if not wholly recovered. There was recognition, even fire, in his big black eyes. Venters was overjoyed. He sat by the black for a long time. Black Star presently labored to his feet with a heave and a groan, shook himself, and snorted for water. Venters repaired to the little pool he had found, filled his sombrero, and gave the racer a drink. Black Star gulped it at one draught, as if it were but a drop, and pushed his nose into the hat and snorted for more. Venters now led Night down to drink, and after a further time Black Star also. Then the blacks began to graze.

The sorrel had wandered off down the sage between the trail and the cañon. Once or twice he disappeared in little swales. Finally Venters concluded Wrangle had grazed far enough, and, taking his lasso, he went to fetch him back. In crossing from one ridge to another he saw where the horse had made muddy a pool of water. It occurred to Venters then that Wrangle had drunk his fill, and did not seem the worse for it, and might be anything but easy to catch. And, true enough, he could not come within roping reach of the sorrel. He tried for an hour, and gave up in disgust. Wrangle did not seem so wild as simply perverse. In a quandary Venters returned to the other horses, hoping much, yet doubting more, that when Wrangle had grazed to suit himself he might be caught.

As the afternoon wore away Venters's concern diminished, yet he kept close watch on the blacks and the trail and the sage. There was no telling of what Jerry Card might be capable. Venters sullenly acquiesced to the idea that the rider had been too quick and too shrewd for him. Strangely and doggedly, however, Venters clung to his foreboding of Card's downfall.

The wind died away; the red sun topped the far distant western rise of slope; and the long, creeping purple shadows lengthened. The rims of the cañons gleamed crimson and the deep clefts appeared to belch forth blue smoke. Silence enfolded the scene.

It was broken by a horrid, long-drawn scream of a horse and the thudding of heavy hoofs. Venters sprang erect and wheeled south. Along the cañon rim, near the edge, came Wrangle, once more in thundering flight.

Venters gasped in amazement. Had the wild sorrel gone mad? His head was high and twisted, in a most singular position for a running horse. Suddenly Venters descried a frog-like shape clinging to Wrangle's neck. Jerry Card! Somehow he had straddled Wrangle and now stuck like a huge burr. But it was his strange position and the sorrel's wild scream that shook Venters's nerves. Wrangle was pounding toward the turn where the trail went down. He plunged onward like a blind horse. More than one of his leaps took him to the very edge of the precipice.

Jerry Card was bent forward with his teeth fast in the front of Wrangle's nose! Venters saw it, and there flashed over him a memory of this trick of a few desperate riders. He even thought of one rider who had worn off his teeth in this terrible hold to break or control desperate horses. Wrangle had indeed gone mad. The marvel was what guided him. Was it the half-brute, the more than half-horse instinct of Jerry Card? Whatever the mystery, it was true. And in a few more rods Jerry would have the sorrel turning into the trail leading down into the cañon.

'No – Jerry!' whispered Venters, stepping forward and throwing up the rifle. He tried to catch the little humped, frog-like shape over the sights. It was moving too fast; it was too small. Yet Venters shot once . . . twice . . . the third time . . . four times . . . five! All wasted shots and precious seconds!

With a deep-muttered curse Venters caught Wrangle through the sights and pulled the trigger. Plainly he heard the bullet thud. Wrangle uttered a horrible strangling sound. In swift death action he whirled, and with one last splendid leap he cleared the cañon rim. And he whirled downward with the little frog-like shape clinging to his neck!

There was a pause which seemed never ending, a shock, and an instant's silence.

Then up rolled a heavy crash, a long roar of sliding rocks dying away in distant echo, then silence unbroken.

Wrangle's race was run.

CHAPTER EIGHTEEN
Oldring's Knell

SOME FORTY HOURS OR more later Venters created a commotion in Cottonwoods by riding down the main street on Black Star and leading Bells and Night. He had come upon Bells grazing near the body of a dead rustler, the only incident of his quick ride into the village.

Nothing was farther from Venters's mind than bravado. No thought came to him of the defiance and boldness of riding Jane Withersteen's racers straight into the arch-plotter's stronghold. He wanted men to see the famous Arabians; he wanted men to see them dirty and dusty, bearing all the signs of having been driven to their limit; he wanted men to see and to know that the thieves who had ridden them out into the sage had not ridden them back. Venters had come for that and for more – he wanted to meet Tull face to face; if not Tull, then Dyer; if not Dyer, then anyone in the secret of these master conspirators. Such was Venters's passion. The meeting with the rustlers, the unprovoked attack upon him, the spilling of blood, the recognition of Jerry Card and the horses, the race, and that last plunge of mad Wrangle – all these things, fuel on fuel to the smoldering fire, had kindled and swelled and leaped into living flame. He could have shot Dyer in the midst of his religious services at the altar; he could have killed Tull in front of wives and babes.

He walked the three racers down the broad, green-bordered village road. He heard the murmur of running water from Amber Spring. Bitter waters for Jane Withersteen! Men and women stopped to gaze at him and the horses. All knew him; all knew the blacks and the bay. As well as if it had been spoken, Venters read in the faces of men the intelligence that Jane Withersteen's Arabians had been known to have been stolen. Venters reined in and halted before Dyer's residence. It was a low, long, stone structure resembling Withersteen House. The spacious front yard was green and luxuriant with grass and flowers; gravel walks led to the huge porch; a well-trimmed hedge of purple sage separated the yard from the church grounds; birds sang in the trees; water flowed musically along the walks; and there were glad, careless shouts of children. For Venters the beauty of this home, and the serenity and its apparent happiness, all turned red and black. For Venters a shade over-spread the lawn, the flowers, the old vine-clad stone house. In the music of the singing birds, in the murmur of the running water, he heard an ominous sound. Quiet beauty – sweet music – innocent laughter! By what monstrous abortion of fate did these abide in the shadow of Dyer?

Venters rode on and stopped before Tull's cottage. Women stared at him with white faces and then flew from the porch. Tull himself appeared at the door, bent low, craning his neck. His dark face flashed out of sight; the door banged; a heavy bar dropped with a hollow sound.

Venters shook Black Star's bridle, and, sharply trotting, led the other horses to the center of the village. Here at the intersecting streets and in front of the stores he halted once more. The usual lounging atmosphere of that prominent corner was not now in evidence. Riders and ranchers and villagers broke up what must have been absorbing conversation. There was a rush of many feet, and then the walk was lined with faces.

Venters's glance swept down the line of silent stone-faced men. He recognized many riders and villagers, but none of those he had hoped to meet. There was no expression in the faces turned toward him. All of them knew him, most were inimical, but there were few who were not burning with curiosity and wonder in regard to the return of Jane Withersteen's racers. Yet all were silent. Here were the familiar characteristics – masked feeling – strange secretiveness – expressionless expression of mystery and hidden power.

'Has anybody here seen Jerry Card?' queried Venters, in a loud voice.

In reply there came not a word, not a nod or shake of head, not so much as dropping eye or twitching lip – nothing but a quiet, stony stare.

'Been under the knife? You've a fine knife-wielder here – one Tull, I believe! . . . Maybe you've all had your tongues cut out?'

This passionate sarcasm of Venters brought no response, and the stony calm was as oil on the fire within him.

'I see some of you pack guns, too!' he added, in biting scorn. In the long, tense pause, strung keenly as a tight wire, he sat motionless on Black Star. 'All right,' he went on. 'Then let some of you take this message to Tull. Tell him I've seen Jerry Card! . . . Tell him Jerry Card *will never return!*'

Thereupon, in the same dead calm, Venters backed Black Star away from the curb, into the street, and out of range. He was ready now to ride up to Withersteen House and turn the racers over to Jane.

'Hello, Venters!' a familiar voice cried, hoarsely, and he saw a man running toward him. It was the rider Judkins who came up and gripped Venters's hand. 'Venters, I could hev dropped when I seen them hosses. But thet sight ain't a marker to the looks of you. What's wrong? Hev you gone crazy? You must be crazy to ride in here this way – with them hosses – talkin' thet way about Tull an' Jerry Card.'

'Jud, I'm not crazy – only mad clean through,' replied Venters.

'Wal, now, Bern, I'm glad to hear some of your old self in your voice. Fer when you come up you looked like the corpse of a dead rider with fire fer eyes. You hed thet crowd too stiff fer throwin' guns. Come, we've got to hev a talk. Let's go up the lane. We ain't much safe here.'

Judkins mounted Bells and rode with Venters up to the cottonwood grove. Here they dismounted and went among the trees.

'Let's hear from you first,' said Judkins. 'You fetched back them hosses. Thet *is* the trick. An', of course, you got Jerry the same as you got Horne.'

'Horne!'

'Sure. He was found dead yesterday all chewed by coyotes, an' he'd been shot plumb center.'

'Where was he found?'

'At the split down the trail – you know where Oldrin's cattle trail runs off north from the trail to the pass.'

'That's where I met Jerry and the rustlers. What was Horne doing with them? I thought Horne was an honest cattle-man.'

'Lord – Bern, don't ask me thet! I'm all muddled now tryin' to figure things.'

Venters told of the fight and the race with Jerry Card and its tragic conclusion.

'I knowed it! I knowed all along that Wrangle was the best hoss!' exclaimed Judkins, with his lean face working and his eyes lighting. 'Thet was a race! Lord, I'd like to hev seen Wrangle jump the cliff with Jerry. An' thet was good-bye to the grandest hoss an' rider ever on the sage! . . . But, Bern, after you got the hosses why'd you want to bolt right in Tull's face?'

'I want him to know. An' if I can get to him I'll – '

'You can't get near Tull,' interrupted Judkins. 'Thet vigilante bunch hev taken to bein' bodyguard for Tull an' Dyer, too.'

'Hasn't Lassiter made a break yet?' inquired Venters, curiously.

'Naw!' replied Judkins, scornfully. 'Jane turned his head. He's mad in love over her – follers her like a dog. He ain't no more Lassiter! He's lost his nerve; he doesn't look like the same feller. It's village talk. Everybody knows it. He hasn't thrown a gun, an' he won't!'

'Jud, I'll bet he does,' replied Venters, earnestly. 'Remember what I say. This Lassiter is something more than a gun-man. Jud, he's big – he's great! . . . I feel that in him. God help Tull and Dyer when Lassiter does go after them. For horses and riders and stone walls won't save them.'

'Wal, hev it your way, Bern. I hope you're right. Nat'rully I've been some sore on Lassiter fer gittin' soft. But I ain't denyin' his nerve, or whatever's great in him thet sort of paralyzes people. No later 'n this mornin' I seen him saunterin' down the lane, quiet an' slow. An' like his guns he comes black – *black*, thet's Lassiter. Wal, the crowd on the corner never batted an eye, an' I'll gamble my hoss thet there wasn't one who hed a heartbeat till Lassiter got by. He went in Shell's saloon, an' as there wasn't no gun play I had to go in, too. An' there, darn my pictures, if Lassiter wasn't standin' to the bar, drinkin' an' talkin' with Oldrin'.'

'*Oldring!*' whispered Venters. His voice, as all fire and pulse within him, seemed to freeze.

'Let go my arm!' exclaimed Judkins. 'Thet's my bad arm. Sure it was Oldrin'. What the hell's wrong with you, anyway? Venters, I tell you somethin's wrong. You're whiter'n a sheet. You can't be *scared* of the rustler. I don't believe you've got a scare in you. Wal, now, jest let me talk. You know I like to talk, an' if I'm slow I allus git there sometime. As I said, Lassiter was talkin' chummy with Oldrin'. There wasn't no hard feelin's. An' the gang wasn't payin' no pertic'lar attention. But like a cat watchin' a mouse I hed my eyes on them two fellers. It was strange to me, thet confab. I'm gittin' to think a lot, fer a feller who doesn't know much. There's been some queer deals lately an' this seemed to me the queerest. These men stood to the bar alone, an' so close their big gun-hilts butted together. I seen Oldrin' was some surprised at first, an' Lassiter was cool as ice. They talked, an' presently at somethin' Lassiter said the rustler bawled out a curse, an' then he jest fell up against the bar, an' sagged there. The gang in the saloon looked around an' laughed, an' thet's about all. Finally Oldrin' turned, and it was easy to see somethin' hed shook him. Yes, sir, thet big rustler – you know he's as broad as he is long, an' the powerfulest build of a man – yes, sir, the nerve had been taken out of him. Then, after a little, he began to talk an' said a lot to Lassiter, an' by an' by it didn't take much of an eye to see thet Lassiter was gittin' hit hard. I never seen him anyway but cooler'n ice – till then. He seemed to be hit harder'n Oldrin', only he didn't roar out thet way. He jest kind of sunk in, an' looked an' looked, an' he didn't see a livin' soul in thet saloon. Then he sort of come to, an' shakin' hands – mind you, *shakin' hands* with Oldrin' – he went out. I couldn't help thinkin' how easy even a boy could hev dropped the great gun-man then! . . . Wal, the rustler stood at the bar fer a long time, an' he was seein' things far off, too; then he come to an' roared for whisky, an' gulped a drink thet was big enough to drown me.'

'Is Oldring here now?' whispered Venters. He could not speak above a whisper. Judkins's story had been meaningless to him.

'He's at Shell's yet. Bern, I hevn't told you yet thet the rustlers hev been raisin' hell. They shot up Stone Bridge an' Glaze, an' fer three days they've been here drinkin' an' gamblin' an' throwin' of gold. These rustlers hev a pile of gold. If it was gold dust or nugget gold I'd hev reason to think, but it's new coin gold, as if it had jest come from the United States treasury. An' the coin's genuine. Thet's all been proved. The truth is Oldrin's on a rampage. A while back he lost his Masked Rider, an' they say he's wild about thet. I'm wonderin' if Lassiter could hev told the rustler anythin' about thet little masked, hard-ridin' devil! Ride! He was most as good as Jerry Card. An', Bern, I've been wonderin' if you know – '

'Judkins, you're a good fellow,' interrupted Venters. 'Some day I'll tell you a story. I've no time now. Take the horses to Jane.'

Judkins stared, and then, muttering to himself, he mounted Bells, and stared again at Venters, and then, leading the other horses, he rode into the grove and disappeared.

Once, long before, on the night Venters had carried Bess through the cañon and up into Surprise Valley, he had experienced the strangeness of faculties singularly, tinglingly acute. And now the same sensation recurred. But it was different in that he felt cold, frozen, mechanical, incapable of free thought, and all about him seemed unreal, aloof, remote. He hid his rifle in the sage, marking its exact location with extreme care. Then he faced down the lane and strode toward the center of the village. Perceptions flashed upon him, the faint, cold touch of the breeze, a cold, silvery tinkle of flowing water, a cold sun shining out of a cold sky, song of birds and laugh of children, coldly distant. Cold and intangible were all things in earth and heaven. Colder and tighter stretched the skin over his face; colder and harder grew the polished butts of his guns; colder and steadier became his hands as he wiped the clammy sweat from his face or reached low to his gun-sheaths. Men meeting him in the walk gave him wide berth. In front of Bevin's store a crowd melted apart for his passage, and their faces and whispers were faces and whispers of a dream. He turned a corner to meet Tull face to face, eye to eye. As once before he had seen this man pale to a ghastly, livid white, so again he saw the change. Tull stopped in his tracks, with right hand raised and shaking. Suddenly it dropped, and he seemed to glide aside, to pass out of Venters's sight. Next he saw many horses with bridles down – all clean-limbed, dark bays or blacks – rustlers' horses! Loud voices and boisterous laughter, rattle of dice and scrape of chair and clink of gold, burst in mingled din from an open doorway. He stepped inside.

With the sight of smoke-hazed room and drinking, cursing, gambling, dark-visaged men, reality once more dawned upon Venters.

His entrance had been unnoticed, and he bent his gaze upon the drinkers at the bar. Dark-clothed, dark-faced men they all were, burned by the sun, bow-legged as were most riders of the sage, but neither lean nor gaunt. Then Venters's gaze passed to the tables, and swiftly it swept over the hard-featured gamesters, to alight upon the huge, shaggy, black head of the rustler chief.

'*Oldring!*' he cried, and to him his voice seemed to split a bell in his ears.

It stilled the din.

That silence suddenly broke to the scrape and crash of Oldring's chair as he rose; and then, while he passed, a great gloomy figure, again the thronged room stilled in silence yet deeper.

'Oldring, a word with you!' continued Venters.

'Ho! What's this?' boomed Oldring, in frowning scrutiny.

'Come outside, alone. A word for you – *from your Masked Rider!*'

Oldring kicked a chair out of his way and lunged forward with a stamp of heavy boot that jarred the floor. He waved down his muttering, rising men.

Venters backed out of the door and waited, hearing, as no sound had ever before struck into his soul, the rapid, heavy steps of the rustler.

Oldring appeared, and Venters had one glimpse of his great breadth and bulk, his gold-buckled belt with hanging guns, his high-top boots with gold spurs. In that moment Venters had a strange, unintelligible curiosity to see Oldring alive. The rustler's broad brow, his large black eyes, his sweeping beard, as dark as the wing of a raven, his enormous width of shoulder and depth of chest, his whole splendid presence so wonderfully charged with vitality and force and strength, seemed to afford Venters an unutterable fiendish joy because for that magnificent manhood and life he meant cold and sudden death.

'Oldring, Bess is alive! But she's dead to you – dead to the life you made her lead – dead as you will be in one second!'

Swift as lightning Venters's glance dropped from Oldring's rolling eyes to his hands. One of them, the right, swept out, then toward his gun – and Venters shot him through the heart.

Slowly Oldring sank to his knees, and the hand, dragging at his gun, fell away. Venters's strangely acute faculties grasped the meaning of that limp arm, of the swaying hulk, of the gasp and heave, of the quivering beard. But was that awful spirit in the black eyes only one of vitality?

'Man – *why* – didn't – *you* – wait? Bess – was – ' Oldring's whisper died under his beard, and with a heavy lurch he fell forward.

Bounding swiftly away, Venters fled around the corner, across the street, and, leaping a hedge, he ran through the yard, orchard, and garden to the sage. Here, under cover of the tall brush, he turned west and ran on to the place where he had hidden his rifle. Securing that, he again set out into a run, and circling through the sage, came up behind Jane Withersteen's stable and corrals. With laboring, dripping chest, and pain as of a knife thrust in his side, he stopped to regain his breath, and while resting his eyes roved around in search of a horse. Doors and windows of the stable were open wide and had a deserted look. One dejected, lonely burro stood in the near corral. Strange indeed was the silence brooding over the once happy, noisy home of Jane Withersteen's pets.

He went into the corral, exercising care to leave no tracks, and led the burro to the watering-trough. Venters, though not thirsty, drank till he could drink no more. Then, leading the burro over hard ground, he struck into the sage and down the slope.

He strode swiftly, turning from time to time to scan the slope for riders. His head just topped the level of sage-brush, and the burro could not have been seen at all. Slowly the green of Cottonwoods sank behind the slope, and at last a wavering line of purple sage met the blue of sky.

To avoid being seen, to get away, to hide his trail – these were the sole ideas in his mind as he headed for Deception Pass; and he directed all his acuteness of eye and ear, and the keenness of a rider's judgment for distance and ground, to stern accomplishment of the task. He kept to the sage far to the left of the trail leading into the Pass. He walked ten miles and looked back a thousand times. Always the graceful, purple wave of sage remained wide and lonely, a clear, undotted waste. Coming to a stretch of rocky ground, he took advantage of it to cross the trail and then continued down on the right. At length he persuaded himself that he would be able to see riders mounted on horses before they could see him on the little burro, and he rode bareback.

Hour by hour the tireless burro kept to his faithful, steady trot. The sun sank and the long shadows lengthened down the slope. Moving veils of purple twilight crept out of the hollows and, mustering and forming on the levels, soon merged and shaded into night. Venters guided the burro nearer to the trail, so that he could see its white line from the ridges, and rode on through the hours.

Once down in the Pass without leaving a trail, he would hold himself safe for the time being. When late in the night he reached the break in the sage, he sent the burro down ahead of him, and started an avalanche that all but buried the animal at the bottom of the trail. Bruised and battered as he was, he had a moment's elation, for he had hidden his tracks. Once more he mounted the burro and rode on. The hour was the blackest of the night when he made the thicket which inclosed his old camp. Here he turned the burro loose in the grass near the spring, and then lay down on his old bed of leaves.

He felt only vaguely, as outside things, the ache and burn and throb of the muscles of his body. But a dammed-up torrent of emotion at last burst its bounds, and the hour that saw his release from immediate action was one that confounded him in the reaction of his spirit. He suffered without understanding why. He caught glimpses into himself, into unlit darkness of soul. The fire that had blistered him and the cold which had frozen him now united in one torturing possession of his mind and heart, and like a fiery steed with ice-shod feet, ranged his being, ran rioting through his blood, trampling the resurging good, dragging ever at the evil.

Out of the subsiding chaos came a clear question. What had happened? He had left the valley to go to Cottonwoods. Why? It seemed that he had gone to kill a man – Oldring! The name riveted his consciousness upon the one man of all men upon earth whom he had wanted to meet. He had met the rustler. Venters recalled the smoky haze of the saloon, the dark-visaged men, the huge Oldring. He saw him step out of the door, a splendid specimen of manhood, a handsome giant with purple-black and sweeping beard. He remembered inquisitive gaze of falcon eyes. He heard himself repeating: 'Oldring, Bess is alive! But she's dead to you,' and he felt himself jerk, and his ears throbbed to the thunder of a gun, and he saw the giant sink slowly to his knees. Was that only the vitality of him – that awful light in the eyes – only the hard-dying life of a tremendously powerful brute? A broken whisper, strange as death: *Man – why – didn't – you wait! Bess – was –* And Oldring plunged face forward, dead.

'I killed him,' cried Venters, in remembering shock. 'But it wasn't *that.* Ah, the look in his eyes and his whisper!'

Herein lay the secret that had clamored to him through all the tumult and stress of his emotions. What a look in the eyes of a man shot through the heart! It had been neither hate nor ferocity nor fear of men nor fear of death. It had been no passionate, glinting spirit of a fearless foe, willing shot for shot, life for life, but lacking physical power. Distinctly recalled now, never to be forgotten, Venters saw in Oldring's magnificent eyes the rolling of great, glad surprise – softness – love! Then came a shadow and the terrible superhuman striving of his spirit to speak. Oldring, shot through the heart, had fought and forced back death, not for a moment in which to shoot or curse, but to whisper strange words.

What words for a dying man to whisper! Why had not Venters waited? For what? That was no plea for life. It was a regret that there was not a moment of life left in which to speak. Bess was – Herein lay renewed torture for Venters. What had Bess been to Oldring? The old question, like a specter, stalked from its grave to haunt him. He had overlooked, he had forgiven, he had loved, and he had forgotten; and now, out of the mystery of a dying man's whisper rose again that perverse, unsatisfied, jealous uncertainty. Bess had loved that splendid, black-crowned giant – by her own confession she had loved him; and in Venters's soul again flamed up the jealous hell. Then into the clamoring hell burst the shot that had killed Oldring, and it rang in a wild, fiendish gladness, a hateful, vengeful joy. That passed to the memory of the love and light in Oldring's eyes and the mystery in his whisper. So the changing, swaying emotions fluctuated in Venters's heart.

This was the climax of his year of suffering and the crucial struggle of his life. And when the gray dawn came he rose, a gloomy, almost heartbroken man, but victor over evil passions. He could not change the past; and, even if he had not loved Bess with all his soul, he had grown into a man who would not change the future he had planned for her. Only, and once for all, he must know the truth, know the worst, stifle all these insistent doubts and subtle hopes and jealous fancies, and kill the past by knowing truly what Bess had been to Oldring. For that matter, he knew – he had always known, but he must hear it spoken. Then, when they had safely gotten out of that wild country to take up a new and an absorbing life, she would forget, she would be happy, and through that, in the years to come, he could not but find life worth living.

All day he rode slowly and cautiously up the Pass, taking time to peer around corners, to pick out hard ground and grassy patches, and to make sure there was no one in pursuit. In the night sometime he came to the smooth, scrawled rocks dividing the valley, and here set the burro at liberty. He walked beyond, climbed the slope and the dim, starlit gorge. Then, weary to the point of exhaustion, he crept into a shallow cave and fell asleep.

In the morning, when he descended the trail, he found the sun was pouring a golden stream of light through the arch of the great stone bridge. Surprise Valley, like a valley of dreams, lay mystically soft and beautiful, awakening to the golden flood which rolling away its slumberous bands of mist, brightening its walled faces.

While yet far off he discerned Bess moving under the silver spruces, and soon the barking of the dogs told him that they had seen him. He heard the mocking-birds singing in the trees, and then the twittering of the quail. Ring and Whitie came bounding toward him, and behind them ran Bess, her hands outstretched.

'Bern! You're back! You're back!' she cried, in joy that rang of her loneliness.

'Yes, I'm back,' he said, as she rushed to meet him.

She had reached out for him when suddenly, as she saw him closely, something checked her, and as quickly all her joy fled, and with it her color, leaving her pale and trembling.

'Oh! What's happened?'

'A good deal has happened, Bess. I don't need to tell you what. And I'm played out. Worn out in mind more than body.'

'Dear – you look strange to me!' faltered Bess.

'Never mind that. I'm all right. There's nothing for you to be scared about. Things are going to turn out just as we have planned. As soon as I'm rested we'll make a break to get out of the country. Only now, right now, I must know the truth about you.'

'Truth about me?' echoed Bess, shrinkingly. She seemed to be casting back into her mind for a forgotten key. Venters himself, as he saw her, received a pang.

'Yes – the truth. Bess, don't misunderstand. I haven't changed that way. I love you still. I'll love you more afterward. Life will be just as sweet – sweeter to us. We'll be – be married as soon as ever we can. We'll be happy – but there's a devil in me. A perverse, jealous devil! Then I've queer fancies. I forgot for a long time. Now all those fiendish little whispers of doubt and faith and fear and hope come torturing me again. I've got to kill them with the truth.'

'I'll tell you anything you want to know,' she replied, frankly.

'Then, by Heaven! we'll have it over and done with! . . . Bess – did Oldring love you?'

'Certainly he did.'

'Did – you love him?'

'Of course. I told you so.'

'How can you tell it so lightly?' cried Venters, passionately. 'Haven't you any sense of – of – ' He choked back speech. He felt the rush of pain and passion. He seized her in rude, strong hands and drew her close. He looked straight into her dark-blue eyes. They were shadowing with the old wistful light, but they were as clear as the limpid water of the spring. They were earnest, solemn in unutterable love and faith and abnegation. Venters shivered. He knew he was looking into her soul. He knew she could not lie in that moment; but that she might tell the truth, looking at him with those eyes, almost killed his belief in purity.

'What are – what were you to – to Oldring?' he panted, fiercely.

'I am his daughter,' she replied, instantly.

Venters slowly let go of her. There was a violent break in the force of his feeling – then creeping blankness.

'What – was it – you said?' he asked, in a kind of dull wonder.

'I am his daughter.'

'Oldring's daughter?' queried Venters, with life gathering in his voice.

'Yes.'

With a passionately awakening start he grasped her hands and drew her close.

'All the time – you've been Oldring's daughter?'

'Yes, of course all the time – always.'

'But Bess, you told me – you let me think – I made out you were – a – so – so ashamed.'

'It is my shame,' she said, with voice deep and full, and now the scarlet fired her cheek. 'I told you – I'm nothing – nameless – just Bess, Oldring's girl!'

'I know – I remember. But I never thought – ' he went on, hurriedly, huskily. 'That time – when you lay dying – you prayed – you – somehow I got the idea you were bad.'

'Bad?' she asked, with a little laugh.

She looked up with a faint smile of bewilderment and the absolute unconsciousness of a child. Venters gasped in the gathering might of the truth. She did not understand his meaning.

'Bess! Bess!' He clasped her in his arms, hiding her eyes against his breast. She must not see his face in that moment. And he held her while he looked out across the valley. In his dim and blinded sight, in the blur of golden light and moving mist, he saw Oldring. She was the rustler's nameless daughter. Oldring had loved her. He had so guarded her, so kept her from women and men and knowledge of life that her mind was as a child's. That was part of the secret – part of the mystery. That was the wonderful truth. Not only was she not bad, but good, pure, innocent above all innocence in the world – the innocence of lonely girlhood.

He saw Oldring's magnificent eyes, inquisitive, searching – softening. He saw them flare in amaze, in gladness, with love, then suddenly strain in terrible effort of will. He heard Oldring whisper and saw him sway like a log and fall. Then a million bellowing, thundering voices – gunshots of conscience, thunderbolts of remorse – dinned horribly in his ears. He had killed Bess's father. Then a rushing wind filled his ears like the moan of wind in the cliffs, a knell indeed – Oldring's knell.

He dropped to his knees and hid his face against Bess, and grasped her with hands of a drowning man.

'My God! . . . My God! . . . Oh, Bess! . . . Forgive me! Never mind what I've done – what I've thought. But forgive me. I'll give you my life. I'll live for you. I'll love you. Oh, I do love you as no man ever loved a woman. I want you to know – to remember that I fought a fight for you – however blind I was. I thought – I thought – never mind what I thought – but I loved you – I asked you to marry me. Let that – let me have that to hug to my heart. Oh, Bess, I was driven! And I might have known! I could not rest nor sleep till I had this mystery solved. God! how things work out!'

'Bern, you're weak – trembling – you talk wildly.' cried Bess. 'You've overdone your strength. There's nothing to forgive. There's no mystery except your love for me. You have come back to me!'

And she clasped his head tenderly in her arms and pressed it closely to her throbbing breast.

CHAPTER NINETEEN

Fay

AT THE HOME OF JANE Withersteen Little Fay was climbing Lassiter's knee.

'Does oo love me?' she asked.

Lassiter, who was as serious with Fay as he was gentle and loving, assured her in earnest and elaborate speech that he was her devoted subject. Fay looked thoughtful and appeared to be debating the duplicity of men or searching for a supreme test to prove this cavalier.

'Does oo love my new muvver?' she asked, with a bewildering suddenness.

Jane Withersteen laughed, and for the first time in many a day she felt a stir of her pulse and warmth in her cheek.

It was a still drowsy summer of afternoon, and the three were sitting in the shade of the wooded knoll that faced the sage-slope. Little Fay's brief spell of unhappy longing for her mother – the childish, mystic gloom – had passed, and now where Fay was there were prattle and laughter and glee. She had emerged from sorrow to be the incarnation of joy and loveliness. She had grown supernaturally sweet and beautiful. For Jane Withersteen, the child was an answer to prayer, a blessing, a possession infinitely more precious than all she had lost. For Lassiter, Jane divined that little Fay had become a religion.

'Does oo love my new muvver?' repeated Fay.

Lassiter's answer to this was a modest and sincere affirmative.

'Why don't oo marry my new muvver an' be my favver?'

Of the thousands of questions put by little Fay to Lassiter that was the first he had been unable to answer.

'Fay – Fay, don't ask questions like that,' said Jane.

'Why?'

'Because,' replied Jane. And she found it strangely embarrassing to meet the child's gaze. It seemed to her that Fay's violet eyes looked through her with piercing wisdom.

'Oo love him, don't oo?'

'Dear child – run and play,' said Jane, 'but don't go too far. Don't go from this little hill.'

Fay pranced off wildly, joyous over freedom that had not been granted her for weeks.

'Jane, why are children more sincere than grown-up persons?' asked Lassiter.

'Are they?'

'I reckon so. Little Fay there – she sees things as they appear on the face. An Indian does that. So does a dog. An' an Indian an' a dog are most of the time right in what they see. Mebbe a child is always right.'

'Well, what does Fay see?' asked Jane.

'I reckon you know. I wonder what goes on in Fay's mind when she sees part of the truth with the wise eyes of a child, an' wantin' to know more, meets with strange falseness from you? Wait! You are false in a way, though you're the best woman I ever knew. What I want to say is this. Fay has taken you're pretendin' to – to care for me for the thing it looks on the face. An' her little formin' mind asks questions. An' the answers she gets are different from the looks of things. So she'll grow up, gradually takin' on that falseness, an' be like the rest of women, an' men, too. An' the truth of this falseness to life is proved by your appearin' to love me when you don't. Things aren't what they seem.'

'Lassiter, you're right. A child should be told the absolute truth. But – is that possible? I haven't been able to do it, and all my life I've loved the truth, and I've prided myself upon being truthful. Maybe that was only egotism. I'm learning much, my friend. Some of those blinding scales have fallen from my eyes. And – as to caring for you, I think I care a great deal. How much, how little, I couldn't say. My heart is almost broken, Lassiter. So now is not a good time to judge of affection. I can still play and be merry with Fay. I can still dream. But when I attempt serious thought I'm dazed. I don't think. I don't care any more. I don't pray! . . . Think of that my friend! But in spite of my numb feeling I believe I'll rise out of all this dark agony a better woman, with greater love of man and God. I'm on the rack now; I'm senseless to all but pain, and growing dead to that. Sooner or later I shall rise out of this stupor. I'm waiting the hour.'

'It'll soon come, Jane,' replied Lassiter, soberly. 'Then I'm afraid for you. Years are terrible things, an' for years you've been bound. Habit of years is strong as life itself. Somehow, though, I believe as you – that you'll come out of it all a finer woman. I'm waitin' too. An' I'm wonderin' – I reckon, Jane, that marriage between us is out of all human reason?'

'Lassiter! . . . My dear friend! . . . It's impossible for us to marry.'

'Why – as Fay says?' inquired Lassiter, with gentle persistence.

'Why! I never thought why. But it's not possible. I am Jane, daughter of Withersteen. My father would rise out of his grave. I'm of Mormon birth. I'm being broken. But I'm still a Mormon woman. And you – you are Lassiter!'

'Mebbe I'm not so much Lassiter as I used to be.'

'What was it you said? Habit of years is strong as life itself! You can't change the one habit – the purpose of your life. For you still pack those black guns! You still nurse your passion for blood.'

A smile, like a shadow, flickered across his face.

'No.'

'Lassiter, I lied to you. But I beg of you – don't you lie to me. I've great respect for you. I believe you're softened toward most, perhaps all, my people except – But when I speak of your purpose, your hate, your guns, I have only him in mind. I don't believe you've changed.'

For answer he unbuckled the heavy cartridge-belt, and laid it with the heavy, swing gun-sheaths in her lap.

'Lassiter!' Jane whispered, as she gazed from him to the black, cold guns. Without them he appeared shorn of strength, defenseless, a smaller man. Was she Delilah? Swiftly, conscious of only one motive – refusal to see this man called craven by his enemies – she rose, and with blundering fingers buckled the belt round his waist where it belonged.

'Lassiter, *I* am the coward.'

'Come with me out of Utah – where I can put away my guns an' be a man,' he said. 'I reckon I'll prove it to you then! Come! You've got Black Star back, an' Night an' Bells. Let's take the racers an' little Fay, an' ride out of Utah. The hosses an' the child are all you have left. Come!'

'No, no, Lassiter. I'll never leave Utah. What would I do in the world with my broken fortunes and my broken heart? I'll never leave these purple slopes I love so well.'

'I reckon I ought to've knowed that. Presently you'll be livin' down here in a hovel, an' presently Jane Withersteen will be a memory. I only wanted to have a chance to show you how a man – *any* man – can be better 'n he was. If we left Utah I could prove – I reckon I could prove this thing you call love. It's strange, an' hell an' heaven at once, Jane Withersteen. 'Pears to me that you've thrown away your big heart on love – love of religion an' duty an' church-men, an' riders an' poor families an' poor children! Yet you can't see what love is – how it changes a person! . . . Listen, an' in tellin' you Milly Erne's story I'll show you how love changed her.

'Milly an' me was children when our family moved from Missouri to Texas, an' we growed up in Texas ways same as if we'd been born there. We had been poor, an' there we prospered. In time the little village where we went became a town,

an' strangers an' new families kept movin' in. Milly was the belle them days. I can
see her now, a little girl no bigger 'n a bird, an' as pretty. She had the finest eyes,
dark blue-black when she was excited, an' beautiful all the time. You remember
Milly's eyes! An' she had light-brown hair with streaks of gold, an' a mouth that
every feller wanted to kiss.

'An' about the time Milly was the prettiest an' the sweetest, along came a young
minister who began to ride some of a race with the other fellers for Milly. An' he
won. Milly had always been strong on religion, an' when she met Frank Erne she
went in heart an' soul for the salvation of souls. Fact was, Milly, through study of
the Bible an' attendin' church an' revivals, went a little out of her head. It didn't
worry the old folks none, an' the only worry to me was Milly's ever-lastin' prayin'
an' workin' to save my soul. She never converted me, but we was the best of
comrades, an' I reckon no brother an' sister ever loved each other better. Well,
Frank Erne an' me hit up a great friendship. He was a strappin' feller, good to look
at, an' had the most pleasin' ways. His religion never bothered me, for he could
hunt an' fish an' ride an' be a good feller. After buffalo once, he come pretty near
to savin' my life. We got to be thick as brothers, an' he was the only man I ever
seen who I thought was good enough for Milly. An' the day they were married I got
drunk for the only time in my life.

'Soon after that I left home – it seems Milly was the only one who could keep me
home – an' I went to the bad, as to prosperin'. I saw some pretty hard life in the
Pan Handle, an' then I went North. In them days Kansas an' Nebraska was as bad,
come to think of it, as these days right here on the border of Utah. I got to be
pretty handy with guns. An' there wasn't many riders as could beat me ridin'. An' I
can say all modest-like that I never seen the white man who could track a hoss or a
steer or a man with me. Afore I knowed it two years slipped by, an' all at once I got
homesick, an' pulled a bridle south.

'Things at home had changed. I never got over that home-comin'. Mother was
dead an' in her grave. Father was a silent, broken man, killed already on his feet.
Frank Erne was a ghost of his old self, through with workin', through with
preachin', almost through with livin', an' Milly was gone! . . . It was a long time
before I got the story. Father had no mind left, an' Frank Erne was *afraid* to talk. So
I had to pick up what'd happened from different people.

'It 'pears that soon after I left home another preacher come to the little town.
An' he an' Frank become rivals. This feller was different from Frank. He preached
some other kind of religion, and he was quick an' passionate, where Frank was
slow an' mild. He went after people, women specially. In looks he couldn't
compare to Frank Erne, but he had power over women. He had a voice, an' he
talked an' talked an' preached an' preached. Milly fell under his influence. She
became mightily interested in his religion. Frank had patience with her, as was his
way, an' let her be as interested as she liked. All religions were devoted to one
God, he said, an' it wouldn't hurt Milly none to study a different point of view. So
the new preacher often called on Milly, an' sometimes in Frank's absence. Frank
was a cattle-man between Sundays.

'Along about this time an incident come off that I couldn't get much light on. A
stranger come to town, an' was seen with the preacher. This stranger was a big
man with an eye like blue ice, an' a beard of gold. He had money, an' he 'peared a
man of mystery, an' the town went to buzzin' when he disappeared about the same
time as a young woman known to be mightily interested in the new preacher's
religion. Then, presently, along comes a man from somewheres in Illinois, an' he
up an' spots this preacher as a famous Mormon proselyter. That ri'led Frank Erne

as nothin' ever before, an' from rivals they come to be bitter enemies. An' it ended in Frank goin' to the meetin'-house where Milly was listenin', an before her an' everybody else he called that preacher – called him, well, almost as hard as Venters called Tull here sometime back. An' Frank followed up that call with a hoss-whippin', an' he drove the proselyter out of town.

'People noticed, so 'twas said, that Milly's sweet disposition changed. Some said it was because she would soon become a mother, an' others said she was pinin' after the new religion. An' there was women who said right out that she was pinin' after the Mormon. Anyway, one mornin' Frank rode in from one of his trips, to find Milly gone. He had no real near neighbors – livin' a little out of town – but those who was nearest said a wagon had gone by in the night, an' they thought it stopped at her door. Well, tracks always tell, an' there was the wagon tracks an' hoss tracks an' man tracks. The news spread like wildfire that Milly had run off from her husband. Everybody but Frank believed it an' wasn't slow in tellin' why she run off. Mother had always hated that strange streak of Milly's, takin' up with the new religion as she had, an' she believed Milly ran of with the Mormon. That hastened mother's death, an' she died unforgivin'. Father wasn't the kind to bow down under disgrace or misfortune, but he had surpassin' love for Milly, an' the loss of her broke him.

'From the minute I heard of Milly's disappearance I never believed she went off of her own free will. I knew Milly, an' I knew she *couldn't* have done that. I stayed at home awhile, tryin' to make Frank Erne talk. But if he knowed anythin' then he wouldn't tell it. So I set out to find Milly. An' I tried to get on the trail of that proselyter. I knew if I ever struck a town he'd visited that I'd get a trail. I knew, too, that nothin' short of hell would stop his proselytin'. An' I rode from town to town. I had a blind faith that somethin' was guidin' me. An' as the weeks an' months went by I growed into a strange sort of a man, I guess. Anyway, people were afraid of me. Two years after that, way over in a corner of Texas, I struck a town where my man had been. He'd jest left. People said he came to that town *without* a woman. I back-trailed my man through Arkansas an' Mississippi, an' the old trail got hot again in Texas. I found the town where he first went after leavin' home. An' here I got track of Milly. I found a cabin where she had given birth to her baby. There was no way to tell whether she'd been kept a prisoner or not. The feller who owned the place was a mean, silent sort of a skunk, an' as I was leavin' I jest took a chance an' left my mark on him. Then I went home again.

'It was to find that I hadn't any home, no more. Father had been dead a year. Frank Erne still lived in the house where Milly had left him. I stayed with him awhile, an' I grew old watchin' him. His farm had gone to weed, his cattle had strayed or been rustled, his house weathered till it wouldn't keep out rain nor wind. An' Frank set on the porch and whittled sticks, an' day by day wasted away. There was times when he ranted about like a crazy man, but mostly he was always sittin' an' starin' with eyes that made a man curse. I figured Frank had a secret fear that I needed to know. An' when I told him I'd trailed Milly for near three years an' had got trace of her, an' saw where she'd had her baby, I thought he would drop dead at my feet. An' when he'd come round more natural-like he begged me to *give up* the trail. But he wouldn't explain. So I let him alone, an' watched him day an' night.

'An' I found there was one thing still precious to him, an' it was a little drawer where he kept his papers. This was in the room where he slept. An' it 'peared he seldom slept. But after bein' patient I got the contents of that drawer an' found two letters from Milly. One was a long letter written a few months after her disappearance. She had been bound an' gagged an' dragged away from her home by three men, an' she named them – Hurd, Metzger, Slack. They was strangers to her. She was taken to the little town where I found trace of her two years after. But she didn't send the letter from that town. There she was penned in. 'Peared that the proselyter, who had, of course, come on the scene, was not runnin' any risks of losin' her. She went on to say that for a time she was out of her head, an' when she got right again all that kept her alive was the baby. It was a beautiful baby, she said, an' all she thought an' dreamed of was somehow to get baby back to its father, an' then she'd thankfully lay down and die. An' the letter ended abrupt, in the middle of a sentence, an' it wasn't signed.

'The second letter was written more than two years after the first. It was from Salt Lake City. It simply said that Milly had heard her brother was on her trail. She asked Frank to tell her brother to give up the search because if he didn't she would suffer in a way too horrible to tell. She didn't beg. She just stated a fact an' made the simple request. An' she ended that letter by sayin' she would soon leave Salt Lake City with the man she had come to love, an' would never be heard of again.

'I recognized Milly's handwritin', an' I recognized her way of puttin' things. But that second letter told me of some great change in her. Ponderin' over it, I felt at last she'd either come to love that feller an' his religion, or some terrible fear made her lie an' say so. I couldn't be sure which. But, of course, I meant to find out. I'll say here, if I'd known Mormons then as I do now I'd left Milly to her fate. For mebbe she was right about what she'd suffer if I kept on her trail. But I was young an' wild them days. First I went to the town where she'd first been taken, an' I went to the place where she'd been kept. I got that skunk who owned the place, an' took him out in the woods, an' made him tell all he knowed. That wasn't much as to length, but it was pure hell's-fire in substance. This time I left him some incapacitated for any more skunk work short of hell. Then I hit the trail for Utah.

'That was fourteen years ago. I saw the incomin' of most of the Mormons. It was a wild country an' a wild time. I rode from town to town, village to village, ranch to ranch, camp to camp, I never stayed long in one place. I never had but one idea. I never rested. Four years went by, an' I knowed every trail in northern Utah. I kept on an' as time went by, an' I'd begun to grow old in my search, I had firmer, blinder faith in whatever was guidin' me. Once I read about a feller who sailed the seven seas an' traveled the world, an' he had a story to tell, an' whenever he seen the man to whom he must tell that story he knowed him on sight. I was like that, only I had a question to ask. An' always I knew the man of whom I must ask. So I never really lost the trail, though for years it was the dimmest trail ever followed by any man.

'Then come a change in my luck. Along in Central Utah I rounded up Hurd, an' I whispered somethin' in his ear, an' watched his face, an' then throwed a gun against his bowels. An' he died with his teeth so tight shut that I couldn't have pried them open with a knife. Slack an' Metzger that same year both heard me whisper the same question, an' neither would they speak a word when they lay dyin'. Long before I'd learned no man of this breed or class – or God knows what – would give up any secrets! I had to see in a man's fear of death the connections with Milly Erne's fate. An' as the years passed at long intervals I would find such a man.

'So as I drifted on the long trail down into southern Utah my name preceded me, an' I had to meet a people prepared for me, an' ready with guns. They made me a gun-man. An' that suited me. In all this time signs of the proselyter an' the giant with the blue-ice eyes an' the gold beard seemed to fade dimmer out of the trail. Only twice in ten years did I find a trace of the mysterious man who had visited the proselyter at my home village. What he had to do with Milly's fate was beyond all hope for me to hear, unless my guidin' spirit led me to him! As for the other man, I knew, as sure as I breathed an' the stars shone an' the wind blew, that I'd meet him some day.

'Eighteen years I've been on the trail. An' it led me to the last lonely villages of the Utah border. Eighteen years! . . . I feel pretty old now. I was only twenty when I hit that trail. Well, as I told you, back here a ways a Gentile said Jane Withersteen could tell me about Milly Erne an' show me her grave!'

The low voice ceased, and Lassiter slowly turned his sombrero round and round, and appeared to be counting the silver ornaments on the band. Jane, leaning toward him, sat as if petrified, listening intently, waiting to hear more. She could have shrieked, but power of tongue and lips were denied her. She saw only this sad, gray, passion-worn man, and she heard only the faint rustling of the leaves.

'Well, I came to Cottonwoods,' went on Lassiter, 'an' you showed me Milly's grave. An' though your teeth have been shut tighter'n them of all the dead men lyin' back along that trail, jest the same you told me the secret I've lived these eighteen years to hear! Jane, I said you'd tell me without ever me askin'. I didn't need to ask my question here. The day, you remember, when that fat party throwed a gun on me in your court, an' – '

'Oh! Hush!' whispered Jane, blindly holding up her hands.

'*I seen in your face that Dyer, now a bishop, was the proselyter who ruined Milly Erne!*'

For an instant Jane Withersteen's brain was a whirling chaos, and she recovered to find herself grasping at Lassiter like one drowning. And as if by a lightning stroke she sprang from her dull apathy into exquisite torture.

'*It's a lie!* Lassiter! No, no!' she moaned. 'I swear – you're wrong!'

'Stop! You'd perjure yourself! But I'll spare you that. You poor woman! Still blind! Still faithful! . . . Listen. I *know.* Let that settle it. An' I give up my purpose!'

'What is it – you say?'

'I give up my purpose. I've come to see an' feel differently. I can't help poor Milly. An' I've outgrowed revenge. I've come to see I can be no judge for men. I can't kill a man jest for hate. Hate ain't the same with me since I loved you and little Fay.'

'Lassiter! You mean you won't kill him?' Jane whispered.

'No.'

'For my sake?'

'I reckon. I can't understand, but I'll respect your feelin's.'

'Because you – oh, because you love me? . . . Eighteen years! You were that terrible Lassiter! And *now* – because you love me?'

'That's it, Jane.'

'Oh, you'll make me love you! How can I help but love you? My heart must be stone. But – oh, Lassiter, wait, wait! Give me time. I'm not what I was. Once it was so easy to love. Now it's easy to hate. Wait! My faith in God – *some* God – still lives. By it I see happier times for you, poor passion-swayed wanderer! For me – a miserable, broken woman. I loved your sister Milly. I *will* love you. I can't have fallen so low – I can't be so abandoned by God – that I've no love left to give you. Wait! Let us forget Milly's sad life. Ah, I knew it as no one else on earth! There's one thing I shall tell you – if you are at my death-bed, but I can't speak now.'

'I reckon I don't want to hear no more,' said Lassiter.

Jane leaned against him; as if some pent-up force had rent its way out, she fell into a paroxysm of weeping. Lassiter held her in silent sympathy. By degrees she regained composure, and she was rising, sensible of being relieved of a weighty burden, when a sudden start on Lassiter's part alarmed her.

'I heard hosses – hosses with muffled hoofs!' he said; and he got up guardedly.

'Where's Fay?' asked Jane, hurriedly glancing round the shady knoll. The bright-haired child, who had appeared to be close all the time, was not in sight.

'Fay!' called Jane.

No answering shout of glee. No patter of flying feet. Jane saw Lassiter stiffen.

'Fay – oh – Fay!' Jane almost screamed.

The leaves quivered and rustled; a lonesome cricket chirped in the grass; a bee hummed by. The silence of the waning afternoon breathed hateful portent. It terrified Jane. When had silence been so infernal?

'She's – only – strayed – out – of – earshot,' faltered Jane, looking at Lassiter.

Pale, rigid as a statue, the rider stood, not in listening, searching posture, but in one of doomed certainty. Suddenly he grasped Jane with an iron hand, and, turning his face from her gaze, he strode with her from the knoll.

'See – Fay played here last – a house of stones an' sticks . . . An' here's a corral of pebbles with leaves for hosses,' said Lassiter, stridently, and pointed to the ground. 'Back an' forth she trailed . . . See, she's buried somethin' – a dead grasshopper – there's a tombstone . . . here she went, chasin' a lizard – see the tiny streaked trail . . . she pulled bark off this cottonwood . . . look in the dust of the path – the letters you taught her – she's drawn pictures of birds an' hosses an' people . . . Look, a cross! Oh, Jane, *your* cross!'

Lassiter dragged Jane on, and as if from a book read the meaning of little Fay's trail. All the way down the knoll. through the shrubbery, round and round a cottonwood. Fay's vagrant fancy left records of her sweet musings and innocent play. Long had she lingered round a bird-nest to leave therein the gaudy wing of a butterfly. Long had she played beside the running stream, sending adrift vessels freighted with pebbly cargo. Then she had wandered through the deep grass, her tiny feet scarcely turning a fragile blade, and she had dreamed beside some old faded flowers. Thus her steps led her into the broad lane. The little dimpled imprints of her bare feet showed clean-cut in the dust; they went a little way down the lane; and then, at a point where they stopped, the great tracks of a man led out from the shrubbery and returned.

CHAPTER TWENTY

Lassiter's Way

FOOTPRINTS TOLD THE story of little Fay's abduction. In anguish Jane Withersteen turned speechlessly to Lassiter, and, confirming her fears, she saw him gray-faced, aged all in a moment, stricken as if by a mortal blow.

Then all her life seemed to fall about her in wreck and ruin.

'It's all over,' she heard her voice whisper. 'It's ended. I'm going – I'm going –'

'Where?' demanded Lassiter, suddenly looming darkly over her.

'To – to those cruel men – '

'Speak names!' thundered Lassiter.

'To Bishop Dyer – to Tull,' went on Jane, shocked into obedience.

'Well – what for?'

'I want little Fay. I can't live without her. They've stolen her as they stole Milly Erne's child. I must have little Fay. I want only her. I give up. I'll go and tell Bishop Dyer – I'm broken. I'll tell him I'm ready for the yoke – only give me back Fay – and – I'll marry Tull!'

'*Never!*' hissed Lassiter.

His long arm leaped at her. Almost running, he dragged her under the cottonwoods, across the court, into the huge hall of Withersteen House, and he shut the door with a force that jarred the heavy walls. Black Star and Night and Bells, since their return, had been locked in this hall, and now they stamped on the stone floor.

Lassiter released Jane and like a dizzy man swayed from her with a hoarse cry and leaned shaking against a table where he kept his rider's accoutrements. He began to fumble in his saddle-bags. His action brought a clinking, metallic sound – the rattling of gun-cartridges. His fingers trembled as he slipped cartridges into an extra belt. But as he buckled it over the one he habitually wore his hands became steady. This second belt contained two guns, smaller than the black ones swinging low, and he slipped them round so that his coat hid them. Then he fell to swift action. Jane Withersteen watched him, fascinated but uncomprehending; and she saw him rapidly saddle Black Star and Night. Then he drew her into the light of the huge window, standing over her, gripping her arm with fingers like cold steel.

'Yes, Jane, it's ended – but you're not goin' to Dyer! . . . *I'm goin' instead!*'

Looking at him – he was so terrible of aspect – she could not comprehend his words. Who was this man with the face gray as death, with eyes that would have made her shriek had she the strength, with the strange, ruthlessly bitter lips? Where was the gentle Lassiter? What was this presence in the hall, about him, about her – this cold, invisible presence?

'Yes, it's ended, Jane,' he was saying, so awfully quiet and cool and implacable, 'an' I'm goin' to make a little call. I'll lock you in here, an' when I get back have the saddle-bags full of meat an' bread. An' be ready to ride!'

'Lassiter!' cried Jane.

Desperately she tried to meet his gray eyes, in vain; desperately she tried again, fought herself as feeling and thought resurged in torment, and she succeeded; and then she knew.

'No – no – no!' she wailed. 'You said you'd foregone your vengeance. You promised not to kill Bishop Dyer.'

'If you want to talk to me about him – leave off the Bishop. I don't understand that name, or its use.'

'Oh, hadn't you foregone your vengeance on – on Dyer?'

'Yes.'

'But – your actions – your words – your guns – your terrible looks! . . . They don't seem foregoing vengeance?'

'Jane, now it's justice.'

'You'll – kill him?'

'If God lets me live another hour! If not God – then the devil who drives me!'

'You'll kill him – for yourself – for your vengeful hate?'

'No!'

'For Milly Erne's sake?'

'No.'

'For little Fay's?'

'No!'

'Oh – for whose?'

'For yours!'

'His blood on my soul!' whispered Jane, and she fell to her knees. This was the long-pending hour of fruition. And the habit of years – the religious passion of her life – leaped from lethargy, and the long months of gradual drifting to doubt were as if they had never been. 'If you spill his blood it'll be on my soul – and on my father's. Listen.' And she clasped his knees, and clung there as he tried to raise her. 'Listen. Am I nothing to you?'

'Woman – don't trifle at words! I love you! An' I'll soon prove it!'

'I'll give myself to you – I'll ride away with you – marry you, if only you'll spare him?'

His answer was a cold, ringing, terrible laugh.

'Lassiter – I'll love you. Spare him!'

'No!'

She sprang up in despairing, breaking spirit, and encircled his neck with her arms, and held him in an embrace that he strove vainly to loosen. 'Lassiter, would you kill me? I'm fighting my last fight for the principles of my youth – love of religion, love of father. You don't know – you can't guess the truth, and I can't speak it! I'm losing all. I'm changing. All I've gone through is nothing to this hour. Pity me – help me in my weakness. You're strong again – oh, so cruelly, coldly strong! You're killing me. I see you – feel you as some other Lassiter! My master, be merciful – spare him!'

His answer was a ruthless smile.

She clung closer to him, and leaned her panting breast on him, and lifted her face to his. 'Lassiter, I do love you! It's leaped out of my agony. It comes suddenly with a terrible blow of truth. You are a man! I never knew it till now. Some wonderful change came to me when you buckled on these guns and showed that gray, awful face. I loved you then. All my life I've loved, but never as now. No woman can love like a broken woman. If it were not for one thing – just one thing – and yet! I can't speak it – I'd glory in your manhood – the lion in you that means to slay for me. Believe me – and spare Dyer. Be merciful – great as it's in you to be great . . . Oh, listen and believe – I have nothing, but I'm a woman – a beautiful woman, Lassiter – a passionate, loving woman – and I love you! Take me – hide me in some wild place – and love me and mend my broken heart. Spare him and take me away.'

She lifted her face closer and closer to his, until their lips nearly touched, and she hung upon his neck, and with strength almost spent pressed and still pressed her palpitating body to his.

'Kiss me!' she whispered, blindly.

'No – not at your price!' he answered. His voice had changed or she had lost clearness of hearing.

'Kiss me! . . . Are you a man? Kiss me and save me!'

'Jane, you never played fair with me. But now you're blisterin' your lips – blackenin' your soul with lies!'

'By the memory of my mother – by my Bible – no! No, I have no Bible! But by my hope of heaven I swear I love you!'

Lassiter's gray lips formed soundless words that meant even her love could not avail to bend his will. As if the hold of her arms was that of a child's he loosened it and stepped away.

'Wait! Don't go! Oh, hear a last word! . . . May a more just and merciful God than the God I was taught to worship judge me – forgive me – save me! For I can no longer keep silent! . . . Lassiter, in pleading for Dyer I've been pleading more for my father. My father was a Mormon master, close to the leaders of the church. It was my father who sent Dyer out to proselyte. It was my father who had the blue-ice eye and the beard of gold. It was my father you got trace of in the past years. Truly, Dyer ruined Milly Erne – dragged her from her home – to Utah – to Cottonwoods. *But it was for my father!* If Milly Erne was ever wife of a Mormon that Mormon was my father! I never knew – never will know whether or not she was a wife. Blind I may be, Lassiter – fanatically faithful to a false religion I may have been, but I know justice, and my father is beyond human justice. Surely he is meeting just punishment – somewhere. Always it has appalled me – the thought of your killing Dyer for my father's sins. So I have prayed!'

'Jane, the past is dead. In my love for you I forgot the past. This thing I'm about to do ain't for myself or Milly or Fay. It's not because of anythin' that ever happened in the past, but for what is happenin' right *now*. *It's for you!* . . . An' listen. Since I was a boy I've never thanked God for anythin'. If there is a God – an' I've come to believe it – I thank Him now for the years that made me Lassiter! . . . I can reach down an' feel these big guns, an' know what I can do with them. An', Jane, only one of the miracles Dyer professes to believe in can save him!'

Again for Jane Withersteen came the spinning of her brain in darkness, and as she whirled in endless chaos she seemed to be falling at the feet of a luminous figure – a man – Lassiter – who had saved her from herself, who could not be changed, who would slay rightfully. Then she slipped into utter blackness.

When she recovered from her faint she became aware that she was lying on a couch near the window in her sitting-room. Her brow felt damp and cold and wet; someone was chafing her hands; she recognized Judkins, and then saw that his lean, hard face wore the hue and look of excessive agitation.

'Judkins!' Her voice broke weakly.

'Aw, Miss Withersteen, you're comin' round fine. Now jest lay still a little. You're all right; everythin's all right.'

'Where is – he?'

'Who?'

'Lassiter!'

'You needn't worry none about him.'

'Where is he? Tell me – instantly.'

'Wal, he's in the other room patchin' up a few triflin' bullet-holes.'

'Ah! . . . Bishop Dyer?'

'When I seen him last – a matter of half an hour ago, he was on his knees. He was some busy, *but* he wasn't prayin'!'

'How strangely you talk! I'll sit up. I'm – well, strong again. Tell me. Dyer on his knees! What was he doing?'

'Wal, beggin' your pardon fer blunt talk, Miss Withersteen, Dyer was on his knees an' *not* prayin'. You remember his big, broad hands? You've seen 'em raised in blessin' over old gray men an' little curly-headed children like – like Fay Larkin! Come to think of thet, I disremember ever hearin' of his liftin' his big hands in blessin' over a *woman*. Wal, when I seen him last – jest a little while ago – he was on his knees, *not* prayin', as I remarked – an' he was pressin' his big hands over some bigger wounds.'

'Man, you drive me mad! Did Lassiter kill Dyer?'

'Yes.'

'Did he kill Tull?'

'No. Tull's out of the village with most of his riders. He's expected back before evenin'. Lassiter will hev to git away before Tull an' his riders come in. It's sure death fer him here. An' wuss for you, too, Miss Withersteen. There'll be some of an uprisin' when Tull gits back.'

'I shall ride away with Lassiter. Judkins, tell me all you saw – all you know about this killing.' She realized, without wonder or amaze, how Judkins's one word, affirming the death of Dyer – that the catastrophe had fallen – had completed the change whereby she had been molded or beaten or broken into another woman. She felt calm, slightly cold, strong as she had not been strong since the first shadow fell upon her.

'I jest saw about all of it, Miss Withersteen, an' I'll be glad to tell you if you'll only hev patience with me,' said Judkins, earnestly. 'You see, I've been pecooliarly interested, an' nat'rully I'm some excited. An' I talk a lot thet mebbe ain't necessary, but I can't help thet.

'I was at the meetin'-house where Dyer was holdin' court. You know he allus acts as magistrate an' judge when Tull's away. An' the trial was fer tryin' what's left of my boy riders – thet helped me hold your cattle – fer a lot of hatched-up things the boys never did. We're used to thet, an' the boys wouldn't hev minded bein' locked up fer a while, or hevin' to dig ditches, or whatever the judge laid down. You see, I divided the gold you give me among all my boys, an' they all hid it, an' they all feel rich. Howsomever, court was adjourned before the judge passed sentence. Yes, ma'am, court was adjourned some strange an' quick, much as if lightnin' hed struck the meetin'-house.

'I hed trouble attendin' the trial, but I got in. There was a good many people there, all my boys, an' Judge Dyer with his several clerks. Also he hed with him the five riders who've been guardin' him pretty close of late. They was Carter, Wright, Jengessen, an' two new riders from Stone Bridge. I didn't hear their names, but I heard they was handy men with guns an' they looked more like rustlers than riders. Anyway, there they was, the five all in a row.

'Judge Dyer was tellin' Willie Kern, one of my best an' steadiest boys – Dyer was tellin' him how there was a ditch opened near Willie's home lettin' water through his lot, where it hadn't ought to go. An' Willie was tryin' to git a word in to prove he wasn't at home all the day it happened – which was true, as I know – but Willie couldn't git a word in, an' then Judge Dyer went on layin' down the law. An' all at once he happened to look down the long room. An' if ever any man turned to stone he was thet man.

'Nat'rully I looked back to see what hed acted so powerful strange on the judge. An' there, half-way up the room, in the middle of the wide aisle, stood Lassiter! All white an' black he looked an' I can't think of anythin' he resembled, onless it's death. Venters made thet same room some still an' chilly when he called Tull; but this was different. I give my word, Miss Withersteen, thet I went cold to my very marrow. I don't know why. But Lassiter has a way about him thet's awful. He spoke a word – a name – I couldn't understand it, though he spoke clear as a bell. I was too excited, mebbe. Judge Dyer must hev understood it, an' a lot more thet was mystery to me, fer he pitched forward out of his chair right on to the platform.

'Then them five riders, Dyer's bodyguards, they jumped up, an' two of them thet I found out afterward were the strangers from Stone Bridge, they piled right out of a winder, so quick you couldn't catch your breath. It was plain they wasn't Mormons.

'Jengessen, Carter, an' Wright eyed Lassiter, for what must hev been a second an' seemed like an hour, an' they went white an' strung. But they didn't weaken nor lose their nerve.

'I hed a good look at Lassiter. He stood sort of stiff, bendin' a little, an' both his arms were crooked, an' his hands looked like a hawk's claws. But there ain't no tellin' how his eyes looked. I know this, though, an' thet is his eyes could read the mind of any man about to throw a gun. An' in watchin' him, of course, I couldn't see the three men go fer their guns. An' though I was lookin' right at Lassiter – lookin' hard – I couldn't see how he drawed. He was quicker'n eyesight – thet's all. But I seen the red spurtin' of his guns, an' heard his shots jest the very littlest instant before I heard the shots of the riders. An' when I turned, Wright an' Carter was down, an' Jengessen, who's tough like a steer, was pullin' the trigger of a wabblin' gun. But it was plain he was shot through, plumb center. An' sudden he fell with a crash, an' his gun clattered on the floor.

'Then there was a hell of a silence. Nobody breathed. Sartin I didn't, anyway. I saw Lassiter slip a smokin' gun back in a belt. But he hadn't throwed either of the big black guns, an' I thought thet strange. An' all this was happenin' quick – you can't imagine how quick.

'There come a scrapin' on the floor an' Dyer got up, his face like lead. I wanted to watch Lassiter, but Dyer's face, onct I seen it like thet, glued my eyes. I seen him go fer his gun – why, I could hev done better, quicker – an' then there was a thunderin' shot from Lassiter, an' it hit Dyer's right arm, an' his gun went off as it dropped. He looked at Lassiter like a cornered sage-wolf, an' sort of howled, an' reached down fer his gun. He'd jest picked it off the floor an' was raisin' it when another thunderin' shot almost tore thet arm off – so it seemed to me. The gun dropped again an' he went down on his knees, kind of flounderin' after it. It was some strange an' terrible to see his awful earnestness. Why would such a man cling so to life? Anyway, he got the gun with left hand an' was raisin' it, pullin' trigger in his madness, when the third thunderin' shot hit his left arm, an' he dropped the gun again. But thet left arm wasn't useless yet, fer he grabbed up the gun, an' with a shakin' aim thet would hev been pitiful to me – in any other man – he began to shoot. One wild bullet struck a man twenty feet from Lassiter. An' it killed thet man, as I seen afterward. Then come a bunch of thunderin' shots – nine I calkilated after, fer they come so quick I couldn't count them – an' I knew Lassiter hed turned the black guns loose on Dyer.

'I'm tellin' you straight, Miss Withersteen, fer I want you to know. Afterward you'll git over it. I've seen some soul-rackin' scenes on this Utah border, but this was the awfulest. I remember I closed my eyes, an' fer a minute I thought of the strangest things, out of place there, such as you'd never dream would come to mind. I saw the sage, an' runnin' hosses – an' thet's the beautifulest sight to me – an' I saw dim things in the dark, an' there was a kind of hummin' in my ears. An' I remember distinctly – fer it was what made all these things whirl out of my mind an' opened my eyes – I remember distinctly it was the smell of gunpowder.

'The court had about adjourned fer thet judge. He was on his knees, an' he wasn't prayin'. He was gaspin' an' trying' to press his big, floppin', crippled hands over his body. Lassiter had sent all those last thunderin' shots through his body. Thet was Lassiter's way.

'An' Lassiter spoke, an' if I ever forgit his words I'll never forgit the sound of his voice.

' "*Proselyter*, I reckon you'd better call quick on thet God who reveals Hisself to you on earth, because He won't be visitin' the place you're goin' to!"

'An' then I seen Dyer look at his big, hangin' hands thet wasn't big enough fer the last work he set them to. An' he looked up at Lassiter. An' then he stared horrible at somethin' thet wasn't Lassiter, nor anyone there, nor the room, nor the branches of purple sage peepin' into the winder. Whatever he seen, it was with the look of a man who *discovers* somethin' too late. Thet's a terrible look! . . . An' with a horrible *understandin'* cry he slid forward on his face.'

Judkins paused in his narrative, breathing heavily while he wiped his perspiring brow.

'Thet's about all,' he concluded. 'Lassiter left the meetin'-house an' I hurried to catch up with him. He was bleedin' from three gunshots, none of them much to bother him. An' we come right up here. I found you layin' in the hall, an' I hed to work some over you.'

Jane Withersteen offered up no prayer for Dyer's soul.

Lassiter's step sounded in the hall – the familiar soft, silver-clinking step – and she heard it with thrilling new emotions in which was a vague joy in her very fear of him. The door opened, and she saw him, the old Lassiter, slow, easy, gentle, cool, yet not exactly the same Lassiter. She rose, and for a moment her eyes blurred and swam in tears.

'Are you – all – all right?' she asked, tremulously.

'I reckon.'

'Lassiter, I'll ride away with you. Hide me till danger is past – till we are forgotten – then take me where you will. Your people shall be my people, and your God my God!'

He kissed her hand with the quaint grace and courtesy that came to him in rare moments.

'Black Star an' Night are ready,' he said, simply.

His quiet mention of the black racers spurred Jane to action. Hurrying to her room, she changed to her rider's suit, packed her jewelry, and the gold that was left, and all the woman's apparel for which there was space in the saddle-bags, and then returned to the hall. Black Star stamped his iron-shod hoofs and tossed his beautiful head, and eyed her with knowing eyes.

'Judkins, I give Bells to you,' said Jane. 'I hope you will always keep him and be good to him.'

Judkins mumbled thanks that he could not speak fluently, and his eyes flashed.

Lassiter strapped Jane's saddle-bags upon Black Star, and led the racers out into the court.

'Judkins, you ride with Jane out into the sage. If you see any riders comin' shout quick twice. An', Jane, *don't look back!* I'll catch up soon. We'll get to the break into the Pass before midnight, an' then wait until mornin' to go down.'

Black Star bent his graceful neck and bowed his noble head, and his broad shoulders yielded as he knelt for Jane to mount.

She rode out of the court beside Judkins, through the grove, across the wide lane into the sage, and she realized that she was leaving Withersteen House forever, and she did not look back. A strange, dreamy, calm peace pervaded her soul. Her doom had fallen upon her, but, instead of finding life no longer worth living she found it doubly significant, full of sweetness as the western breeze, beautiful and unknown as the sage-slope stretching its purple sunset shadows before her. She became aware of Judkins's hand touching hers; she heard him speak a husky good-bye; then into the place of Bells shot the dead-black, keen, racy nose of Night, and she knew Lassiter rode beside her.

'Don't – look – back!' he said, and his voice, too, was not clear.

Facing straight ahead, seeing only the waving, shadowy sage, Jane held out her gauntleted hand, to feel it enclosed in strong clasp. So she rode on without a backward glance at the beautiful grove of Cottonwoods. She did not seem to think of the past, of what she left forever, but of the color and mystery and wildness of the sage-slope leading down to Deception Pass, and of the future. She watched the shadows lengthen down the slope; she felt the cool west wind sweeping by from the rear; and she wondered at low, yellow clouds sailing swiftly over her and beyond.

'Don't – look – back!' said Lassiter.

Thick-driving belts of smoke traveled by on the wind, and with it came a strong, pungent odor of burning wood.

Lassiter had fired Withersteen House! But Jane did not look back.

A misty veil obscured the clear, searching gaze she had kept steadfastly upon the purple slope and the dim lines of cañons. It passed, as passed the rolling clouds of smoke, and she saw the valley deepening into the shades of twilight. Night came on, swift as the fleet racers, and stars peeped out to brighten and grow, and the huge, windy, eastern heave of sage-level paled under a rising moon and turned to silver. Blanched in moonlight, the sage yet seemed to hold its hue of purple and was infinitely more wild and lonely. So the night hours wore on, and Jane Withersteen never once looked back.

CHAPTER TWENTY-ONE

Black Star and Night

THE TIME HAD COME FOR Venters and Bess to leave their retreat. They were at great pains to choose the few things they would be able to carry with them on the journey out of Utah.

'Bern, whatever kind of a pack's this, anyhow?' questioned Bess, rising from her work with reddened face.

Venters, absorbed in his own task, did not look up at all, and in reply said he had brought so much from Cottonwoods that he did not recollect the half of it.

'A woman packed this!' Bess exclaimed.

He scarcely caught her meaning, but the peculiar tone of her voice caused him instantly to rise, and he saw Bess on her knees before an open pack which he recognized as the one given him by Jane.

'By George!' he ejaculated, guiltily, and then a sight of Bess's face he laughed outright.

'A woman packed this,' she repeated, fixing woeful, tragic eyes on him.

'Well, is that a crime?'

'There – there is a woman, after all!'

'Now Bess – '

'You've lied to me!'

Then and there Venters found it imperative to postpone work for the present. All her life Bess had been isolated, but she had inherited certain elements of the eternal feminine.

'But there *was* a woman and you *did* lie to me,' she kept repeating, after he had explained.

'What of that? Bess, I'll get angry at you in a moment. Remember you've been pent up all your life. I venture to say that if you'd been out in the world you'd have had a dozen sweethearts and had told many a lie before this.'

'I wouldn't anything of the kind,' declared Bess, indignantly.

'Well – perhaps not a lie. But you'd have had the sweethearts. You couldn't have helped that – being so pretty.'

This remark appeared to be a very clever and fortunate one; and the work of selecting and then of stowing all the packs in the cave went on without further interruption.

Venters closed up the opening of the cave with a thatch of willows and aspens, so that not even a bird or a rat could get in to the sacks of grain. And this work was in order with the precaution habitually observed by him. He might not be able to get out of Utah, and have to return to the valley. But he owed it to Bess to make the attempt, and in case they were compelled to turn back he wanted to find that fine store of food and grain intact. The outfit of implements and utensils he packed away in another cave.

'Bess, we have enough to live here all our lives,' he said once, dreamily.

'Shall I go roll Balancing Rock?' she asked, in light speech, but with deep-blue fire in her eyes.

'No – no.'

'Ah, you don't forget the gold and the world,' she signed.

'Child, you forget the beautiful dresses and the travel – and everything.'

'Oh, I want to go. But I want to stay!'

'I feel the same way.'

They let the eight calves out of the corral, and kept only two of the burros Venters had brought from Cottonwoods. These they intended to hide. Bess freed all her pets – the quail and rabbits and foxes.

The last sunset and twilight and night were both the sweetest and saddest they had ever spent in Surprise Valley. Morning brought keen exhilaration and excitement. When Venters had saddled the two burros, strapped on the light packs and the two canteens, the sunlight was dispersing the lazy shadows from the valley. Taking a last look at the caves and the silver spruces, Venters and Bess made a reluctant start, leading the burros. Ring and Whitie looked keen and knowing. Something seemed to drag at Venters's feet and he noticed Bess lagged behind. Never had the climb from terrace to bridge appeared so long.

Not till they reached the opening of the gorge did they stop to rest and take one last look at the valley. The tremendous arch of stone curved clear and sharp in outline against the morning sky. And through it streaked the golden shaft. The valley seemed an enchanted circle of glorious veils of gold and wraiths of white and silver haze and dim, blue, moving shade – beautiful and wild and unreal as a dream.

'We – we – can – th – think of it – always – re – re – member,' sobbed Bess.

'Hush! Don't cry. Our valley has only fitted us for a better life somewhere. Come!'

They entered the gorge and he closed the willow gate. From rosy, golden morning light they passed into cool, dense gloom. The burros pattered up the trail with little hollow-cracking steps. And the gorge widened to narrow outlet and the gloom lightened to gray. At the divide they halted for another rest. Venters's keen, remembering gaze searched Balancing Rock, and the long incline, and the cracked toppling walls, but failed to note the slightest change.

The dogs led the descent; then came Bess leading her burro; then Venters leading his. Bess kept her eyes bent downward. Venters, however, had an irresistible desire to look upward at Balancing Rock. It had always haunted him, and now he wondered if he were really to get through the outlet before the huge stone thundered down. He fancied that would be a miracle. Every few steps he answered to the strange, nervous fear and turned to make sure the rock still stood like a giant statue. And, as he descended, it grew dimmer in his sight. It changed form; it swayed; it nodded darkly; and at last, in his heightened fancy, he saw it heave and roll. As in a dream when he felt himself falling yet knew he would never fall, so he saw this long-standing thunderbolt of the little stone-men plunge down to close forever the outlet to Deception Pass.

And while he was giving way to unaccountable dread imaginations the descent was accomplished without mishap.

'I'm glad that's over,' he said, breathing more freely. 'I hope I'm by that hanging rock for good and all. Since almost the moment I first saw it I've had an idea that it was waiting for me. Now, when it does fall, if I'm thousands of miles away, I'll hear it.'

With the first glimpses of the smooth slope leading down to the grotesque cedars and out to the Pass, Venters's cool nerve returned. One long survey to the left, then one to the right, satisfied his caution. Leading the burros down to the spur of the rock, he halted at the steep incline.

'Bess, here's the bad place, the place I told you about, with the cut steps. You start down, leading your burro. Take your time and hold on to him if you slip. I've got a rope on him and a half-hitch on this point of rock, so I can let him down safely. Coming up here was a killing job. But it'll be easy going down.'

Both burros passed down the difficult stairs cut by the cliff-dwellers, and did it without a misstep. After that the descent down the slope and over the mile of scrawled, ribbed, and ridged rock required only careful guidance, and Venters got the burros to level ground in a condition that caused him to congratulate himself.

'Oh, if we only had Wrangle!' exclaimed Venters. 'But we're lucky. That's the worst of our trail passed. We've only men to fear now. If we get up in the sage we can hide and slip along like coyotes.'

They mounted and rode west through the valley and entered the cañon. From time to time Venters walked, leading his burro. When they got by all the cañons and gullies opening into the Pass they went faster and with fewer halts. Venters did not confide in Bess the alarming fact that he had seen horses and smoke less than a mile up one of the intersecting cañons. He did not talk at all. And long after he had passed this cañon and felt secure once more in the certainty that they had been unobserved he never relaxed his watchfulness. But he did not walk any more, and he kept the burros at a steady trot. Night fell before they reached the last water in the Pass and they made camp by starlight. Venters did not want the burros to stray, so he tied them with long halters in the grass near the spring. Bess, tired out and silent, laid her head in a saddle and went to sleep between the two dogs. Venters did not close his eyes. The cañon silence appeared full of the low, continuous hum of insects. He listened until the hum grew into a roar, and then, breaking the spell, once more he heard it low and clear. He watched the stars and the moving shadows, and always his glance returned to the girl's dimly pale face. And he remembered how white and still it had once looked in the starlight. And again stern thought fought his strange fancies. Would all his labor and his love be for naught? Would he lose her, after all? Did calamity lurk on that long upland trail through the sage? Why should his heart swell and throb with nameless fear? He listened to the silence, and told himself that in the broad light of day he could dispel this leaden-weighted dread.

At the first hint of gray over the eastern rim he awoke Bess, saddled the burros, and began the day's travel. He wanted to get out of the Pass before there was any chance of riders coming down. They gained the break as the first red rays of the rising sun colored the rim.

For once, so eager was he to get up to level ground, he did not send Ring or Whitie in advance. Encouraging Bess to hurry, pulling at his patient, plodding burro, he climbed the soft, steep trail.

Brighter and brighter grew the light. He mounted the last broken edge of rim to have the sun-fired, purple sage-slope burst upon him as a glory. Bess panted up to his side, tugging on the halter of her burro.

'We're up!' he cried, joyously. 'There's not a dot on the sage. We're safe. We'll not be seen! Oh, Bess – '

Ring growled and sniffed the keen air and bristled. Venters clutched at his rifle. Whitie sometimes made a mistake, but Ring never. The dull thud of hoofs almost deprived Venters of power to turn and see from where disaster threatened. He felt his eyes dilate as he stared at Lassiter leading Black Star and Night out of the sage, with Jane Withersteen, in rider's costume, close beside them.

For an instant Venters felt himself whirl dizzily in the center of vast circles of sage. He recovered partially, enough to see Lassiter standing with a glad smile and Jane riveted in astonishment.

'Why, Bern!' she exclaimed. 'How good it is to see you! We're riding away, you see. The storm burst – and I'm a ruined woman! . . . I thought you were alone.'

Venters, unable to speak for consternation, and bewildered out of all sense of what he ought or ought not to do, simply stared at Jane.

'Son, where are you bound for?' asked Lassiter.

'Not safe – where I was. I'm – we're going out of Utah – back East,' he found tongue to say.

'I reckon this meetin's the luckiest thing that ever happened to you an' to me – an' to Jane – an' to Bess,' said Lassiter, coolly.

'*Bess!*' cried Jane, with a sudden leap of blood to her pale cheek.

It was entirely beyond Venters to see any luck in that meeting.

Jane Withersteen took one flashing, woman's glance at Bess's scarlet face, at her slender, shapely form.

'Venters! is this a girl – a woman?' she questioned, in a voice that stung. 'Yes.'

'Did you have her in that wonderful valley?'

'Yes, but Jane – '

'All the time you were gone?'

'Yes, but I couldn't tell – '

'Was it for *her* you asked me to give you supplies? Was it for *her* that you wanted to make your valley a paradise?'

'Oh – Jane – '

'Answer me.'

'Yes.'

'Oh, you liar!' And with these passionate words Jane Withersteen succumbed to fury. For the second time in her life she fell into the ungovernable rage that had been her father's weakness. And it was worse than his, for she was a jealous woman – jealous even of her friends.

As best he could, he bore the brunt of her anger. It was not only his deceit to her that she visited upon him, but her betrayal by religion, by life itself.

Her passion, like fire at white heat, consumed itself in little time. Her physical strength failed, and still her spirit attempted to go on in magnificent denunciation of those who had wronged her. Like a tree cut deep into its roots, she began to quiver and shake, and her anger weakened into despair. And her ringing voice sank into a broken, husky whisper. Then, spent and pitiable, upheld by Lassiter's arm, she turned and hid her face in Black Star's mane.

Numb as Venters was when at length Jane Withersteen lifted her head and looked at him, he yet suffered a pang.

'Jane, the girl is innocent!' he cried.

'Can you expect me to believe that?' she asked, with weary, bitter eyes.

'I'm not that kind of a liar. And you know it. If I lied – if I kept silent when honor should have made me speak, it was to spare you. I came to Cottonwoods to tell you. But I couldn't add to your pain. I intended to tell you I had come to love this girl. But, Jane, I hadn't forgotten how good you were to me. I haven't changed at all toward you. I prize your friendship as I always have. But, however it may look to you – don't be unjust. The girl is innocent. Ask Lassiter.'

'Jane, she's jest as sweet an' innocent as little Fay,' said Lassiter. There was a faint smile upon his face and a beautiful light.

Venters saw, and knew that Lassiter saw, how Jane Withersteen's tortured soul wrestled with hate and threw it – with scorn, doubt, suspicion, and overcame all.

'Bern, if in my misery I accused you unjustly, I crave forgiveness,' she said. 'I'm not what I once was. Tell me – who is this girl?'

'Jane, she is Oldring's daughter, and his Masked Rider. Lassiter will tell you how I shot her for a rustler, saved her life – all the story. It's a strange story, Jane, as wild as the sage. But it's true – true as her innocence. That you must believe!'

'Oldring's Masked Rider! Oldring's daughter!' exclaimed Jane. 'And she's innocent! You ask me to believe much. If this girl is – is what you say, how could she be going away with the man who killed her father?'

'Why did you tell that?' cried Venters, passionately.

Jane's question had roused Bess out of stupefaction. Her eyes suddenly darkened and dilated. She stepped toward Venters and held up both hands as if to ward off a blow.

'Did – did you kill Oldring?'

'I did, Bess, and I hate myself for it. But you know I never dreamed he was your father. I thought he'd wronged you. I killed him when I was madly jealous.'

For a moment Bess was shocked into silence.

'But he was my father!' she broke out, at last. 'And now I must go back – I can't go with you. It's all over – that beautiful dream. Oh, I *knew* it couldn't come true. You can't take me now.'

'If you forgive me, Bess, it'll all come right in the end!' implored Venters.

'It can't be right. I'll go back. After all, I loved him. He was good to me. I can't forget that.'

'If you go back to Oldring's men I'll follow you, and then they'll kill me,' said Venters, hoarsely.

'Oh no, Bern, you'll not come. Let me go. It's best for you to forget me. I've brought you only pain and dishonor.'

She did not weep. But the sweet bloom and life died out of her face. She looked haggard and sad, all at once stunted; and her hands dropped listlessly; and her head drooped in slow, final acceptance of a hopeless fate.

'Jane, look there!' cried Venters, in despairing grief. 'Need you have told her? Where was all your kindness of heart? This girl has had a wretched, lonely life. And I'd found a way to make her happy. You've killed it. You've killed something sweet and pure and hopeful, just as sure as you breathe.'

'Oh, Bern! It was a slip. I never thought – I never thought!' replied Jane. 'How could I tell she didn't know?'

Lassiter suddenly moved forward, and with the beautiful light on his face now strangely luminous, he looked at Jane and Venters and then let his soft, bright gaze rest on Bess.

'Well, I reckon you've all had your say, an' now it's Lassiter's turn. Why, I was jest prayin' for this meetin'. Bess, jest look here.'

Gently he touched her arm and turned her to face the others, and then outspread his great hand to disclose a shiny, battered gold locket.

'Open it,' he said, with a singularly rich voice.

Bess complied, but listlessly.

'Jane – Venters – come closer,' went on Lassiter. 'Take a look at the picture. Don't you know the woman?'

Jane, after one glance, drew back.

'Milly Erne!' she cried, wonderingly.

Venters, with tingling pulse, with something growing on him, recognized in the faded miniature portrait the eyes of Milly Erne.

'Yes, that's Milly,' said Lassiter, softly. 'Bess, did you ever see her face – look hard – with all your heart an' soul?'

'The eyes seem to haunt me,' whispered Bess. 'Oh, I can't remember – they're eyes of my dreams – but – but – '

Lassiter's strong arm went round her and he bent his head.

'Child, I thought you'd remember her eyes. They're the same beautiful eyes you'd see if you looked in a mirror or a clear spring. They're your mother's eyes. You are Milly Erne's child. Your name is Elizabeth Erne. You're not Oldring's daughter. You're the daughter of Frank Erne, a man once my best friend. Look! Here's his picture beside Milly's. He was handsome, an' as fine an' gallant a Southern gentleman as I ever seen. Frank come of an old family. You come of the best of blood, lass, an' blood tells.'

Bess slipped through his arm to her knees and hugged the locket to her bosom, and lifted wonderful, yearning eyes.

'It – can't – be – true!'

'Thank God, lass, it is true,' replied Lassiter. 'Jane an' Bern here – they both recognize Milly. They see Milly in you. They're so knocked out they can't tell you, that's all.'

'Who are you?' whispered Bess.

'I reckon I'm Milly's brother an' your uncle! . . . Uncle Jim! Ain't that fine?'

'Oh, I can't believe – Don't raise me! Bern, let me kneel. I see truth in your face – in Miss Withersteen's. But let me hear it all – on my knees. Tell me how it's true!'

'Well, Elizabeth, listen,' said Lassiter. 'Before you was born your father made a mortal enemy of a Mormon named Dyer. They was both ministers an' come to be rivals. Dyer stole your mother away from her home. She gave birth to you in Texas eighteen years ago. Then she was taken to Utah, from place to place, an' finally to the last border settlement – Cottonwoods. You was about three years old when you was taken away from Milly. She never knew what had become of you. But she lived a good while hopin' and prayin' to have you again. Then she gave up an' died. An' I may as well put in here your father died ten years ago. Well, I spent my time tracin' Milly, an' some months back I landed in Cottonwoods. An' jest lately I learned all about you. I had a talk with Oldrin' an' told him you was dead, an' he told me what I had so long been wantin' to know. It was Dyer, of course, who stole you from Milly. Part reason he was sore because Milly refused to give you Mormon teachin', but mostly he still hated Frank Erne so infernally that he made a deal with Oldrin' to take you an' bring you up as an infamous rustler an' rustler's girl. The idea was to break Frank Erne's heart if he ever came to Utah – to show him his daughter with a band of low rustlers. Well – Oldrin' took you, brought you up from childhood, an' then made you his Masked Rider. He made you infamous. He kept that part of the contract, but he learned to love you as a daughter an' never let any but his own men know you was a girl. I heard him say that with my own ears, an' I saw his big eyes grow dim. He told me how he had guarded you always, kept you locked up in his absence, was always at your side or near you on those rides that made you famous on the sage. He said he an' an old rustler whom he trusted had taught you how to read an' write. They selected the books for you. Dyer had wanted you brought up the vilest of the vile! An' Oldrin' brought you up the innocentest of the innocent. He said you didn't know what vileness was. I can hear his big voice tremble now as he said it. He told me how the men – rustlers an' outlaws – who from time to time tried to approach you familiarly – he told me how he shot them dead. I'm tellin' you this 'specially because you've showed such shame – sayin' you was nameless an' all that. Nothin' on earth can be wronger than that idea of yours. An' the truth of it is here. Oldrin' swore to me that if Dyer died, releasin' the contract, he intended to hunt up your father an' give you back to him. It seems Oldrin' wasn't all bad, an' he sure loved you.'

Venters leaned forward in passionate remorse.

'Oh, Bess! I know Lassiter speaks the truth. For when I shot Oldring he dropped to his knees and fought with unearthly power to speak. And he said: "Man – why – didn't – you – wait? Bess was – " Then he fell dead. And I've been haunted by his look and words. Oh, Bess, what a strange, splendid thing for Oldring to do! It all seems impossible. But, dear, you really are not what you thought.'

'Elizabeth Erne!' cried Jane Withersteen. 'I loved your mother and I see her in you!'

What had been incredible from the lips of men became, in the tone, look, and gesture of a woman, a wonderful truth for Bess. With little tremblings of all her slender body she rocked to and fro on her knees. The yearning wistfulness of her eyes changed to solemn splendor of joy. She believed. She was realizing happiness. And as the process of thought was slow, so were the variations of her expression. Her eyes reflected the transformation of her soul. Dark, brooding, hopeless belief – clouds of gloom – drifted, paled, vanished in glorious light. An exquisite rose flush – a glow – shone from her face as she slowly began to rise from her knees. A spitit uplifted her. All that she had held as base dropped from her.

Venters watched her in joy too deep for words. By it he divined something of what Lassiter's revelation meant to Bess, but he knew he could only faintly understand. That moment when she seemed to be lifted by some spiritual transfiguration was the most beautiful moment of his life. She stood with parted, quivering lips, with hands tightly clasping the locket to her heaving breast. A new conscious pride of worth dignified the old, wild, free grace and poise.

'Uncle Jim!' she said, tremulously, with a different smile from any Venters had ever seen on her face.

Lassiter took her into his arms.

'I reckon. It's powerful fine to hear that,' replied Lassiter, unsteadily.

Venters, feeling his eyes grow hot and wet, turned away, and found himself looking at Jane Withersteen. He had almost forgotten her presence. Tenderness and sympathy were fast hiding traces of her agitation. Venters read her mind – felt the reaction of her noble heart – saw the joy she was beginning to feel at the happiness of others. And suddenly blinded, choked by his emotions, he turned from her also. He knew what she would do presently; she would make some magnificent amend for her anger; she would give some manifestation of her love; probably all in a moment, as she had loved Milly Erne, so would she love Elizabeth Erne.

"Pears to me, folks, that we'd better talk a little serious now,' remarked Lassiter, at length. 'Time flies.'

'You're right, replied Venters, instantly. 'I'd forgotten time – place – danger. Lassiter, you're riding away. Jane's leaving Withersteen House?'

'Forever,' replied Jane.

'I fired Withersteen House,' said Lassiter.

'Dyer?' questioned Venters, sharply.

'I reckon where Dyer's gone there won't be any kidnappin' of girls.'

'Ah! I knew it. I told Judkins – And Tull?' went on Venters, passionately.

'Tull wasn't around when I broke loose. By now he's likely on our trail with his riders.'

'Lassiter, you're going into the Pass to hide till all this storm blows over?'

'I reckon that's Jane's idea. I'm thinkin' the storm'll be a powerful long time blowin' over. I was comin' to join you in Surprise Valley. You'll go back now with me?'

'No. I want to take Bess out of Utah. Lassiter, Bess found gold in the valley. We've a saddle-bag full of gold. If we can reach Sterling – '

'Man! how're you ever goin' to do that? Sterlin' is a hundred miles.'

'My plan is to ride on, keeping a sharp lookout. Somewhere up the trail we'll take to the sage and go round Cottonwoods and then hit the trail again.'

'It's a bad plan. You'll kill the burros in two days.'

'Then we'll walk.'

'That's more bad an' worse. Better go back down the Pass with me.'

'Lassiter, this girl has been hidden all her life in that lonely place,' went on Venters. 'Oldring's men are hunting me. We'd not be safe there any longer. Even if we would be I'd take this chance to get her out. I want to marry her. She shall have some of the pleasures of life – see cities and people. We've gold – we'll be rich. Why, life opens sweet for both of us. And, by Heaven! I'll get her out or lose my life in the attempt!'

'I reckon if you go on with them burros you'll lose your life all right. Tull will have riders all over this sage. You can't get out on them burros. It's a fool idea. That's not doin' best by the girl. Come with me an' take chances on the rustlers.'

Lassiter's cool arguments made Venters waver, not in determination to go, but in hope of success.

'Bess, I want you to know. Lassiter says the trip's almost useless now. I'm afraid he's right. We've got about one chance in a hundred to go through. Shall we take it? Shall we go on?'

'We'll go on,' replied Bess.

'That settles it, Lassiter.'

Lassiter spread wide his hands, as if to signify he could do no more, and his face clouded.

Venters felt a touch on his elbow. Jane stood beside him with a hand on his arm. She was smiling. Something radiated from her, and like an electric current accelerated the motion of his blood.

'Bern, you'd be right to die rather than not take Elizabeth out of Utah – out of this wild country. You must do it. You'll show her the great world, with all its wonders. Think how little she has seen! Think what delight is in store for her! You have gold; you will be free; you will make her happy. What a glorious prospect! I share it with you. I'll think of you – dream of you – pray for you.'

'Thank you, Jane,' replied Venters, trying to steady his voice. 'It looks bright. Oh, if we were only across that wide, open waste of sage!'

'Bern, the trip's as good as made. It'll be safe – easy. It'll be a glorious ride,' she said, softly.

Venters stared. Had Jane's troubles made her insane? Lassiter, too, acted queerly, all at once beginning to turn his sombrero round with hands that actually shook.

'You are a rider. She is a rider. This will be the ride of your lives,' added Jane, in that same soft undertone, almost as if she were musing to herself.

'Jane!' he cried.

'I give you Black Star and Night!'

'*Black Star and Night!*' he echoed.

'It's done. Lassiter, put our saddle-bags on the burros.'

Only when Lassiter moved swiftly to execute her bidding did Venters's clogged brain grasp at literal meanings. He leaped to catch Lassiter's busy hands.

'No, no! What are you doing?' he demanded, in a kind of fury. 'I won't take her racers. What do you think I am? It'd be monstrous. Lassiter! stop it, I say! . . . You've got her to save. You've miles and miles to go. Tull is trailing you. There are rustlers in the Pass. Give me back that saddle-bag!'

'Son – cool down,' returned Lassiter, in a voice he might have used to a child. But the grip with which he tore away Venters's grasping hands was that of a giant. 'Listen – you fool boy! Jane's sized up the situation. The burros'll do for us. We'll sneak along an' hide. I'll take your dogs an' your rifle. Why, it's the trick. The blacks are yours, an' sure as I can throw a gun you're goin' to ride safe out of the sage.'

'Jane – stop him – please stop him,' gasped Venters. 'I've lost my strength. I can't do – anything. This's hell for me! Can't you see that? I've ruined you – it was through me you lost all. You've only Black Star and Night left. You love these horses. Oh! I know how you must love them now! And – you're trying to give them to me. To help me out of Utah! To save the girl I love!'

'That will be my glory.'

Then in the white, rapt face, in the unfathomable eyes, Venters saw Jane Withersteen in a supreme moment. This moment was one wherein she reached up to the height for which her noble soul had ever yearned. He, after disrupting the calm tenor of her peace, after bringing down on her head the implacable hostility of her churchmen, after teaching her a bitter lesson of life – he was to be her salvation. And he turned away again, this time shaken to the core of his soul. Jane

Withersteen was the incarnation of selflessness. He experienced wonder and terror, exquisite pain and rapture. What were all the shocks life had dealt him compared to the thought of such loyal and generous friendship?

And instantly, as if by some divine insight, he knew himself in the remaking – tried, found wanting; but stronger, better, surer – and he wheeled to Jane Withersteen, eager, joyous, passionate, wild, exalted. He bent to her; he left tears and kisses on her hands.

'Jane, I – I can't find words – now,' he said. 'I'm beyond words. Only – I understand. And I'll take the blacks.'

'Don't be losin' no more time,' cut in Lassiter. 'I ain't certain, but I think I seen a speck up the sage-slope. Mebbe I was mistaken. But, anyway, we must all be movin'. I've shortened the stirrups on Black Star. Put Bess on him.'

Jane Withersteen held out her arms.

'Elizabeth Erne!' she cried, and Bess flew to her.

How inconceivably strange and beautiful it was for Venters to see Bess clasped to Jane Withersteen's breast!

Then he leaped astride Night.

'Venters, ride straight on up the slope,' Lassiter was saying, 'an' if you don't meet any riders keep on till you're a few miles from the village, then cut off in the sage an' go round to the trail. But you'll most likely meet riders with Tull. Jest keep right on till you're just out of gunshot an' then make your cut-off into the sage. They'll ride after you, but it won't be no use. You can ride, an' Bess can ride. When you're out of reach turn on round to the west, an' hit the trail somewhere. Save the hosses all you can, but don't be afraid. Black Star and Night are good for a hundred miles before sundown, if you have to push them. You can get to Sterlin' by night if you want. But better make it along about tomorrow mornin'. When you get through the notch on the Glaze trail, swing to the right. You'll be able to see both Glaze an' Stone Bridge. Keep away from them villages. You won't run no risk of meetin' any of Oldrin's rustlers from Sterlin' on. You'll find water in them deep hollows north of the Notch. There's an old trail there, not much used, an' it leads to Sterlin'. That's your trail. An' one thing more. If Tull pushes you – or keeps on persistent-like, for a few miles – jest let the blacks out an' lose him an' his riders.'

'Lassiter, may we meet again!' said Venters, in a deep voice.

'Son, it ain't likely – it ain't likely. Well, Bess Oldrin' – Masked Rider – Elizabeth Erne – now you climb on Black Star. I've heard you could ride. Well, every rider loves a good hoss. An', lass, there never was but one that could beat Black Star.'

'Ah, Lassiter, there never was any horse that could beat Black Star,' said Jane, with the old pride.

'I often wondered – mebbe Venters rode out that race when he brought back the blacks. Son, was Wrangle the best hoss?'

'No, Lassiter,' replied Venters. For this lie he had his reward in Jane's quick smile.

'Well, well, my hoss-sense ain't always right. An' here I'm talkin' a lot, wastin' time. It ain't so easy to find an' lose a pretty niece all in one hour! Elizabeth – good-bye!'

'Oh, Uncle Jim! . . . Good-bye!'

'Elizabeth Erne, be happy! Good-bye,' said Jane.

'Good-bye – oh – good-bye!'

In lithe, supple action Bess swung up to Black Star's saddle.

'Jane Withersteen! . . . Good-bye!' called Venters hoarsely.
'Bern – Bess – riders of the purple sage – good-bye!'

TWENTY-TWO

Riders of the Purple Sage

BLACK STAR AND NIGHT, answering to spur, swept swiftly westward along the white, slow-rising, sage-bordered trail. Venters heard a mournful howl from Ring, but Whitie was silent. The blacks settled into their fleet, long-striding gallop. The wind sweetly fanned Venters's hot face. From the summit of the first low-swelling ridge he looked back. Lassiter waved his hand; Jane waved her scarf. Venters replied by standing in his stirrups and holding high his sombrero. Then the dip of the ridge hid them. From the height of the next he turned once more. Lassiter, Jane, and the burros had disappeared. They had gone down into the Pass. Venters felt a sensation of irreparable loss.

'Bern – look!' called Bess, pointing up the long slope.

A small, dark, moving dot split the line where purple sage met blue sky. That dot was a band of riders.

'Pull the black, Bess.'

They slowed from gallop to canter, then to trot. The fresh and eager horses did not like the check.

'Bern, Black Star has great eyesight.'

'I wonder if they're Tull's riders. They might be rustlers. But it's all the same to us.'

The black dot grew to a dark patch moving under low dust-clouds. It grew all the time, though very slowly. There were long periods when it was in plain sight, and intervals when it dropped behind the sage. The blacks trotted for half an hour, for another half-hour, and still the moving patch appeared to stay on the horizon line. Gradually, however, as time passed, it began to enlarge, to crrep down the slope, to encroach upon the intervening distance.

'Bess, what do you make them out?' asked Venters. 'I don't think they're rustlers.'

'They're sage-riders,' replied Bess. 'I see a white horse and several grays. Rustlers seldom ride any horses but bays and blacks.'

'That white horse is Tull's. Pull the black, Bess. I'll get down and cinch up. We're in for some riding. Are you afraid?'

'Not now,' answered the girl, smiling.

'You needn't be. Bess, you don't weigh enough to make Black Star know you're on him. I won't be able to stay with you. You'll leave Tull and his riders as if they were standing still.'

'How about you?'

'Never fear. If I can't stay with you I can still laugh at Tull.'

'Look, Bern! They've stopped on that ridge. They see us.'

'Yes. But we're too far yet for them to make out who we are. They'll recognize the blacks first. We've passed most of the ridges and the thickest sage. Now, when I give the word, let Black Star go and ride!'

Venters calculated that a mile or more still intervened between them and the riders. They were approaching at a swift canter. Soon Venters recognized Tull's white horse, and concluded that the riders had likewise recognized Black Star and Night. But it would be impossible for Tull yet to see that the blacks were not ridden by Lassiter and Jane. Venters noted that Tull and the line of horsemen, perhaps ten or twelve in number, stopped several times and evidently looked hard down the slope. It must have been a puzzling circumstance for Tull. Venters laughed grimly at the thought of what Tull's rage would be when he finally discovered the trick. Venters meant to sheer out into the sage before Tull could possibly be sure who rode the blacks.

The gap closed to a distance of half a mile. Tull halted. His riders came up and formed a dark group around him. Venters thought he saw him wave his arms, and was certain of it when the riders dashed into the sage, to right and left of the trail. Tull had anticipated just the move held in mind by Venters.

'Now Bess!' shouted Venters. 'Strike north. Go round those riders and turn west.'

Black Star sailed over the low sage, and in few leaps got into his stride and was running. Venters spurred Night after him. It was hard going in the sage. The horses could run as well there, but keen eyesight and judgment must constantly be used by the riders in choosing ground. And continuous swerving from aisle to aisle between the brush, and leaping little washes and mounds of the pack-rats, and breaking through sage, made rough riding. When Venters had turned into a long aisle he had time to look up at Tull's riders. They were now strung out into an extended line riding northeast. And, as Venters and Bess were holding due north, this meant, if the horses of Tull and his riders had the speed and the staying power, they would head the blacks and turn them back down the slope. Tull's men were not saving their mounts; they were driving them desperately. Venters feared only an accident to Black Star or Night, and skillful riding would mitigate possibility of that. One glance ahead served to show him that Bess could pick a course through the sage as well as he. She looked neither back nor at the running riders, and bent forward over Black Star's neck and studied the ground ahead.

It struck Venters, presently, after he had glanced up from time to time, that Bess was drawing away from him as he had expected. He had, however, only thought of the light weight Black Star was carrying and of his superior speed; he saw now that the black was being ridden as never before, except when Jerry Card lost the race to Wrangle. How easily, gracefully, naturally, Bess sat at her saddle! She could ride! Suddenly Venters remembered she had said she could ride. But he had not dreamed she was capable of such superb horsemanship. Then all at once, flashing over him, thrilling him, came the recollection that Bess was Oldring's Masked Rider.

He forgot Tull – the running riders – the race. He let Night have a free rein and felt him lengthen out to suit himself, knowing he would keep to Black Star's course, knowing that he had been chosen by the best rider now on the upland sage. For Jerry Card was dead. And fame had rivaled him with only one rider, and that was the slender girl who now swung so easily with Black Star's stride. Venters had abhorred her notoriety, but now he took passionate pride in her skill, her daring, her power over a horse. And he delved into his memory, recalling famous rides which he had heard related in the villages and round the camp-fires. Oldring's Masked Rider! Many times this strange rider, at once well known and unknown, had escaped pursuers by matchless riding. He had run the gauntlet of

vigilantes down the main street of Stone Bridge, leaving dead horses and dead
rustlers behind. He had jumped his horse over the Gerber Wash, a deep, wide
ravine separating the fields of Glaze from the wild sage. He had been surrounded
north of Sterling; and he had broken through the line. How often had been told
the story of day stampedes, of night raids, of pursuit, and then how the Masked
Rider, swift as the wind, was gone in the sage! A fleet, dark horse – a slender, dark
form – a black mask – a driving run down the slope – a dot on the purple sage – a
shadowy, muffled steed disappearing in the night!

And this Masked Rider of the uplands had been Elizabeth Erne!

The sweet sage wind rushed in Venters's face and sang a song in his ears. He
heard the dull, rapid beat of Night's hoofs; he saw Black Star drawing away,
farther and farther. He realized both horses were swinging to the west. Then
gunshots in the rear reminded him of Tull. Venters looked back. Far to the side,
dropping behind, trooped the riders. They were shooting. Venters saw no puffs of
dust, heard no whistling bullets. He was out of range. When he looked back again
Tull's riders had given up pursuit. The best they could do, no doubt, had been to
get near enough to recognize who really rode the blacks. Venters saw Tull
drooping in his saddle.

Then Venters pulled Night out of his running stride. Those few miles had
scarcely warmed the black, but Venters wished to save him. Bess turned, and,
though she was far away, Venters caught the white glint of her waving hand. He
held Night to a trot and rode on, seeing Bess and Black Star, and the sloping
upward stretch of sage, and from time to time the receding black riders behind.
Soon they disappeared behind a ridge, and he turned no more. They would go
back to Lassiter's trail and follow it, and follow in vain. So Venters rode on, with
the wind growing sweeter to taste and smell, and the purple sage richer and the sky
bluer in his sight; and the song in his ears ringing. By and by Bess halted to wait for
him, and he knew she had come to the trail. When he reached her it was to smile
at sight of her standing with arms round Black Star's neck.

'Oh, Bern! I love him!' she cried. 'He's beautiful; he knows; and how he can
run! I've had fast horses. But Black Star! . . . Wrangle never beat him!'

'I'm wondering if I didn't dream that. Bess, the blacks are grand. What it must
have cost Jane – ah! – well, when we get out of this wild country with Star and
Night, back to my old home in Illinois, we'll buy a beautiful farm with meadows
and springs and cool shade. There we'll turn the horses free – free to roam and
browse and drink – never to feel a spur again – never to be ridden!'

'I would like that,' said Bess.

They rested. Then, mounting, they rode side by side up the white trail. The sun
rose higher behind them. Far to the left a low line of green marked the site of
Cottonwoods. Venters looked once and looked no more. Bess gazed only straight
ahead. They put the blacks to the long, swinging rider's canter, and at times
pulled them to a trot, and occasionally to a walk. The hours passed, the miles
slipped behind, and the wall of rock loomed in the fore. The Notch opened wide.
It was a rugged, stony pass, but with level and open trail, and Venters and Bess ran
the blacks through it. An old trail led off to the right, taking the line of the wall,
and this Venters knew to be the trail mentioned by Lassiter.

The little hamlet, Glaze, a white and green patch in the vast waste of purple,
lay miles down a slope much like the Cottonwoods slope, only this descended to
the west. And miles farther west a faint green spot marked the location of Stone
Bridge. All the rest of that world was seemingly smooth, undulating sage, with no
ragged lines of canōns to accentuate its wildness.

'Bess, we're safe – we're free!' said Venters. 'We're alone on the sage. We're half way to Sterling.'

'Ah! I wonder how it is with Lassiter and Miss Withersteen.'

'Never fear, Bess. He'll outwit Tull. He'll get away and hide her safely. He might climb into Surprise Valley, but I don't think he'll go so far.'

'Bern, will we ever find any place like our beautiful valley?'

'No. But, dear, listen. We'll go back some day, after years – ten years. Then we'll be forgotten. And our valley will be just as we left it.'

'What if Balancing Rock falls and closes the outlet to the Pass?'

'I've thought of that. I'll pack in ropes and ropes. And if the outlet's closed we'll climb up the cliffs and over them to the valley and go down on rope ladders. It could be done. I know just where to make the climb, and I'll never forget.'

'Oh, yes, let us go back!'

'It's something sweet to look forward to. Bess, it's like all the future looks to me.'

'Call me – Elizabeth,' she said shyly.

'Elizabeth Erne! It's a beautiful name. But I'll never forget Bess. Do you know – have you thought that very soon – by this time tomorrow – you will be Elizabeth Venters?'

So they rode on down the old trail. And the sun sloped to the west, and a golden sheen lay on the sage. The hours sped now; the afternoon waned. Often they rested the horses. The glisten of a pool of water in a hollow caught Venters's eye, and here he unsaddled the blacks and let them roll and drink and browse. When he and Bess rode up out of the hollow the sun was low, a crimson ball, and the valley seemed veiled in purple fire and smoke. It was that short time when the sun appeared to rest before setting, and silence, like a cloak of invisible life, lay heavy on all that shimmering world of sage.

They watched the sun begin to bury its red curve under the dark horizon.

'We'll ride on till late,' he said. 'Then you can sleep a little, while I watch and graze the horses. And we'll ride into Sterling early tomorrow. We'll be married! . . . We'll be in time to catch the stage. We'll tie Black Star and Night behind – and then – for a country not wild and terrible like this!'

'Oh, Bern! . . . But look! The sun is setting on the sage – the last time for us till we dare come again to the Utah border. Ten years! Oh, Bern, look, so you will never forget!'

Slumbering, fading purple fire burned over the undulating sage ridges. Long streaks and bars and shafts and spears fringed the far western slope. Drifting, golden veils mingled with low, purple shadows. Colors and shades changed in slow, wondrous transformation.

Suddenly Venters was startled by a low, rumbling roar – so low that it was like the roar in a sea-shell.

'Bess, did you hear anything?' he whispered.

'No.'

'Listen! . . . Maybe I only imagined . . . Ah!'

Out of the east or north, from remote distance, breathed an infinitely low, continuously long sound – deep, weird, detonating, thundering, deadening – dying.

TWENTY-THREE

The Fall of Balancing Rock

THROUGH TEAR-BLURRED sight Jane Withersteen watched Venters and Elizabeth Erne and the black racers disappear over the ridge of sage.

'They're gone!' said Lassiter. 'An' they're safe now. An' there'll be a day of their comin' happy lives but what they'll remember Jane Withersteen an' – an' Uncle Jim! . . . I reckon, Jane, we'd better be on our way.'

The burros obediently wheeled and started down the break with little, cautious steps, but Lassiter had to leash the whining dogs and lead them. Jane felt herself bound in a feeling that was neither listlessness nor indifference, yet which rendered her incapable of interest. She was still strong in body, but emotionally tired. That hour at the entrance to Deception Pass had been the climax of her suffering – the flood of her wrath – the last of her sacrifice – the supremacy of her love – and the attainment of peace. She thought that if she had little Fay she would not ask any more of life.

Like an automaton she followed Lassiter down the steep trail of dust and bits of weathered stone; and when the little slides moved with her or piled around her knees she experienced no alarm. Vague relief came to her in the sense of being enclosed between dark stone walls, deep hidden from the glare of sun, from the glistening sage. Lassiter lengthened the stirrup straps on one of the burros and bade her mount and ride close to him. She was to keep the burro from cracking his little hard hoofs on stones. Then she was riding on between dark, gleaming walls. There were quiet and rest and coolness in this canōn. She noted indifferently that they passed close under shady, bulging shelves of cliff, through patches of grass and sage and thicket and groves of slender trees, and over white, pebbly washes, and around masses of broken rock. The burros trotted tirelessly; the dogs, once more free, pattered tirelessly; and Lassiter led on with never a stop, and at every open place he looked back. The shade under the walls gave place to sunlight. And presently they came to a dense thicket of slender trees, through which they passed to rich, green grass and water. Here Lassiter rested the burros for a little while, but he was restless, uneasy, silent, always listening, peering under the trees. She dully reflected that enemies were behind them – before them; still the thought awakened no dread or concern or interest.

At his bidding she mounted and rode on close to the heels of his burro. The canōn narrowed; the walls lifted their rugged rims higher; and the sun shone down hot from the center of the blue stream of sky above. Lassiter traveled slower, with more exceeding care as to the ground he chose, and he kept speaking low to the dogs. They were now hunting-dogs – keen, alert, suspicious, sniffing the warm breeze. The monotony of the yellow walls broke in change of color and smooth surface, and the rugged outline of rims grew craggy. Splits appeared in deep breaks, and gorges running at right angles, and then the Pass opened wide at a junction of intersecting canōns.

Lassiter dismounted, led his burro, called the dogs close, and proceeded at snail pace through dark masses of rock and dense thickets under the left wall. Long he watched and listened before venturing to cross the mouths of side canōns. At length he halted, tied his burro, lifted a warning hand to Jane, and then slipped away among the boulders, and, followed by the stealthy dogs, disappeared from sight. The time he remained absent was neither short nor long to Jane Withersteen.

When he reached her side again he was pale, and his lips were set in a hard line, and his gray eyes glittered coldly. Bidding her dismount, he led the burros into a covert of stones and cedars, and tied them.

'Jane, I've run into the fellers I've been lookin' for, an' I'm goin' after them,' he said.

'Why?' she asked.

'I reckon I won't take time to tell you.'

'Couldn't we slip by without being seen?'

'Likely enough. But that ain't my game. An' I'd like to know, in case I don't come back, what you'll do.'

'What can I do?'

'I reckon you can go back to Tull. Or stay in the Pass an' be taken off by rustlers. Which'll you do?'

'I don't know. I can't think very well. But I believe I'd rather be taken off by rustlers.'

Lassiter sat down, put his head in his hands, and remained for a few moments in what appeared to be deep and painful thought. When he lifted his face it was haggard, lined, cold as sculptured marble.

'I'll go. I only mentioned that chance of my not comin' back. I'm pretty sure to come.'

'Need you risk so much? Must you fight more? Haven't you shed enough blood?'

'I'd like to tell you why I'm goin',' he continued, in coldness he had seldom used to her. She remarked it, but it was the same to her as if he had spoken with his old gentle warmth. 'But I reckon I won't. Only, I'll say that mercy an' goodness, such as is in you, though they're the grand things in human nature, can't be lived up to on this Utah border. Life's hell out here. You think – or you used to think – that your religion made this life heaven. Mebbe them scales on your eyes has dropped now, Jane, I wouldn't have you no different, an' that's why I'm goin' to try to hide you somewhere in this Pass. I'd like to hide many more women, for I've come to see there are more like you among your people. An' I'd like you to see jest how hard an' cruel this border life is. It's bloody. You'd think churches an' churchmen would make it better. They make it worse. You give names to things – bishops, elders, ministers, Mormonism, duty, faith, glory. You dream – or you're driven mad. I'm a man, an' I know. I name fanatics, followers, blind women, oppressors, thieves, ranchers, rustlers, riders. An' we have – what you've lived through these last months. It can't be helped. But it can't last always. An' remember this – some day the border'll be better, cleaner, for the ways of men like Lassiter!'

She saw him shake his tall form erect, look at her strangely and steadfastly, and then, noiselessly, stealthily slip away amid the rocks and trees. Ring and Whitie, not being bidden to follow, remained with Jane. She felt extreme weariness, yet somehow it did not seem to be of her body. And she sat down in the shade and tried to think. She saw a creeping lizard, cactus flowers, the drooping burros, the resting dogs, an eagle high over a yellow crag. Once the meanest flower, a color, the flight of a bee, or any living thing had given her deepest joy. Lassiter had gone off, yielding to his incurable blood lust, probably to his own death; and she was sorry, but there was no feeling in her sorrow.

Suddenly from the mouth of the canõn just beyond her rang out a clear, sharp report of a rifle. Echoes clapped. Then followed a piercingly high yell of anguish, quickly breaking. Again echoes clapped, in grim imitation. Dull revolver shots –

hoarse yells – pound of hoofs – shrill neighs of horses – commingling of echoes – and again silence! Lassiter must be busily engaged, thought Jane, and no chill trembled over her, no blanching tightened her skin. Yes, the border was a bloody place. But life had always been bloody. Men were blood-spillers. Phases of the history of the world flashed through her mind – Greek and Roman wars, dark, mediaeval times, the crimes in the name of religion. On sea, on land, everywhere – shooting, stabbing, cursing, clashing, fighting men! Greed, power, oppression, fanaticism, love, hate, revenge, justice, freedom – for these, men killed one another.

She lay there under the cedars, gazing up through the delicate lacelike foliage at the blue sky, and she thought and wondered and did not care.

More rattling shots disturbed the noonday quiet. She heard a sliding of weathered rock, a hoarse shout of warning, a yell of alarm, again the clear, sharp crack of the rifle, and another cry that was a cry of death. Then rifle reports pierced a dull volley of revolver shots. Bullets whizzed over Jane's hiding-place; one struck a stone and whined away in the air. After that, for a time, succeeded desultory shots; and then they ceased under long, thundering fire from heavier guns.

Sooner or later, then, Jane heard the cracking of horses' hoofs on the stones, and the sound came nearer and nearer. Silence intervened until Lassiter's soft, jingling step assured her of his approach. When he appeared he was covered with blood.

'All right, Jane,' he said. 'I come back. An' don't worry.'

With water from a canteen he washed the blood from his face and hands.

'Jane, hurry now. Tear my scarf in two, an' tie up these places. That hole through my hand is some inconvenient, worse'n this cut over my ear. There – you're doin' fine! Not a bit nervous – no tremblin'. I reckon I ain't done your courage justice. I'm glad you're brave jest now – you'll need to be. Well, I was hid pretty good, enough to keep them from shootin' me deep, but they was slingin' lead close all the time. I used up all the rifle shells, an' then I went after them. Mebbe you heard. It was then I got hit. I had to use up every shell in my own guns, an' they did, too, as I seen. Rustlers an' Mormons, Jane! An' now I'm packin' five bullet holes in my carcass, an' guns without shells. Hurry, now.'

He unstrapped the saddle-bags from the burros, slipped the saddles and let them lie, turned the burros loose, and, calling the dogs, led the way through stones and cedars to an open where two horses stood.

'Jane, are you strong?' he asked.

'I think so. I'm not tired,' Jane replied.

'I don't mean that way. Can you bear up?'

'I think I can bear anything.'

'I reckon you look a little cold an' thick. So I'm preparing you.'

'For what?'

'I didn't tell you why I jest had to go after them fellers. I couldn't tell you. I believe you'd have died. But I can tell you now – if you'll bear up under a shock?'

'Go on, my friend.'

'*I've got little Fay!* Alive – bad hurt – but she'll live!'

Jane Witherseen's dead-locked feeling, rent by Lassiter's deep, quivering voice, leaped into an agony of sensitive life.

'Here,' he added, and showed her where little Fay lay on the grass.

Unable to speak, unable to stand, Jane dropped on her knees. By that long, beautiful golden hair Jane recognized the beloved Fay. But Fay's loveliness was gone. Her face was drawn and looked old with grief. But she was not dead –

her heart beat – and Jane Withersteen gathered strength and lived again.

'You see I jest had to go after Fay,' Lassiter was saying, as he knelt to bathe her little pale face. 'But I reckon I don't want no more choices like the one I had to make. There was a crippled feller in that bunch, Jane. Mebbe Venters crippled him. Anyway, that's why they were holdin' up here. I seen little Fay first thing, an' was hard put to it to figure out a way to get her. An' I wanted hosses, too. I had to take chances. So I crawled close to their camp. One feller jumped a hoss with little Fay, an' when I shot him, of course she dropped. She's stunned an' bruised – she fell right on her head. Jane, she's comin' to! She ain't bad hurt!'

Fay's long lashes fluttered; her eyes opened. At first they seemed glazed over. They looked dazed by pain. Then they quickened, darkened, to shine with intelligence – bewilderment – memory – and sudden wonderful joy.

'Muvver – Jane!' she whispered.

'Oh, little Fay, little Fay!' cried Jane, lifting, clasping the child to her.

'Now, we've got to rustle!' said Lassiter, in grim coolness. 'Jane, look down the Pass!'

Across the mounds of rock and sage Jane caught sight of a band of riders filing out of the narrow neck of the Pass; and in the lead was a white horse, which, even at a distance of a mile or more, she knew.

'Tull!' she almost screamed.

'I reckon. But, Jane, we've still got the game in our hands. They're ridin' tired hosses. Venters likely give them a chase. He wouldn't forget that. An' we've fresh hosses.'

Hurriedly he strapped on the saddle-bags, gave quick glance to girths and cinches and stirrups, then leaped astride.

'Lift little Fay up,' he said.

With shaking arms Jane complied.

'Get back your nerve, woman! This's life or death now. Mind that. Climb up! Keep your wits. Stick close to me. Watch where your hoss's goin' an' ride!'

Somehow Jane mounted; somehow found strength to hold the reins, to spur, to cling on, to ride. A horrible quaking, craven fear possessed her soul. Lassiter led the swift flight across the wide space, over washes, through sage, into a narrow cañon where the rapid clatter of hoofs rapped sharply from the walls. The wind roared in her ears; the gleaming cliffs swept by; trail and sage and grass moved under her. Lassiter's bandaged, blood-stained face turned to her; he shouted encouragement; he looked back down the Pass; he spurred his horse. Jane clung on, spurring likewise. And the horses settled from hard, furious gallop into a long-striding, driving run. She had never ridden at anything like that pace; desperately she tried to get the swing of the horse, to be of some help to him in that race, to see the best of the ground and guide him into it. But she failed of everything except to keep her seat in the saddle, and to spur and spur. At times she closed her eyes, unable to bear sight of Fay's golden curls streaming in the wind. She could not pray; she could not rail; she no longer cared for herself. All of life, of good, of use in the world, of hope in heaven centered in Lassiter's ride with little Fay to safety. She would have tried to turn the iron-jawed brute she rode; she would have given herself to that relentless, dark-browed Tull. But she knew Lassiter would turn with her, so she rode on and on.

Whether that run was of moments or hours Jane Withersteen could not tell. Lassiter's horse covered her with froth that blew back in white streams. Both horses ran their limit, were allowed to slow down in time to save them, and went on dripping, heaving, staggering.

'Oh, Lassiter, we must run – we must run!'

He looked back, saying nothing. The bandage had blown from his head, and blood trickled down his face. He was bowing under the strain of injuries, of the ride, of his burden. Yet how cool and gray he looked – how intrepid!

The horses walked, trotted, galloped, ran, to fall again to walk. Hours sped or dragged. Time was an instant – an eternity. Jane Withersteen felt hell pursuing her, and dared not look back for fear she would fall from her horse.

'Oh, Lassiter! Is he coming?'

The grim rider looked over his shoulder, but said no word. Little Fay's golden hair floated on the breeze. The sun shone; the walls gleamed; the sage glistened. And then it seemed the sun vanished, the walls shaded, the sage paled. The horses walked – trotted – galloped – ran – to fall again to walk. Shadows gathered under shelving cliffs. The canōn turned, brightened, opened into long, wide, wall-enclosed valley. Again the sun, lowering in the west, reddened the sage. Far ahead round, scrawled stone appeared to block the Pass.

'Bear up, Jane, bear up!' called Lassiter. 'It's our game, if you don't weaken.'

'Lassiter! Go on – alone! Save little Fay!'

'Only with you!'

'Oh! – I'm a coward – a miserable coward! I can't fight or think or hope or pray! I'm lost! Oh, Lassiter, look back! Is he coming? I'll not – hold out – '

'Keep your breath, woman, an' ride not for yourself or for me, but for Fay!'

A last breaking run across the sage brought Lassiter's horse to a walk.

'He's done,' said the rider.

'Oh, no – no!' moaned Jane.

'Look back, Jane, look back. Three – four miles we've come across this valley, an' no Tull yet in sight. Only a few more miles!'

Jane looked back over the long stretch of sage, and found the narrow gap in the wall, out of which came a file of dark horses with a white horse in the lead. Sight of the riders acted upon Jane as a stimulant. The weight of cold, horrible terror lessened. And, gazing forward at the dogs, at Lassiter's limping horse, at the blood on his face, at the rocks growing nearer, last at Fay's golden hair, the ice left her veins, and slowly, strangely, she gained hold of strength that she believed would see her to the safety Lassiter promised. And, as she gazed, Lassiter's horse stumbled and fell.

He swung his legs and slipped from the saddle.

'Jane, take the child,' he said, and lifted Fay up. Jane clasped her with arms suddenly strong.

'They're gainin',' went on Lassiter, as he watched the pursuing riders. 'But we'll beat 'em yet.'

Turning with Jane's bridle in his hand, he was about to start when he saw the saddle-bag on the fallen horse.

'I've jest about got time,' he muttered, and with swift fingers that did not blunder or fumble he loosened the bag and threw it over his shoulder. Then he started to run, leading Jane's horse, and he ran, and trotted, and walked, and ran again. Close ahead now Jane saw a rise of bare rock. Lassiter reached it, searched along the base, and, finding a low place, dragged the weary horse up and over round, smooth stone. Looking backward, Jane saw Tull's white horse not a mile distant, with riders strung out in a long line behind him. Looking forward, she saw more valley to the right, and to the left a towering cliff. Lassiter pulled the horse and kept on.

Little Fay lay in her arms with wide-open eyes – eyes which were still shadowed by pain, but no longer fixed, glazed in terror. The golden curls blew across Jane's lips; the little hands feebly clasped her arm; a ghost of a troubled, trustful smile hovered round the sweet lips. And Jane Withersteen awoke to the spirit of a lioness.

Lassiter was leading the horse up a smooth slope toward cedar-trees of twisted and bleached appearance. Among these he halted.

'Jane, give me the girl an' get down,' he said. As if it wrenched him he unbuckled the empty black guns with a strange air of finality. He then received Fay in his arms and stood a moment looking backward. Tull's white horse mounted the ridge of round stone, and several bays or blacks followed. 'I wonder what he'll think when he sees them empty guns. Jane, bring your saddle-bag and climb after me.'

A glistening, wonderful bare slope, with little holes, swelled up and up to lose itself in a frowning yellow cliff. Jane closely watched her steps and climbed behind Lassiter. He moved slowly. Perhaps he was only husbanding his strength. But she saw drops of blood on the stone, and then she knew. They climbed and climbed without looking back. Her breast labored; she began to feel as if little points of fiery steel were penetrating her side into her lungs. She heard the panting of Lassiter and the quicker panting of the dogs.

'Wait – here,' he said.

Before her rose a bulge of stone, nicked with little cut steps, and above that a corner of yellow wall, and overhanging that a vast, ponderous cliff.

The dogs pattered up, disappeared round the corner. Lassiter mounted the steps with Fay, and he swayed like a drunken man, and he too disappeared. But instantly he returned alone, and half ran, half slipped down to her.

Then from below pealed up hoarse shouts of angry men. Tull and several of his riders had reached the spot where Lassiter had parted with his guns.

'You'll need that breath – mebbe!' said Lassiter, facing downward, with glittering eyes.

'Now, Jane, the last pull,' he went on. 'Walk up them little steps. I'll follow an' steady you. Don't think. Jest go. Little Fay's above. Her eyes are open. She jest said to me, "Where's muvver Jane?"'

Without a fear or a tremor or a slip or a touch of Lassiter's hand Jane Withersteen walked up that ladder of cut steps.

He pushed her round the corner of wall. Fay lay with wide staring eyes, in the shade of a gloomy wall. The dogs waited. Lassiter picked up the child and turned into a dark cleft. It zigzagged. It widened. It opened. Jane was amazed at a wonderfully smooth and steep incline leading up between ruined, splintered, toppling walls. A red haze from the setting sun filled this passage. Lassiter climbed with slow, measured steps, and blood dripped from him to make splotches on the white stone. Jane tried not to step in his blood, but was compelled, for she found no other footing. The saddle-bag began to drag her down; she gasped for breath; she thought her heart was bursting. Slower, slower yet the rider climbed, whistling as he breathed. The incline widened. Huge pinnacles and monuments of stone stood alone, leaning fearfully. Red sunset haze shone through cracks where the wall had split. Jane did not look high, but she felt the overshadowing of broken rims above. She felt it was a fearful, menacing place. And she climbed on in heartrending effort. And she fell beside Lassiter and Fay at the top of the incline in a narrow, smooth divide.

He staggered to his feet – staggered to a huge, leaning rock that rested on a small pedestal. He put his hand on it – the hand that had been shot through – and Jane saw blood drip from the ragged hole. Then he fell.

'Jane – I – can't – do – it!' he whispered.

'What?'

'Roll the – stone! . . . All my – life I've loved – to roll stones – an' now I – can't!'

'What of it? You talk strangely. Why roll that stone?'

'I planned to – fetch you here – to roll this stone. See! It'll smash the crags – loosen the walls – close the outlet!'

As Jane Withersteen gazed down that long incline, walled in by crumbling cliffs, awaiting only the slightest jar to make them fall asunder, she saw Tull appear at the bottom and begin to climb. A rider followed him – another – and another.

'See! Tull! The riders!'

'Yes – they'll get us – now.'

'Why? Haven't you got strength left to roll the stone?'

'Jane – it ain't that – I've lost my nerve!'

'You! . . . Lassiter!'

'I wanted to roll it – meant to – but I – can't. Venters's valley is down behind here. We could – live there. But if I roll the stone – we're shut in for always I don't dare. I'm thinkin' of you!'

'Lassiter! Roll the stone!' she cried.

He arose, tottering, but with set face, and again he placed the bloody hand on the Balancing Rock. Jane Withersteen gazed from him down the passageway. Tull was climbing. Almost, she thought, she saw his dark, relentless face. Behind him more riders climbed. What did they mean for Fay – for Lassiter – for herself?

'Roll the stone! . . . Lassiter, I love you!'

Under all his deathly pallor, and the blood, and the iron of seared cheek and lined brow, worked a great change. He placed both hands on the rock and then leaned his shoulder there and braced his powerful body.

'ROLL THE STONE!'

It stirred, it groaned, it grated, it moved; and with a slow grinding, as of wrathful relief, began to lean. It had waited ages to fall, and now was slow in starting. Then, as if suddenly instinct with life, it leaped hurtlingly down to alight on the steep incline, to bound more swiftly into the air, to gather momentum, to plunge into the lofty leaning crag below. The crag thundered into atoms. A wave of air – a splitting shock! Dust shrouded the sunset red of shaking rims; dust shrouded Tull as he fell on his knees with uplifted arms. Shafts and monuments and sections of wall fell majestically.

From the depths there arose a long-drawn rumbling roar. The outlet to Deception Pass closed forever.

TENNESSEE'S PARTNER

THE LUCK OF ROARING CAMP

BY

BRET HARTE

Tennessee's Partner

I DO NOT THINK THAT we ever knew his real name. Our ignorance of it certainly never gave us any social inconvenience, for at Sandy Bar in 1854 most men were christened anew. Sometimes these appellatives were derived from some distinctiveness of dress, as in the case of 'Dungaree Jack'; or from some peculiarity of habit, as shown in 'Saleratus Bill,' so called from an undue proportion of that chemical in his daily bread; or from some unlucky slip, as exhibited in 'The Iron Pirate,' a mild, inoffensive man, who earned that baleful title by his unfortunate mispronunciation of the term 'iron pyrites.' Perhaps this may have been the beginning of a rude heraldry; but I am constrained to think that it was because a man's real name in that day rested solely upon his own unsupported statement. 'Call yourself Clifford, do you?' said Boston, addressing a timid newcomer with infinite scorn; 'hell is full of such Cliffords!' He then introduced the unfortunate man, whose name happened to be really Clifford, as 'Jaybird Charley' – an unhallowed inspiration of the moment that clung to him ever after.

But to return to Tennessee's Partner, whom we never knew by any other than this relative title. That he had ever existed as a separate and distinct individuality we only learned later. It seems that in 1853 he left Poker Flat to go to San Francisco, ostensibly to procure a wife. He never got any farther than Stockton. At that place he was attracted by a young person who waited upon the table at the hotel where he took his meals. One morning he said something to her which caused her to smile not unkindly, to somewhat coquettishly break a plate of toast over his upturned, serious, simple face, and to retreat to the kitchen. He followed her, and emerged a few moments later, covered with more toast and victory. That day week they were married by a justice of the peace, and returned to Poker Flat. I am aware that something more might be made of this episode, but I prefer to tell it as it was current at Sandy Bar – in the gulches and bar-rooms – where all sentiment was modified by a strong sense of humor.

Of their married felicity but little is known, perhaps for the reason that Tennessee, then living with his partner, one day took occasion to say something to the bride on his own account, at which, it is said, she smiled not unkindly and chastely retreated – this time as far as Marysville, where Tennessee followed her, and where they went to housekeeping without the aid of a justice of the peace. Tennessee's Partner took the loss of his wife simply and seriously, as was his fashion. But to everybody's surprise, when Tennessee one day returned from Marysville, without his partner's wife – she having smiled and retreated with somebody else – Tennessee's Partner was the first man to shake his hand and greet him with affection. The boys who had gathered in the canyon to see the shooting were naturally indignant. Their indignation might have found vent in sarcasm but for a certain look in Tennessee's Partner's eye that indicated a lack of humorous appreciation. In fact, he was a grave man, with a steady application to practical detail which was unpleasant in a difficulty.

Meanwhile a popular feeling against Tennessee had grown up on the Bar. He was known to be a gambler; he was suspected to be a thief. In these suspicions Tennessee's Partner was equally compromised; his continued intimacy with Tennessee after the affair above quoted could only be accounted for on the hypothesis of a copartnership of crime. At last Tennessee's guilt became flagrant. One day he overtook a stranger on his way to Red Dog. The stranger afterward related that Tennessee beguiled the time with interesting anecdote and reminiscence, but illogically concluded the interview in the following words: 'And now, young man, I'll trouble you for your knife, your pistols, and your money. You see your weppings might get you into trouble at Red Dog, and your money's a temptation to the evilly disposed. I think you said your address was San Francisco. I shall endeavor to call.' It may be stated here that Tennessee had a fine flow of humor, which no business preoccupation could wholly subdue.

This exploit was his last. Red Dog and Sandy Bar made common cause against the highwayman. Tennessee was hunted in very much the same fashion as his prototype, the grizzly. As the toils closed around him, he made a desperate dash through the Bar, emptying his revolver at the crowd before the Arcade Saloon, and so on up Grizzly Canyon; but at its farther extremity he was stopped by a small man on a gray horse. The men looked at each other a moment in silence. Both were fearless, both self-possessed and independent, and both types of a civilization that in the seventeenth century would have been called heroic, but in the nineteenth simply 'reckless.'

'What have you got there? – I call,' said Tennessee quietly.

'Two bowers and an ace,' said the stranger quietly, showing two revolvers and a bowie knife.

'That takes me,' returned Tennessee; and with this gambler's epigram, he threw away his useless pistol and rode back with his captor.

It was a warm night. The cool breeze which usually sprang up with the going down of the sun behind the chaparral-crested mountain was that evening withheld from Sandy Bar. The little canyon was stifling with heated resinous odors, and the decaying driftwood on the Bar sent forth faint sickening exhalations. The feverishness of day and its fierce passions still filled the camp. Lights moved restlessly along the bank of the river, striking no answering reflection from its tawny current. Against the blackness of the pines the windows of the old loft above the express office stood out staringly bright; and through their curtainless panes the loungers below could see the forms of those who were even then deciding the fate of Tennessee. And above all this, etched on the dark firmament, rose the Sierra, remote and passionless, crowned with remoter passionless stars.

The trial of Tennessee was conducted as fairly as was consistent with a judge and jury who felt themselves to some extent obliged to justify, in their verdict, the previous irregularities of arrest and indictment. The law of Sandy Bar was implacable, but not vengeful. The excitement and personal feeling of the chase were over; with Tennessee safe in their hands, they were ready to listen patiently to any defense, which they were already satisfied was insufficient. There being no doubt in their own minds, they were willing to give the prisoner the benefit of any that might exist. Secure in the hypothesis that he ought to be hanged on general principles, they indulged him with more latitude of defense than his reckless hardihood seemed to ask. The Judge appeared to be more anxious than the prisoner, who, otherwise unconcerned, evidently took a grim pleasure in the responsibility he had created. 'I don't take any hand in this yer game,' had been his invariable but good-humored reply to all questions. The Judge – who was also his captor – for a moment vaguely regretted that he had not shot him 'on sight' that morning, but presently dismissed this human weakness as unworthy of the judicial mind. Nevertheless, when there was a tap at the door, and it was said that Tennessee's Partner was there on behalf of the prisoner, he was admitted at once without question. Perhaps the younger members of the jury, to whom the proceedings were becoming irksomely thoughtful, hailed him as a relief.

For he was not, certainly, an imposing figure. Short and stout, with a square face, sunburned into a preternatural redness, clad in a loose duck 'jumper' and trousers streaked and splashed with red soil, his aspect under any circumstances would have been quaint, and was now even ridiculous. As he stooped to deposit at his feet a heavy carpetbag he was carrying, it became obvious, from partially developed legends and inscriptions, that the material with which his trousers had been patched had been originally intended for a less ambitious covering. Yet he advanced with great gravity, and after shaking the hand of each person in the room with labored cordiality, he wiped his serious perplexed face on a red bandana handkerchief, a shade lighter than his complexion, laid his powerful hand upon the table to steady himself, and thus addressed the Judge:

'I was passin' by,' he began, by way of apology, 'and I thought I'd just step in and see how things was gittin' on with Tennessee thar – my pardner. It's a hot night. I disremember any sich weather before on the Bar.'

He paused a moment, but nobody volunteering any other meteorological recollection, he again had recourse to his pocket handkerchief, and for some moments mopped his face diligently.

'Have you anything to say on behalf of the prisoner?' said the Judge finally.

'Thet's it,' said Tennessee's Partner, in a tone of relief. 'I come yar as Tennessee's pardner – knowing him nigh on four year, off and on, wet and dry, in luck and out o' luck. His ways ain't aller my ways, but thar ain't any p'ints in that young man, thar ain't any liveliness as he's been up to, as I don't know. And you sez to me, sez you – confidential-like, and between man and man – sez you, "Do you know anything in his behalf?" and I sez to you, sez I – confidential-like, as between man and man – "What should a man know of his pardner?" '

'Is this all you have to say?' asked the Judge impatiently, feeling, perhaps, that a dangerous sympathy of humor was beginning to humanize the court.

'Thet's so,' continued Tennessee's Partner. 'It ain't for me to say anything agin' him. And now, what's the case? Here's Tennessee wants money, wants it bad, and doesn't like to ask it of his old pardner. Well, what does Tennessee do? He lays for a stranger, and he fetches that stranger; and you lays for *him*, and you fetches *him*; and the honors is easy. And I put it to you, bein' a fa'r-minded man, and to you, gentlemen all, as fa'r-minded men, ef this isn't so.'

'Prisoner,' said the Judge, interrupting, 'have you any questions to ask this man?'

'No! no!' continued Tennessee's Partner hastily. 'I play this yer hand alone. To come down to the bedrock, it's just this: Tennessee thar has played it pretty rough and expensivelike on a stranger, and on this yer camp. And now, what's the fair thing? Some would say more, some would say less. Here's seventeen hundred dollars in coarse gold and a watch – it's about all my pile – and call it square!' And before a hand could be raised to prevent him, he had emptied the contents of the carpetbag upon the table.

For a moment his life was in jeopardy. One or two men sprang to their feet, several hands groped for hidden weapons, and a suggestion to 'throw him from the window' was only overridden by a gesture from the Judge. Tennessee laughed. And apparently oblivious of the excitement, Tennessee's Partner improved the opportunity to mop his face again with his handkerchief.

When order was restored, and the man was made to understand by the use of forcible figures and rhetoric that Tennessee's offense could not be condoned by money, his face took a more serious and sanguinary hue, and those who were nearest to him noticed that his rough hand trembled slightly on the table. He hesitated a moment as he slowly returned the gold to the carpetbag, as if he had not yet entirely caught the elevated sense of justice which swayed the tribunal, and was perplexed with the belief that he had not offered enough. Then he turned to the Judge, and saying, 'This yer is a lone hand, played alone, and without any pardner,' he bowed to the jury and was about to withdraw, when the Judge called him back:

'If you have anything to say to Tennessee, you had better say it now.'

For the first time that evening the eyes of the prisoner and his strange advocate met. Tennessee smiled, showed his white teeth, and saying, 'Euchred, old man!' held out his hand. Tennessee's Partner took it in his own, and saying, 'I just dropped in as I was passin' to see how things was gettin' on,' let the hand passively fall, and adding that 'it was a warm night,' again mopped his face with his handkerchief, and without another word withdrew.

The two men never again met each other alive. For the unparalleled insult of a bribe offered to Judge Lynch – who, whether bigoted, weak, or narrow, was at least incorruptible – firmly fixed in the mind of that mythical personage any wavering determination of Tennessee's fate; and at the break of day he was marched, closely guarded, to meet it at the top of Marley's Hill.

How he met it, how cool he was, how he refused to say anything, how perfect were the arrangements of the committee, were all duly reported, with the addition of a warning moral and example to all future evildoers, in the Red Dog Clarion by its editor, who was present, and to whose vigorous English I cheerfully refer the reader. But the beauty of that midsummer morning, the blessed amity of earth and air and sky, the awakened life of the free woods and hills, the joyous renewal and promise of Nature, and above all, the infinite serenity that thrilled through each, was not reported, as not being a part of the social lesson. And yet, when the weak and foolish deed was done, and a life, with its possibilities and responsibilities, had passed out of the misshapen thing that dangled between earth and sky, the birds sang, the flowers bloomed, the sun shone, as cheerily as before; and possibly the Red Dog Clarion was right.

Tennessee's Partner was not in the group that surrounded the ominous tree. But as they turned to disperse, attention was drawn to the singular appearance of a motionless donkey cart halted at the side of the road. As they approached, they at once recognized the venerable Jenny and the two-wheeled cart as the property of Tennessee's Partner, used by him in carrying dirt from his claim; and a few paces distant the owner of the equipage himself, sitting under a buckeye tree, wiping the perspiration from his glowing face. In answer to an inquiry, he said he had come for the body of the 'diseased,' 'if it was all the same to the committee.' He didn't wish to 'hurry anything;' he could 'wait.' He was not working that day; and when the gentlemen were done with the 'diseased,' he would take him. 'Ef thar is any present,' he added in his simple, serious way, 'as would care to jine in the fun'l, they kin come.' Perhaps it was from a sense of humor, which I have already intimated was a feature of Sandy Bar – perhaps it was from something even better than that, but two thirds of the loungers accepted the invitation at once.

It was noon when the body of Tennessee was delivered into the hands of his partner. As the cart drew up to the fatal tree, we noticed that it contained a rough oblong box – apparently made from a section of sluicing – and half filled with bark and the tassels of pine. The cart was further decorated with slips of willow and made fragrant with buckeye blossoms. When the body was deposited in the box, Tennessee's Partner drew over it a piece of tarred canvas, and gravely mounting the narrow seat in front with his feet upon the shafts, urged the little donkey forward. The equipage moved slowly on, at that decorous pace which was habitual with Jenny even under less solemn circumstances. The men – half curiously, half jestingly, but all good-humoredly – strolled along beside the cart, some in advance, some a little in the rear of the homely catalfalque. But whether from the narrowing of the road or some present sense of decorum, as the cart passed on, the company fell to the rear in couples, keeping step, and otherwise assuming the external show of a formal procession. Jack Folinsbee, who had at the outset played a funeral march in dumb show upon an imaginary trombone, desisted from a lack of sympathy and appreciation – not having, perhaps, your true humorist's capacity to be content with the enjoyment of his own fun.

The way led through Grizzly Canyon, by this time clothed in funeral drapery and shadows. The redwoods, burying their moccasined feet in the red soil, stood in Indian file along the track, trailing an uncouth benediction from their bending boughs upon the passing bier. A hare, surprised into helpless inactivity, sat upright and pulsating in the ferns by the roadside as the cortège went by. Squirrels hastened to gain a secure outlook from higher boughs; and the blue jays, spreading their wings, fluttered before them like outriders, until the outskirts of Sandy Bar were reached, and the solitary cabin of Tennessee's Partner.

Viewed under more favorable circumstances, it would not have been a cheerful place. The unpicturesque site, the rude and unlovely outlines, the unsavory details, which distinguish the nest-building of the California miner, were all here with the dreariness of decay superadded. A few paces from the cabin there was a rough enclosure, which, in the brief days of Tennessee's Partner's matrimonial felicity, had been used as a garden, but was now overgrown with fern. As we approached it, we were surprised to find that what we had taken for a recent attempt at cultivation was the broken soil about an open grave.

The cart was halted before the enclosure, and rejecting the offers of assistance with the same air of simple self-reliance he had displayed throughout, Tennessee's Partner lifted the rough coffin on his back, and deposited it unaided within the shallow grave. He then nailed down the board which served as a lid, and mounting the little mound of earth beside it, took off his hat and slowly mopped his face with his handkerchief. This the crowd felt was a preliminary to speech, and they disposed themselves variously on stumps and boulders, and sat expectant.

'When a man,' began Tennessee's Partner slowly, 'has been running free all day, what's the natural thing for him to do? Why, to come home. And if he ain't in a condition to go home, what can his best friend do? Why, bring him home. And here's Tennessee has been running free, and we brings him home from his wandering.' He paused and picked up a fragment of quartz, rubbed it thoughtfully on his sleeve, and went on: 'It ain't the first time that I've packed him on my back, as you see'd me now. It ain't the first time that I brought him to this yer cabin when he couldn't help himself; it ain't the first time that I and Jinny have waited for him on yon hill, and picked him up and so fetched him home, when he couldn't speak and didn't know me. And now that it's the last time, why' – he paused and rubbed the quartz gently on his sleeve – 'you see it's sort of rough on his pardner. And now, gentlemen,' he added abruptly, picking up his long-handled shovel, 'the fun'l's over; and my thanks, and Tennessee's thanks, to you for your trouble.'

Resisting any proffers of assistance, he began to fill in the grave, turning his back upon the crowd, that after a few moments' hesitation gradually withdrew. As they crossed the little ridge that hid Sandy Bar from view, some, looking back, thought they could see Tennessee's Partner, his work done, sitting upon the grave, his shovel between his knees, and his face buried in his red bandana handkerchief. But it was argued by others that you couldn't tell his face from his handkerchief at that distance, and this point remained undecided.

In the reaction that followed the feverish excitement of the day, Tennessee's Partner was not forgotten. A secret investigation had cleared him of any complicity in Tennessee's guilt, and left only a suspicion of his general sanity. Sandy Bar made a point of calling on him, and proffering various uncouth but well-meant kindnesses. But from that day his rude health and great strength seemed visibly to decline; and when the rainy season fairly set in, and the tiny grass blades were beginning to peep from the rocky mound above Tennessee's grave, he took to his bed.

One night, when the pines beside the cabin were swaying in the storm and trailing their slender fingers over the roof, and the roar and rush of the swollen river were heard below, Tennessee's Partner lifted his head from the pillow, saying, 'It is time to go for Tennessee; I must put Jinny in the cart;' and would have risen from his bed but for the restraint of his attendant. Struggling, he still pursued his singular fancy: 'There, now, steady, Jinny, steady, old girl. How dark it is! Look out for the ruts, and look out for him, too, old gal. Sometimes, you know, when he's blind drunk, he drops down right in the trail. Keep on straight up to the pine on the top of the hill. Thar! I told you so! – thar he is – coming this way, too – all by himself, sober, and his face a-shining. Tennessee! Pardner!'

And so they met.

The Luck of Roaring Camp

THERE WAS COMMOTION IN Roaring Camp. It could not have been a fight, for in 1850 that was not novel enough to have called together the entire settlement. The ditches and claims were not only deserted, but 'Tuttle's grocery' had contributed its gamblers, who, it will be remembered, calmly continued their game the day that French Pete and Kanaka Joe shot each other to death over the bar in the front room. The whole camp was collected before a rude cabin on the outer edge of the clearing. Conversation was carried on in a low tone, but the name of a woman was frequently repeated. It was a name familiar enough to the camp – 'Cherokee Sal.'

Perhaps the less said of her the better. She was a coarse and, it is to be feared, a very sinful woman. But at that time she was the only woman in Roaring Camp, and was just then lying in sore extremity, when she most needed the ministration of her own sex. Dissolute, abandoned, and irreclaimable, she was yet suffering a martyrdom hard enough to bear even when veiled by sympathizing womanhood, but now terrrible in her loneliness. The primal curse had come to her in that original isolation which must have made the punishment of the first transgression so dreadful. It was, perhaps, part of the expiation of her sin that, at a moment when she most lacked her sex's intuitive tenderness and care, she met only the half-contemptuous faces of her masculine associates. Yet a few of the spectators were, I think, touched by her sufferings. Sandy Tipton thought it was 'rough on Sal,' and in the contemplation of her condition, for a moment rose superior to the fact that he had an ace and two bowers in his sleeve.

It will be seen also that the situation was novel. Deaths were by no means uncommon in Roaring Camp, but a birth was a new thing. People had been dismissed the camp effectively, finally, and with no possibility of return; but this was the first time that anybody had been introduced *ab initio*. Hence the excitement.

'You go in there, Stumpy,' said a prominent citizen known as 'Kentuck,' addressing one of the loungers. 'Go in there, and see what you kin do. You've had experience in them things.'

Perhaps there was a fitness in the selection. Stumpy, in other climes, had been the putative head of two families; in fact, it was owing to some legal informality in these proceedings that Roaring Camp – a city of refuge – was indebted to his company. The crowd approved the choice, and Stumpy was wise enough to bow to the majority. The door closed on the extempore surgeon and midwife, and Roaring Camp sat down outside, smoked its pipe, and awaited the issue.

The assemblage numbered about a hundred men. One or two of these were actual fugitives from justice, some were criminal, and all were reckless. Physically they exhibited no indication of their past lives and character. The greatest scamp had a Raphael face, with a profusion of blond hair; Oakhurst, a gambler, had the melancholy air and intellectual abstraction of a Hamlet; the coolest and most courageous man was scarcely over five feet in height, with a soft voice and an embarrassed, timid manner. The term 'roughs' applied to them was a distinction rather than a definition. Perhaps in the minor details of fingers, toes, ears, etc., the camp may have been deficient, but these slight omissions did not detract from their aggregate force. The strongest man had but three fingers on his right hand; the best shot had but one eye.

Such was the physical aspect of the men that were dispersed around the cabin. The camp lay in a triangular valley between two hills and a river. The only outlet was a steep trail over the summit of a hill that faced the cabin, now illuminated by the rising moon. The suffering woman might have seen it from the rude bunk whereon she lay – seen it winding like a silver thread until it was lost in the stars above.

A fire of withered pine boughs added sociability to the gathering. By degrees the natural levity of Roaring Camp returned. Bets were freely offered and taken regarding the result. Three to five that 'Sal would get through with it'; even that the child would survive; side bets as to the sex and complexion of the coming stranger. In the midst of an excited discussion an exclamation came from those nearest the door, and the camp stopped to listen. Above the swaying and moaning of the pines, the swift rush of the river, and the crackling of the fire rose a sharp, querulous cry – a cry unlike anything heard before in the camp. The pines stopped moaning, the river ceased to rush, and the fire to crackle. It seemed as if Nature had stopped to listen too.

The camp rose to its feet as one man! It was proposed to explode a barrel of gunpowder; but in consideration of the situation of the mother, better counsels prevailed, and only a few revolvers were discharged; for whether owing to the rude surgery of the camp, or some other reason, Cherokee Sal was sinking fast. Within an hour she had climbed, as it were, that rugged road that led to the stars, and so passed out of Roaring Camp, its sin and shame, forever. I do not think that the announcement disturbed them much, except in speculation as to the fate of the child. 'Can he live now?' was asked of Stumpy. The answer was doubtful. The only other being of Cherokee Sal's sex and maternal condition in the settlement was an ass. There was some conjecture as to fitness, but the experiment was tried. It was less problematical than the ancient treatment of Romulus and Remus, and apparently as successful.

When these details were completed, which exhausted another hour, the door was opened, and the anxious crowd of men, who had already formed themselves into a queue, entered in single file. Beside the low bunk or shelf, on which the figure of the mother was starkly outlined below the blankets, stood a pine table. On this a candlebox was placed, and within it, swathed in staring red flannel, lay the last arrival at Roaring Camp. Beside the candlebox was placed a hat. Its use was soon indicated. 'Gentlemen,' said Stumpy, with a singular mixture of authority and ex officio complacency – 'gentlemen will please pass in at the front door, round the table, and out at the back door. Them as wishes to contribute anything toward the orphan will find a hat handy.' The first man entered with his hat on; he uncovered, however, as he looked about him, and so unconsciously set an example to the next. In such communities good and bad actions are catching. As the procession filed in comments were audible – criticisms addressed perhaps rather to Stumpy in the character of showman: 'Is that him?' 'Mighty small specimen;' 'Hasn't more'n got the color;' 'Ain't bigger nor a derringer.' The contributions were as characteristic: A silver tobacco box; a doubloon; a navy revolver, silver mounted; a gold specimen; a very beautifully embroidered lady's handkerchief (from Oakhurst the gambler); a diamond breastpin; a diamond ring (suggested by the pin, with the remark from the giver that he 'saw that pin and went two diamonds better'); a slung shot; a Bible (contributor not detected); a golden spur; a silver teaspoon (the initials, I regret to say, were not the giver's); a pair of surgeon's shears; a lancet; a Bank of England note for £5; and about $200 in loose gold and silver coin. During these proceedings Stumpy maintained a silence as impassive as the dead on his left, a gravity as inscrutable as that of the newly born on his right. Only one incident occurred to break the monotony of the curious procession. As Kentuck bent over the candlebox half curiously, the child turned, and, in a spasm of pain, caught at his groping finger and held it fast for a moment. Kentuck looked foolish and embarrassed. Something like a blush tried to assert itself in his weather-beaten cheek. 'The d – d little cuss!' he said, as he extricated his finger, with perhaps more tenderness and care than he might have been deemed capable of showing. He held that finger a little apart from its fellows as he went out, and examined it curiously. The examination provoked the same original remark in regard to the child. In fact, he seemed to enjoy repeating it. 'He rastled with my finger,' he remarked to Tipton, holding up the member, 'the d – d little cuss!'

It was four o'clock before the camp sought repose. A light burnt in the cabin where the watchers sat, for Stumpy did not go to bed that night. Nor did Kentuck. He drank quite freely, and related with great gusto his experience, invariably ending with his characteristic condemnation of the newcomer. It seemed to relieve him of any unjust implication of sentiment, and Kentuck had the weaknesses of the nobler sex. When everybody else had gone to bed, he walked down to the river and whistled reflectively. Then he walked up the gulch past the cabin, still whistling with demonstrative unconcern. At a large redwood tree he paused and retraced his steps, and again passed the cabin. Halfway down to the river's bank he again paused, and then returned and knocked at the door. It was opened by Stumpy. 'How goes it?' said Kentuck, looking past Stumpy toward the candlebox. 'All serene!' replied Stumpy. 'Anything up?' 'Nothing.' There was a pause – an embarrassing one – Stumpy still holding the door. Then Kentuck had recourse to his finger, which he held up to Stumpy. 'Rastled with it – the d – d little cuss,' he said, and retired.

The next day Cherokee Sal had such rude sepulture as Roaring Camp afforded. After her body had been committed to the hillside, there was a formal meeting of the camp to discuss what should be done with her infant. A resolution to adopt it was unanimous and enthusiastic. But an animated discussion in regard to the manner and feasibility of providing for its wants at once sprang up. It was remarkable that the argument partook of none of those fierce personalities with which discussions were usually conducted at Roaring Camp. Tipton proposed that they should send the child to Red Dog – a distance of forty miles – where female attention could be procured. But the unlucky suggestion met with fierce and unanimous opposition. It was evident that no plan which entailed parting from their new acquisition would for a moment be entertained. 'Besides,' said Tom Ryder, 'them fellows at Red Dog would swap it, and ring in somebody else on us.' A disbelief in the honesty of other camps prevailed at Roaring Camp, as in other places.

The introduction of a female nurse in the camp also met with objection. It was argued that no decent woman could be prevailed to accept Roaring Camp as her home, and the speaker urged that 'they didn't want any more of the other kind.' This unkind allusion to the defunct mother, harsh as it may seem, was the first spasm of propriety – the first symptom of the camp's regeneration. Stumpy advanced nothing. Perhaps he felt a certain delicacy in interfering with the selection of a possible successor in office. But when questioned, he averred stoutly that he and 'Jinny' – the mammal before alluded to – could manage to rear the child. There was something original, independent, and heroic about the plan that pleased the camp. Stumpy was retained. Certain articles were sent for to Sacramento. 'Mind,' said the treasurer, as he pressed a bag of gold dust into the expressman's hand, 'the best that can be got – lace, you know, and filigree work and frills – d – n the cost!'

Strange to say, the child thrived. Perhaps the invigorating climate of the mountain camp was compensation for material deficiencies. Nature took the foundling to her broader breast. In that rare atmosphere of the Sierra foothills – that air pungent with balsamic odor, that ethereal cordial at once bracing and exhilarating – he may have found food and nourishment, or a subtle chemistry that transmuted ass's milk to lime and phosphorus. Stumpy inclined to the belief that it was the latter and good nursing. 'Me and that ass,' he would say, 'has been father and mother to him! Don't you,' he would add, apostrophizing the helpless bundle before him, 'never go back on us.'

By the time he was a month old the necessity of giving him a name became apparent. He had generally been known as 'The Kid,' 'Stumpy's Boy,' 'The Coyote' (an allusion of his vocal powers), and even by Kentuck's endearing diminutive of 'The d – d little cuss.' But these were felt to be vague and unsatisfactory, and were at last dismissed under another influence. Gamblers and adventurers are generally superstitious, and Oakhurst one day declared that the baby had brought 'the luck' to Roaring Camp. It was certain that of late they had been successful. 'Luck' was the name agreed upon, with the prefix of Tommy for greater convenience. No allusion was made to the mother, and the father was unknown. 'It's better,' said the philosophical Oakhurst, 'to take a fresh deal all round. Call him Luck, and start him fair.' A day was accordingly set apart for the christening. What was meant by this ceremony the reader may imagine who has already gathered some idea of the reckless irreverence of Roaring Camp. The master of ceremonies was one 'Boston,' a noted wag, and the occasion seemed to promise the greatest facetiousness. This ingenious satirist had spent two days in preparing a burlesque of the Church service, with pointed local allusions. The choir was properly trained, and Sandy Tipton was to stand godfather. But after the procession had marched to the grove with music and banners, and the child had been deposited before a mock altar, Stumpy stepped before the expectant crowd. 'It ain't my style to spoil fun, boys,' said the little man, stoutly eying the faces around him, 'but it strikes me that this thing ain't exactly on the squar. It's playing it pretty low down on this yer baby to ring in fun on him that he ain't goin' to understand. And ef there's goin' to be any godfathers round, I'd like to see who's got any better rights than me.' A silence followed Stumpy's speech. To the credit of all humorists be it said that the first man to acknowledge its justice was the satirist thus stopped of his fun. 'But,' said Stumpy, quickly following up his advantage, 'we're here for a christening, and we'll have it. I proclaim you Thomas Luck, according to the laws of the United States and the State of California, so help me God.' It was the first time that the name of the Deity had been otherwise uttered than profanely in the camp. The form of christening was perhaps ever more ludicrous than the satirist had conceived; but strangely enough, nobody saw it and nobody laughed. 'Tommy' was christened as seriously as he would have been under a Christian roof, and cried and was comforted in as orthodox fashion.

And so the work of regeneration began in Roaring Camp. Almost imperceptibly a change came over the settlement. The cabin assigned to 'Tommy Luck' – or 'The Luck,' as he was more frequently called – first showed signs of improvement. It was kept scrupulously clean and whitewashed. Then it was boarded, clothed, and papered. The rosewood cradle, packed eighty miles by mule, had, in Stumpy's way of putting it, 'sorter killed the rest of the furniture.' So the rehabilitation of the camp became a necessity. The men who were in the habit of lounging in at Stumpy's to see 'how "The Luck" got on' seemed to appreciate the change, and in self-defense the rival establishment of 'Tuttle's grocery' bestirred itself and imported a carpet and mirrors. The reflections of the latter on the appearance of Roaring Camp tended to produce stricter habits of personal cleanliness. Again Stumpy imposed a kind of quarantine upon those who aspired to the honor and privilege of holding The Luck. It was a cruel mortification to Kentuck – who, in the carelessness of a large nature and the habits of frontier life, had begun to regard all garments as a second cuticle, which, like a snake's, only sloughed off through decay – to be debarred this privilege from certain prudential reasons. Yet such was the subtle influence of innovation that he thereafter appeared regularly every afternoon in a clean shirt and face still shining from his ablutions. Nor were moral and social sanitary laws neglected. 'Tommy,' who was supposed to spend his whole existence in a persistent attempt to repose, must not be disturbed by noise. The shouting and yelling, which had gained the camp its infelicitous title, were not permitted within hearing distance of Stumpy's. The men conversed in whispers or smoked with Indian gravity. Profanity was tacitly given up in these sacred precincts, and throughout the camp a popular form of expletive, known as 'D – n the luck!' and 'Curse the luck!' was abandoned, as having a new personal bearing. Vocal music was not interdicted, being supposed to have a soothing, tranquilizing quality; and one song, sung by 'Man-o'-War Jack', an English sailor from her Majesty's Australian colonies, was quite popular as a lullaby. It was a lugubrious recital of the exploits of 'the Arethusa, Seventy-four,' in a muffled minor, ending with a prolonged dying fall at the burden of each verse, 'On b-oo-o-ard of the Arethusa.' It was a fine sight to see Jack holding The Luck, rocking from side to side as if with the motion of a ship, and crooning forth this naval ditty. Either through the peculiar rocking of Jack or the length of his song – it contained ninety stanzas, and was continued with conscientious deliberation to the bitter end – the lullaby generally had the desired effect. At such times the men would lie at full length under the trees in the soft summer twilight, smoking their pipes and drinking in the melodious utterances. An indistinct idea that this was pastoral happiness pervaded the camp. 'This 'ere kind o' think,' said the Cockney Simmons, meditatively reclining on his elbow, 'is 'evingly.' It reminded him of Greenwich.

On the long summer days The Luck was usually carried to the gulch from whence the golden store of Roaring Camp was taken. There, on a blanket spread over pine boughs, he would lie while the men were working in the ditches below. Latterly there was a rude attempt to decorate this bower with flowers and sweet-smelling shrubs, and generally some one would bring him a cluster of wild honeysuckles, azaleas, or the painted blossoms of Las Mariposas. The men had suddenly awakened to the fact that there were beauty and significance in these trifles, which they had so long trodden carelessly beneath their feet. A flake of glittering mica, a fragment of variegated quartz, a bright pebble from the bed of the creek, became beautiful to eyes thus cleared and strengthened, and were invariably put aside for The Luck. It was wonderful how many treasures the woods and hillsides yielded that 'would do for Tommy.' Surrounded by playthings such as never child out of fairyland had before, it is to be hoped that Tommy was content. He appeared to be serenely happy, albeit there was an infantine gravity about him, a contemplative light in his round gray eyes, that sometimes worried Stumpy. He was always tractable and quiet, and it is recorded that once, having crept beyond his 'corral' – a hedge of tessellated pine boughs, which surrounded his bed – he dropped over the bank on his head in the soft earth, and remained with his mottled legs in the air in that position for at least five minutes with unflinching gravity. He was extricated without a murmur. I hesitate to record the many other instances of his sagacity, which rest, unfortunately, upon the statements of prejudiced friends. Some of them were not without a tinge of superstition. 'I crep' up the bank just now,' said Kentuck one day, in a breathless state of excitement, 'and dern my skin if he wasn't a-talking to a jay bird as was a sittin' on his lap. There they was, just as free and sociable as anything you please, a-jawin' at each other just like two cherrybums.' Howbeit, whether creeping over the pine boughs or lying lazily on his back blinking at the leaves above him, to him the birds sang, the squirrels chattered, and the flowers bloomed. Nature was his nurse and playfellow. For him she would let slip between the leaves golden shafts of sunlight that fell just within his grasp; she would send wandering breezes to visit him with the balm of bay and resinous gum; to him the tall redwoods nodded familiarly and sleepily, the bumblebees buzzed, and the rooks cawed a slumbrous accompaniment.

Such was the golden summer of Roaring Camp. They were 'flush times', and the luck was with them. The claims had yielded enormously. The camp was jealous of its privileges and looked suspiciously on strangers. No encouragement was given to immigration, and, to make their seclusion more perfect, the land on either side of the mountain wall that surrounded the camp they duly pre-empted. This, and a reputation for singular proficiency with the revolver, kept the reserve of Roaring Camp inviolate. The expressman – their only connecting link with the surrounding world – sometimes told wonderful stories of the camp. He would say, 'They've a street up there in "Roaring" that would lay over any street in Red Dog. They've got vines and flowers round their houses, and they wash themselves twice a day. But they're mighty rough on strangers, and they worship an Ingin baby.'

With the prosperity of the camp came a desire for further improvement. It was proposed to build a hotel in the following spring, and to invite one or two decent families to reside there for the sake of The Luck, who might perhaps profit by female companionship. The sacrifice that this concession to the sex cost these men, who were fiercely skeptical in regard to its general virtue and usefulness, can only be accounted for by their affection for Tommy. A few still held out. But the resolve could not be carried into effect for three months, and the minority meekly yielded in the hope that something might turn up to prevent it. And it did.

The winter of 1851 will long be remembered in the foothills. The snow lay deep on the Sierras, and every mountain creek became a river, and every river a lake. Each gorge and gulch was transformed into a tumultuous watercourse that descended the hillsides, tearing down giant trees and scattering its drift and debris along the plain. Red Dog had been twice under water, and Roaring Camp had been forewarned. 'Water put the gold into them gulches,' said Stumpy. 'It's been here once and will be here again!' And that night the North Fork suddenly leaped over its banks and swept up the triangular valley of Roaring Camp.

In the confusion of rushing water, crashing trees, and crackling timber, and the darkness which seemed to flow with the water and blot out the fair valley, but little could be done to collect the scattered camp. When the morning broke, the cabin of Stumpy, nearest the river-bank, was gone. Higher up the gulch they found the body of its unlucky owner; but the pride, the hope, the joy, The Luck, of Roaring Camp had disappeared. They were returning with sad hearts when a shout from the bank recalled them.

It was a relief-boat from down the river. They had picked up, they said, a man and an infant, nearly exhausted, about two miles below. Did anybody know them, and did they belong here?

It needed but a glance to show them Kentuck lying there, cruelly crushed and bruised, but still holding The Luck of Roaring Camp in his arms. As they bent over the strangely assorted pair, they saw that the child was cold and pulseless. 'He is dead,' said one. Kentuck opened his eyes. 'Dead?' he repeated feebly. 'Yes, my man, and you are dying too.' A smile lit the eyes of the expiring Kentuck. 'Dying!' he repeated; 'he's a-taking me with him. Tell the boys I've got The Luck with me now;' and the strong man, clinging to the frail babe as a drowning man is said to cling to a straw, drifted away into the shadowy river that flows forever to the unknown sea.

GREAT AMERICAN WRITERS

THE
CABALLERO'S
WAY

THE
PIMIENTA
PANCAKES

A CALL
LOAN

BY

O. HENRY

The Caballero's Way

THE CISCO KID HAD KILLED six men in more or less fair scrimmages, had murdered twice as many (mostly Mexicans), and had winged a larger number whom he modestly forebore to count. Therefore a woman loved him.

The Kid was twenty-five, looked twenty; and a careful insurance company would have estimated the probable time of his demise at, say, twenty-six. His habitat was anywhere between the Frio and the Rio Grande. He killed for the love of it – because he was quick-tempered – to avoid arrest – for his own amusement – any reason that came to his mind would suffice. He had escaped capture because he could shoot five-sixths of a second sooner than any sheriff or ranger in the service, and because he rode a speckled roan horse that knew every cowpath in the mesquite and pear thickets from San Antonio to Matamoras.

Tonia Perez, the girl who loved the Cisco Kid, was half Carmen, half Madonna, and the rest – oh, yes, a woman who is half Carmen and half Madonna can always be something more – the rest, let us say, was humming-bird. She lived in a grass-roofed *jacal* near a little Mexican settlement at the Lone Wolf Crossing of the Frio. With her lived a father or grandfather, a lineal Aztec, somewhat less than a thousand years old, who herded a hundred goats and lived in a continuous drunken dream from drinking *mescal*. Back of the *jacal* a tremendous forest of bristling pear, twenty feet high at its worst, crowded almost to its door. It was along the bewildering maze of this spinous thicket that the speckled roan would bring the Kid to see his girl. And once, clinging like a lizard to the ridge-pole, high up under the peaked grass roof, he had heard Tonia, with her Madonna face and Carmen beauty and humming-bird soul, parley with the sheriff's posse, denying knowledge of her man in her soft *mélange* of Spanish and English.

One day the adjutant-general of the State, who is, *ex officio*, commander of the ranger forces, wrote some sarcastic lines to Captain Duval of Company X, stationed at Laredo, relative to the serene and undisturbed existence led by murderers and desperadoes in the said captain's territory.

The captain turned the color of brick dust under his tan, and forwarded the letter, after adding a few comments, per ranger Private Bill Adamson, to ranger Lieutenant Sandridge, camped at a water hole on the Neuces with a squad of five men in preservation of law and order.

Lieutenant Sandridge turned a beautiful *couleur de rose* through his ordinary strawberry complexion, tucked the letter in his hip pocket, and chewed off the end of his gamboge moustache.

The next morning he saddled his horse and rode alone to the Mexican settlement at the Lone Wolf Crossing of the Frio, twenty miles away.

Six feet two, blond as a Viking, quiet as a deacon, dangerous as a machine gun, Sandridge moved among the *Jacales*, patiently seeking news of the Cisco Kid.

Far more than the law, the Mexicans dreaded the cold and certain vengeance of the lone rider that the ranger sought. It had been one of the Kid's pastimes to shoot Mexicans 'to see them kick': if he demanded from them moribund Terpischorean feats, simply that he might be entertained, what terrible and extreme penalties would be certain to follow should they anger him! One and all they lounged with upturned palms and shrugging shoulders, filling the air with 'quién sabes' and denials of the Kid's acquaintance.

But there was a man named Fink who kept a store at the Crossing – a man of many nationalities, tongues, interests, and ways of thinking.

'No use to ask them Mexicans,' he said to Sandridge. 'They're afraid to tell. This hombre they call the Kid – Goodall is his name, ain't it? – he's been in my store once or twice. I have an idea you might run across him at – but I guess I don't keer to say, myself. I'm two seconds later in pulling a gun than I used to be and the difference is worth thinking about. But this Kid's got a half-Mexican girl at the Crossing that he comes to see. She lives in that jacal a hundred yards down the arroyo at the edge of the pear. Maybe she – no, I don't suppose she would, but that jacal would be a good place to watch, anyway.'

Sandridge rode down to the jacal of Perez. The sun was low, and the broad shade of the great pear thicket already covered the grass-thatched hut. The goats were enclosed for the night in a brush corral near by. A few kids walked the top of it, nibbling the chaparral leaves. The old Mexican lay upon a blanket on the grass, already in a stupor from his mescal, and dreaming, perhaps, of the nights when he and Pizarro touched glasses to their New World fortunes – so old his wrinkled face seemed to proclaim him to be. And in the door of the jacal stood Tonia. And Lieutenant Sandridge sat in his saddle staring at her like a gannet agape at a sailorman.

The Cisco Kid was a vain person, as all eminent and successful assassins are, and his bosom would have been ruffled had he known that at a simple exchange of glances two persons, in whose minds he had been looming large, suddenly abandoned (at least for the time) all thought of him.

Never before had Tonia seen such a man as this. He seemed to be made of sunshine and blood-red tissue and clear weather. He seemed to illuminate the shadow of the pear when he smiled, as though the sun were rising again. The men she had known had been small and dark. Even the Kid, in spite of his achievements, was a stripling no larger than herself, with black straight hair and a cold marble face that chilled the noonday.

As for Tonia, though she sends description to the poorhouse, let her make a millionaire of your fancy. Her blue-black hair, smoothly divided in the middle and bound close to her head, and her large eyes full of the Latin melancholy, gave her the Madonna touch. Her motions and air spoke of the concealed fire and the desire to charm that she inherited from the gitanas of the Basque province. As for the humming-bird part of her, that dwelt in her heart; you could not perceive it unless her bright red skirt and dark blue blouse gave you a symbolic hint of the vagarious bird.

The newly lighted sun-god asked for a drink of water. Tonia brought it from the red jar hanging under the brush shelter. Sandridge considered it necessary to dismount so as to lessen the trouble of her ministrations.

I play no spy; nor do I assume to master the thoughts of any human heart; but I assert, by the chronicler's right, that before a quarter of an hour had sped, Sandridge was teaching her how to plait a six-strand rawhide stake-rope, and Tonia had explained to him that were it not for her little English book that the peripatetic *padre* had given her and the little crippled *chivo*, that she fed from a bottle, she would be very, very lonely indeed.

Which leads to a suspicion that the Kid's fences needed repairing, and that the adjutant-general's sarcasm had fallen upon unproductive soil.

In his camp by the water hole Lieutenant Sandridge announced and reiterated his intention of either causing the Cisco Kid to nibble the black loam of the Frio country prairies or of hailing him before a judge and jury. That sounded business-like. Twice a week he rode over to the Lone Wolf Crossing of the Frio, and directed Tonia's slim, slightly lemon-tinted fingers among the intricacies of the slowly growing lariat. A six-strand plait is hard to learn and easy to teach.

The ranger knew that he might find the Kid there at any visit. He kept his armament ready, and had a frequent eye for the pear thicket at the rear of the *jacal*. Thus he might bring down the kite and the humming-bird with one stone.

While the sunny-haired ornithologist was pursuing his studies the Cisco Kid was also attending to his professional duties. He moodily shot up a saloon in a small cow village on Quintana Creek, killed the town marshal (plugging him neatly in the centre of his tin badge), and then rode away, morose and unsatisfied. No true artist is uplifted by shooting an aged man carrying an old-style .38 bulldog.

On his way the Kid suddenly experienced the yearning that all men feel when wrong-doing loses its keen edge of delight. He yearned for the woman he loved to reassure him that she was his in spite of it. He wanted her to call his bloodthirsti-ness bravery and his cruelty devotion. He wanted Tonia to bring him water from the red jug under the brush shelter, and tell him how the *chivo* was thriving on the bottle.

The Kid turned the speckled roan's head up the ten-mile pear flat that stretches along the Arroyo Hondo until it ends at the Lone Wolf Crossing of the Frio. The roam whickered; for he had a sense of locality and direction equal to that of a belt-line street-car horse; and he knew he would soon be nibbling the rich mesquite grass at the end of a forty-foot stake rope while Ulysses rested his head in Circe's straw-roofed hut.

More weird and lonesome than the journey of an Amazonian explorer is the ride of one through a Texas pear flat. With dismal monotony and startling variety the uncanny and multiform shapes of the cacti lift their twisted trunks and fat, bristly hands to encumber the way. The demon plant, appearing to live without soil or rain, seems to taunt the parched traveler with its lush gray greenness. It warps itself a thousand times about what look to be open and inviting paths, only to lure the rider into blind and impassable spine-defended 'bottoms of the bag,' leaving him to retreat if he can, with the points of the compass whirling in his head.

To be lost in the pear is to die almost the death of the thief on the cross, pierced by nails and with grotesque shapes of all the fiends hovering about.

But it was not so with the Kid and his mount. Winding, twisting, circling, tracing the most fantastic and bewildering trail every picked out, the good roan lessened the distance to the Lone Wolf Crossing with every coil and turn that he made.

While they fared the Kid sang. He knew but one tune and he sang it, as he knew but one code and lived it, and but one girl and loved her. He was a single-minded man of conventional ideas. He had a voice like a coyote with bronchitis, but whenever he chose to sing his song he sang it. It was a conventional song of the camps and trail, running at its beginning as near as may be to these words:

> Don't you monkey with my Lulu girl
> Or I'll tell you what I'll do—

and so on. The roan was inured to it, and did not mind.

But even the poorest singer will, after a certain time, gain his own consent to refrain from contributing to the world's noises. So the Kid, by the time he was within a mile or two of Tonia's *jacal*, had reluctantly allowed his song to die away – not because his vocal performance had become less charming to his own ears, but because his laryngeal muscles were weary.

As though he were in a circus ring the speckled roan wheeled and danced through the labyrinth of pear until at length his rider knew by certain landmarks that the Lone Wolf Crossing was at hand. Then, where the pear was thinner, he caught sight of the grass roof of the *jacal* and the hackberry tree on the edge of the arroyo. A few yards farther the Kid stopped the roan and gazed intently through the prickly openings. Then he dismounted, dropped the roan's reins, and proceeded on foot, stooping and silent, like an Indian. The roan, knowing his part, stood still, making no sound.

The Kid crept noiselessly to the very edge of the pear thicket and reconnoitered between the leaves of a clump of cactus.

Ten yards from his hiding-place, in the shade of the *jacal*, sat his Tonia calmly plaiting a raw-hide lariat. So far she might surely escape condemnation; women have been known, from time to time, to engage in more mischievous occupations. But if all must be told, there is to be added that her head reposed against the broad and comfortable chest of a tall red-and-yellow man, and that his arm was about her, guiding her nimble small fingers that required so many lessons at the intricate six-strand plait.

Sandridge glanced quickly at the dark mass of pear when he heard a slight squeaking sound that was not altogether unfamiliar. A gun-scabbard will make that sound when one grasps the handle of a six-shooter suddenly. But the sound was not repeated; and Tonia's fingers needed close attention.

And then, in the shadow of death, they began to talk of their love; and in the still July afternoon every word they uttered reached the ears of the Kid.

'Remember, then,' said Tonia, 'you must not come again until I send for you. Soon he will be here. A *vaquero* at the *tienda* said today he saw him on the Guadalupe three days ago. When he is that near he always comes. If he comes and finds you here he will kill you. So, for my sake, you must come no more until I send you the word.'

'All right,' said the ranger. 'And then what?'

'And then,' said the girl, 'you must bring your men here and kill him. If not, he will kill you.'

'He ain't a man to surrender, that's sure,' said Sandridge. 'It's kill or be killed for the officer that goes up against Mr Cisco Kid.'

'He must die,' said the girl. 'Otherwise there will not be any peace in the world for thee and me. He has killed many. Let him so die. Bring your men, and give him no chance to escape.'

'You used to think right much of him,' said Sandridge.

Tonia dropped the lariat, twisted herself around, and curved a lemon-tinted arm over the ranger's shoulder.

'But then,' she murmured in liquid Spanish, 'I had not beheld thee, thou great, red mountain of a man! And thou art kind and good, as well as strong. Could one choose him, knowing thee? Let him die; for then I will not be filled with fear by day and night lest he hurt thee or me.'

'How can I know when he comes?' asked Sandridge.

'When he comes,' said Tonia, 'he remains two days, sometimes three. Gregorio, the small son of Old Luisa, the *lavandera*, has a swift pony. I will write a letter to thee and send it by him, saying how it will be best to come upon him. By Gregorio will the letter come. And bring many men with thee, and have such care, oh, dear red one, for the rattlesnake is not quicker to strike that is "*El Chivato*," as they call him, to send a ball from his *pistola*.'

'The Kid's handy with his gun, sure enough,' admitted Sandridge, 'but when I come for him I shall come alone. I'll get him by myself or not at all. The Cap wrote one or two things to me that make me want to do the trick without any help. You let me know when Mr Kid arrives, and I'll do the rest.'

'I will send you the message by the boy Gregorio,' said the girl. 'I knew you were braver than that small slayer of men who never smiles. How could I ever have thought I cared for him?'

It was time for the ranger to ride back to his camp on the water hole. Before he mounted his horse he raised the slight form of Tonia with one arm high from the earth for a parting salute. The drowsy stillness of the torpid summer air still lay thick upon the dreaming afternoon. The smoke from the fire in the *jacal*, where the *frijoles* blubbered in the iron pot, rose straight as a plumb-line above the clay-daubed chimney. No sound or movement disturbed the serenity of the dense pear thicket ten yards away.

When the form of Sandridge had disappeared, loping his big dun down the steep banks of the Frio crossing, the Kid crept back to his own horse, mounted him, and rode back along the tortuous trail he had come.

But not far. He stopped and waited in the silent depths of the pear until half an hour had passed. And then Tonia heard the high, untrue notes of his unmusical singing coming nearer and nearer; and she ran to the edge of the pear to meet him.

The Kid seldom smiled; but he smiled and waved his hat when he saw her. He dismounted, and his girl sprang into his arms. The Kid looked at her fondly. His thick black hair clung to his head like a wrinkled mat. The meeting brought a slight ripple of some undercurrent of feeling to his smooth, dark face that was usually as motionless as a clay mask.

'How's my girl?' he asked, holding her close.

'Sick of waiting so long for you, dear one,' she answered. 'My eyes are dim with always gazing into that devil's pincushion through which you come. And I can see into it such a little way, too. But you are here, beloved one, and I will not scold. *Qué mal muchacho!* not to come to see your *alma* more often. Go in and rest, and let me water your horse and stake him with the long rope. There is cool water in the jar for you.'

The Kid kissed her affectionately.

'Not if the court knows itself do I let a lady stake my horse for me,' said he. 'But if you'll run in, *chica*, and throw a pot of coffee together while I attend to the *caballo*, I'll be a good deal obliged.'

Besides his marksmanship the Kid had another attribute for which he admired himself greatly. He was *muy caballero*, as the Mexicans express it, where the ladies were concerned. For them he had always gentle words and consideration. He could not have spoken a harsh word to a woman. He might ruthlessly slay their husbands and brothers, but he could not have laid the weight of a finger in anger upon a woman. Wherefore many of that interesting division of humanity who had come under the spell of his politeness declared their disbelief in the stories circulated about Mr Kid. One shouldn't believe everything one heard, they said. When confronted by their indignant men folk with proof of the *caballero*'s deeds of infamy, they said maybe he had been driven to it, and that he knew how to treat a lady, anyhow.

Considering this extremely courteous idiosyncrasy of the Kid and the pride that he took in it, one can perceive that the solution of the problem that was presented to him by what he saw and heard from his hiding-place in the pear that afternoon (at least as to one of the actors) must have been obscured by difficulties. And yet one could not think of the Kid overlooking little matters of that kind.

At the end of the short twilight they gathered around a supper of *frijoles*, goat steaks, canned peaches, and coffee, by the light of a lantern in the *jacal*. Afterward, the ancestor, his flock corralled, smoked a cigarette and became a mummy in a gray blanket. Tonia washed the few dishes while the Kid dried them with the flour-sacking towel. Her eyes shone; she chatted volubly of the inconsequent happenings of her small world since the Kid's last visit; it was as all his other home-comings had been.

Then outside Tonia swung in a grass hammock with her guitar and sang sad *canciones de amor*.

'Do you love me just the same, old girl?' asked the Kid, hunting for his cigarette papers.

'Always the same, little one,' said Tonia, her dark eyes lingering upon him.

'I must go over to Fink's,' said the Kid, rising, 'for some tobacco. I thought I had another sack in my coat. I'll be back in a quarter of an hour.'

'Hasten,' said Tonia, 'and tell me – how long shall I call you my own this time? Will you be gone again tomorrow, leaving me to grieve, or will you be longer with your Tonia?'

'Oh, I might stay two or three days this trip,' said the Kid, yawning. 'I've been on the dodge for a month, and I'd like to rest up.'

He was gone half an hour for his tobacco. When he returned Tonia was still lying in the hammock.

'It's funny,' said the Kid, 'how I feel. I feel like there was somebody lying behind every bush and tree waiting to shoot me. I never had mully-grubs like them before. Maybe it's one of them presumptions. I've got half a notion to light out in the morning before day. The Guadalupe country is burning up about that old Dutchman I plugged down there.'

'You are not afraid – no one could make my brave little one fear.'

'Well, I haven't been usually regarded as a jack-rabbit when it comes to scrapping; but I don't want a posse smoking me out when I'm in your *jacal*. Somebody might get hurt that oughtn't to.'

'Remain with your Tonia; no one will find you here.'

The Kid looked keenly into the shadows up and down the arroyo and toward the dim lights of the Mexican village.

'I'll see how it looks later on,' was his decision.

At midnight a horseman rode into the ranger's camp, blazing his way by noisy 'halloes' to indicate a pacific mission. Sandridge and one or two others turned out to investigate the row. The rider announced himself to be Domingo Sales, from the Lone Wolf Crossing. He bore a letter for Señor Sandridge. Old Luisa, the *lavandera*, had persuaded him to bring it, he said, her son Gregorio being too ill of a fever to ride.

Sandridge lighted the camp lantern and read the letter. These were its words:

DEAR ONE:

He has come. Hardly had you ridden away when he came out of the pear. When he first talked he said he would stay three days or more. Then as it grew later he was like a wolf or a fox, and walked about without rest, looking and listening. Soon he said he must leave before daylight when it is dark and stillest. And then he seemed to suspect that I be not true to him. He looked at me so strange that I am frightened. I swear to him that I love him, his own Tonia. Last of all he said I must prove to him I am true. He thinks that even now men are waiting to kill him as he rides from my house. To escape he says he will dress in my clothes, my red skirt and the blue waist I wear and the brown mantilla over the head, and thus ride away. But before that he says that I must put on his clothes, his *pantalones* and *camisa* and hat, and ride away on his horse from the *jacal* as far as the big road beyond the crossing and back again. This before he goes, so he can tell if I am true and if men are hidden to shoot him. It is a terrible thing. An hour before daybreak this is to be. Come, my dear one, and kill this man and take me for your Tonia. Do not try to take hold of him alive, but kill him quickly. Knowing all, you should do that. You must come long before the time and hide yourself in the little shed near the *jacal* where the wagon and saddles are kept. It is dark in there. He will wear my red skirt and blue waist and brown mantilla. I send you a hundred kisses. Come surely and shoot quickly and straight.

THINE OWN TONIA

Sandridge quickly explained to his men the official part of the missive. The rangers protested against his going alone.

'I'll get him easy enough,' said the lieutenant. 'The girl's got him trapped. And don't even think he'll get the drop on me.'

Sandridge saddled his horse and rode to the Lone Wolf Crossing. He tied his big dun in a clump of brush on the arroyo, took his Winchester from his scabbard, and carefully approached the Perez *jacal*. There was only the half of a high moon drifted over by ragged, milk-white gulf clouds.

The wagon-shed was an excellent place for ambush; and the ranger got inside it safely. In the black shadow of the brush shelter in front of the *jacal* he could see a horse tied and hear him impatiently pawing the hard-trodden earth.

He waited almost an hour before two figures came out of the *jacal*. One, in man's clothes, quickly mounted the horse and galloped past the wagon-shed toward the crossing and village. And then the other figure, in skirt, waist, and mantilla over its head, stepped out into the faint moonlight, gazing after the rider. Sandridge thought he would take his chance then before Tonia rode back. He fancied she might not care to see it.

'Throw up your hands,' he ordered, loudly, stepping out of the wagon-shed with his Winchester at his shoulder.

There was a quick turn of the figure, but no movement to obey, so the ranger pumped in the bullets – one – two – three – and then twice more; for you never could be too sure of bringing down the Cisco Kid. There was no danger of missing at ten paces, even in that half moonlight.

The old ancestor, asleep on his blanket, was awakened by the shots. Listening further, he heard a great cry from some man in mortal distress or anguish, and rose up grumbling at the disturbing ways of moderns.

The tall, red ghost of a man burst into the *jacal*, reaching one hand, shaking like a *tule* reed, for the lantern hanging on its nail. The other spread a letter on the table.

'Look at this letter, Perez,' cried the man. 'Who wrote it?'

'*Ah Dios!* it is Señor Sandridge,' mumbled the old man, approaching. '*Pues, señor*, that letter was written by "*El Chivata,*" as he is called – by the man of Tonia. They say he is a bad man; I do not know. While Tonia slept he wrote the letter and sent it by this old hand of mine to Domingo Sales to be brought to you. Is there anything wrong in the letter? I am very old; and I did not know. *Valgame Dios!* it is a very foolish world; and there is nothing in the house to drink – nothing to drink.'

Just then all that Sandridge could think of to do was to go outside and throw himself face downward in the dust by the side of his humming-bird, of whom not a feather fluttered. He was not a *caballero* by instinct, and he could not understand the niceties of revenge.

A mile away the rider who had ridden past the wagon-shed struck up a harsh, untuneful song, the words of which began:

> Don't you monkey with my Lulu girl
> Or I'll tell you what I'll do—

The Pimienta Pancakes

WHILE WE WERE ROUNDING UP a bunch of the Triangle-O cattle in the Frio bottoms a projecting branch of a dead mesquite caught my wooden stirrup and gave my ankle a wrench that laid me up in camp for a week.

On the third day of my compulsory idleness I crawled out near the grub wagon, and reclined helpless under the conversational fire of Judson Odom, the camp cook. Jud was a monologist by nature, whom Destiny, with customary blundering, had set in a profession wherein he was bereaved, for the greater portion of his time, of an audience.

Therefore, I was manna in the desert of Jud's obmutescence.

Betimes I was stirred by invalid longings for something to eat that did not come under the caption of 'grub.' I had visions of the maternal pantry 'deep as first love, and wild with all regret,' and then I asked:

'Jud, can you make pancakes?'

Jud laid down his sixshooter, with which he was preparing to pound an antelope steak, and stood over me in what I felt to be a menacing attitude. He further indorsed my impression that his pose was resentful by fixing upon me with his light blue eyes a look of cold suspicion.

'Say, you,' he said, with candid, though not excessive, choler, 'did you mean that straight, or was you trying to throw the gaff into me? Some of the boys been telling you about me and that pancake racket?'

'No, Jud,' I said, sincerely, 'I meant it. It seems to me I'd swap my pony and saddle for a stack of buttered brown pancakes with some first crop, open kettle, New Orleans sweetening. Was there a story about pancakes?'

Jud was mollified at once when he saw that I had not been dealing in allusions. He brought some mysterious bags and tin boxes from the grub wagon and set them in the shade of the hackberry where I lay reclined. I watched him as he began to arrange them leisurely and untie their many strings.

'No, not a story,' said Jud, as he worked, 'but just the logical disclosures in the case of me and that pink-eyed snoozer from Mired Mule Cañada and Miss Willella Learight. I don't mind telling you.

'I was punching then for old Bill Toomey, on the San Miguel. One day I gets all ensnared up in aspirations for to eat some canned grub that hasn't even mooed or baaed or grunted or been in peck measures. So, I gets on my bronc and pushed the wind for Uncle Emsley Telfair's store at the Pimienta Crossing on the Neuces.

'About three in the afternoon I throwed my bridle over a mesquite limb and walked the last twenty yards into Uncle Emsley's store. I got up on the counter and told Uncle Emsley that the signs pointed to the devastation of the fruit crop of the world. In a minute I had a bag of crackers and a long handled spoon, with an open can each of apricots and pineapples and cherries and green-gages beside of me with

Uncle Emsley busy chopping away with the hatchet at the yellow clings. I was feeling like Adam before the apple stampede, and was digging my spurs into the side of the counter and working with my twenty-four-inch spoon when I happened to look out of the window into the yard of Uncle Emsley's house, which was next to the store.

'There was a girl standing there – an imported girl with fixings on – philandering with a croquet maul and amusing herself by watching my style of encouraging the fruit canning industry.

'I slid off the counter and delivered up my shovel to Uncle Emsley.

' "That's my niece," says he; "Miss Willella Learight, down from Palestine on a visit. Do you want that I should make you acquainted?"

' "The Holy Land," I says to myself, my thought milling some as I tried to run 'em into the corral. "Why not? There was sure angels in Pales – Why yes, Uncle Emsley," I says out loud, "I'd be awful edified to meet Miss Learight."

'So Uncle Emsley took me out in the yard and gave us each other's entitlements.

'I never was shy about women. I never could understand why some men who can break a mustang before breakfast and shave in the dark, get all left-handed and full of perspiration and excuses when they see a bolt of calico draped around what belongs in it. Inside of eight minutes me and Miss Willella was aggravating the croquet balls around as amiable as second cousins. She gave me a dig about the quantity of canned fruit I had eaten, and I got back at her, flat-footed, about how a certain lady named Eve started the fruit trouble in the first free-grass pasture – "Over in Palestine, wasn't it?" says I, as easy and pat as roping a one-year-old.

'That was how I acquired cordiality for the proximities of Miss Willella Learight; and the disposition grew larger as time passed. She was stopping at Pimienta Crossing for her health, which was very good, and for the climate, which was forty per cent hotter than Palestine. I rode over to see her once every week for a while; and then I figured out that if I doubled the number of trips I would see her twice as often.

'One week I slipped in a third trip; and that's where the pancakes and the pink-eyed snoozer busted into the game.

'That evening, while I set on the counter with a peach and two damsons in my mouth, I asked Uncle Emsley how Miss Willella was.

' "Why," says Uncle Emsley, "she's gone riding with Jackson Bird, the sheep man from over at Mired Mule Cañada."

'I swallowed the peach seed and the two damsons seeds. I guess somebody held the counter by the bridle while I got off; and then I walked out straight ahead till I butted against the mesquite where my roan was tied.

' "She's gone riding," I whispered in my bronc's ear, "with Birdstone Jack, the hired mule from Sheep Man's Cañada. Did you get that, old Leather-and-Gallops?"

'That bronc of mine wept, in his way. He'd been raised a cow pony and he didn't care for snoozers.

'I went back and said to Uncle Emsley: "Did you say a sheep man?"

' "I said a sheep man," says Uncle again. "You must have heard tell of Jackson Bird. He's got eight sections of grazing and four thousand head of the finest Merinos south of the Arctic Circle."

'I went out and sat on the ground in the shade of the store and leaned against a prickly pear. I sifted sand into my boots with unthinking hands while I soliloquized a quantity about this bird with the Jackson plumage to his name.

'I never had believed in harming sheep men. I see one, one day, reading a Latin grammar on hossback, and I never touched him! They never irritated me like they do most cowmen. You wouldn't go to work now, and impair and disfigure snoozers, would you, that eat on tables and wear little shoes and speak to you on subjects? I had always let 'em pass, just as you would a jack-rabbit; with a polite word and a guess about the weather, but no stopping to swap canteens. I never thought it was worth while to be hostile with a snoozer. And because I'd been lenient, and let 'em live, here was one going around riding with Miss Willella Learight!

'An hour by sun they come loping back, and stopped at Uncle Emsley's gate. The sheep person helped her off; and they stood throwing each other sentences all sprightful and sagacious for a while. And then this feathered Jackson flies up in his saddle and raises his little stewpot of a hat, and trots off in the direction of his mutton ranch. By this time I had turned the sand out of my boots and unpinned myself from the prickly pear; and by the time he gets half a mile out of Pimienta, I singlefoots up beside him on my bronc.

'I said that snoozer was pink-eyed, but he wasn't. His seeing arrangement was gray enough, but his eye-lashes was pink and his hair was sandy, and that gave you the idea. Sheep man – he wasn't more than a lamb man, anyhow – a little thing with his neck involved in a yellow silk handkerchief, and shoes tied up in bowknots.

' "Afternoon!" says I to him. "You now ride with a equestrian who is commonly called Dead-Moral-Certainty Judson, on account of the way I shoot. When I want a stranger to know me I always introduce myself before the draw, for I never did like to shake hands with ghosts."

' "Ah," says he, just like that – "Ah, I'm glad to know you, Mr Judson. I'm Jackson Bird, from over at Mired Mule Ranch."

'Just then one of my eyes saw a roadrunner skipping down the hill with a young tarantula in his bill, and the other eye noticed a rabbit-hawk sitting on a dead limb in a water-elm. I popped over one after the other with my forty-five just to show him. "Two out of three," said I. "Birds just naturally seem to draw my fire wherever I go."

' "Nice shooting," says the sheep man, without a flutter. "But don't you sometimes ever miss the third shot? Elegant fine rain that was last week for the young grass, Mr Judson," says he.

' "Willie," says I, riding over close to his palfrey, "your infatuated parents may have denounced you by the name of Jackson, but you sure moulted into a twittering Willie – let us slough of this here analysis of rain and the elements, and get down to talk that is outside the vocabulary of parrots. That is a bad habit you have got of riding with young ladies over at Pimienta. I've known birds," says I, "to be served on toast for less than that. Miss Willella," says I, "don't ever want any nest made out of sheep's wool by a tomtit of the Jacksonian branch of ornithology. Now, are you going to quit, or do you wish for me to gallop up against this Dead-Moral-Certainty attachment to my name, which is good for two hyphens and at least one set of funeral obsequies?"

'Jackson Bird flushed up some, and then he laughed.

' "Why, Mr Judson," says he, "you've got the wrong idea. I've called on Miss Learight a few times; but not for the purpose you imagine. My object is purely a gastronomical one."

'I reached for my gun.

' "Any coyote," says I, "that would boast of dishonorable—"

' "Wait a minute," says this Bird, "till I explain. What would I do with a wife? If you ever saw that ranch of mine! I do my own cooking and mending. Eating – that's all the pleasure I get out of sheep raising. Mr Judson, did you ever taste the pancakes that Miss Learight makes?"

' "Me? No," I told him. "I never was advised that she was up to any culinary maneuvers."

' "They're golden sunshine," says he, "honey-browned by the ambrosial fires of Epicurus. I'd give two years of my life to get the recipe for making them pancakes. That's what I went to see Miss Learight for," says Jackson Bird, "but I haven't been able to get it from her. It's an old recipe that's been in the family for seventy-five years. They hand it down from one generation to another, but they don't give it away to outsiders. If I could get that recipe, so I could make them pancakes for myself on my ranch, I'd be a happy man," says Bird.

' "Are you sure," I says to him, "that it ain't the hand that mixes the pancakes that you're after?"

' "Sure," says Jackson. "Miss Learight is a mighty nice girl, but I can assure you my intentions go no further than the gastro—" but he seen my hand going down to my holster and he changed his similitude – "than the desire to procure a copy of the pancake recipe," he finishes.

' "You ain't such a bad little man," says I, trying to be fair. "I was thinking some of making orphans of your sheep, but I'll let you fly away this time. But you stick to pancakes," says I, "as close as the middle one of a stack; and don't go and mistake sentiments for syrup, or there'll be singing at your ranch, and you won't hear it."

' "To convince you that I am sincere," says the sheep man, "I'll ask you to help me. Miss Learight and you being closer friends, maybe she would do for you what she wouldn't for me. If you will get me a copy of that pancake recipe, I give you my word that I'll never call upon her again."

' "That's fair," I says, and I shook hands with Jackson Bird. "I'll get it for you if I can, and glad to oblige." And he turned off down the big pear flat on the Piedra, in the direction of Mired Mule; and I steered north-west for old Bill Toomey's ranch.

'It was five days afterward when I got another chance to ride over to Pimienta. Miss Willella and me passed a gratifying evening at Uncle Emsley's. She sang some, and exasperated the piano quite a lot with quotations from the operas. I gave imitations of a rattlesnake, and told her about Snaky McFee's new way of skinning cows, and described the trip I made to Saint Louis once. We was getting along in one another's estimations fine. Thinks I, if Jackson can now be persuaded to migrate, I win. I recollect his promise about the pancake receipt, and I thinks I will persuade it from Miss Willella and give it to him; and then if I catches Birdie off of Mired Mule again, I'll make him hop the twig.

'So, along about ten o'clock, I put on a wheedling smile and says to Miss Willella: "Now, if there's anything I do like better than the sight of a red steer on green grass it's the taste of a nice hot pancake smothered in sugarhouse molasses."

'Miss Willella gives a little jump on the piano stool, and looked at me curious.

' "Yes," says she, "they're real nice. What did you say was the name of that street in Saint Louis, Mr Odom, where you lost your hat?"

' "Pancake Avenue," says I, with a wink, to show her that I was on about the family receipt, and couldn't be side-corralled off of the subject. "Come now, Miss Willella," I says; "let's hear how you make 'em. Pancakes is just whirling in my head like wagon wheels. Start her off, now – pound of flour, eight dozen eggs, and so on. How does the catalogue of constituents run?"

' "Excuse me for a moment, please," says Willella, and she gives me a quick kind of sideways look, and slides off the stool. She ambled out into the other room and directly Uncle Emsley comes in in his shirt sleeves, with a pitcher of water. He turns around to get a glass on the table, and I see a forty-five in his hip pocket. "Great post-holes!" thinks I, "but here's a family thinks a heap of cooking receipts, protecting it with firearms. I've known outfits that wouldn't do that much by a family feud."

' "Drink this here down," says Uncle Emsley, handing me the glass of water. "You've rid too far today, Jud, and got yourself over-excited. Try to think about something else now."

' "Do you know how to make them pancakes, Uncle Emsley?" I asked.

' "Well, I'm not as apprised in the anatomy of them as some," says Uncle Emsley, "but I reckon you take a sifter of plaster of paris and a little dough and saleratus and corn meal, and mix 'em with eggs and buttermilk as usual. Is old Bill going to ship beeves to Kansas City again this spring, Jud?"

'That was all the pancake specifications I could get that night. I didn't wonder that Jackson Bird found it uphill work. So I dropped the subject and talked with Uncle Emsley a while about hollow-horn and cyclones. And then Miss Willella came and said "Goodnight," and I hit the breeze for the ranch.

'About a week afterward I met Jackson Bird riding out of Pimienta as I rode in, and we stopped in the road for a few frivolous remarks.

' "Got the bill of particulars for them flap-jacks yet?" I asked him.

' "Well, no," says Jackson. "I don't seem to have any success in getting hold of it. Did you try?"

' "I did," says I, "and 'twas like trying to dig a prairie dog out of his hole with a peanut hull. That pancake receipt must be a jooka-lorum, the way they hold on to it."

' "I'm 'most ready to give it up," says Jackson, so discouraged in his pronunci-ations that I felt sorry for him; "but I did want to know how to make them pancakes to eat on my lonely ranch," says he. "I lie awake at nights thinking how good they are."

' "You keep on trying for it," I tells him, "and I'll do the same. One of us is bound to get a rope over its horns before long. Well, so-long, Jacksy."

'You see, by this time we was on the peacefullest of terms. When I saw that he wasn't after Miss Willella I had more endurable contemplations of that sandy-haired snoozer. In order to help out the ambitions of his appetite I kept on trying to get that receipt from Miss Willella. But every time I would say "pancakes" she would get sort of remote and fidgety about the eye, and try to change the subject. If I held her to it she would slide out and round up Uncle Emsley with his pitcher of water and hip-pocket howitzer.

'One day I galloped over to the store with a fine bunch of blue verbenas that I cut out of a herd of wild flowers over on Poisoned Dog Prairie. Uncle Emsley looked at 'em with one eye shut and says:

' "Haven't ye heard the news?"

' "Cattle up?" I asks.

' "Willella and Jackson Bird was married in Palestine yesterday," says he. "Just got a letter this morning."

'I dropped them flowers in a cracker-barrel, and let the news trickle in my ears and down toward my upper left-hand shirt pocket until it got to my feet.

' "Would you mind saying that over again once more, Uncle Emsley?" says I. "Maybe my hearing has got wrong, and you only said that prime heifers was 4.80 on the hoof, or something like that."

' "Married yesterday," says Uncle Emsley, "and gone to Waco and Niagara Falls on a wedding tour. Why, didn't you see none of the signs all along? Jackson Bird has been courting Willella ever since that day he took her out riding."

' "Then," says I, in a kind of a yell, "what was all this zizzaparoola he gives me about pancakes? Tell me *that*."

'When I said "pancakes" Uncle Emsley sort of dodged and stepped back.

' "Somebody's been dealing me pancakes from the bottom of the deck," I says, "and I'll find out. I believe you know. Talk up," says I, "or we'll mix a panful of batter right here."

'I slid over the counter after Uncle Emsley. He grabbed at his gun, but it was in a drawer, and he missed it two inches. I got him by the front of his shirt and shoved him in a corner.

' "Talk pancakes," says I, "or be made into one. Does Miss Willella make 'em?"

' "She never made one in her life and I never saw one," says Uncle Emsley, soothing. "Calm down now, Jud – calm down. You've got excited, and that wound in your head is contaminating your sense of intelligence. Try not to think about pancakes."

' "Uncle Emsley," says I, "I'm not wounded in the head except so far as my natural cogitative instincts run to runts. Jackson Bird told me he was calling on Miss Willella for the purpose of finding out her system of producing pancakes, and he asked me to help him get the bill of lading of the ingredients. I done so, with the results as you see. Have I been sodded down with Johnson grass by a pink-eyed snoozer, or what?"

' "Slack up your grip on my dress shirt," says Uncle Emsley, "and I'll tell you. Yes, it looks like Jackson Bird has gone and humbugged you some. The day after he went riding with Willella he came back and told me and her to watch out for you whenever you go to talking about pancakes. He said you was in camp once where they was cooking flapjacks, and one of the fellows cut you over the head with a frying pan. Jackson said that whenever you got over-hot or excited that would hurt you and made you kind of crazy, and you went raving about pancakes. He told us to just get you worked off of the subject and soothed down, and you wouldn't be dangerous. So, me and Willella done the best by you we knew how. Well, well," says Uncle Emsley, "that Jackson Bird is sure a seldom kind of a snoozer." '

During the progress of Jud's story he had been slowly but deftly combining certain portions of the contents of his sacks and cans. Toward the close of it he set before me the finished product – a pair of red-hot, rich-hued pancakes on a tin plate. From some secret hoarding place he also brought a lump of excellent butter and a bottle of golden syrup.

'How long ago did these things happen?' I asked him.

'Three years,' said Jud. 'They're living on the Mired Mule Ranch now. But I haven't seen either of 'em since. They say Jackson Bird was fixing his ranch fine with rocking chairs and window curtains all the time he was putting me up the pancake tree. Oh, I got over it after a while. But the boys kept the racket up.'

'Did you make these cakes by the famous recipe?' I asked.

'Didn't I tell you there wasn't no receipt?' said Jud. 'The boys hollered pancakes till they got pancake hungry, and I cut this receipt out of a newspaper. How does the truck taste?'

'They're delicious,' I answered. 'Why don't you have some, too, Jud?' I was sure I heard a sigh.

'Me?' said Jud. 'I don't never eat 'em.'

A Call Loan

IN THOSE DAYS THE CATTLEMEN were the anointed. They were the grandees of the grass, kings of the kine, lords of the lea, barons of beef and bone. They might have ridden in golden chariots had their tastes so inclined. The cattleman was caught in a stampede of dollars. It seemed to him that he had more money than was decent. But when he had bought a watch with precious stones set in the case so large that they hurt his ribs, and a California saddle with silver nails and Angora skin *suaderos*, and ordered everybody up to the bar for whisky – what else was there for him to spend money for?

Not so circumscribed in expedient for the reduction of surplus wealth were those lairds of the lariat who had womenfolk to their name. In the breast of the rib-sprung sex the genius of purse lightening may slumber through years of inopportunity, but never, my brothers, does it become extinct.

So, out of the chaparral came Long Bill Longley from the Bar Circle Ranch on the Frio – a wife-driven man – to taste the urban joys of success. Something like half a million dollars he had, with an income steadily increasing.

Long Bill was a graduate of the camp and trail. Luck and thrift, a cool head, and a telescopic eye for mavericks had raised him from cowboy to be a cowman. Then came the boom in cattle, and Fortune, stepping gingerly among the cactus thorns, came and emptied her cornucopia at the doorstep of the ranch.

In the little frontier city of Chaparosa, Longley built a costly residence. Here he became a captive, bound to the chariot of social existence. He was doomed to become a leading citizen. He struggled for a time like a mustang in his first corral, and then he hung up his quirt and spurs. Time hung heavily on his hands. He organized the First National Bank of Chaparosa, and was elected its president.

One day a dyspeptic man, wearing double-magnifying glasses, inserted an official-looking card between the bars of the cashier's window of the First National Bank. Five minutes later the bank force was dancing at the beck and call of a national bank examiner.

This examiner, Mr J. Edgar Todd, proved to be a thorough one.

At the end of it all the examiner put on his hat, and called the president, Mr William R. Longley, into the private office.

'Well, how do you find things?' asked Longley, in his slow, deep tones. 'Any brands in the round-up you didn't like the looks of?'

'The bank checks up all right, Mr Longley,' said Todd; 'and I find your loans in very good shape – with one exception. You are carrying one very bad bit of paper – one that is so bad that I have been thinking that you surely do not realize the serious position it places you in. I refer to a call loan of $10,000 made to Thomas Merwin. Not only is the amount in excess of the maximum sum the bank can loan any individual legally, but it is absolutely without endorsement or security. Thus you have doubly violated the national banking laws, and have laid yourself open to criminal prosecution by the Government. A report of the matter to the Comptroller of the Currency – which I am bound to make – would, I am sure, result in the matter being turned over to the Department of Justice for action. You see what a serious thing it is.'

Bill Longley was leaning his lengthy, slowly moving frame back in his swivel chair. His hands were clasped behind his head, and he turned a little to look the examiner in the face. The examiner was surprised to see a smile creep about the rugged mouth of the banker, and a kindly twinkle in his light-blue eyes. If he saw the seriousness of the affair, it did not show in his countenance.

'Of course, you don't know Tom Merwin,' said Longley, almost genially. 'Yes, I know about that loan. It hasn't any security except Tom Merwin's word. Somehow, I've always found that when a man's word is good, it's the best security there is. Oh, yes, I know the Government doesn't think so. I guess I'll see Tom about that note.'

Mr Todd's dyspepsia seemed to grow suddenly worse. He looked at the chaparral banker through his double-magnifying glasses in amazement.

'You see,' said Longley, easily explaining the thing away, 'Tom heard of 2,000 head of two-year-olds down near Rocky Ford on the Rio Grande that could be had for $8 a head. I reckon 'twas one of old Laendro Garcia's outfits that he had smuggled over, and he wanted to make a quick turn on 'em. Those cattle are worth $15 on the hoof in Kansas City. Tom knew it and I knew it. He had $6,000, and I let him have the $10,000 to make the deal with. His brother Ed took 'em on to market three weeks ago. He ought to be back 'most any day now with the money. When he comes Tom'll pay that note.'

The bank examiner was shocked. It was, perhaps, his duty to step out to the telegraph office and wire the situation to the Comptroller. But he did not. He talked pointedly and effectively to Longley for three minutes. He succeeded in making the banker understand that he stood upon the border of a catastrophe. And then he offered a tiny loophole of escape.

'I am going to Hilldale's tonight,' he told Longley, 'to examine a bank there. I will pass through Chaparosa on my way back. At twelve tomorrow I shall call at this bank. If this loan has been cleared out of the way by that time it will not be mentioned in my report. If not – I will have to do my duty.'

With that the examiner bowed and departed.

The President of the First National lounged in his chair half an hour longer, and then he lit a mild cigar, and went over to Tom Merwin's house. Merwin, a ranchman in brown duck, with a contemplative eye, sat with his feet upon a table, plaiting a rawhide quirt.

'Tom,' said Longley, leaning against the table, 'you heard anything from Ed yet?'

'Not yet,' said Merwin, continuing his plaiting. 'I guess Ed'll be along back now in a few days.'

'There was a bank examiner,' said Longley, 'nosing around our place today, and he bucked a sight about that note of yours. You know I know it's all right, but the thing is against the banking laws. I was pretty sure you'd have paid it off before the bank was examined again, but the son-of-a-gun slipped in on us, Tom. Now, I'm short of cash myself just now, or I'd let you have the money to take it up with. I've got till twelve o'clock tomorrow, and then I've got to show the cash in place of that note or—'

'Or what, Bill?' asked Merwin, as Longley hesitated.

'Well, I suppose it means be jumped on with both of Uncle Sam's feet.'

'I'll try to raise the money for you on time,' said Merwin, interested in his plaiting.

'All right, Tom,' concluded Longley, as he turned toward the door; 'I knew you would if you could.'

Merwin threw down his whip and went to the only other bank in town, a private one, run by Cooper & Craig.

'Cooper,' he said, to the partner by that name, 'I've got to have $10,000 to-day or tomorrow. I've got a house and lot here that's worth about $6,000 and that's all the actual collateral. But I've got a cattle deal on that's sure to bring me in more than that much profit within a few days.'

Cooper began to cough.

'Now, for God's sake don't say no,' said Merwin. 'I owe that much money on a call loan. It's been called, and the man that called it is a man I've laid on the same blanket with in cow-camps and ranger-camps for ten years. He can call anything I've got. He can call the blood out of my veins and it'll come. He's got to have the money. He's in a devil of a – Well, he needs the money, and I've got to get it for him. You know my word's good, Cooper.'

'No doubt of it,' assented Cooper, urbanely, 'but I've a partner, you know. I'm not free in making loans. And even if you had the best security in your hands, Merwin, we couldn't accommodate you in less than a week. We're just making a shipment of $15,000 to Myer Brothers in Rockdell, to buy cotton with. It goes down on the narrow gauge tonight. That leaves our cash quite short at present. Sorry we can't arrange it for you.'

Merwin went back to his little bar office and plaited at his quirt again. About four o'clock in the afternoon he went to the First National and leaned over the railing of Longley's desk.

'I'll try to get that money for you tonight – I mean tomorrow, Bill.'

'All right, Tom,' said Longley, quietly.

At nine o'clock that night Tom Merwin stepped cautiously out of the small frame house in which he lived. It was near the edge of the little town, and few citizens were in the neighborhood at that hour. Merwin wore two six-shooters in a belt and a slouch hat. He moved swiftly down a lonely street, and then followed the sandy road that ran parallel to the narrow-gauge track until he reached the water-tank, two miles below the town. There Tom Merwin stopped, tied a black silk handkerchief about the lower part of his face, and pulled his hat down low.

In ten minutes the night train for Rockdell pulled up at the tank, having come from Chaparosa.

With a gun in each hand Merwin raised himself from behind a clump of chaparral and started for the engine. But before he had taken three steps, two long, strong arms clasped him from behind, and he was lifted from his feet and thrown, face downward, upon the grass. There was a heavy knee pressing against his back, and an iron hand grasping each of his wrists. He was held thus, like a child, until the engine had taken water, and until the train had moved, with accelerating speed, out of sight. Then he was released, and rose to his feet to face Bill Longley.

'The case never needed to be fixed up this way, Tom,' said Longley. 'I saw Cooper this evening, and he told me what you and him talked about. Then I went down to your house tonight and saw you come out with your guns on, and I followed you. Let's go back, Tom.'

They walked away together, side by side.

"Twas the only chance I saw,' said Merwin, presently. 'You called your loan, and I tried to answer you. Now, what'll you do, Bill, if they sock it to you?'

'What would you have done if they'd socked it to you?' was the answer Longley made.

'I never thought I'd lay in a bush to stick up a train,' remarked Merwin; 'but a call loan's different. A call's a call with me. We've got twelve hours yet, Bill, before his spy jumps on to you. We've got to raise them spondulicks somehow. Maybe we can – Great Sam Houston! do you hear that?'

Merwin broke into a run, and Longley kept with him, hearing only a rather pleasing whistle somewhere in the night rendering the lugubrious air of 'The Cowboy's Lament.'

'It's the only tune he knows,' shouted Merwin, as he ran. 'I'll bet—'

They were at the door of Merwin's house. He kicked it open and fell over an old valise lying in the middle of the floor. A sunburned, firmjawed youth, stained by travel, lay upon the bed puffing at a brown cigarette.

'What's the word, Ed?' gasped Merwin.

'So, so,' drawled that capable youngster. 'Just got in on the 9:30. Sold the bunch for fifteen, straight. Now, buddy, you want to quit kickin' a valise around that's got $29,000 in greenbacks in its in'ards.'

THE LAST OF THE MOHICANS

(AN EXTRACT)

BY

JAMES FENIMORE COOPER

Before these fields were shorn and tilled,
  Full to the brim our rivers flowed;
The melody of waters filled
  The fresh and boundless wood;
And torrents dashed, and rivulets played,
  And fountains spouted in the shade.

Bryant, 'An Indian at the Burial-Place
  of His Fathers,' 11. 67–72.

LEAVING THE UNSUSPECTING Heyward, and his confiding companions, to penetrate still deeper into a forest that contained such treacherous inmates, we must use an author's privilege, and shift the scene a few miles to the westward of the place where we have last seen them.

On that day, two men were lingering on the banks of a small but rapid stream, within an hour's journey of the encampment of Webb, like those who awaited the appearance of an absent person, or the approach of some expected event. The vast canopy of woods spread itself to the margin of the river, overhanging the water, and shadowing its dark current with a deeper hue. The rays of the sun were beginning to grow less fierce, and the intense heat of the day was lessened, as the cooler vapors of the springs and fountains rose above their leafy beds, and rested in the atmosphere. Still that breathing silence, which marks the drowsy sultriness of an American landscape in July, pervaded the secluded spot, interrupted, only, by the low voices of the men, the occasional and lazy tap of a wood-pecker, the discordant cry of some gaudy jay, or a swelling on the ear, from the dull roar of a distant water-fall.

These feeble and broken sounds were, however, too familiar to the foresters, to draw their attention from the more interesting matter of their dialogue. While one of these loiterers showed the red skin and wild accoutrements of a native of the woods, the other exhibited, through the mask of his rude and nearly savage equipments, the brighter, though sunburnt and long-faded complexion of one who might claim descent from a European parentage. The former was seated on the end of a mossy log, in a posture that permitted him to heighten the effect of his earnest language, by the calm but expressive gestures of an Indian, engaged in debate. His body, which was nearly naked, presented a terrific emblem of death, drawn in intermingled colors of white and black. His closely shaved head, on which no other hair than the well known and chivalrous scalping tuft* was

*The North American warrior caused the hair to be plucked from his whole body; a small tuft, only, was left on the crown of his head, in order that his enemy might avail himself of it, in wrenching off the scalp in the event of his fall. The scalp was the only admissible trophy of victory. Thus, it was deemed

preserved, was without ornament of any kind, with the exception of a solitary eagle's plume, that crossed his crown, and depended over the left shoulder. A tomahawk and scalping-knife, of English manufacture, were in his girdle; while a short military rifle, of that sort with which the policy of the whites armed their savage allies, lay carelessly across his bare and sinewy knee. The expanded chest, full-formed limbs, and grave countenance of this warrior, would denote that he had reached the vigor of his days, though no symptoms of decay appeared to have yet weakened his manhood.

The frame of the white man, judging by such parts as were not concealed by his clothes, was like that of one who had known hardships and exertion from his earliest youth. His person, though muscular, was rather attenuated than full; but every nerve and muscle appeared strung and indurated, by unremitted exposure and toil. He wore a hunting-shirt of forest green, fringed with faded yellow,† and a summer cap, of skins which had been shorn of their fur. He also bore a knife in a girdle of wampum, like that which confined the scanty garments of the Indian, but no tomahawk. His moccasins were ornamented after the gay fashion of the natives, while the only part of his under dress which appeared below the hunting-frock, was a pair of buckskin leggings, that laced at the sides, and which were gartered above the knees, with the sinews of a deer. A pouch and horn completed his personal accoutrements, though a rifle of great length,‡ which the theory of the more ingenious whites had taught them, was the most dangerous of all fire-arms, leaned against a neighboring sapling. The eye of the hunter, or scout, whichever he might be, was small, quick, keen, and restless, roving while he spoke, on every side of him, as if in quest of game, or distrusting the sudden approach of some lurking enemy. Notwithstanding these symptoms of habitual suspicion, his countenance was not only without guile, but at the moment at which he is introduced, it was charged with an expression of sturdy honesty.

'Even your traditions make the case in my favor, Chingachgook,' he said, speaking in the tongue which was known to all the natives who formerly inhabited the country between the Hudson and the Potomack, and of which we shall give a free translation for the benefit of the reader; endeavoring, at the same time, to preserve some of the peculiarities, both of the individual and of the language. 'Your fathers came from the setting sun, crossed the big river,* fought the people of the country, and took the land; and mine came from the red sky of the morning, over the salt lake, and did their work much after the fashion that had been set them by yours; then let God judge the matter between us, and friends spare their words!'

'My fathers fought with the naked red-man!' returned the Indian, sternly, in the same language. 'Is there no difference, Hawk-eye, between the stone-headed arrow of the warrior, and the leaden bullet with which you kill?'

'There is reason in an Indian, though nature has made him with a red skin!' said

more important to obtain the scalp than to kill the man. Some tribes lay great stress on the honor of striking a dead body. These practices have nearly disappeared among the Indians of the Atlantic states. [1831]

†The hunting-shirt is a picturesque smock-frock, being shorter, and ornamented with fringes and tassels. The colors are intended to imitate the hues of the wood, with a view to concealment. Many corps of American riflemen have been thus attired; and the dress is one of the most striking of modern times. The hunting shirt is frequently white. [1831]

‡The rifle of the army is short; that of the hunter is always long. [1831]

*The Mississippi. The scout alludes to a tradition which is very popular among the tribes of the Atlantic states. Evidence of their Asiatic origin is deduced from the circumstance, though great uncertainty hangs over the whole history of the Indians. [1831]

the white man, shaking his head, like one on whom such an appeal to his justice was not thrown away. For a moment he appeared to be conscious of having the worst of the argument, then rallying again, he answered the objection of his antagonist in the best manner his limited information would allow: 'I am no scholar, and I care not who knows it; but judging from what I have seen at deer chaces, and squirrel hunts, of the sparks below, I should think a rifle in the hands of their grandfathers, was not so dangerous as a hickory bow, and a good flint-head might be, if drawn with Indian judgment, and sent by an Indian eye.'

'You have the story told by your fathers,' returned the other, coldly waving his hand. 'What say your old men? do they tell the young warriors, that the pale-faces met the red-men, painted for war and armed with the stone hatchet or wooden gun?'

'I am not a prejudiced man, nor one who vaunts himself on his natural privileges, though the worst enemy I have on earth, and he is an Iroquois, daren't deny that I am genuine white,' the scout replied, surveying, with secret satisfaction, the faded color of his bony and sinewy hand; 'and I am willing to own that my people have many ways, of which, as an honest man, I can't approve. It is one of their customs to write in books what they have done and seen, instead of telling them in their villages, where the lie can be given to the face of a cowardly boaster, and the brave soldier can call on his comrades to witness for the truth of his words. In consequence of this bad fashion, a man who is too conscientious to misspend his days among the women, in learning the names of black marks, may never hear of the deeds of his fathers, nor feel a pride in striving to outdo them. For myself, I conclude all the Bumppos could shoot; for I have a natural turn with a rifle, which must have been handed down from generation to generation, as our holy commandments tell us, all good and evil gifts are bestowed; though I should be loth to answer for other people in such a matter. But every story has its two sides; so I ask you, Chingachgook, what passed, according to the traditions of the red men, when our fathers first met?'

A silence of a minute succeeded, during which the Indian sat mute; then, full of the dignity of his office, he commenced his brief tale, with a solemnity that served to heighten its appearance of truth.

'Listen, Hawk-eye, and your ear shall drink no lie. 'Tis what my fathers have said, and what the Mohicans have done.' He hesitated a single instant, and bending a cautious glance towards his companion, he continued in a manner that was divided between interrogation and assertion – 'does not this stream at our feet, run towards the summer, until its waters grow salt, and the current flows upward!'

'It can't be denied, that your traditions tell you true in both these matters,' said the white man; 'for I have been there, and have seen them; though, why water, which is so sweet in the shade, should become bitter in the sun, is an alteration for which I have never been able to account.'

'And the current!' demanded the Indian, who expected his reply with that sort of interest that a man feels in the confirmation of testimony, at which he marvels even while he respects it; 'the fathers of Chingachgook have not lied!'

'The Holy Bible is not more true, and that is the truest thing in nature. They call this up-stream current the tide, which is a thing soon explained, and clear enough. Six hours the waters run in, and six hours they run out, and the reason is this; when there is higher water in the sea than in the river, they run in, until the river gets to be highest, and then it runs out again.'

'The waters in the woods, and on the great lakes, run downward until they lie like my hand,' said the Indian, stretching the limb horizontally before him, 'and then they run no more.'

'No honest man will deny it,' said the scout, a little nettled at the implied distrust of his explanation of the mystery of the tides; 'and I grant that it is true on the small scale, and where the land is level. But every thing depends on what scale you look at things. Now, on the small scale, the 'arth is level; but on the large scale it is round. In this manner, pools and ponds, and even the great fresh water lakes, may be stagnant, as you and I both know they are, having seen them; but when you come to spread water over a great tract, like the sea, where the earth is round, how in reason can the water be quiet? You might as well expect the river to lie still on the brink of those black rocks a mile above us, though your own ears tell you that it is tumbling over them at this very moment!'

If unsatisfied by the philosophy of his companion, the Indian was far too dignified to betray his unbelief. His listened like one who was convinced, and resumed his narrative in his former solemn manner.

'We came from the place where the sun is hid at night, over great plains where the buffaloes live, until we reached the big river. There we fought the Alligewi, till the ground was red with their blood. From the banks of the big river to the shores of the salt lake, there was none to meet us. The Maquas followed at a distance. We said the country should be ours from the place where the water runs up no longer, on this stream, to a river, twenty suns' journey toward the summer. The land we had taken like warriors, we kept like men. We drove the Maquas into the woods with the bears. They only tasted salt at the licks; they drew no fish from the great lake: we threw them the bones.'

'All this I have heard and believe,' said the white man, observing that the Indian paused; 'but it was long before the English came into the country.'

'A pine grew then, where this chestnut now stands. The first pale faces who came among us spoke no English. They came in a large canoe, when my fathers had buried the tomahawk with the red men around them. Then, Hawk-eye,' he continued, betraying his deep emotion, only by permitting his voice to fall to those low, guttural tones, which render his language, as spoken at times, so very musical; 'then, Hawk-eye, we were one people, and we were happy. The salt lake gave us its fish, the wood its deer, and the air its birds. We took wives who bore us children; we worshipped the Great Spirit; and we kept the Maquas beyond the sound of our songs of triumph!'

'Know you any thing of your own family, at that time?' demanded the white. 'But you are a just man for an Indian! and as I suppose you hold their gifts, your fathers must have been brave warriors, and wise men at the council fire.'

'My tribe is the grandfather of nations, but I am an unmixed man. The blood of chiefs is in my veins, where it must stay for ever. The Dutch landed, and gave my people the fire-water; they drank until the heavens and the earth seemed to meet, and they foolishly thought they had found the Great Spirit. Then they parted with their land. Foot by foot, they were driven back from the shores, until I, that am a chief and a Sagamore, have never seen the sun shine but through trees, and have never visited the graves of my fathers.'

'Graves bring solemn feelings over the mind,' returned the scout, a good deal touched at the calm suffering of his companion; 'and they often aid a man in his good intentions, though, for myself, I expect to leave my own bones unburied, to bleach in the woods, or to be torn asunder by the wolves. But where are to be found those of your race who came to their kin in the Delaware country, so many summers since?'

'Where are the blossoms of those summers! – falling, one by one: so all of my family departed, each in his turn, to the land of spirits. I am on the hill-top, and must go down into the valley; and when Uncas follows in my footsteps, there will no longer be any of the blood of the Sagamores, for my boy is the last of the Mohicans.'

'Uncas is here!' said another voice, in the same soft, guttural tones, near his elbow; 'who speaks to Uncas?'

The white man loosened his knife in its leathern sheath, and made an involuntary movement of the hand towards his rifle, at this sudden interruption, but the Indian sat composed, and without turning his head at the unexpected sounds.

At the next instant, a youthful warrior passed between them, with a noiseless step, and seated himself on the bank of the rapid stream. No exclamation of surprise escaped the father, nor was any question asked or reply given for several minutes, each appearing to await the moment, when he might speak, without betraying womanish curiosity or childish impatience. The white man seemed to take counsel from their customs, and relinquishing his grasp of the rifle, he also remained silent and reserved. At length Chingachgook turned his eyes slowly towards his son, and demanded—

'Do the Maquas dare to leave the print of their moccasins in these woods?'

'I have been on their trail,' replied the young Indian, 'and know that they number as many as the fingers of my two hands; but they lie hid like cowards.'

'The thieves are outlying for scalps and plunder!' said the white man, whom we shall call Hawk-eye, after the manner of his companions. 'That busy Frenchman, Montcalm, will send his spies into our very camp, but he will know what road we travel!'

''Tis enough!' returned the father, glancing his eye towards the setting sun; 'they shall be driven like deer from their bushes. Hawkeye, let us eat tonight, and show the Maquas that we are men tomorrow.'

'I am as ready to do the one as the other; but to fight the Iroquois, 'tis necessary to find the skulkers; and to eat, 'tis necessary to get the game – talk of the devil and he will come; there is a pair of the biggest antlers I have seen this season, moving the bushes below the hill! Now, Uncas,' he continued in a half whisper, and laughing with a kind of inward sound, like one who had learnt to be watchful, 'I will bet my charger three times full of powder, against a foot of wampum, that I take him atwixt the eyes, and nearer to the right than to the left.'

'It cannot be!' said the young Indian, springing to his feet with youthful eagerness; 'all but the tips of his horns are hid!'

'He's a boy!' said the white man, shaking his head while he spoke, and addressing the father. 'Does he think when a hunter sees a part of the creatur, he can't tell where the rest of him should be!'

Adjusting his rifle, he was about to make an exhibition of that skill, on which he so much valued himself, when the warrior struck up the piece with his hand, saying,

'Hawk-eye! will you fight the Maquas?'

'These Indians know the nature of the woods, as it might be by instinct!' returned the scout, dropping his rifle, and turning away like a man who was convinced of his error. 'I must leave the buck to your arrow, Uncas, or we may kill a deer for them thieves, the Iroquois, to eat.'

The instant the father seconded this intimation by an expressive gesture of the hand, Uncas threw himself on the ground, and approached the animal with wary movements. When, within a few yards of the cover, he fitted an arrow to his bow with the utmost care, while the antlers moved, as if their owner snuffed an enemy in the tainted air. In another moment the twang of the cord was heard, a white streak was seen glancing into the bushes, and the wounded buck plunged from the cover, to the very feet of his hidden enemy. Avoiding the horns of the infuriated animal, Uncas darted to his side, and passed his knife across the throat, when bounding to the edge of the river, it fell, dying the waters with its blood.

''Twas done with Indian skill,' said the scout, laughing inwardly, but with vast satisfaction; 'and 'twas a pretty sight to behold! Though an arrow is a near shot, and needs a knife to finish the work.'

'Hugh!' ejaculated his companion, turning quickly, like a hound who scented his game.

'By the Lord, there is a drove of them!' exclaimed the scout, whose eyes began to glisten with the ardour of his usual occupation; 'if they come within range of a bullet, I will drop one, though the whole Six Nations should be lurking within sound! What do you hear, Chingachgook? for to my ears the woods are dumb.'

'There is but one deer, and he is dead,' said the Indian, bending his body, till his ear nearly touched the earth. 'I hear the sounds of feet!'

'Perhaps the wolves have driven the buck to shelter, and are following on his trail.'

'No. The horses of white men are coming!' returned the other, raising himself with dignity, and resuming his seat on the log with his former composure. 'Hawk-eye, they are your brothers; speak to them.'

'That will I, and in English that the king needn't be ashamed to answer,' returned the hunter, speaking in the language of which he boasted; 'but I see nothing, nor do I hear the sounds of man or beast; 'tis strange that an Indian should understand white sounds better than a man, who, his very enemies will own, has no cross in his blood, although he may have lived with the red skins long enough to be suspected! Ha! there goes something like the cracking of a dry stick, too – now I hear the bushes move – yes, yes, there is a trampling that I mistook for the falls – and – but here they come themselves; God keep them from the Iroquois!'

> Well, go thy way; thou shalt not from this grove,
> Till I torment thee for this injury.
> *A Midsummer Night's Dream*, II. i. 146–147

THE WORDS WERE STILL in the mouth of the scout, when the leader of the party, whose approaching footsteps had caught the vigilant ear of the Indian, came openly into view. A beaten path, such as those made by the periodical passage of the deer, wound through a little glen at no great distance, and struck the river at the point where the white man and his red companions had posted themselves. Along this track the travellers, who had produced a surprise so unusual in the depths of the forest, advanced slowly towards the hunter, who was in front of his associates, in readiness to receive them.

'Who comes?' demanded the scout, throwing his rifle carelessly across his left arm, and keeping the fore finger of his right hand on the trigger, though he avoided all appearance of menace in the act – 'Who comes hither, among the beasts and dangers of the wilderness?'

'Believers in religion, and friends to the law and to the king,' returned he who rode foremost. 'Men who have journeyed since the rising sun, in the shades of this forest, without nourishment, and are sadly tired of their wayfaring.'

'You are, then, lost,' interrupted the hunter, 'and have found how helpless 'tis not to know whether to take the right hand or the left?'

'Even so; sucking babes are not more dependent on those who guide them, than we who are of larger growth, and who may now be said to possess the stature without the knowledge of men. Know you the distance to a post of the crown called William Henry?'

'Hoot!' shouted the scout, who did not spare his open laughter, though, instantly checking the dangerous sounds, he indulged his merriment at less risk of being overheard by any lurking enemies. 'You are as much off the scent as a hound would be, with Horican atwixt him and the deer! William Henry, man! if you are friends to the king, and have business with the army, your better way would be to follow the river down to Edward, and lay the matter before Webb; who tarries there, instead of pushing into the defiles, and driving this saucy Frenchman back across Champlain, into his den again.'

Before the stranger could make any reply to this unexpected proposition, another horseman dashed the bushes aside, and leaped his charger into the pathway in front of his companion.

'What, then, may be our distance from Fort Edward?' demanded a new speaker; 'the place you advise us to seek we left this morning, and our destination is the head of the lake.'

'Then you must have lost your eyesight afore losing your way, for the road across the portage is cut to a good two rods, and is as grand a path, I calculate, as any that runs into London, or even before the palace of the king himself.'

'We will not dispute concerning the excellence of the passage,' returned Heyward, smiling, for, as the reader has anticipated, it was he. 'It is enough, for the present, that we trusted to an Indian guide to take us by a nearer, though blinder path, and that we are deceived in his knowledge. In plain words, we know not where we are.'

'An Indian lost in the woods!' said the scout, shaking his head doubtingly; 'when the sun is scorching the tree tops, and the water courses are full; when the moss on every beech he sees, will tell him in which quarter the north star will shine at night! The woods are full of deer paths which run to the streams and licks, places well known to every body; nor have the geese done their flight to the Canada waters, altogether! 'Tis strange that an Indian should be lost atwixt Horican and the bend in the river! Is he a Mohawk?'

'Not by birth, though adopted in that tribe; I think his birth place was farther north, and he is one of those you call a Huron.'

'Hugh!' exclaimed the two companions of the scout, who had continued until this part of the dialogue, seated, immoveable, and apparently indifferent to what passed, but who now sprang to their feet with an activity and interest that had evidently gotten the better of their reserve, by surprise.

'A Huron!' repeated the sturdy scout, once more shaking his head in open distrust; 'they are a thievish race, nor do I care by whom they are adopted; you can never make any thing of them but skulks and vagabonds. Since you trusted yourself to the care of one of that nation, I only wonder that you have not fallen in with more.'

'Of that there is little danger, since William Henry is so many miles in our front. You forget that I have told you our guide is now a Mohawk, and that he serves with our forces as a friend.'

'And I tell you that he who is born a Mingo will die a Mingo,' returned the other, positively. 'A Mohawk! No, give me a Delaware or a Mohican for honesty; and when they will fight, which they won't all do, having suffered their cunning enemies, the Maquas, to make them women – but when they will fight at all, look to a Delaware or a Mohican for a warrior!'

'Enough of this,' said Heyward, impatiently; 'I wish not to inquire into the character of a man that I know, and to whom you must be a stranger. You have not yet answered my question; what is our distance from the main army at Edward?'

'It seems that may depend on who is your guide. One would think such a horse as that might get over a good deal of ground atwixt sun-up and sun-down.'

'I wish no contention of idle words with you, friend,' said Heyward, curbing his dissatisfied manner, and speaking in a more gentle voice; 'if you will tell me the distance to Fort Edward, and conduct me thither, your labor shall not go without its reward.'

'And in so doing, how know I that I don't guide an enemy, and a spy of Montcalm, to the works of the army? It is not every man who can speak the English tongue that is an honest subject.'

'If you serve with the troops of whom I judge you to be a scout, you should know of such a regiment of the king as the 60th.'

'The 60th! you can tell me little of the Royal Americans that I don't know, though I do wear a hunting shirt, instead of a scarlet jacket.'

'Well, then, among other things, you may know the name of its major?'

'Its major!' interrupted the hunter, elevating his body like one who was proud of his trust. 'If there is a man in the country who knows Major Effingham, he stands before you.'

'It is a corps which has many majors; the gentleman you name is the senior, but I speak of the junior of them all; he who commands the companies in garrison at William Henry.'

'Yes, yes, I have heard that a young gentleman of vast riches, from one of the provinces far south, has got the place. He is over young, too, to hold such rank, and to be put above men whose heads are beginning to bleach; and yet they say he is a soldier in his knowledge, and a gallant gentleman!'

'Whatever he may be, or however he may be qualified for his rank, he now speaks to you, and of course can be no enemy to dread.'

The scout regarded Heyward in surprise, and then lifting his cap, he answered, in a tone less confident than before – though still expressing doubt –

'I have heard a party was to leave the encampment, this morning, for the lake shore?'

'You have heard the truth; but I preferred a nearer route, trusting to the knowledge of the Indian I mentioned.'

'And he deceived you, and then deserted?'

'Neither, as I believe; certainly not the latter, for he is to be found in the rear.'

'I should like to look at the creatur; if it is a true Iroquois I can tell him by his knavish look, and by his paint,' said the scout, stepping past the charger of Heyward, and entering the path behind the mare of the singing master, whose foal had taken advantage of the halt to exact the maternal contribution. After shoving aside the bushes, and proceeding a few paces, he encountered the females, who awaited the result of the conference with anxiety, and not entirely without apprehension. Behind these, the runner leaned against a tree, where he stood the close examination of the scout with an air unmoved, though with a look so dark and savage, that it might in itself excite fear. Satisfied with his scrutiny, the hunter soon left him. As he repassed the females, he paused a moment to gaze upon their beauty, answering to the smile and nod of Alice with a look of open pleasure. Thence he went to the side of the motherly animal, and spending a minute in a fruitless inquiry into the character of her rider, he shook his head and returned to Heyward. .

'A Mingo is a Mingo, and God having made him so, neither the Mohawks nor any other tribe can alter him,' he said, when he had regained his former position. 'If we were alone, and you would leave that noble horse at the mercy of the wolves tonight, I could show you the way to Edward myself within an hour, for it lies only about an hour's journey hence; but with such ladies in your company, 'tis impossible!'

'And why? they are fatigued, but they are quite equal to a ride of a few more miles.'

''Tis a natural impossibility!' repeated the scout; 'I wouldn't walk a mile in these woods after night gets into them, in company with that runner, for the best rifle in the colonies. They are full of outlying Iroquois, and your mongrel Mohawk knows where to find them too well, to be my companion.'

'Think you so,' said Heyward, leaning forward in the saddle, and dropping his voice nearly to a whisper; 'I confess I have not been without my own suspicions, though I have endeavored to conceal them, and affected a confidence I have not always felt, on account of my companions. It was because I suspected him, that I would follow no longer; making him, as you see, follow me.'

'I knew he was one of the cheats as soon as I laid eyes on him!' returned the scout, placing a finger on his nose in sign of caution. 'The thief is leaning against the foot of the sugar sapling that you can see over them bushes; his right leg is in a line with the bark of the tree, and,' tapping his rifle, 'I can take him, from where I stand, between the ankle and the knee, with a single shot, putting an end to his tramping through the woods for at least a month to come. If I should go back to him, the cunning varmint would suspect something, and be dodging through the trees like any frightened deer.'

'It will not do. He may be innocent, and I dislike the act. Though, if I felt confident of his treachery' –

''Tis a safe thing to calculate on the knavery of an Iroquois,' said the scout, throwing his rifle forward, by a sort of instinctive movement.

'Hold!' interrupted Heyward; 'it will not do – we must think of some other scheme; – and yet, I have much reason to believe the rascal has deceived me.'

The hunter, who had already abandoned his intention of maiming the runner, mused a moment, and then made a gesture, which instantly brought his two red companions to his side. They spoke together earnestly in the Delaware language, though in an under tone, and by the gestures of the white man, which were frequently directed towards the top of the sapling, it was evident he pointed out the situation of their hidden enemy. His companions were not long in comprehending his wishes, and laying aside their fire-arms, they parted, taking opposite sides of the path, and burying themselves in the thicket, with such cautious movements, that their steps were inaudible.

'Now go you back,' said the hunter, speaking again to Heyward, 'and hold the imp in talk; these Mohicans here, will take him, without breaking his paint.'

'Nay,' said Heyward, proudly, 'I will seize him myself.'

'Hist! what could you do, mounted, against an Indian, in the bushes?'

'I will dismount.'

'And, think you, when he saw one of your feet out of the stirrup, he would wait for the other to be free! Whoever comes into the woods to deal with the natives, must use Indian fashions, if he would wish to prosper in his undertakings. Go, then; talk openly to the miscreant, and seem to believe him the truest friend you have on 'arth.'

Heyward prepared to comply, though with strong disgust at the nature of the office he was compelled to execute. Each moment, however, pressed upon him a conviction of the critical situation in which he had suffered his invaluable trust to be involved, through his own confidence. The sun had already disappeared, and the woods, suddenly deprived of his light,* were assuming a dusky hue, which keenly reminded him, that the hour the savage usually chose for his most barbarous and remorseless acts of vengeance or hostility, was speedily drawing near. Stimulated by apprehension, he left the scout, who immediately entered into a loud conversation with the stranger that had so unceremoniously enlisted himself in the party of travellers that morning. In passing his gentler companions, Heyward uttered a few words of encouragement, and was pleased to find that, though fatigued with the exercise of the day, they appeared to entertain no suspicion that their present embarrassment was other than the result of accident. Giving them reason to believe he was merely employed in a consultation concerning the future route, he spurred his charger, and drew the reins again when the animal had carried him within a few yards of the place, where the sullen runner still stood leaning against the tree.

'You may see, Magua,' he said, endeavoring to assume an air of freedom and confidence, 'that the night is closing around us, and yet we are no nearer to William Henry than when we left the encampment of Webb, with the rising sun. You have missed the way, nor have I been more fortunate. But, happily, we have fallen in with a hunter, he whom you hear talking to the singer, that is acquainted with the deer-paths and by-ways of the woods, and who promises to lead us to a place where we may rest securely till the morning.'

The Indian riveted his glowing eyes on Heyward as he asked, in his imperfect English, 'Is he alone?'

'Alone!' hesitatingly answered Heyward, to whom deception was too new to be assumed without embarrassment. 'Oh! not alone, surely, Magua, for you know that we are with him.'

'Then le Renard Subtil will go,' returned the runner, coolly raising his little wallet from the place where it had lain at his feet; 'and the pale faces will see none but their own color.'

'Go! Whom call you le Renard?'

''Tis the name his Canada fathers have given to Magua,' returned the runner, with an air that manifested his pride at the distinction. 'Night is the same as day to le Subtil, when Munro waits for him.'

'And what account will le Renard give the chief of William Henry concerning his daughters? will he dare to tell the hot-blooded Scotsman that his children are left without a guide, though Magua promised to be one?'

*The scene of this tale was in the 42d degree of latitude, where the twilight is never of long continuance. [1831]

'Though the gray head has a loud voice, and a long arm, le Renard will not hear him or feel him in the woods.'

'But what will the Mohawks say! They will make him petticoats, and bid him stay in the wigwam with the women, for he is no longer to be trusted with the business of a man.'

'Le Subtil knows the path to the great lakes, and he can find the bones of his fathers,' was the answer of the unmoved runner.

'Enough, Magua,' said Heyward; 'are we not friends! why should there be bitter words between us? Munro has promised you a gift for your services when performed, and I shall be your debtor for another. Rest your weary limbs, then, and open your wallet to eat. We have a few moments to spare; let us not waste them in talk like wrangling women. When the ladies are refreshed we will proceed.'

'The pale faces make themselves dogs to their women,' muttered the Indian, in his native language, 'and when they want to eat, their warriors must lay aside the tomahawk to feed their laziness.'

'What say you, Renard?'

'Le Subtil says it is good.'

The Indian then fastened his eyes keenly on the open countenance of Heyward, but meeting his glance, he turned them quickly away, and seating himself deliberately on the ground, he drew forth the remnant of some former repast, and began to eat, though not without first bending his looks slowly and cautiously around him.

'This is well,' continued Heyward; 'and le Renard will have strength and sight to find the path in the morning;' – he paused, for sounds like the snapping of a dried stick, and the rustling of leaves, rose from the adjacent bushes, but recollecting himself instantly he continued – 'we must be moving before the sun is seen, or Montcalm may lie in our path, and shut us out from the fortress.'

The hand of Magua dropped from his mouth to his side, and though his eyes were fastened on the ground, his head was turned aside, his nostrils expanded, and his ears seemed even to stand more erect than usual, giving to him the appearance of a statue that was made to represent intense attention.

Heyward, who watched his movements with a vigilant eye, carelessly extricated one of his feet from the stirrup, while he passed a hand towards the bear-skin covering of his holsters. Every effort to detect the point most regarded by the runner, was completely frustrated by the tremulous glances of his organs, which seemed not to rest a single instant on any particular object, and which, at the same time, could be hardly said to move. While he hesitated how to proceed, le Subtil cautiously raised himself to his feet, though with a motion so slow and guarded, that not the slightest noise was produced by the change. Heyward felt it had now become incumbent on him to act. Throwing his leg over the saddle, he dismounted, with a determination to advance and seize his treacherous companion, trusting the result to his own manhood. In order, however, to prevent unnecessary alarm, he still preserved an air of calmness and friendship.

'Le Renard Subtil does not eat,' he said, using the appellation he had found most flattering to the vanity of the Indian. 'His corn is not well parched, and it seems dry. Let me examine; perhaps something may be found among my own provisions that will help his appetite.'

Magua held out the wallet to the proffer of the other. He even suffered their hands to meet, without betraying the least emotion, or varying his riveted attitude of attention. But when he felt the fingers of Heyward moving gently along his own naked arm, he struck up the limb of the young man, and uttering a piercing cry, as he darted beneath it, plunged, at a single bound, into the opposite thicket. At the next instant, the form of Chingachgook appeared from the bushes, looking like a spectre in its paint, and glided across the path in swift pursuit. Next followed the shout of Uncas, when the woods were lighted by a sudden flash, that was accompanied by the sharp report of the hunter's rifle.

> —'In such a night,
> Did Thisbe fearfully o'ertrip the dew;
> And saw the lion's shadow ere himself.'—
>   *The Merchant of Venice,* V. i. 7–8

THE SUDDENNESS OF THE FLIGHT of his guide, and the wild cries of the pursuers, caused Heyward to remain fixed, for a few moments, in inactive surprise. Then recollecting the importance of securing the fugitive, he dashed aside the surrounding bushes, and pressed eagerly forward to lend his aid in the chase. Before he had, however, proceeded a hundred yards, he met the three foresters already returning from their unsuccessful pursuit.

'Why so soon disheartened!' he exclaimed; 'the scoundrel must be concealed behind some of these trees, and may yet be secured. We are not safe while he goes at large.'

'Would you set a cloud to chase the wind?' returned the disappointed scout; 'I heard the imp, brushing over the dry leaves, like a black snake, and blinking a glimpse of him, just over ag'in yon big pine, I pulled as it might be on the scent; but 'twouldn't do! and yet for a reasoning aim, if any body but myself had touched the trigger, I should call it a quick sight; and I may be accounted to have experience in these matters, and one who ought to know. Look at this sumach; its leaves are red, though every body knows the fruit is in the yellow blossom, in the month of July!'

''Tis the blood of le Subtil! he is hurt, and may yet fall!'

'No, no,' returned the scout, in decided disapprobation of this opinion, 'I rubbed the bark off a limb, perhaps, but the creatur leaped the longer for it. A rifle bullet acts on a running animal, when it barks him, much the same as one of your spurs on a horse; that is, it quickens motion, and puts life into the flesh, instead of taking it away. But when it cuts the ragged hole, after a bound or two, there is, commonly, a stagnation of further leaping, be it Indian or be it deer!'

'We are four able bodies, to one wounded man!'

'Is life grievous to you?' interrupted the scout. 'Yonder red devil would draw you within swing of the tomahawks of his comrades, before you were heated in the chase. It was an unthoughtful act, in a man who has so often slept with the war-whoop ringing in the air, to let off his piece, within sound of an ambushment! But, then it was a natural temptation! 'twas very natural! Come, friends, let us move our station, and in such a fashion, too, as will throw the cunning of a Mingo on a wrong scent, or our scalps will be drying in the wind in front of Montcalm's marquee, ag'in this hour tomorrow.'

This appalling declaration, which the scout uttered with the cool assurance of a man who fully comprehended, while he did not fear to face the danger, served to remind Heyward of the importance of the charge with which he himself had been intrusted. Glancing his eyes around, with a vain effort to pierce the gloom that was thickening beneath the leafy arches of the forest, he felt as if, cut off from human aid, his unresisting companions would soon lie at the entire mercy of those barbarous enemies, who, like beasts of prey, only waited till the gathering darkness might render their blows more fatally certain. His awakened imagination, deluded by the deceptive light, converted each waving bush, or the fragment of some fallen tree, into human forms, and twenty times he fancied he could distinguish the horrid visages of his lurking foes, peering from their hiding places, in never-ceasing watchfulness of the movements of his party. Looking upward, he found that the thin fleecy clouds, which evening had painted on the blue sky, were already losing their faintest tints of rose-color, while the embedded stream which glided past the spot where he stood, was to be traced only by the dark boundary of its wooded banks.

'What is to be done?' he said, feeling the utter helplessness of doubt in such a pressing strait; 'desert me not, for God's sake! remain to defend those I escort, and freely name your own reward!'

His companions, who conversed apart in the language of their tribe, heeded not this sudden and earnest appeal. Though their dialogue was maintained in low and cautious sounds, but little above a whisper, Heyward, who now approached, could easily distinguish the earnest tones of the younger warrior, from the more deliberate speeches of his seniors. It was evident, that they debated on the propriety of some measure, that nearly concerned the welfare of the travellers. Yielding to his powerful interest in the subject, and impatient of a delay that seemed fraught with so much additional danger, Heyward drew still nigher to the dusky groupe, with an intention of making his offers of compensation more definite, when the white man, motioning with his hand as if he conceded the disputed point, turned away, saying in a sort of soliloquy, and in the English tongue:—

'Uncas is right! it would not be the act of men, to leave such harmless things to their fate, even though it breaks up the harboring place for ever. If you would save these tender blossoms from the fangs of the worst of sarpents, gentleman, you have neither time to lose nor resolution to throw away!'

'How can such a wish be doubted! have I not already offered'—

'Offer your prayers to Him, who can give us wisdom to carcumvent the cunning of the devils who fill these woods,' calmly interrupted the scout, 'but spare your offers of money, which neither you may live to realize, nor I to profit by. These Mohicans and I, will do what man's thoughts can invent, to keep such flowers, which, though so sweet, were never made for the wilderness, from harm, and that without hope of any other recompense but such as God always gives to upright dealings. First, you must promise two things, both in your own name, and for your friends, or without serving you, we shall only injure ourselves!'

'Name them.'

'The one is to be still as these sleeping woods, let what will happen; and the other, is to keep the place where we shall take you forever a secret from all mortal men.'

'I will do my utmost to see both these conditions fulfilled.'

'Then follow, for we are losing moments that are as precious as the heart's blood to a stricken deer!'

Heyward could distinguish the impatient gesture of the scout, through the increasing shadows of the evening, and he moved in his footsteps, swiftly, towards the place where he had left the remainder of his party. When they rejoined the expecting and anxious females, he briefly acquainted them with the conditions of their new guide, and with the necessity that existed for their hushing every apprehension, in instant and serious exertions. Although his alarming communication was not received without much secret terror by the listeners, his earnest and impressive manner, aided perhaps by the nature of the danger, succeeded in bracing their nerves to undergo some unlooked for and unusual trial. Silently, and without a moment's delay, they permitted him to assist them from their saddles, when they descended, quickly, to the water's edge, where the scout had collected the rest of the party, more by the agency of his expressive gestures than by any use of words.

'What to do with these dumb creaturs!' muttered the white man, on whom the sole control of their future movements appeared to devolve; 'it would be time lost to cut their throats, and cast them into the river; and to leave them here, would be to tell the Mingoes that they have not far to seek to find their owners!'

'Then give them their bridles, and let them range the woods!' Heyward ventured to suggest.

'No; it would be better to mislead the imps, and make them believe they must equal a horse's speed to run down their chase. Ay, ay, that will blind their fire-balls of eyes! Chingach – Hist! what stirs the bush?'

'The colt.'

'That colt, at least, must die,' muttered the scout, grasping at the mane of the nimble beast, which easily eluded his hand; 'Uncas, your arrows!'

'Hold!' exclaimed the proprietor of the condemned animal, aloud, without regard to the whispering tones used by the others; 'spare the foal of Miriam! it is the comely offspring of a faithful dam, and would, willingly, injure naught.'

'When men struggle for the single life God has given them,' said the scout, sternly, 'even their own kind seem no more than the beasts of the wood. If you speak again, I shall leave you to the mercy of the Maquas! Draw to your arrow's head, Uncas; we have no time for second blows!'

The low, muttering sounds of his threatening voice, were still audible, when the wounded foal, first rearing on its hinder legs, plunged forward to its knees. It was met by Chingachgook, whose knife passed across its throat quicker than thought, and then precipitating the motion of the struggling victim, he dashed it into the river, down whose stream it glided away, gasping audibly for breath with its ebbing life. This deed of apparent cruelty, but of real necessity, fell upon the spirits of the travellers, like a terrific warning of the peril in which they stood, heightened, as it was, by the calm though steady resolution of the actors in the scene. The sisters shuddered, and clung closer to each other, while Heyward, instinctively, laid his hand on one of the pistols he had just drawn from their holsters, as he placed himself between his charge and those dense shadows, that seemed to draw an impenetrable veil before the bosom of the forest.

The Indians, however, hesitated not a moment, but taking the bridles, they led the frightened and reluctant horses into the bed of the river.

At a short distance from the shore, they turned, and were soon concealed by the projection of the bank, under the brow of which they moved, in a direction opposite to the course of the waters. In the mean time, the scout drew a canoe of bark from its place of concealment beneath some low bushes, whose branches were waving with the eddies of the current, into which he silently motioned for the females to enter. They complied without hesitation, though many a fearful and anxious glance was thrown behind them, towards the thickening gloom, which now lay like a dark barrier along the margin of the stream.

So soon as Cora and Alice were seated, the scout, without regarding the element, directed Heyward to support one side of the frail vessel, and posting himself at the other, they bore it up against the stream, followed by the dejected owner of the dead foal. In this manner they proceeded, for many rods, in a silence that was only interrupted by the rippling of the water, as its eddies played around them, or the low dash made by their own cautious footsteps. Heyward yielded the guidance of the canoe, implicitly, to the scout, who approached or receded from the shore, to avoid the fragments of rocks, or deeper parts of the river, with a readiness that showed his knowledge of the route they held. Occasionally he would stop; and in the midst of a breathing stillness, that the dull but increasing roar of the waterfall only served to render more impressive, he would listen with painful intenseness to catch any sounds that might arise from the slumbering forest. When assured that all was still, and unable to detect, even by the aid of his practiced senses, any sign of his approaching foes, he would deliberately resume his slow and guarded progress. At length they reached a point in the river, where the roving eye of Heyward became riveted on a cluster of black objects, collected at a spot where the high bank threw a deeper shadow than usual on the dark waters. Hesitating to advance, he pointed out the place to the attention of his companion.

'Ay,' returned the composed scout, 'the Indians have hid the beasts with the judgment of natives! Water leaves no trail, and an owl's eyes would be blinded by the darkness of such a hole.'

The whole party was soon reunited, and another consultation was held between the scout and his new comrades, during which, they, whose fates depended on the faith and ingenuity of these unknown foresters, had a little leisure to observe their situation more minutely.

The river was confined between high and cragged rocks, one of which impended above the spot where the canoe rested. As these, again, were surmounted by tall trees, which appeared to totter on the brows of the precipice, it gave the stream the appearance of running through a deep and narrow dell. All beneath the fantastic limbs and ragged tree-tops, which were, here and there, dimly painted against the starry zenith, lay alike in shadowed obscurity. Behind them, the curvature of the banks soon bounded the view, by the same dark and wooded outline; but in front, and apparently at no great distance, the water seemed piled against the heavens, whence it tumbled into caverns, out of which issued those sullen sounds, that had loaded the evening atmosphere. It seemed, in truth, to be a spot devoted to seclusion, and the sisters imbibed a soothing impression of security, as they gazed upon its romantic, though not unappalling beauties. A general movement among their conductors, however, soon recalled them from a contemplation of the wild charms that night had assisted to lend the place, to a painful sense of their real peril.

The horses had been secured to some scattering shrubs that grew in the fissures of the rocks, where, standing in the water, they were left to pass the night. The scout directed Heyward and his disconsolate fellow travellers to seat themselves in the forward end of the canoe, and took possession of the other himself, as erect and steady as if he floated in a vessel of much firmer materials. The Indians warily retraced their steps towards the place they had left, when the scout, placing his pole against a rock, by a powerful shove, sent his frail bark directly into the centre of the turbulent stream. For many minutes the struggle between the light bubble in which they floated, and the swift current, was severe and doubtful. Forbidden to stir even a hand, and almost afraid to breathe, lest they should expose the frail fabric to the fury of the stream, the passengers watched the glancing waters in feverish suspense. Twenty times they thought the whirling eddies were sweeping them to destruction, when the master-hand of their pilot would bring the bows of the canoe to stem the rapid. A long, a vigorous, and, as it appeared to the females, a desperate effort, closed the struggle. Just as Alice veiled her eyes in horror, under the impression that they were about to be swept within the vortex at the foot of the cataract, the canoe floated, stationary, at the side of a flat rock, that lay on a level with the water.

'Where are we? and what is next to be done?' demanded Heyward, perceiving that the exertions of the scout had ceased.

'You are at the foot of Glenn's,' returned the other, speaking aloud, without fear of consequences, within the roar of the cataract; 'and the next thing is to make a steady landing, lest the canoe upset, and you should go down again the hard road we have travelled, faster than you came up; 'tis a hard rift to stem, when the river is a little swelled; and five is an unnatural number to keep dry in the hurry-skurry, with a little birchen bark, and gum. There, go you all on the rock, and I will bring up the Mohicans with the venison. A man had better sleep without his scalp, than famish in the midst of plenty.'

His passengers gladly complied with these directions. As the last foot touched the rock, the canoe whirled from its station, when the tall form of the scout was seen, for an instant, gliding above the waters, before it disappeared in the impenetrable darkness that rested on the bed of the river. Left by their guide, the travellers remained a few minutes in helpless ignorance, afraid even to move along the broken rocks, lest a false step should precipitate them down some one of the many deep and roaring caverns, into which the water seemed to tumble, on every side of them. Their suspense, however, was soon relieved; for, aided by the skill of the natives, the canoe shot back into the eddy, and floated again at the side of the low rock, before they thought the scout had even time to rejoin his companions.

'We are now fortified, garrisoned, and provisioned,' cried Heyward, cheerfully, 'and may set Montcalm and his allies at defiance. How, now, my vigilant sentinel, can you see any thing of those you call the Iroquois on the main land?'

'I call them Iroquois, because to me every native, who speaks a foreign tongue, is accounted an enemy, though he may pretend to serve the king! If Webb wants faith and honesty in an Indian, let him bring out the tribes of the Delawares, and send these greedy and lying Mohawks and Oneidas, with their six nations of varlets, where in nature they belong, among the French!'

'We should then exchange a warlike for a useless friend! I have heard that the Delawares have laid aside the hatchet, and are content to be called women!'

'Ay, shame on the Hollanders* and Iroquois, who carcumvented them by their deviltries into such a treaty! But I have known them for twenty years, and I call him liar, that says cowardly blood runs in the veins of a Delaware. You have driven their tribes from the sea-shore, and would now believe what their enemies say, that you may sleep at night upon an easy pillow. No, no; to me, every Indian who speaks a foreign tongue is an Iroquois, whether the castle† of his tribe be in Canada or be in York.'

Heyward perceiving that the stubborn adherence of the scout to the cause of his

*The reader will remember that New York was originally a colony of the Dutch. [1831]
†The principal villages of the Indian are still called 'castles' by the whites of New York. 'Oneida castle' is no more than a scattered hamlet; but the name is in general use. [1831]

friends the Delawares or Mohicans, for they were branches of the same numerous people, was likely to prolong a useless discussion, changed the subject.

'Treaty or no treaty, I know full well, that your two companions are brave and cautious warriors! have they heard or seen any thing of our enemies?'

'An Indian is a mortal to be felt afore he is seen,' returned the scout, ascending the rock, and throwing the deer carelessly down. 'I trust to other signs than such as come in at the eye, when I am outlying on the trail of the Mingoes.'

'Do your ears tell you that they have traced our retreat?'

'I should be sorry to think they had, though this is a spot that stout courage might hold for a smart skrimmage. I will not deny, however, but the horses cowered when I passed them, as though they scented the wolves; and a wolf is a beast that is apt to hover about an Indian ambushment, craving the offals of the deer the savages kill.'

'You forget the buck at your feet! or, may we not owe their visit to the dead colt? Ha! what noise is that!'

'Poor Miriam,' murmured the stranger; 'thy foal was foreordained to become a prey to ravenous beasts!' Then suddenly lifting up his voice amid the eternal din of the waters, he sang aloud—

'First born of Egypt, smite did he,
Of mankind, and of beast also;
O Egypt! wonders sent 'midst thee,
On Pharoah and his servants too!'

'The death of the colt sits heavy on the heart of its owner,' said the scout; 'but it's a good sign to see a man account upon his dumb friends. He has the religion of the matter, in believing what is to happen will happen; and with such a consolation, it wont be long afore he submits to the rationality of killing a four-footed beast, to save the lives of human men. It may be as you say,' he continued, reverting to the purport of Heyward's last remark; 'and the greater the reason why we should cut our steaks, and let the carcass drive down the stream, or we shall have the pack howling along the cliffs, begruding every mouthful we swallow. Besides, though the Delaware tongue is the same as a book to the Iroquois, the cunning varlets are quick enough at understanding the reason of a wolf's howl.'

The scout, whilst making his remarks, was busied in collecting certain necessary implements; as he concluded, he moved silently by the groupe of travellers, accompanied by the Mohicans, who seemed to comprehend his intentions with instinctive readiness, when the whole three disappeared in succession, seeming to vanish against the dark face of a perpendicular rock, that rose to the height of a few yards, within as many feet of the water's edge.

'Those strains that once did sweet in Zion glide;
He wales a portion with judicious care;
And let us worship God, he says, with solemn air.'
                    Burns, 'The Cotter's Saturday Night,' 11.106–108.

HEYWARD, AND HIS FEMALE COMPANIONS, witnessed this mysterious movement with secret uneasiness; for, though the conduct of the white man had hitherto been above reproach, his rude equipments, blunt address, and strong antipathies, together with the character of his silent associates, were all causes for exciting distrust in minds that had been so recently alarmed by Indian treachery. The stranger alone disregarded the passing incidents. He seated himself on a projection of the rocks, whence he gave no other signs of consciousness, than by the struggles of his spirit, as manifested in frequent and heavy sighs. Smothered voices were next heard, as though men called to each other in the bowels of the earth, when a sudden light flashed upon those without, and laid bare the much prized secret of the place.

At the farther extremity of a narrow, deep, cavern in the rock, whose length appeared much extended by the perspective and the nature of the light by which it was seen, was seated the scout, holding a blazing knot of pine. The strong glare of the fire fell full upon his sturdy, weather-beaten countenance and forest attire, lending an air of romantic wildness to the aspect of an individual, who, seen by the sober light of day, would have exhibited the peculiarities of a man remarkable for the strangeness of his dress, the iron-like inflexibility of his frame, and the singular compound of quick, vigilant sagacity, and of exquisite simplicity, that by turns usurped the possession of his muscular features. At a little distance in advance stood Uncas, his whole person thrown powerfully into view. The travellers anxiously regarded the upright, flexible figure of the young Mohican, graceful and unrestrained in the attitudes and movements of nature. Though his person was more than usually skreened by a green and fringed hunting shirt, like that of the white man, there was no concealment to his dark, glancing, fearless eye, alike terrible and calm; the bold outline of his high, haughty features, pure in their native red; or to the dignified elevation of his receding forehead, together with all the finest proportions of a noble head, bared to the generous scalping tuft. It was the first opportunity possessed by Duncan and his companions, to view the marked lineaments of either of their Indian attendants, and each individual of the party felt relieved from a burthen of doubt, as the proud and determined, though wild, expression of the features of the young warrior forced itself on their notice. They felt it might be a being partially benighted in the vale of ignorance, but it could not be one who would willingly devote his rich natural gifts to the purposes of wanton treachery. The ingenuous Alice gazed at his free air and proud carriage, as she would have looked upon some precious relic of the Grecian chisel, to which life had been imparted, by the intervention of a miracle; while Heyward, though accustomed to see the perfection of form which abounds among the uncorrupted natives, openly expressed his admiration at such an unblemished specimen of the noblest proportions of man.

'I could sleep in peace,' whispered Alice, in reply, 'with such a fearless and generous looking youth for my sentinel. Surely, Duncan, those cruel murders, those terrific scenes of torture, of which we read and hear so much, are never acted in the presence of such as he!'

'This, certainly, is a rare and brilliant instance of those natural qualities, in which these peculiar people are said to excel,' he answered. 'I agree with you, Alice, in thinking that such a front and eye were formed rather to intimidate than to deceive; but let us not practice a deception on ourselves, by expecting any other exhibition of what we esteem virtue, than according to the fashion of a savage. As bright examples of great qualities are but too uncommon among christians, so are they singular and solitary with the Indians; though, for the honor of our common nature, neither are incapable of producing them. Let us then hope, that this Mohican may not disappoint our wishes, but prove, what his looks assert him to be, a brave and constant friend.'

'Now Major Heyward speaks, as Major Heyward should,' said Cora; 'who, that looks at this creature of nature, remembers the shades of his skin!'

A short, and apparently an embarrassed, silence succeeded this remark, which was interrupted by the scout calling to them aloud, to enter.

'This fire begins to show too bright a flame,' he continued, as they complied, 'and might light the Mingoes to our undoing.' Uncas, drop the blanket, and show the knaves its dark side. This is not such a supper as a major of the Royal Americans has a right to expect, but I've known stout detachments of the corps glad to eat their venison raw, and without a relish too. * Here, you see, we have plenty of salt, and can make a quick broil. There's fresh saxafrax boughs for the ladies to sit on, which may not be as proud as their my-hog-guinea chairs, but which sends up a sweeter flavor than the skin of any hog can do, be it of Guinea, or be it of any other land. Come, friend, dont be mournful for the colt; 'twas an innocent thing, and had not seen much hardship. Its death will save the creatur many a sore back and weary foot!'

Uncas did as the other had directed, and when the voice of Hawk-eye ceased, the roar of the cataract sounded like the rumbling of distant thunder.

'Are we quite safe in this cavern?' demanded Heyward. 'Is there no danger of surprise? A single armed man, at its entrance, would hold us at his mercy.'

A spectral looking figure stalked from out of the darkness behind the scout, and seizing a blazing brand, held it towards the further extremity of their place of retreat. Alice uttered a faint shriek, and even Cora rose to her feet, as this appalling object moved into the light; but a single word from Heyward calmed them, with the assurance it was only their attendant, Chingachgook, who, lifting another blanket, discovered that the cavern had two outlets. Then, holding the brand, he crossed a deep, narrow chasm in the rocks, which ran at right angles with the passage they were in, but which, unlike that, was open to the heavens, and entered another cave, answering to the description of the first, in every essential particular.

'Such old foxes as Chingachgook and myself, are not often caught in a burrow with one hole,' said Hawk-eye, laughing; 'you can easily see the cunning of the place – the rock is black limestone, which every body knows is soft; it makes no uncomfortable pillow, where brush and pine wood is scarce; well, the fall was once a few yards below us, and I dare to say was, in its time, as regular and as handsome a sheet of water as any along the Hudson. But old age is a great injury to good looks, as these sweet young ladies have yet to l'arn! The place is sadly changed! These

---

* In vulgar parlance the condiments of a repast are called by the American 'a relish,' substituting the thing for its effect. These provincial terms are frequently put in the mouths of the speakers, according to their several conditions in life. Most of them are of local use, and others quite peculiar to the particular class of men to which the character belongs. In the present instance, the scout uses the word with immediate reference to the 'salt,' with which his own party was so fortunate as to be provided. [1831]

rocks are full of cracks, and in some places, they are softer than at othersome, and the water has worked out deep hollows for itself, until it has fallen back, ay, some hundred feet, breaking here, and wearing there, until the falls have neither shape nor consistency.'

'In what part of them are we?' asked Heyward.

'Why, we are nigh by the spot that Providence first placed them at, but where, it seems, they were too rebellious to stay. The rock proved softer on either side of us, and so they left the centre of the river bare and dry, first working out these two little holes for us to hide in.'

'We are then on an island?'

'Ay! there are the falls on two sides of us, and the river above and below. If you had daylight, it would be worth the trouble to step up on the height of this rock, and look at the perversity of the water! It falls by no rule at all; sometimes it leaps, sometimes it tumbles; there, it skips; here, it shoots; in one place 'tis white as snow, and in another 'tis green as grass; hereabouts, it pitches into deep hollows, that rumble and quake the 'arth; and thereaway, it ripples and sings like a brook, fashioning whirlpools and gullies in the old stone, as if 'twas no harder than trodden clay. The whole design of the river seems disconcerted. First it runs smoothly, as if meaning to go down the descent as things were ordered; then it angles about and faces the shores; nor are there places wanting, where it looks backward, as if unwilling to leave the wilderness, to mingle with the salt! Ay, lady, the fine cobweb-looking cloth you wear at your throat, is coarse, and like a fish net, to little spots I can show you, where the river fabricates all sorts of images, as if, having broke loose from order, it would try its hand at every thing. And yet what does it amount to! After the water has been suffered to have its will for a time, like a headstrong man, it is gathered together by the hand that made it, and a few rods below you may see it all, flowing on steadily towards the sea, as was foreordained from the first foundation of the 'arth!'

While his auditors received a cheering assurance of the security of their place of concealment, from this untutored description of Glenn's,[*] they were much inclined to judge differently from Hawk-eye, of its wild beauties. But they were not in a situation to suffer their thoughts to dwell on the charms of natural objects; and, as the scout had not found it necessary to cease his culinary labors while he spoke, unless to point out, with a broken fork, the direction of some particularly obnoxious point in the rebellious stream, they now suffered their attention to be drawn to the necessary though more vulgar consideration of their supper.

The repast, which was greatly aided by the addition of a few delicacies, that Heyward had the precaution to bring with him, when they left their horses, was exceedingly refreshing to the wearied party. Uncas acted as attendant to the females, performing all the little offices within his power, with a mixture of dignity and anxious grace, that served to amuse Heyward, who well knew that it was an utter innovation on the Indian customs, which forbid their warriors to descend to any menial employment, especially in favor of their women. As the rites of

[*]Glenn's Falls are on the Hudson, some forty or fifty miles above the head of tide, or the place where that river becomes navigable for sloops. The description of this picturesque and remarkable little cataract, as given by the scout, is sufficiently correct, though the application of the water to the uses of civilized life has materially injured its beauties. The rocky island and the two caverns are well known to every traveller, since the former sustains a pier of a bridge, which is now thrown across the river, immediately above the fall. In explanation of the taste of Hawk-eye, it should be remembered that men always prize that most which is least enjoyed. Thus, in a new country, the woods and other objects, which in an old country would be maintained at great cost, are gotten rid of, simply with a view of 'improving' as it is called. [1831]

hospitality were, however, considered sacred among them, this little departure from the dignity of manhood excited no audible comment. Had there been one there sufficiently disengaged to become a close observer, he might have fancied that the services of the young chief were not entirely impartial. That, while he tendered to Alice the gourd of sweet water, and the venison in a trencher, neatly carved from the knot of the pepperage, with sufficient courtesy, in performing the same offices to her sister, his dark eye lingered on her rich, speaking, countenance. Once or twice he was compelled to speak, to command the attention of those he served. In such cases, he made use of English, broken and imperfect, but sufficiently intelligible, and which he rendered so mild and musical, by his* deep, guttural voice, that it never failed to cause both ladies to look up in admiration and astonishment. In the course of these civilities, a few sentences were exchanged, that served to establish the appearance of an amicable intercourse between the parties.

In the meanwhile, the gravity of Chingachgook remained immovable. He had seated himself more within the circle of light, where the frequent, uneasy glances of his guests were better enabled to separate the natural expression of his face, from the artificial terrors of the warpaint. They found a strong resemblance between father and son, with the difference that might be expected from age and hardships. The fierceness of his countenance now seemed to slumber, and in its place was to be seen the quiet, vacant composure, which distinguishes an Indian warrior, when his faculties are not required for any of the greater purposes of his existence. It was, however, easy to be seen, by the occasional gleams that shot across his swarthy visage, that it was only necessary to arouse his passions in order to give full effect to the terrific device which he had adopted to intimidate his enemies. On the other hand, the quick, roving eye of the scout seldom rested. He ate and drank with an appetite that no sense of danger could disturb, but his vigilance seemed never to desert him. Twenty times the gourd or the venison was suspended before his lips, while his head was turned aside, as though he listened to some distant and distrusted sounds – a movement that never failed to recall his guests from regarding the novelties of their situation, to a recollection of the alarming reasons that had driven them to seek it. As these frequent pauses were never followed by any remark, the momentary uneasiness they created quickly passed away, and for a time was forgotten.

'Come, friend,' said Hawk-eye, drawing out a keg from beneath a cover of leaves, towards the close of the repast, and addressing the stranger who sat at his elbow, doing great justice to his culinary skill, 'try a little spruce; 'twill wash away all thoughts of the colt, and quicken the life in your bosom. I drink to our better friendship, hoping that a little horseflesh may leave no heart-burnings atween us. How do you name yourself?'

'Gamut – David Gamut,' returned the singing-master, preparing to wash down his sorrows, in a powerful draught of the woodsman's high-flavored and well-laced compound.

'A very good name, and, I dare say, handed down from honest forefathers. I'm an admirator of names, though the Christian fashions fall far below savage customs in this particular. The biggest coward I ever knew was called Lyon; and his wife, Patience, would scold you out of hearing in less time than a hunted deer would run a rod. With an Indian 'tis a matter of conscience; what he calls himself, he generally is – not that Chingachgook, which signifies big sarpent, is really a

*The meaning of Indian words is much governed by the emphasis and tones. [1826]

snake, big or little; but that he understands the windings and turnings of human natur, and is silent, and strikes his enemies when they least expect him. What may be your calling?'

'I am an unworthy instructor in the art of psalmody.'

'Anan!'

'I teach singing to the youths of the Connecticut levy.'

'You might be better employed. The young hounds go laughing and singing too much already through the woods, when they ought not to breathe louder than a fox in his cover. Can you use the smooth bore, or handle the rifle?'

'Praised be God, I have never had occasion to meddle with murderous implements!'

'Perhaps you understand the compass, and lay down the water courses and mountains of the wilderness on paper, in order that they who follow may find places by their given names?'

'I practice no such employment.'

'You have a pair of legs that might make a long path seem short! you journey sometimes, I fancy, with tidings for the general.'

'Never; I follow no other than my own high vocation, which is instruction in sacred music!'

"Tis a strange calling!' muttered Hawk-eye, with an inward laugh, 'to go through life, like a cat-bird, mocking all the ups and downs that may happen to come out of other men's throats. Well, friend, I suppose it is your gift, and mustn't be denied any more than if 'twas shooting, or some other better inclination. Let us hear what you can do in that way; 'twill be a friendly manner of saying good night, for 'tis time these ladies should be getting strength for a hard and a long push, in the pride of the morning, afore the Maquas are stirring.'

'With joyful pleasure do I consent,' said David, adjusting his iron-rimmed spectacles, and producing his beloved little volume, which he immediately tendered to Alice. 'What can be more fitting and consolatory, than to offer up evening praise after a day of such exceeding jeopardy!'

Alice smiled; but regarding Heyward, she blushed and hesitated.

'Indulge yourself,' he whispered; 'ought not the suggestion of the worthy namesake of the Psalmist to have its weight at such a moment?'

Encouraged by his opinion, Alice did what her pious inclinations and her keen relish for gentle sounds, had before so strongly urged. The book was open at a hymn not ill adapted to their situation, and in which the poet, no longer goaded by his desire to excel the inspired King of Israel, had discovered some chastened and respectable powers. Cora betrayed a disposition to support her sister, and the sacred song proceeded, after the indispensable preliminaries of the pitch-pipe and the tune had been duly attended to by the methodical David.

The air was solemn and slow. At times it rose to the fullest compass of the rich voices of the females, who hung over their little book in holy excitement, and again it sunk so low, that the rushing of the waters ran through their melody like a hollow accompaniment. The natural taste and true ear of David, governed and modified the sounds to suit their confined cavern, every crevice and cranny of which was filled with the thrilling notes of their flexible voices. The Indians riveted their eyes on the rocks, and listened with an attention that seemed to turn them into stone. But the scout, who had placed his chin in his hand, with an expression of cold indifference, gradually suffered his rigid features to relax, until, as verse succeeded verse, he felt his iron nature subdued, while his recollection was carried back to boyhood, when his ears had been accustomed to listen to similar sounds of praise, in the settlements of the colony. His roving eyes began to moisten, and before the hymn was ended, scalding tears rolled out of fountains that had long seemed dry, and followed each other down those cheeks that had oftener felt the storms of heaven, than any testimonials of weakness. The singers were dwelling on one of those low, dying chords, which the ear devours with such greedy rapture, as if conscious that it is about to lose them, when a cry, that seemed neither human, nor earthly, rose in the outward air, penetrating not only the recesses of the cavern, but to the inmost hearts of all who heard it. It was followed by a stillness apparently as deep as if the waters had been checked in their furious progress at such a horrid and unusual interruption.

'What is it?' murmured Alice, after a few moments of terrible suspense.

'What is it?' repeated Heyward, aloud.

Neither Hawk-eye, nor the Indians, made any reply. They listened, as if expecting the sound would be repeated, with a manner that expressed their own astonishment. At length, they spoke together, earnestly, in the Delaware language, when Uncas, passing by the inner and most concealed aperture, cautiously left the cavern. When he had gone, the scout first spoke in English.

'What it is, or what it is not, none here can tell; though two of us have ranged the woods for more than thirty years! I did believe there was no cry that Indian or beast could make, that my ears had not heard; but this has proved that I was only a vain and conceited mortal.'

'Was it not, then, the shout the warriors make when they wish to intimidate their enemies?' asked Cora, who stood drawing her veil about her person, with a calmness to which her agitated sister was a stranger.

'No, no; this was bad, and shocking, and had a sort of unhuman sound; but when you once hear the war-whoop, you will never mistake it for any thing else! Well, Uncas!' speaking in the Delaware to the young chief as he re-entered, 'what see you? do our lights shine through the blankets?'

The answer was short, and apparently decided, being given in the same tongue.

'There is nothing to be seen without,' continued Hawk-eye, shaking his head in discontent; 'and our hiding-place is still in darkness! Pass into the other cave, you that need it, and seek for sleep; we must be afoot long before the sun, and make the most of our time to get to Edward, while the Mingoes are taking their morning nap.'

Cora set the example of compliance, with a steadiness that taught the more timid Alice the necessity of obedience. Before leaving the place, however, she whispered a request to Duncan that he would follow. Uncas raised the blanket for their passage, and as the sisters turned to thank him for this act of attention, they saw the scout seated again before the dying embers, with his face resting on his hands, in a manner which showed how deeply he brooded on the unaccountable interruption, which had broken up their evening devotions.

Heyward took with him a blazing knot, which threw a dim light through the narrow vista of their new apartment. Placing it in a favorable position, he joined the females, who now found themselves alone with him, for the first time since they had left the friendly ramparts of fort Edward.

'Leave us not, Duncan,' said Alice; 'we cannot sleep in such a place as this, with that horrid cry still ringing in our ears!'

'First let us examine into the security of your fortress,' he answered, 'and then we will speak of rest.'

He approached the farther end of the cavern, to an outlet, which, like the others, was concealed by blankets, and removing the thick skreen, breathed the fresh and reviving air from the cataract. One arm of the river flowed through a deep, narrow ravine, which its current had worn in the soft rock, directly beneath his feet, forming an effectual defence, as he believed, against any danger from that quarter; the water, a few rods above them, plunging, glancing, and sweeping along, in its most violent and broken manner.

'Nature has made an impenetrable barrier on this side,' he continued, pointing down the perpendicular declivity into the dark current, before he dropped the blanket; 'and as you know that good men and true, are on guard in front, I see no reason why the advice of our honest host should be disregarded. I am certain Cora will join me in saying, that sleep is necessary to you both!'

'Cora may submit to the justice of your opinion, though she cannot put it in practice,' returned the elder sister, who had placed herself by the side of Alice, on a couch of sassafras; 'there would be other causes to chase away sleep, though we had been spared the shock of this mysterious noise. Ask yourself, Heyward, can daughters forget the anxiety a father must endure, whose children lodge, he knows not where or how, in such a wilderness, and in the midst of so many perils!'

'He is a soldier, and knows how to estimate the chances of the woods.'

'He is a father, and cannot deny his nature.'

'How kind has he ever been to all my follies! how tender and indulgent to all my wishes!' sobbed Alice. 'We have been selfish, sister, in urging our visit at such hazard!'

'I may have been rash in pressing his consent in a moment of so much embarrassment, but I would have proved to him, that however others might neglect him, in his strait, his children at least were faithful!'

'When he heard of your arrival at Edward,' said Heyward, kindly, 'there was a powerful struggle in his bosom between fear and love; though the latter, heightened, if possible, by so long a separation, quickly prevailed. "It is the spirit of my noble minded Cora that leads them, Duncan," he said, "and I will not balk it. Would to God, that he who holds the honor of our royal master in his guardianship, would show but half her firmness." '

'And did he not speak of me, Heyward?' demanded Alice, with jealous affection. 'Surely, he forgot not altogether his little Elsie!'

'That were impossible,' returned the young man; 'he called you by a thousand endearing epithets, that I may not presume to use, but to the justice of which I can warmly testify. Once, indeed, he said—'

Duncan ceased speaking; for while his eyes were rivetted on those of Alice, who had turned towards him with the eagerness of filial affection, to catch his words, the same strong, horrid cry, as before, filled the air, and rendered him mute. A long, breathless silence succeeded, during which, each looked at the others in fearful expectation of hearing the sound repeated. At length, the blanket was slowly raised, and the scout stood in the aperture with a countenance whose firmness evidently began to give way, before a mystery that seemed to threaten some danger, against which all his cunning and experience might prove of no avail.

'They do not sleep.
On yonder cliffs, a grisly band,
I see them sit.'

                    Gray, 'The Bard,' I.3 [Epode I.] 11. 43–45.

''TWOULD BE NEGLECTING a warning that is given for our good, to lie hid any longer,' said Hawk-eye, 'when such sounds are raised in the forest! These gentle ones may keep close, but the Mohicans and I will watch upon the rock, where I suppose a major of the 60th would wish to keep us company.'

'Is then our danger so pressing?' asked Cora.

'He who makes strange sounds, and gives them out for man's information, alone knows our danger. I should think myself wicked unto rebellion against his will, was I to burrow with such warnings in the air! Even the weak soul, who passes his days in singing, is stirred by the cry, and, as he says, is "ready to go forth to the battle." If 'twere only a battle, it would be a thing understood by us all, and easily managed; but I have heard that when such shrieks are atween heaven and 'arth, it betokens another sort of warfare!'

'If all our reasons for fear, my friend, are confined to such as proceed from supernatural causes, we have but little occasion to be alarmed,' continued the undisturbed Cora; 'are you certain that our enemies have not invented some new and ingenious method to strike us with terror, that their conquest may become more easy?'

'Lady,' returned the scout, solemnly, 'I have listened to all the sounds of the woods for thirty years, as a man will listen, whose life and death depend on the quickness of his ears. There is no whine of the panther; no whistle of the cat-bird; nor any invention of the devilish Mingoes, that can cheat me! I have heard the forest moan like mortal men, in their affliction; often, and again, have I listened to the wind playing its music in the branches of the girdled trees; and I have heard the lightning cracking in the air, like the snapping of blazing brush, as it spitted forth sparks and forked flames; but never have I thought that I heard more than the pleasure of him, who sported with the things of his hand. But neither the Mohicans, nor I, who am a white man without a cross, can explain the cry just heard. We, therefore, believe it a sign given for our good.'

'It is extraordinary!' said Heyward, taking his pistols from the place where he had laid them, on entering; 'be it a sign of peace, or a signal of war, it must be looked to. Lead the way, my friend; I follow.'

On issuing from their place of confinement, the whole party instantly experienced a grateful renovation of spirits, by exchanging the pent air of the hiding place, for the cool and invigorating atmosphere, which played around the whirlpools and pitches of the cataract. A heavy opening breeze swept along the surface of the river, and seemed to drive the roar of the falls into the recesses of their own caverns, whence it issued heavily and constant, like thunder rumbling beyond the distant hills. The moon had risen, and its light was already glancing here and there on the waters above them; but the extremity of the rock where they stood still lay in shadow. With the exception of the sounds produced by the rushing waters, and an occasional breathing of the air, as it murmured past them, in fitful currents, the scene was as still as night and solitude could make it. In vain were the eyes of each individual bent along the opposite shores, in quest of some signs of life, that might explain the nature of the interruption they had heard.

Their anxious and eager looks were baffled by the deceptive light, or rested only on naked rocks, and straight and immovable trees.

'Here is nothing to be seen but the gloom and quiet of a lovely evening,' whispered Duncan; 'how much should we prize such a scene, and all this breathing solitude, at any other moment, Cora! Fancy yourselves in security, and what now, perhaps, increases your terror, may be made conducive to enjoyment—'

'Listen!' interrupted Alice.

The caution was unnecessary. Once more the same sound arose, as if from the bed of the river, and having broken out of the narrow bounds of the cliffs, was heard undulating through the forest, in distant and dying cadences.

'Can any here give a name to such a cry?' demanded Hawk-eye, when the last echo was lost in the woods; 'if so, let him speak; for myself, I judge it not to belong to 'arth!'

'Here, then, is one who can undeceive you,' said Duncan; 'I know the sound full well, for often have I heard it on the field of battle, and in situations which are frequent in a soldier's life. 'Tis the horrid shriek that a horse will give in his agony; oftener drawn from him in pain, though sometimes in terror. My charger is either a prey to the beasts of the forest, or he sees his danger without the power to avoid it. The sound might deceive me in the cavern, but in the open air I know it too well to be wrong.'

The scout and his companions listened to this simple explanation with the interest of men, who imbibe new ideas, at the same time that they get rid of old ones, which had proved disagreeable inmates. The two latter uttered their usual and expressive exclamation, 'hugh!' as the truth first glanced upon their minds, while the former, after a short musing pause, took on himself to reply.

'I cannot deny your words,' he said; 'for I am little skilled in horses, though born where they abound. The wolves must be hovering above their heads on the bank, and the timorsome creatures are calling on man for help, in the best manner they are able. Uncas' – he spoke in Delaware – 'Uncas, drop down in the canoe, and whirl a brand among the pack; or fear may do what the wolves can't get at to perform, and leave us without horses in the morning, when we shall have so much need to journey swiftly!'

The young native had already descended to the water, to comply, when a long howl was raised on the edge of the river, and was borne swiftly off into the depths of the forest, as though the beasts, of their own accord, were abandoning their prey, in sudden terror. Uncas, with instinctive quickness, receded, and the three foresters held another of their low, earnest conferences.

'We have been like hunters who have lost the points of the heavens, and from whom the sun has been hid for days,' said Hawk-eye, turning away from his companions; 'now we begin again to know the signs of our course, and the paths are cleared from briars! Seat yourselves in the shade, which the moon throws from yonder beech – 'tis thicker than that of the pines – and let us wait for that which the Lord may choose to send next. Let all your conversation be in whispers; though it would be better, and perhaps, in the end, wiser, if each one held discourse with his own thoughts for a time.'

The manner of the scout was seriously impressive, though no longer distinguished by any signs of unmanly apprehension. It was evident, that his momentary weakness had vanished with the explanation of a mystery, which his own experience had not served to fathom; and though he now felt all the realities of their actual condition, that he was prepared to meet them with the energy of his hardy nature. This feeling seemed also common to the natives, who placed themselves in positions which commanded a full view of both shores, while their own persons were effectually concealed from observation. In such circumstances, common prudence dictated that Heyward, and his companions, should imitate a caution that proceeded from so intelligent a source. The young man drew a pile of the sassafras from the cave, and placing it in the chasm which separated the two caverns, it was occupied by the sisters; who were thus protected by the rocks from any missiles, while their anxiety was relieved by the assurance that no danger could approach without a warning. Heyward himself was posted at hand, so near that he might communicate with his companions without raising his voice to a dangerous elevation; while David, in imitation of the woodsmen, bestowed his person in such a manner among the fissures of the rocks, that his ungainly limbs were no longer offensive to the eye.

In this manner, hours passed by without further interruption. The moon reached the zenith, and shed its mild light, perpendicularly, on the lovely sight of the sisters, slumbering peacefully in each other's arms. Duncan cast the wide shawl of Cora before a spectacle he so much loved to contemplate, and then suffered his own head to seek a pillow on the rock. David began to utter sounds that would have shocked his delicate organs in more wakeful moments; in short, all but Hawk-eye and the Mohicans lost every idea of consciousness, in uncontrollable drowsiness. But the watchfulness of these vigilant protectors, neither tired nor slumbered. Immovable as that rock, of which each appeared to form a part, they lay, with their eyes roving, without intermission, along the dark margin of trees that bounded the adjacent shores of the narrow stream. Not a sound escaped them; the most subtle examination could not have told they breathed. It was evident, that this excess of caution proceeded, from an experience, that no subtlety on the part of their enemies could deceive. It was, however, continued without any apparent consequences, until the moon had set, and a pale streak above the tree tops, at the bend of the river, a little below, announced the approach of day.

Then, for the first time, Hawk-eye was seen to stir. He crawled along the rock, and shook Duncan from his heavy slumbers.

'Now is the time to journey,' he whispered; 'awake the gentle ones, and be ready to get into the canoe when I bring it to the landing place.'

'Have you had a quiet night?' said Heyward; 'for myself, I believe sleep has gotten the better of my vigilance.'

'All is yet still as midnight. Be silent, but be quick.'

By this time Duncan was thoroughly awake, and he immediately lifted the shawl from the sleeping females. The motion caused Cora to raise her hand as if to repulse him, while Alice murmured, in her soft, gentle voice, 'No, no, dear father, we were not deserted; Duncan was with us.'

'Yes, sweet innocence,' whispered the youth; 'Duncan is here, and while life continue, or danger remain, he will never quit thee. Cora! Alice! awake! The hour has come to move!'

A loud shriek from the younger of the sisters, and the form of the other standing upright before him, in bewildered horror, was the unexpected answer he received. While the words were still on the lips of Heyward, there had arisen such a tumult of yells and cries, as served to drive the swift currents of his own blood, back from its bounding course into the fountains of his heart. It seemed, for near a minute, as if the demons of hell had possessed themselves of the air about them, and were venting their savage humors in barbarous sounds. The cries came from no particular direction, though it was evident they filled the woods, and, as the appalled listeners easily imagined, the caverns of the falls, the rocks, the bed of the river, and the upper air. David raised his tall person in the midst of the infernal din, with a hand on either ear, exclaiming—

'Whence comes this discord! Has hell broke loose, that man should utter sounds like these!'

The bright flashes, and the quick reports of a dozen rifles, from the opposite banks of the stream, followed this incautious exposure of his person, and left the unfortunate singing master, senseless, on that rock where he had been so long slumbering. The Mohicans boldly sent back the intimidating yell of their enemies, who raised a shout of savage triumph at the fall of Gamut. The flash of rifles was then quick and close between them, but either party was too well skilled to leave even a limb exposed to the hostile aim. Duncan listened with intense anxiety for the strokes of the paddle, believing that flight was now their only refuge. The river glanced by with its ordinary velocity, but the canoe was no where to be seen on its dark waters. He had just fancied they were cruelly deserted by the scout, as a stream of flame issued from the rock beneath him, and a fierce yell, blended with a shriek of agony, announced that the messenger of death, hurled from the fatal weapon of Hawk-eye had found a victim. At this slight repulse the assailants instantly withdrew and, gradually, the place became as still as before the sudden tumult.

Duncan seized the favorable moment to spring to the body of Gamut, which he bore within the shelter of the narrow chasm that protected the sisters. In another minute the whole party was collected in this spot of comparative safety.

'The poor fellow has saved his scalp,' said Hawk-eye, coolly passing his hand over the head of David; 'but he is a proof that a man may be born with too long a tongue! 'Twas downright madness to show six feet of flesh and blood, on a naked rock, to the raging savages. I only wonder he has escaped with life.'

'Is he not dead!' demanded Cora, in a voice whose husky tones showed how powerfully, natural horror struggled with her assumed firmness. 'Can we do aught to assist the wretched man?'

'No, no! the life is in his heart yet, and after he has slept awhile he will come to himself, and be a wiser man for it, till the hour of his real time shall come,' returned Hawk-eye, casting another oblique glance at the insensible body, while he filled his charger with admirable nicety. 'Carry him in, Uncas, and lay him on the saxafrax. The longer his nap lasts the better it will be for him; as I doubt whether he can find a proper cover for such a shape on these rocks; and singing won't do any good with the Iroquois.'

'You believe, then, the attack will be renewed?' asked Heyward.

'Do I expect a hungry wolf will satisfy his craving with a mouthful! They have lost a man, and 'tis their fashion, when they meet a loss, and fail in the surprise, to fall back; but we shall have them on again, with new expedients to circumvent us, and master our scalps. Our main hope,' he continued, raising his rugged countenance, across which a shade of anxiety just then passed like a darkening cloud, 'will be to keep the rock until Munro can send a party to our help! God send it may be soon, and under a leader that knows the Indian customs!'

'You hear our probable fortunes, Cora,' said Duncan; 'and you know we have every thing to hope from the anxiety and experience of your father. Come, then, with Alice, into this cavern, where you, at least, will be safe from the murderous rifles of our enemies, and where you may bestow a care suited to your gentle natures, on our unfortunate comrade.'

The sisters followed him into the outer cave, where David was beginning, by his sighs, to give symptoms of returning consciousness, and, then, commending the wounded man to their attention, he immediately prepared to leave them.

'Duncan!' said the tremulous voice of Cora, when he had reached the mouth of the cavern. He turned, and beheld the speaker, whose color had changed to a deadly paleness, and whose lip quivered, gazing after him, with an expression of interest which immediately recalled him to her side. 'Remember, Duncan, how necessary your safety is to our own – how you bear a father's sacred trust – how much depends on your discretion and care – in short,' she added, while the tell-tale blood stole over her features, crimsoning her very temples, 'how very deservedly dear you are to all of the name of Munro.'

'If any thing could add to my own base love of life,' said Heyward, suffering his unconscious eyes to wander to the youthful form of the silent Alice; 'it would be so kind an assurance. As major of the 60th, our honest host will tell you I must take my share of the fray; but our task will be easy; it is merely to keep these blood-hounds at bay for a few hours.'

Without waiting for reply, he tore himself from the presence of the sisters, and joined the scout and his companions, who still lay within the protection of the little chasm, between the two caves.

'I tell you, Uncas,' said the former, as Heyward joined them, 'you are wasteful of your powder, and the kick of the rifle disconcerts your aim! Little powder, light lead, and a long arm, seldom fail of bringing the death screech from a Mingo! At least, such has been my experience with the creaturs. Come, friends; let us to our covers, for no man can tell when or where a Maqua* will strike his blow!'

The Indians silently repaired to their appointed stations, which were fissures in the rocks, whence they could command the approaches to the foot of the falls. In the centre of the little island, a few short and stunted pines had found root, forming a thicket, into which Hawk-eye darted, with the swiftness of a deer, followed by the active Duncan. Here they secured themselves, as well as circumstances would permit, among the shrubs and fragments of stone that were scattered about the place. Above them was a bare, rounded rock, on each side of which the water played its gambols, and plunged into the abysses beneath, in the manner already described. As the day had now dawned, the opposite shores no longer presented a confused outline, but they were able to look into the woods, and distinguish objects, beneath the canopy of gloomy pines.

A long and anxious watch succeeded, but without any further evidences of a renewed attack, and Duncan began to hope that their fire had proved more fatal than was supposed, and that their enemies had been effectually repulsed. When he ventured to utter this impression to his companion, it was met by Hawk-eye with an incredulous shake of the head.

'You know not the nature of a Maqua, if you think he is so easily beaten back, without a scalp!' he answered. 'If there was one of the imps yelling this morning, there were forty! and they know our number and quality too well to give up the chase so soon. Hist! look into the water above, just where it breaks over the rocks. I am no mortal, if the risky devils haven't swam down upon the very pitch, and as bad luck would have it, they have hit the head of the island! Hist! man, keep close! or the hair will be off your crown in the turning of a knife!'

Heyward lifted his head from the cover, and beheld what he justly considered a prodigy of rashness and skill. The river had worn away the edge of the soft rock in

---

* It will be observed that Hawk-eye applies different names to his enemies. Mingo and Maqua are terms of contempt, and Iroquois is a name given by the French. The Indians rarely use the same name when different tribes speak of each other. [1831]

such a manner, as to render its first pitch less abrupt and perpendicular, than is usual at waterfalls. With no other guide than the ripple of the stream where it met the head of the island, a party of their insatiable foes had ventured into the current, and swam down upon this point, knowing the ready access it would give, if successful, to their intended victims. As Hawk-eye ceased speaking, four human heads could be seen peering above a few logs of drift wood, that had lodged on these naked rocks, and which had probably suggested the idea of the practicability of the hazardous undertaking. At the next moment, a fifth form was seen floating over the green edge of the fall, a little from the line of the island. The savage struggled powerfully to gain the point of safety, and favored by the glancing water, he was already stretching forth an arm to meet the grasp of his companions, when he shot away again with the whirling current, appeared to rise into the air, with uplifted arms, and starting eye-balls, and fell, with a sullen plunge, into that deep and yawning abyss over which he hovered. A single, wild, despairing shriek, rose from the cavern, and all was hushed again as the grave.

The first generous impulse of Duncan, was to rush to the rescue of the hapless wretch, but he felt himself bound to the spot, by the iron grasp of the immoveable scout.

'Would ye bring certain death upon us, by telling the Mingoes where we lie?' demanded Hawk-eye, sternly; ''tis a charge of powder saved, and ammunition is as precious now as breath to a worried deer! Freshen the priming of your pistols – the mist of the falls is apt to dampen the brimstone – and stand firm for a close struggle, while I fire on their rush.'

He placed a finger in his mouth, and drew a long, shrill whistle, which was answered from the rocks, that were guarded by the Mohicans. Duncan caught glimpses of heads above the scattered drift wood, as this signal rose on the air, but they disappeared again as suddenly as they had glanced upon his sight. A low, rustling sound, next drew his attention behind him, and turning his head, he beheld Uncas within a few feet, creeping to his side. Hawk-eye spoke to him in Delaware, when the young chief took his position with singular caution, and undisturbed coolness. To Heyward this was a moment of feverish and impatient suspense; though the scout saw fit to select it as a fit occasion to read a lecture to his more youthful associates, on the art of using firearms with discretion.

'Of all we'pons,' he commenced, 'the long barrelled, true grooved, soft met-alled rifle, is the most dangerous in skillful hands, though it wants a strong arm, a quick eye, and great judgment in charging, to put forth all its beauties. The gunsmiths can have but little insight into their trade, when they make their fowling-pieces and short horsemens'—'

He was interrupted by the low, but expressive 'hugh' of Uncas.

'I see them, boy, I see them!' continued Hawk-eye; 'they are gathering for the rush, or they would keep their dingy backs below the logs. Well, let them,' he added, examining his flint; 'the leading man certainly comes on to his death, though it should be Montcalm himself!'

At that moment the woods were filled with another burst of cries, and, at the signal, four savages sprang from the cover of the drift wood. Heyward felt a burning desire to rush forward to meet them, so intense was the delirious anxiety of the moment, but he was restrained by the deliberate examples of the scout and Uncas. When their foes, who leaped over the black rocks that divided them, with long bounds, uttering the wildest yells, were within a few rods, the rifle of Hawk-eye slowly rose among the shrubs, and poured out its fatal contents. The foremost

Indian bounded like a stricken deer, and fell headlong among the clefts of the island.

'Now, Uncas!' cried the scout, drawing his long knife, while his quick eyes began to flash with ardour, 'take the last of the screeching imps; of the other two we are sartain!'

He was obeyed; and but two enemies remained to be overcome. Heyward had given one of his pistols to Hawk-eye, and together they rushed down a little declivity towards their foes; they discharged their weapons at the same instant, and equally without success.

'I know'd it! and I said it!' muttered the scout, whirling the despised little implement over the falls, with bitter disdain. 'Come on, ye bloody minded hellhounds! ye meet a man without a cross!'

The words were barely uttered, when he encountered a savage of gigantic stature, and of the fiercest mien. At the same moment, Duncan found himself engaged with the other, in a similar contest of hand to hand. With ready skill, Hawk-eye and his antagonist each grasped that uplifted arm of the other, which held the dangerous knife. For near a minute, they stood looking one another in the eye, and gradually exerting the power of their muscles for the mastery. At length, the toughened sinews of the white man prevailed over the less practised limbs of the native. The arm of the latter slowly gave way before the increasing force of the scout, who suddenly wresting his armed hand from the grasp of his foe, drove the sharp weapon through his naked bosom to the heart. In the meantime, Heyward had been pressed in a more deadly struggle. His slight sword was snapped in the first encounter. As he was destitute of any other means of defence, his safety now depended entirely on bodily strength and resolution. Though deficient in neither of these qualities, he had met an enemy every way his equal. Happily, he soon succeeded in disarming his adversary, whose knife fell on the rock at their feet, and from this moment it became a fierce struggle, who should cast the other over the dizzy height, into a neighboring cavern of the falls. Every successive struggle brought them nearer to the verge, where Duncan perceived the final and conquering effort must be made. Each of the combatants threw all his energies into that effort, and the result was, that both tottered on the brink of the precipice. Heyward felt the grasp of the other at his throat, and saw the grim smile the savage gave, under the revengeful hope that he hurried his enemy to a fate similar to his own, as he felt his body slowly yielding to a resistless power, and the young man experienced the passing agony of such a moment in all its horrors. At that instant of extreme danger, a dark hand and glancing knife appeared before him; the Indian released his hold, as the blood flowed freely from around the severed tendons of his wrist; and while Duncan was drawn backward by the saving arm of Uncas, his charmed eyes were still riveted on the fierce and disappointed countenance of his foe, who fell sullenly and disappointed down the irrecoverable precipice.

'To cover! to cover!' cried Hawk-eye, who just then had despatched his enemy; 'to cover, for your lives! the work is but half-ended!'

The young Mohican gave a shout of triumph, and followed by Duncan, he glided up the acclivity they had descended to the combat, and sought the friendly shelter of the rocks and shrubs.

'They linger yet,
Avengers of their native land.'
Gray, 'The Bard,' I.3. [Epode I.] 11.45–46.

THE WARNING CALL OF THE SCOUT was not uttered without occasion. During the occurrence of the deadly encounter just related, the roar of the falls was unbroken by any human sound whatever. It would seem, that interest in the result had kept the natives, on the opposite shores, in breathless suspense, while the quick evolutions and swift changes in the positions of the combatants, effectually prevented a fire, that might prove dangerous alike to friend and enemy. But the moment the struggle was decided, a yell arose, as fierce and savage as wild and revengeful passions could throw into the air. It was followed by the swift flashes of the rifles, which sent their leaden messengers across the rock in vollies, as though the assailants would pour out their impotent fury on the insensible scene of the fatal contest.

A steady, though deliberate, return was made from the rifle of Chingachgook, who had maintained his post throughout the fray with unmoved resolution. When the triumphant shout of Uncas was borne to his ears, the gratified father had raised his voice in a single responsive cry, after which his busy piece alone proved that he still guarded his pass with unwearied diligence. In this manner many minutes flew by with the swiftness of thought; the rifles of the assailants speaking, at times, in rattling vollies, and at others, in occasional, scattering shots. Though the rock, the trees, and the shrubs, were cut and torn in a hundred places around the besieged, their cover was so close, and so rigidly maintained, that, as yet, David had been the only sufferer in their little band.

'Let them burn their powder,' said the deliberate scout, while bullet after bullet whizzed by the place where he securely lay; 'there will be a fine gathering of lead when it is over, and I fancy the imps will tire of the sport, afore these old stones cry out for mercy! Uncas, boy, you waste the kernels by overcharging; and a kicking rifle never carries a true bullet. I told you to take that loping miscreant under the line of white paint; now, if your bullet went a hair's breadth, it went two inches above it. The life lies low in a Mingo, and humanity teaches us to make a quick end of the sarpents.'

A quiet smile lighted the haughty features of the young Mohican, betraying his knowledge of the English language, as well as of the other's meaning, but he suffered it to pass away without vindication or reply.

'I cannot permit you to accuse Uncas of want of judgment or of skill,' said Duncan; 'he saved my life in the coolest and readiest manner, and he has made a friend who never will require to be reminded of the debt he owes.'

Uncas partly raised his body, and offered his hand to the grasp of Heyward. During this act of friendship, the two young men exchanged looks of intelligence, which caused Duncan to forget the character and condition of his wild associate. In the meanwhile, Hawk-eye, who looked on this burst of youthful feeling with a cool but kind regard, made the following reply:

'Life is an obligation which friends often owe to each other in the wilderness. I dare say I may have served Uncas some such turn myself before now; and I very well remember, that he has stood between me and death five different times: three times from the Mingoes, once in crossing Horican, and—'

'That bullet was better aimed than common!' exclaimed Duncan, involuntarily shrinking from a shot which struck the rock at his side with a smart rebound.

Hawk-eye laid his hand on the shapeless metal, and shook his head, as he examined it, saying, 'Falling lead is never flattened! had it come from the clouds this might have happened!'

But the rifle of Uncas was deliberately raised toward the heavens, directing the eyes of his companions to a point, where the mystery was immediately explained. A ragged oak grew on the right bank of the river, nearly opposite to their position, which, seeking the freedom of the open space, had inclined so far forward, that its upper branches overhung that arm of the stream which flowed nearest to its own shore. Among the topmost leaves, which scantily concealed the gnarled and stunted limbs, a savage was nestled, partly concealed by the trunk of the tree, and partly exposed, as though looking down upon them, to ascertain the effect produced by his treacherous aim.

'These devils will scale heaven to circumvent us to our ruin,' said Hawk-eye; 'keep him in play, boy, until I can bring "kill-deer" to bear, when we will try his metal on each side of the tree at once.'

Uncas delayed his fire until the scout uttered the word. The rifles flashed, the leaves and bark of the oak flew into the air, and were scattered by the wind, but the Indian answered their assault by a taunting laugh, sending down upon them another bullet in return, that struck the cap of Hawk-eye from his head. Once more the savage yells burst out of the woods, and the leaden hail whistled above the heads of the besieged, as if to confine them to a place where they might become easy victims to the enterprise of the warrior who had mounted the tree.

'This must be looked to!' said the scout, glancing about him with an anxious eye. 'Uncas, call up your father; we have need of all our we'pons to bring the cunning varment from his roost.'

The signal was instantly given; and, before Hawk-eye had reloaded his rifle, they were joined by Chingachgook. When his son pointed out to the experienced warrior the situation of their dangerous enemy, the usual exclamatory 'hugh,' burst from his lips; after which, no further expression of surprise or alarm was suffered to escape him. Hawk-eye and the Mohicans conversed earnestly together in Delaware for a few moments, when each quietly took his post, in order to execute the plan they had speedily devised.

The warrior in the oak had maintained a quick, though ineffectual, fire, from the moment of his discovery. But his aim was interrupted by the vigilance of his enemies, whose rifles instantaneously bore on any part of his person that was left exposed. Still his bullets fell in the centre of the crouching party. The clothes of Heyward, which rendered him peculiarly conspicuous, were repeatedly cut, and once blood was drawn from a slight wound in his arm.

At length, emboldened by the long and patient watchfulness of his enemies, the Huron attempted a better and more fatal aim. The quick eyes of the Mohicans caught the dark line of his lower limbs incautiously exposed through the thin foliage, a few inches from the trunk of the tree. Their rifles made a common report, when, sinking on his wounded limb, part of the body of the savage came into view. Swift as thought, Hawk-eye seized the advantage, and discharged his fatal weapon into the top of the oak. The leaves were unusually agitated; the dangerous rifle fell from its commanding elevation, and after a few moments of vain struggling, the form of the savage was seen swinging in the wind, while he still grasped a ragged and naked branch of the tree with hands clenched in desperation.

'Give him, in pity, give him, the contents of another rifle!' cried Duncan, turning away his eyes in horror from the spectacle of a fellow creature in such awful jeopardy.

'Not a karnel!' exclaimed the obdurate Hawk-eye; 'his death is certain, and we
have no powder to spare, for Indian fights, sometimes, last for days; 'tis their
scalps, or ours! – and God, who made us, has put into our natures the craving to
keep the skin on the head!'

Against this stern and unyielding morality, supported, as it was, by such visible
policy, there was no appeal. From that moment the yells in the forest once more
ceased, the fire was suffered to decline, and all eyes, those of friends, as well as
enemies, became fixed on the hopeless condition of the wretch, who was dangling
between heaven and earth. The body yielded to the currents of air, and though no
murmur or groan escaped the victim, there were instants when he grimly faced his
foes, and the anguish of cold despair might be traced, through the intervening
distance, in possession of his swarthy lineaments. Three several times the scout
raised his piece in mercy, and as often prudence getting the better of his intention,
it was again silently lowered. At length, one hand of the Huron lost its hold, and
dropped exhausted to his side. A desperate and fruitless struggle to recover the
branch succeeded, and then the savage was seen for a fleeting instant, grasping
wildly at the empty air. The lightning is not quicker than was the flame from the
rifle of Hawk-eye; the limbs of the victim trembled and contracted, the head fell to
the bosom, and the body parted the foaming waters, like lead, when the element
closed above it, in its ceaseless velocity, and every vestige of the unhappy Huron
was lost for ever.

No shout of triumph succeeded this important advantage, but even the
Mohicans gazed at each other in silent horror. A single yell burst from the woods,
and all was again still. Hawk-eye, who alone appeared to reason on the occasion,
shook his head, at his own momentary weakness, even uttering his self-
disapprobation aloud.

"Twas the last charge in my horn, and the last bullet in my pouch, and 'twas the
act of a boy!' he said; 'what mattered it whether he struck the rock living or dead!
feeling would soon be over. Uncas, lad, go down to the canoe, and bring up the
big horn; it is all the powder we have left, and we shall need it to the last grain, or I
am ignorant of the Mingo nature.'

The young Mohican complied, leaving the scout turning over the useless
contents of his pouch, and shaking the empty horn with renewed discontent.
From this unsatisfactory examination, however, he was soon called by a loud and
piercing exclamation from Uncas, that sounded even to the unpractised ears of
Duncan, as the signal of some new and unexpected calamity. Every thought filled
with apprehension for the precious treasure he had concealed in the cavern, the
young man started to his feet, totally regardless of the hazard he incurred by such
an exposure. As if actuated by a common impulse, his movement was imitated by
his companions, and, together, they rushed down the pass to the friendly chasm,
with a rapidity that rendered the scattering fire of their enemies perfectly
harmless. The unwonted cry had brought the sisters, together with the wounded
David, from their place of refuge, and the whole party, at a single glance, was
made acquainted with the nature of the disaster, that had disturbed even the
practiced stoicism of their youthful Indian protector.

At a short distance from the rock, their little bark was to be seen floating across
the eddy, towards the swift current of the river, in a manner which proved that its
course was directed by some hidden agent. The instant this unwelcome sight
caught the eye of the scout, his rifle was levelled, as by instinct, but the barrel gave
no answer to the bright sparks of the flint.

"Tis too late, 'tis too late!' Hawk-eye exclaimed, dropping the useless piece, in bitter disappointment; 'the miscreant has struck the rapid, and had we powder, it could hardly send the lead swifter than he now goes!'

The adventurous Huron raised his head above the shelter of the canoe, and while it glided swiftly down the stream, he waved his hand, and gave forth the shout, which was the known signal of success. His cry was answered by a yell, and a laugh from the woods, as tauntingly exulting as if fifty demons were uttering their blasphemies at the fall of some Christian soul.

'Well may you laugh, ye children of the devil!' said the scout, seating himself on a projection of the rock, and suffering his gun to fall neglected at his feet, 'for the three quickest and truest rifles in these woods, are no better than so many stalks of mullen, or the last year's horns of a buck!'

'What is to be done?' demanded Duncan, losing the first feeling of disappointment, in a more manly desire for exertion; 'what will become of us?'

Hawk-eye made no other reply than by passing his finger around the crown of his head, in a manner so significant, that none who witnessed the action could mistake its meaning.

'Surely, surely, our case is not so desperate!' exclaimed the youth; 'the Hurons are not here; we may make good the caverns; we may oppose their landing.'

'With what?' coolly demanded the scout. 'The arrows of Uncas, or such tears as women shed! No, no; you are young, and rich, and have friends, and at such an age I know it is hard to die! but,' glancing his eyes at the Mohicans, 'let us remember, we are men without a cross, and let us teach these natives of the forest, that white blood can run as freely as red, when the appointed hour is come.'

Duncan turned quickly in the direction indicated by the other's eyes, and read a confirmation of his worst apprehensions in the conduct of the Indians. Chingachgook, placing himself in a dignified posture on another fragment of the rock, had already laid aside his knife and tomahawk, and was in the act of taking the eagle's plume from his head, and smoothing the solitary tuft of hair, in readiness to perform its last and revolting office. His countenance was composed, though thoughtful, while his dark, gleaming eyes, were gradually losing the fierceness of the combat in an expression better suited to the change he expected, momentarily, to undergo.

'Our case is not, cannot, be so hopeless!' said Duncan; 'even at this very moment succour may be at hand. I see no enemies! they have sickened of a struggle, in which they risk so much with so little prospect of gain!'

'It may be a minute, or it may be an hour, afore the wily sarpents steal upon us, and it's quite in natur for them to be lying within hearing at this very moment,' said Hawk-eye; 'but come they will, and in such a fashion as will leave us nothing to hope! Chingachgook' – he spoke in Delaware – 'my brother, we have fought our last battle together, and the Maquas will triumph in the death of the sage man of the Mohicans, and of the pale face, whose eyes can make night as day, and level the clouds to the mists of the springs!'

'Let the Mingo women go weep over their slain!' returned the Indian, with characteristic pride, and unmoved firmness; 'the great snake of the Mohicans has coiled himself in their wigwams, and has poisoned their triumph with the wailings of children, whose fathers have not returned! Eleven warriors lie hid from the graves of their tribe, since the snows have melted, and none will tell where to find them, when the tongue of Chingachgook shall be silent! Let them draw the sharpest knife, and whirl the swiftest tomahawk, for their bitterest enemy is in their hands. Uncas, topmost branch of a noble trunk, call on the cowards to hasten, or their hearts will soften, and they will change to women!'

'They look among the fishes for their dead!' returned the low, soft voice of the youthful chieftain; 'the Hurons float with the slimy eels! They drop from the oaks like fruit that is ready to be eaten! and the Delawares laugh!'

'Ay, ay,' muttered the scout, who had listened to this peculiar burst of the natives with deep attention; 'they have warmed their Indian feelings, and they'll soon provoke the Maquas to give them a speedy end. As for me, who am of the whole blood of the whites, it is befitting that I should die as becomes my color, with no words of scoffing in my mouth, and without bitterness at the heart!'

'Why die at all!' said Cora, advancing from the place where natural horror had, until this moment, held her riveted to the rock; 'the path is open on every side; fly, then, to the woods, and call on God for succour! Go, brave men, we owe you too much already; let us no longer involve you in our hapless fortunes!'

'You but little know the craft of the Iroquois, lady, if you judge they have left the path open to the woods!' returned Hawk-eye, who, however, immediately added in his simplicity; 'the down stream current, it is certain, might soon sweep us beyond the reach of their rifles, or the sounds of their voices.'

'Then try the river. Why linger, to add to the number of the victims of our merciless enemies?'

'Why!' repeated the scout, looking about him proudly, 'because it is better for a man to die at peace with himself, than to live haunted by an evil conscience! What answer could we give to Munro, when he asked us, where and how we left his children?'

'Go to him, and say, that you left them with a message to hasten to their aid,' returned Cora, advancing nigher to the scout, in her generous ardour; 'that the Hurons bear them into the northern wilds, but that by vigilance and speed they may yet be rescued; and if, after all, it should please heaven, that his assistance come too late, bear to him,' she continued, her voice gradually lowering, until it seemed nearly choked, 'the love, the blessings, the final prayers of his daughters, and bid him not mourn their early fate, but to look forward with humble confidence to the Christian's goal to meet his children.'

The hard, weather-beaten features of the scout began to work, and when she had ended, he dropped his chin to his hand, like a man musing profoundly on the nature of the proposal.

'There is reason in her words!' at length broke from his compressed and trembling limps; 'ay, and they bear the spirit of christianity; what might be right and proper in a red skin, may be sinful in a man who has not even a cross in blood to plead for his ignorance. Chingachgook! Uncas! hear you the talk of the dark-eyed woman!'

He now spoke in Delaware to his companions, and his address, though calm and deliberate, seemed very decided. The elder Mohican heard him with deep gravity, and appeared to ponder on his words, as though he felt the importance of their import. After a moment of hesitation, he waved his hand in assent, and uttered the English word 'good,' with the peculiar emphasis of his people. Then, replacing his knife and tomahawk in his girdle, the warrior moved silently to the edge of the rock most concealed from the banks of the river. Here he paused a moment, pointed significantly to the woods below, and saying a few words in his own language, as if indicating his intended route, he dropped into the water, and sunk from before the eyes of the witnesses of his movements.

The scout delayed his departure to speak to the generous girl, whose breathing became lighter as she saw the success of her remonstrance.

'Wisdom is sometimes given to the young, as well as to the old,' he said; 'and what you have spoken is wise, not to call it by a better word. If you are led into the woods, that is, such of you as may be spared for a while, break the twigs on the bushes as you pass, and make the marks of your trail, as broad as you can, when, if mortal eyes can see them, depend on having a friend who will follow to the ends of the 'arth afore he desarts you.'

He gave Cora an affectionate shake of the hand, lifted his rifle, and after regarding it a moment with melancholy solicitude, laid it carefully aside, and descended to the place where Chingachgook had just disappeared. For an instant he hung suspended by the rock; and looking about him, with a countenance of peculiar care, he added, bitterly, 'Had the powder held out, this disgrace could never have befallen!' then, loosening his hold, the water closed above his head, and he also became lost to view.

All eyes were now turned on Uncas, who stood leaning against the ragged rock, in immoveable composure. After waiting a short time, Cora pointed down the river, and said—

'Your friends have not been seen, and are now, most probably, in safety; is it not time for you to follow?'

'Uncas will stay,' the young Mohican calmly answered, in English.

'To increase the horror of our capture, and to diminish the chances of our release! Go, generous young man,' Cora continued, lowering her eyes under the gaze of the Mohican, and, perhaps, with an intuitive consciousness of her power; 'go to my father, as I have said, and be the most confidential of my messengers. Tell him to trust you with the means to buy the freedom of his daughters. Go; 'tis my wish, 'tis my prayer, that you will go!'

The settled, calm, look of the young chief, changed to an expression of gloom, but he no longer hesitated. With a noiseless step he crossed the rock, and dropped into the troubled stream. Hardly a breath was drawn by those he left behind, until they caught a glimpse of his head emerging for air, far down the current, when he again sunk, and was seen no more.

These sudden and apparently successful experiments had all taken place in a few minutes of that time, which had now become so precious. After the last look at Uncas, Cora turned, and, with a quivering lip, addressed herself to Heyward:

'I have heard of your boasted skill in the water, too, Duncan,' she said; 'follow, then, the wise example set you by these simple and faithful beings.'

'Is such the faith that Cora Munro would exact from her protector,' said the young man, smiling, mournfully, but with bitterness.

'This is not a time for idle subtleties and false opinions,' she answered; 'but a moment when every duty should be equally considered. To us you can be of no further service here, but your precious life may be saved for other and nearer friends.'

He made no reply, though his eyes fell wistfully on the beautiful form of Alice, who was clinging to his arm with the dependency of an infant.

'Consider,' continued Cora, after a pause, during which she seemed to struggle with a pang, even more acute than any that her fears had excited, 'that the worst to us can be but death; a tribute that all must pay at the good time of God's appointment.'

'There are evils worse than death,' said Duncan, speaking hoarsely, and as if fretful at her importunity, 'but which the presence of one who would die in your behalf may avert.'

Cora ceased her entreaties, and veiling her face in her shawl, drew the nearly insensible Alice after her into the deepest recess of the inner cavern.

'Be gay securely;
Dispel, my fair, with smiles, the tim'rous cloud,
That hangs on thy clear brow.'
Gray, Agrippina, A Tragedy, Sc.II. 196–97.

THE SUDDEN AND ALMOST MAGICAL change, from the stirring incidents of the combat, to the stillness that now reigned around him, acted on the heated imagination of Heyward like some exciting dream. While all the images and events he had witnessed remained deeply impressed on his memory, he felt a difficulty in persuading himself of their truth. Still ignorant of the fate of those who had trusted to the aid of the swift current, he at first listened intently to any signal, or sounds of alarm, which might announce the good or evil fortune of their hazardous undertaking. His attention was, however, bestowed in vain; for with the disappearance of Uncas, every sign of the adventurers had been lost, leaving him in total uncertainty of their fate.

In a moment of such painful doubt, Duncan did not hesitate to look about him, without consulting that protection from the rocks which just before had been so necessary to his safety. Every effort, however, to detect the least evidence of the approach of their hidden enemies, was as fruitless as the inquiry after his late companions. The wooded banks of the river seemed again deserted by every thing possessing animal life. The uproar which had so lately echoed through the vaults of the forest was gone, leaving the rush of the waters to swell and sink on the currents of the air, in the unmingled sweetness of nature. A fish-hawk, which, secure on the topmost branches of a dead pine, had been a distant spectator of the fray, now stooped from his high and ragged perch, and soared, in wide sweeps, above his prey; while a jay, whose noisy voice had been stilled by the hoarser cries of the savages, ventured again to open his discordant throat, as though once more in undisturbed possession of his wild domains. Duncan caught from these natural accompaniments of the solitary scene a glimmering of hope, and he began to rally his faculties to renewed exertions, with something like a reviving confidence of success.

'The Hurons are not to be seen,' he said, addressing David, who had by no means recovered from the effects of the stunning blow he had received; 'let us conceal ourselves in the cavern, and trust the rest to Providence.'

'I remember to have united with two comely maidens, in lifting up our voices in praise and thanksgiving,' returned the bewildered singing-master; 'since which time I have been visited by a heavy judgment for my sins. I have been mocked with the likeness of sleep, while sounds of discord have rent my ears; such as might manifest the fullness of time, and that nature had forgotten her harmony.'

'Poor fellow! thine own period was, in truth, near its accomplishment! But arouse, and come with me; I will lead you where all other sounds, but those of your own psalmody, shall be excluded.'

'There is melody in the fall of the cataract, and the rushing of many waters is sweet to the senses!' said David, pressing his hand confusedly on his brow. 'Is not the air yet filled with shrieks and cries, as though the departed spirits of the damned—'

'Not now, not now,' interrupted the impatient Heyward, 'they have ceased; and they who raised them, I trust in God, they are gone too! every thing but the water is still and at peace; in, then, where you may create those sounds you love so well to hear.'

David smiled sadly, though not without a momentary gleam of pleasure, at this allusion to his beloved vocation. He no longer hesitated to be led to a spot, which promised such unalloyed gratification to his wearied senses; and, leaning on the arm of his companion, he entered the narrow mouth of the cave. Duncan seized a pile of the sassafras, which he drew before the passage, studiously concealing every appearance of an aperture. Within this fragile barrier he arranged the blankets abandoned by the foresters, darkening the inner extremity of the cavern, while its outer received a chastened light from the narrow ravine, through which one arm of the river rushed, to form the junction with its sister branch, a few rods below.

'I like not that principle of the natives, which teaches them to submit without a struggle, in emergencies that appear desperate,' he said, while busied in this employment; 'our own maxim, which says, "while life remains there is hope," is more consoling, and better suited to a soldier's temperament. To you, Cora, I will urge no words of idle encouragement; your own fortitude and undisturbed reason, will teach you all that may become your sex; but cannot we dry the tears of that trembling weeper on your bosom?'

'I am calmer, Duncan,' said Alice, raising herself from the arms of her sister, and forcing an appearance of composure through her tears; 'much calmer, now. Surely, in this hidden spot, we are safe, we are secret, free from injury; we will hope every thing from those generous men, who have risked so much already in our behalf.'

'Now does our gentle Alice speak like a daughter of Munro!' said Heyward, pausing to press her hand as he passed towards the outer entrance of the cavern. 'With two such examples of courage before him, a man would be ashamed to prove other than a hero.' He then seated himself in the centre of the cavern, grasping his remaining pistol with a hand convulsively clenched, while his contracted and frowning eye announced the sullen desperation of his purpose. 'The Hurons, if they come, may not gain our position so easily as they think,' he lowly muttered; and dropping his head back against the rock, he seemed to await the result in patience, though his gaze was unceasingly bent on the open avenue to their place of retreat.

With the last sound of his voice, a deep, a long, and almost breathless silence succeeded. The fresh air of the morning had penetrated the recess, and its influence was gradually felt on the spirits of its inmates. As minute after minute passed by, leaving them in undisturbed security, the insinuating feeling of hope was gradually gaining possession of every bosom, though each one felt reluctant to give utterance to expectations that the next moment might so fearfully destroy.

David alone formed an exception to these varying emotions. A gleam of light from the opening crossed his wan countenance, and fell upon the pages of the little volume, whose leaves he was again occupied in turning, as if searching for some song more fitted to their condition than any that had yet met his eye. He was most probably acting all this time under a confused recollection of the promised consolation of Duncan. At length, it would seem, his patient industry found its reward; for, without explanation or apology, he pronounced aloud the words 'Isle of Wight,' drew a long, sweet sound from his pitch-pipe, and then ran through the preliminary modulations of the air, whose name he had just mentioned, with the sweeter tones of his own musical voice.

'May not this prove dangerous?' asked Cora, glancing her dark eye at Major Heyward.

'Poor fellow! his voice is too feeble to be heard amid the din of the falls,' was the answer; 'besides, the cavern will prove his friend. Let him indulge his passion, since it may be done without hazard.'

'Isle of Wight!' repeated David, looking about him with that dignity with which he had long been wont to silence the whispering echoes of his school; "tis a brave tune, and set to solemn words; let it be sung with meet respect!'

After allowing a moment of stillness to enforce his discipline, the voice of the singer was heard, in low, murmuring syllables, gradually stealing on the ear, until it filled the narrow vault, with sounds, rendered trebly thrilling by the feeble and tremulous utterance produced by his debility. The melody which no weakness could destroy, gradually wrought its sweet influence on the senses of those who heard it. It even prevailed over the miserable travesty of the song of David, which the singer had selected from a volume of similar effusions, and caused the sense to be forgotten, in the insinuating harmony of the sounds. Alice unconsciously dried her tears, and bent her melting eyes on the pallid features of Gamut, with an expression of chastened delight, that she neither affected, nor wished to conceal. Cora bestowed an approving smile on the pious efforts of the namesake of the Jewish prince, and Heywood soon turned his steady, stern, look from the outlet of the cavern, to fasten it, with a milder character, on the face of David, or to meet the wandering beams which at moments strayed from the humid eyes of Alice. The open sympathy of the listeners stirred the spirit of the votary of music, whose voiced regained its richness and volume, without losing that touching softness which proved its secret charm. Exerting his renovated powers to their utmost, he was yet filling the arches of the cave with long and full tones, when a yell burst into the air without, that instantly stilled his pious strains, choking his voice suddenly, as though his heart had literally bounded into the passage of his throat.

'We are lost!' exclaimed Alice, throwing herself into the arms of Cora.

'Not yet, not yet,' returned the agitated but undaunted Heyward; 'the sound came from the centre of the island, and it has been produced by the sight of their dead companions. We are not yet discovered, and there is still hope.'

Faint and almost despairing as was the prospect of escape, the words of Duncan were not thrown away, for it awakened the powers of the sisters in such a manner, that they awaited the result in silence. A second yell soon followed the first, when a rush of voices was heard pouring down the island, from its upper to its lower extremity, until they reached the naked rock above the caverns, where, after a shout of savage triumph, the air continued full of horrible cries and screams, such as man alone can utter, and he only when in a state of the fiercest barbarity.

The sounds quickly spread around them in every direction. Some called to their fellows from the water's edge, and were answered from the heights above. Cries were heard in the startling vicinity of the chasm between the two caves, which mingled with hoarser yells that arose out of the abyss of the deep ravine. In short, so rapidly had the savage sounds diffused themselves over the barren rock, that it was not difficult for the anxious listeners to imagine that they could be heard beneath, as, in truth, they were above, and on every side of them.

In the midst of this tumult, a triumphant yell was raised within a few yards of the hidden entrance to the cave. Heyward abandoned every hope, with the belief it was the signal that they were discovered. Again the impression passed away, as he heard the voices collect near the spot where the white man had so reluctantly abandoned his rifle. Amid the jargon of the Indian dialects that he now plainly heard, it was easy to distinguish not only words, but sentences in the patois of the Canadas. A burst of voices had shouted, simultaneously, 'la Longue Carabine!' causing the opposite woods to re-echo with a name which, Heyward well remembered, had been given by his enemies to a celebrated hunter and scout of the English camp, and who he now learnt, for the first time, had been his late companion.

'La Longue Carabine! la Longue Carabine!' passed from mouth to mouth, until the whole band appeared to be collected around a trophy, which would seem to announce the death of its formidable owner. After a vociferous consultation, which was, at times, deafened by bursts of savage joy, they again separated, filling the air with the name of a foe, whose body, Heyward could collect from their expressions, they hoped to find concealed in some crevice of the island.

'Now,' he whispered to the trembling sisters, 'now is the moment of uncertainty! if our place of retreat escape this scrutiny, we are still safe! In every event, we are assured, by what has fallen from our enemies, that our friends have escaped, and in two short hours we may look for succour from Webb.'

There were now a few minutes of fearful stillness, during which Heyward well knew that the savages conducted their search with greater vigilance and method. More than once he could distinguish their footsteps, as they brushed the sassafras, causing the faded leaves to rustle, and the branches to snap. At length, the pile yielded a little, a corner of a blanket fell, and a faint ray of light gleamed into the inner part of the cave. Cora folded Alice to her bosom in agony, and Duncan sprang to his feet. A shout was at that moment heard, as if issuing from the centre of the rock, announcing that the neighboring cavern had at length been entered. In a minute, the number and loudness of the voices indicated that the whole party was collected in and around that secret place.

As the inner passages to the two caves were so close to each other, Duncan, believing that escape was no longer possible, passed David and the sisters, to place himself between the latter and the first onset of the terrible meeting. Grown desperate by his situation, he drew nigh the slight barrier which separated him only by a few feet from his relentless pursuers, and placing his face to the casual opening, he even looked out, with a sort of desperate indifference, on their movements.

Within reach of his arm was the brawny shoulder of a gigantic Indian, whose deep and authoritative voice appeared to give directions to the proceedings of his fellows. Beyond him again, Duncan could look into the vault opposite, which was filled with savages, upturning and rifling the humble furniture of the scout. The wound of David had died the leaves of sassafras with a color, that the natives well knew was anticipating the season. Over this sign of their success, they set up a howl, like an opening from so many hounds, who had recovered a lost trail. After this yell of victory, they tore up the fragrant bed of the cavern, and bore the branches into the chasm, scattering the boughs, as if they suspected them of concealing the person of the man they had so long hated and feared. One fierce and wild looking warrior, approached the chief, bearing a load of the brush, and pointing, exultingly, to the deep red stains with which it was sprinkled, uttered his joy in Indian yells, whose meaning Heyward was only enabled to comprehend, by the frequent repetition of the name of 'la Longue Carabine!' When his triumph had ceased, he cast the brush on the slight heap that Duncan had made before the entrance of the second cavern, and closed the view. His example was followed by others; who, as they drew the branches from the cave of the scout, threw them into one pile, adding unconsciously to the security of those they sought. The very slightness of the defence was its chief merit, for no one thought of disturbing a mass of brush, which all of them believed, in that moment of hurry and confusion, had been accidentally raised by the hands of their own party.

As the blankets yielded before the outward pressure, and the branches settled into the fissure of the rock by their own weight, forming a compact body, Duncan once more breathed freely. With a light step, and lighter heart, he returned to the centre of the cave, and took the place he had left, where he could command a view of the opening next the river. While he was in the act of making his movement, the Indians, as if changing their purpose by a common impulse, broke away from the chasm in a body, and were heard rushing up the island again, towards the point, whence they had originally descended. Here another wailing cry betrayed that they were again collected around the bodies of their dead comrades.

Duncan now ventured to look at his companions; for, during the most critical moments of their danger, he had been apprehensive that the anxiety of his countenance might communicate some additional alarm, to those who were so little able to sustain it.

'They are gone, Cora!' he whispered; 'Alice, they are returned whence they came, and we are saved! To heaven, that has alone delivered us from the grasp of so merciless an enemy, be all the praise!'

'Then to heaven will I return my thanks!' exclaimed the younger sister, rising from the encircling arms of Cora, and casting herself, with enthusiastic gratitude, on the naked rock, 'to that heaven who has spared the tears of a gray-headed father; has saved the lives of those I so much love—'

Both Heyward, and the more tempered Cora, witnessed the act of involuntary emotion with powerful sympathy, the former secretly believing that piety had never worn a form so lovely, as it had now assumed in the youthful person of Alice. Her eyes were radiant with the glow of grateful feelings; the flush of her beauty was again seated on her cheeks, and her whole soul seemed ready and anxious to pour out its thanksgivings, through the medium of her eloquent features. But when her lips moved, the words they should have uttered appeared frozen by some new and sudden chill. Her bloom gave place to the paleness of death; her soft and melting eyes grew hard, and seemed contracting with horror; while those hands, which she had raised, clasped in each other, towards heaven, dropped in horizontal lines before her, the fingers pointing forward in convulsed motion. Heyward turned the instant she gave a direction to his suspicions, and, peering just above the ledge which formed the threshold of the open outlet of the cavern, he beheld the malignant, fierce, and savage features of le Renard Subtil.

In that moment of surprise, the self-possession of Heyward did not desert him. He observed by the vacant expression of the Indian's countenance, that his eye, accustomed to the open air, had not yet been able to penetrate the dusky light which pervaded the depth of the cavern. He had even thought of retreating beyond the curvature in the natural wall, which might still conceal him and his companions, when, by the sudden gleam of intelligence that shot across the features of the savage, he saw it was too late, and that they were betrayed.

The look of exultation and brutal triumph which announced this terrible truth, was irresistibly irritating. Forgetful of every thing but the impulses of his hot blood, Duncan levelled his pistol and fired. The report of the weapon made the cavern bellow like an eruption from a volcano, and when the smoke, it vomited, had been driven away before the current of air which issued from the ravine, the place so lately occupied by the features of his treacherous guide was vacant. Rushing to the outlet, Heyward caught a glimpse of his dark figure, stealing around a low and narrow ledge, which soon hid him entirely from sight.

Among the savages, a frightful stillness succeeded the explosion, which had

THE LAST OF THE MOHICANS

just been heard bursting from the bowels of the rock. But when le Renard raised his voice in a long and intelligible whoop, it was answered by a spontaneous yell from the mouth of every Indian within hearing of the sound. The clamorous noises again rushed down the island, and before Duncan had time to recover from the shock, his feeble barrier of brush was scattered to the winds, the cavern was entered at both its extremities, and he and his companions were dragged from their shelter, and borne into the day, where they stood surrounded by the whole band of the triumphant Hurons.

'I fear we shall outsleep the coming morn,
As much as we this night have overwatched!'
A *Midsummer Night's Dream*, V. i. 365–366.

THE INSTANT THE SHOCK of this sudden misfortune had abated, Duncan began to make his observations on the appearance and proceedings of their captors. Contrary to the usages of the natives in the wantonness of their success, they had respected, not only the persons of the trembling sisters, but his own. The rich ornaments of his military attire, had indeed been repeatedly handled by different individuals of the tribe, with eyes expressing a savage longing to possess the baubles, but before the customary violence could be resorted to, a mandate, in the authoritative voice of the large warrior already mentioned, stayed the uplifted hand, and convinced Heyward that they were to be reserved for some object of particular moment.

While, however, these manifestations of weakness were exhibited by the young and vain of the party, the more experienced warriors continued their search throughout both caverns, with an activity that denoted they were far from being satisfied with those fruits of their conquest, which had already been brought to light. Unable to discover any new victim, these diligent workers of vengeance soon approached their male prisoners, pronouncing the name of 'la Longue Carabine,' with a fierceness that could not easily be mistaken. Duncan affected not to comprehend the meaning of their repeated and violent interrogatories, while his companion was spared the effort of a similar deception, by his ignorance of French. Wearied, at length, by their importunities, and apprehensive of irritating his captors by too stubborn a silence, the former looked about him in quest of Magua, who might interpret his answers to questions which were, at each moment, becoming more earnest and threatening.

The conduct of this savage had formed a solitary exception to that of all his fellows. While the others were busily occupied in seeking to gratify their childish passion for finery, by plundering even the miserable effects of the scout, or had been searching, with such blood-thirsty vengeance in their looks, for their absent owner, le Renard had stood at a little distance from the prisoners, with a demeanor so quiet and satisfied, as to betray, that he had already effected the grand purpose of his treachery. When the eyes of Heyward first met those of his recent guide, he turned them away, in horror, at the sinister though calm look he encountered. Conquering his disgust, however, he was able, with an averted face, to address his successful enemy:

'Le Renard Subtil is too much of a warrior,' said the reluctant Heyward, 'to refuse telling an unarmed man what his conquerors say.'

'They ask for the hunter who knows the paths through the woods,' returned Magua, in his broken English, laying his hand, at the same time, with a ferocious smile, on the bundle of leaves, with which a wound on his own shoulder was bandaged; 'la Longue Carabine! his rifle is good, and his eye never shut; but, like the short gun of the white chief, it is nothing against the life of le Subtil!'

'Le Renard is too brave to remember the hurts received in war, or the hands that gave them!'

'Was it war, when the tired Indian rested at the sugar tree, to taste his corn! who filled the bushes with creeping enemies! who drew the knife! whose tongue was peace, while his heart was colored with blood! Did Magua say that the hatchet was out of the ground, and that his hand had dug it up?'

As Duncan dared not retort upon his accuser, by reminding him of his own premeditated treachery, and disdained to deprecate his resentment by any words of apology, he remained silent. Magua seemed also content to rest the controversy, as well as all further communication, there, for he resumed the leaning attitude against the rock, from which, in momentary energy, he had arisen. But the cry of 'la Longue Carabine,' was renewed, the instant the impatient savages perceived that the short dialogue was ended.

'You hear,' said Magua, with stubborn indifference; 'the red Hurons call for the life of the "long rifle," or they will have the blood of them that keep him hid!'

'He is gone – escaped; he is far beyond their reach.'

Renard smiled with cold contempt, as he answered:

'When the white man dies, he thinks he is at peace; but the red men know how to torture even the ghosts of their enemies. Where is his body? Let the Hurons see his scalp!'

'He is not dead, but escaped.'

Magua shook his head incredulously.

'Is he a bird, to spread his wings; or is he a fish, to swim without air! The white chief reads in his books, and he believes the Hurons are fools!'

'Though no fish, the "long rifle" can swim. He floated down the stream when the powder was all burnt, and when the eyes of the Hurons were behind a cloud.'

'And why did the white chief stay?' demanded the still incredulous Indian. 'Is he a stone, that goes to the bottom, or does the scalp burn his head?'

'That I am not a stone, your dead comrade, who fell into the falls, might answer, were the life still in him,' said the provoked young man, using, in his anger, that boastful language which was most likely to excite the admiration of an Indian. 'The white man thinks none but cowards desert their women.'

Magua uttered a few words, inaudibly, between his teeth, before he continued, aloud—

'Can the Delawares swim, too, as well as crawl in the bushes? Where is "le Gros Serpent"?'

Duncan, who perceived by the use of these Canadian appellations, that his late companions were much better known to his enemies than to himself, answered, reluctantly: 'He also is gone down with the water.'

' "Le Cerf Agile" is not here?'

'I know not whom you call the "nimble deer," ' said Duncan, gladly profiting by any excuse to create delay.

'Uncas,' returned Magua, pronouncing the Delaware name with even greater difficulty than he spoke his English words. ' "Bounding elk" is what the white man says when he calls to the young Mohican.'

'Here is some confusion in names between us, le Renard,' said Duncan, hoping to provoke a discussion. 'Daim is the French for deer, and cerf for stag; élan is the true term, when one would speak of an elk.'

'Yes,' muttered the Indian, in his native tongue; 'the pale faces are prattling women! they have two words for each thing, while a red skin will make the sound of his voice speak for him.' Then changing his language, he continued, adhering to the imperfect nomenclature of his provincial instructers. 'The deer is swift, but weak; the elk is swift, but strong; and the son of "le serpent" is "le cerf agile." Has he leaped the river to the woods?'

'If you mean the younger Delaware, he too is gone down with the water.'

As there was nothing improbable to an Indian, in the manner of the escape, Magua admitted the truth of what he had heard, with a readiness that afforded additional evidence how little he would prize such worthless captives. With his companions, however, the feeling was manifestly different.

The Hurons had awaited the result of this short dialogue with characteristic patience, and with a silence, that increased, until there was a general stillness in the band. When Heyward ceased to speak, they turned their eyes, as one man, on Magua, demanding, in this expressive manner, an explanation of what had been said. Their interpreter pointed to the river, and made them acquainted with the result, as much by the action as by the few words he uttered. When the fact was generally understood, the savages raised a frightful yell, which declared the extent of their disappointment. Some ran furiously to the water's edge, beating the air with frantic gestures, while others spat upon the element, to resent the supposed treason it had committed against their acknowledged rights as conquerors. A few, and they not the least powerful and terrific of the band, threw lowering looks, in which the fiercest passion was only tempered by habitual self-command, at those captives who still remained in their power; while one or two even gave vent to their malignant feelings by the most menacing gestures, against which neither the sex, nor the beauty of the sisters, was any protection. The young soldier made a desperate, but fruitless, effort to spring to the side of Alice, when he saw the dark hand of a savage twisted in the rich tresses, which were flowing in volumes over her shoulders, while a knife was passed around the head from which they fell, as if to denote the horrid manner in which it was about to be robbed of its beautiful ornament. But his hands were bound, and at the first movement he made, he felt the grasp of the powerful Indian, who directed the band, pressing his shoulder like a vice. Immediately conscious how unavailing any struggle against such an overwhelming force must prove, he submitted to his fate, encouraging his gentle companions, by a few low and tender assurances, that the natives seldom failed to threaten more than they performed.

But, while Duncan resorted to these words of consolation, to quiet the apprehensions of the sisters, he was not so weak as to deceive himself. He well knew that the authority of an Indian chief was so little conventional, that it was oftener maintained by physical superiority, than by any moral supremacy he might possess. The danger was, therefore, magnified exactly in proportion to the number of the savage spirits by which they were surrounded. The most positive mandate from him, who seemed the acknowledged leader, was liable to be violated, at each moment, by any rash hand that might choose to sacrifice a victim to the manes of some dead friend or relative. While, therefore, he sustained an outward appearance of calmness and fortitude, his heart leaped into his throat, whenever any of their fierce captors drew nigher than common to the helpless sisters, or fastened one of their sullen wandering looks on those fragile forms, which were so little able to resist the slightest assault.

His apprehensions were however greatly relieved, when he saw that the leader had summoned his warriors to himself in council. Their deliberations were short, and it would seem, by the silence of most of the party, the decision unanimous. By the frequency with which the few speakers pointed in the direction of the encampment of Webb, it was apparent they dreaded the approach of danger from that quarter. This consideration probably hastened their determination, and quickened the subsequent movements.

During this short conference, Heyward finding a respite from his greatest fears, had leisure to admire the cautious manner in which the Hurons had made their approaches, even after hostilities had ceased.

It has already been stated, that the upper half of the island was a naked rock, and destitute of any other defences than a few scattering logs of drift wood. They had selected this point to make their descent, having borne the canoe through the wood, around the cataract, for that purpose. Placing their arms in the little vessel, a dozen men, clinging to its sides, had trusted themselves to the direction of the canoe, which was controlled by two of the most skilful warriors, in attitudes, that enabled them to command a view of the dangerous passage. Favored by this arrangement, they touched the head of the island, at that point which had proved so fatal to their first adventurers, but with the advantages of superior numbers, and the possession of fire arms. That such had been the manner of their descent, was rendered quite apparent to Duncan, for they now bore the light bark from the upper end of the rock, and placed it in the water, near the mouth of the outer cavern. As soon as this change was made, the leader made signs to the prisoners to descend and enter.

As resistance was impossible, and remonstrance useless, Heyward set the example of submission, by leading the way into the canoe, where he was soon seated with the sisters, and the still wondering David. Notwithstanding the Hurons were necessarily ignorant of the little channels among the eddies and rapids of the stream, they knew the common signs of such a navigation too well, to commit any material blunder. When the pilot chosen for the task of guiding the canoe had taken his station, the whole band plunged again into the river, the vessel glided down the current, and in a few moments the captives found themselves on the south bank of the stream, nearly opposite to the point where they had struck it, the preceding evening.

Here was held another short but earnest consultation, during which, the horses, to whose panic their owners ascribed their heaviest misfortune, were led from the cover of the woods, and brought to the sheltered spot. The band now divided. The great chief, so often mentioned, mounting the charger of Heyward, led the way directly across the river, followed by most of his people, and disappeared in the woods, leaving the prisoners in charge of six savages, at whose head was le Renard Subtil. Duncan witnessed all their movements with renewed uneasiness.

He had been fond of believing, from the uncommon forbearance of the savages, that he was reserved as a prisoner, to be delivered to Montcalm. As the thoughts of those who are in misery seldom slumber, and the invention is never more lively, than when it is stimulated by hope, however feeble and remote, he had even imagined that the parental feelings of Munro were to be made instrumental in seducing him from his duty to the king. For though the French commander bore a high character for courage and enterprise, he was also thought to be expert in those political practices, which do not always respect the nicer obligations of morality, and which so generally disgraced the European diplomacy of that period.

All those busy and ingenious speculations were now annihilated by the conduct of his captors. That portion of the band who had followed the huge warrior, took the route towards the foot of the Horican, and no other expectation was left for himself and companions, than that they were to be retained as hopeless captives by their savage conquerors. Anxious to know the worst, and willing, in such an emergency, to try the potency of gold, he overcame his reluctance to speak to Magua. Addressing himself to his former guide, who had now assumed the authority and manner of one who was to direct the future movements of the party, he said, in tones as friendly and confiding as he could assume—

'I would speak to Magua, what is fit only for so great a chief to hear.'

The Indian turned his eyes on the young soldier, scornfully, as he answered—'Speak; trees have no ears!'

'But the red Hurons are not deaf; and counsel that is fit for the great men of a nation, would make the young warriors drunk. If Magua will not listen, the officer of the king knows how to be silent.'

The savage spoke carelessly to his comrades, who were busied, after their awkward manner, in preparing the horses for the reception of the sisters, and moved a little to one side, whither, by a cautious gesture, he induced Heyward to follow.

'Now speak,' he said; 'if the words are such as Magua should hear.'

'Le Renard Subtil has proved himself worthy of the honorable name given to him by his Canada fathers,' commenced Heyward; 'I see his wisdom, and all that he has done for us, and shall remember it, when the hour to reward him arrives. Yes! Renard has proved that he is not only a great chief in council, but one who knows how to deceive his enemies!'

'What has Renard done?' coldly demanded the Indian.

'What! has he not seen that the woods were filled with outlying parties of the enemies, and that the serpent could not steal through them without being seen? Then, did he not lose his path, to blind the eyes of the Hurons? Did he not pretend to go back to his tribe, who had treated him ill, and driven him from their wigwams, like a dog? And, when we saw what he wished to do, did we not aid him, by making a false face, that the Hurons might think the white man believed that his friend was his enemy? Is not all this true? And when le Subtil had shut the eyes and stopped the ears of his nation by his wisdom, did they not forget that they had once done him wrong, and forced him to flee to the Mohawks? And did they not leave him on the south side of the river, with their prisoners, while they have gone foolishly on the north? Does not Renard mean to turn like a fox on his footsteps, and carry to the rich and gray headed Scotchman, his daughters? Yes, Magua, I see it all, and I have already been thinking how so much wisdom and honesty should be repaid. First, the chief of William Henry will give as a great chief should, for such a service. The medal* of Magua will no longer be of tin, but of beaten gold; his horn will run over with powder; dollars will be as plenty in his pouch, as pebbles on the shore of Horican; and the deer will lick his hand, for they will know

---

*It has long been a practice with the whites to conciliate the important men, of the Indians, by presenting medals, which are worn in the place of their own rude ornaments. Those given by the English generally bear the impression of the reigning king, and those given by the Americans that of the president. [1831]

it to be vain to fly from the rifle he will carry! As for myself, I know not how to exceed the gratitude of the Scotchman, but I – yes, I will—'

'What will the young chief, who comes from towards the sun, give?' demanded the Huron, observing that Heyward hesitated in his desire to end the enumeration of benefits with that which might form the climax of an Indian's wishes.

'He will make the fire-water from the islands in the salt lake, flow before the wigwam of Magua, until the heart of the Indian shall be lighter than the feathers of the humming-bird, and his breath sweeter than the wild honeysuckle.'

Le Renard had listened gravely as Heyward slowly proceeded in this subtle speech. When the young man mentioned the artifice he supposed the Indian to have practiced on his own nation, the countenance of the listener was veiled in an expression of cautious gravity. At the allusion to the injury which Duncan affected to believe had driven the Huron from his native tribe, a gleam of such ungovernable ferocity flashed from the other's eyes, as induced the adventurous speaker to believe he had struck the proper chord. And by the time he reached the part where he so artfully blended the thirst of vengeance with the desire of gain, he had, at least, obtained a command of the deepest attention of the savage. The question put by le Renard had been calm, and with all the dignity of an Indian; but it was quite apparent, by the thoughtful expression of the listener's countenance, that the answer was most cunningly devised. The Huron mused a few moments, and then laying his hand on the rude bandages of his wounded shoulder, he said, some with energy—

'Do friends make such marks?'

'Would "la Longue Carabine" cut one so light on an enemy?'

'Do the Delawares crawl upon those they love like snakes, twisting themselves to strike?'

'Would "le Gros Serpent" have been heard by the ears of one he wished to be deaf?'

'Does the white chief burn his powder in the faces of his brothers?'

'Does he ever miss his aim, when seriously bent to kill?' returned Duncan, smiling with well acted sincerity.

Another long and deliberative pause succeeded these sententious questions and ready replies. Duncan saw that the Indian hesitated. In order to complete his victory, he was in the act of recommencing the enumeration of the rewards, when Magua made an expressive gesture, and said—

'Enough; le Renard is a wise chief, and he what he does will be seen. Go, and keep the mouth shut. When Magua speaks, it will be the time to answer.'

Heyward, perceiving that the eyes of his companion were warily fastened on the rest of the band, fell back immediately, in order to avoid the appearance of any suspicious confederacy with their leader. Magua approached the horses, and affected to be well pleased with the diligence and ingenuity of his comrades. He then signed to Heyward to assist the sisters into the saddles, for he seldom deigned to use the English tongue, unless urged by some motive of more than usual moment.

There was no longer any plausible pretext for delay, and Duncan was obliged, however reluctantly, to comply. As he performed this office, he whispered his reviving hopes in the ears of the trembling females, who, through dread of encountering the savage countenances of their captors, seldom raised their eyes from the ground. The mare of David had been taken with the followers of the large chief; in consequence, its owner, as well as Duncan, were compelled to journey on foot. The latter did not, however, so much regret this circumstance, as it might enable him to retard the speed of the party – for he still turned his longing looks in the direction of fort Edward, in the vain expectation of catching some sound from that quarter of the forest, which might denote the approach of succour.

When all were prepared, Magua made the signal to proceed, advancing in front, to lead the party in person. Next followed David, who was gradually coming to a true sense of his condition, as the effects of the wound becamed less and less apparent. The sisters rode in his rear, with Heyward at their side, while the Indians flanked the party, and brought up the close of the march, with a caution that seemed never to tire.

In this manner they proceeded in uninterrupted silence, except when Heyward addressed some solitary word of comfort to the females, or David gave vent to the moanings of his spirit, in piteous exclamations, which he intended should express the humility of resignation. Their direction lay towards the south, and in a course nearly opposite to the road to William Henry. Notwithstanding this apparent adherence in Magua to the original determination of his conquerors, Heyward could not believe his tempting bait was so soon forgotten; and he knew the windings of an Indian path too well, to suppose that its apparent course led directly to its object, when artifice was at all necessary. Mile after mile was, however, passed through the boundless woods in this painful manner, without any prospect of a termination to their journey. Heyward watched the sun, as he darted his meridian rays through the branches of the trees, and pined for the moment when the policy of Magua should change their route to one more favorable to his hopes. Sometimes he fancied that the wary savage, despairing of passing the army of Montcalm, in safety, was holding his way towards a well known border settlement, where a distinguished officer of the crown, and a favored friend of the Six Nations, held his large possessions, as well as his usual residence. To be delivered into the hands of Sir William Johnson, was far preferable to being led into the wilds of Canada; but in order to effect even the former, it would be necessary to traverse the forest for many weary leagues, each step of which was carrying him further from the scene of the war, and, consequently, from the post, not only of honor, but of duty.

Cora alone remembered the parting injunctions of the scout, and whenever an opportunity offered, she stretched forth her arm to bend aside the twigs that met her hands. But the vigilance of the Indians rendered this act of precaution both difficult and dangerous. She was often defeated in her purpose, by encountering their watchful eyes, when it became necessary to feign an alarm she did not feel, and occupy the limb, by some gesture of feminine apprehension. Once, and once only, was she completely successful; when she broke down the bough of a large sumach, and, by a sudden thought, let her glove fall at the same instant. This sign intended for those that might follow, was observed by one of her conductors, who restored the glove, broke the remaining branches of the bush in such a manner, that it appeared to proceed from the struggling of some beast in its branches, and then laid his hand on his tomahawk, with a look so significant, that it put an effectual end to these stolen memorials of their passage.

As there were horses, to leave the prints of their footsteps, in both bands of the Indians, this interruption cut off any probable hopes of assistance being conveyed through the means of their trail.

Heyward would have ventured a remonstrance, had there been any thing encouraging in the gloomy reserve of Magua. But the savage, during all this time, seldom turned to look at his followers, and never spoke. With the sun for his only guide, or aided by such blind marks as are only known to the sagacity of a native, he held his way along the barrens of pine, through occasional little fertile vales, across brooks and rivulets, and over undulating hills, with the accuracy of instinct, and nearly with the directness of a bird. He never seemed to hesitate. Whether the path was hardly distinguishable, whether it disappeared, or whether it lay beaten and plain before him, made no sensible difference in his speed or certainty. It seemed as if fatigue could not affect him. Whenever the eyes of the wearied travellers rose from the decayed leaves over which they trode, his dark form was to be seen glancing among the stems of the trees in front, his head immoveably fastened in a forward position, with the light plume on its crest, fluttering in a current of air, made solely by the swiftness of his own motion.

But all this diligence and speed was not without an object. After crossing a low vale, through which a gushing brook meandered, he suddenly ascended a hill, so steep and difficult of ascent, that the sisters were compelled to alight, in order to follow. When the summit was gained, they found themselves on a level spot, but thinly covered with trees, under one of which Magua had thrown his dark form, as if willing and ready to seek that rest, which was so much needed by the whole party.

—'Cursed be my tribe,
If I forgive him.'
The Merchant of Venice, I. iii. 51–52.

THE INDIAN HAD SELECTED for this desirable purpose, one of those steep, pyramidal hills, which bear a strong resemblance to artificial mounds, and which so frequently occur in the valleys of America. The one in question was high, and precipitous; its top flattened, as usual; but with one of its sides more than ordinarily irregular. It possessed no other apparent advantages for a resting place, than in its elevation and form, which might render defence easy, and surprise nearly impossible. As Heyward, however, no longer expected that rescue, which time and distance now rendered so improbable, he regarded these little peculiarities with an eye devoid of interest, devoting himself entirely to the comfort and condolence of his feebler companions. The Narragansets were suffered to browse on the branches of the trees and shrubs, that were thinly scattered over the summit of the hill, while the remains of their provisions were spread under the shade of a beech, that stretched its horizontal limbs like a canopy above them.

Notwithstanding the swiftness of their flight, one of the Indians had found an opportunity to strike a straggling fawn with an arrow, and had borne the more preferable fragments of the victim, patiently on his shoulders, to the stopping place. Without any aid from the science of cookery, he was immediately employed, in common with his fellows, in gorging himself with this digestable sustenance. Magua alone sat apart, without participating in the revolting meal, and apparently buried in the deepest thought.

This abstinence, so remarkable in an Indian, when he possessed the means of satisfying hunger, at length attracted the notice of Heyward. The young man willingly believed that the Huron deliberated on the most eligible manner of eluding the vigilance of his associates. With a view to assist his plans by any suggestion of his own, and to strengthen the temptation, he left the beech, and straggled, as if without an object, to the spot where le Renard was seated.

'Has not Magua kept the sun in his face long enough to escape all danger from the Canadians?' he asked, as though no longer doubtful of the good intelligence established between them; 'and will not the chief of William Henry be better pleased to see his daughters before another night may have hardened his heart to their loss, to make him less liberal in his reward?'

'Do the pale faces love their children less in the morning than at night?' asked the Indian, coldly.

'By no means,' returned Heyward, anxious to recall his error, if he had made one; 'the white man may, and does often, forget the burial place of his fathers; he sometimes ceases to remember those he should love, and has promised to cherish; but the affection of a parent for his child is never permitted to die.'

'And is the heart of the white-headed chief soft, and will he think of the babes that his squaws have given him? He is hard to his warriors, and his eyes are made of stone!'

'He is severe to the idle and wicked, but to the sober and deserving he is a leader, both just and humane. I have known many fond and tender parents, but never have I seen a man whose heart was softer towards his child. You have seen the gray-head in front of his warriors, Magua, but I have seen his eyes swimming in water, when he spoke of those children who are now in your power!'

Heyward paused, for he knew not how to construe the remarkable expression that gleamed across the swarthy features of the attentive Indian. At first it seemed as if the remembrance of the promised reward grew vivid in his mind, while he listened to the sources of parental feeling which were to assure its possession; but as Duncan proceeded, the expression of joy became so fiercely malignant, that it was impossible not to apprehend it proceeded from some passion more sinister than avarice.

'Go,' said the Huron, suppressing the alarming exhibition in an instant, in a death-like calmness of countenance; 'go to the dark-haired daughter, and say, Magua waits to speak. The father will remember what the child promises.'

Duncan, who interpreted this speech to express a wish for some additional pledge that the promised gifts should not be withheld, slowly and reluctantly repaired to the place where the sisters were now resting from their fatigue, to communicate its purport to Cora.

'You understand the nature of an Indian's wishes,' he concluded, as he led her towards the place where she was expected, 'and must be prodigal of your offers of powder and blankets. Ardent spirits are, however, the most prized by such as he; nor would it be amiss to add some boon from your own hand, with that grace you so well know how to practice. Remember, Cora, that on your presence of mind and ingenuity, even your life, as well as that of Alice, may in some measure depend.'

'Heyward, and yours!'

'Mine is of little moment; it is already sold to my king, and is a prize to be seized by any enemy who may possess the power. I have no father to expect me, and but few friends to lament a fate, which I have courted with the unsatiable longings of youth after distinction. But, hush; we approach the Indian. Magua, the lady, with whom you wish to speak, is here.'

The Indian rose slowly from his seat, and stood for near a minute silent and motionless. He then sighed with his hand for Heyward to retire, saying, coldly—

'When the Huron talks to the women, his tribe shut their ears.'

Duncan still lingering, as if refusing to comply, Cora said, with a calm smile—
'You hear, Heyward, and delicacy at least should urge you to retire. Go to
Alice, and comfort her with our reviving prospects.'

She waited until he had departed, and then turning to the native, with the
dignity of her sex, in her voice and manner, she added: 'What would le Renard say
to the daughter of Munro?'

'Listen,' said the Indian, laying his hand firmly upon her arm, as if willing to
draw her utmost attention to his words; a movement that Cora as firmly, but
quietly repulsed, by extricating the limb from his grasp – 'Magua was born a chief
and a warrior among the red Hurons of the lakes; he saw the suns of twenty
summers make the snows of twenty winters run off in the streams, before he saw a
pale-face; and he was happy! Then his Canada fathers came into the woods, and
taught him to drink the fire-water, and he became a rascal. The Hurons drove him
from the graves of his fathers, as they would chase the hunted buffalo. He ran
down the shores of the lakes, and followed their outlet to the "city of cannon."
There he hunted and fished, till the people chased him again through the woods
into the arms of his enemies. The chief, who was born a Huron, was at last a
warrior among the Mohawks!'

'Something like this I had heard before,' said Cora, observing that he paused to
suppress those passions which began to burn with too bright a flame, as he recalled
the recollection of his supposed injuries.

'Was it the fault of le Renard that his head was not made of rock? Who gave him
the fire-water? who made him a villain? 'Twas the pale-faces, the people of your
own color.'

'And am I answerable that thoughtless and unprincipled men exist, whose
shades of countenance may resemble mine?' Cora calmly demanded of the excited
savage.

'No; Magua is a man, and not a fool; such as you never open their lips to the
burning stream; the Great Spirit has given you wisdom!'

'What then have I to do, or say, in the matter of your misfortunes, not to say of
your errors?'

'Listen,' repeated the Indian, resuming his earnest attitude; 'when his English
and French fathers dug up the hatchet, le Renard struck the war-post of the
Mohawks, and went out against his own nation. The pale-faces have driven the
red-skins from their hunting grounds, and now, when they fight, a white man
leads the way. The old chief at Horican, your father, was the great captain of our
war party. He said to the Mohawks do this, and do that, and he was minded. He
made a law, that if an Indian swallowed the fire-water, and came into the cloth
wigwams of his warriors, it should not be forgotten. Magua foolishly opened his
mouth, and the hot liquor led him into the cabin of Munro. What did the gray-
head? let his daughter say.'

'He forgot not his words, and did justice, by punishing the offender,' said the
undaunted daughter.

'Justice!' repeated the Indian, casting an oblique glance of the most ferocious
expression at her unyielding countenance; 'is it justice to make evil, and then
punish for it! Magua was not himself; it was the fire-water that spoke and acted for
him! but Munro did not believe it. The Huron chief was tied up before all the pale-
faced warriors, and whipped like a dog.'

Cora remained silent, for she knew not how to palliate this imprudent severity
on the part of her father, in a manner to suit the comprehension of an Indian.

'See!' continued Magua, tearing aside the slight calico that very imperfectly concealed his painted breast; 'here are scars given by knives and bullets – of these a warrior may boast before his nation; but the gray-head has left marks on the back of the Huron chief, that he must hide, like a squaw, under this painted cloth of the whites.'

'I had thought,' resumed Cora, 'that an Indian warrior was patient, and that his spirit felt not, and knew not, the pain his body suffered?'

'When the Chippewas tied Magua to the stake, and cut this gash,' said the other, laying his finger on a deep scar, 'the Huron laughed in their faces, and told them, women struck so light! His spirit was then in the clouds! But when he felt the blows of Munro, his spirit lay under the birch. The spirit of a Huron is never drunk; it remembers for ever!'

'But it may be appeased. If my father has done you this injustice, show him how an Indian can forgive an injury, and take back his daughters. You have heard from Major Heyward—'

Magua shook his head, forbidding the repetition of offers he so much despised.

'What would you have,' continued Cora, after a most painful pause, while the conviction forced itself on her mind, that the too sanguine and generous Duncan had been cruelly deceived by the cunning of the savage.

'What a Huron loves – good for bad; bad for bad!'

'You would then revenge the injury inflicted by Munro, on his helpless daughters. Would it not be more like a man to go before his face, and take the satisfaction of a warrior?'

'The arms of the pale-faces are long, and their knives sharp!' returned the savage, with a malignant laugh; 'why should le Renard go among the muskets of his warriors, when he holds the spirit of the gray-head in his hand?'

'Name your intention, Magua,' said Cora, struggling with herself to speak with steady calmness. 'Is it to lead us prisoners to the woods, or do you contemplate even some greater evil? Is there no reward, no means of palliating the injury, and of softening your heart? At least, release my gentle sister, and pour out all your malice on me. Purchase wealth by her safety, and satisfy your revenge with a single victim. The loss of both his daughters might bring the aged man to his grave, and where would then be the satisfaction of le Renard?'

'Listen,' said the Indian again. 'The light eyes can go back to the Horican, and tell the old chief what has been done, if the dark-haired woman will swear, by the Great Spirit of her fathers, to tell no lie.'

'What must I promise?' demanded Cora, still maintaining a secret ascendancy over the fierce native, by the collected and feminine dignity of her presence.

'When Magua left his people, his wife was given to another chief; he has now made friends with the Hurons, and will go back to the graves of his tribe, on the shores of the great lake. Let the daughter of the English chief follow, and live in his wigwam for ever.'

However revolting a proposal of such a character might prove to Cora, she retained, notwithstanding her powerful disgust, sufficient self-command to reply, without betraying the weakness.

'And what pleasure would Magua find in sharing his cabin with a wife he did not love; one who would be of a nation and color different from his own? It would be better to take the gold of Munro, and buy the heart of some Huron maid with his gifts.'

The Indian made no reply for near a minute, but bent his fierce looks on the countenance of Cora, in such wavering glances, that her eyes sunk with shame, under an impression, that, for the first time, they had encountered an expression

JAMES FENIMORE COOPER

that no chaste female might endure. While she was shrinking within herself, in dread of having her ears wounded by some proposal still more shocking than the last, the voice of Magua answered, in its tones of deepest malignancy—

'When the blows scorched the back of the Huron, he would know where to find a woman to feel the smart. The daughter of Munro would draw his water, hoe his corn, and cook his venison. The body of the gray-head would sleep among his cannon, but his heart would lie within reach of the knife of le Subtil.'

'Monster! well dost thou deserve thy treacherous name!' cried Cora, in an ungovernable burst of filial indignation. 'None but a fiend could meditate such vengeance! But thou overratest thy power! You shall find it is, in truth, the heart of Munro you hold, and that it will defy your utmost malice!'

The Indian answered this bold defiance by a ghastly smile, that showed an unaltered purpose, while he motioned her away, as if to close the conference, for ever. Cora, already regretting her precipitation, was obliged to comply; for Magua instantly left the spot, and approached his gluttonous comrades. Heyward flew to the side of the agitated female, and demanded the result of a dialogue, that he had watched at a distance with so much interest. But unwilling to alarm the fears of Alice, she evaded a direct reply, betraying only by her countenance her utter want of success, and keeping her anxious looks fastened on the slightest movements of their captors. To the reiterated and earnest questions of her sister, concerning their probable destination, she made no other answer, than by pointing towards the dark groupe, with an agitation she could not control, and murmuring, as she folded Alice to her bosom—

'There, there; read our fortunes in their faces; we shall see! we shall see!'

The action, and the choked utterance of Cora, spoke more impressively than any words, and quickly drew the attention of her companions on that spot, where her own was riveted with an intenseness, that nothing but the importance of the stake could create.

When Magua reached the cluster of lolling savages, who, gorged with their disgusting meal, lay stretched on the earth, in brutal indulgence, he commenced speaking with the dignity of an Indian chief. The first syllables he uttered, had the effect to cause his listeners to raise themselves in attitudes of respectful attention. As the Huron used his native language, the prisoners, notwithstanding the caution of the natives had kept them within the swing of their tomahawks, could only conjecture the substance of his harangue, from the nature of those significant gestures with which an Indian always illustrates his eloquence.

At first, the language, as well as the action of Magua, appeared calm and deliberative. When he had succeeded in sufficiently awakening the attention of his comrades, Heyward fancied, by his pointing so frequently toward the direction of the great lakes, that he spoke of the land of their fathers, and of their distant tribe. Frequent indications of applause escaped the listeners, who, as they uttered the expressive 'hugh!' looked at each other in commendation of the speaker. Le Renard was too skilful to neglect his advantage. He now spoke of the long and painful route by which they had left those spacious hunting grounds and villages, to come and battle against the enemies of their Canadian fathers. He enumerated the warriors of the party; their several merits; their frequent services to the nation; their wounds, and the number of the scalps they had taken. Whenever he alluded to any present, (and the subtle Indian neglected none), the dark countenance of the flattered individual gleamed with exultation, nor did he even hesitate to assert the truth of the words, by gestures of applause and confirmation. Then the voice of the speaker fell, and lost the loud, animated tones of triumph with which he had enumerated their deeds of success and victory. He described the cataract of Glenn's; the impregnable position of its rocky island, with its caverns, and its numerous rapids and whirlpools; he named the name of 'la Longue Carabine,' and paused until the forest beneath them had sent up the last echo of a loud and long yell, with which the hated appellation was received. He pointed toward the youthful military captive, and described the death of a favorite warrior, who had been precipitated into the deep ravine by his hand. He not only mentioned the fate of him who, hanging between heaven and earth, had presented such a spectacle of horror to the whole band, but he acted anew the terrors of his situation, his resolution and his death, on the branches of a sapling; and, finally, he rapidly recounted the manner in which each of their friends had fallen, never failing to touch upon their courage, and their most acknowledged virtues. When this recital of events was ended, his voice once more changed, and became plaintive, and even musical, in its low, guttural sounds. He now spoke of the wives and children of the slain; their destitution; their misery, both physical and moral; their distance; and, at last, of their unavenged wrongs. Then suddenly lifting his voice to a pitch of terrific energy, he concluded, by demanding—

'Are the Hurons dogs, to bear this? Who shall say to the wife of Menowgua, that the fishes have his scalp, and that his nation have not taken revenge! Who will dare meet the mother of Wassawattimie, that scornful woman, with his hands clean! What shall be said to the old men, when they ask us for scalps, and we have not a hair from a white head to give them! The women will point their fingers at us. There is a dark spot on the names of the Hurons, and it must be hid in blood!—'

His voice was no longer audible in the burst of rage, which now broke into the air, as if the wood, instead of containing so small a band, was filled with their nation. During the foregoing address, the progress of the speaker was too plainly read by those most interested in his success, through the medium of the countenances of the men he addressed. They had answered his melancholy and mourning, by sympathy and sorrow; his assertions, by gestures of confirmation; and his boastings, with the exultation of savages. When he spoke of courage, their looks were firm and responsive; when he alluded to their injuries, their eyes kindled with fury; when he mentioned the taunts of the women, they dropped their heads in shame; but when he pointed out their means of vengeance, he struck a chord which never failed to thrill in the breast of an Indian. With the first intimation that it was within their reach, the whole band sprang upon their feet, as one man, and giving utterance to their rage in the most frantic cries, they rushed upon their prisoners in a body, with drawn knives and uplifted tomahawks. Heyward threw himself between the sisters and the foremost, whom he grappled with a desperate strength that for a moment checked his violence. This unexpected resistance gave Magua time to interpose, and with rapid enunciation and animated gestures, he drew the attention of the band again to himself. In that language he knew so well how to assume, he diverted his comrades from their instant purpose, and invited them to prolong the misery of their victims. His proposal was received with acclamations, and executed with the swiftness of thought.

Two powerful warriors cast themselves on Heyward, while another was occupied in securing the less active singing-master. Neither of the captives, however, submitted without a desperate though fruitless struggle. Even David hurled his assailant to the earth; nor was Heyward secured, until the victory over his companion enabled the Indians to direct their united force to that object. He was then bound and fastened to the body of the sapling, on whose branches Magua had acted the pantomime of the falling Huron. When the young soldier regained his recollection, he had the painful certainty before his eyes, that a common fate was intended for the whole party. On his right was Cora, in a durance similar to his own, pale and agitated, but with an eye, whose steady look still read the proceedings of their enemies. On his left, the withes which bound her to a pine, performed that office for Alice which her trembling limbs refused, and alone kept her fragile form from sinking. Her hands were clasped before her in prayer, but instead of looking upward to that power which alone could rescue them, her unconscious looks wandered to the countenance of Duncan, with infantile dependency. David had contended; and the novelty of the circumstance held him silent, in deliberation, on the propriety of the unusual occurrence.

The vengeance of the Hurons had now taken a new direction, and they prepared to execute it, with that barbarous ingenuity, with which they were familiarized by the practice of centuries. Some sought knots, to raise the blazing pile; one was riving the splinters of pine, in order to pierce the flesh of their captives with the burning fragments; and others bent the tops of two saplings to the earth, in order to suspend Heyward by the arms between the recoiling branches. But the vengeance of Magua sought a deeper and a more malignant enjoyment.

While the less refined monsters of the band prepared, before the eyes of those who were to suffer, these well known and vulgar means of torture, he approached Cora, and pointed out, with the most malign expression of countenance, the speedy fate that awaited her—

'Ha!' he added, 'what says the daughter of Munro? Her head is too good to find a pillow in the wigwam of le Renard; will she like it better when it rolls about this hill, a plaything for the wolves? Her bosom cannot nurse the children of a Huron; she will see it spit upon by Indians!'

'What means the monster!' demanded the astonished Heyward.

'Nothing!' was the firm reply. 'He is a savage, a barbarous and ignorant savage, and knows not what he does. Let us find leisure, with our dying breath, to ask for him penitence and pardon.'

'Pardon!' echoed the fierce Huron, mistaking, in his anger, the meaning of her words; 'the memory of an Indian is longer than the arm of the pale-faces; his mercy shorter than their justice! Say; shall I send the yellow-hair to her father, and will you follow Magua to the great lakes, to carry his water, and feed him with corn?'

Cora beckoned him away, with an emotion of disgust she could not control.

'Leave me,' she said, with a solemnity that for a moment checked the barbarity of the Indian; 'you mingle bitterness in my prayers; you stand between me and my God!'

The slight impression produced on the savage was, however, soon forgotten, and he continued pointing, with taunting irony, towards Alice.

'Look! the child weeps! She is young to die! Send her to Munro, to comb his gray hairs, and keep life in the heart of the old man.'

Cora could not resist the desire to look upon her youthful sister, in whose eyes she met an imploring glance, that betrayed the longings of nature.

'What says he, dearest Cora?' asked the trembling voice of Alice. 'Did he speak of sending me to our father?'

For many moments the elder sister looked upon the younger, with a countenance that wavered with powerful and contending emotions. At length she spoke, though her tones had lost their rich and calm fulness, in an expression of tenderness, that seemed maternal.

'Alice,' she said, 'the Huron offers us both life – nay, more than both; he offers to restore Duncan – our invaluable Duncan, as well as you, to our friends – to our father – to our heart-stricken, childless father, if I will bow down this rebellious, stubborn pride of mine, and consent—'

Her voice became choked, and clasping her hands, she looked upward, as if seeking, in her agony, intelligence from a wisdom that was infinite.

'Say on,' cried Alice; 'to what, dearest Cora? Oh! that the proffer were made to me! to save you, to cheer our aged father! to restore Duncan, how cheerfully could I die!'

'Die!' repeated Cora, with a calmer and firmer voice, 'that were easy! Perhaps the alternative may not be less so. He would have me,' she continued, her accents sinking under a deep consciousness of the degradation of the proposal, 'follow him to the wilderness; to go to the habitations of the Hurons; to remain there: in short, to become his wife! Speak then, Alice; child of my affections! sister of my love! And you too, Major Heyward, aid my weak reason with your counsel. Is life to be purchased by such a sacrifice? Will you, Alice, receive it at my hands, at such a price? And *you*, Duncan; guide me; control me between you; for I am wholly yours.'

'Would I!' echoed the indignant and astonished youth. 'Cora! Cora! you jest with our misery! Name not the horrid alternative again; the thought itself is worse than a thousand deaths.'

'That such would be *your* answer, I well knew!' exclaimed Cora, her cheeks flushing, and her dark eyes once more sparkling with the lingering emotions of a woman. 'What says my Alice? for her will I submit without another murmur.'

Although both Heyward and Cora listened with painful suspense and the deepest attention, no sounds were heard in reply. It appeared as if the delicate and sensitive form of Alice had shrunk into itself, as she listened to this proposal. Her arms had fallen lengthwise before her, the fingers moving in slight convulsions; her head dropped upon her bosom, and her whole person seemed suspended against the tree, looking like some beautiful emblem of the wounded delicacy of her sex, devoid of animation, and yet keenly conscious. In a few moments, however, her head began to move slowly, in a sign of deep, unconquerable disapprobation.

'No, no, no; better that we die, as we have lived, together!'

'Then die!' shouted Magua, hurling his tomahawk with violence at the unresisting speaker, and gnashing his teeth with a rage that could no longer be bridled, at this sudden exhibition of firmness in the one he believed the weakest of the party. The axe cleaved the air in front of Heyward, and cutting some of the flowing ringlets of Alice, quivered in the tree above her head. The sight maddened Duncan to desperation. Collecting all his energies in one effort, he snapped the twigs which bound him, and rushed upon another savage, who was preparing, with loud yells, and a more deliberate aim, to repeat the blow. They encountered, grappled, and fell to the earth together. The naked body of his antagonist, afforded Heyward no means of holding his adversary, who glided from his grasp, and rose again with one knee on his chest, pressing him down with the weight of a giant. Duncan already saw the knife gleaming in the air, when a whistling sound swept past him, and was rather accompanied, than followed, by the sharp crack of a rifle. He felt his breast relieved from the load it had endured; he saw the savage expression of his adversary's countenance change to a look of vacant wildness, when the Indian fell dead on the faded leaves by his side.

> 'Clo. – I am gone, sir,
> And anon, sir,
> I'll be with you again.'
>
> *Twelfth Night, IV. ii. 120–122.*

THE HURONS STOOD AGHAST at this sudden visitation of death on one of their band. But, as they regarded the fatal accuracy of an aim, which had dared to immolate an enemy, at so much hazard to a friend, the name of 'la Longue Carabine' burst simultaneously from every lip, and was succeeded by a wild and a sort of plaintive howl. The cry was answered by a loud shout from a little thicket, where the incautious party had piled their arms; and, at the next moment, Hawk-eye, too eager to load the rifle he had regained, was seen advancing upon them, brandishing the clubbed weapon, and cutting the air with wide and powerful sweeps. Bold and rapid as was the progress of the scout, it was exceeded by that of a light and vigorous form, which bounding past him, leaped with incredible activity and daring, into the very centre of the Hurons, where it stood, whirling a tomahawk, and flourishing a glittering knife, with fearful menaces, in front of Cora. Quicker than the thoughts could follow these unexpected and audacious movements, an image, armed in the emblematic panoply of death, glided before their eyes, and assumed a threatening attitude at the other's side. The savage tormentors recoiled before these warlike intruders, and uttered, as they appeared, in such quick succession, the often repeated and peculiar exclamation of surprise, followed by the well known and dreaded appellations of—

'Le Cerf Agile! le Gros Serpent!'

But the wary and vigilant leader of the Hurons, was not so easily disconcerted. Casting his keen eyes around the little plain, he comprehended the nature of the assault, at a glance, and encouraging his followers by his voice, as well as by his example, he unsheathed his long and dangerous knife, and rushed, with a loud whoop, upon the expecting Chingachgook. It was the signal for a general combat. Neither party had fire-arms, and the contest was to be decided in the deadliest manner; hand to hand, with weapons of offence, and none of defence.

Uncas answered the whoop, and leaping on an enemy, with a single, well-directed blow of his tomahawk, cleft him to the brain. Heyward tore the weapon of Magua from the sapling, and rushed eagerly towards the fray. As the combatants were now equal in number, each singled an opponent from the adverse band. The rush and blows passed with the fury of a whirlwind, and the swiftness of lightning. Hawk-eye soon got another enemy within reach of his arm, and with one sweep of his formidable weapon, he beat down the slight and inartificial defences of his antagonist, crushing him to the earth with the blow. Heyward ventured to hurl the tomahawk he had seized, too ardent to await the moment of closing. It struck the Indian he had selected on the forehead, and checked for an instant his onward rush. Encouraged by this slight advantage, the impetuous young man continued his onset, and sprang upon his enemy with naked hands. A single instant was sufficient to assure him of the rashness of the measure, for he immediately found himself fully engaged, with all his activity and courage, in endeavoring to ward the desperate thrusts made with the knife of the Huron. Unable longer to foil an enemy so alert and vigilant, he threw his arms about him, and succeeded in pinning the limbs of the other to his side, with an iron grasp, but one that was far too exhausting to himself to continue long. In this extremity he heard a voice near him, shouting—

'Extarminate the varlets! no quarter to an accursed Mingo!'

At the next moment, the breech of Hawk-eye's rifle fell on the naked head of his adversary, whose muscles appeared to wither under the shock, as he sunk from the arms of Duncan, flexible and motionless.

When Uncas had brained his first antagonist, he turned, like a hungry lion, to seek another. The fifth and only Huron disengaged at the first onset, had paused a moment, and then seeing that all around him were employed in the deadly strife, he had sought, with hellish vengeance, to complete the baffled work of revenge. Raising a shout of triumph, he had sprung towards the defenceless Cora, sending his keen axe, as the dreadful precursor of his approach. The tomahawk grazed her shoulder, and cutting the withes which bound her to the tree, left the maiden at liberty to fly. She eluded the grasp of the savage, and reckless of her own safety, threw herself on the bosom of Alice, striving, with convulsed and ill-directed fingers, to tear asunder the twigs which confined the person of her sister. Any other than a monster would have relented at such an act of generous devotion to the best and purest affection; but the breast of the Huron was a stranger to any sympathy. Seizing Cora by the rich tresses which fell in confusion about her form, he tore her from her frantic hold, and bowed her down with brutal violence to her knees. The savage drew the flowing curls through his hand, and raising them on high with an outstretched arm, he passed the knife around the exquisitely moulded head of this victim, with a taunting and exulting laugh. But he purchased this moment of fierce gratification, with the loss of the fatal opportunity. It was just then the sight caught the eye of Uncas. Bounding from his footsteps, he appeared for an instant darting through the air, and descending in a ball he fell on the chest of his enemy, driving him many yards from the spot, headlong and prostrate. The violence of the exertion cast the young Mohican at his side. They arose together, fought, and bled, each in his turn. But the conflict was soon decided; the tomahawk of Heyward, and the rifle of Hawk-eye, descended on the skull of the Huron, at the same moment that the knife of Uncas reached his heart.

The battle was now entirely terminated, with the exception of the protracted struggle between 'le Renard Subtil' and 'le Gros Serpent.' Well did these barbarous warriors prove that they deserved those significant names, which had been bestowed for deeds in former wars. When they engaged, some little time was lost in eluding the quick and vigorous thrusts which had been aimed at their lives. Suddenly darting on each other, they closed, and came to the earth, twisted together, like twining serpents, in pliant and subtle folds. At the moment when the victors found themselves unoccupied, the spot where these experienced and desperate combatants lay, could only be distinguished by a cloud of dust and leaves, which moved from the centre of the little plain towards its boundary, as if raised by the passage of a whirlwind. Urged by the different motives of filial affection, friendship, and gratitude, Heyward and his companions rushed with one accord to the place, encircling the little canopy of dust which hung above the warriors. In vain did Uncas dart around the cloud, with a wish to strike his knife into the heart of his father's foe; the threatening rifle of Hawk-eye was raised and suspended in vain; while Duncan endeavored to seize the limbs of the Huron, with hands that appeared to have lost their power. Covered, as they were, with dust and blood, the swift evolutions of the combatants seemed to incorporate their bodies into one. The death-like looking figure of the Mohican, and the dark form of the Huron, gleamed before their eyes in such quick and confused succession, that the friends of the former knew not where nor when to plant the succouring blow. It is true, there were short and fleeting moments, when the fiery eyes of Magua were seen glittering, like the fabled organs of the basilisk, through the dusty wreath by which he was enveloped, and he read by those short and deadly glances, the fate of the combat in the presence of his enemies; ere, however, any hostile hand could descend on his devoted head, its place was filled by the scowling visage of Chingachgook. In this manner, the scene of the combat was removed from the centre of the little plain to its verge. The Mohican now found an opportunity to make a powerful thrust with his knife; Magua suddenly relinquished his grasp, and fell backward, without motion, and, seemingly, without life. His adversary leaped on his feet, making the arches of the forest ring with the sounds of triumph.

'Well done for the Delawares! victory to the Mohican!' cried Hawk-eye, once more elevating the butt of the long and fatal rifle; 'a finishing blow from a man without a cross, will never tell against his honor, nor rob him of his right to the scalp!'

But, at the very moment when the dangerous weapon was in the act of descending, the subtle Huron rolled swiftly from beneath the danger, over the edge of the precipice, and falling on his feet, was seen leaping, with a single bound, into the centre of a thicket of low bushes, which clung along its sides. The Delawares, who had believed their enemy dead, uttered their exclamation of surprise, and were following with speed and clamor, like hounds in open view of the deer, when a shrill and peculiar cry from the scout, instantly changed their purpose, and recalled them to the summit of the hill.

''Twas like himself!' cried the inveterate forester, whose prejudices contributed so largely to veil his natural sense of justice in all matters which concerned the Mingoes; 'a lying and deceitful varlet as he is! An honest Delaware now, being fairly vanquished, would have laid still, and been knocked on the head, but these knavish Maquas cling to life like so many cats-o'-the-mountain. Let him go – let him go; 'tis but one man, and he without the rifle or bow, many a long mile from his French commerades; and, like a rattler that has lost his fangs, he can do no farther mischief, until such time as he, and we too, may leave the prints of our moccasins over a long reach of sandy plain. See, Uncas,' he added, in Delaware, 'your father is flaying the scalps already! It may be well to go round and feel the vagabonds that are left, or we may have another of them loping through the woods, and screeching like any jay that has been winged!'

So saying, the honest, but implacable scout, made the circuit of the dead, into whose senseless bosoms he thrust his long knife, with as much coolness, as though they had been so many brute carcasses. He had, however, been anticipated by the elder Mohican, who had already torn the emblems of victory from the unresisting heads of the slain.

But Uncas, denying his habits, we had almost said his nature, flew with instinctive delicacy, accompanied by Heyward to the assistance of the females, and quickly releasing Alice, placed her in the arms of Cora. We shall not attempt to describe the gratitude to the Almighty Disposer of events which glowed in the bosoms of the sisters, who were thus unexpectedly restored to life, and to each other. Their thanksgivings were deep and silent; the offerings of their gentle spirits, burning brightest and purest on the secret altars of their hearts; and their renovated and more earthly feelings exhibiting themselves in long and fervent, though speechless caresses. As Alice rose from her knees, where she had sunk, by the side of Cora, she threw herself on the bosom of the latter, and sobbed aloud the name of their aged father, while her soft, dove-like eyes, sparkled with the rays of hope.

'We are saved! we are saved!' she murmured; 'to return to the arms of our dear, dear father, and his heart will not be broken with grief! And you too, Cora, my sister; my more than sister, my mother; you too are spared! and Duncan,' she added, looking round upon the youth, with a smile of ineffable innocence, 'even our own brave and noble Duncan has escaped without a hurt!'

To these ardent and nearly incoherent words, Cora made no other answer than by straining the youthful speaker to her heart, as she bent over her, in melting tenderness. The manhood of Heyward felt no shame, in dropping tears over this spectacle of affectionate rapture; and Uncas stood, fresh and blood-stained from the combat, a calm, and, apparently, an unmoved looker-on, it is true, but with eyes that had already lost their fierceness, and were beaming with a sympathy, that elevated him far above the intelligence, and advanced him probably centuries before the practices of his nation.

During this display of emotions so natural in their situation, Hawk-eye, whose vigilant distrust had satisfied itself that the Hurons, who disfigured the heavenly scene, no longer possessed the power to interrupt its harmony, approached David, and liberated him from the bonds he had, until that moment, endured with the most exemplary patience.

'There,' exclaimed the scout, casting the last withe behind him, 'you are once more master of your own limbs, though you seem not to use them with much greater judgment than that, in which they were first fashioned. If advice from one who is not older than yourself, but who, having lived most of his time in the wilderness, may be said to have experience beyond his years, will give no offence, you are welcome to my thoughts; and these are, to part with the little tooting instrument in your jacket to the first fool you meet with, and buy some useful we'pon with the money, if it be only the barrel of a horseman's pistol. By industry and care, you might thus come to some prefarment; for by this time, I should think, your eyes would plainly tell you, that a carrion crow is a better bird than a mocking thresher. The one will, at least, remove foul sights from before the face of man, while the other is only good to brew disturbances in the woods, by cheating the ears of all that hear them.'

'Arms and clarion for the battle, but the song of thanksgiving to the victory!' answered the liberated David. 'Friend,' he added, thrusting forth his lean, delicate hand, toward Hawk-eye, in kindness, while his eyes twinkled and grew moist, 'I thank thee that the hairs of my head still grow where they were first rooted by Providence; for, though those of other men may be more glossy and curling, I have ever found mine own well suited to the brain they shelter. That I did not join myself to the battle, was less owing to disinclination, than to the bonds of the heathen. Valiant and skilful hast thou proved thyself in the conflict, and I hereby thank thee, before proceeding to discharge other and more important duties, because thou hast proved thyself well worthy of a Christian's praise!'

'The thing is but a trifle, and what you may often see, if you tarry long among us,' returned the scout, a good deal softened toward the man of song, by this unequivocal expression of gratitude. 'I have got back my old companion, "kill-deer," ' he added, striking his hand on the breech of his rifle, 'and that in itself is a victory. These Iroquois are cunning, but they outwitted themselves when they placed their firearms out of reach; and had Uncas, or his father, been gifted with only their common Indian patience, we should have come in upon the knaves with three bullets instead of one, and that would have made a finish of the whole pack; yon lopeing varlet, as well as his commerades. But 'twas all fore-ordered, and for the best!'

'Thou sayest well,' returned David, 'and hast caught the true spirit of christianity. He that is to be saved will be saved, and he that is predestined to be damned will be damned! This is the doctrine of truth, and most consoling and refreshing it is to the true believer.'

The scout, who by this time was seated, examining into the state of his rifle with a species of parental assiduity, now looked up at the other in a displeasure that he did not affect to conceal, roughly interrupting further speech.

'Doctrine, or no doctrine,' said the sturdy woodsman, "tis the belief of knaves, and the curse of an honest man! I can credit that yonder Huron was to fall by my hand, for with my own eyes have I seen it; but nothing short of being a witness, will cause me to think he has met with any reward, or that Chingachgook, there, will be condemned at the final day.'

'You have no warranty for such an audacious doctrine, nor any covenant to support it,' cried David, who was deeply tinctured with the subtle distinctions, which, in his time, and more especially in his province, had been drawn around the beautiful simplicity of revelation, by endeavoring to penetrate the awful mystery of the divine nature, supplying faith by self-sufficiency, and by consequence, involving those who reasoned from such human dogmas in absurdities and doubt; 'your temple is reared on the sands, and the first tempest will wash away its foundation. I demand your authorities for such an uncharitable assertion; (like other advocates of a system, David was not always accurate in his use of terms.) Name chapter and verse; in which of the holy books do you find language to support you?'

'Book!' repeated Hawk-eye, with singular and ill-concealed disdain; 'do you take me for a whimpering boy, at the apron string of one of your old gals; and this good rifle on my knee for the feather of a goose's wing, my ox's horn for a bottle of ink, and my leathern pouch for a cross-barred handkercher to carry my dinner! Book! what have such as I, who am a warrior of the wilderness, though a man without a cross, to do with books! I never read but in one, and the words that are written there are too simple and too plain to need much schooling; though I may boast that of forty long and hard working years.'

'What call you the volume?' said David, misconceiving the other's meaning.

"Tis open before your eyes,' returned the scout; 'and he who owns it is not a niggard of its use. I have heard it said, that there are men who read in books, to convince themselves there is a God! I know not but man may so deform his works in the settlements, as to leave that which is so clear in the wilderness, a matter of doubt among traders and priests. If any such there be, and he will follow me from sun to sun, through the windings of the forest, he shall see enough to teach him that he is a fool, and that the greatest of his folly lies in striving to rise to the level of one he can never equal, be it in goodness, or be it in power.'

The instant David discovered that he battled with a disputant who imbibed his faith from the lights of nature, eschewing all subtleties of doctrine, he willingly abandoned a controversy, from which he believed neither profit nor credit was to be derived. While the scout was speaking, he had also seated himself, and producing the ready little volume, and the iron-rimmed spectacles, he prepared to discharge a duty, which nothing but the unexpected assault he had received in his orthodoxy, could have so long suspended. He was, in truth, a minstrel of the western continent, of a much later day, certainly, than those gifted bards, who formerly sung the profane renown of baron and prince, but after the spirit of his own age and country; and he was now prepared to exercise the cunning of his craft, in celebration of, or rather in thanksgiving for, the recent victory. He waited patiently for Hawk-eye to cease, then lifting his eyes, together with his voice, he said, aloud—

'I invite you, friends, to join in praise for this signal deliverance from the hands of barbarians and infidels, to the comfortable and solemn tones of the tune, called "Northampton."'

He next named the page and verse where the rhymes selected were to be found, and applied the pitch-pipe to his lips, with the decent gravity, that he had been wont to use in the temple. This time he was, however, without any accompaniment, for the sisters were just then pouring out those tender effusions of affection, which have been already alluded to. Nothing deterred by the smallness of his audience, which, in truth, consisted only of the discontented scout, he raised his voice, commencing and ending the sacred song, without accident or interruption of any kind.

Hawk-eye listened, while he coolly adjusted his flint and reloaded his rifle, but the sounds wanting the extraneous assistance of scene and sympathy, failed to awaken his slumbering emotions. Never minstrel, or by whatever more suitable name David should be known, drew upon his talents in the presence of more insensible auditors; though considering the singleness and sincerity of his motive, it is probable that no bard of profane song ever uttered notes that ascended so near to that throne, where all homage and praise is due. The scout shook his head, and muttering some intelligible words, among which 'Throat' and 'Iroquois,' were alone audible, he walked away, to collect and to examine into the state of the captured arsenal of the Hurons. In this office he was now joined by Chingachgook, who found his own, as well as the rifle of his son, among the arms. Even Heyward and David were furnished with weapons, nor was ammunition wanting to render them all effectual.

When the foresters had made their selection, and distributed their prizes, the scout announced, that the hour had arrived when it was necessary to move. By this time the song of Gamut had ceased, and the sisters had learned to still the exhibition of their emotions. Aided by Duncan and the younger Mohican, the two latter descended the precipitous sides of the hill which they had so lately ascended, under so very different auspices, and whose summit had so nearly proved the scene of their massacre. At the foot, they found the Narragansets browsing the herbage of the bushes, and having mounted, they followed the movements of a guide, who, in the most deadly straits, had so often proved himself their friend. The journey was, however, short. Hawk-eye, leaving the blind path that the Hurons had followed, turned short to his right, and entering the thicket, he crossed a babbling brook, and halted in a narrow dell, under the shade of a few water elms. Their distance from the base of the fatal hill was but a few rods, and the steeds had been serviceable only in crossing the shallow stream.

The scout and the Indians appeared to be familiar with the sequestered place where they now were; for, leaning their rifles against the trees, they commenced throwing aside the dried leaves, and opening the blue clay, out of which a clear and sparkling spring of bright, glancing water, quickly bubbled. The white man then looked about him, as though seeking for some object, which was not to be found as readily as he expected—

'Them careless imps, the Mohawks, with their Tuscarora and Onondaga brethren, have been here slaking their thirst,' he muttered, 'and the vagabonds have thrown away the gourd! This is the way with benefits, when they are bestowed on such disremembering hounds! Here has the Lord laid his hand, in the midst of the howling wilderness, for their good, and raised a fountain of water from the bowels of the 'arth, that might laugh at the richest shop of apothecary's ware in all the colonies; and see! the knaves have trodden in the clay, and deformed the cleanliness of the place, as though they were brute beasts, instead of human men!'

Uncas silently extended towards him the desired gourd, which the spleen of Hawk-eye had hitherto prevented him from observing, on a branch of an elm. Filling it with water, he retired a short distance, to a place where the ground was more firm and dry; here he coolly seated himself, and after taking a long, and, apparently, a grateful draught, he commenced a very strict examination of the fragments of food left by the Hurons, which had hung in a wallet on his arm.

'Thank you, lad,' he continued, returning the empty gourd to Uncas; 'now we will see how these rampaging Hurons lived, when outlying in ambushments. Look at this! The varlets know the better pieces of the deer, and one would think they might carve and roast a saddle, equal to the best cook in the land! But every thing is raw, for them Iroquois are thorough savages. Uncas, take my steel, and kindle a fire; a mouthful of a tender broil will give natur a helping hand, after so long a trail.'

Heyward, perceiving that their guides now set about their repast in sober earnest, assisted the ladies to alight, and placed himself at their side, not unwilling to enjoy a few moments of grateful rest, after the bloody scene he had just gone through. While the culinary process was in hand, curiosity induced him to inquire into the circumstances which had led to their timely and unexpected rescue—

'How is it that we see you so soon, my generous friend,' he asked, 'and without aid from the garrison of Edward?'

'Had we gone to the bend in the river, we might have been in time to rake the leaves over your bodies, but too late to have saved your scalps,' coolly answered the scout. 'No, no; instead of throwing away strength and opportunity by crossing to the fort, we lay by, under the bank of the Hudson, waiting to watch the movements of the Hurons.'

'You were, then, witnesses of all that passed!'

'Not of all; for Indian sight is too keen to be easily cheated, and we kept close. A difficult matter it was, too, to keep this Mohican boy snug in the ambushment! Ah! Uncas, Uncas, your behavior was more like that of a curious woman, than of a warrior on his scent!'

Uncas permitted his eyes to turn for an instant on the sturdy countenance of the speaker, but he neither spoke, nor gave any indication of repentance. On the contrary, Heyward thought the manner of the young Mohican was disdainful, if not a little fierce, and that he suppressed passions that were ready to explode, as much in compliment to the listeners, as from the deference he usually paid to his white associate.

'You saw our capture?' Heyward next demanded.

'We heard it,' was the significant answer. 'An Indian yell is plain language to men who have passed their days in the woods. But when you landed, we were driven to crawl, like sarpents, beneath the leaves; and then we lost sight of you entirely, until we placed eyes on you again trussed to the trees, and ready bound for an Indian massacre.'

'Our rescue was the deed of Providence! It was nearly a miracle that you did not mistake the path, for the Hurons divided, and each band had its horses!'

'Ay! there we were thrown off the scent, and might, indeed, have lost the trail, had it not been for Uncas; we took the path, however, that led into the wilderness; for we judged, and judged rightly, that the savages would hold that course with their prisoners. But when we had followed it for many miles, without finding a single twig broken, as I had advised, my mind misgave me; especially as all the footsteps had the prints of moccasins.'

'Our captors had the precaution to see us shod like themselves,' said Duncan, raising a foot, and exhibiting the buskin he wore.

'Ay! 'twas judgmatical, and like themselves; though we were too expart to be thrown from a trail by so common an invention.'

'To what then are we indebted for our safety?'

'To what, as a white man who has no taint of Indian blood, I should be ashamed to own; to the judgment of the young Mohican, in matters which I should know better than he, but which I can now hardly believe to be true, though my own eyes tell me it is so.'

''Tis extraordinary! will you not name the reason?'

'Uncas was bold enough to say, that the beasts ridden by the gentle ones,' continued Hawk-eye, glancing his eyes, not without curious interest on the fillies of the ladies, 'planted the legs of one side on the ground at the same time, which is contrary to the movements of all trotting four-footed animals of my knowledge, except the bear! And yet here are horses that always journey in this manner, as my own eyes have seen, and as their trail has shown for twenty long miles!'

''Tis the merit of the animal! They come from the shores of Narraganset Bay, in the small province of Providence Plantations, and are celebrated for their hardihood, and the ease of this peculiar movement; though other horses are not unfrequently trained to the same.'

'It may be – it may be,' said Hawk-eye, who had listened with singular attention to this explanation; 'though I am a man who has the full blood of the whites, my judgment in deer and beaver is greater than in beasts of burthen. Major Effingham has many noble chargers, but I have never seen one travel after such a sideling gait!'

'True, for he would value the animals for very different properties. Still, is this a breed highly esteemed, and as you witness, much honored with the burthens it is often destined to bear.'

The Mohicans had suspended their operations about the glimmering fire, to listen, and when Duncan had done, they looked at each other significantly, the father uttering the never-failing exclamation of surprise. The scout ruminated, like a man digesting his newly acquired knowledge, and once more stole a curious glance at the horses.

'I dare to say there are even stranger sights to be seen in the settlements!' he said, at length; 'natur is sadly abused by man, when he once gets the mastery. But, go sideling, or go straight, Uncas had seen the movement, and their trail led us on to the broken bush. The outer branch, near the prints of one of the horses, was bent upward, as a lady breaks a flower from its stem, but all the rest were ragged and broken down, as if the strong hand of a man had been tearing them! So I concluded, that the cunning varments had seen the twig bent, and had torn the rest, to make us believe a buck had been feeling the boughs with his antlers.'

'I do believe your sagacity did not deceive you; for some such thing occurred!'

'That was easy to see,' added the scout, in no degree conscious of having exhibited any extraordinary sagacity; 'and a very different matter it was from a waddling horse! It then struck me the Mingoes would push for this spring, for the knaves well know the vartue of its waters!'

'Is it, then, so famous?' demanded Heyward, examining, with a more curious eye, the secluded dell, with its bubbling fountain, surrounded, as it was, by earth of a deep dingy brown.

'Few red-skins, who travel south and east of the great lakes, but have heard of its qualities. Will you taste for yourself?'

Heyward took the gourd, and after swallowing a little of the water, threw it aside with grimaces of discontent. The scout laughed in his silent, but heartfelt manner, and shook his head with vast satisfaction.

'Ah! you want the flavor that one gets by habit; the time was when I liked it as little as yourself; but I have come to my taste, and I now crave it, as a deer does the licks.* Your high spiced wines are not better liked than a red-skin relishes this water; especially when his natur is ailing. But Uncas has made his fire, and it is time we think of eating, for our journey is long, and all before us.'

Interrupting the dialogue by this abrupt transition, the scout had instant recourse to the fragments of food, which had escaped the voracity of the Hurons. A very summary process completed the simple cookery, when he and the Mohicans commenced their humble meal, with the silence and characteristic diligence of men, who ate in order to enable themselves to endure great and unremitting toil.

When this necessary, and, happily, grateful duty had been performed, each of the foresters stooped and took a long and parting draught, at that solitary and silent spring,* around which and its sister fountains, within fifty years, the wealth, beauty, and talents, of a hemisphere, were to assemble in throngs, in pursuit of health and pleasure. Then Hawk-eye announced his determination to proceed. The sisters resumed their saddles; Duncan and David grasped their rifles, and followed on their footsteps; the scout leading the advance, and the Mohicans bringing up the rear. The whole party moved swiftly through the narrow path, towards the north, leaving the healing waters to mingle unheeded with the adjacent brook, and the bodies of the dead to fester on the neighboring mount, without the rites of sepulture; a fate but too common to the warriors of the woods, to excite either commiseration or comment.

> 'I'll seek a readier path.'
>
> *Parnell, 'A Night-Piece on Death,' 1. 7.*

THE ROUTE TAKEN BY Hawk-eye lay across those sandy plains, relieved by occasional valleys and swells of land, which had been traversed by their party on the morning of the same day, with the baffled Magua for their guide. The sun had now fallen low towards the distant mountains, and as their journey lay through the interminable forest, the heat was no longer oppressive. Their progress, in

---

*Many of the animals of the American forests resort to those spots where salt springs are found. These are called 'licks' or 'salt licks,' in the language of the country, from the circumstance that the quadruped is often obliged to lick the earth, in order to obtain the saline particles. These licks are great places of resort with the hunters, who way-lay their game near the paths that lead to them. [1831]

*The scene of the foregoing incidents is on the spot where the village of Ballston now stands; one of the two principal watering places of America. [1831]

consequence, was proportionate, and long before the twilight gathered about them, they had made good many toilsome miles, on their return.

The hunter, like the savage whose place he filled, seemed to select among the blind signs of their wild route with a species of instinct, seldom abating his speed, and never pausing to deliberate. A rapid and oblique glance at the moss on the trees, with an occasional upward gaze towards the setting sun, or a steady but passing look at the direction of the numerous water courses, through which he waded, were sufficient to determine his path, and remove his greatest difficulties. In the mean time, the forest began to change its hues, losing that lively green which had embellished its arches, in the graver light, which is the usual precursor of the close of day.

While the eyes of the sisters were endeavoring to catch glimpses, through the trees, of the flood of golden glory, which formed a glittering halo around the sun, tinging here and there, with ruby streaks, or bordering with narrow edgings of shining yellow, a mass of clouds that lay piled at no great distance above the western hills, Hawk-eye turned suddenly, and pointing upward towards the gorgeous heavens, he spoke.

'Yonder is the signal given to man to seek his food and natural rest,' he said; 'better and wiser would it be, if he could understand the signs of nature, and take a lesson from the fowls of the air, and the beasts of the fields! Our night, however, will soon be over, for, with the moon, we must be up and moving again. I remember to have fout the Maquas hereaways, in the first war in which I ever drew blood from man; and we threw up a work of blocks, to keep the ravenous varments from handling our scalps. If my marks do not fail me, we shall find the place a few rods further to our left.'

Without waiting for an assent, or, indeed, for any reply, the sturdy hunter moved boldly into a dense thicket of young chestnuts, shoving aside the branches of the exuberant shoots which nearly covered the ground, like a man who expected, at each step, to discover some object he had formerly known. The recollection of the scout did not deceive him. After penetrating through the brush, matted as it was with briars, for a few hundred feet, he entered an open space, that surrounded a low, green hillock, which was crowned by the decayed block-house in question. This rude and neglected building was one of those deserted works, which, having been thrown up on an emergency, had been abandoned with the disappearance of danger, and was now quietly crumbling in the solitude of the forest, neglected, and nearly forgotten, like the circumstances which had caused it to be reared. Such memorials of the passage and struggles of man are yet frequent throughout the broad barrier of wilderness, which once separated the hostile provinces, and form a species of ruins, that are intimately associated with the recollections of colonial history, and which are in appropriate keeping with the gloomy character of the surrounding scenery. * The roof of bark

---

* Some years since, the writer was shooting in the vicinity of the ruins of Fort Oswego, which stands on the shores of Lake Ontario. His game was deer, and his chase a forest that stretched, with little interruption, fifty miles inland. Unexpectedly he came upon six or eight ladders lying in the woods within a short distance of each other. They were rudely made and much decayed. Wondering what could have assembled so many of these instruments in such a place, he sought an old man who resided near for the explanation.

During the war of 1776 Fort Oswego was held by the British. An expedition had been sent two hundred miles through the wilderness to surprise the fort. It appears that the Americans, on reaching the spot named, which was within a mile or two of the fort, first learned that they were expected, and in great danger of being cut off. They threw away their scaling ladders, and made a rapid retreat. These ladders had lain unmolested thirty years, in the spot where they had thus been cast. [1831]

had long since fallen and mingled with the soil, but the huge logs of pine, which had been hastily thrown together, still preserved their relative positions, though one angle of the work had given way under the pressure, and threatened a speedy downfall to the remainder of the rustic edifice. While Heyward and his companions hesitated to approach a building so decayed, Hawk-eye and the Indians entered within the low walls, not only without fear, but with obvious interest. While the former surveyed the ruins, both internally and externally, with the curiosity of one whose recollections were reviving at each moment, Chingachgook related to his son, in the language of the Delawares, and with the pride of a conqueror, the brief history of the skirmish which had been fought in his youth, in that secluded spot. A strain of melancholy, however, blended with his triumph, rendering his voice, as usual, soft and musical.

In the mean time, the sisters gladly dismounted, and prepared to enjoy their halt in the coolness of the evening, and in a security which they believed nothing but the beasts of the forest could invade.

'Would not our resting-place have been more retired, my worthy friend,' demanded the more vigilant Duncan, perceiving that the scout had already finished his short survey, 'had we chosen a spot less known, and one more rarely visited than this?'

'Few live who know the block-house was ever raised,' was the slow and musing answer, "tis not often that books are made, and narratives written, of such a skrimmage as was here fout atween the Mohicans and the Mohawks, in a war of their own waging. I was then a younker, and went out with the Delawares, because I know'd they were a scandalized and wronged race. Forty days and forty nights did the imps crave our blood around this pile of logs, which I designed and partly reared, being, as you'll remember, no Indian myself, but a man without a cross. The Delawares lent themselves to the work, and we made it good, ten to twenty, until our numbers were nearly equal, and then we sallied out upon the hounds, and not a man of them ever got back to tell the fate of his party. Yes, yes; I was then young, and new to the sight of blood, and not relishing the thought that creatures who had spirits like myself, should lay on the naked ground, to be torn asunder by beasts, or to bleach in the rains, I buried the dead with my own hands, under that very little hillock, where you have placed yourselves; and no bad seat does it make neither, though it be raised by the bones of mortal men.'

Heyward and the sisters arose on the instant from the grassy sepulchre; nor could the two latter, notwithstanding the terrific scenes they had so recently passed through, entirely suppress an emotion of natural horror, when they found themselves in such familiar contact with the grave of the dead Mohawks. The gray light, the gloomy little area of dark grass, surrounded by its border of brush, beyond which the pines rose, in breathing silence, apparently, into the very clouds, and the death-like stillness of the vast forest, were all in unison to deepen such a sensation.

'They are gone, and they are harmless,' continued Hawk-eye, waving his hand, with a melancholy smile, at their manifest alarm; 'they'll never shout the warwhoop, nor strike a blow with the tomahawk, again! And of all those who aided in placing them where they lie, Chingachgook and I only are living! The brothers and family of the Mohican formed our war party, and you see before you, all that are now left of his race.'

The eyes of the listeners involuntarily sought the forms of the Indians, with a compassionate interest in their desolate fortune. Their dark persons were still to be seen within the shadows of the block-house, the son listening to the relation of his father, with that sort of intenseness, which would be created by a narrative, that redounded so much to the honor of those, whose names he had long revered for their courage and savage virtues.

'I had thought the Delawares a pacific people,' said Duncan, 'and that they never waged war in person; trusting the defence of their lands to those very Mohawks that you slew!'

"Tis true in part,' returned the scout, 'and yet, at the bottom, 'tis a wicked lie. Such a treaty was made in ages gone by, through the deviltries of the Dutchers, who wished to disarm the natives that had the best right to the country, where they had settled themselves. The Mohicans, though a part of the same nation, having to deal with the English, never entered into the silly bargain, but kept to their manhood; as in truth did the Delawares, when their eyes were opened to their folly. You see before you, a chief of the great Mohican Sagamores! Once his family could chase their deer over tracts of country wider than that which belongs to the Albany Patteroon, without crossing brook or hill, that was not their own; but what is left to their descendant! He may find his six feet of earth, when God chooses; and keep it in peace, perhaps, if he has a friend who will take the pains to sink his head so low, that the ploughshares cannot reach it!'

'Enough!' said Heyward, apprehensive that the subject might lead to a discussion that would interrupt the harmony, so necessary to the preservation of his fair companions; 'we have journeyed far, and few among us are blest with forms like that of yours, which seems to know neither fatigue nor weakness.'

'The sinews and bones of a man carry me through it all,' said the hunter, surveying his muscular limbs with a simplicity that betrayed the honest pleasure the compliment afforded him; 'there are larger and heavier men to be found in the settlements, but you might travel many days in a city, before you could meet one able to walk fifty miles without stopping to take breath, or who has kept the hounds within hearing during a chase of hours. However, as flesh and blood are not always the same, it is quite reasonable to suppose, that the gentle ones are willing to rest, after all they have seen and done this day. Uncas, clear out the spring, while your father and I make a cover for their tender heads of these chestnut shoots, and a bed of grass and leaves.'

The dialogue ceased, while the hunter and his companions busied themselves in preparations for the comfort and protection of those they guided. A spring, which many long years before had induced the natives to select the place for their temporary fortification, was soon cleared of leaves, and a fountain of crystal gushed from the bed, diffusing its waters over the verdant hillock. A corner of the building was then roofed in such a manner, as to exclude the heavy dew of the climate, and piles of sweet shrubs and dried leaves were laid beneath it, for the sisters to repose on.

While the diligent woodsmen were employed in this manner, Cora and Alice partook of that refreshment, which duty required, much more than inclination prompted, them to accept. They then retired within the walls, and first offering up their thanksgivings for past mercies, and petitioning for a continuance of the Divine favor throughout the coming night, they laid their tender forms on the fragrant couch, and in spite of recollection and forebodings, soon sunk into those slumbers which nature so imperiously demanded, and which were sweetened by hopes for the morrow. Duncan had prepared himself to pass the night in watchfulness, near them, just without the ruin; but the scout, perceiving his intention, pointed towards Chingachgook, as he coolly disposed his own person on the grass, and said—

'The eyes of a white man are too heavy, and too blind, for such a watch as this! The Mohican will be our sentinel; therefore, let us sleep.'

'I proved myself a sluggard on my post during the past night,' said Heyward, 'and have less need of repose than you, who did more credit to the character of a soldier. Let all the party seek their rest, then, while I hold the guard.'

'If we lay among the white tents of the 60th, and in front of an enemy like the French, I could not ask for a better watchman,' returned the scout; 'but in the darkness, and among the signs of the wilderness, your judgment would be like the folly of a child, and your vigilance thrown away. Do, then, like Uncas and myself; sleep, and sleep in safety.'

Heyward perceived, in truth, that the younger Indian had thrown his form on the side of the hillock, while they were talking, like one who sought to make the most of the time allotted to rest, and that his example had been followed by David, whose voice literally 'clove to his jaws' with the fever of his wound, heightened, as it was, by their toilsome march. Unwilling to prolong a useless discussion, the young man affected to comply, by posting his back against the logs of the block-house, in a half-recumbent posture, though resolutely determined, in his own mind, not to close an eye until he had delivered his precious charge into the arms of Munro himself. Hawk-eye, believing he had prevailed, soon fell asleep, and a silence as deep as the solitude in which they had found it, pervaded the retired spot.

For many minutes Duncan succeeded in keeping his senses on the alert, and alive to every moaning sound that arose from the forest. His vision became more acute, as the shades of evening settled on the place, and even after the stars were glimmering above his head, he was able to distinguish the recumbent forms of his companions, as they lay stretched on the grass, and to note the person of Chingachgook, who sat upright, and motionless as one of the trees, which formed the dark barrier on every side of them. He still heard the gentle breathings of the sisters, who lay within a few feet of him, and not a leaf was ruffled by the passing air, of which his ear did not detect the whispering sound. At length, however, the mournful notes of a whip-poor-will, became blended with the moanings of an owl; his heavy eyes occasionally sought the bright rays of the stars, and then he fancied he saw them through the fallen lids. At instants of momentary wakefulness, he mistook a bush for his associate sentinel; his head next sunk upon his shoulder, which, in its turn, sought the support of the ground; and, finally, his whole person became relaxed and pliant, and the young man sunk into a deep sleep, dreaming that he was a knight of ancient chivalry, holding his midnight vigils before the tent of a re-captured princess, whose favor he did not despair of gaining, by such a proof of devotion and watchfulness.

How long the tired Duncan lay in this insensible state he never knew himself, but his slumbering visions had been long lost in total forgetfulness, when he was awakened by a light tap on the shoulder. Aroused by this signal, slight as it was, he sprang upon his feet, with a confused recollection of the self-imposed duty he had assumed with the commencement of the night—

'Who comes?' he demanded, feeling for his sword, at the place where it was usually suspended. 'Speak! friend or enemy?'

'Friend,' replied the low voice of Chingachgook; who, pointing upward at the luminary which was shedding its mild light through the opening in the trees, directly on their bivouac, immediately added, in his rude English, 'moon comes, and white man's fort far – far off; time to move, when sleep shuts both eyes of the Frenchman!'

'You say true! call up your friends, and bridle the horses, while I prepare my own companions for the march.'

'We are awake, Duncan,' said the soft, silvery tones of Alice within the building, 'and ready to travel very fast, after so refreshing a sleep; but you have watched through the tedious night, in our behalf, after having endured so much fatigue the livelong day!'

'Say, rather, I would have watched, but my treacherous eyes betrayed me; twice have I proved myself unfit for the trust I bear.'

'Nay, Duncan, deny it not,' interrupted the smiling Alice, issuing from the shadows of the building into the light of the moon, in all the loveliness of her freshened beauty; 'I know you to be a heedless one, when self is the object of your care, and but too vigilant in favor of others. Can we not tarry here a little longer, while you find the rest you need. Cheerfully, most cheerfully, will Cora and I keep the vigils, while you, and all these brave men, endeavor to snatch a little sleep!'

'If shame could cure me of my drowsiness, I should never close an eye again,' said the uneasy youth, gazing at the ingenuous countenance of Alice, where, however, in its sweet solicitude, he read nothing to confirm his half awakened suspicion. 'It is but too true, that after leading you into danger by my heedlessness, I have not even the merit of guarding your pillows, as should become a soldier.'

'No one but Duncan himself, should accuse Duncan of such a weakness. Go, then, and sleep; believe me, neither of us, weak girls as we are, will betray our watch.'

The young man was relieved from the awkwardness of making any further protestations of his own demerits, by an exclamation from Chingachgook, and the attitude of riveted attention assumed by his son.

'The Mohicans hear an enemy!' whispered Hawk-eye, who, by this time, in common with the whole party, was awake and stirring. 'They scent danger in the wind!'

'God forbid!' exclaimed Heyward. 'Surely, we have had enough of bloodshed!'

While he spoke, however, the young soldier seized his rifle, and advancing towards the front, prepared to atone for his venial remissness, by freely exposing his life in defense of those he attended.

''Tis some creature of the forest prowling around us in quest of food!' he said, in a whisper, as soon as the low, and, apparently, distant sounds, which had startled the Mohicans, reached his own ears.

'Hist!' returned the attentive scout; ''tis man; even I can now tell his tread, poor as my senses are, when compared to an Indian's! That scampering Huron has fallen in with one of Montcalm's outlying parties, and they have struck upon our trail. I shouldn't like myself to spill more human blood in this spot,' he added, looking around with anxiety in his features, at the dim objects by which he was surrounded; 'but what must be, must! Lead the horses into the block-house, Uncas; and, friends, do you follow to the same shelter. Poor and old as it is, it offers a cover, and has rung with the crack of a rifle afore tonight!'

He was instantly obeyed, the Mohicans leading the Narragansets within the ruin, whither the whole party repaired, with the most guarded silence.

The sounds of approaching footsteps were now too distinctly audible, to leave any doubts as to the nature of the interruption. They were soon mingled with voices, calling to each other, in an Indian dialect, which the hunter, in a whisper, affirmed to Heyward, was the language of the Hurons. When the party reached the point where the horses had entered the thicket which surrounded the block-house, they were evidently at fault, having lost those marks which, until that moment, had directed their pursuit.

It would seem by the voices that twenty men were soon collected at that one spot, mingling their different opinions and advice, in noisy clamor.

'The knaves know our weakness,' whispered Hawk-eye, who stood by the side of Heyward, in deep shade, looking through an opening in the logs, 'or they wouldn't indulge their idleness in such a squaw's march. Listen to the reptiles! each man among them seems to have two tongues, and but a single leg!'

Duncan, brave as he was in the combat, could not, in such a moment of painful suspense, make any reply to the cool and characteristic remark of the scout. He only grasped his rifle more firmly, and fastened his eyes upon the narrow opening, through which he gazed upon the moonlight view with increasing anxiety. The deeper tones of one who spoke as having authority, were next heard, amid a silence that denoted the respect with which his orders, or rather advice, was received. After which, by the rustling of leaves, and cracking of dried twigs, it was apparent the savages were separating in pursuit of the lost trail. Fortunately for the pursued, the light of the moon, while it shed a flood of mild lustre, upon the little area around the ruin, was not sufficiently strong to penetrate the deep arches of the forest, where the objects still lay in deceptive shadow. The search proved fruitless; for so short and sudden had been the passage from the faint path the travellers had journeyed into the thicket, that every trace of their footsteps was lost in the obscurity of the woods.

It was not long, however, before the restless savages were heard beating the brush, and gradually approaching the inner edge of that dense border of young chestnuts, which encircled the little area.

'They are coming!' muttered Heyward, endeavoring to thrust his rifle through the chink in the logs; 'let us fire on their approach!'

'Keep every thing in the shade,' returned the scout; 'the snapping of a flint, or even the smell of a single karnel of the brimstone, would bring the hungry varlets upon us in a body. Should it please God, that we must give battle for the scalps, trust to the experience of men who know the ways of the savages, and who are not often backward when the war-whoop is howled.'

Duncan cast his eyes behind him, and saw that the trembling sisters were cowering in the far corner of the building, while the Mohicans stood in the shadow, like two upright posts, ready, and apparently willing, to strike, when the blow should be needed. Curbing his impatience, he again looked out upon the area, and awaited the result in silence. At that instant the thicket opened, and a tall and armed Huron advanced a few paces into the open space. As he gazed upon the silent block-house, the moon fell full upon his swarthy countenance, and betrayed its surprise and curiosity. He made the exclamation, which usually accompanies the former emotion in an Indian, and calling in a low voice, soon drew a companion to his side.

These children of the woods stood together for several moments, pointing at the crumbling edifice, and conversing in the unintelligible language of their tribe. They then approached, though with slow and cautious steps, pausing every instant to look at the building, like startled deer, whose curiosity struggled powerfully with their awakened apprehensions for the mastery. The foot of one of them suddenly rested on the mound, and he stooped to examine its nature. At this moment, Heyward observed that the scout loosened his knife in its sheath, and lowered the muzzle of his rifle. Imitating these movements, the young man prepared himself for the struggle, which now seemed inevitable.

The savages were so near, that the least motion in one of the horses, or even a breath louder than common, would have betrayed the fugitives. But, in discovering the character of the mound, the attention of the Hurons appeared directed to a different object. They spoke together, and the sounds of their voices were low and solemn, as if influenced by a reverence that was deeply blended with awe. Then they drew warily back, keeping their eyes riveted on the ruin, as if they expected to see the apparitions of the dead issue from its silent walls, until having reached the boundary of the area, they moved slowly into the thicket, and disappeared.

Hawk-eye dropped the breech of his rifle to the earth, and drawing a long, free breath, exclaimed, in an audible whisper—

'Ay! they respect the dead, and it has this time saved their own lives, and it may be, the lives of better men too!'

Heyward lent his attention, for a single moment, to his companion, but without replying, he again turned towards those who just then interested him more. He heard the two Hurons leave the bushes, and it was soon plain that all the pursuers were gathered about them, in deep attention to their report. After a few minutes of earnest and solemn dialogue, altogether different from the noisy clamor with which they had first collected about the spot, the sounds grew fainter, and more distant, and finally were lost in the depths of the forest.

Hawk-eye waited until a signal from the listening Chingachgook assured him, that every sound from the retiring party was completely swallowed by the distance, when he motioned to Heyward to lead forth the horses, and to assist the sisters into their saddles. The instant this was done, they issued through the broken gate-way, and stealing out by a direction opposite to the one by which they had entered, they quitted the spot, the sisters casting furtive glances at the silent grave and crumbling ruin, as they left the soft light of the moon, to bury themselves in the gloom of the woods.

'*Guard.* – Qui est là?
Puc. – Paisans, pauvres gens de France.'

I Henry VI, III. ii. 13–14.

DURING THE RAPID MOVEMENT from the block-house, and until the party was deeply buried in the forest, each individual was too much interested in the escape, to hazard a word even in whispers. The scout resumed his post in the advance, though his steps, after he had thrown a safe distance between himself and his enemies, were more deliberate than in their previous march, in consequence of his utter ignorance of the localities of the surrounding woods. More than once he halted to consult with his confederates, the Mohicans, pointing upwards at the moon, and examining the barks of the tree with care. In these brief pauses, Heyward and the sisters listened, with senses rendered doubly acute by the danger, to detect any symptoms which might announce the proximity of their foes. At such moments, it seemed as if a vast range of country lay buried in eternal sleep; not the least sound arising from the forest, unless it was the distant and scarcely audible rippling of a water-course. Birds, beasts, and man, appeared to slumber alike, if, indeed, any of the latter were to be found in that wide tract of wilderness.

But the sounds of the rivulet, feeble and murmuring as they were, relieved the guides at once from no trifling embarrassment, and towards it they immediately held their way.

When the banks of the little stream were gained, Hawk-eye made another halt; and, taking the moccasins from his feet, he invited Heyward and Gamut to follow his example. He then entered the water, and for near an hour they travelled in the bed of the brook, leaving no trail. The moon had already sunk into an immense pile of black clouds, which lay impending above the western horizon, when they issued from the low and devious water-course to rise, again, to the light and level of the sandy but wooded plain. Here the scout seemed to be once more at home, for he held on his way, with the certainty and diligence of a man, who moved in the security of his own knowledge. The path soon became more uneven, and the travellers could plainly perceive, that the mountains drew nigher to them on each hand, and that they were, in truth, about entering one of their gorges. Suddenly, Hawk-eye made a pause, and waiting until he was joined by the whole party, he spoke; though in tones so low and cautious, that they added to the solemnity of his words, in the quiet and darkness of the place.

'It is easy to know the path-ways, and to find the licks and water-courses of the wilderness,' he said; 'but who that saw this spot, could venture to say, that a mighty army was at rest among yonder silent trees and barren mountains!'

'We are then at no great distance from William Henry?' said Heyward, advancing nigher to the scout.

'It is yet a long and weary path, and when and where to strike it, is now our greatest difficulty. See,' he said, pointing through the trees towards a spot where a little basin of water reflected the stars from its placid bosom, 'here is the "bloody pond;" and I am on ground that I have not only often travelled, but over which I have fou't the enemy, from the rising to the setting sun!'

'Ha! that sheet of dull and weary water, then, is the sepulchre of the brave men who fell in the contest! I have heard it named, but never have I stood on its banks before!'

'Three battles did we make with the Dutch Frenchman* in a day!' continued Hawk-eye, pursuing the train of his own thoughts, rather than replying to the remark of Duncan. 'He met us hard by, in our outward march to ambush his advance, and scattered us, like driven deer, through the defile, to the shores of Horican. Then we rallied behind our fallen trees, and made head against him, under Sir William – who was made Sir William for that very deed; and well did we pay him for the disgrace of the morning! Hundreds of Frenchmen saw the sun that day for the last time; and even their leader, Dieskau himself, fell into our hands, so cut and torn with the lead, that he has gone back to his own country, unfit for further acts in war.'

''Twas a noble repulse!' exclaimed Heyward in the heat of his youthful ardour; 'the fame of it reached us early in our southern army.'

'Ay! but it did not end there. I was sent by Major Effingham, at Sir William's own bidding, to out-flank the French, and carry the tidings of their disaster across the portage, to the fort on the Hudson. Just hereaway, where you see the trees rise into a mountain swell, I met a party coming down to our aid, and I led them where the enemy were taking their meal, little dreaming that they had not finished the bloody work of the day.'

*Baron Dieskau, a German, in the service of France. A few years previously to the period of the tale, this officer was defeated by Sir William Johnson of Johnstown, New York, on the shores of Lake George. [1831]

'And you surprised them!'

'If death can be a surprise to men who are thinking only of the cravings of their appetites! we gave them but little breathing time, for they had borne hard upon us in the fight of the morning, and there were few in our party who had not lost friend or relative by their hands. When all was over, the dead, and some say the dying, were cast into that little pond. These eyes have seen its waters colored with blood, as natural water never yet flowed from the bowels of the 'arth.'

'It was a convenient, and, I trust, will prove a peaceful grave for a soldier! You have, then, seen much service on this frontier?'

'I!' said the scout, erecting his tall person with an air of military pride; 'there are not many echoes among these hills that haven't rung with the crack of my rifle, nor is there the space of a square mile atwixt Horican and the river, that "kill-deer" hasn't dropped a living body on, be it an enemy, or be it a brute beast. As for the grave there, being as quiet as you mention, it is another matter. There are them in the camp, who say and think, man to lie still, should not be buried while the breath is in the body; and certain it is, that in the hurry of that evening, the doctors had but little time to say who was living, and who was dead. Hist! see you nothing walking on the shore of the pond?'

''Tis not probable that any are as houseless as ourselves, in this dreary forest.'

'Such as he may care but little for house or shelter, and night dew can never wet a body that passes its days in the water!' returned the scout, grasping the shoulder of Heyward, with such convulsive strength, as to make the young soldier painfully sensible how much superstitious terror had gotten the mastery of a man usually so dauntless.

'By heaven! there is a human form, and it approaches! stand to your arms, my friends, for we know not whom we encounter.'

'Qui vive?' demanded a stern, quick voice, which sounded like a challenge from another world, issuing out of that solitary and solemn place.

'What says it?' whispered the scout; 'it speaks neither Indian nor English!'

'Qui vive?' repeated the same voice, which was quickly followed by the rattling of arms, and a menacing attitude.

'France,' cried Heyward, advancing from the shadow of the trees, to the shore of the pond, within a few yards of the sentinel.

'D'où venez-vous – où allez-vous d'aussi bonne heure?' demanded the grenadier, in the language, and with the accent of a man from old France.

'Je viens de la découverte, et je vais me coucher.'

'Etes vous officier du roi?'

'Sans doute, mon camarade; me prends-tu pour un provincial! Je suis capitaine de chasseurs (Heyward well knew that the other was of a regiment in the line) – j'ai ici, avec moi, les filles du commandant de la fortification. Aha! tu en as entendu parler! je les ai fait prisonnières près de l'autre fort, et je les conduis au général.'

'Ma foi! mesdames; j'en suis fâché pour vous,' exclaimed the young soldier, touching his cap with grace; 'mais – fortune de guerre! vous trouverez notre général un brave homme, et bien poli avec les dames.'

'C'est le caractère des gens de guerre,' said Cora, with admirable self-possession; 'Adieu, mon ami; je vous souhaiterais un devoir plus agréable, à remplir.'

The soldier made a low and humble acknowledgment for her civility; and Heyward adding a 'bonne nuit, mon camarade,' they moved deliberately forward; leaving the sentinel pacing the banks of the silent pond, little suspecting an enemy of so much effrontery, and humming to himself those words which were recalled to his mind by the sight of women, and, perhaps, by recollections of his own distant and beautiful France—

'Vive le vin, vive l'amour,'&c.&c.

''Tis well you understood the knave!' whispered the scout, when they had gained a little distance from the place, and letting his rifle fall into the hollow of his arm again; 'I soon saw that he was one of them uneasy Frenchers, and well for him it was, that his speech was friendly, and his wishes kind; or a place might have been found for his bones amongst those of his countrymen.'

He was interrupted by a long and heavy groan, which arose from the little basin, as though, in truth, the spirits of the departed lingered about their watery sepulchre.

'Surely, it was of flesh!' continued the scout; 'no spirit could handle its arms so steadily!'

'It *was* of flesh, but whether the poor fellow still belongs to this world, may well be doubted,' said Heyward, glancing his eyes around him, and missing Chingach-gook from their little band. Another groan, more faint than the former, was succeeded by a heavy and sullen plunge into the water, and all was as still again, as if the borders of the dreary pool had never been awakened from the silence of creation. While they yet hesitated in uncertainty, the form of the Indian was seen gliding out of the thicket. As the chief rejoined them, with one hand he attached the reeking scalp of the unfortunate young Frenchman to his girdle, and with the other he replaced the knife and tomahawk that had drunk his blood. He then took his wonted station, with the air of a man who believed he had done a deed of merit.

The scout dropped one end of his rifle to the earth, and leaning his hands on the other, he stood musing in profound silence. Then shaking his head in a mournful manner, he muttered—

''Twould have been a cruel and an inhuman act for a white-skin; but 'tis the gift and natur of an Indian, and I suppose it should not be denied! I could wish, though, it had befallen an accursed Mingo, rather than that gay, young boy, from the old countries!'

'Enough!' said Heyward, apprehensive the unconscious sisters might compre-hend the nature of the detention, and conquering his disgust by a train of reflections very much like that of the hunter; ''tis done, and though better it were left undone, cannot be amended. You see we are, too obviously, within the sentinels of the enemy; what course do you propose to follow?'

'Yes,' said Hawk-eye, rousing himself again, ''tis, as you say, too late to harbor further thoughts about it! Ay, the French have gathered around the fort in good earnest, and we have a delicate needle to thread in passing them.'

'And but little time to do it in,' added Heyward; glancing his eyes upward, towards the bank of vapor that concealed the setting moon.

'And little time to do it in!' repeated the scout. 'The thing may be done in two fashions, by the help of Providence, without which it may not be done at all!'

'Name them quickly, for time presses.'

'One would be, to dismount the gentle ones, and let their beasts range the plain; by sending the Mohicans in front, we might then cut a lane through their sentries, and enter the fort over the dead bodies.'

'It will not do – it will not do!' interrupted the generous Heyward; 'a soldier might force his way in this manner, but never with such a convoy.'

"Twould be, indeed, a bloody path for such tender feet to wade in!' returned the equally reluctant scout, 'but I thought it befitting my manhood to name it. We must then turn on our trail, and get without the line of their look-outs, when we will bend short to the west, and enter the mountains; where I can hide you, so that all the devil's hounds in Montcalm's pay would be thrown off the scent, for months to come.'

'Let it be done, and that instantly.'

Further words were unnecessary; for Hawk-eye, merely uttering the mandate to 'follow,' moved along the route, by which they had just entered their present, critical, and even dangerous situation. Their progress, like their late dialogue, was guarded, and without noise; for none knew at what moment a passing patrol, or a crouching picquet, of the enemy, might rise upon their path. As they held their silent way along the margin of the pond, again, Heyward and the scout stole furtive glances at its appalling dreariness. They looked in vain for the form they had so recently seen stalking along its silent shores, while a low and regular wash of the little waves, by announcing that the waters were not yet subsided, furnished a frightful memorial of the deed of blood they had just witnessed. Like all that passing and gloomy scene, the low basin, however, quickly melted in the darkness, and became blended with the mass of black objects in the rear of the travellers.

Hawk-eye soon deviated from the line of their retreat, and striking off towards the mountains which form the western boundary of the narrow plain, he led his followers, with steep steps, deep within the shadows, that were cast from their high and broken summits. The route was now painful; lying over ground ragged with rocks, and intersected with ravines, and their progress proportionately slow. Bleak and black hills lay on every side of them, compensating, in some degree, for the additional toil of the march, by the sense of security they imparted. At length the party began slowly to rise a steep and rugged ascent, by a path that curiously wound among rocks and trees, avoiding the one, and supported by the other, in a manner that showed it had been devised by men long practiced in the arts of the wilderness. As they gradually rose from the level of the valleys, the thick darkness which usually precedes the approach of day, began to disperse, and objects were seen in the plain and palpable colors with which they had been gifted by nature. When they issued from the stunted woods which clung to the barren sides of the mountain, upon a flat and mossy rock, that formed its summit, they met the morning, as it came blushing above the green pines of a hill, that lay on the opposite side of the valley of the Horican.

The scout now told the sisters to dismount, and taking the bridles from the mouths and the saddles off the backs of the jaded beasts, he turned them loose, to glean a scanty subsistence, among the shrubs and meager herbage of that elevated region.

'Go,' he said, 'and seek your food where natur gives it you; and beware that you become not food to ravenous wolves yourselves, among these hills.'

'Have we no further need of them?' demanded Heyward.

'See, and judge with your own eyes,' said the scout, advancing towards the eastern brow of the mountain, whither he beckoned for the whole party to follow; 'if it was as easy to look into the heart of man, as it is to spy out the nakedness of Montcalm's camp from this spot, hypocrites would grow scarce, and the cunning of a Mingo might prove a losing game, compared to the honesty of a Delaware.'

When the travellers had reached the verge of the precipice, they saw, at a glance, the truth of the scout's declaration, and the admirable foresight with which he had led them to their commanding station.

The mountain on which they stood, elevated perhaps a thousand feet in the air, was a high cone, that rose a little in advance of that range which stretches for miles along the western shores of the lake, until meeting its sister piles, beyond the water, it ran off towards the Canadas, in confused and broken masses of rock, thinly sprinkled with evergreens. Immediately at the feet of the party the southern shore of the Horican swept in a broad semi-circle, from mountain to mountain, marking a wide strand, that soon rose into an uneven and somewhat elevated plain. To the north, stretched the limpid, and, as it appeared from that dizzy height, the narrow sheet of the 'holy lake,' indented with numberless bays, embellished by fantastic head-lands, and dotted with countless islands. At the distance of a few leagues, the bed of the waters became lost among mountains, or was wrapped in the masses of vapor, that came slowly rolling along their bosom, before a light morning air. But a narrow opening between the crests of the hills, pointed out the passage by which they found their way still farther north, to spread their pure and ample sheets again, before pouring out their tribute into the distant Champlain. To the south stretched the defile, or, rather, broken plain, so often mentioned. For several miles, in this direction, the mountains appeared reluctant to yield their dominion, but within reach of the eye they diverged, and finally melted into the level and sandy lands, across which we have accompanied our adventurers in their double journey. Along both ranges of hills, which bounded the opposite sides of the lake and valley, clouds of light vapor were rising in spiral wreaths from the uninhabited woods, looking like the smokes of hidden cottages, or rolled lazily down the declivities, to mingle with the fogs of the lower land. A single, solitary, snow-white cloud, floated above the valley, and marked the spot, beneath which lay the silent pool of the 'bloody pond.'

Directly on the shore of the lake, and nearer to its western than to its eastern margin, lay the extensive earthen ramparts and low buildings of William Henry. Two of the sweeping bastions appeared to rest on the water, which washed their bases, while a deep ditch and extensive morasses guarded its other sides and angles. The land had been cleared of wood for a reasonable distance around the work, but every other part of the scene lay in the green livery of nature, except where the limpid water mellowed the view, or the bold rocks thrust their black and naked heads above the undulating outlines of the mountain ranges. In its front, might be seen the scattered sentinels, who held a weary watch against their numerous foes; and within the walls themselves, the travellers looked down upon men still drowsy with a night of vigilance. Towards the south-east, but in immediate contact with the fort, was an entrenched camp, posted on a rocky eminence, that would have been far more eligible for the work itself, in which Hawk-eye pointed out the presence of those auxiliary regiments that had so recently left the Hudson, in their company. From the woods, a little farther to the south, rose numerous dark and lurid smokes, that were easily to be distinguished from the purer exhalations of the springs, and which the scout also showed to Heyward, as evidences that the enemy lay in force in that direction.

But the spectacle which most concerned the young soldier, was on the western bank of the lake, though quite near to its southern termination. On a stripe of land, which appeared, from his stand, too narrow to contain such an army, but which, in truth, extended many hundreds of yards from the shores of the Horican to the base of the mountain, were to be seen the white tents and military engines of an encampment of ten thousand men. Batteries were already thrown up in their front, and even while the spectators above them were looking down, with such different emotions, on a scene, which lay like a map beneath their feet, the roar of artillery rose from the valley, and passed off, in thundering echoes, along the eastern hills.

'Morning is just touching them below,' said the deliberate and musing scout, 'and the watchers have a mind to wake up the sleepers by the sound of cannon. We are a few hours too late! Montcalm has already filled the woods with his accursed Iroquois.'

'The place is, indeed, invested,' returned Duncan; 'but is there no expedient by which we may enter? capture in the works would be far preferable to falling, again, into the hands of roving Indians.'

'See!' exclaimed the scout, unconsciously directing the attention of Cora to the quarters of her own father, 'how that shot has made the stones fly from the side of the commandant's house! Ay! these Frenchers will pull it to pieces faster than it was put together, solid and thick enough it be!'

'Heyward, I sicken at the sight of danger, that I cannot share,' said the undaunted but anxious daughter. 'Let us go to Montcalm, and demand admission; he dare not deny a child the boon!'

'You would scarce find the tent of the Frenchman with the hair on your head!' said the blunt scout. 'If I had but one of the thousand boats which lie empty along that shore, it might be done. Ha! here will soon be an end of the firing, for yonder comes a fog that will turn day to night, and make an Indian arrow more dangerous than a moulded cannon. Now, if you are equal to the work, and will follow, I will make a push; for I long to get down into that camp, if it be only to scatter some Mingo dogs, that I see lurking in the skirts of yonder thicket of birch.'

'We are equal!' said Cora, firmly; 'on such an errand we will follow to any danger!'

The scout turned to her with a smile of honest and cordial approbation, as he answered—

'I would I had a thousand men, of brawny limbs and quick eyes, that feared death as little as you! I'd send them jabbering Frenchers back into their den again, afore the week was ended, howling like so many fettered hounds, or hungry wolves. But stir,' he added, turning from her to the rest of the party, 'the fog comes rolling down so fast, we shall have but just the time to meet it on the plain, and use it as a cover. Remember, if any accident should befall me, to keep the air blowing on your left cheeks – or, rather, follow the Mohicans; they'd scent their way, be it in day, or be it at night.'

He then waved his hand for them to follow, and threw himself down the steep declivity, with free but careful footsteps. Heyward assisted the sisters to descend, and in a few minutes they were all far down a mountain, whose sides they had climbed with so much toil and pain.

The direction taken by Hawk-eye soon brought the travellers to the level of the plain, nearly opposite to a sally-port, in the western curtain of the fort, which lay, itself, at the distance of about half a mile from the point where he halted, to allow Duncan to come up with his charge. In their eagerness, and favored by the nature of the ground, they had anticipated the fog, which was rolling heavily down the lake, and it became necessary to pause, until the mists had wrapped the camp of the enemy in their fleecy mantle. The Mohicans profited by the delay, to steal out of the woods, and to make a survey of surrounding objects. They were followed, at a little distance, by the scout, with a view to profit early by their report, and to obtain some faint knowledge for himself of the more immediate localities.

In a very few moments he returned, his face reddened with vexation, while he muttered his disappointment in words of no very gentle import.

'Here, has the cunning Frenchman been posting a picquet directly in our path,' he said; 'red-skins and whites; and we shall be as likely to fall into their midst, as to pass them in the fog!'

'Cannot we make a circuit to avoid the danger,' asked Heyward, 'and come into our path again when it is past?'

'Who that once bends from the line of his march, in a fog, can tell when or how to turn to find it again! The mists of Horican are not like the curls from a peace-pipe, or the smoke which settles above a mosquetoe fire!'

He was yet speaking, when a crashing sound was heard, and a cannon ball entered the thicket, striking the body of a sapling, and rebounding to the earth, its force being much expended by previous resistance. The Indians followed instantly like busy attendants on the terrible messenger, and Uncas commenced speaking earnestly, and with much action, in the Delaware tongue.

'It may be so, lad,' muttered the scout, when he had ended; 'for desperate fevers are not to be treated like a tooth-ache. Come, then, the fog is shutting in.'

'Stop!' cried Heyward; 'first explain your expectations.'

"Tis soon done, and a small hope it is; but it is better than nothing. This shot that you see,' added the scout, kicking the harmless iron with his foot, 'has ploughed the 'arth in its road from the fort, and we shall hunt for the furrow it has made, when all other signs may fail. No more words, but follow; or the fog may leave us in the middle of our path, a mark for both armies to shoot at.'

Heyward perceiving that, in fact, a crisis had arrived, when acts were more required than words, placed himself between the sisters, and drew them swiftly forward, keeping the dim figure of their leader in his eye. It was soon apparent that Hawk-eye had not magnified the power of the fog, for before they had proceeded twenty yards, it was difficult for the different individuals of the party to distinguish each other, in the vapor.

They had made their little circuit to the left, and were already inclining again towards the right, having, as Heyward thought, got over nearly half the distance to the friendly works, when his ears were saluted with the fierce summons, apparently within twenty feet of them, of—

'Qui va là?'

'Push on!' whispered the scout, once more bending to the left.

'Push on!' repeated Heyward; when the summons was renewed by a dozen voices, each of which seemed charged with menace.

'C'est moi,' cried Duncan, dragging, rather than leading, those he supported, swiftly, onward.

'Bête! qui? moi!'

'Ami de la France.'

'Tu m'as plus l'air d'un ennemi de la France; arrete! ou pardieu je te ferai ami du diable. Non! feu; camarades; feu!'

The order was instantly obeyed, and the fog was stirred by the explosion of fifty muskets. Happily, the aim was bad, and the bullets cut the air in a direction a little different from that taken by the fugitives; though still so nigh them, that to the unpractised ears of David and the two females, it appeared as if they whistled within a few inches of the organs. The outcry was renewed, and the order, not only to fire again, but to pursue, was too plainly audible. When Heyward briefly explained the meaning of the words they heard, Hawk-eye halted, and spoke with quick decision and great firmness.

'Let us deliver our fire,' he said; 'they will believe it a sortie, and give way; or they will wait for reinforcements.'

The scheme was well conceived, but failed in its effect. The instant the French heard the pieces, it seemed as if the plain was alive with men, muskets rattling along its whole extent, from the shores of the lake to the farthest boundary of the woods.

'We shall draw their entire army upon us, and bring on a general assault,' said Duncan. 'Lead on my friend, for your own life, and ours!'

The scout seemed willing to comply; but, in the hurry of the moment, and in the change of position, he had lost the direction. In vain he turned either cheek towards the light air; they felt equally cool. In this dilemma, Uncas lighted on the furrow of the cannon ball, where it had cut the ground in three adjacent ant-hills.

'Give me the range!' said Hawk-eye, bending to catch a glimpse of the direction, and then instantly moving onward.

Cries, oaths, voices calling to each other, and the reports of muskets, were now quick and incessant, and, apparently, on every side of them. Suddenly, a strong glare of light flashed across the scene, the fog rolled upward in thick wreaths, and several cannon belched across the plain, and the roar was thrown heavily back from the bellowing echoes of the mountain.

''Tis from the fort!' exclaimed Hawk-eye, turning short on his tracks; 'and we, like stricken fools, were rushing to the woods, under the very knives of the Maquas.'

The instant their mistake was rectified, the whole party retraced the error with the utmost diligence. Duncan willingly relinquished the support of Cora to the arm of Uncas, and Cora as readily accepted the welcome assistance. Men, hot and angry in pursuit, were evidently on their footsteps, and each instant threatened their capture, if not their destruction.

'Point de quartier, aux coquins!' cried an eager pursuer, who seemed to direct the operations of the enemy.

'Stand firm, and be ready, my gallant 60ths!' suddenly exclaimed a voice above them; 'wait to see the enemy; fire low, and sweep the glacis.'

'Father! father!' exclaimed a piercing cry from out the mist; 'it is I! Alice! thy own Elsie! spare, oh! save, your daughters!'

'Hold!' shouted the former speaker, in the awful tones of parental agony, the sound reaching even to the woods, and rolling back in solemn echo. ''Tis she! God has restored me my children! Throw open the sally-port; to the field, 60ths, to the field; pull not a trigger, lest ye kill my lambs! Drive off these dogs of France with your steel.'

Duncan heard the grating of the rusty hinges, and darting to the spot, directed by the sound, he met a long line of dark-red warriors, passing swiftly towards the glacis. He knew them for his own battalion of the Royal Americans, and flying to their head, soon swept every trace of his pursuers from before the works.

For an instant, Cora and Alice had stood trembling and bewildered by this unexpected desertion; but, before either had leisure for speech, or even thought, an officer of gigantic frame, whose locks were bleached with years and service, but whose air of military grandeur had been rather softened than destroyed by time, rushed out of the body of the mist, and folded them to his bosom, while large, scalding tears rolled down his pale and wrinkled cheeks, and he exclaimed, in the peculiar accent of Scotland—

'For this I thank thee, Lord! Let danger come as it will, thy servant is now prepared!'

'Then go we in, to know his embassy;
Which I could, with a ready guess, declare,
Before the Frenchman speak a word of it.'
Henry V, I.i.95–97.

A FEW SUCCEEDING DAYS were passed amid the privations, the uproar, and the dangers of the siege, which was vigorously pressed by a power, against whose approaches Munro possessed no competent means of resistance. It appeared as if Webb, with his army, which lay slumbering on the banks of the Hudson, had utterly forgotten the strait to which his countrymen were reduced. Montcalm had filled the woods of the portage with his savages, every yell and whoop from whom rang through the British encampment, chilling the hearts of men, who were already but too much disposed to magnify the danger.

Not so, however, with the besieged. Animated by the words, and stimulated by the examples of their leaders, they had found their courage, and maintained their ancient reputation, with a zeal that did justice to the stern character of their commander. As if satisfied with the toil of marching through the wilderness to encounter his enemy, the French general, though of approved skill, had neglected to seize the adjacent mountains; whence the besieged might have been exterminated with impunity, and which, in the more modern warfare of the country, would not have been neglected for a single hour. This sort of contempt for eminences, or rather dread of the labor of ascending them, might have been termed the besetting weakness of the warfare of the period. It originated in the simplicity of the Indian contests, in which, from the nature of the combats, and the density of the forests, fortresses were rare, and artillery next to useless. The carelessness engendered by these usages, descended even to the war of the revolution, and lost the states the important fortress of Ticonderoga, opening a way for the army of Burgoyne, into what was then the bosom of the country. We look back at this ignorance, or infatuation, which ever it may be called, with wonder, knowing that the neglect of an eminence, whose difficulties, like those of Mount Defiance, had been so greatly exaggerated, would, at the present time, prove fatal to the reputation of the engineer who had planned the works at their base, or to that of the general, whose lot it was to defend them.

The tourist, the valetudinarian, or the amateur of the beauties of nature, who, in the train of his four-in-hand, now rolls through the scenes we have attempted to describe, in quest of information, health, or pleasure, or floats steadily towards his object on those artificial waters, which have sprung up under the administration of a statesman,* who has dared to stake his political character on the hazardous issue, is not to suppose that his ancestors traversed those hills, or struggled with the same currents with equal facility. The transportation of a single heavy gun, was often considered equal to a victory gained; if happily the difficulties of the passage had not so far separated it from its necessary concomitants, the ammunition, as to render it no more than a useless tube of unwieldy iron.

The evils of this state of things pressed heavily on the fortunes of the resolute Scotsman, who now defended William Henry. Though his adversary neglected the hills, he had planted his batteries with judgment on the plain, and caused them to be served with vigor and skill. Against this assault, the besieged could

---

*Evidently the late de Witt Clinton, who died governor of New York, in 1828. [1831]

only oppose the imperfect and hasty preparations of a fortress in the wilderness.

It was in the afternoon of the fifth day of the siege, and the fourth of his own service in it, that Major Heyward profited by a parley that had just been beaten, by repairing to the ramparts of one of the water bastions, to breathe the cool air from the lake, and to take a survey of the progress of the siege. He was alone, if the solitary sentinel who paced the mound be excepted; for the artillerists had hastened also to profit by the temporary suspension of their arduous duties. The evening was delightfully calm, and the light air from the limpid water fresh and soothing. It seemed as if, with the termination to the roar of artillery, and the plunging of shot, nature had also seized the moment to assume her mildest and most captivating form. The sun poured down his parting glory on the scene, without the oppression of those fierce rays that belong to the climate and the season. The mountains looked green, and fresh, and lovely; tempered with the milder light, or softened in shadow, as thin vapors floated between them and the sun. The numerous islands rested on the bosom of the Horican, some low and sunken, as if imbedded in the waters, and others appearing to hover above the element, in little hillocks of green velvet; among which the fishermen of the beleaguering army peacefully rowed their skiffs, or floated at rest on the glassy mirror, in quiet pursuit of their employment.

The scene was at once animated and still. All that pertained to nature was sweet, or simply grand; while those parts which depended on the temper and movements of man, were lively and playful.

Two little spotless flags were abroad, the one on a salient angle of the fort, and the other on the advanced battery of the besiegers; emblems of the truce which existed, not only to the acts, but it would seem, also, to the enmity of the combatants. Behind these, again, swung, heavily opening and closing in silken folds, the rival standards of England and France.

A hundred gay and thoughtless young Frenchmen were drawing a net to the pebbly beach, within dangerous proximity to the sullen but silent cannon of the fort, while the eastern mountain was sending back the loud shouts and gay merriment that attended their sport. Some were rushing eagerly to enjoy the aquatic games of the lake, and others were already toiling their way up the neighboring hills, with the restless curiosity of their nation. To all these sports and pursuits, those of the enemy who watched the besieged, and the besieged themselves, were, however, merely the idle, though sympathizing spectators. Here and there a picquet had, indeed, raised a song, or mingled in a dance, which had drawn the dusky savages around them, from their lairs in the forest. In short, every thing wore rather the appearance of a day of pleasure, than of an hour stolen from the dangers and toil of a bloody and vindictive warfare.

Duncan had stood in a musing attitude, contemplating this scene a few minutes, when his eyes were directed to the glacis in front of the sally-port, already mentioned, by the sounds of approaching footsteps. He walked to an angle of the bastion, and beheld the scout advancing, under the custody of a French officer, to the body of the fort. The countenance of Hawk-eye was haggard and care-worn, and his air dejected, as though he felt the deepest degradation at having fallen into the power of his enemies. He was without his favorite weapon, and his arms were even bound behind him with thongs, made of the skin of a deer. The arrival of flags, to cover the messengers of summons, had occurred so often of late, that when Heyward first threw his careless glance on this groupe, he expected to see another of the officers of the enemy, charged with a similar office; but the instant he recognized the tall person, and still sturdy, though downcast, features of his friend, the woodsman, he started with surprise, and turned to descend from the bastion into the bosom of the work.

The sounds of other voices, however, caught his attention, and for a moment caused him to forget his purpose. At the inner angle of the mound, he met the sisters, walking along the parapet, in search, like himself, of air and relief from confinement. They had not met since that painful moment when he deserted them, on the plain, only to assure their safety. He had parted from them, worn with care, and jaded with fatigue; he now saw them refreshed and blooming, though timid and anxious. Under such an inducement, it will cause no surprise, that the young man lost sight, for a time, of other objects, in order to address them. He was, however, anticipated by the voice of the ingenuous and youthful Alice.

'Ah! thou truant! thou recreant knight! he who abandons his damsels in the very lists!' she cried; 'here have we been days, nay, ages, expecting you at our feet, imploring mercy and forgetfulness of your craven backsliding, or, I should rather say, back-running – for verily you fled in a manner that no stricken deer, as our worthy friend the scout would say, could equal!'

'You know that Alice means our thanks and our blessings,' added the graver and more thoughtful Cora. 'In truth, we have a little wondered why you should so rigidly absent yourself from a place, where the gratitude of the daughters might receive the support of a parent's thanks.'

'Your father himself could tell you, that though absent from your presence, I have not been altogether forgetful of your safety,' returned the young man; 'the mastery of yonder village of huts,' pointing to the neighboring entrenched camp, 'has been keenly disputed; and he who holds it, is sure to be possessed of this fort, and that which it contains. My days and nights have all been passed there, since we separated, because I thought that duty called me thither. But,' he added, with an air of chagrin, which he endeavored, though unsuccessfully, to conceal, 'had I been aware, that what I then believed a soldier's conduct, could be so construed, shame would have been added to the list of reasons.'

'Heyward! – Duncan!' exclaimed Alice, bending forward to read his half-averted countenance, until a lock of her golden hair rested on her flushed cheek, and nearly concealed the tear that had started to her eye; 'did I think this idle tongue of mine had pained you, I would silence it for ever! Cora can say, if Cora would, how justly we have prized your services, and how deep – I had almost said, how fervent – is our gratitude!'

'And will Cora attest the truth of this?' cried Duncan, suffering the cloud to be chased from his countenance by a smile of open pleasure. 'What says our graver sister? Will she find an excuse for the neglect of the knight, in the duty of a soldier?'

Cora made no immediate answer, but turned her face toward the water, as if looking on the sheet of the Horican. When she did bend her dark eyes on the young man, they were yet filled with an expression of anguish that at once drove every thought but that of kind solicitude from his mind.

'You are not well, dearest Miss Munro!' he exclaimed; 'we have trifled, while you are in suffering!'

''Tis nothing,' she answered, refusing his offered support, with feminine reserve. 'That I cannot see the sunny side of the picture of life, like this artless but ardent enthusiast,' she added, laying her hand lightly, but affectionately, on the arm of her sister, 'is the penalty of experience, and, perhaps, the misfortune of my nature. See,' she continued, as if determined to shake off infirmity, in a sense of duty; 'look around you, Major Heyward, and tell me what a prospect is this, for the daughter of a soldier, whose greatest happiness is his honor and his military renown?'

'Neither ought nor shall be tarnished by circumstances, over which he has had no control,' Duncan warmly replied. 'But your words recall me to my own duty. I go now to your gallant father, to hear his determination in matters of the last moment to the defence. God bless you in every fortune, noble – Cora – I may, and must call you.' She frankly gave him her hand, though her lip quivered, and her cheeks gradually became of an ashy paleness. 'In every fortune, I know you will be an ornament and honor to your sex. Alice, adieu' – his tone changed from admiration to tenderness – 'adieu, Alice; we shall soon meet again; as conquerors, I trust, and amid rejoicings!'

Without waiting for an answer from either, the young man threw himself down the grassy steps of the bastion, and moving rapidly across the parade, he was quickly in the presence of their father. Munro was pacing his narrow apartment with a disturbed air, and gigantic strides, as Duncan entered.

'You have anticipated my wishes, Major Heyward,' he said; 'I was about to request this favor.'

'I am sorry to see, sir, that the messenger I so warmly recommended, has returned in custody of the French! I hope there is no reason to distrust his fidelity?'

'The fidelity of the "Long Rifle" is well known to me,' returned Munro, 'and is above suspicion; though his usual good fortune seems, at least, to have failed. Montcalm has got him, and with the accursed politeness of his nation, he has sent him in with a doleful tale, of "knowing how I valued the fellow, he could not think of retaining him." A jesuitical way, that, Major Duncan Heyward, of telling a man of his misfortunes!'

'But the general and his succour?—'

'Did ye look to the south as ye entered, and could ye not see them!' said the old soldier, laughing bitterly. 'Hoot! hoot! you're an impatient boy, sir, and cannot give the gentlemen leisure for their march!'

'They are coming then? The scout has said as much?'

'When? and by what path? for the dunce has omitted to tell me this! There is a letter, it would seem, too; and that is the only agreeable part of the matter. For the customary attentions of your Marquis of Montcalm – I warrant me, Duncan, that he of Lothian would buy a dozen such marquessates – but, if the news of the letter were bad, the gentility of this French monsieur would certainly compel him to let us know it!'

'He keeps the letter, then, while he releases the messenger?'

'Ay, that does he, and all for the sake of what you call your "bonhommie." I would venture, if the truth was known, the fellow's grandfather taught the noble science of dancing!'

'But what says the scout? he has eyes and ears, and a tongue! what verbal report does he make?'

'Oh! sir, he is not wanting in natural organs, and he is free to tell all that he has seen and heard. The whole amount is this: there is a fort of his majesty's on the banks of the Hudson, called Edward, in honor of his gracious highness of York, you'll know, and it is well filled with armed men, as such a work should be!'

'But there was no movement, no signs, of any intention to advance to our relief?'

'There were the morning and evening parades, and when one of the provincial loons – you'll know, Duncan, you're half a Scotsman yourself – when one of them dropped his powder over his porretch, if it touched the coals, it just burnt!' Then suddenly changing his bitter, ironical manner, to one more grave and thoughtful, he continued; 'and yet there might, and must be, something in that letter, which it would be well to know!'

'Our decision should be speedy,' said Duncan, gladly availing himself of this change of humor, to press the more important objects of their interview; 'I cannot conceal from you, sir, that the camp will not be much longer tenable; and I am sorry to add, that things appear no better in the fort; – more than half the guns are bursted.'

'And how should it be otherwise! some were fished from the bottom of the lake; some have been rusting in the woods since the discovery of the country; and some were never guns at all – mere privateersmen's playthings! Do you think, sir, you can have Woolwich Warren in the midst of a wilderness; three thousand miles from Great Britain!'

'The walls are crumbling about our ears, and provisions begin to fail us,' continued Heyward, without regarding this new burst of indignation; 'even the men show signs of discontent and alarm.'

'Major Heyward,' said Munro, turning to his youthful associate with the dignity of his years and superior rank; 'I should have served his majesty for half a century, and earned these gray hairs, in vain, were I ignorant of all you say, and of the pressing nature of our circumstances; still, there is every thing due to the honor of the king's arms, and something to ourselves. While there is hope of succour, this fortress will I defend, though it be to be done with pebbles gathered on the lake shore. It is a sight of the letter, therefore, that we want, that we may know the intentions of the man, the Earl of London has left among us as his substitute.'

'And can I be of service in the matter.'

'Sir, you can; the Marquis of Montcalm has, in addition to his other civilities, invited me to a personal interview between the works and his own camp; in order, as he says, to impart some additional information. Now, I think it would not be wise to show any undue solicitude to meet him, and I would employ you, an officer of rank, as my substitute; for it would but ill comport with the honor of Scotland, to let it be said, one of her gentlemen was outdone in civility, by a native of any other country on earth!'

Without assuming the supererogatory task of entering into a discussion of the comparative merits of national courtesy, Duncan cheerfully assented to supply the place of the veteran, in the approaching interview. A long and confidential communication now succeeded, during which the young man received some additional insight into his duty, from the experience and native acuteness of his commander, and then the former took his leave.

As Duncan could only act as the representative of the commandant of the fort, the ceremonies which should have accompanied a meeting between the heads of the adverse forces, were of course dispensed with. The truce still existed, and with a roll and beat of the drum, and covered by a little white flag, Duncan left the sally-port, within ten minutes after his instructions were ended. He was received by the French officer in advance, with the usual formalities, and immediately accompanied to the distant marquee of the renowned soldier, who led the forces of France.

The general of the enemy received the youthful messenger, surrounded by his principal officers, and by a swarthy band of the native chiefs, who had followed him to the field, with the warriors of their several tribes. Heyward paused short, when, in glancing his eyes rapidly over the dark groupe of the latter, he beheld the malignant countenance of Magua, regarding him with the calm but sullen attention which marked the expression of that subtle savage. A slight exclamation of surprise even burst from the lips of the young man; but, instantly recollecting his errand, and the presence in which he stood, he suppressed every appearance of emotion, and turned to the hostile leader, who had already advanced a step to receive him.

The Marquis of Montcalm was, at the period of which we write, in the flower of his age, and it may be added, in the zenith of his fortunes. But even in that enviable situation, he was affable, and distinguished as much for his attention to the forms of courtesy, as for that chivalrous courage, which, only two short years afterwards, induced him to throw away his life, on the plains of Abraham. Duncan, in turning his eyes from the malign expression of Magua, suffered them to rest with pleasure on the smiling and polished features, and the noble, military air of the French general.

'Monsieur,' said the latter, 'J'ai beaucoup de plaisir à – bah! ou èst cet interprête?'

'Je crois, monsieur, qu'il ne sera pas nécessaire,' Heyward modestly replied; 'je parle un peu Français.'

'Ah! j'en suis bien aise,' said Montcalm, taking Duncan familiarly by the arm, and leading him deep into the marquee, a little out of earshot; 'je déteste ces fripons-là; on se sait jamais sur quel piè, on est avec eux. Eh, bien! monsieur,' he continued, still speaking in French; 'though I should have been proud of receiving your commandant, I am very happy that he has seen proper to employ an officer so distinguished, and who, I am sure, is so amiable, as yourself.'

Duncan bowed low, pleased with the compliment, in spite of a most heroic determination to suffer no artifice to lure him into forgetfulness of the interests of his prince; and Montcalm, after a pause of a moment, as if to collect his thoughts, proceeded—

'Your commandant is a brave man, and well qualified to repel my assaults. Mais, monsieur, is it not time to begin to take more counsel of humanity, and less of your own courage? The one as strongly characterizes the hero, as the other!'

'We consider the qualities as inseparable,' returned Duncan, smiling; 'but, while we find in the vigor of your excellency, every motive to stimulate the one, we can, as yet, see no particular call for the exercise of the other.'

Montcalm, in his turn, slightly bowed, but it was with the air of a man too practised to remember the language of flattery. After musing a moment, he added—

'It is possible my glasses have deceived me, and that your works resist our cannon better than I had supposed. You know our force?'

'Our accounts vary,' said Duncan, carelessly; 'the highest, however, has not exceeded twenty thousand men.'

The Frenchman bit his lip, and fastened his eyes keenly on the other, as if to read his thoughts; then, with a readiness peculiar to himself, he continued, as if assenting to the truth of an enumeration, which quite doubled his army—

'It is a poor compliment to the vigilance of us soldiers, monsieur, that, do what we will, we never can conceal our numbers. If it were to be done at all, one would believe it might succeed in these woods. Though you think it too soon to listen to the calls of humanity,' he added, smiling, archly, 'I may be permitted to believe that gallantry is not forgotten by one so young as yourself. The daughters of the commandant, I learn, have passed into the fort, since it was invested?'

'It is true, monsieur; but so far from weakening our efforts, they set us an example of courage in their own fortitude. Were nothing but resolution necessary to repel so accomplished a soldier, as M. de Montcalm, I would gladly trust the defence of William Henry to the elder of those ladies.'

'We have a wise ordinance in our Salique laws, which says, "the crown of France shall never degrade the lance to the distaff," ' said Montcalm, dryly, and with a little hauteur; but, instantly adding, with his former frank and easy air, 'as all the nobler qualities are hereditary, I can easily credit you; though, as I said before, courage has its limits, and humanity must not be forgotten. I trust, monsieur, you come authorized to treat for the surrender of the place?'

'Has your excellency found our defense so feeble, as to believe the measure necessary!'

'I should be sorry to have the defense protracted in such a manner, as to irritate my red friends there,' continued Montcalm, glancing his eyes at the groupe of grave and attentive Indians, without attending to the other's question; 'I find it difficult, even now, to limit them to the usages of war.'

Heyward was silent; for a painful recollection of the dangers he had so recently escaped came over his mind, and recalled the images of those defenceless beings, who had shared in all his sufferings.

'Ces messieurs-là,' said Montcalm, following up the advantage which he conceived he had gained, 'are most formidable when baffled; and it is unnecessary to tell you, with what difficulty they are restrained in their anger. Eh bien, monsieur! shall we speak of the terms?'

'I fear your excellency has been deceived as to the strength of William Henry, and the resources of its garrison!'

'I have not set down before Quebec, but an earthen work, that is defended by twenty-three hundred gallant men,' was the laconic reply.

'Our mounds are earthen, certainly – nor are they seated on the rocks of Cape Diamond; – but they stand on that shore which proved so destructive to Dieskau, and his army. There is also a powerful force within a few hours' march of us, which we account upon as part of our means.'

'Some six or eight thousand men,' returned Montcalm, with much apparent indifference, 'whom their leader, wisely, judges to be safer in their works, than in the field.'

It was now Heyward's turn to bite his lip with vexation, as the other so coolly alluded to a force which the young man knew to be overrated. Both mused a little while in silence, when Montcalm renewed the conversation, in a way that showed he believed the visit of his guest was, solely, to propose terms of capitulation. On the other hand, Heyward began to throw sundry inducements in the way of the French general, to betray the discoveries he had made through the intercepted letter. The artifice of neither, however, succeeded; and, after a protracted and fruitless interview, Duncan took his leave, favorably impressed with an opinion of the courtesy and talents of the enemy's captain, but as ignorant of what he came to learn, as when he arrived. Montcalm followed him as far as the entrance of the marquee, renewing his invitations to the commandant of the fort, to give him an immediate meeting in the open ground, between the two armies.

There they separated, and Duncan returned to the advanced post of the French, accompanied as before; whence he instantly proceeded to the fort, and to the quarters of his own commander.